THE CITY AND THE SHIP

The "Brain Ship" Megabook Series

Brain Ships
The Ship Who Searched
by Anne McCaffrey & Mercedes Lackey
Partnership
by Anne McCaffrey & Margaret Ball

The Ship Who Saved the Worlds
The Ship Who Won
by Anne McCaffrey & Jody Lynn Nye
The Ship Errant
by Jody Lynn Nye

The City and the Ship
The City Who Fought
by Anne McCaffrey & S.M. Stirling
The Ship Avenged
by S.M. Stirling

THE
CITY AND THE SHIP
THE

ANNE McCAFFREY
S.M. STIRLING

THE CITY AND THE SHIP

This is a work of fiction. All the characters and events portrayed in this book are fictional, and any resemblance to real people or incidents is purely coincidental.

A Baen Books Original MegaBook

Baen Publishing Enterprises
P.O. Box 1403
Riverdale, NY 10471
www.baen.com

ISBN: 0-7434-7189-X

Cover art by Stephen Hickman

First Megabook printing, March 2004

Library of Congress Cataloging-in-Publication Data

McCaffrey, Anne.
  [City who fought]
  The city and the ship / Anne McCaffrey, S.M. Stirling.
  p. cm. -- (The "brain ship" megabook series)
  "A Baen Books original megabook"--T.p. verso.
  ISBN 0-7434-7189-X
  1. Space ships--Fiction. 2. Space warfare--Fiction. 3. Science fiction, American. I. Stirling, S.M. II. Stirling, S. M. Ship avenged. III. Title. IV. Series.

PS3563.A255C56 2004
813'.54--dc22

                                              2003027415

Distributed by Simon & Schuster
1230 Avenue of the Americas
New York, NY 10020

Production by Windhaven Press, Auburn, NH
Printed in the United States of America

10 9 8 7 6 5 4 3 2 1

CONTENTS

The City Who Fought
by Anne McCaffrey and S.M. Stirling   1

The Ship Avenged
by S.M. Stirling   351

THE
CITY AND THE SHIP

THE CITY WHO FOUGHT

Anne McCaffrey & S. M. Stirling

PROLOGUE

"HOW LONG?" AMOS ben Sierra Nueva said desperately.

"Another forty-five minutes, esteemed sir," the technician answered in a voice flat with focused concentration.

Amos touched the pickup in his ear and turned back to the low hills ahead. They were covered in pine forest, or had been, until about an hour ago. Now they were burning, a furnace of resin-fueled candles fifty meters high. The invaders had barred their own way with the blast of beam-fire from the aircraft, but they seemed lazily indifferent about inflicting casualties on their own forces. The Bethelite noble-man ground his teeth in fury at that lordly disdain; unfortunately, it seemed justified.

For now. Most of the resistance to the Kolnari invasion had come from Bethel's planetary constabulary, and the Guardians of the Temple. Those few who didn't see the invasion as punishment for the sins of godless young Amos ben Sierra Nueva and his followers had, of course, resisted. The faithful had effectively offered their throats to the pirate knife. Sheer luck that Amos and those follow-ers had been preparing even if their efforts had been made against the day when the Guardians came for *them.*

"Everything is in place, my brother," said the man beside Amos in the rear seat of the pickup. Joseph ben Said was a commoner— worse than that, a bastard from the slums of Keriss—but he had been the first of Amos' followers, and had proved to be the most loyal.

Not to mention certain skills, Amos reminded himself.

"Take me forward to the bunker," he said, and cut off Joseph's protest with a brusque chop of his hand.

The gunner behind the pintle-mounted launcher swayed as the driver gunned the fans and slid the vehicle down the dirt track. He was inexperienced; they all were. The Second Revelation had trained in secret with their hoarded weapons, preparing for the Second Exodus to Al Mina. Official Temple policy held there was no need to venture beyond Bethel when three centuries of valiant breeding left the Chosen still thin on the ground in the initial area of settlement. There had been no time to acquire much real skill with the tools of destruction. The measures had been insurance, really, in case the Elders actually were willing to use force to prevent the settlement of the Saffron system's other habitable planet.

Ahead, the fire throbbed and roared. The pines were a native variety; candlestick trees, they were called. They were explosively flammable this time of year, and the air was thick with the heavy resinous smoke. Dust spurted from under the car as they swung behind the bunker, just now thrown up with farming machines and covered with raw dirt. The driver backed and then let the vehicle settle on its flexible skirt, keeping the fans running and the gunner's line of sight just over the top of the mound.

"Good man," Amos said, thumping him on the shoulder before he hopped down and ducked to enter the bunker.

A display film had been tacked to one wall. It showed footage from a pickup located a kilometer down the road. Half a dozen men and women in coveralls and caps were talking into communicators or hovering over a schematic display on a rickety camp table. In the bunker, the air was full of a crackling tension, louder to the nerves than the burning forest was to the ears. Amos nodded to . . . *the officer,* he reminded himself. No longer friends and retainers, but warriors.

"They are coming," Rachel bint Damscus said.

Her plain bony face was tightly impassive. She was an info-systems specialist, rare for a woman on Bethel, where most females held to traditional feminine careers like medicine or literature. Joseph made her a formal bow.

"You are well, lady?" he said.

She gave a curt nod, then turned back to Amos. "They hit the forest with some sort of indirect-fire incendiary weapon, and now they are advancing through it. Powered vehicles. Fusion-bubble neutrino signatures, fairly heavy ones."

"They probably do not know how common bad fires are here," Amos said. He worked a tongue in a mouth gone dry. Bethel vehicles used stressed-storage batteries.

Rachel was holding up well, better than he had expected. She had a violent temper, and he suspected a buried streak of hysteria. She was also a claustrophobe: the bunker would add that distress to her burdens. The more credit to her, for conquering her phobia.

"They thought to mask their approach in the flames," he said aloud.

Their first ambush had killed several of the invader infantry. Even a few hours had shown how the strangers reacted to a challenge: strike back immediately with overwhelming power. He cleared his throat and asked calmly:

"How far are they from the mine?"

"Two kilometers and closing. Closing at twenty kph. Onscreen."

The view through the screen tacked to the wall trembled. That meant something was shaking the ground under the pickup, even though it was spiked to solid rock. Hills rose on either side ahead, everything on fire except for the narrow stream and the road beside it, down at the base of the massive granite slopes. Shapes were moving through the burning trees on the lower slopes. Dull-gleaming shapes, hard to make out against the background, as if the surfaces were adapting themselves, chameleon-fashion, as they moved. Low turtle-backed outlines, with long weapons jutting from their sloped forward plates, the barrels built up from coils or rings, some sort of wave-guide or electromagnetic launcher.

One fighting vehicle pivoted. The muzzle flashed, bright even through the hot-iron glow of the fires. The viewscreen fogged slightly as a pickup was blasted into plasma, then cleared as the system compensated by spreading input from the others.

"Well, that gives us a clue to the sensitivity of their detectors," Joseph said. He leaned forward. "Everyone is out of there?"

"Falling back to the launching ground. There is nobody within fifteen kilometers," Rachel said. "We are closest."

"Do it, then," Amos said.

She touched a control surface. The screen flashed white and went blank. Half a second later an actinic glare flashed through the bunker, reflected in from the rear entrance but still bright enough to make their goggles darken protectively. Sound and shock followed in a few heart-beats: a roar like God returning in anger, an earthquake rumble through the soil, then a wave of heat and pressure making their ears pop.

"So Keriss died," Rachel said absently, to herself. "Tamik saw it. He said the flash was like the sword of God, and the waves a kilometer high when they broke over the Peninsula mountains."

"Everyone leave," Amos said quietly, glancing down at the watch woven into his sleeve. There was nothing else to say. Rachel's family had lived in Keriss, the capital city of Bethel. So had most of Amos' surviving kindred, and Joseph's, if he had any. "We will rendezvous in forty minutes at the shuttle." He paused. "And, Rachel?"

"Yes, sir?"

"Well done. Very well done."

When they left the bunker, the pillar of cloud was already flattening out high in the stratosphere.

CHAPTER ONE

"SSS." THE SENSOR OVERWATCH AI filtered a possible message out of the interstellar background and passed it through to the controller of Station SSS-900.

"Hissing again, are we?" Simeon muttered absently at the subprogram, and turned his attention back to the simulacrum.

Napoleon had just pushed the British north of Nottingham. Wounded, exhausted soldiers sprawled across the fields where the defeated army camped, as the rain drained down, gray skies darkening over trampled muddy fields. Away across the rolling landscape fires still flickered, where dead men lay gaping around smashed cannon. The women were out with lanterns, looking for their husbands and sons.

A dispatch rider came clattering up to Wellesley's tent with news of the Jacobin uprisings in Birmingham and Manchester, and a landing of the Irish rebels. The big beak-nosed man stood in the open flap of the tent as the dripping militiaman saluted clumsily and handed over the dispatches, blinking in the driving rain.

"The devil with it," he muttered, turning to the map-table within and unfolding the heavy wax-sealed papers. "It's too bad. If we'd won that last battle . . . if wishes were horses, beggars would ride. Still, it was a damned near-run thing—a very near thing."

He looked up. "You are to inform His Majesty that he and the royal family must take ship for India immediately. These—" he extended the reports from his folding desk "—are for Viceroy Arnold in Calcutta."

I concede, the computer said.

"Of course," Simeon answered smugly.

He switched his primary visual focus from simulation back to the lounge and looked down at the big holotable. An excellent model for use in war-gaming, the map of England was scattered with unit symbols. Finer and finer detail could be obtained by magnifying individual sectors—right down to the animate models of soldiers and horses. Or tanks and artillery, for some of the other games. He focused: on a horse tiredly nipping at its neighbor on the picket line, on the stubbled gap-toothed face of a sentry yawning.

"SSS."

"What is that?" Simeon asked.

The answer floated up into his awareness from the peripherals; tightbeam signal, modulated subspace waves, picked up by one of the passive buoys out on the fringes of the system. A subroutine had flagged it as possibly interesting.

Hmmm, he thought. *Odd.* It *might* just be the last fading noise from a leaking mini-singularity about to go pop. The things tended to cluster in this area, which was full of third-generation stars and black holes, though this one tasted like a signal. The problem with that was that there was nothing much *out* that way; nothing listed as inhabited for better than two hundred lights. Certainly no traffic into the sphere of Space Station Simeon-900-X's operations. He would have to see if anything more came of it. Presumably if someone was calling, they would try again.

Idly, he ran a checklist of station functions. Life-support was nominal, of course; any variation of *that* was red-flagged. One hundred seventy-two craft of various sorts from the liner *Altair* to barge-tugs were currently docked. Twenty-seven megatons of various mineral powders were in transit, in storage, or undergoing processing in SSS-900-X's attendant fabrication modules. Two new tugs were under construction in the yard. A civic election was underway, with Anita de Chong-Markowitz leading for council-rep in station sector three, the entertainment decks. *Death in the Twenty-First* was still billing as most popular holo of the month. Simeon sneered mentally, with a wistful overtone. Historical dramas were impossible for a serious scholar to watch because the manufacturers would *not* do their research.

It was not necessary to investigate much more in detail. With the connectors, shellperson Simeon *was* SSS-900-X. Little awareness remained of the stunted body inside its titanium shell in the central column of the lounge. He *was* the station, and any weakness or failure was, like pain, intense and personal. As far as his kinesthetic sense was concerned, *he* was a metal tube a kilometer long, with two huge globes attached on either end.

The *Altair* was in. Simeon had docked the incoming ship with his usual efficiency but without his usual close scrutiny. He deliberately turned his attention away from disembarking passengers, refusing to study their faces, especially the faces of the women.

Radon's replacement as Simeon's brawn was on this ship, and all he knew was her work record and her name. *Channa Hap.* Probably from Hawking Alpha Proxima Station, Hap being a common surname for those born in that ancient and wealthy community. He wasn't entirely sure. He'd fought Radon's retirement too hard to have much personal interest in his replacement. *All right, I was sulking,* he told himself. *Time to get with the program.* He'd established a subroutine to trash the applications of replacements. That hadn't been personal, merely a ploy.

He hadn't wanted her, but they were stuck with each other now.

Liners docked at the north polar aspect of the two linked globes that made up the station. The tube was a kilometer long and half that wide, more than enough for the replenishment feeds and a debarkation lounge fancy enough to satisfy the station's collective vanity: twenty meters on a side and fifteen high, lined with murals, walled and floored with exotic space-mined stone, with information kiosks and everything else a visitor needed to feel at home.

"I'm Channa Hap," a woman said to one of the kiosks. "I need directions to Control Central."

So that's her. Long high-cheekboned face, medium-length curling dark hair.

"You are expected, Ms. Hap," the terminal said. It had a mellow, commanding voice synthed from several of Simeon's favorite actors, some of whom dated back to the twenty-fourth century. "Do you wish transportation?"

"If there's no hurry, I'll walk. Might as well get used to the new home."

"This way, please."

She nodded. Simeon froze the visual and studied her; tall, athletic.

Dressed plainly in a coverall, but she had *presence.* Nice figure, too, if you liked subtle curves and rolling muscle. *A fox.*

In an amazingly short time the door-chime signaled a request for admittance. Feeling as nervous as he had when meeting his first brawn, Simeon said, "Come," and the door swished open.

Channa entered. He closed in on the viewer to what he thought of as normal conversational distance. That was an advantage some-times, since softshells couldn't get to their psychologically comfort-able distance with you. She had delicate, clear-cut features and earnest dark eyes, and the curly black hair was swept back from her face in a disciplined no-nonsense fashion. *A vid-show heroine. Perfect!* he thought. *I'll get things off on the right foot.* He switched on a screen with his own "face"—the way he'd imagined it, ruggedly handsome with a tan, a Heidelberg dueling scar, level gray eyes, close-cropped blond hair and a *Centauri Jets* fan cap—and spoke aloud:

"Hubba-hubba!"

The dark eyes widened slightly, "Excuse me?"

He laughed, "That's ancient Earth slang for 'sexy lady.'"

"I see."

The words were so clipped Simeon could almost hear them ping on the deck as they fell through a short silence.

Ah, geesh, he thought, *this is going really well.* "Um, I meant it as a compliment." *Why didn't they send me a male brawn?* he asked himself, conveniently forgetting his request form. Male bonding he knew about.

"Yes, of course," she said coolly. "It's just not a type of compli-ment that I'm particularly fond of receiving."

She's got a nice voice, Simeon thought uneasily. *Pity she seems to be a bitch.* "What sort of compliments *do* you accept?" he asked in a tone of forced jocularity which wasn't easy to manage through a digital speaker.

"I accept those that deal with my quick learning ability, and my efficiency, or that acknowledge I'm doing a good job," she said, moving further into the room and taking a seat before his column. Until she had finished speaking, she did not look directly at him.

"The sort of compliment you'd give a servo-mechanism, if you gave servo-mechanisms compliments," he said.

"Exactly." She smiled sweetly and folded her hands.

"You've an interesting attitude, Ms. Hap," he said, laying a little stress on the ancient honorific. *If she wants to get formal, I'll show her formal.* "Most of the women I've worked with didn't object to an occasional compliment on their appearance."

She raised her brows slightly and cocked her head. "Perhaps if they objected you simply dismissed it as being part of an 'attitude.'"

I could cry, if I could cry, Simeon thought. He'd gotten lonely these last weeks without Tell Radon. He'd begun to anticipate the *fun* he'd been going to have with a new brawn. Someone to talk to. . . . How could they have matched him with this . . . ice princess? They knew he was easy going, sure, but he'd given them a very good idea of what he was looking for in a brawn. Exact specifications, which Channa Hap hadn't met, fully. Was someone in Central taking advantage of his good nature, somehow hoping he could straighten her out, or maybe loosen her up?

"I find *your* attitude rather interesting," she murmured, narrowing her eyes. "Have you checked your hormone levels recently?"

"That's a rather personal remark. . . ." *Maybe they just want me to blast her out an airlock when nobody's looking.*

"'Sexy lady' isn't?" She smiled and raised a sardonic brow.

"That was a compliment, intended to put you at ease. Have you checked your own hormone levels lately?"

There was silence.

After a moment she sat forward and looked at him levelly. "Look, even though it hardly seems worth the trouble of officially submitting my orders to you, on a practical level we may as well just admit that, for the time being, we're stuck with each other. You need a brawn and I'm here. I'm well trained, experienced and hard working. We don't have to love each other to work together."

"True, but it gets a little cold trying to maintain your distance with someone you see every day. It would be a *lot* easier if we could be friends. Look, why don't we just erase what just happened and start over? Whaddaya say?"

She pursed her lips, then smiled. "I'm game. But let's start slow, and we'll avoid the personal remarks for the time being, okay?" She cocked her head at him and raised an eyebrow. "You start."

"Hello, you must be Channa Hap. Welcome to the SSS-900-C."

"Thank you. I hope I'm not interrupting."

"Nah, I always have time for a pret . . . colleague." He detected a slight narrowing of her eyes. "My, you sure are efficient looking."

"Well, and so are you, you're so *steely* and all."

"Funny, I was just about to say the same thing about you."

She stood up. "This isn't going to work."

"My fault. I shouldn't have said that. Look, you must be tired from all the travel you've been doing. Why don't you settle in, look around, relax a little—things might look different."

"This has nothing to do with my being tired or your hormones. . . ."

"What is this fixation you have with my hormones?"

"Shut-up-and-listen-to-me." Channa was giving him a look that he could almost feel. She paused and held up her hands, sitting down again. "Just listen," she said earnestly. "I think that it would be best if we put our cards on the table. I haven't studied your files in full yet," she admitted with a tired smile. "I just couldn't make myself do it. But I do know quite a bit about you." She leaned back and crossed her long legs. "I know that you have a fair amount of influence and a lot of contacts at Central Admin. And I know that you called on just about all of them in the matter of your brawn replacement." She gave him a severe look. "You made yourself famous on just about every level."

He was a little lost here. He *had* kicked up quite a fuss when they forcibly retired Tell Radon, but what did it have to do with her?

"In case you're wondering why I'm bringing this up," she continued.

Geeeze, Simeon thought, *that's eerie! She can't possibly read my mind. Can she?*

"It may interest you to know that I have my own contacts at Admin. And they've told me that you came up with a list of qualifications that were extremely hard to fill. In fact, I was the only candidate who did fit them, with the glaring exception of the age qualification. I hear that I'm four years too young for this post."

"Well, you see . . ."

"Excuse me, I'm not finished. I was also told that you went over my service records looking for black marks, and that when you couldn't find them, you went looking for shadows that you could pretend were black marks. . . ."

"Hey! I don't know who you were talking to."

"Bear with me a few moments longer," Channa said, holding up one finger. "Then you can have your say. I'm not going anywhere." She looked at his image on the screen for a moment with narrowed eyes, and when he remained silent she nodded. "I've been told that all you need do to ruin the day of almost any Admin executive is to mention my name. The feeling you appear to have left behind you as the smoke cleared on this was that where there's smoke, there's fire. And that if you, well-known and respected brain that you are, would object so strenuously to my assignment to the SSS-900, despite the fact that I fit all but one of your many qualifications, then there must indeed be something seriously wrong with me."

"Oh." He honestly hadn't thought about that. He'd been so intent on saving Tell from forced retirement that no other considerations had seemed important. Channa Hap as a person had never entered into his thoughts.

Channa continued speaking, "I told myself that it probably wasn't personal."

God, it's weird the way she can pick up on my thoughts like that!

"I told myself to keep an open mind. If you had only greeted me as a fellow professional, then I think I could have let the whole mess be forgotten. But the first words out of your speakers show that either you can't discern the difference between a compliment and a lip-smacking, smarmy, personal remark, or your campaign to get rid of me continues."

"Now wait a minute!" Simeon said. She opened her mouth to speak and he overrode her. "It's my turn. Okay, you said I'd get a turn and I'm taking it." She raised her brows and gave him an open-handed gesture, giving him the floor. "I don't know who your informant is, but they've got it all wrong. I'm going to assume that you know the system well enough to realize that whoever came up for consideration was going to be gone over with a fine-tooth comb. A space station the size of a small city requires versatility. I'm going to assume that you're mature enough to know that twenty-six is very young for this posting. Tell was thirty-eight when we came here, and that's the general age I was looking for. I don't think, given the importance of the SSS-900, that I'm being unreasonable. But, I suppose that to someone uninformed, the in-depth investigation could look like a campaign to discredit you. That was honestly not my intention, nor is it my intention now. If my greeting was a little too familiar, I apologize, but I had no way of knowing what dark suspicions you were harboring. I'm really very open, Ms. Hap."

She smiled amiably and nodded. "Mmhm. This entire charming explanation of yours is predicated on the assumption that my informant is someone's secretary." She shook her head sadly. "No."

Gulp, maybe I did go a little far.... "Um..."

"You can rest easy," she assured him. "I'm very good at what I do. As you well know, I have an almost perfect record...."

Actually, you do have a perfect record, Simeon thought miserably.

" ... so, whether we actually get along or not, the station won't suffer. And I promise you that I'm not going to just up and disappear on you once you've gotten used to me. Because I have it *on good* authority that, after what you've done to my career and reputation, I'd have to bribe and sleep my way into a secondary assignment on the meanest asteroid-mining outpost at the farthest reaches of the explored galaxy." She rose and said, "I'd like to look at my quarters now."

"Yeah ... just," Simeon slid the door to the brawn's quarters open, "just settle in. We'll work this out, Ms. Hap—you'll see. I'm not as bad as you seem to think I am. I'll check out your allegations and see if I can make things right. Okay?"

She looked from the open door to Simeon and back again. She sighed as she walked to the door. "No, I think it would be better if you just left things alone for a while."

"Ms. Hap," Simeon called. She turned. "When a new brawn comes aboard, station protocol recommends a little informal gathering of the department heads. I've arranged one for this evening at 20:00. That is, if that's all right with you?"

She nodded and smiled. "I think that's a great idea." The door to her room slid shut behind her.

CHAPTER TWO

"I CAN'T KEEP her level! I can't keep her level!"

Amos ben Sierra Nueva leaned forward, gripping the edge of the console as if he could force strength down the commlink and the beam to the stricken transport.

"Do not panic, Shintev," he said, firm but calm. "You are too close to your destination for panic."

Panic seemed to be the order of the day. The bridge of the *Exodus*—a minor substation control center for three hundred years—was in pandemonium as the refugee technicians struggled to activate and improvise. There was a hissing puncture right through the pressure hull where they had slammed a steel tube for the coaxial feeds to Guiyon's shell. None of the big cargo-bay doors were operable so they had had to lash the surface-to-ship transporters to the exterior of the ancient ship and climb in through service-hatch doors. The air was thin and cold, dim with the emergency lighting, full of the smell of fear and sweat and scorched insulation.

"Excellent sir. I think that the enemy has detected us," a voice said from one corner.

"You *think*?"

"I am not sure!" the technician wailed, on the brink of tears. "They are moving . . . yes! They have detected us!"

Amos' head whipped around. Then the link from the last shuttle began to transmit only a long high-pitched scream. He looked back

15

again to see a face rammed into the pickup, plastered there by centrifugal force. Flesh and pooling blood rippled across the screen before it blanked out.

"They are gone," Amos said into the sudden hush. "Decouple the remaining shuttles. Prepare for boost."

Another chorus of screams protested that they were not ready.

"The engines are on-line," Guiyon's calm deep voice said. "That will suffice for now."

Amos turned and punched an override. "Prepare for acceleration! Acceleration in ten seconds from mark. Mark!"

A speck of light blossomed across one of the exterior fields.

"They got Shintev," somebody whispered. An extra-orbital fighter, bouncing across the surface of the troposphere like a skipped stone had gotten close enough to launch a seeker missile at the out-of-control shuttle.

"Attend to your duty!" Amos snapped. *Later there will be time for prayers, and for tears.*

Force pushed at the ancient ship. Humming and snapping sounds vibrated through the hull. Exterior feeds showed gantries and constructs bending and breaking under a strain they had never been intended to endure. The ground-to-orbit shuttles were breaking away as well, and a few figures in spacesuits.

Damnation, Amos thought, looking away. *They were warned!* So many lives rested on his shoulders.

The great cloud-girdled shape of Bethel began to shrink in the rear viewscreen. The visible face of the planet was obscured by dust and flame from the fighting. Acceleration flattened him into his chair as he read figures from the flickering screens.

"Guiyon!" he said. "We are moving too slowly!"

"Peace, Amos. I am trying to—yes, I am venting the life-support tanks." Tens of thousands of kilotons of water were jettisoned. "That will help us. And hinder the enemy."

"What force pursues us?"

"Five ships of small to moderate size. I think they are the enemy sentinels. None other are in position or rigged for pursuit."

"Will they be able to intercept?"

"I do not know. But I must stress the engines, and there will be casualties among the passengers."

"Do what must be done."

The weight pressing into his body increased until his bones creaked from the gravity that the antique compensators could not handle. The actual gravity would crush.

Behind the *Exodus,* half the universe vanished in a blaze of drive energies. The hull did not *hum* anymore: it creaked, with occasional rending and crashing noises as components which had weakened or reset during the long years as an orbital station came apart under the stress and crashed sternwards. Somewhere a child called for its mother, again and again.

"What can we do?" Amos asked.

"Little, until we clear the gravity well," Guiyon answered. "Pray, perhaps, since that was your custom?"

One by one, the refugees lifted voices in chant.

Patsy Sue Coburn glanced over at a silk-clad Channa Hap. Channa was sipping champagne and listening politely to a medical officer who had backed her into a corner to tell a story that seemed to involve a lot of cutting motions. The room was full of station bigwigs, section representatives, department heads, company reps, merchanter captains, the odd artist or entertainer. Trays floated about at shoulder height, loaded with beverages, canapés, and stimulants. Everyone seemed filled with a new enthusiasm for conversations they'd had a hundred times before, as if the new brawn had reinvigorated old topics. Patsy Sue felt the warmth of Florian Gusky's presence even before his deep voice rumbled softly in her ear.

"So . . . what do you think of the new girl?"

Patsy looked at him out of the corner of her bottle-green eyes and flicked back her long blond hair. His jaw was thrust forward and his thick neck was hunched into heavy shoulders, accentuating the rugged cast of his features. A big man and nearly as tough as he thought he was. Gusky was an enthusiast for Revival Games, particularly rugby; he looked ready to tackle Channa.

Or stomp on her with cleats, she thought. "I think the new *woman's* elegant," Patsy replied. *And makes me wish I'd been a little more restrained,* she added to herself. Her own Junoesque figure was squeezed into a tight red sheath with a deep cleavage and a slit skirt. Her ash-blond hair—her own natural coloring with the barest tint of help from modern technology—was woven with ropes of black pearls.

"I think she's a snob," Gusky said decisively.

"She seems a bit reserved," Patsy allowed. *Who wouldn't be, dropped into this mill-and-swill?*

"She seems shallow."

"What *is* yer problem? Y' lookin' at the woman like you think she's got the legs of a cockroach under that gown. I've neva known you to make snap judgments. Do you know somethin' that needs tellin'?"

He looked into his drink, frowning. "No . . . it's just . . . Simeon's awfully quiet." He looked up at her with concern in his brown eyes. "That's just not like him."

She grinned and flicked her blond bangs aside. "Well, this will be quite an adjustment fer him after all," she said. "He an' Tell Radon were together for decades. Maybe he's missin' him and doesn't feel like bein' at a party."

Gus nodded, pursing his lips. "Yeah, or maybe he wants to give her a chance to shine. . . ."

They both looked down for a moment and shuffled their feet. They looked up at the same moment and said, "Simeon?" simultaneously, and then burst out laughing.

"You called?" The familiar image bloomed on a screen beside them.

"Ah! Oh, hi, Sim, we, uh . . . we . . ."

"We were just saying you're kinda quiet tonight," Gus finished.

"Well, with most of my senior staff here at the party, I'm sort of pulling double-duty," Simeon said listlessly. "Excuse me," and he was gone.

Patsy and Gus looked at each other in amazement, then turned to take a new look at Channa Hap, now being introduced to a cargo specialist.

Gus shook his head. "What did she *do* to him?"

Patsy smiled. "Trimmed his sails good and proper."

"This was not a match made in Paradise," Gus muttered.

"Oh, I dunno," Patsy said, narrowing her green eyes thoughtfully. "The woman has style, Gus. This place could use some style. Look at this party. When was the last time you came to Simeon's place and got somethin' besides beer and pretzels?"

Gus looked at her in amazement. "What's that supposed to mean? Are you telling me you can be bought with the right canapés?"

"No. Chocolate truffles maybe, but not synthesized fish eggs on carbo wafers." At his growl she continued more seriously. "What I'm sayin' is, this place is more like a boys' camp than the hub of culture and science and business that it could be. She'll shake us up all right, but maybe that's a good thing. It's goin' to get a lot more interestin' around here."

He went back to glowering. Patsy went over to Channa to compliment her choice of the Rovolodorus' Second Celestial Suite as background music.

"Glad you like it, Ms. Coburn," Channa said. Her smile had the slightly artificial quality of someone who has spent the last few hours fending off would-be favor seekers. "You're from Larabie, though, aren't you?"

"I left," Patsy replied. "Didn't like the down-home music there, and I get so *sick* of the *Miner's Rant* and the other Pioneer Stomp stuff Simeon plays. No offense, Simeon."

"*None taken*," a voice said out of the air, the "n" fading into silence.

Channa's next smile was more genuine. "I'd have thought the chief environmentalist would be in favor of stability," she said.

"I get so *sick* of watchin' algae breed," Patsy said, and they both laughed. "Maybe that's why I had four husbands in a row—just to show I wasn't a unicellular organism."

"Goodnight," Channa called as the door swished shut behind the last departing guest. The big circular room looked even larger with the crowd gone; the holos on the walls had reset to restful underwater scenes with tropical fish.

She turned toward Simeon's screen image on the pillar—a brain's body was *there*, after all, and it had become a matter of courtesy in brawns to address that position even if the brain could hear them anywhere on the station. She stood a moment leisurely studying the large Sinosian tapestry that was tastefully draped across his column.

"That's a lovely hanging," she said at last. "I've been admiring it all evening." She clasped her hands behind her back and walked slowly towards him. "Thank you," she said softly. "This party was very pleasant, Simeon, and a thoughtful gesture."

Once you loosened up a little, Simeon thought in some surprise, *you were fun, too. If I can just keep you half-tanked, we might be able to get along.*

"Well, everyone is more relaxed at this sort of gathering," he said, "divorced from their official positions. You get to see the social side before you have to contend with the professional."

She nodded. "I had just enough time before they got here to glance at everyone's records. I didn't want to make the same mistake with them that I made with you."

"You didn't read my records?"

"No," she said archly, "I wanted to be surprised."

"So did I," he admitted.

She laughed. "Then I guess we do have something in common after all. We can both screw up. Goodnight, Simeon."

Smiling, she gave one last wave at the column as she went into her room.

She has a nice laugh, Simeon thought, as the door swished closed behind her.

Phew, Channa thought.

She thought again, and took several recondite pieces of equipment out of her bag.

When these showed that the sensors in the walls weren't activated, she was slightly ashamed of herself for being so uncharitable about Simeon.

"There is no chance of repairing it?" Amos ben Sierra Nueva said.

"Crapulous none," the technician rasped. "Esteemed sir," he added, wiping at the lubricating fluid on his cheek.

They both backed out of the corridor and dogged the hatchway. A subliminal hum surrounded them; Amos was alone among the refugees in knowing that was a bad sign. Misaligned drive, no surprise after the colony ship had spent three centuries doubling as an orbital station. It was a miracle that the engines functioned at all, and a tribute to the engineers of the Central Worlds. A double miracle that they were holding up under the unnatural stress of maintaining subspace speeds past redline for so long. Guiyon's doing.

"We will just have to economize on oxygen," Amos said firmly.

"Stop *breathing?*" the technician asked.

"Coldsleep," Amos replied. "That will cut down our consumption by at least half. A small crew can manage the ship. It was designed so. Guiyon could run it alone, if need be."

Sweat from more than the exertion of crawling along disused passageways glistened on the man's brown skin. Amos forced himself to breath normally as he walked back to the command deck. His chest felt heavy but it was impossible to detect any CO_2 buildup yet. *Purely psychological,* he told himself sternly.

"There is no chance of repairing the machinery," he said to the assembled command group. A few of them grunted as if struck. "At the current rate, we will exhaust the available air supplies two-thirds of the way to our destination."

"*Why* was the ship not properly maintained?" someone half shouted.

"Because this was an orbital station with unlimited supplies and an algae tank!" Amos snapped, then brought himself back under control. Of necessity, they had had to dump the excess water in the tanks. Too much mass to haul when speed is essential. "We lost more supplies, too, when the enemy hulled us."

"This is our situation," he said, deliberately calm. "We have to deal with it. A hundred lives and the fate of Bethel depend upon it."

They all nodded. There was no way the Kolnari fleet could have been kept secret, even in backwaters like the Saffron system, if there were any witnesses after they left a world. Given time on Bethel, they would hide their tracks the same way.

"What . . . what about coldsleep?" Rachel said, licking her lips.

"A possibility presently to be considered," Amos said. "Guiyon?"

The brain's voice sounded inhumanly detached as always. There were four centuries of experience behind him, and abilities no softperson could ever match. Amos shuddered slightly. *Abomination* was the most charitable term the Faith used for such as he. *Control yourself,* Amos chided. *Guiyon rescued us all. He is our only hope.* The stress was bringing back archaic fears.

"Marginal," Guiyon said. "Possible. We should concentrate all the personnel in one or two compartments, pump the atmosphere from the others back into reserve, and begin coldsleep treatments immediately." He paused. "We are not properly equipped—internal temperature control is very uncertain. There is a risk of substantial casualties."

"Do it," Amos said, with the ring of authority in his voice. He could sense the others relaxing. The menace was still there, but someone was taking steps. *Now, if only I had an authority figure,* he thought wryly. *I suppose the responsibility has to stop somewhere.* "And may God have mercy upon us."

"Amen."

Amos waited until the others had filed out to begin reorganizing the hundred-odd refugees.

"The enemy?" he asked softly.

"Four ships," Guiyon replied. "One turned back, I think, with engine problems—there were discontinuities in its emissions. The remainder are gaining slowly. I am running the engines over the specifications as it is, but they were never designed for this sort of usage. My estimate is that we have escaped so far because the Kolnari ships are carrying extra fuel mass and sublight maneuver engines. They are also not redlining their propulsion systems."

"Will we have enough lead-time to reach Rigel Base?"

"That is impossible to calculate," Guiyon said. His voice was slowly taking on an extra tinge of animation, like a piece of rusty machinery that turned more smoothly when warmed up after long disuse. "Too much depends on intervening factors—mass density in the interstellar medium, the enemy's actions, and what awaits us. We still have several possible destinations, but there may have been changes since the last update. My data is very old."

"As God wills," Amos said reflexively.

"Indeed."

The data-input jumped and fizzled through the jury-rigged inputs. Pain jagged along Guiyon's nerves in sympathy with the overstressed fabric of the ship. Anxiety ate at him as sector after sector went blank, a spreading numbness like leprosy.

Behind him, the rosette of pursuing Kolnari ships was mostly hidden by the blaze of his own drive energies. The sleeting energetic particles of their beam-weapons were not probing and eroding at the drive coils of the ancient, crumbling vessel. Ghost memories of the ship when it was young and strong haunted him, confusing his responses. His own nutrient and oxygen feeds kept slipping past redline, and each time the emergency adjustments took longer to swing the indicators back.

We will not make Rigel Base, Guiyon knew. He would not, and the ship would not. And if they could, the softshells on board most certainly would not. *I must select an alternate destination.*

If there is one.

CHAPTER THREE

"IS IT REALLY necessary to inspect in person, Ms. Hap?" the detection systems chief said. "We have a virtual system for remotes," he went on helpfully.

"No substitute for hands on," Channa said with determined cheerfulness.

She reached up to the hatchway and chinned herself, sliding into the narrow inspection corridor. "Hand me up the toolkit, will you?"

Two hours later the chief stood rigidly as Channa finished her checklist. His skin was a muddy gray under the natural brown, and he seemed to be shaking slightly.

"... and deviations are more than *thirty percent* beyond approved," she said crisply.

"Ms. Hap"—the luckless bureaucrat said, trying to cut in once more—"those long-range systems are purely backup. They haven't been used since the SSS was commissioned!" At her raised eyebrow, he continued hurriedly, "Besides, I'm understaffed, and—"

"Chief Doak," she went on. "Regular personal inspections are standard procedure in all installations of this type. I don't *care* if the equipment is used infrequently. Backups exist for an *emergency* when they had better be able to perform the functions for which they were designed. And I *don't care* if you send in the remotes every so often. Machinery does what you tell it to do, whether that's the right thing or not. Experienced technicians are supposed to have a feel for their

23

equipment. Your people obviously don't. This isn't satisfactory. Is that understood?"

"Yes, Ms. Hap," he said woodenly.

Bitch, she read in his eye. *That's fine. You have your right to an opinion of me, and I have a right to expect you to do your work,* she thought, turning and striding briskly for the door.

"I don't care what anyone says, Ms. Hap. I think you're going to do a great job."

It was one of the communications technicians. Channa smiled pleasantly at her and said softly, noting her name tag. "Frankly, Ms. . . . Foss, I don't give a damn *what* you think. I'm only concerned with the quality of your work. Which, at the moment, you're not doing." She continued down the corridor.

"Excuse me." Simeon said to Channa when she was out of earshot.

"Yes?"

"Did you have to be so nasty to her?"

"Simeon, it would be unprofessional of me to allow people to choose up sides like that. *We* can chew out a section chief, but interfering in the chain of command is petty and divisive and causes morale problems. Perhaps I'm not going to be here very long, and I'm unwilling to leave that sort of mess for someone else to sort out. You've got to nip these things in the bud."

"Nipping is one thing. You cut her off at the knees."

"Oh, I see. You think I was unkind."

"You *were*! In fact, you were downright cruel."

Channa stood a moment, hands on hips, looking down thoughtfully. Then she shifted her weight and crossed her arms. "Simeon, I noticed that Tell Radon was here twelve years longer than standard retirement date."

"He wasn't ready to go," Simeon replied suspiciously.

"But six years ago he submitted his resignation."

"He changed his mind and withdrew it. I wasn't about to force him out. He's a friend."

"Un-hunh. Well, when I glanced over some of the meeting records for the last few years, I couldn't help but notice that everyone behaved as though he wasn't there. On the infrequent occasions when he did make a contribution, it was immediately questioned. Or don't the words 'Is that right, Simeon' sound familiar?"

"So what are you getting at?"

"I'm getting at the basic difference in our styles, Simeon. When I'm cruel, it's to prevent more pain further down the line. When you're cruel, it's to get your own way."

"*What!*"

"Surely you know that consideration for a friend can go both ways? Maybe Tell Radon stayed because he knew you would prefer it that way. You've had things your own way around here for quite a long while now. I don't imagine you were looking forward to breaking in someone new. Some stranger who might want to do things *their* way instead of using the nice, smooth routines you've worked out over time."

"Where are you getting this bullshit?"

She shrugged. "It's that or you just got so used to seeing him humiliated on a daily basis that you didn't notice it anymore. Either way, it probably felt the same to him."

"I know him, Hap; you don't. If Tell had a problem, he would have said something. Why would he suffer in silence when he knew he could come to me?"

"Have you looked at the recordings?"

"I don't *have* to look at anything. I was there."

"They'll confirm what I've said, you know."

You corycium-plated bitch! "Has it occurred to you that you're biased? You've been finding fault with me since we said hello. Let me tell you something, omniscient one, you can't get a good impression of Tell from the recs. He hated the damn meetings. 'Hell,' he used to say, 'these frigging meetings make my brain melt.' He *rarely* spoke at meetings. They just weren't his style."

"Was it customary to question his every comment when he did speak?"

"You're making a simple request for confirmation sound like attempted murder."

Channa bit her lower lip. "Simeon, the recs will confirm that what I saw is there, very plain to see, unmistakable, clear, obvious. You might find a review of the meeting recs illuminating. Okay?"

After a moment's reflection, something in Simeon opened like an eye and he saw a bitter twist to Tell Radon's mouth. Tell had always described it as "gas," but . . .

"You fight dirty, Channa," he said.

She blushed, but her expression remained hostile. "I'm angry," she said honestly. "My career is in ribbons because you wanted him to stay on. So when I saw ..." She bit her lip again. Then she went on more calmly. "You have to be careful how you use expressions like, 'you cut her off at the knees' and 'you were cruel,' around me. It tends to set me off. Also, you could have taken me at my word instead of turning self-righteous."

"Yeah ... I'll remember that." He paused. "Y'know, if you're really so hot to get out of here, I'll back your transfer request to the hilt. Since I didn't get what I asked for last time, I figure I'm still owed a few favors—"

"Ho no. The last time you backed someone to the hilt, the hilt ended up protruding from between *my* shoulder blades. Thank you so much. Now that I think about it, I intend to give Central Admin plenty of time to forget this mess and my starring role in it. You're stuck with me for a couple of years, at least, so you'd better get used to it. Oh, on the subject of overlooking things ..."

"Yeah?" *What now? Is there dust on the light fixtures?*

"I came face to face with a little boy in one of the aft engineering compartments."

Silence.

"What? No comment? Does this mean that you know about him? After all, you *are* able to view all areas of the station."

In the silence that followed, she walked over to the wall and leaned casually against it. "He was gone before I could react. But you know what's really strange? There is *nothing* on file about such a kid." The silence lengthened. "Simeon?" she asked with some asperity.

"A little boy?"

"Yes, Simeon, about twelve years old—Standard—give or take a couple of years. In the aft power compartment. A restricted area, I believe. A kid who looks and smells like a Sondee mud-puppy. Whose child is he? What can you tell me about him? Don't even try to tell me you know nothing. Kids don't acquire a patina of dirt like that overnight. He also looked like he'd been eating regularly, if not well. So someone's been looking out for him ... minimally."

I don't think saying "You're cute when you're angry" would be a very good idea right now, Simeon thought. He froze her image and scanned it for temperature variations and pupil dilation. She was angry on behalf of an abandoned child rather than at him. *Which makes a nice change.*

Besides, he could use an ally with this problem.

"He calls himself Joat," Simeon confessed with a sigh. "I don't know how long he's been here. I discovered him by accident myself. He's mechanically brilliant. The area he's staked out as his own just stopped needing repairs. That's probably the only reason I investigated. I mean, there are enough squeaky wheels around here. Why take notice of one that's quiet? Then I noticed that the last repair made in that section was two years ago. I got curious about nothing ever going wrong. So I went on a prowl, using mobile bugs, and kept, well, softpersons refer to it as seeing things out of the corner of their eyes. I always thought that had something to do with blinking, you know, eyelashes getting in your line of sight or something. But I kept see- ing these flickers of movement and I *don't* blink. By turning up my sound reception I could sometimes hear little scrapes and movement, but there was a sort of 'white noise' masking it. It seemed unlikely that everything else in the area was running perfectly with the excep- tion of my sensors, so I decided to do a stakeout. Eventually, he got careless and wandered into my line of sight. The first time I spoke to him, blip, he disappeared. It was a long time before I could get him to talk to me. You'll note I said talk, not trust. He's incredibly wary. I can't believe he was clumsy enough to let you see him."

"Two *years*?"

Leave it to you, you bitchoid, to pick out the pertinent information. "I said the last logged repair was two years ago. It's been known to happen. What can I say? Somewhere from two years to two months, who knows?"

"Who is he, Simeon?"

"His story is that he ran away from a tramp freighter. Joat told me that the captain won him from his uncle in a card game. I know, I know, that sort of thing's illegal, but it *does* happen out here in the boonies. The tramp left abruptly and went somewhere not listed. Joat has never had it soft, but apparently, the captain he ran from was of a different order of brutality altogether."

Channa wrinkled her nose. "Sounds like something out of Dickens."

"Yeah, well, the more things change . . ." and he left the sentence dangling. "What are you going to do?" he asked warily. After his first, disastrously wrong, impression, Channa hadn't struck him as a bleed- ing heart. Would she suggest flooding the compartment to flush the poor kid out?

"We've got to get him out of there. We can't leave a little boy in a dangerous *and* restricted area. It's illegal at best and irresponsible by any standard."

"He's been badly hurt and frightened, Channa. He doesn't want to be with people. The little guy can barely tolerate me. He likes machinery better than people, and I qualify as a borderline case. Besides, even *I* can't find him if he really doesn't want to be found. Maybe we should leave him alone for the time being. He's where he wants to be."

Channa looked up with her jaw set. "Simeon, no child *wants* to be alone in the dark and the cold of a power room, or wherever he's lodged himself. He needs and deserves to be taken care of! It's his right."

"I agree in principle, but I think he needs more time. I'll take the responsibility."

"What does that mean?"

"I'll take full and complete responsibility for what happens to him."

Channa brightened. "Really?"

"Yeah, really."

"Okay," she said, "I'll call up some information on adoption procedures and we can get doings underway."

"*What?*" *I'm always screaming* what? *at this woman. I'm beginning to feel like a demented parrot.*

"Well, what else did you mean when you said you would accept responsibility?"

"That, if anything goes wrong, I'll answer for it." *I swear, if I had hair I'd tear it out. Softshells have some advantages after all. But, what is this . . . this . . . wench* trying to do to me?

"Great! If he gets killed or maimed, you'll accept a discommodation? Well, how big of you!" Channa cut Simeon off when he began to splutter a protest. "By now you should know that I listen to what you say, even when *you* don't. I promise you, Simeon. I will *always* call you on it when you try to shut me up or fob me off. You're not going to shuffle this one off, buddy. I won't let you."

"What are you talking about? I didn't put him in this situation. I want to help the kid. Hell, I *am* helping. I just don't see any need to rush him. The fact that you saw him may mean that he's almost ready to come out on his own. I'm certainly opposed to coercing him. Geeeze but you're hostile! You're so willing to believe the worst about me that every time I talk to you I feel like my circuits are being realigned. Am I really such an evil bastard? Or," and he changed his tone from plaintive to trenchant, "could it be that you really are the most bloody-minded, impossible woman I have ever met?"

"Oh, Simeon," she drawled, "you have no idea how difficult I can be. Just cross me if you want to find out."

A chill settled in Simeon's mind. *Does that mean that so far she's been reasonable? Gah!*

"You're about to become a father, Simeon. That's what full and complete responsibility for a child means. Congratulations, it's a boy. *If* your word is good."

"They're not going to let me adopt a kid."

"Why not? You've been extensively tested for emotional stability, you have a responsible job. You even appear to care very much about his feelings. Do you think such a wounded child, of his age, is going to have prospective parents lining up to take care of him? I think you've got a very good chance."

She clapped her hands and rubbed them together gleefully. "So . . . let's get to work on it."

Mart'an presented the menu with a flourish and left them with a bow.

Channa looked around wide-eyed at the dimly lit, subdued elegance of the Perimeter Restaurant. There were even actual beeswax candles burning on the tables; a fortune for material and air-bills both.

No pleasure like spending somebody else's money, she thought. The Perimeter was paying; something of a goodwill gesture. And it *was* logical for her to get acquainted with one of the station's premier tourist attractions.

SSS-900's finest restaurant was just down from the north-polar docking extension; the outer wall was a hundred-meter sheet of synthmet set on clear. Stars rolled huge and bright beyond—fixed stars and the frosty arch of the Snakeshead Nebula, and the bright moving points of light that were shuttles and tugs. Within, the floor was of glossy black stone set with squares of gold—SSS-900 processed a lot of gold as a by-product—and the tables were made of real and precious wood, glossy under the snowy linen tablecloths. Waiters moved amid a quiet chinking of silverware, savory smells wafting from the platters they carried. A live orchestra played something soft and ancient.

"Stars and comets—a little rich for this outposter!" Channa said. "I'd *heard* of the Perimeter, but somehow I never expected to actually come here."

Patsy grinned. "C'mon now, Hawking Station wasn't an asteroid minin' center. Leastwise, not of the sort our sainted Simeon cut his teeth on."

"Well, no . . . but I couldn't afford anything like this when I was at home. Didn't have the time, either. After I graduated and started pulling assignments, I've been mostly at outposts. *Worse* than Simeon's."

Waiters filled water glasses, laid their napkins in their laps, brought warm rolls and softened butter. *Everything except brush our teeth and massage our feet,* Channa thought. It was a little unnerving. Most places you asked for the selection, told the table what you wanted, and a float brought the meal to you. The sheer *expense* of having live human beings do all this!

"I'd never've et in here if it weren't on the station's ticket," Patsy confessed in a whisper during a lull in the service. "Or unless a date was *really* tryin' to impress me. More relaxin' with another female— you kin concentrate on the food without insultin' 'em."

"If this weren't complimentary, I wouldn't be here now, either."

They grinned at each other.

"Well, thank you fer invitin' me," Patsy said. "I woulda thought you might invite that med-tech you were talkin' to last night."

"Please, I'm looking forward to this meal. I won't be able to eat if I remember him. Have you heard some of his anecdotes?"

"All of 'em," Patsy said, nodding solemnly. "You've a point thar, ma'am. Chaundra's a nice enough feller, but his stomach's a mite too strong fer me."

"Besides, you and I have similar taste in music. You can always talk to someone who likes the same music."

Talk they did, touching on everything from Geranian folk ballads to eighteenth-century Earth composers, eventually matching the personnel of the station to various types of music.

"Simeon? Straight honky-tonk, no question," Channa said firmly.

Patsy laughed. "Oh, c'mon, Channa, there's unplumbed depths there. He's not that simple. It's just that the minin' center assignment came at an impressionable age fer him. Rough, tough rockjack, you know. His public image."

"Well." She looked down at the menu. It provided motion holos of the dishes as she ran her finger down the page. "I'll start with these grumawns, first, in the fiery sauce. Cleardrop soup. Grilled rack of jumbuk from Mother Hutton's World—good grief, they *do* have everything here!—baby carrots, salad. Spun pastry bluet confection for dessert, with Port Royal coffee. Castiliari brandy."

"Sounds good. I'll go with the jumbuk too, but . . . hmm. Fennel-leek soup first. Wine?"

"I don't usually—" Channa began.

"If I might suggest?" Mart'an appeared at their table. *Appeared*, Channa thought, as if he'd blinked out of some hypothetical sub-space. "The Mon'rach '97 to begin with, a half-bottle. Then, with the main course, a Hosborg estate-bottled '85. I'll open it now so it can breathe."

"Sure," Channa said, then sighed with pleasure. "You know, I *was* looking forward to the Perimeter, ever since they told me SSS-900 would be—"

"SSS-900-*C*, now, Ms. Hap."

Channa blushed. "—would be my next assignment."

The first course arrived. The pink grumawns were coiled steaming on top of a bed of fragrant saffron rice, the sauce to one side. Channa took a sip of the wine, chilled and with a faint scent of violets, then lifted one grumawn on the end of a two-tined fork.

"I *did* do a lot of work today," she murmured to herself. She opened her mouth, and—

The Confederate armor was grinding through the woods and fields north of Indianapolis. The burning city cast a pall of smoke into the sky behind them. Diesel engines pig-grunted as the smooth low-slung shapes of the tanks and tank-destroyers crashed through brush and twelve-foot high cornstalks, past the flaming shards of a farmhouse and barns. The long 90mm barrels of the tank guns swung toward the thin strung-out lines of the Union convoys, caught in the flank as they attempted to switch front. The fighting vehicles surged back on their tracks at each monster *crack* of high-velocity cannon fire, and the air filled with the bitter scent of cordite. Chaos spread through the blue ranks as tracer and cannon fire sent trucks exploding into globes of magenta fire. A Northern tank dissolved, the turret flipping up like a frying-pan, a hundred meters into the air.

Behind the fighting vehicles, long lines of men in gray uniforms followed, advancing with their semiautomatic rifles carried at the port. Here and there an officer carried a sword, or the Stars and Bars fluttered from a staff.

"Now!" General Fitzroy Anson-Hugh Beauregard III said into the bulky mike hung from his vehicle helmet.

His command tank was a little back from the edge of the combat,

hull down; the general stood head-and-shoulders out of the commander's cupola. The turret pivoted under him, the massive casting
moving smoothly on its bearing race. The long cannon fired in a flash
that seared his vision, just as the opening salvos of artillery went by
overhead. Down along the road, tall poplar-shapes of black dirt
gouted skyward. Another explosion shook the earth and sent heavy
vehicles pinwheeling like a child's models under a careless boot; the
command-tank's round had hit the tracked carrier for a Unionist self-
propelled gun.

The general nodded. "Nothing to stop us short of the Lakes," he
said. Nothing to stop them linking up with the British Guards
Armored Corps, driving southeast out of occupied Detroit, cutting
the Union in two. . . .

"Conceded," Florian Gusky said, and lifted the visor of the simulation helmet. He sighed heavily and took a pull of his beer, then
looked around the room as though surprised to find himself alone
with Simeon, blinking away the consciousness of a world and war
that had never been. There was a slight sheen of sweat on his heavy-
browed face and he worked the thick muscles of his shoulders to
loosen the tension.

"You could play it out to the end," Simeon's image said from a
screen above his desk.

"No dam' point. You've whipped my butt in that simulation *twice*,
from both Union and Confederate sides."

"I could take a handicap," Simeon said with much less enthusiasm, Gus noted.

So he nodded. The last time he had beaten Simeon was in a Caesar
vs. Rommel match on the site of Carthage, with the shellperson
commanding Caesar's spear-armed host against Panzers and Stukas.
Even then he had inflicted embarrassing casualties.

"Where is she?" Gus asked. There was no need to identify the
female in question.

"She's dining at the Perimeter."

Gus raised his eyebrows in astonishment. "The Perimeter? That's
some salary she gets." The Perimeter attracted two sets of guests: the
rich, and spacers looking to blow six months' pay on one night.

Simeon laughed. "Nah, she's a guest of the management. Patsy's
with her."

"Yeah, Patsy likes her," Gus said, his tone indicating that this revealed a serious and heretofore unsuspected flaw in Patsy's character. "Can you see them?"

"Yup."

"What're they doing?"

"Talking."

"About us?"

"I don't know. I'm not listening. Now they're laughing."

"They're talking about us, alright," Gus said gloomily.

"Geesh, Gus, let's get back to the game."

There was a plaintive edge to Simeon's voice. Gus reached for the helmet and then stopped, a slow grin creasing his heavy features.

"Isn't it about time we had a drill?" he said, thoughtfully.

"We just had one. About four hours ago, remember?"

"When I was in the Navy we had 'em six times a day, sometimes," Gus replied.

He knew that Simeon badly wanted to pull Navy duty. Only a few staff-and-command vessels used shell controllers and Simeon didn't rate, yet. In the meantime, he put a lot of weight on Gus' experience as a fire-control officer on a patrol frigate. That had been some time ago—Florian Gusky had spent a decade's hard work clawing his way up to regional security chief for Namakuri-Singh, the big drive-systems firm—but Simeon had a bad case of military romanticism. *And real talent,* he told himself without envy of the brain's abilities.

"I know it's early," Gus went on persuasively, "but it's important not to have predictable intervals. So we don't get complacent."

"Well . . ."

"I'd love to see the look on their faces."

"Since you put it that way—"

Channa started as the klaxons rang. They sounded like no other she had ever heard, a harsh repeated *ouuuuga-ouuuuga* sound. The elegant minuet of movement among the waiters turned to an inelegant but efficient scramble for the exits; some moved to assist guests. Thick slabs hissed up out of the floor along the outer wall and the lights flared bright.

"BREACH IN THE PRESSURE HULL!" a harsh male voice tone announced. "EMERGENCY PERSONNEL TO THEIR STATIONS. SECURE ALL SUBSECTION REFUGE AREAS."

Patsy stood and looked at her barely touched entree with dismay. "Damn! That's the second time this shift!" She threw her napkin down with disgust. "Simeon pulls these drills like a boy kickin' over an anthill to see the bugs scurry."

"Simeon!" Channa shouted.

"Yeah?" The klaxons dimmed in a globe around them.

"Is this a genuine emergency or just a test?"

"Excuse me, brawn-o'-mine, but you're not supposed to be privy to that information." There was the hint of a smug smile in the brain's voice.

"If you think I'm getting up from the best meal that's ever been put in front of me just because you're feeling your oats, you've got another thing coming. Cut it!"

As the klaxon abruptly ceased, people stopped, puzzled, and milled around uncertainly.

"Tell them it's over, Simeon. Don't just leave them standing there."

"This has been a test," Simeon informed them in the feminine tones he used for such announcements. "Return to your stations. This has been a test."

"We will discuss this later," Channa assured him icily. "Overdoing drills is dangerous, irresponsible and generally counterproductive."

Ah, hell, Simeon thought exhaustedly, *why did I listen to you, Gus? I don't think you like the looks on their faces after all, buddy. I know I don't.* He wondered what he could do to make it impossible for her to gain access to him for the next week.

Patsy sat down slowly, her wide eyes fixed on Channa's flushed countenance. "You really don't lahk him, do ya?" she said with some astonishment.

Channa looked at her blandly. "Whatever makes you say that?"

Patsy shook her head. "Just a hunch."

Channa sighed and smiled ruefully. "Well, to be fair, there may be a touch of 'transference' there. You see, I've always wanted to work planet-side. I love the feel of wind in my hair and rain on my face. I enjoy splashing in an ocean, and the feel of earth under my feet. So, for the past two years I've been campaigning for a particular assignment." She looked up at Patsy inquiringly. "Have you ever been to Senalgal?"

Patsy nodded and smiled warmly in reminiscence. "I sher have. I had my first honeymoon thar. What a gorgeous place! Beautiful beaches, warm ocean, flowers eve'rwhar, and the *food*. I'd love to live thar, at least fer a while." She sighed. "So, go on."

"Well, as you can imagine, the competition was incredible. I'd been through twelve interviews, including one with Ita Secand, the city-manager of Kelta, whom I would have been working with. God! What I wouldn't give to work with her. She's witty, charming, sophisticated. I felt that I could learn so much from her. It had come down to two of us, myself and someone else."

She shook her head. "I never did know who the other candidate was, but my feeling was that it was going to be an extremely difficult choice. When suddenly, after holding on for twelve years, Tell Radon decides that he has to retire right now! And that sweet little plum, that was almost in my hand, was snatched away so fast it left scorch marks on my nail polish. 'You're station born and bred,' they told me. 'You're perfect for this assignment,' they said. 'It's an extremely important and prestigious post,' they assured me. Rurrrgh! As the saying goes, I could just spit."

Patsy looked at Channa's bitter face.

"It's a gyp, alright. Looks like yer skills ah goin' against you instead of helpin' you out. So, maybe you ah takin' it out on Simeon jest a teensy bit?" She grinned and held up a hand that measured out a micrometer between thumb and forefinger. "Hey, maybe that's good fer him. Now, I think," she placed a hand on her bosom, "that we need you mo'n Senalgal does. I mean, Senalgal's gonna be special whoever runs it, right? But a station, well, it can be just a big ol' factory with the wrong people in charge. You don't need Ita Secand t' teach you to be witty and sophisticated—you already ah. We need some a' that right here, Ms. Hap, an I'm not kiddin'."

Channa blushed and grinned, taking a sip of her wine to hide her embarrassment.

"Well, thank you. That's quite a challenge you've set me," she murmured, and changed the subject. "Who was that big, handsome, gray-haired fellow you were talking to last night? Somehow I never met him."

"Florian Gusty?"

"*Florian?*"

"We call him Gus."

"I can see why."

Patsy smiled warmly. "He's quite a guy—a retired Navy man, a crack navigator. The stories he's got . . . I mean to tell you, mmhm."

"I see he's spoken for," Channa said with a grin.

"Not so you'd notice," Pasty said primly. "I admit I lahk him, though. I jus' love to heah him talk. When I was a kid, I thought I'd do what he did. You know, join the Navy and scour the universe of evil doers, jus' like some ferocious holo-hero." She sighed. "But heah I am, nothin' but an algae-herder."

"An algae-herder?" Channa asked in amusement. "Algae travel in herds?"

"Oh, you know what I mean. Instead of doin' somethin' adventurous, I'm just watchin' these bubblin' vats o' goop. The excitement is not goin' to give me ulcers." She sighed. "Sometimes I wish fer a *real* disaster. Something special."

Channa looked at her seriously. "Be careful what you wish for," she said. "You may get it."

Channa hummed tunelessly as she filled out the adoption forms, looking perfectly content and at peace with the world. The sound irritated Simeon excessively. True, he could in a sense "leave" the area and had done so. But he kept coming back, as though to a blown circuit; drawn to the irritant, checking again and again to see if anything had changed.

Finally he said, "You seem happy." *Hap. Happy. Bet that would bug her* bad.

"I love filling out forms," she said. "The more complex the better."

Somehow it figures, Simeon thought. *When you became a brawn, the universe lost a great tax auditor.*

"Filling out your side of this is no problem," she said. "Your whole life is on file. But I'm going to have to talk to the child soon."

"I can do that," he said defensively. *I can also fill out the damn forms, in half the time or less and without making obnoxious noises.*

She turned to look at the column that held him. "Simeon . . . while I grant you that we should be as delicate as possible." She paused and gestured helplessly. "I've . . . *we've,* got to get him to Medical. We've got to prove, by retinal patterns and gene analysis, that he exists at all. You know how bureaus are: no tickee, no washee. We've got to do a recorded interview of him. So he's got to emerge, fully grown—well, almost—from the engineering compartments and into the real world," she concluded in a rush.

"Okay, I'll talk to him."

"Simeon," she hesitated, "why don't you introduce us? I mean, you can discuss the adoption with him. I can stay out of sight nearby until he wants to meet me."

She's being conciliatory, he realized. *Why doesn't this reassure me?* He forced down nonexistent hackles and replied in a neutral tone. "Sure, why not?"

Channa could hear them talking from where she sat against the cold bulkhead.

"You want to adopt me?" a young voice asked in disbelief. A yearning hope sounded through it.

"Yeah," Simeon said, surprised to find that he was getting to like the idea.

Joat's head popped into Simeon's line of sight, seemingly from out of nowhere.

"You can't do that," he said with complete certainty, voice flat again. "They won't let you adopt a kid. You're not real."

Simeon was taken aback. "What do you mean I'm not real?"

Joat's young face was lit with amused wonder. "I hate to be the one to break your bubble, but who's going to let a computer adopt a kid?"

"Where did you get the idea that I'm *just* a computer?" Simeon demanded with a hard edge to his tone.

Channa bit down on the fleshy part of her hand. *That kid doesn't pull his punches,* she thought. *Poor Simeon brain, though, does the offended dignity bit well . . .* She stifled the rising guffaw with a swallow. An audible reaction would be out of place. Definitely.

"*You* told me," Joat informed him, exasperation creeping into his voice. "You said 'I am, in effect, the station.' That means you're a machine. I've heard about AIs and voice-address systems."

To both his observers, his voice was conciliatory but his expression reflected an inner anxiety that maybe this computer was losing its tiny mind.

And he probably thinks that would be very *interesting, the station computer losing function,* Simeon thought in exasperation. *Kids!*

He had noted that, while Joat could keep his voice disciplined, his expression revealed his real feelings. Simeon wondered if he could maintain that duality in the presence of the visually-advantaged. Not that he, Simeon, was in any way visually-*dis*advantaged. Quite the opposite, as Joat would learn soon enough. "Joat, I think it's time that notion got altered. There's someone nearby I'd like you to meet. She's known as a brawn, and she's my mobile partner." *Which was true as far as it went,* Simeon amended.

Joat's face went wary. "I don't want to meet anybody," he muttered sullenly, looking cautiously around him. "She, you said?" Another pause. "No, I don't want to meet *anyone.*"

"But we've already met, sort of," Channa called out.

Joat vanished instantly.

"He's gone," Simeon said.

"No, he's not," Channa contradicted. "He's nearby. Joat? Simeon is a real person, as real as you or me. But he *is* connected to the station in such a way that the station is an extension of his body. I'd be happy to tell you about it."

No answer but a receptivity which she could almost feel beyond her in the narrow access aisle.

"Well," she began, "shellpeople were created as a means of enabling the disadvantaged to live as normal a life as possible. At first that was limited to the creation of miniaturized tongue or digital controls, or body braces. The extension of such devices was to encapsulate the entire body, though some people still think it's just the person's brain—because they're called 'brains.' Despite popular fiction, such an inhumanity is not permitted. Simeon is there, body, mind and . . ." She paused and then realized that she couldn't permit personal opinion to corrupt the explanation. " . . . heart. Simeon is a real person complete with his natural body but he is also this station-city in the sense that instead of walking about it, he has sensors that gather information for him and he controls every function of the station from his central location."

"Where is—" Joat paused, too, struggling to comprehend the concept "—he? He is a he, isn't he?"

"I'm as masculine as you," Simeon said, accustomed to such an explanation of shellpeople but wishing to underline his *humanity.* He did note that his voice had dropped further down the baritone level he used. *Well, why not?*

"Oh!"

"Instead of having to give orders to subordinates," Channa went on, "to, say, check the life-support systems, or Airlock 40, or order an emergency drill, he can do it himself more quickly and more thoroughly than any independently mobile person could."

"And I don't need to sleep, so I'm on call all the time." Simeon couldn't resist adding that.

"Never sleep?" Joat was either appalled or awed.

"I don't require rest, although I do like relaxation and I have a hobby. . . ."

"Not now, Simeon, although—" and there was a smile in Channa's voice "—I admit that that makes you more human."

"Were you human . . . I mean, were you . . . did you live like one of us?" Joat asked.

"I am human, not a mutant, or a humanoid, Joat," Simeon said reassuringly. "But something happened when I was born, and I'd never have been able to walk, talk, or even live very long unless the process of encapsulating had been invented. Usually it's babies that become shellpeople. We are more psychologically adjusted to our situation than adults. Though sometimes pre-puberty accident victims work out well as shellpeople. I can look forward to a long and very useful life. But I'm human for all of that."

"Very human," Channa replied in a droll voice.

Simeon didn't quite like the implications, but at least she *said* the right things.

"And *you* run the city?"

"I do, having instantaneous access to every computerized aspect of such a large and multi-function space station as well as peripheral monitoring devices in a network to control traffic in and out."

"I thought brains only ran ships," Joat said after a long pause.

"Oh, some do, of course," Simeon said, slightly patronizing, "but I was specially chosen and trained for this demanding sort of work." He ignored the delicate snort from Channa that somehow reminded him he'd started out his management career in a less prestigious assignment. "Do you understand now that I *am* human?"

"I guess so," was Joat's unenthusiastic reply. "You've been in that shell since you were a *baby?*"

"Wouldn't be anywhere else," Simeon said proudly, letting his voice ring with a sincerity no shellperson ever had to counterfeit.

There was a slightly longer pause. "Then it's not true, what I heard?" Joat began tentatively.

"Depends on what you heard," Channa said, having learned in academy the long list of atrocities supposedly enacted.

"That they put orphaned kids in boxes?"

"*Absolutely not!*" Channa and Simeon chorused in loud unison.

"That's totally inaccurate," Channa said firmly. "It's the sort of mean thing people say to scare kids, though. The program won't accept perfectly healthy bodies. To begin with, the medical costs and education are incredibly expensive. So is the maintenance for shellpersons. But it's better than depriving a sound mind of life because the body won't function normally. Don't you think so?"

Silence greeted that query.

"And if you've also heard the one about taking the brains from the homeless or displaced—no, that is definitely not permitted, either."

"You're sure?"

"Sure!" Simeon and Channa replied firmly.

"And we should know," Channa went on. "I had to spend four years in academy to learn how to deal with shellpeople, of all types."

Which, Simeon knew, *was another backhanded slam at him. Did she never let up?* One thing was sure, Joat's misinformation made him more determined than ever to adopt the boy and give him such security that that sort of macabre stuff would be forgotten.

"And, no matter what sort of spaceflot you've been told, Central Worlds doesn't make slaves of people," Channa was saying at her most emphatic. "The very idea sends chills up my spine."

"Not even criminals?"

"Especially not criminals," Channa said with a little laugh. "With all the power available to a shellperson, you may be very sure Central Worlds makes certain that they are psychologically conditioned to a high ethical and moral standard."

"What's this e'tical?" Joat asked.

"Code of conduct," Simeon said, "probity, honesty, dedication to duty, *personal* integrity of the highest standard."

"And you *own* this station?" Joat asked, his voice tinged with awe.

Channa laughed in surprise at that assumption.

"I wish," Simeon said fervently.

"Remember my mentioning that creating and training a shellperson is expensive? I wasn't kidding. By the time Simeon graduated from training, he had an enormous debt to pay off to Central Worlds."

"Hunh. Thought you said they weren't slaves."

"They're not. Every shellperson has the right to pay off their debt and become a free agent. A good many shippersons do and then they own themselves. A management shellperson, like Simeon, will often get their debt picked up by a corporation, and when they've worked off the debt, they work under contract."

"Are you paid off, Simeon?"

"No, though my contract fee is generous enough. But, as I mentioned, I have hobbies . . ."

"Like what?" Joat asked.

"I've got a great sword and dagger collection which includes a genuine Civil War flag, a regimental eagle."

"Hey, way cool! Got any *guns*?"

What is it with some males? Channa thought.

"Yeah," Simeon said eagerly. "I've got a real Brown Bess flintlock, and an M22. And one of the first backpack lasers ever issued!"

"No shit!" Joat said, seeming to forget Channa's presence for a moment. His voice sounded louder, as if he was drifting back from whatever refuge he had bolted towards. "All sorts of old weapons, eh?"

"You name it. A Roman gladius, even."

"A what?"

"Good question," Channa said.

"Shortsword. Over three thousand years old," Simeon broke in. A pause. "Of course, it could be a reproduction. If so, it's *still* in awfully good shape for an artifact of that age. I can trace it back at least five hundred years' provenance. The records say it was first owned by the legendary collector Pawgitti, then dug up out of the ruins of his villa."

My throat is getting hoarse, Channa realized an hour later. *Amazing what he knows.* Joat had probably neatly escaped formal education, but had acquired a jackdaw's treasure chest of information about his keener interests. Anger awoke in her. It was criminal that a mind like Joat's had been ignored, like a weed in a corner lot. Or the barbaric way in which pre-shell handicapped were ignored as non-productive persons. Joat wasn't just interested in showing that he knew things that she didn't, either. There was a naked hunger to *learn* in his voice. Closer and closer . . . She could see a little huddled shadow and an occasional glint of his eyes as he turned his head.

"And weapons are merely a part of what I've been collecting over the years," Simeon was saying. "I've got great strategy games—whole boards . . ."

Channa was shocked. Simeon would adopt the kid as a games partner? Then she realized he was only sweetening the pot.

"I don't know of a shellperson who has adopted, but I think it would be to your advantage, Joat. Certainly it would mean security and a place to call your own instead of ducking from one hidey-hole to the next when inspection teams go through. You'd have regular meals, and you could go to engineering school."

Channa heard a soft "yeah" from out of the cold darkness.

"Think it over tonight, why don't you?" Simeon said. "Tomorrow you can come up and scan the room I can assign you. Maybe have dinner with Channa and talk about it some more."

"Yeah," came more clearly from out of the darkness.

"Okay," Simeon's voice was pleased. "If you have any questions tonight, just speak 'em out, and I'll answer."

CHAPTER FOUR

IT'S AN HONOR to win the trust of a child, Simeon thought, *especially one who's been through what this kid has. I don't think I've ever been quite this happy.* He intuited that the feeling approximated what the word "tickled" meant, and he also thought that this was what it felt like to smile. Since Joat had moved in, he'd been trying to empathize more with the softperson worldview.

Of course, there have *been some surprises. . . .*

Seen for the first time by the full light of day-cycle floros, Joat was not prepossessing. Short for his age, scrawny to the point of emaciation, with huge blue eyes in a face that might have been any color short of black under the gray, ground-in coating of grime and machine oil. The mouse-brown hair had been hacked off and was standing up in tufts. The clothing was an adult-sized coverall with the arms and legs cut off to fit. An air of sullen suspicion accompanied a pungent odor.

"I've never run across the name, 'Joat' before," Channa began casually. "It doesn't give a clue about where you're from the way that some names do. I use 'Hap' as a surname because I was born on Hawking Alpha Proxima Station, for example."

"Joat's *my* name." Joat answered, sticking his chin out aggressively. "I gave it to myself. It means 'jack-of-all-trades,' 'cause that's what I do, some of everything."

"So it's a nickname," Channa said. "Shall we put you down on the form as Jack, then?"

Joat looked at her with cool contempt. "Why? That's a *boy's* name."

"You're a . . . girl?" Simeon asked, bringing the "g" sound up from the depths of his diaphragm and managing to split the word in several astonished syllables.

"What's wrong with that? *She's* a girl!" Joat declared defensively, pointing at Channa, as though ducking responsibility.

Channa burbled with heavily suppressed laughter before she managed some reassurance. "Hey, it's all right that you're a girl. It's just that . . . All that dirt . . ." Channa couldn't risk continuing in that vein and switched abruptly " . . . is an effective disguise."

"Good disguise," Joat said proudly. "Bad idea to let people know when you're a girl. Can cause you trouble. But, since you say I gotta go to a medic," she paused to look questioningly at Channa who nodded, "best you don't look surprised then." She grinned slyly and then looked over at Simeon's column. "You really didn't know?"

"Not a clue," he said wonderingly, and Joat giggled with pleasure. "Hmm. According to the biological studies I had, it's not easy to tell with the pre-pubescent . . . dressed or in disguise."

"*I* can always tell," Joat said with some contempt for his ignorance. "You're a softshell."

"You *sure* you're not a computer?"

"Yes, I *am*—stop teasing!"

Joat grinned unrepentantly. Simeon felt an unfamiliar sensation and tried to identify it. *A flutter in the ribcage?* he thought wonderingly.

"Why haven't they answered the tight-beam?" Simeon asked nervously a week later. "I *sent* everything. The forms were all correct."

"It's a bureaucracy," Channa said soothingly.

"Oh? That's supposed to *reassure* me?" Simeon said. A moment later: "Why is Joat's room always a mess? I send in the servos twice a day and it's still in a maximum-entropy state."

"It's called 'adolescence,' Simeon," Channa said. "At least she seems to be settling in at school."

Simeon's image winced. Joat had unexpectedly cleaned up as pretty, though she had wrinkled her nose when he'd mentioned *that*. She seemed to trust him—Channa as well—to a limited extent. Any further social interfacing was . . . lacking.

"She gets in too many fights," he said. She also fought very, very dirty. He winced again when he thought of the places some blows, kicks and punches had landed.

"She's not used to interacting except as a potential victim," Channa replied. "I don't think she's ever been with anyone in her own age group. She certainly doesn't know the local rituals. She's an outsider—practically a feral child. We're lucky she can respond to other human beings at all."

An awkward silence fell for a moment. Unspoken: *and she didn't think you were human when she met you.*

"She's learned about daily showers," Simeon pointed out helpfully.

"Oh, there's good stuff in Joat," and Channa grimaced. "Even if her brand of ethics is unusual, at least she's consistent in applying it. All she needs is some security and a chance."

"Isn't that all *anybody* needs?"

Several hours later, Simeon still glowed with satisfaction in their accomplishments with Joat. *This, being a father thing, is great,* he thought, and wanned measurably towards Channa. *I've got to thank her.*

For the first time since she had arrived, Simeon looked into her quarters and was surprised at how, in that short time—under two weeks, although it seemed like more—it had changed from the spartan chamber Tell Radon had occupied. She had tinted the walls a soft, off-pink and had put "paint-chips" into the permanently installed frame-projectors. The jewel-bright colors and romantic images of the pre-Raphaelites, Alma-Tadema and Maxfield Parrish glowed from the walls, along with some modern Mintoro reproductions. The bedspread was an icy gray satin on which were scattered embroidered pillows of peach and gray and blue.

"Say, Channa," he said in tones of pleased approval, "I like what you've done with the room."

Channa emerged from the bathroom clad in a blue silk robe trimmed with lace, a brush in her hand and swept out of her quarters into the main lounge without saying a word. She stopped in front of Simeon's column and crossed her arms, her eyes blazing. All Simeon's warm feelings fell into cold ash as he looked out at her. Maybe if he didn't say anything, she'd go away and not say whatever it was that was burning inside her eyes. *Nah, when have I ever been that lucky where she's concerned?*

Her body was rigid, though her shoulders twitched and her lips opened several time. He'd better say something to stem the acid eruption.

Using as casual and complimentary tone as he could manage, he said, "You have very romantic tastes, Channa," which seemed to reduce her blazing eyes a degree or two. He'd never know why he continued: perhaps sheer mischief to get a little of his own back. "Though your bed looks amazingly like an ice cube."

She blinked in astonishment and he thought, *A hit! A very palpable hit!* But then she took a deep breath.

"I did not think," she said, every word precise and polished, "that it would be necessary to actually say this, *but* since I must, I shall. Because we got off on the wrong foot and I did *not* trust you, I swept my quarters for active scanners." She crossed her arms. "You will please," she went on with careful emphasis, "not ever enter my quarters without knocking and requesting admittance, *and* waiting for my express permission to enter. Is that clear, Simeon?"

"I apologize, Channa. Of course you're right. I got careless, all those years with Tell."

"As to the quality of my taste . . ." she said in a voice even more brittle than before.

Oh please, he thought, *for once, just once, shut up and let it go.*

" . . . it's none of your business." She glared at him. "Given your own preference for interior decoration," she said indicating his sword and dagger collection, "I'd say you have titanium gall to make snarky remarks about mine."

"But I like it. I said I liked it!"

"And what," she continued unheeding, "would someone with such a morbid fascination with humanity's lapses into ritualized slaughter know about romance anyway?"

Simeon was dumbstruck. "I've never . . . thought of my interest in military history as a 'morbid fascination.' I am genuinely fascinated by strategy and military tactics. But to call it morbid, well, romance and morbidity have a long and interesting relationship."

She sighed with exasperation. "Let's just say that while *both* can be morbid, romance and militarism make uncomfortable . . ." and she winced " . . . bedfellows."

"Channa, some of the most romantic people in history have been military personnel. Doesn't the very word 'warrior' conjure up romantic images?"

She shook her head discouragingly. "Not to me!"

"Not even 'knights in shining armor?' "

She groaned. "Look, Simeon, it's late and I'm tired. Let's just say that I don't like my privacy invaded at any time, by anyone." Her lips curled in a slight rueful grin. "But I think I overreacted a tad. Especially when you made fun of my decor."

"Well, you might wait till you're actually *being* made fun of before you start clawing pieces out of people."

"Sorry."

"Romance has its place," he murmured.

She smiled sardonically and raised one eyebrow. "With all due respect, Simeon, I doubt that romance has crossed your mind. Real, genuine romance, with its aspects of tenderness and sentiment are, if you'll excuse me, beyond your ken."

There was more challenge than honest regret in her voice, and he took offense. "Because I'm a shellperson?" he asked, fairly purring with suppressed anger.

Channa's jaw dropped. "N-no, of course not!" she said, stammering slightly. Then she caught herself and shook her hairbrush at him. "What a nasty, evil, slimy debater's trick! You know perfectly well that I never even thought of that! What I meant was that so far in our acquaintance, you have yet to demonstrate that you are sensitive, or idealistic or . . . well, tender. Passion, now—I think you've very effectively conceptualized raw, basic, animal passion. Which does not exist in the same universe as romance."

"Let me tell you something, Ms. Hap. I'm well aware that romance happens in the mind and the soul and the heart. I know that it isn't necessarily a physical thing. Remember Heloise and Abelard . . ."

"Great warrior couple, were they?" she asked smiling.

He sighed to himself. *What do they teach them in university these days?* "Not they, milady. I see I must persuade you beyond any measure of doubt. You've put me on my mettle." She cocked her head at him. "I shall court you, *belle dame sans merci,* and win your heart."

She laughed aloud in astonishment. "You've got your work cut out for you. I may like the romantical—as decor—but I'm no dewy-eyed sentimentalist and not at all susceptible."

"Oh, so you're seduction-proof, are you?"

"I'm not even going to dignify that with an answer. Goodnight, Simeon."

"Goodnight, Channa," he said quietly as she left without another word.

Not susceptible, eh, Happy baby? Well, get ready for it, sweetheart— you're in for the time of your life! You want romance? I'll give you

*romance, little lady, in such subtle and clever portions, you won't realize
that you're being wooed by a very personal phantom lover.*

He settled down to consider his strategy. Softshells could rely on
physical attraction for starters; that was impossible for him, of course.

How to begin, he wondered. *Well, with Channa, I suppose I could
start with deft cooperation and nineteenth-century manners. I'd better look into the mores of Hawking Alpha Proxima Station and see
what their courting customs are. Nothing so blatant as gifts right off,
hmmm. Ah-ha! Music! After all, it hath charms to soothe the savage beast, or breast. Both apply in this case. Now, I'll just access her
musical repertoire—which doesn't invade her privacy, merely her overt
records . . .*

"Hey, Simeon, what's going on?" Joat said, turning from her breakfast to stare at his column.

"Going on, my dear?" Simeon said.

"Yeah, going on. All of a sudden you're so smooth you'd make a
wombat puke, and Channa looks as if she'd just found a dead body,
a long-time dead body."

Channa snorted suddenly. Since she was in the middle of a
mouthful of coffee, the results were spectacular. Joat silently offered
her a napkin as she coughed and sputtered.

"You're imagining things," Simeon replied, with a touch of asperity.
He shifted into a mellow tone: "Are you all right, Channa?"

"What's wrong with Simeon?" Patsy asked, sotto voce. They were
in the shadow of an impeller pump, and the vibration would make
voice-pickup difficult.

"Wrong?" Channa said, frowning.

"Yeah, he's *agreein'* all the time."

"Now that you mention it . . ."

The woman from Larabie shrugged. "Don't look a gift horse in
the mouth, Chan. But, if you do, check the teeth fer file-marks."

Chief Administrator Claren gave a final keystroke.

"That's the projections matched against the past five years," he said.
"You'll note turnover is a little high, but on a transit station, it's
difficult to keep people."

Channa frowned. "I'd think it would be easier here," she said. "More
big-city facilities."

"Also easier to leave," Claren pointed out, nodding towards the large passenger terminal.

"We should do more in the way of social and cultural activities," Channa said. "The contingency fund would cover it, and in the long run, such amenities pay for themselves and then some. There are a *lot* of mining and exploration sectors around here"—which was exactly why SSS-900-C had been established in the middle of the cluster of mineral-rich fifth-generation suns—"and their people need leisure activities just as much as their equipment and ships need servicing. The Perimeter's a gold mine for its owners and for the station, to name your only real star attraction. If the outposters could get entertainment and commissary supplies in a range from cheap to expensive, they wouldn't need to travel further in towards Center. This whole area would take a big step further toward being *part* of the Central Worlds and not just a primitive frontier zone."

"Exactly, Ms. Hap," Claren said. He was a mousy-looking little man, with thinning black hair combed back over his head. He dressed like a humorist's caricature of a bureaucrat, down to the keypad holder on his belt. "It's what I've been saying for years."

"What do you think, Simeon?" Channa asked.

"Sounds good to me," the affable city manager replied.

Claren coughed violently; one of his hovering assistants scurried forward with a glass of water.

Channa waited until he had recovered. "Surprise you, did he?"

"Surprise me? Me? No, no, something caught in my throat. Air's dry, I think." He hastily swallowed another sip of water to reinforce that interpretation. "Now, here," and his fingers flew over the key of his terminal, "are some plans we've had pending, with the projected—"

"Answer the question, please, Administrator Claren," she said firmly but quietly. She might be new, but she could recognize "sign now, *please*," when she heard it.

"Well, ah, this isn't the first time these specific projects have been put forward," Claren said. "But, ah, there has never been a sufficiently positive reaction to implement the schemes. Until now, that is. It's a pleasure to work with someone who can appreciate planning ahead and is so naturally decisive. Ahhhhh, oh dear." His voice trailed off.

Channa's took on a steely note. "Changed our mind, have we, Simeon?"

"This station wasn't in a position to plunge into such an ambitious project. Much less have the incentive," Simeon replied smoothly. "Tell was a roughneck like me. Neither of us had the background for coordinating such enterprises. Here, anyway."

Channa turned, subliminally aware of something moving through the air behind her. It was a message tray, floating at elbow height. The domed top folded back, revealing chilled glasses and a frosted, uncorked bottle of a fine vintage. A single red rose lay on the white napery. Her lips grew thin but, as she saw Claren watching her closely and knew that she must be flushing, she controlled her impulse to sling the bottle at the sensor that linked Simeon to this office.

"Yes, by all means let us drink to the success of this undertaking, Claren," she said and began to pour.

Facetiously, she lifted her glass towards the sensor and sipped, mildly surprised at the dry crisp taste. "Hmm. Not a bad white! Didn't know you had it in you, Simeon."

"I'm not without a few talents of mine own," he replied, wishing there was an imager in Claren's office so he could project the suave smile he was feeling.

She downed the rest of the glass, replacing it on the float. "If you'd just transfer the plans to my terminal, Administrator Claren, I can peruse them at my leisure." Then she strode purposefully out of the office.

She was storming by the time she got to their lounge. "I bet you think you were being *subtle*! *Subtle* like colliding with an asteroid, you—" She swung around to the screen which he had prudently left blank, giving her anger no focus. Then she began to hear the sounds filling the room.

Simeon delightedly watched her expression gradually alter from livid to astonished and finally to enchanted as the lilting sounds of the Reticulan mating croon filled the lounge. The sounds were long, low, dreamy. There was no formal melody, but somehow the theme suggested the stillness of deep forest and dew falling like liquid diamond in streaks of sunlight dazzling through the leaves.

Channa stood still for a moment. She winced slightly as the door closed with an audible swoosh, annoyed that any other sound marred the perfection of what she was hearing. Then, stepping carefully, as though fearful that cloth brushing against cloth or shoe against carpet might cause her to lose a precious second of the complex music that surrounded her, she walked to a chair. She sat down so slowly she seemed to float down to it, scarcely seemed to breathe as she absorbed the music.

My first impression of her was correct, Simeon thought, watching Channa. *She* is *a fox!* Then, peering more closely, he wasn't so sure, for her eyes were half-closed, starred with tears, and his acute vision let him see the skin of her face relaxing, smoothing out. *She doesn't look that foxy now! In fact, she looks kinda . . . sweet.*

When the croon had drifted off into a serene silence, she sat without moving. Then she closed her eyes and slowly leaned back, clasping her hands before her. When she opened her eyes, they shone and her voice was husky.

"Oh, Simeon . . . I can forgive you a lot of tricks for *that!* I might even kiss you. In appreciation, of course. That was so beautiful. Thank you," and she smiled.

Simeon modulated his voice so that there was a "smile" in his tones when he answered her. "You're welcome. Do you happen to know what that was?" He didn't think she was likely to, but he kept *that* out of his tone.

She wiped an eye and said, "I've never had the opportunity to hear one, but that has to be a Reticulan croon."

"You're right about that," Simeon said with satisfaction. "But I'll bet you'll never guess who performed it." He tried hard to keep any smugness out of his voice.

"Now, how would I know *who* sang, much less who could, beside Reticulans, and they're on the other side of this galaxy. Oh! It couldn't be . . ." Her eyes went round in awed surprise. "Not *Helva*? She's supposed to be able to sing them. But . . . you . . . and Helva, the ship who sings?"

"None other." Simeon was gratified by her reaction.

"You know her?"

"Indeed I do," and Simeon allowed himself to speak with considerable pride. "She drops by every now and then to visit—" he couldn't resist a little pause for effect "—me. We discuss and exchange contemporary music from all parts of the galaxy. Since there are so few recordings of Reticulan croons—which we shellpeople enjoy so much—she herself made me a gift of this one." The memory of his thrill at receiving such a prize colored his tone.

Channa smiled in response. "Finally read my personnel tape, did you?"

"Well, I'd love to say that I'm just terribly perceptive, but music's mentioned as a significant interest. I just thought this particular recording might please, too."

"Oooh," she said with a quaver in her laugh, "music hath charms department? As you said not long ago," and there was an edge of combined sarcasm and chagrin, "you have a few talents." Then she added brightly, "Do you sing, too? That's not mentioned in your personals."

Simeon made a throat-clearing, clearly self-deprecating sound. "I am *not* like Helva and make no claims to musical discrimination. I listen to what I like, but I don't know if I'll like something until I hear it."

"So what else have you heard and liked?" she asked, relaxed in the afterglow of the beautiful croon. "Besides rockjack, that is?"

His tone was embarrassed. "I really don't *like* Rant much. I just got used to it, you know. The guys on those early mining belt assignments I had didn't play anything else. Most of what I *like* turns out to be classical or operatic."

"Me, too," she said, smiling towards his column with a kindliness he had not seen in her before. "Well, if Helva liked you enough to give you that superb Reticulan recording, and you actually *admit* to a preference for classical and operatic, perhaps we should call a truce?"

"A truce? Do we need one?"

She narrowed her eyes. "In a manner of speaking, we do. We have struck a few sparks." She grinned. "A mutual appreciation of music is so far probably the firmest common ground between us. Halfway through secondary school, I realized that my best friends were also my choirmates." She leaned toward the column, with the first intimacy she had so far shown him. "We used to produce and cast ghost operas."

"You did what?"

"We'd choose a subject or theme, and a composer, then select a cast. The rules said that composer and cast have to be dead."

"Really? How bizarre!" Simeon paused to consider the notion. "Do go on."

"We'd start with . . . the name of this opera. Say, 'Rasputin.' Have you heard of him?" The merry tone of her voice was subtly teasing, challenging him.

"Of course, I have. He's often credited with being the indirect cause of a successful revolution."

She regarded his column with a wry expression. "You would know about him if he caused a war, wouldn't you?"

"Do we, or don't we have a truce?"

"We do," she said, holding up both hands in surrender.

"Who writes this 'Rasputin' opera?"

"Oh, Verdi," she said instantly. "Such a grand theme as well as that particular time would appeal to him. Don't you think? Now, you tell me who should play the lead."

Simeon accessed the necessary historical information from his files. "In the available likenesses of him, Rasputin has enormous eyes and a riveting gaze, so we want a singer who's physically powerful and dramatically able to do justice to such a role. How about !Tlac Suc, the Sendee tenor?"

"Eh . . . he does have a compelling gaze, I grant you, and his eyes are large. But don't you think he has a few too many of them? Besides he's only retired, not dead."

Simeon flipped back a massive leap in the research file. "Um, Placido Domingo?"

"I know of him! He lived in a time blessed with great tenors. He's perfect! Tall, lean, big brown eyes and what a voice. Nice choice, Simeon."

"And he's dead, too."

"I can see it now," she said, standing suddenly and clutching histrionically at her throat. "They poison him, you see," and then she flung her arms wide, "and he sings! They stab him," she mimed a thrust to the bosom, before flinging her arms wide again, "and he sings! They drown him," she flapped her arms as though splashing frantically, then placed both hands on her heart, "and he sings! They shoot him," she staggered to Simeon's column and leaned her back against it.

"Channa, he's got to stop singing sometime."

She raised a finger, "Sotto voce, he sings, 'it is over.'" She slid down the column into a graceful art-deco position, "And he dies." Her head flopped forward and her hands dangled loosely from her wrists.

The com chimed and the screen cleared, allowing communications specialist Keri Holen an unobstructed view of Channa slumped at the base of Simeon's column. "Oh! What's hap . . . I mean, Ms. Hap! Simeon, is she all right?"

Channa was instantly on her feet, palm up in a calming gesture. "I'm fine," she said, serenely adjusting her tunic blouse. "What is it?"

"Uh . . . a message from Child Welfare on Central, from a Ms. Dorgan. If it's convenient, she's scheduled a conference call for 1600 today."

"Perfect," Simeon said, "tell her thank you," and he broke the connection.

"I thank the powers that be that wasn't Ms. Dorgan herself," Channa said nervously.

"I like that 'if it's convenient,'" Simeon said, musingly. "Channa, have *you* ever replied, 'No, it's damned inconvenient?'"

Channa regarded him with a singularly blank expression. "No, actually I haven't. But then, in my branch of the service, it shouldn't ever be!"

Simeon studied Joat nervously, wondering if they should have dressed her differently. All the other children her age wore the same shapeless clothes, disgusting and often raucous color combinations, but not necessarily what the prudent guardian would recommend for this kind of interview. The com chimed.

Too late, he thought. Channa seemed calm, but then Channa always seemed calm. *Odd when she can exude such depths of hostility. . . .* Still, she always did them with a controlled and icy demeanor. Yeah, Channa was fine. Joat's hands were clasped in her lap. *Poor kid, her knuckles are white.* But otherwise she seemed composed. *I'm fine, too,* he thought. *I'm not calm, but I'm fine.*

Ms. Dorgan studied them from the screen, like a teacher assessing a class of delinquents, then smiled, a tight, superior little smile. Her hair was gray, cut short, combed in a simple disciplined style. She wore a severe dark blue suit with a prim white blouse and no jewelry. The view of background behind her was official and equally unsoftened by anything even remotely unofficial.

I'll bet she starches her bras, Simeon thought. He remembered Patsy Sue using that expression: entirely appropriate right now.

Ms. Dorgan nodded to Channa, then fastened her cold little eyes on Joat. "Hello, dear," she said in syrupy tones. "I'm Ms. Dorgan, your case-worker."

Joat's face had hardened to wariness, her whole body going rigid. Simeon wondered how his nutrient fluid had suddenly gone so cold, but he didn't dare divert an erg of his attention away from these proceedings. He didn't even dare reassure Joat. She mumbled a barely audible "hello" in response.

"Well, dear, you made some very impressive scores on the tests. Did you know that?"

A nearly inaudible "no" answered her.

Ms. Dorgan glanced down at something below the screen's range, and then her right hand became visible, probably pressing the button to scroll her file forward.

"You are, however, considerably behind your age group in a good many subjects, with the exception of mathematics and mechanicals, where you positively excel." That much was said with some genuine enthusiasm. "You've no idea the excitement you've generated in some quarters. I think you may now anticipate a much brighter future than your past may have led you to expect, dear."

Simeon spoke for the first time, keeping his promise to his protégé. "Joat wants to study engineering. You obviously concur that she has a unique talent in that field."

Ms. Dorgan's studied smile wavered and the tendons on her neck stood out with the strain of not obviously peering around the room. "You are the . . . shellperson?" She seemed to hold her thin lips away from the word as though it might soil them. Her eyes roved between Channa and Joat as though hoping one of them might be ventriloquising the male voice.

"Yes. I am Simeon, the SSS-900-C. I'm applying to adopt Joat as a full daughter and full relation."

Ms. Dorgan's hand delicately brushed a strand of hair back into place.

"Yes, well, as to that," she raised her brows as though surprised that he had spoken at all, "you realize that other prospective parents have put in applications for children with Joat's potential. We usually give preference to couples." There was a faint emphasis on the final word. She fingered her collar nervously. "In Joan's case . . ."

"Joat," said Joat, Simeon and Channa in unison.

"Joat's case, I've shown her file to a quantum-lattice engineer, who is a professor of my acquaintance, and he immediately expressed an interest in her. He's extremely enthusiastic about tutoring someone of such promise. He's married, too, on a life-contract with a poet. Such a situation would have many advantages for the child."

Simeon watched Joat's face go white. "As a station manager, I am intimately acquainted with a variety of sciences, including regular updates on state-of-the-art, so I am quite capable of tutoring her, on the practical level she prefers, in any specialty that interests her.

Relax, Joat. Ms. Gorgon's merely mentioning options and possibilities."

The case-worker loudly cleared her throat. "My name, Station Manager Simeon, is Dorgan, with a D. Which reminds me, Joat, somewhere on the application, ah, here it is, it says that your name is an acronym for 'jack-of-all-trades.' Where 'Jack' was a gender-inappropriate first name, 'Jill' was substituted. How would you feel about being called Jill?"

"About the same as I'd feel about being called shit," Joat replied, every inch the belligerent corridor-kid now, scornful and angry; no trace of her earlier diffidence remaining. "And I wouldn't answer to it 'cause it's not my name."

"Joat!" Channa gasped.

"Don't you see it, Simeon, Channa?" Joat said, her blue eyes sparkling with contempt. "This is all a joke! This ol' Ms. *Organ . . .*"

"Dorgan, if you please."

" . . . bitch has made up her mind. What are we wasting our time and credit talkin' to her for?"

"Calm down, Joat," Simeon said. "Let's not jump to conclusions yet. Ms. Dorgan, although I have unlimited communication links, my time is heavily scheduled, and I was assured by the authorities that this was merely a formality. Shall we move to settling the details now?"

Slightly pink in the cheeks, Ms. Dorgan took a deep breath and released it in a small huff.

"I can't believe that you would persist in this application, knowing that a human couple is interested in the child. It would be one thing if no one wanted her, but that is not the case. In the first place, since she's at a very sensitive stage of development, there is no way that someone like you could appreciate what she's going through."

"Because Simeon is male?" Channa asked quietly.

"Because he is a shellperson. My dear Ms. Hap, as a professional brawn, you are surely well-acquainted with the peculiarities of these persons. Why deny that they are practically a different species? With no real understanding of what it's like to be independently mobile? How could he possibly raise an *active, growing* child?" The slight emphasis on the two adjectives made Channa clench her teeth in disgust. Dorgan's question was also rhetorical.

"Well, now, Joat," Simeon drawled, heavily borrowing from Patsy Sue again, "I guess you were right. Ms. Gorgon had made up her mind before she saw us."

"That's Dorgan," the case-worker said, leaning heavily on the "d."

"Toldja," Joat said, "ol' Ms. Organ's already decided."

"Dorgan. *Dorgan.* DORGAN!"

"Stop it! All three of you." Channa cast her glare over Simeon's column, Joat's flushed face, and finally settled it on the Child Welfare representative. "You have some very strange ideas about shell-people, Ms. Dorgan, with a D. My advice would be to consider carefully before you make any more bigoted remarks. I particularly resent your denying Simeon his intrinsic humanity. I've never met a shellperson who wasn't at *least* as able and responsible as a softperson. And indisputably more ethical! In fact, your remarks indicate active prejudice on your part. Prejudice which is, I might remind you, legally actionable."

Ms. Dorgan raised her chin. "There's no need, no need at all, Ms. Hap, to make threats. No doubt it is due to your long association with such persons that you no longer consider them ... abnormal." Before Channa could get over sputtering at that, the case-worker smiled smugly. "In the child's best interests, I'm afraid that I shall have to deny this petition. I shall make arrangements for her transport to Central, where, after a short stay at our orphan facility, she will no doubt be adopted by a *proper* family." Still smiling she broke the connection.

"Well?" Simeon almost shouted into the ensuing silence. "You're not going to let her have the last word on this, are you?"

"Don't she have it? Far's this orphan child's concerned?" Joat demanded bitterly. "I knew this'd happen. I *told* myself this'd happen. But you two trained brains were both so damned *sure.*" She sneered as she counted off her points. "You knew just where to go and just who to talk to and just what to do. But you know what? You don't know ANYTHING! But after all, how could you?" she asked her eyes beginning to fill with tears. "Everything's always gone your way. Everything's always just been handed to you." She started to sob. "Shells, education, food, a living place. Well, they don't get handed out, lemme tell ya. And look what you've done to *me*! Now they know I exist and where I am, and they're coming to get me! For all I know, that lattice engineer wants to play diddly on my lattice work. Only he's human and a professor and's got an 'in' with *her.* You got me into this, but I'm sure not waiting for you to get me out. I'm not goin' anywhere with *nobody* I don't want to!" Her voice had reached scream level before she pivoted and ran from the lounge.

"Joat!" Channa moved to follow her, but Simeon closed the door in her face. "Simeon!" she said in disbelief.

"Let her go, Channa. What could you do now? Lock her in her room until they come for her?" Channa looked as though he'd struck her. "She needs time and privacy. She needs to feel in control again. Let her alone."

"There *are* things we can do, Simeon. I'm not going to let that woman win. We can go over her head in Child Welfare. We can appeal to SPRIM and Double M for help. You taped that interview, didn't you?"

He laughed, for once pleased to see her so combative. "Yes, I did, and won't the Mutant Minorities and the Society for the Preservation of the Rights of Intelligent Minorities dump on La Gorgon for her attitudes! Good thinking, Channa. I'm this very moment apprising them of this incident. Y'know, this could even be fun."

Late that night, Simeon noticed that a light came on in Channa's quarters. He had assiduously kept to his promise, but the faint glow under the door was plainly visible. *Well, to anyone with photonscanners like mine,* he amended. Still, he was observing the principle of the thing.

Channa heard a chiming sound and, after a surprised pause, called out, "Hello?"

Simeon's voice, carefully adjusted to low audibility, answered from the lounge, "May I come in?"

She smiled and laid aside the reader she'd picked up. "Yes, you may."

She lay in bed, looking tousled and sleepy. Simeon thought that she looked little more than a kid herself. "Can't sleep?" he asked.

She shook her head, "I keep thinking of Joat, alone down there in the dark."

"Joat's been asleep for hours."

"How do you know that? She might still be crying her heart out for all we know."

"I know because I can hear little Joat-sized snores issuing from one of her favorite haunts."

"She didn't turn on her sound-scrubber?"

"Nope. She *was* upset!"

"No, she was thoughtful. She is becoming more civilized if she didn't want us to worry." And Channa laughed in relief, then sobered.

"She's such a good kid. She really didn't deserve Gorgon on her case. Look, Simeon, B & B's are considered couples by Central Worlds. Our contracts tend to last a lot longer than mere marriages. If I stayed on for say, ten years and applied for joint custody with you, most of Gorgon's objections would be invalid."

"Joint custody, huh? Well, Gorgon can't say a female brawn isn't a good role model. I've got comlines hotting up, but what I don't know is how many others at Child Welfare suffer from Dorgan's prejudice. I'd hate to see you make such a 'supreme sacrifice' for nothing. Fighting Ms. Gorgon through the bureaucracy won't turn us to stone, but it could bore our brains into oatmeal."

Channa gave a little "tsh" of scorn. "It's not like I've got anywhere else to go."

"I know, I heard about Senalgal. Sorry, Channa. I know what it's like to lose an assignment you'd sell your soul to get."

She raised her eyebrows inquiringly. "What was it for you, if you don't mind my asking—a planet-based city, a scout ship? Or maybe you looked as high as a whole planet?"

"I've *got* a city, more or less. Definitely not a scout ship. The brain/brawn scout ship is too claustrophobic and limited. I like dealing with a lot of people. I enjoy the give and take of various personalities and situations. More challenge on a station this size. I love being challenged."

"Not a city, not a ship. You're after a planet?"

"No, I wouldn't want *that* much responsibility. And a planet's too sedentary. But a ship, definitely, so I could get around a lot."

"Ah," she said, making the connection between his leisure interests and the only ship assignment that applied, "a Space Navy command-ship." She cocked her head. "Are you in line for one?"

"Theoretically, yes. I've applied and what do I get? 'You're too important where you are,'" he began in a singsong monotone, "'You're too perfect where you are, there's no one else as well-trained as you are for such a highly specialized situation.' I've always," he added wryly, "considered SSS-900-C to be a temporary assignment."

"Forty years is temporary?"

"With shellpersons, of course it is."

"Maybe we aren't so imperfectly matched after all." She paused a moment, then in a flippant tone added, "With Joat to sweeten the deal, I don't think I would regard staying here as a 'supreme sacrifice.' Ugh! Orphan facility, indeed! Pick her up? Like some sort of a package?" She peered out of her room towards his column. "Do you think we stand a chance of reversing Dorgan's decision?"

Simeon wouldn't have taken bets, but he had barely tackled the task. On the up side, he felt something deep inside him beginning to uncoil. "With a B & B partnership, we have a chance. I appreciate your willingness to consider one very much, Channa. Right now though, dear lady, why don't you sleep on it?"

She sighed. "Mm, but I'm restless, and," she played with an edge of the reader, "there's nothing I really want to read."

"Then," he said, gently dimming the lights, "I shall recite a bedtime poem for you. Settle in." He waited until she had scooted down and adjusted covers and pillows, smiling as she did so. He began, "We who with songs beguile your pilgrimage . . ." Her eyes closed, and gradually she drifted off to sleep as Simeon recited.

" . . . softly through the silence beat the bells,
Along the golden road to Samarkand."

CHAPTER FIVE

CHANNA EMERGED INTO the lounge, heading for the table and her morning coffee. A wave of sound struck her—very much a wave, like plunging into a curling jade-green wall that seized her and bore her back towards the beach.

She couldn't help but recognize the music as "The Triumphal March" from *The Empress of Ganymede* by User.

She paused with a slight frown when she realized that she had unconsciously altered her stride to suit the march tempo. She stopped, and her pause was the length of a measure. She laughed when she realized it. "Does this mean I get to be queen today?"

"Actually, after your restless night, I decided something upbeat would suit."

"Well, I sure got off on the right foot, then," she said with a sound approximating a giggle.

Simeon was pleased. Last night their relationship really had turned a corner. They were going to be all right.

"So, a good morning to you, Simeon," she said with an impish smile.

"And a good morning right back atcha, as Patsy Sue would say."

Channa's appreciative smile faded slowly into a frown. "I'd consider it a real good morning if I could see and speak to Joat as soon as possible. I'm very worried that she might jump ship on us, and that would ruin every step of progress we've made with her."

"Wish I could oblige you on that, Channa, but I don't know where she is now. She turned on her sound-scrubber early this morning and effectively vanished." He hurried on when Channa's face showed her disappointment clearly. "I don't think she'd leave on two counts. One, she knows her way intimately between the skins of this station, and it's certainly big enough for her to change hidey-holes on an hourly basis if necessary. And two, none of the ships undocking today are the type she could stow away on or hire out on. I've got every sensor tuned to her registered patterns, and I've discreetly alerted key personnel."

Channa nodded and went to her console, pulling the notescreen towards her. "Then we had better get to work. SPRIM ought to be moving on that dispatch you sent off last night." Her anxiety lifted at Simeon's knowing chuckle. She ran her fingers in a tattoo on the console. "And I suspect Child Welfare won't like being on their hit list."

"Hit list?" Simeon spoke with some alarm. "Are they that way inclined?" He didn't wish Ms. Dorgan any *physical* harm.

"The way SPRIM execs rave about *humanocentric chauvinism* is enough to turn even a tolerant person into a xenophobe. They've got money and they're tireless in ensuring protection. That slur she made on shellpeople, well . . . And the MM make SPRIM look like a quilting party."

"Quilting party?" Simeon searched his lexicon for the term.

"Old-fashioned way to spend a productive and socializing evening," she explained absently.

"Oh. Not much we can do until they get back to us, I suppose."

Simeon sounded unhappy. Channa quirked a corner of her mouth.

"We can't go in with lasers blazing and slag Child Welfare Central, if that's what you mean. If the station had full self-government, they wouldn't be able to mess with us—so let's concentrate on station business for now, shall we?" She cleared her throat. "I've been going over your accounts, Simeon, and I've got to say that you have some *weird* entries. For example, tucked away in the fourth quarter is the notation 'stuff.' You'll have to be more specific than 'stuff.'"

"Why? 'Stuff' is acceptable to the accountants," he said in a facetious tone.

"I'm not an accountant. I'm supposed to be your partner. Would you explain 'stuff'?"

"It's like this, Channa, I buy things that interest me. Me, Simeon, not the station master brain." Never mind that that also accounted for why he hadn't paid off his natal debt to Central Worlds. *So I'm a pack rat. Is that her business now?*

Far out in space, Simeon's peripheral monitors, the ring of sensors that warned of incoming traffic, began to transmit information that suggested a very large object was headed their way. From the ripples it caused in subspace, it was very large or very fast or both. He split his attention between her and the alert, and sent a communicator pulse in the direction of the disturbance. There were strict rules on how to approach a station. Approaching unheralded broke half a dozen regs and invariably caused stiff credit penalties.

Respond to hailing, he transmitted. **Respond immediately.**

"Well, we've got this inspection and audit coming up in two weeks," he heard Channa saying in a firm let's-not-beat-about-the-bush tone. "We have *got* to have everything shipshape and Bristol fashion, partner."

He did appreciate that she subtly reminded him of her promise to help with Joat, but this was no time for petty details.

"I don't *have* a ship shape, Channa," he muttered in his distraction, "but I do have something very unusual out there, approaching me without due protocol."

Visual information was now reaching him. Dropping out of interstellar transit and approaching at . . . *Great Ghu, .17 c!* A large vessel whose profile did not fit any known human ship. The basic hull-form was spherical, but carried a web of crazy-quilt additions, constructions of girder and latticework. Some of them looked as if they had been slashed off short with energy beams, and the outpoints were *tattered.* People were generally not sloppy with cutting tools. Enemies were. Simeon relayed a standard "please identify" message and put the tug bays on standby.

"Nor am I abristle," he continued to Channa. "The inspectors will be when they come, though."

Channa groaned. "Even for you that was lame. You're being unusually ridiculous, Simeon. You know the mentality that goes with these inspections—sentence first, trial afterwards."

"In other words, off with our heads, if they could reach mine."

"And us running as fast as we can to stay in one place, too. Which capability you also don't have. Now, since this is my first time with you . . ."

"Oh, Channa . . . pant, pant."

"Simeon," she said warningly. "I know where the controls for your hormone balance are."

"Heh heh, sorry. What's the worst they can do to me? Send me back to asteroidic purgatory? Like I told you, I'm only on temporary duty here anyway."

Channa had been running a scan. "There are twelve entries for the word 'stuff'! You want this to be a temporary assignment? Well, you may get your wish."

"It's not a wish, my dear, I never said 'I wish they'd take me away from here and put me anywhere else.' I've a very definite destination in mind, as you so astutely concluded the other evening. If I had my druthers, I'd be running a command ship and waging star wars on the Axial Perimeter. But," and he gave a huge audible sigh, "who believes in wishes anymore?"

"You do, with all your war games and tactical daydreams."

The approaching ship still had not responded, nor was it dumping speed as fast as it should. In fact, whoever was in command had waited much too long to begin doing so. The flare of drive energies should be blanking out that whole quadrant, and the neutrino flux was barely enough for a pile just ticking over. Simeon came to a disagreeable conclusion.

"Whoa, there, Channa. We've got stuff, not mine, coming in to make mince of us if we're not careful. Have a look?"

Simeon slapped up a main screen view of the intruder bearing down on them. Surprise and alarm held her motionless for only a split second before she reacted.

"I'm alerting the perimeter guard," she said, wiping her previous program and inputting the new.

"Right!" Although he already had, two sources of the same alert emphasized the emergency. "I'm busy calculating how to cushion the impact of that great hulking mass whistling towards us. I hope they know where the brakes are." Nice to have a brawn to share emergency work. The station personnel should get used to dealing with her.

Stabbing the alert button on the main console, Channa then called up a finer resolution of the object, which to her appeared to be a darker mass against the black of space.

"Unannounced arrival!" She transmitted the image to the personnel on perimeter traffic control, alerting them to the pertinent vector and ordering them to begin rerouting incoming traffic.

"How do you know it's *whistling* toward us?" she asked in as calm a voice as he was using while her fingers flew over the controls. "There's no sound in space."

Simeon could detect just a micro-tremor of fear in her noncommittal tone. "If I think it whistles," he answered, "it whistles."

"Perimeter says it's like nothing they've ever seen before either and—" she paused and licked her lips "—it's about to cut a broad swath through the proper traffic pattern."

Simeon took full control of the traffic control boards. He could see and respond to the necessary changes in traffic patterns faster than any unshelled human. He was simultaneously redirecting and responding to dozens of ships.

Suddenly Channa started cursing. "Damn their eyes and innards! These damned civilians are asking questions instead of doing what they're supposed to in emergency routines. Now you see why I didn't like you calling those false alarms. No one's paying a blind bit of attention to this *genuine* emergency! Wolf-cryer!"

"I've put it on every public screen. They'll know it's no drill," Simeon said, his voice velvet with malice, "and it's coming straight at us. I don't think it'll stop."

I didn't realize you could banter when you're terrified, he thought with tight control, though it helped being able to set your analogue of adrenal glands.

Channa stared, stunned, as the screen filled with the alien ship. "You haven't activated the repel screen? Hit it for God's sake!" She pressed her rocker switch just a fraction of a second behind Simeon.

Joat gritted her teeth and wiped eyes and nose on the back of her sleeve. It was a good shirt, and clean. *Dumb,* she told herself fiercely. *Dumb, dumb, dumb bitch, dumb gash, just like the captain told you you were.* Especially when he was drunk. He'd always been worse then.

She turned her attention back to the little computer. It was the best she'd ever been able to steal, a real Spuglish; jacked into the station system right now, with the skipper-unit she'd cobbled up to keep the station from knowing just where or why.

Ship schedules / departures / outsystem, she told it. Machines didn't lie to you! You could trust machines and, if they didn't do what they were supposed to, it wasn't because they had lied. Maths and machinery could be believed.

A barking sob broke through her lips, spattering drops on the screen. She bit down on her hand until the pain and the taste of her own blood let her continue. Then she wiped the machine down with the tail of her shirt. Machines didn't let you down, either.

Departures, the computer said. **Look, Joat, you don't have to leave here. Trust me, we're—**

"No!" she screamed.

Joat stuffed the scramblers into her pockets and went off down the duct at a scrambling crawl, ignoring projections and brackets that only slightly impeded her progress. The motions were reflexive, with a graceless efficiency.

Nobody's going to give me away again, she thought. *Get me used to eating regular and school and everything, then give me away!* The thought went round and round in her head, filling it, so that it was minutes before the klaxon penetrated her self-absorption.

"Oh, shit," she whispered in a still small voice, listening. Then she turned and went back the way she came, faster still. The computer was back there, and without it, she wouldn't be able to find out what was really going on.

Her spacesuit was there, too. This sounded serious.

"THIS IS NO DRILL! REPEAT, THIS IS NO DRILL!" The words rang down the corridors and hallspaces, without the melodramatic klaxons Simeon had always used. "Nonessential personnel report to secure areas. Report to secure areas. Prepare for breach of hull integrity."

This time the citizens of the SSS-900-C listened, hastening into suits, gathering children and pets and heading for the central core or section shelters. Crews pelted onto their ships, even as moorings were detached and entry locks irised shut and each "all on board" signal was relayed to Simeon. Emergency crews flocked to their assigned stations. Infirmary patients who could not be moved were placed in individual, independently powered life-support units. All too soon, most of the citizens of SSS-900-C could only wait, imagining their station crushed like an egg as the invader plowed into them.

Simeon worked frantically, ordering ships of all sizes out of the projected path of the incoming ship, brutally suppressing the knowledge that ships with ordinary, unshelled pilots could barely handle the split second timing he was asking of them. So far, so good—no one out there seemed destined to die today. For a heart-stopping moment he thought the alien might be decelerating, but the blaze of energies sputtered and died. *It's only shed 7% of relative velocity,* he calculated dismally. *Not nearly enough.*

"Why didn't they program mobility?"

"Who?" Channa asked distractedly. "Where?"

"In me! In this station! I can't duck! I've no weaponry to blast it out of my way. I can't even fend off such mass. All I can do is watch. What lasers I've got can just about handle a decent-sized meteor. The best I can do is warm up his hull a little, and I have to wait till he's up my ass to do it! Damn! This station is like a paraplegic space-ship!"

"Whoa! Did you see that?" Channa shouted. The mass had seemed to deliberately veer aside from an ordinary asteroid miner vessel, something the miner pilot himself probably couldn't have done. "Watch," she said, "there! Did you see? It jigged just a bit to miss that incoming ferry traffic. It *is* being guided."

"But by what?" Simeon asked. He ran calculations on the ballistics of those maneuvers. The deviations were *absolutely* minimal for the effect. "It's traveling so fast now, no human pilot could stop it and stay conscious. They don't answer any radio messages. They're ignoring the damn warning flares. Shit, maybe they think we're welcoming them. Ah, *good*!"

"But they are decelerating again, Simeon," Channa said, glancing up from her own screens to the main viewer before she went back to other chores which she had assumed.

"Yeah, marginally longer this time. No, cutting out—no, decelerating *again*. Rate of energy-release . . . God, but they're still not dumping enough velocity! And still on a collision course!" His voice went slightly wild. "They must *want* to destroy me!"

"I don't see any weapons," Channa said, trying to finish her current task in time.

"Who can tell in that jumble of struts and boxes and crap! Besides, that thing *itself* is a weapon." Simeon had just one card to play and at exactly the right moment for maximum effect. "You're not even suited up, partner. At least take shelter in my shaft core, Channa."

She shook her head, "Not till I'm through evacuating the alien quadrant. 'Sides, those Letheans scare easily enough as it is without me appearing in full gear."

She had managed at last to get through to the leader of the Lethe contingent. A people so formal that emergencies required a ceremony,

mercifully brief, for deferring the usual endless courtesies in favor
of survival. Had Channa not performed the ceremony and explained
the situation to them, they would have died rather than commit such
a breach of manners as assuming that something was actually wrong.
She broke the connection at last and exclaimed, "Joat!"

"She has a suit," Simeon said, "first thing I gave her. She's probably in it right now. Why aren't you?"

She dashed for the cabinet holding her space suit and began to
struggle into it.

"Come to me, Channa," he said, in a wildly facetious tone, "come,
touch the hard, male core of my innermost being."

"Ee-yuck, is that the sort of romance you've been studying? Try
another mode."

"When I've world enough and time, lovely one, but have a look
at what I've managed to arrange as stop signs."

Seemingly from out of nowhere, three communications satellites
came diving towards the incoming ship, two striking it head on
and one slightly astern. Whole sections of the scaffolding and outer
skin of the derelict sublimed in white flashes that expanded into
circles with zero-g perfection. The alien ship was not slowed—there
was too much kinetic energy in that mass—but its vector altered
slightly.

"Comsats aren't supposed to be able to move like that!" Channa
exclaimed tightly. Simeon's sensors could hear the pounding of her
heart, analyze the ketones her sweat-damp skin was emitting. Fear
under hard control. *The lady has guts,* he thought.

"A little something I cooked up on my own," he said smugly.

"Cooked in the wrong sort of pot, you crazy loon. Without those
satellites, we'll be out of communication with half the universe for
weeks."

"Channa, if I hadn't done that we'd be out of communication with
the all of the universe permanently. Besides, my satellite tactic
worked!"

Channa looked up at the main monitor and saw that the projected
vector had skewed slightly. "Not enough," she muttered. "Please don't
use any more of our comm satellites like billiard balls, Simeon. If
we do survive this, they'll be needed more than ever."

"Oh-oh," Simeon muttered.

"Oh-oh?" she repeated anxiously.

It means, I screwed the pooch, Channa, Simeon thought. Aloud he went on. "*SS Conrad*, dump your carrier modules and get out of that sector. You are now directly in the path of the incoming ship."

"No-can-do SSS-900-C. I've got a full load here. The company'll have my ass if I desert it."

"The company'll have to hold a seance to get it, then, 'cause if you stay put, you're about to become immortal. Jump it!"

"Now!" Channa shouted. "It's less than two k-thousand kilometers from you. Now, dammit!"

"No shit!" the pilot shouted and disconnected the "cab," the crew quarters and control section of the ship, from the much larger freight storage sections.

They watched the tiny cab move with agonizing slowness across the seemingly endless bow of the strange ship.

"Down on station horizon," Simeon instructed, "ninety-degrees, straight down."

"Down? You want me to stop? With that bastard coming right for me! Are you crazy?"

"It's your only chance, buddy. She's shallow on the bottom but, by Ghu, is she wide! Show me what kind of pilot you are! Not what kind of smear you'll make."

Obediently, the little ship flared energy, applying thrust at right-angles to its previous vector. Its path shifted, slowly at first and then with growing speed like a bell-curve graph across a computer screen. Slowly, slowly, descending, a bright spot against the ever larger mass approaching them.

"Oh shit, oh shit," the captain whispered desperately. "Help?"

The intruder was less than a kilometer away, now, from the cab which looked like a white pin-point against the black hull of the stranger. At half a kilometer it cleared the leading edge of the incoming ship and the pilot began to laugh wildly.

"Keep going," Simeon ordered sharply, to be heard through the hysteria. "It's about to hit your freighter. Keep moving till I tell you to stop."

"It's ore," the captain gasped though he sounded more as if he was weeping, "iron ore. Nickel-iron-carboniferous, in ten-kilo globules."

Aw, crap! Simeon thought, as the intruder struck the freighter with majestic slowness. The forward third of its hull vanished in the fireball, and so did much of the freighter's cargo. The energy-release and spectrographic analysis would tell him a good deal about the composition. Right now he had millions of special delivery meteors pouring down from the breached holds onto his station. Great example of Newtonian physics, action and reaction.

The collision had, serendipitously, damped much of the incoming ship's remaining velocity, but the fragments of ship and cargo had picked it up for themselves. He tracked the myriad trajectories of the space flotsam and relayed the information to the ships in the scatter area, directing them into still more impossible flight patterns. He assigned the computer responsibility for tracking and blasting the larger chunks of ore with the station's lasers. No problems with dispersion when the stuff was in your face. On the other hand, there was one hell of a lot of it. Simeon set the computer to figuring out just how much would get through.

He realized that Channa was staring at the monitor in horrified fascination. "Hey Hap, Happy baby, get in the shaft core."

"Why?" she asked. "It's stopping."

"Slowing, yes, but if it so much as kisses me on the cheek, it'll breach the station and you're on a one-way trip to the nebula. We need you here, so shaft me baby."

"Shaft yourself," she said. "It has come to a complete cessation of forward movement."

A final flare of energy left the *aft* third of the intruder's hull slumping and melting, the drive cores and conduction vanes white-hot and misting titanium-rutile monofiber.

"So it has," Simeon said mildly.

Channa gave a giddy whoop and slumped against the central shaft, trying to wipe at the sweat that filmed her face. Her glove clacked against the faceplate of her helmet.

"Dead, stock still," he said, feeling intense relief. "Relative to the station, that is."

With a glance at his column, Channa hit the disconnect switch and the red warning lights stopped flashing. Simeon began to announce stand-down to Condition Yellow in dulcet, paternal tones. Channa took off her helmet and began to confer with the Lethe leader, reestablishing the usual formal relations.

When at last they disconnected from their various crucial chores, Channa looked at her incoming electronic messages and laughed. "By God, but we're a resilient species. Look at these."

Simeon scanned them and laughed, too. "I haven't even finished flushing the excess adrenalin from my system and they're already complaining about lost cargo and insurance. I love the human race. We're consistently more concerned with trivia than serious threats."

"And we're not even out of danger, are we?"

"Out of mortal danger. That thing could have totaled us. The ore will cause a lot of trouble and expense, so let's maintain Condition Yellow for a while."

That would keep nonessentials out of the exterior compartments, mostly industrial areas anyway, and everyone in suits with helmets in reach and within sprinting distance of the shelters. Megacredits of money were being lost, of course, most of which would be paid by Lloyds' Interstellar.

Channa was examining the strange ship on a close screen.

"Next question is who, or what's, aboard."

"And if there's anything left of the pilot captain," Simeon added, "who's broken regulations I didn't know existed till now. I sent out a dozen probes to secure available information on what's left. Ah! Input!"

The main screen blanked, and then displayed a schematic of the strange craft, shifting to a three-dimensional model as the computers extrapolated.

"So that's what it looked like before it started hitting things and melting down its drives," Simeon murmured as brain and brawn surveyed an elongated sphere amid its tangle of extensions. "And now I'll subtract what doesn't appear to be part of the original construction."

The resulting model didn't look much like the slagged ruin tumbling slowly through space in the real-time image that Simeon kept up in the lower right-hand corner of the screen. Channa leaned forward and frowned at such an unfamiliar design. *Huge* it certainly was. At least eighty kilotons mass, with extravagant ship-bays and airlocks, old-fashioned cooling vanes around the equator . . .

"That looks like human construction," she said thoughtfully, "Just not any model I've ever seen or heard about." Human civilization had been unified at the beginning of starflight and their ships bore a family resemblance.

"It does look vaguely human-made," Simeon agreed, "but I can't even find a match in historical files of *Jane's All the Galaxy's Spaceships* for the last century. The composition is odd, too; metal-metal fiber matrix. Ferrous alloys. No comparable design for the last *two* centuries. Hmmm."

"Something?"

"This." He called up an image beside the reconstructed ship.

"Close but no cigar," Channa said.

"That's the last of a line of heavy transports—that one was a Central Worlds space-navy troop-transport. Designers were Dauvig-ishipili and Sons. They used to make a lot of military craft, operated on stations out of the New Lieutas system. See, there *is* some use to being a military historian. Ah, *here.*"

The image changed and now there was a virtual one-to-one match.

"Colonial transport," Simeon said. "They stopped building them about three hundred years ago, so it could be up to four hundred years old. Original capacity was ten thousand colonists, in coldsleep of course, with a crew of thirty. There were a lot of odd little colonies back then, people looking for places where they could practice as weird a religion as they wanted and not have the Central Worlds bugging them. The few that survived are still pretty flaky. Are you surprised to learn that the ship-class was called the *Manifest Destiny* vehicle? A few of the later models had brain controllers before Central Worlds put a stop to that practice on humane grounds. Some of those minor cults were—" he made a brief pause to consult his lexicon "—aberrant! Hmm, and I'd bet this one got transmogrified into an orbital station. Look at all that stuff!"

"Your kind of 'stuff'?" asked Channa ingenuously.

"Gadgetry," he amended in a firm, this-is-serious voice, "plastered on the exterior: observation stuff, transmission stuff, the usual. And intended to be used in orbit. I mean, who would try to fly any ship with all that crap sticking out? For starters, the thrust axis wouldn't be through the center of mass anymore, so for starters, it's unbalanced."

Channa scanned through more probe transmissions, including some views taken by the perimeter sensors as the hulk barreled in, so they could see the havoc caused by collision and too-rapid deceleration.

"They may have had cause for their precipitous intrusion," she said, and froze a view of the stubs of the radar and radio antennas. "Those look like battle damage to me."

"Hmmm." Simeon did a rapid close-scan and match with the naval records in his files. "You're right, Channa-mine. Transmission antennae sheared off so they couldn't have responded to our hails. Whoever shot those darts knew his stuff, and their most vulnerable points.

See the long star-shaped ripple patterns in the hull? And those long sort of fuzzy distortions clustered in the rear third of the hull? Those are beamers at extreme range, I'd say. Hard to tell 'cause it's so messed up." He spoke more slowly, in an almost somber tone. "Hell, Channa, beamers like that are naval ordnance weapons. The real thing." *Oh, boy, this is not like a simulation* at all. "Somebody was trying to *destroy* that ship."

"While the victims were desperate enough to fly close to blind and totally deaf," Channa said. That was *not* a safe thing to do, even in the vastness of interstellar space. "My next intelligent question is, did they escape? Or are they still being pursued?"

"Ahead of you there, partner," Simeon replied, feeling slightly smug that he had anticipated her. "I can't detect anything coming in on the same vector." He heaved an audible sigh of relief that coincided with hers. "Or . . . no, they *were* blind. The pursuit could have dropped off long ago, and they wouldn't have had any way to tell. But we'd better establish who and why. If, and it's a big if, there's anyone alive in there now to tell us the facts. I'm not inclined to be charitable. For all we know, they could be pirates or hijackers, and they were running from Central Worlds' naval pursuit. Either way, they came within centimeters of smashing us to a smithereen."

"Smithereens," Channa said thoughtfully, "because it's fragments they are and they have to be plural to be dangerous. I rather discount their being illegals. *Something* real deadly must have pushed them to run in a craft that unspaceworthy. Something that came to their planet suddenly. Why else wouldn't they take the time to cut away that mass clinging to the ship? Maybe their sun went nova. Anyway," she said briskly, "if there are people on board, they're in bad shape and what have you been doing to rescue and/or apprehend them?"

"Ahem, Channa-mine. You're the mobile half of this partnership. Remember? So go be brawn for me. And be careful!"

Channa paused. "Ah, yes, so I am. Thank you for reminding me of that!" Her tone was brightly brittle. "Somehow this wasn't the sort of duty I thought came along with this assignment."

"Well, it has!" he said, making his voice lilt. "Hate to have caused you to get into that clumsy suit for no reason at all."

She lifted her helmet.

"Thatta girl!" Simeon said rather patronizingly. She ignored him. "Oh, and Channa?"

"What?"

"Before you lock your helmet, do switch on your implant."

"Ah!" She touched the switch grounded in bone just behind her ear, the contact responding only to her individual bio-energy. "Are you receiving?"

"Check."

"Can I go now?" she said rather patronizingly.

"Check."

"And mate, Simy baby."

"Got it," Joat muttered to herself as she rescued the computer from the shadowed ledge and turned it on, fingers clumsy in the space suit gloves. Joat had become well-acquainted with the station's drills but, with survival skills as finely honed as hers were, she had put the suit on when the klaxon sounded Red Alert. Besides, she'd had a chance to time just how fast she could get into the flippin' thing.

"Wow!" was her reaction to the activity the computer duly reported. "Fardling A wow!" The system was taking in some heavy data, converting it and feeding it to Simeon the way it transferred data from the pickups, though never in this density or complexity. "Heavy read!"

Joat did her best to follow, but the speed was too much. Then, *"Got* it." Now the main computer was also encoding it for her little friend. She fiddled to get a finer tuning, get rid of the drivel, giving her the visual and aural stuff. She reared back in surprise, hitting her head on the metal bulkhead but ignoring the pain as she realized what she now had.

Hey, this is from Channa. Strange, heavy strange—I'm getting what she's seeing. She must have an implant to input directly to Simeon like this. And what Channa was seeing made Joat feel a little more charitable towards her. Channa wasn't squishstuff, her private term for organic tissue.

"Beats hacking in to the holo system any day," Joat muttered, eyes glued to the miniature screen. She squirmed into a more comfortable position, plopped down a purloined pillow so she wouldn't slam her head again, braced her feet against the roof of the duct, plugged the earphone into the helmet outlet, and absorbed the action.

"Real-time adventure holo!" Perfect, apart from a wavering line down one side of the picture-cube that must represent breathing and life-signs and stuff. "Go, Channa, go!"

CHAPTER SIX

STATION-BORN AND BRED, Channa had gone space-walking as soon as she was old enough to fit into a juvenile suit. But there the difference between her Hawking Alpha Proxima Station days and now ended.

Theoretically, she knew that SSS-900-C was at the edge of the Shiva Nebula. Trade routes crossed here, carrying processed ores essential for drive-core manufacture. As the ship which had brought her had approached the dumbbell-shaped station, she'd watched the process on her cabin's screen with great interest. But theory, and that shipboard view in complete safety, had not prepared her for the great arc of pearly mist that filled her vision plate; mist glowing with scores of proto-suns in a score of colors.

"Spectacular, ain't it?" Patsy asked.

Channa came to herself with a start. "What are *you* doing out here?"

"This tug's my emergency station," she said, grinning broadly inside her bubble helmet. "The algae'll keep right on breedin' for a while without me, randy little bastards. An' I'm a right good tug pilot, too."

"Believe you, ma'am," Channa said, throwing a salute from her bubbled temple. *What's Simeon on about? He's got a fleet—of sorts— to command.* "Let's go."

In turn, they slid down into the cramped cabin of the tug and plugged suit feeds into the ship system. The tugs were stripped-down little vessels, just a powerplant and drive with minimal controls;

wedge-shaped, with grapnel fields and an inflatable habitat for taking survivors in their dual role as rescue vessels. The docking bay and the cabin itself were open to vacuum, but she felt a low whining as Patsy brought the drive up and lifted them out. There was the usual disorienting lurch as they passed out of station gravity. Now the only weight was acceleration, and the barbell shape of the station was a huge bulk *below* them instead of behind. Her senses tried to tell her she was climbing vertically in a gravity field, then yielded to training as she made herself ignore up and down for the omni-directional outlook that was most useful in space.

"Vectoring in," Patsy said into her helmet mike.

Other tugs were drifting motes of light, fireflies against the blackness. The analogy remained in force as they circled the drifting hulk of the intruder; it was *big*. Forward was a frayed mass of tendrils, and the rear still glowed red-white, heat slow to radiate in vacuum.

"Readings?" Channa asked. Her nose itched; it always did when she had a helmet on.

Simeon's voice answered her. "Main power system went out when they burned their drive," he said. "Be careful about that, by the way— it's radiating gamma, real museum piece. Main internal gravity field's down. There are localized auxiliary systems still operating amidships, and traces of water vapor and atmosphere. There might be a chamber in there still running life-support."

Channa scanned the bridge section of the ship again. The instruments available in the cockpit of the tug were basically little more than sophisticated motion detectors.

"I can't get a thing," she said in frustration. "Am I missing something?"

"Not much," Simeon told her. "There's too much dirt out there, which'll confuse readings. See if you can get aboard."

"Right," she said, and looked down the hull toward the equator where the shuttle bays should be located. "Bring us in there, Patsy."

Channa flicked an indicator light on the hull. They sank gradually, until the ancient ship filled half the sky.

"Don't build 'em like this anymore," Patsy said as they beheld shuttle bay doors which were easily two hundred meters long, big enough to accommodate a small liner.

"They don't have to," Channa answered absently. Drive cores were a lot cheaper and safer nowadays, which made ships this size obsolete. "Somebody did *not* like them."

This close in, the scars on the hull were enormous, metal heated to melting with a slagged look around the edges of the cuts, but miraculously there didn't seem to be much structural damage as they swung further into the bay.

"They *have* to be alive," Channa murmured. "Nothing could kill people this lucky."

"Except running out of luck," Simeon said grimly.

"There is that." She came at last to a smaller shuttle bay and attempted to open the portal with several standard call codes. "Simeon, what does the library suggest we use for a ship this old? I'm not getting any response with the usual ones."

"Three one seven, three one seven five?"

"Tried it, nothing."

Simeon relayed several more codes.

"Nothing's working," she said in disgust. "Could they have locked them?"

"Hard to say until we're sure they're crazy or not. Try another bay. That one might just be inoperative."

She had Patsy fly out and down the massive ship's side until they came to another shuttle bay. It, too, refused her admittance.

"This is ridiculous," she said in exasperation. "They got in, so there has to be an operable entrance!"

"Considering the visible damage, maybe you'd have more luck with a service hatch. There're close to a hundred of them and only six shuttle bays. Try something midship."

"That's a good idea," she said, feeling more optimistic with such odds. "Just in case, what do we use for a can opener? We don't want any survivors dead of old age before we reach them."

The very first hatch they tried opened, about half a meter. Channa looked at it, Simeon looked at it through her eyes via the implant which connected directly to her optic nerve.

"You're not that big, but you're also not that small," he said with a wistful note.

"I'm putting us down," Patsy said. "Contact." A faint *clunk* came through the metal of the tug as the fields gripped the big hull.

"And I'm going to try and effect entry. I think it's wide enough." Channa told Simeon.

"Just you be very careful, Channa-mine . . ."

"For Ghu's sake, Simeon, I've been space-walking since I was five. I'm a stickfoot."

"Yeah, but I don't think your station ever experienced a hostile attack. And there's all that flying junk! Could knock you right off the hull . . . or smear you across it."

"You do know how to give a girl confidence. I'm going, Simeon, and that's that." She muttered to herself about titanium twits and agoraphobic asses as she prepared to leave the tug. Patsy Sue at least gave her a cheerful grin and a thumbs-up. "We need to know what or who's in there."

"No problem," Patsy cut in, reaching into the toolbox under the pilot's seat. Her hand came out with the ugly black shape of an arc pistol.

Channa looked around, her jaw dropped. "Aren't those illegal?"

Patsy waggled the pronged muzzle. "Not on Larabie, they ain't."

Channa shook her head, then picked up where she'd left off. "You know, Simeon, they *do* give us brawns training. I've done search-and-rescue before."

"How often?"

"Once. My inexperience will only make me more cautious. I can *do* this, Simeon. Once I'm inside maybe I can do something to widen the hatch opening. Direct some of the other tugs this way so I'll have reinforcements nearby, if I need them."

Patsy waggled the arc pistol, apparently accustomed to the weight of the weapon.

"Assuming it's needed," Channa added cheerfully. "Have you got any positive life readings, partner?" she asked as she eased herself with practised care out of the tug. With one hand on a hull bracket, she let herself drift to the hull where the stickfield of her boots held her safely.

"According to my sensors, nobody's conscious. But there *might* be—"

"Stop being so reassuring," she said facetiously. "Have you got a medical team ready?"

"We were just getting to know each other," he said regretfully.

Channa paused, caught by the emotion in his voice. "You are the most *manipulative* creature it has ever been my misfortune to meet," she said coldly, clipping a reel of optical fiber to her suit. Simeon sighed. "Look, I'm not a total idiot. The tug will shield me on one side, and I'm only two strides away from the hatch."

"Me? Manipulative? I'm *supposed* to keep my brawn from risking its fluffy little tail."

Carefully breaking boot contact, she took the first step to the hatch, and the second. Then clipped both feet free and floated neatly to the opening to examine it more closely. The magnetic grapple built into the left forearm of her suit twitched, with a feeling like a light push. The contact disk flicked out, trailing braided monofilament, and impacted on the door of the bay. She activated the switch that reeled her in. Patsy followed with an expert somersault leap that landed her less than an arm's length from her friend.

"Showoff," Channa said.

"You ain't the only one with walk experience," Patsy said. Her voice was light, but the arc pistol was ready as she peered within the half-open hatch. "Coburn to rescue squad. We're about to enter the Hulk. Stand by."

Channa licked dry lips. *It's the suit air,* she told herself firmly. *Always too dry.* She spoke aloud to Simeon. "You're just jealous of me, Bellona Rockjaw, heroine of the space frontier."

"I'm right there with you, Channa," Simeon said with a trace of wistfulness in his voice.

"Hmmph."

She struggled to get through the narrow opening, grunting with effort.

"Do not get stuck," he advised her.

Channa started to giggle. "Do not make me laugh," she admonished. "And stop reading my mind."

With the unpleasant sensation of metal and plastic scraping against each other, she pushed through at last. The chamber had held maintenance equipment of some sort long ago; there were feeds and racks for EVA suits, and empty toolholders. Only a single strip lit the dim interior. On the hullside wall was a massive, clumsy-looking airlock, and a blinking row of readouts beside it.

"Some systems still active," she said. "Patsy, prop yourself against the frame and see if you can't push the hatch door open."

"Nevah get through iffen I doan," the older woman muttered. "Makes me wish I were flat-chested, too."

"She is not," Simeon replied vehemently.

Channa grinned, but Patsy Sue was busy getting herself into position in the hatchway, attaching her filament to the inside of the hatch before she grabbed the top of the frame with both hands and gave a mighty heave. The hatch did not so much as budge a millimeter.

"No, it's jammed tighter'n . . . nemmind. You got a polarizin' face-plate?" Patsy asked.

"Standard."

"Okay. I'll try somethin' subtle."

Coburn stepped back, raised the arc pistol and fired four times. The bar of actinic blue-white light was soundless in vacuum, but a fog of metal particles exploded outward like glittering donuts centered on the aiming points. Patsy nodded in satisfaction and twisted herself around to brace her feet on the hatch and grip two handhold loops on the hull nearby. Channa could hear her give a grunt of effort, and the hatchway flipped out into space, tumbling end-over-end.

"Nice brand of subtle you wield," Channa said.

"Think nothin' of it," Patsy said, pretending to blow smoke off the arc pistol's barrel. "Any luck?"

Channa bent over the touchpad beside the airlock. "Not much. Ah, that's got it. Simeon, how's the transmission holding up?"

"Loud and clear, since Patsy got the door out of the way. I may lose Patsy's signal further inside. Maybe you should wait? There're four more tugs closing in on your position."

Channa ignored the pleading note, not without a pang of guilt. *But what the hell, the situation is irresistible,* she admitted. She had been trained as an administrator-partner-troubleshooter, but most of the time, circumstances were fairly conventional. Not boring; she wouldn't have made it through brawn training if she were bored with it. On the other hand, she wouldn't have been picked if there weren't an element of the adventurer in her psychological profile.

"String this, would you, Patsy?" she said, passing over the reel. The optical fiber was encased in woven tungsten-filament, with receptor-booster chips at intervals. Barely thicker than thread, it had a breaking strain of several tons. Tacked to the wall behind them, neither her implants nor Patsy's suit communits could fade out. Patsy welded the outer end to the hull beside the hatch, using the spot heater in her construction suit's gauntlet.

"Ready?" Channa said, taking a deep breath.

"Surely am." Patsy came up behind her, arc pistol ready.

"Standing by," Simeon said.

The keypad lights blinked green and amber. "I think it's saying there's some doubt about the atmosphere," Channa said. "It's definitely pressurized in there." She attached a sensor line to the surface.

"They're in trouble," Simeon said. "Hear that whining?" Channa shook her head, and felt him boost the audio pickups of her helmet. A faint tooth-grating sound came through.

"What *is* that?"

"That's the main internal drive cores," Simeon replied grimly. "The powerplant's down, but they're still superconducting. The alloys they used back then were tough. They built 'em more redundant then, too."

"Which means?"

"Which means . . . to stop this thing, the pilot put everything the powerplant had into the drive. The exterior coils blew before it could go all out. Now the internal coil's going to go."

"Bad news," Patsy said.

"It's going to blow?" Channa asked apprehensively. The energies needed to move megatons between stars were *immense*.

Simeon listened. "Not *just* yet, but soon. Building, but the noise will be considerably more audible before I'd panic. Get that inner hatch open, woman! I'll send the troops. You've got about thirty minutes before you *have* to be off."

The interior airlock slid open. The two women kept their helmets firmly on as it slid down again and the air hissed in. Channa looked down at the readouts on her sleeve and punched for analysis.

"Oxygen's down, CO_2's way up," she said grimly. "*Necrotic ketones,* or so it says—decay products. I'd hate to have to breathe this stuff. Could *anyone* breath it and live?"

"Depends on natural tolerances," Patsy replied. "And it might not be bad further in." Being an environmental maintenance specialist, she knew the parameters. "From the volume of n.k.'s, their scrubbers must have been down for a while."

The inner hatch of the airlock slid open. Now that they were no longer in a soundless vacuum, the exterior pickups of their suits relayed the hiss. Unfortunately, a high-pitched whine was now equally audible: the kind that made the hair on your arms lift up. Channa looked down the long corridor, shabby with age and dim with the emergency glowstrips' ghostly blue light.

Flies buzzed around them. Patsy slapped one against the wall.

"Blowflies," she said after a good look. There was a faint quaver in her voice. "Had 'em on the ranch."

"Sound pickup says there are live ones down there," Channa said. "Let's go."

✧   ✧   ✧

Doctor Chaundra's hands flew over his keypad as he made notes. He was a smallish brown-skinned man with delicate bones and a precise, scholarly manner.

"Fifty maximum, you say?"

Simeon switched back to the implant data filling another part of his consciousness. Channa's breathing sounded ragged; her heartbeat was elevated, and the stomach-acid level indicated suppressed nausea. Simeon wasn't surprised. The things she was seeing made *him* feel a little sick in an entirely nonphysical way that was still highly unpleasant.

"Short-term, improvised attempt at coldsleep," she said, voice struggling for the objectivity of a report. He looked at the tangle of cobbled-together equipment around living and dead. "Probably to cut down on air consumption. Heavy equipment failures."

The latest chamber held mostly dead ones, eyes fallen in and dried lips shrunk back over grinning teeth. Maggots, too. Some of the corpses were children, dead children nestled against dead mothers. In a few, the maggots gave a ghastly semblance of life, moving the swollen, blackened limbs. About the only mercy was the elastic nets that held living and dead down to the pallets on the deck or to the bunks. Evidently someone had foreseen that the interior gravity fields might go. Simeon imagined walking into one of those chambers and finding the putrefying bodies floating loose. . . .

"This one—" Channa began, swallowing and bending over a body that was either still alive or only recently dead. Drifting maggots brushed the surface of her faceplate and clung wetly, writhing. She retched, then forced herself to brush them away.

A *chunngggg* sound echoed through the still air. "What was that?"

Simeon split his viewpoint yet again. The rescue ship hovering off the side of the hulk had launched a missile carrying a large-diameter hose and attached to a pumping system: a force-deck system which punched through the hull and sealed itself.

"Air harpoon," he said. "We'll be pumping in a second."

"I kin hear it," Patsy said from the corridor. Her arc gun crashed, opening a sealed door. "More in heah. 'Bout the same."

"With fifty living, we should have no trouble," the doctor was saying to Simeon in the safe, clean sickbay office. Chaundra tapped for a closeup on one of the recordings, looking at the life-signs readouts beside the wasted face of a refugee. "Coldsleep dosed, the old partial method; very unsafe dosage, and oxygen deprivation. Dehydration, starvation, but mostly inadequate air. Hmm."

He blinked. "Physical type? Sometimes there is genetic divergence on isolated colonies. I must check. These look to be of sudeuropan race—archaic type, very pure. We should evacuate them as soon as possible."

"I'm working on it," Simeon said with controlled passion. *I'm never going to look at battlefield reconstructions quite the same way again,* he thought.

Through Channa's ears, he heard feet clacking in the corridor outside, stickfields in the suit shoes substituting for gravity. The volunteers came in briskly enough, inflatable rescue bubbles in their hands, then halted in disbelief. One tried to control his retching for a moment and then went into an excruciating and dangerous fit of vomiting inside a closed helmet. His squadmates removed it, only to have his paroxysm grow worse as the stink hit his nostrils. The luckless volunteer went into the first of the bubbles.

"Get moving!" Channa ordered. Only Simeon could hear the tremors in her voice beyond the range of normal ears. "The living ones are marked with a slash of yellow from a cargo checker. Use plasma feeds, the emergency antidotes, and get them *out* of here. These people belong in regeneration. *Now!*"

Raggedly, then with gathering speed, the stationers moved to their work. Channa escaped back into the corridor, exhaling a breath she had not been conscious of holding. Simeon was profoundly thankful she had not tried cracking her suit seals when the air hose went in. It would take months of vacuum to get the stink out of this ship. Much more time than the vessel had. The final fire of the interior coils would at least cleanse it.

"How long?" she asked.

"Not less than an hour, not more than three," he replied. "I think the pirate hypothesis is out."

Channa nodded jerkily; too many families and children. Pirates were much more common in fiction than in fact, anyway. Bodies floated in the next chamber down, and medics working over the three living before transferring them to life bubbles.

"Ms. Hap, I'm !Tez Kle." The Sendee wore a medical assistant's arm-flash on his suit.

Channa glanced at him in surprise. Not many aliens chose to

specialize in Terran medicine. Of course, Sondee were rather humanoid, if you managed to ignore the four eyes—two large and golden about where eyes should be, and two more above the whorled ridges that served as ears; you could *not* sneak up on a Sendee— and the lack of any facial features apart from a nostril slit and round suckerlike mouth. They had lovely voices, with far more vocal range and control than a human.

She came up beside the bubbles. "You're in charge?" He nodded. "Let me give you a hand," she said.

The first figure she turned to had reddish-black hair, a short muscular man with a square face. She released his restraints and lifted him, then gave him a gentle shove into the body-length sack, sealed it and activated it. His color seemed to improve immediately. She turned to his companion and froze.

"Channa, your vital signs just did the strangest little jig. What's the problem?" Simeon asked.

This young man was tall, close to two meters, broad-shouldered and slim-hipped, shapely and muscular as an athlete. He had a clean, classically perfect profile, with firmly molded chin and sensitive mouth. His delicately curving cheekbones were brushed by long dark lashes, the corners of his eyes tilted upwards. His long hair was blue-black, curling back from his high intelligent forehead to fall almost to his shoulders.

Channa sighed in admiration, then caught herself. *This stud is so handsome even being sick makes him look good.*

"Oh ho," Simeon crowed. "Very nice, Channa, but if you don't put Adonis there in his sack, he's going to go a very unflattering shade of blue."

"Em . . . right." She unbuckled the man and sealed him in his sack, connecting the two bags together. Then she tugged them behind her to the lock where she turned them over to the waiting med-techs. The goods-transporter's hold was filled with floating, jostling sacks while Channa and the med-tech chief stood in the lock, checking their sensors for heart-beats.

"Guess we got them all," !Tez Kle said. "But I don't think we can save them all. We left those we were certain we couldn't help," he said apologetically.

"Nothing else you could do," Channa told him. "We don't have time for anything else. Go," she said, and slapped his shoulder. "I've got a tug outside." She sealed the end of the caterpillar lock behind him and waited impatiently for the pilot to retract it. "Damn, I wish we could have gotten to the bridge."

"You and Patsy give it a try," Simeon answered. "Every bit of data will help, but we're cutting it a little close. I'm positioning tugs to push that wreck away from the station and *soon*."

Channa looked up sharply. "It's still a danger to you?"

"Nothing this brain can't handle," Simeon said blithely. "You do what you can, brawn."

She looked down at the notescreen tethered at her waist, studying the map of the ship's interior which she had managed to acquire from its own data banks, archaic as they were.

"I'll try through here," she said, struggling with the toggles of the hatch. "It'd be the more direct route, if it's open. If it isn't, I'll rendezvous with Patsy immediately."

"I need some people for tug and detonations work," Simeon announced. "It's going to be dicey."

The assembly room beneath the south-polar docking bay was full of second-wave volunteers, those not needed or qualified for the emergency medical work. Every single one stepped forward. Despite the seriousness of the situation, Simeon found time for a grim internal smile. *That old line's worked its challenge since Gilgamesh,* he thought, proving that even the oldest books on military psychology were right. People were *very* reluctant to appear frightened in front of others, especially their friends. He called the roll of those he needed. They were already suited up, helmets under their arms. Gus, of course, and six of the more experienced tug pilots, with six of the mining explosives experts who had been taking R & R on the SSS. "Thank you and I thank all the rest of you, too."

As soon as the room emptied of all but the participants, he began the briefing with the truth.

"That ship is going to blow. The engines, by the sound of them, are critically unbalanced, redlining far off scale. We've got the survivors off her. But we've *got* to get her far enough from the station so that when she goes, she won't take us with her. That's not the only problem. We've got to be sure she'll break into the smallest possible fragments and that they are thrown in a favorable dispersal pattern."

The explosives men grinned at each other. "Easiest thing in the world, Simeon," their spokesman said with a rakish smile. "If you know what you're doing."

"We do," one of the others said, thumping the spokesman jovially on the back. The man didn't so much as rock on his toes.

"That's good to know, guys! Can you tug pilots match their skill by redlining your engines a little to pull her as far away from us as you can?"

"Hell, Simeon," Gus said, "you oughta know we'd have no trouble doing that little thing for you."

"I'll be monitoring and *should* be able to give you fair warning to get yourselves clear." He paused a moment, anxious despite their obvious disregard for the inherent dangers. "Have I made the situation clear?"

Gus grinned. "Couldn't be clearer, station man," he said, giving his broad shoulders a preparatory twitch in response to the challenge. "And we don't have much time for further chatter!"

Another voice broke in: Patsy's. Simeon keyed her visual transmission to one of the ready-room screens; she was back in the control seat of her tug.

"My, ain't the *machismo* level high around here? You got one tug already in place, Simeon—mine. Count me in, too."

Gus winced. "Look, Patsy, we're in very deep, ah—"

"Very deep shit," she finished, grinning at him. "Ah *know* the words, Gus."

Everybody laughed. Simeon looked them over and stifled a wave of bitter longing. A military commander of any stature led his troops from the front, not from an impervious titanium column. *Don't worry, if they fail you'll be the only one left to say what happened, thanks to that same titanium column. If you can live with your conscience, that is.*

"I'll keep my eye on the coils and give you enough warning to peel off," Simeon promised.

Almost simultaneously, helmets covered the faces of this small band of heroes.

"This is taking more time than it's worth," Channa said in disgust, giving the control panel a final thump with her fist. The door valved open.

"Damn! And I thought that was a station legend," she said. "Does it work for you, Simeon?"

"Having a servo whack me with a wrench to make me work properly?" he asked. "No, not often. The bridge ought to be right down there. And *hurry.*"

"How are we handling the demolition?" she asked him, stepping through the half-open door and trotting down the darkened way, her helmet light fanning ahead. Mercifully, no bodies floated about this section.

"I've got a team rigging explosives all around the ship to blow it to," he paused, his own nerves making him play the clown, "smithereens. Real, genuine, non-station piercing smithereens. It would be disgraceful, utterly disgraceful, to get holed by flying debris after surviving this morning, don't you think? Ah, the tug volunteers are in place, ready to grapple. Ah! They've broken her out of orbital inertia."

Movement was not obvious this far in the bowels of the dying ship. "Who's in charge of the team?" Channa asked.

"Gus."

"Patsy said he was a good pilot," Channa commented. "Soon as I finish here, I'll join her. Is she still standing by at the hatch?"

"She is, to pick you up and bring you straight back to the station with any information you discover."

"I can scan the info back to you, Sim-mate, but first I have to find it, you know." She stumbled over some jumble piled in the corridor and recovered herself.

"You and Patsy get *straight* back here. I can't have my brawn risking her neck when . . ."

"Simeon," she said reasonably, "brawns are supposed to risk their necks for their brains. And if you, the station, are at risk, *I* am required to reduce that risk any way possible. This time I can do it by helping tug the risk away from here. Have I made myself clear on this point?"

"I don't like it," Simeon said in a disgruntled mumble. "Foolish risk."

"Thank you for your input, but Simeon . . ."

"Yeah?"

"Don't you *ever* try to forbid me to do the job I'm here to do. You got that?"

"Right in the forehead, sweetheart."

"Not quite where I was aiming, but it'll do," Channa said.

"If you get through to the bridge of that ship, can I *ask* you for a download?" Simeon said plaintively.

"Why else am I penetrating this about-to-blow-up wreck?" Channa said. "Patsy, you read me?"

"Welcome to the pahty, Channa," came Patsy's cheerful voice.

"You don't mind my crashing?"

Patsy laughed. "Watch yoah choice of words, girl."

"I just noticed something," Channa said, slowing her pace.

"What?"

"Paper. What's all this *paper* doing around?" There were sheets of it drifting down the corridor and sticking with static attraction to the rubbery walls.

"This lumbering hulk must be filled with gear so ancient it's exotic," Simeon said.

"*Paper* storage?" she said dubiously.

"Maybe they regressed."

"Could it originally have been piloted by a shellperson?" Channa asked, suddenly jumping to some conclusions that ought to have been more obvious to both herself and Simeon. If she got the edge on him on this one . . .

"Highly unlikely," Simeon said patronizingly. "B & B ships weren't that common then. All of these little back-of-beyond colonies were literally a shot in the dark, too risky to expend us on. C'mon, forward is to your right, one more passage to reach that control room."

"Aye, sir," she said. She worked her way forward, past leaking pipes and the occasionally sparking control boxes, ruptured by the overloads of the catastrophic deceleration.

"Paper," Channa said in wonder, wishing she could touch the valuable substance with her bare hands.

"And books! At least I think that's what I saw when you glanced into that corner. No, further right. Yes! Books!"

"No time for browsing now," Channa said firmly.

"Right," he said. "Antiquarian reflex, sorry."

"Ah, I am now at the control room," she said.

It was large and circular; most of the consoles were under shrink-shrouds of plastic that looked rigid with age. Raw, hasty jury-rigs had restored a few panels to functionality. She had to duck under festoons of cable which were draped to and fro with no noticeable pattern. In the dimming light, she saw jury-rigged control boxes taped to consoles. The whole bridge seemed to have been reconstructed with mad abandon.

"Ghu! They flew this thing?" Simeon exclaimed. *They must have been crazy,* he thought and cocked a weather-ear to the sound from the engine. "The log," Simeon reminded her. "Though I'm inclined to doubt that this outfit has anything that fancy. Strip the data bank, too. We want any information we can get."

"You tell me how to retrieve information from this archaic mess and you've got it," she answered, peering from workstation to workstation, trying to figure which one might access the main banks.

"I've got to go a long way back in my own files to find something comparable," he said. "There're only three centuries of buggering-up to decode but . . . ah, try the second console to your right. About the only one they hadn't been trying to use."

She drew the information feedline out of her glove and pressed it over the inductor surface. The screen beside it clicked to life and began flowing with a spaghetti-complex web of symbols.

"Oh, my oh my," Simeon muttered.

"Problems, Sim?"

"Nothing ol' Simeon can't handle," he said. "But the code is *old*. I don't have anything that esoteric on file. Nothing I can't eventually decipher."

"Don't let your modesty run away with you," she muttered, looking down at her wrist chrono. *Plenty of time,* she thought. *I hope.*

"I'm just cracking the interface and downloading it to decode at leisure," Simeon replied. "Don't get your tits in a tizzy."

"*What* did you say?"

"Old slang," he replied blandly.

"Another antiquarian reflex, no doubt," she said archly.

"Touché. Okay, got it," he said, "Get out of there."

"Gawd-*damn* this thing!" Patsy said in frustration.

The tug was presenting its broad rear surface to the ancient colony ship. Channa scanned carefully on visual and deep-magnetic, looking for a place to engage their grapple.

"Time is a factor here, Ms. Hap." Gus's voice was a little testy. Aligning an extra tug in the pattern had taken more time than anticipated.

"I just got up here, Mr. Gusky. I'm looking for a flat spot among these struts. I can see why you gave it a pass. It's a mess. Wait, I think I see something now, it's . . ." She looked again and increased the magnification. "Bloody *hell*!" she cried.

"Crap!" Simeon's voice overrode hers. It took the others a few moments longer.

"I don't believe it," Channa whispered.

"What?" Patsy demanded. "What do you see?"

"It's a shell. There's a shellperson out there, strapped to the hull."

"Are you sure?" Gus' voice cut in. "Look, everyone else is in place, we have to get this thing away from the station—"

Simeon ordered in a roar that nearly fractured eardrums. "BELAY THAT, GUSKY!" A moment of stunned silence followed. "Check it out, Channa. Now!"

"Aye, aye, sir," Channa said even as she strobed a landing spot where Patsy could set the tug down. "Yes, Mr. Gusky, it's a shellperson all right. Granted, it doesn't look like anything you're likely to have seen, but brawns learn to recognize 'em all."

She hoped Simeon never had occasion to bellow like that again, with the decibels going off the gauge. Understandable, of course, or at least to her. If brains had a collective nightmare, it was being cut off from their equipment and left helpless. Attached to their leads and machinery, a shellperson was the next thing to immortal, a high-tech demigod in this world. Cut off from it, they were cripples. *Spam-in-a-can*, as the obscene joke had it. Neither Simeon nor she were capable of abandoning a shellperson, even if its occupant should prove dead.

"Gus, why don't you set the haul in motion," Channa said, knowing her priorities had just shifted. "Patsy and I will get this shellperson off."

She anchored the grapple just above the shell and as quickly as possible, reeled the tug to it. She studied the shell in the monitor as she drew closer. "It's inward facing, they did that right at least."

"Fardling *right*?" Simeon cursed. "Did it right? There is nothing *right* about this. What kind of shit-for-brains *did* this? That shellperson was lodged on the *exterior of the hull*! Anything could have happened to him or her! Bastards, bastards, *bastards*. Get him out of there!"

Channa heard the cold passion in Simeon's voice and recognized another aspect of him, one his often diffident manner and sometimes boyish enthusiasms had masked. Shellpeople were as individual as normals. Why had she thought him shallow, even trivial? Because of his fascination with ancient wars and weaponry?

"I'm on my way, Simeon," she said. "Gusky, step on it. We'll get out of your way. This won't take long."

"It had better not," the ex-Navy man said, his voice still carrying a trace of resentment. "Wilco. Out."

The surge of acceleration was faint but definite as the bulky vessel began to move. Channa locked a safety line to her suit before she swung down to the pitted, corroded surface of the hull and began to thread her way through the crazed jungle of beam-fused girders that covered it like fungus. The light had the absolute white-and-shadow of space, but the froth where vaporized metal had recondensed looked out of place.

I'm too used to things being new and functional, she told herself at a level below the machine-efficient movements of hands and feet. Fear coiled at a deeper level still, shouting that she was risking two living humans for a shellperson who could have died long ago. Brawn training overrode that trickle of fear almost before she noticed. A shellperson could *not* be left, not while a brawn could remove him.

"Is the brain alraht?" Patsy asked.

"Can't tell yet," Channa told her. Off to her left a white light flashed and the metal toned beneath her feet.

"What was that?" she half-squawked.

"Iron ore," Gus said. "She's moving into the dispersal cone of that load of balled ore. There's a lot of that crap out here. Hurry."

I'm hurrying, I'm hurrying, Channa thought. The shell was a shape like a metal egg split down the middle, with a tangle of feed lines and telemetry jacked into opened access panels. Three more winks of light as ore struck at hundreds of kps further down the derelict's hull, then a whole cluster. Debris flipped away into space with leisurely grace.

"Channa . . ." Simeon began. The rage was out of his voice, replaced by fear for her. Somehow that warmed Channa despite the cold clamp she'd put on her feelings.

"Can't be helped," she said and planted her own grapple at the top of the shell, just beside the lugs.

"It's a different design from mine," Simeon told her. "I'm doing a search now to see where you can put a heavy magnet without interrupting anything vital."

"Fine," she said distractedly. "Looks like they just took a dozen loops of wire cable and tack-welded it to hold the shell down. Talk about improvisation!"

Simeon watched her hands as she used a small laser to cut through one of the cables lashing the capsule to the hull. It broke free and the shell fell away from the hull slightly, fine wires floating like roots in a glass of water. *God, it looks so naked,* he thought helplessly.

Channa's gaze had passed over the code name incised on the shell so he could read it. PMG-266-S, a low number brain of very advanced years. *Guiyon.* The name floated up out of deep storage where all the names of his kind rested. A managerial sort. Working for the Colonial Department as it was, back then. Paid off his contract and dropped out of touch, presumed rogue. A hermit.

"He's a two-hundred series," he told her. "Now put the grapple dead center, upper side."

Channa used a remote control device to lower one of the smaller grapples from the tug, gingerly placing it as directed. Then she returned to cutting cables. She was working on the next to last one when a pebble-sized piece of ore struck the back of her helmet, hard enough to knock her sideways and to burn straight through her air regulator from left to right. Simeon saw specks of plastic spin off in the wake of the tiny meteor. The exterior view from the tug's pick-ups showed metal glowing white-hot.

"Channa!" Simeon called. The med-readouts flashed unconscious-ness. He overrode the suit and ordered it to inject stimulants, a horse-dose, anything to buy her time.

"Oww." Channa jerked and then shook herself, hauling back on the safety line until her feet touched the surface of the ship. A red light flashed on the inside of her faceplate and the message:

"System failure—air regulation. Ten minutes emergency supply only" appeared. It was replaced by 10:00. Then 09:59, and the seconds scrolled down inexorably.

"Channa, you okay? Should Ah git down there?"

"No!" Channa rasped. "Keep ready for lift."

Simeon called. "Channa, get inside."

"I'm almost finished," she said gruffly.

"Now," he said.

She ignored him. He watched the cable part, and her hands reached for the last one. From another view he watched the ancient colony ship being dragged away at an ever increasing acceleration.

"Channa! Get your ass in that tug now!"

"Shut—*up!*" she snapped.

The final cable parted and the shell swung free. For the first time, Simeon saw that the feeder line was damaged. *No,* he thought.

08:38.

Channa began to disconnect the shell's input leads. It was diffi-cult work in the unwieldy suit gloves, but her long-fingered hands moved with careful delicacy. She closed the valve on the broken feeder line.

"Might not be too bad," she muttered. "There'll be an interior backup. Probably ruptured when they stopped."

Then she keyed the remote to reel them both back to the tug at a careful pace, holding on to the exterior lugs and using her feet to fend them off random projections. The shell went *ter-unnnggg* against the light-load grapnels up near the apex of the stubby wedge; the mechanical claws closed on the hard alloy with immovable pressure.

06:58.

She turned and pivoted around a handhold and dove feetfirst into the control seat.

"Get yo' suit plugged in!" Patsy snapped, beating Simeon by nanoseconds.

"Can't. This is a standard EVA suit, the input valve's upstream of the break. Get moving, we have to help haul this thing!"

"Negative," Simeon said. "Make tracks back to the station, Patsy."

"*Negative on that.*" Channa said. "If we don't get this hulk far enough away, there won't be a station to go back to."

Patsy bit her lip and touched the controls. The tug sprang straight up, the derelict shrinking from sky-spanning vastness to child's model size in seconds as the great soft hand of acceleration shoved at them.

"Then you plant that grapnel field," she said urgently. "We can help the boost with our own rise. But when that's done, we're goin' *home*, girl."

Channa began the adjustments. The tug was designed for straightforward long slow pulls, not this redline-everything race against disaster. She must balance the uneven pull that might shred the tug's structure and compensate for the hulk's weakness by intuition as much as anything. Who knew what structural members had given way within? It would do very little good to rip a large segment of it loose. . . . The giant ship began to grow slightly smaller.

She glanced at the readout. "I hate these clock things," she said fiercely. "They must have been created by a sadist. I'm going to *know* when I run out of air."

"Stop talking," Simeon ordered, "you're wasting oxygen. When that clock has flipped over another thirty seconds, *you* return to station!"

Gus' command rang through the conversation. "*Synchronize release, slave controls to mine as Patsy cuts loose.*"

Channa keyed it in. "Five seconds. *Mark.*"

Patsy cursed with scatological inventiveness as the little craft surged. Then it flipped end-for-end and the space behind them paled as the drive worked to shed velocity. They would have to kill their delta-V away from the station before they could return.

"*Priority,*" she barked over the open circuit. "Everyone git outta my way, 'cause I ain't stoppin'!"

Deceleration turned to acceleration again. Channa wheezed a protest as her ribs clamped down on her lungs.

04:11.

Simeon's monologue took on a frantic note. He forced his mind not to calculate times, with an effort that almost banished fear.

Keep her informed, he thought: " . . . madness to have attempted that sort of linkage. The nutrients might have given out on the trip. It depends on when the feeder line was damaged. *I* might be responsible for that. It could have happened when I hit them with the satellites. What do you think? No, don't answer, save your air. I know we won't be able to tell anyway until we examine him.

"What kind of people are these?" he asked for perhaps the twentieth time. "Could they be pirates who stole the brain? Then why didn't they bring it inside? The access-way? Sure, that must be it, they couldn't get it through the hatch. Still, a shellperson is a valuable resource. You'd think they try to protect him more if they *had* to leave him outside. It could be some kind of punitive measure by an insane religious sect. Nah, Central would never assign a brain to a group like that, it wouldn't make sense." He began to curse again. "Hey, Channa, stop rolling your eyes like that. You're making me dizzy." The circling increased in tempo. "Okay, okay, I'll change the subject. Sheesh, take away a woman's ability to talk . . ." Channa closed her eyes. "I was *joking,* Channa." Her eyes remained closed. "You're getting close to the station. You're going to need to see where you're going. Remember what it's like out there." No change. "Okay, I apologize. It was a stupid, ignorant remark and I regret it. I didn't even mean it. Bad joke, okay?"

She opened her eyes.

03:01.

She was midway between the receding colony-ship and the station.

"I estimate that you'll run out of air three minutes before you reach the station," Simeon said. "But, if you take the most direct route, that unfortunately will take you right through the thickest concentration of spilled ore."

"Shit!" Patsy hissed. "Tell me somethin' Ah don't know!"

Channa fought down an oxygen wasting sigh. "Play safe?"

"Then you'll fall short by four minutes, eight seconds."

"Play safe. Don't want a shell full a holes."

Simeon was silent for a moment, feeding the pilot instructions for avoiding the worst of the ore-meteor cloud.

"You've got more guts than sense, Channa."

Patsy closed one eye and laughed. "Mind now, Ah didn't say Ah didn't like it, Ah was just remarkin' on it." She opened her eye. "Y'hold on now, we're goin' through like a scalded armadillo."

Channa's breathing began to rasp; psychological, but it wasted air. *Oh, God, don't let her die*, he thought. *That shell's hanging out there. Is the mass of the tug enough to shield him from debris?*

Even one pebble of ore at the right angle and all her sacrifice would be for nothing. Simeon knew Channa was about to undergo an experience that would feel like dying. Humans could survive for several minutes without air—hours, sometimes, in cold water. The length of time to brain death was utterly unpredictable but oxygen deprivation might cause brain damage.

Despite a very real and intense anxiety about Channa, his thoughts inexorably returned to the shell . . . to Guiyon. *He's alone in the dark,* Simeon said to himself, *Channa's got Patsy, and me.* Sensory deprivation would make every second feel like a subjective hour, and the backups would keep the shellperson conscious until the last precious molecules of nutrient were gone. Simeon wished desperately that he could spare hum the nightmare.

"Headache," Channa gasped. "*Hurts.*" Her head lolled, would have fallen forward if the savage high-G acceleration had allowed it.

Her breathing was rasping louder now and not psychosomatic. It was instinct—the hindbrain telling the lungs that they were suffocating. The readouts showed an adrenaline surge, just the wrong thing. Reflexes older than her remote reptile ancestors were preparing the body to fight free of whatever barred it from air.

"Hang on, Channa, hang on," Simeon chanted. Then: "Can't you go any *faster?*"

"Not 'lessn you want this here tug smeared all over the loadin' bay," Patsy said grimly.

"Isn't inertia wonderful?" Gusky muttered to himself, looking down again at the readings, *fourteen kps and building.* Not very fast, but the battered remnant of the hulk still massed multiple kilotons.

"Bit of a paradox," one of the volunteer miners said. "I want this thing as far from the station as I can get it—but I want to be as far away from it as possible myself."

"Ho. Ho. Ho," Gusky said. "Number three, you're a little off synch. Don't waste our delta-V."

"What's our safety margin, Gus?"

"That depends on when Simeon tells us to cut and run." *I'm really, really sorry I got you mad at me, Simeon!* "I'd like to get twenty klicks from the station before we drop the thing. But, what can I tell ya? If she blows without warning, if the explosives don't do what they're supposed to, if we don't get far enough away before she goes . . . actually, I don't think we *have* a safety margin."

"Sorry I asked."

"Hmph."

Simeon's voice broke in. "Prepare to drop in one minute seven seconds from mark. *Mark.* Get it right, Gus."

"Yeah," said one of the miners who had rigged the charges, "that thing has to stay in the same attitude. Charges won't be half as effective if it's tumbling."

"Roger that," Simeon said. No time for a linkup. They'd have to listen, *really* carefully. "Everyone got that mark?"

A chorus of affirmatives. Gusky licked sweat from his upper lip. He'd never told Simeon, exactly, but his five-year hitch in the Navy had been pretty uneventful: patrols, exercises, showing the flag, mapping expeditions. The most nerve-wracking moments had been the fleet handball competitions and surprise inspections.

"You pull the trigger, right?" he said.

"You got it, buddy," Simeon replied. His voice had less timbre, less humanity to it than usual.

"I hate being reassured in a voice that calm."

I've got other things on my mind. "Channa's suit got hit. She's running out of air."

"Oh." *I screwed the pooch again, goddammit.* "Sorry."

"Get ready."

The tugs were arrayed around the great tattered bulk of the intruder ship like the legs of a starfish, linked by the invisible bonds of the grapnel fields. Gusky kept the rear-field screen on at a steady 25x magnification. When the fields released, the image of the hulk seemed to disappear into a point-source of light in less than a heart-beat. Vision went gray at the edges, before the engines cycled down to something bearable. Tugs necessarily had high power-to-weight ratios. Then the shrinking dot of the derelict blinked with colorless fire.

Gusky cycled the screen to higher magnification. "Phew," he said gustily. The charges had cut the remaining forward section loose from the half-melted engine compartment and its core. Joined to the power module, whatever parts of the ship did not vaporize would be hyper-velocity shrapnel in all directions. With a klick or so distance and a vector away from the station, much less could go wrong. Blast is less dangerous without an atmosphere to propagate in. There is noth-ing to carry the shock wave except the actual gases of the explosion and they disperse rapidly. Given minimal luck, the explosion would just kick what was left of the hulk further away.

"When will it—"

The screen blanked protectively. So did his faceplate and the for-ward ports of the tug's cabin. Beside him the copilot flung his hand up in useless reflex. Even from the rear, the intensity of light was overwhelming.

"*Did it work?*" Gusky called as visibility returned. That was not as reassuring as it could have been. Half the sensors and telltales on the board were blinking red.

"Sorry." This time Simeon *did* sound sorry. "That ship . . . the engines were so old, the parameters were different . . . There's a lot more secondary radiation and subflux than I thought there would be."

"Thanks," Gusky said facetiously. "All right, people, report."

"I've got a flux in my drive cores I can't damp," one of the vol-unteers said immediately. "Induction, I guess. Getting worse."

"Let me see it," Gusky said, surprised at his own calm. This was much better than waiting; there wasn't *time* to be worried. "All right, you've got a feedback loop there and it's past redline. Set your controls for maximum acceleration at ninety degrees to the ecliptic with a one-minute delay, then bail out."

"*Hey, this is my tug.*" the volunteer wailed.

"It's going to be your ball of incandescent gas in about ten min-utes," Gusky said grimly. "Or hot gas that includes you. Take your pick."

Simeon cut in. "Station will pick up full replacement costs."

"Lobachevsy and Wong, you're closest," Gusky said, "pick 'em up!" Gusky's pickups showed the luckless volunteers jetting away on backpack and their craft streaking for deep space on autopilot. "The rest of you, dump me some data."

"Yessir, Admiral," one replied dryly.

The information dutifully came in. "Okay, Lobachevsky, Wong, you look functional, sort of. Take the others with overstrained drives in tow, and we'll go back nice and slow and easy." *With several millions' worth of tug that just became so much scrap. Suddenly boring routine becomes very attractive as a way of life. War games are excitement enough.*

He touched the control surfaces to establish a tight line circuit to the station. "Simeon, what about us?"

"Let's put it this way, Gus. None of you are going to die. But some of you aren't going to be very happy for a while, either. Sickbay will be crowded." A long pause. "Congratulations."

Gus grinned; half of that was relief from raw fear. Everyone who lives in space is afraid of decompression, which is why many become agoraphobic planetside. Those who do much EVA work or serve on warships develop a similar fear of radiation, which has the added terror of killing insidiously. On the other hand, most dangers in space either kill cleanly or let live.

"You're welcome," the big man continued. "What about Channa?"

Patsy's voice joined in. "She's gonna be fahn. Hey, Gus," she went on lazily, "you thaink people will respect us for this?"

Gusky keyed for the visuals. He got a double view, overhead from the docking chamber where the tug rested in its cradle and from the vehicle itself. Both showed Channa Hap being carried off in a floating stretcher.

"Phew. Glad she made it okay."

"Yayuh, mah sentiments exactly. Got a good one thar."

Gusky nodded. *On station, Channa acted like a cryonic bitch,* he thought, *but she's there when it comes down to cases.* This was the worst emergency SSS-900 had faced in the time he'd been here. *SSS-900-C,* he reminded himself.

"I dunno," he said, "*I* never respected anyone who led from the rear."

She laughed. "Hey! This might get us a nice rest cure somewhar pretty. We could go tagetha." She made the last a question.

"If any two parts of us are still stuck together when this is over, Patsy, you got a date."

"Unh-hunh!" she said enthusiastically.

Hey, first base, Gusky thought. After thirty months of ritualized sparring so routine it had gotten to be as comfortably low-key as playing war games with Simeon. *That is, if I'm not sick as a puke once sickbay gets through with me.* Doctor Chaundra believed in repairing you *rapidly.* In some circles he was known as "Kill or Cure Chaundra."

"I need a drink," he said solemnly.

"Ah'll buy," Patsy said.

CHAPTER SEVEN

CHANNA WOKE TO an excruciating, high-pitched wailing.

The engines! she thought. *I'm still on the derelict! I've got to get out of here!*

She lifted her head with a gasp and laid it back down again with a heartfelt groan. *This has to be a fatal headache,* she thought, *nobody could feel like this and live.*

The ceiling overhead was a soothing pale blue as were the privacy screens around her. There was a vase of flowers on the bedside table and a bank of portable equipment on the other side, quietly talking to itself and occasionally waving a sensor probe over her body. A suit of working clothes, overtights and jacket and belt, were draped on a clothes stand at the foot of the bed. The air had a slight, pleasant scent of cedar.

Sickbay, she thought. The ambience was unmistakable.

The wailing went on and on, sometimes breaking into sharp yelps. *I hope I live long enough to kill whoever is making that racket.*

"Who *is* that?" she finally demanded.

"Ah, Channa," said Simeon in a voice as soft as rain water.

Channa sighed and closed her eyes again. It was restful, and her body was beginning to accept that she was alive and in no danger. Which was a difficult thing, if you'd gone under deeply concerned about your chances of ever waking up again.

"Welcome back to the living," said a flatter voice with a lilting singsong accent. There was a sound of movement.

She opened her eyes to see Doctor Chaundra leaning over her. He had his professional expression on; a sort of antiseptic smile, nothing like the genuine enthusiasm he showed in a social situation talking about his specialty. Channa managed the complex procedure of smiling and wincing simultaneously.

"My head," she said in a croaking voice, feebly raising a shaking hand to rub her brow.

"Got just the thing," he said. He touched the angle of her throat with an injector. It hissed and she felt a touch of cold.

Almost instantly, the pain boring its way into her brain began to fade. "Oh, Ghu! that's better." She licked dry lips.

"No, I have merely blocked the pain," the doctor said pedantically. "The organic damage is minimal but will take several days to heal."

"Thirsty?" She raised her brows in pathetic query.

Chaundra poured a glass of water from a bedside carafe, put in a straw and handed it to her.

She sucked greedily on the straw, mindful of her head position, and handed him the empty glass. "More," she demanded. He refilled it, and she drained it again almost as soon as he handed it to her. The wailer took off again. Channa frowned. "Who's that badly hurt?"

He grimaced. "She's one of the people we evacuated from the ship; the first one awake. We don't know who she is. She's done nothing but shriek since she woke up. To answer your other question, no, she's not badly hurt. She's dehydrated, and probably has a headache like yours from that, and she had a bloody nose from the abrupt deceleration."

There was an especially violent shriek and the sound of something metal tipping over and of things scattering. Voices murmured soothing words in edged tones.

"If she can scream like that with a headache like the one I woke up with, she's crazy," Channa said.

Chaundra nodded. "That, too, is a possibility, but I feel that she is presently venting hysteria as a by-product of coldsleep." He sighed. "The earliest methods sometimes had the effect of suppressing basic inhibition."

"Can't you give her something?" Simeon asked from a wall mike. "That sound has just gone from pathetic to seriously annoying."

"No," the medical chief replied. "Or rather, I'd prefer not to immediately. They drugged themselves rather heavily, indeed, presumably to keep their oxygen consumption down. I've no idea for how long a period of time, but from their physical condition, it must have been too long." He gave another of his sighs. "I'd really rather not put anything else into her system. Especially since many of the substances they used seem to have been past recommended shelf life, or discontinued types, or both."

"They say that if someone gets hysterical, a simple slap across—" Simeon began.

Chaundra interrupted him. "I am thinking that has more to do with relieving the frustration of the listeners than the distress of the patient," he said with a resigned smile.

"You're a saint, Doctor," Channa told him. Actually she knew that he was a pacifist widower with a passion for surgery, but no matter. "But I'm not. So, before I'm compelled to go over there and knock the little git through the wall, I'd like to get out of here."

He smiled and touched the machine. It waved more probes over her, prodding in two or three sensitive places. The readouts had him nodding almost at once. "Yes, you can be going now."

She stood with a satisfied sigh. "Um, is there anyone coherent awake yet?"

"Yes, a young man. He's still more than a bit groggy, so we haven't let him up yet. He wants to help this girl."

"Can't you put him on a pallet or in a chair and push him over there?" Simeon asked. "It might help both of them."

"Depends," Chaundra said, "on how he's doing."

"Just seeing him might help her," Channa suggested.

"Worth a try," Chaundra shrugged and grabbed a float chair from a cluster of them by the door. "Over here," he said and Channa followed, pulling on a dressing gown.

The man in question was the beautiful lad she herself had packed up. Simeon watched Channa's pupils enlarge and decided that she was probably responding even more enthusiastically than she had on the ship. *Pheromones,* he told himself wisely. *And fewer distractions.*

The young man had raised himself up on one elbow, a slight sweat glistening on his shapely brow. He looked at them with distress in his light blue eyes.

"Please, let me go to her," he pleaded. His accent was exquisite, his voice a light baritone. The language was recognizable Standard, although the vowels had an archaic tonality.

From the look on her face, Simeon decided that Channa would

have taken him to hell if he wanted to go. Simeon wanted him off the station.

Guys like him cause more trouble than beautiful females, Simeon thought. *On the other hand, if he can shut that screamer up, I'll put him on the payroll.*

Channa and Chaundra helped the Adonis into the chair and pushed him over to the pallet where the young woman lay. He reached out for her hand and began stroking it.

She had waist-length dark hair and a pale, bony face with plain features and high cheekbones. Long, gold-lashed eyes of a dark blue that was almost black stared at him, her screeches cut off for a blissful moment of silence. Then the whites showed all round the iris of her eyes, and before Channa or Chaundra could stop her, she had grabbed the carafe from the table beside her and was swinging it at him.

"You did this! You could have killed me! *I almost died!*"

The metal carafe connected with his temple in a sickening smack. The young man slid bonelessly from the chair while, not content with the damage she'd just inflicted, the girl strove to climb over the safety railings on the side of her pallet, shrieking that it was his fault, all his fault. Then she began to sob with equal vigor. "My love, my love, what have they done to you?"

Chaundra's interns and head nurse leaped for the pallet in well-choreographed unison. This infirmary saw a lot of visiting miners, still high on various recreational chemicals, not to mention plain old-fashioned ethanol, so they knew what to do. One pinned her arms and another slapped an injector on the nearest portion of her flailing body. Instantly she slumped into unconsciousness.

"Doctor," Simeon said firmly, "put that girl in restraints until she returns to rationality. She can blame me for this one."

"You have it," Chaundra said. The nurses buckled the unconscious woman onto her pallet but were too professional to show the slightest trace of vindictiveness as they tightened the straps. Chaundra bent over the unconscious man.

"Glancing blow after all," he said, pulling up one eyelid. "Should regain consciousness soon."

"I'll be in my quarters, Doctor," Channa said, and gathering up her clothing, walked wearily to an elevator. She entered and leaned against a wall, dosing her eyes.

"You okay?" Simeon asked anxiously.

She smiled. "I'm very okay, thank you." She opened her eyes and straightened, rolling her shoulders to loosen the kinks. "I'm still thirsty," she said, "and hungry, and alive." Then she widened her eyes in dismay. "How could I forget? The brain, did he make it?"

Simeon paused. "No."

Channa slumped and covered her face with her hands. She looked up, her lips pressed tightly together for the rest of the ascent. Then she asked quietly, "Have you had a chance to find out anything about our survivors?"

"Not as much as I'd hoped to, but I did find out something about the shellperson. He was Planetary Manager Guiyon. Last assigned to a colony planet called Bethel, orbiting the sun GK728, known locally as Saffron. I informed Central Worlds of his . . . death: beyond the call of duty, I'd say. They told me what they had on record. After his original contract ended, he just stayed on, apparently for no other reason than he liked Saffron's pretty yellow color.

"Bethel's seemingly just an undistinguished colony of no great population, located a little off the beaten path, more than a bit xenophobic in their attitudes. They won't trade with nonhumans, for example. It was established about three hundred years ago by a tightly knit, religiously oriented group. Hmmm." Simeon paused. "In three hundred years, a religion could develop any number of nasty kinks. The refugees may have been cast out. They may have left voluntarily to establish another base for their sect. I don't have that information." He continued softly. "Guiyon must have been there a long, long time. A long time and a long way to die like that, alone in the dark."

His final words were said in the merest whisper and Channa felt tears pricking at her eyes. It was fitting for a brawn to mourn a brain. She let her tears fall. She could. Simeon couldn't.

She left the elevator and entered the lounge, dropping weakly into the nearest comfortable chair. She leaned her head back and closed her eyes, letting the tears fall. For a long time she and Simeon observed silence.

"What about the data we got from the bridge?" she said at last, wiping her eyes again with the back of her hand. "Was it blank?"

"I, uh, can't read it," Simeon said. Under the grief, embarrassment tinged his voice. "The codes are *ancient*. In fact, it may not be a code, it may be a language. One I don't have on record, which means it must have been extinct before spaceflight and in limited use even then."

Channa began to laugh, suppressing it with effort before it took her over. She stifled it with a groan. "I'm almost afraid to ask this but . . ." and she found herself glancing at his column for reassurance. "What's the report on the people we rescued? Besides the screamer."

"Forty of the fifty we found survived to reach the station."

"Oh, Ghu!" she said and sat forward, her arms crossed on her knees, her forehead resting on them. "We didn't have time to count the dead, did we? Damn! We could at least have done that!" She sat back again and looked around the room bitterly, as though resenting its comfortable, unchanged appearance.

"I know," Simeon told her. "I feel that I've failed."

"You aren't the only one," she said, and sobbed once. She placed her hand over her mouth, pressing hard, to stifle any others that might follow. After a moment she spoke again in a thick voice. "And the station?"

"That came out all right," he said, and gave her a report long enough for her to regain control: good news in the fortunate lack of injury to station personnel, lack of any real structural damage to the station or traffic, with the notable exception of the ore carrier. He reported that incoming ships were huddled on the far side of the station—just in case—and ended with an invitation to the party being thrown by the tug pilot volunteers for anyone who wanted to come. By the time he was finished, Channa was struggling to keep her eyes open.

"I never thought I'd see the day when I was too drained to debauch," she said in a hoarse voice. "I must be getting old."

"Cut yourself some slack, kid," Simeon said, reverting to his juvenile affectation. "You *did* actually die. Subjectively, I mean. I think it's a bit much to expect to be in a partying mood two hours after being brought back to life. Remember, the slogan is 'eat, drink and be merry for *tomorrow* we may die.' So you're covered."

Channa managed a weak grin.

She looks awful, he thought with concern, *and she probably looks exactly like she feels.* "How would it be if I sent something down in your name, champagne or something?"

"Perfect," she said weakly, but with feeling.

"And you must eat something. Doc Chaundra said you'd feel better for it. It'll stave off a return of the headache."

"I'm for that." She rose, reeling slightly on her way to the small galley to find whatever was easiest to prepare. She was staring into a cupboard, not even registering what she was looking at, when the door to the lounge swooshed open. She stumbled out to see who it was and arrived in time to see Mart'an, himself, and a bevy of waiters sweep into the main lounge.

"Ah, my dear and valiant mademoiselle!" He snapped his heels together and bowed crisply from the waist. "I salute you. We of the Perimeter Restauran' would like to thank you for your extraordinary bravery which has saved the station." His arm swept out gracefully, indicating the serving trolley. "A mere token of our esteem, I know, but we put our hearts into everything that we prepare, and this evening, I think that we have even surpassed ourselves. As our gratitude is surpassing." He bowed again, a more modest version, with his right hand spread across his heart.

Channa smiled stupidly at him for a moment until she could gather enough of her wits together to tell him that he was very kind.

He offered her his arm and led her to a chair. Instantly his cohorts flowed into action. A table was brought, a cloth spread, service laid, wine poured, napkin spread and food appeared on her plate. The arrangement alone was a work of art. Simeon recognized actual Terran truffles decorating the appetizer and the entree was no less than *carre d'agneau Mistral.* A file said the recipe was by Escoffier, Mart'an's boyhood hero.

I bet they'd chew it for her if she asked them to, Simeon thought, amused.

"Ah, Monsieur Simeon." Mart'an exhaled a tragic sigh, his face wearing the blank expression softshells adopted when addressing someone unseen. "How we wish we could offer a similar tribute to you."

Simeon put his likeness up on his column-screen, made it smile appreciatively and bow slightly. "By coming to the aid of my brawn in this manner, monsieur, you are serving both myself and the station superbly. I cannot begin to express my appreciation."

Channa's eyes widened; her mouth, however, was fully occupied.

Ha! he thought, triumphantly. *Didn't think I had it in me, didja, Happy? Diplomacy 'R Us.*

"I wonder," he said confidentially to Mart'an, "if it would be possible for you to clear away at a later time? Ms. Hap is extremely weary and I need to bring her up to speed on station business before she retires. . . ."

"Of, course," Mart'an said heartily. With a flutter of his hands, he gathered his magic minions together and the whole group departed as smoothly as they had arrived.

Channa sipped her wine with an appreciative glow on her face.

"Go easy on that," he cautioned her. "I know you're thirsty, but water would be a better choice."

"Yes, Dad." She picked up her fork and began eating again, chewing appreciatively. "Too bad you can't taste foods, but I assure you this lamb is deeelicious." She rolled her eyes. "So, bring me up to speed. What else is there to crown today's glad tidings?"

"Nothing more really," he said, "except that the computer has finally regurgitated a translation program for me. The language *was* extinct—Chuvash, whatever that is. The AI worked back from loanwords of known languages, but it's warning me that there are gaps in vocabulary and most certainly in shades of meaning . . ."

"What does Central Worlds say about this disaster?" She yawned deeply. "Or don't we have enough comsat capability left?"

"I gave them an outline of events and the reappearance of . . . Guiyon. They were more concerned that I was still operational. Which I am. They expect a full report, of course, but I'm hoping to include more information about the ship. They can wait. They've the bones of the matter."

"Any news on Joat?"

"Nothing specific," he said with a sigh. "With everyone suited up, it was impossible to tell who was who. Not all suits have nametags and skill-codes. I haven't heard a sound from the engineering section."

"Well, I want to be sure she's all right," Channa said, exploding in angry anxiety. "You open up a channel down there and tell her that we need to know if she made it. One lousy 'yes, I did' will be sufficient." She picked up her fork again but was merely pushing food around the plate, her expression almost sulky.

Simeon regarded her with a mildly exasperated mental smile. When she was tired, Channa was amazingly like Joat. Sending the necessary discreet query, he was also relieved to have received a prompt reply, though he puzzled over Joat's odd undertone.

"She made it. I told her one word would do it, and she gave me two. Quote, *I'm okay,* end-quote. You should try to get some rest, Channa." A pause. "No, wait a minute. She's adding something. Oh, really? Quote, *Tell Channa she did a neato job.*"

Unutterably relieved, Channa pushed the table aside. Somehow, knowing that Joat was safe released the tension that had kept her going so long. Like a robot, she moved toward her quarters, made it to the door before she stopped, holding onto the frame.

"Simeon," she said, looking over her shoulder at his column, her head of its own accord resting against the cool metal panel, "I am your brawn, remember. You are required to inform me of any untoward incident. Yes?"

"Yes, ma'am," he said meekly.

She nodded sharply: a "you'd better" gesture, and entered her quarters. The bed beckoned irresistibly; she had a dreamlike memory of fumbling with the sickbay wrapper and crawling onto the bed, of a servo pulling the covers up around her. Soft music hummed her to sleep.

"Good morning," Simeon greeted her the next day. "You look rested," he said. *I'm learning,* he congratulated himself, *I didn't say, you looked like hell on a rampage last night, or even, you look a lot better, I'm acquiring sensitivity,* he thought smugly, suppressing the thought that she had made him so. *Hope it doesn't wreck my style.*

"I feel rested, too," she said in some surprise. "After yesterday, I'm surprised I woke up today. You didn't," and her tone became suspicious, "let me oversleep?"

The essential Channa has not altered overnight! "Nothing new to report. I'm still parsing through the language, but it's odds on we'll get more out of the passengers than the logs."

"How are they? Anybody else awake yet?"

"Doctor Chaundra says that poor bastard the screeching Valkyrie cold-cocked is their leader, name of Amos ben Sierra Nueva. The valkyrie is Rachel bint Damscus. I knew you'd like to put names to the face . . . es," he added hurriedly, not wishing to single the man out for her attention in any way. "The doc says he'll be able to join us at the meeting."

"Who else?"

"Leader Amos and his sidekick, a guy called Joseph ben Said."

Channa took a sip of the coffee she'd made. "When are they due here?"

"We've a station officers meeting in about an hour. Chaundra, too, if someone's not critical. Whenever we've finished that, I'll call down for Sierra Nueva and this Joseph fellow."

"Do me a favor," Channa said, "call him Amos, would you please? Sierra Nueva makes him sound like one of those dances that are supposed to make your blood boil and your libido unhinge."

"You got it. We don't want forbidden passions running riot all over the station, now do we?"

"Well," she said with a grin, wiggling her eyebrows suggestively, "that part's negotiable."

Well, well, Channa ma belle, nothing like dying to loosen a person up, eh? Let's hope the "mellow" lasts a while in you.

He noticed a visitor in the corridor and opened the door before the boy outside could ring for admittance: a tall thin twelve-year-old, dark and slender of face but with green eyes and a reddish tint to his brown hair. The boy stood there a moment startled, his mouth a perfect O.

"Come on in," Simeon invited. Channa looked up from her notescreen and reinforced the welcome.

"Uh, hi," the kid said nervously. Simeon noted that he walked with a cane. "I'm Seld Chaundra? I'm in Joat's class?"

"Oh, really?" Simeon said helpfully.

"Yeah." Seld's free hand bunched the material of his trouser leg. "Um, is she here?"

"Not at the moment," Channa told him, resting her chin on her fist. "We'll give her a message," and Channa added a mental *I think.* "Is there a problem?"

"Oh, no," he shook his head in wide-eyed denial. "It's just . . . Well, she wasn't in class today and I was worried that she might of got hurt or something yesterday."

"That's very kind of you," Channa said approvingly. "But she came through . . . okay!"

"We'll tell her that you were asking about her, Seld," Simeon told him.

"Will she be in school tomorrow?"

"Quite possibly," Simeon said mendaciously. "I'll let her know you were asking for her and tell her to contact you. Does she have your call code?"

"Yes, sir, she does, sir." Like all station-born youngsters, Seld was not unaccustomed to Simeon speaking from the nearest sound cube, but he had the good manners to bow to the column. "Sorry to have bothered you." He waved at Channa and stepped back through the door.

"Well!" Channa said, pleased. "She has a peer who cares enough about her well-being to beard you in your lair."

"You think that's enough to entice her back out?"

Channa deliberated. "I think it will certainly alter her thinking. When you're sure no one cares about you, it's easy to be depressed and feel hopeless. Go on," she said with an encouraging smile at his column, "tell her Seld was here, worried she might have been hurt, and looking for her in class."

"Yeah, he's okay—Seld is, sort of," Joat said. "Bit of a kid, y'know?"

"Chronologically speaking," Simeon remarked blandly, "you're a kid yourself."

Joat laughed with more than a trace of bitterness; it was a sound like a yelping coyote. "Never had the time or chance to be one. So it's a little late, like, to expect me to act like one."

Silence fell in the improvised nest at the intersection of the ducts, but the girl heard just the softest sigh of regret issue from Simeon.

Softie, she thought, with a rueful affection. Even if he was . . . what was the jingle? Spam-in-a-can? *Nice guy,* she decided. *He needs someone to look after him.* Besides Channa Hap, that was. Channa might be his brawn, but she seemed to have looked after everyone else yesterday instead of him.

"Yeah, Seld's not a bad osco. Sorta knows his way around a keyboard, in a kid sorta way. Can't fight worth shit, though."

"He says they miss you at school," Simeon replied noncommittally.

Joat gave a second bark of sour laughter. "Not that bitchite Louise Koprekni, she doesn't."

"Pushing her face in the toilet bowl was a bit extreme, wasn't it, Joat?"

"She said I smelled."

"You *did* smell. Then! That's about the time you considered regular washing wasn't such a bizarre notion."

Joat's lower lip stuck out, and she turned back to her keyboard and the collection of miscellaneous electronic junk which Simeon had been trying to identify.

"What's that you're contrapting?" Simeon asked.

"Riffler."

"Dare I ask what a riffler is?" *Do I want to know?*

"Ultrasonic. Pops the caps." At Simeon's interrogative sound, she explained. "Bursts the capillaries, like, you know, instant really, really bad sunburn?"

"It what?" Then he modified his tone to a more conversational level. "We hadn't planned on dragging you out, you know."

"I didn't figure you would."

"You haven't . . . ah . . . tried it out, have you?"

"Not yet."

"How will you know it works?"

"It will!" The confidence in that reply was unnerving.

"Is it . . . umm . . ."

"Wouldn't kill anyone, but it'll sure make 'em think twice about following me."

"Ah, I see."

His visual picked up just the hint of a grin as Joat bent her head to continue her handiwork.

"Some things," she said cryptically.

Silence fell again. Conversations with Joat reminded Simeon of documentaries he had seen of catching trout by hand. You had to be very patient to succeed.

"Looks like trouble coming," she said neutrally.

"Trouble's *over*," Simeon said. "Look, Joat, I do apologize for not checking on you during the alert, but . . ."

"No need. You gave me a suit, remember. That was all I needed," Joat pointed out reasonably. "Something threatens you, the station, we're all in deep kimchee. Right? Much better you spent your time keeping us from getting in so deep we have to shovel our way out."

"You've an extremely realistic attitude, Joat," Simeon said, with a certain tone of admiration for the independence in her that also worried him.

"I'm no sap," Joat announced with satisfaction. "Troubles don't come by ones and twos, either—you get 'em by kilobyte loads. *I'll* be ready." She patted the riffler.

"I'm sure you will," Simeon replied soothingly.

"Yuh. See you at dinner."

"At dinner?" He sounded surprised but that pleased her. "Umm, yes, see you then," he added, doing a good job of sounding casual.

Joat whistled soundlessly to herself as she felt Simeon's attention withdraw—most of it, at least. She also switched on the white-noise maker and the scrambler she'd rigged up. She was no longer *completely* sure they worked, Simeon having had enough of a look at her contrivances to perhaps neutralize them. Not that he'd have had time to bother about her with so much else on his mind these days. Even a brain had some limitations.

She didn't want an audience while she reran the stuff she'd recorded during Channa's exploits on the intruder ship. First she screened something that had come in on the Central datablip just today. The watchman program Joat set up had cut it out and routed it to her system automatically.

Stretching luxuriously, she popped the tab on a can of near-beer. She stayed away from the real thing because it made her feel loggy and squiff. She bit a big hunk off a chocolate nut bar, grinning around the mouthful with vindictive delight as the scene played on.

A crowd surrounded the obviously official building and their chant ran shrill and menacing as they waved their placards which bore the same message they chanted.

"Dorgan the bigot! Dorgan out! Dorgan the bigot! Dorgan out!"

The ground-floor windows have been shattered and a line of riot-armed police were holding the SPRIM demonstrators at bay. The visual shifted to an interior room where Ms. Dorgan of the Child Welfare department, looking rumpled and alarmed, was gesticulating wildly.

"And I *categorically deny* saying that shellpeople are unnatural abominations with no right to live!" she wailed. "Or that they make me want to puke!"

Joat grinned. She wanted to be a systems engineer when she grew up—or maybe even a brawn—but editing was a nice hobby. Editing transmissions of recorded conversations sent to SPRIM and MM, for example. Channa had the right idea, but adults had no *enthusiasm* for taking an idea and running with it.

"Like the teacher said," she muttered, taking another mouthful. "I gotta lot of buried hostility I got to learn to express."

"I felt a good deal like screaming myself," Joseph said.

Amos sighed and lowered himself into a chair. Once Joseph insisted, the doctor here—a man, oddly enough—had moved him into a small suite, with a private sitting room.

Apparently private, he reminded himself, though there might well be listening devices. Otherwise, it had the common strangeness of everything here, like soft synthetics for the walls which could alter

shade or suddenly turn themselves into view screens. He had commanded that the space-scene transform itself into something more
restful, and the holograph had turned to a neutral brown solidity.
In its way, that made him uneasy too. What *appeared* to be plain bare
plastic was obviously anything but.

"It is difficult to believe that we are safe," he said, rubbing a hand
over his face, which had grown enough beard to rasp. He resolved
to ask for a sonic, or the local equivalent. "To be frank, my brother,
I never expected to wake again."

"Neither did I," Joseph said, prowling with slow restlessness. The
gravity was slightly higher than Bethel, just enough to be noticeable.
"But we do not know that we are safe—even from the Kolnari."

Amos looked up sharply. "We do not?"

"The shell—Guiyon," Joseph amended, at Amos' frown "—said that
it—"

"He." Amos compressed his lips firmly after that correction; the
more so since he himself had never felt entirely easy with Guiyon.

Guiyon saved us, he remembered. More than that. Guiyon had been
the first to listen to his youthful doubts without recoiling in horror
and ordering him to do penance. Only families descended from the
Prophet were allowed speech with the Planetary Manager. Most
Bethelites thought that entity was at best legend, at worst an abomination of the infidel. *I am too old to believe in nursery tales,* Amos
thought. He was a man now, with many depending on him.

"He," Joseph said, making a soothing gesture with both hands. "He
intended to take us to Rigel base. This is not Rigel."

"No," Amos conceded. "SSS-900-C. Although they seem reluctant
to tell us more."

"Understandable, sir. Would *you* immediately trust fugitives who
came so close to destroying them, though *we* knew it not? However,
there are things they cannot *help* but tell us."

"Yes," Amos said slowly. "For one, that this is no military base."

"Just so, my brother. These are a peaceful people." At Amos'
dubious look, he went on. "I was raised dockside, you will remember. I know more of traders and trading than most. These are *respectable* merchants and spacefarers, by their own ethics, if not by Bethel
customs. Dockside, we would have called them easy marks."

They looked at each other, haunted by what neither would mention first. Amos took hold of himself. A respectable, an ethical people
deserved the truth.

"And we cannot know if the Kolnari still pursue," Amos whispered. Sickness tugged at the pit of his stomach. *To achieve safety, even for so few, and jeopardize in turn their saviors.* "We must talk to them!"

CHAPTER EIGHT

"ALL THINGS CONSIDERED, we didn't come out of the day too badly at all," Chief Administrator Claren said, once more running his stylus down his notescreen to be sure he'd missed nothing.

Ducking her head, Channa managed to hide a yawn. Meetings were meat and drink to Claren. When he had the opportunity to trot out his careful graphs and statistics for an audience, he positively glowed and inflated. *Like a plain girl who's just been asked to dance by a high-school hero,* she thought mordantly.

"We're down about three million credits," she pointed out, reaching for the water carafe.

Two section chiefs sprang to fill the glass for her: fame was already a bit wearing. The meeting was supposed to have started as a working breakfast. Plates and crumbs were scattered around the table. Gusky was there too, looking a little pale—either from the medications, or from the party. Not only was he prominent in his own business, he was a section representative and, with the recent favorable publicity, looked likely to be re-elected.

Patsy was filing a fingernail. "Somebody has ta pony up the expenses," she pointed out. "Fer example, we commandeered equipment from Namakuri-Singh—who arh *not* known to be a charitable organization."

Gusky grunted. "*I* commandeered the equipment which will have to be replaced, which you, Simeon, authorized me to use."

"Not me personally. The station!" Simeon said sharply. Brains

115

116   Anne McCaffrey & S.M. Stirling

tended to be sensitive about personal debt, having had to pay off such a whacking great amount for their early care and education. "No one could say that I didn't do everything possible to minimize damage. Loss of the tugs was unavoidable and *the station* is morally obligated to compensate their owners for the loss. Which, Claren, we *will* recoup from Lloyd's, invoking the *force majeur* clause."

"Yes, yes, of course, it will," Claren muttered, making a quick notation.

"The other unavoidable losses and damages which we've discussed today are going to wipe out the contingency fund."

"It will?" Gus asked unhappy.

"Yes, it will," Claren agreed in a lugubrious tone of voice.

"In a good cause," Simeon said briskly.

"On this Lloyd's claim," Gus went on, "we'll be dealing with bureaucrats, bureaucratic accountants at that. *Government* bureaucratic accountants, with lawyers in tow."

"The withered hand on the controls," Simeon intoned.

"We could just rely on their decency, good nature and inherent generosity," Gus suggested. Even Claren laughed at that.

Channa shuddered. "So we should be prepared for accusations of mismanagement and hand-wringing over the cost of every rivet, bolt and coupling." She affected a nasal tone. "Didn't you realize that seventeen-point-three seconds boost would have done just as well as seventeen-point-seven?"

Chief Administrator Claren assured them that his entries would be meticulously checked, all forms would be properly made out, filed on time and to the proper bureaus.

"I won't go so far as to guarantee prompt or even early payment," he said, allowing himself a very small smile, "given that we'll be dealing with departments over which I have no control. But, I can promise you that I will do my best, and that is very good indeed."

There was a rumble of agreement.

"At least *we*," Channa said firmly, "can authorize immediate release of the contingency fund to private persons who suffered damage and loss, or have to make repairs germane to station functions. Claren, just get the claims into the insurance companies as soon as you can."

"Good luck," said the owner of a minerals company in a wry tone. "I've noticed they're always more enthusiastic about collecting premiums than paying claims."

That brought another chuckle. Channa turned to the pillar and

Simeon's image. "As far as the station exterior damage is concerned, isn't there a relevant clause in the station's charter that guarantees immediate repairs?"

"Hmmm." The holo turned static for a moment before Simeon smiled. "Yes, as a matter of fact—emergency expenses for maintaining station integrity and saving life and limb are covered under the general station contract with Lloyd's. We ought to be able to cover everything."

"Excellent," Claren said, tapping at his keyboard.

"'Nuther li'l thing. Fo' all them drills, Simeon, when we was supposed to know what to do iffen thar was a real one, thar was a mighty lot of folks ended up runnin' around like scalded roosters. Ought to be fined, to remind 'em to pay attention."

"Fined? Yes, fined! Fine. Good notion, Patsy," Simeon said. "And the longer they've been on station and should know better, the heavier the fine. Pinch a pocket, mark the memory. What bothers me is *why* didn't they know where they were supposed to be. I call these drills— even if you're always complaining about them—often enough for everyone to know exactly where to go and what to do. Their names are always checked off on the roster, so why the hell were they running around bumping into walls?"

"Aw, thar's allus some folk who panic, Simeon," Patsy said. "Mos' of us was whar we shoulda been. And Lord knows, we got it all done, din we?" Patsy said.

"I'm inclined to think that perhaps we should give them the benefit of the doubt here," Channa put in. "But perhaps you should keep an eye on the group leaders, in the event that they just automatically check off every name on their list without verifying that everyone is in position and accounted for."

"Assign them a buddy," Gus said. "If they're too helpless to know where to go and how to get there, make it a joint responsibility."

"Should be the group leaders," Chaundra said in a disgusted tone.

"Joint responsibility! Excellent," Simeon said, "just like B & B teams."

The resolution was passed unanimously.

"Move that we break for lunch," somebody said. "It's 1300."

"Seconded," Channa said. "I think I need a full stomach to hear what our guests have to say. Spaceflot suggests they've got a fairly lurid set of adventures to tell us. Any objections? Adjourned."

❖   ❖   ❖

A little different from last night, eh Happy? Simeon watched as Channa munched on her thin sandwich. He hoped she was comparing this fare with the feast Mart'an had spread for her. The deck commissary was *not* up to Perimeter standards, although Gus claimed that they did an acceptable late-night pizza.

"So, brief us with what you know, Simeon, about our latest arrivals," Gus said.

Simeon made a throat-clearing sound. "Data base describes 'em as a 'tightly knit, religiously oriented group' in origin," he said. "Judaeo-Sufi Buddhist roots."

"Wow," Patsy said. "Thassa mouthful. But do they believe in God?"

Wondering looks, sage nods and quizzical "ooh's" went around the table.

"Probably worshipping snails and marrying their siblings, or some such genetically stupid custom," Vickers said. The station security chief was a short, rather squat woman from New Newfoundland. "Buddhists, you said? No wonder they nearly crashed us. That kind don't know much about mechanical stuff."

"Wait, just a precise minute." Doctor Chaundra held up a protesting hand. "To begin with, I saw no medical indications of dangerous inbreeding. They may have *looked* as if they didn't comprehend directions or our comments, but they were all dazed from their experiences. They are needing rest and recuperation, but under that is health. Genetic diversity is low, but there are few recessives. I would hazard that they must have had a good screening program to begin with. The group is above the norm. One or two may have endocrine behavioral problems from the coldsleep drugs. They administered drugs well beyond their storage lives. The Bethelite leader is a very articulate man, educated and intelligent.

"Although," he went on, with a slight frown, "he has not been particularly communicative."

"Unfortunately, education and intelligence don't always go hand in hand," Simeon commented. "It's not that I've got my heart set on the 'religious fanatics drive the heretics away' scenario, but it does fit the little I've been able to decipher of Guiyon's log. Phrases like, 'Damn rockheaded elders who said immorality and doubt in the young had brought doom'; 'told them their children had a right to live'; 'feared some of them might betray us'; 'escaped as best we could'; and saddest of all, 'had to leave some behind to face death.'"

Patsy put down her sandwich. "I'm not hungry anymore."

"Nor am I," Channa said grimly. "It's time to get this from the mouths of the horses."

Stallion, you mean, Simeon remarked very privately.

Amos ben Sierra Nueva was accompanied by the smaller, thick-set man who had been found beside him on the colony ship. Two of Vickers' guards were discreetly in attendance, more to guide the floatchairs than guard.

They're weak as kittens, Simeon thought, *not to mention unarmed and with no place else to go and nothing to go there in.* Station personnel developed a special kind of paranoia as a survival trait: nothing, no one must harm their station. Any station, no matter how state-of-the-art and safety conscious, was totally vulnerable. Had he, in innocence, welcomed aboard terrorists fleeing 'rockheaded' elders? Oddly enough, the presence of Guiyon argued against that possibility.

As their chairs thumped softly off their air cushions to the floor, the two strangers looked with impassive expressions at those seated around the table.

Simeon heard Patsy murmuring under her breath; very faintly, almost subvocalizing. He focused, upping the gain on his receptors:

"*Oh, my oh my, that one is pretty,*" she was saying. "*My oh my oh my.*"

Patsy's obvious interest in the man did not surprise Simeon but it did suggest he might have an entirely different problem on his hands. However, if Patsy's charms should win Amos, Simeon could relax. Then he caught Channa, glancing surreptitiously at Amos' classic profile, slightly clouded with a worry that only gave him a more Jovian solemnity. Then, seeing the look exchanged between Amos and Joseph, Simeon wondered hopefully if the short, muscular man was his boyfriend.

"Dr. Chaundra says that we mustn't tire you," Simeon said by way of calling the meeting to order, "but we'd appreciate your filling us in on a few details."

Amos gave a start, and his eyes widened as he suddenly looked up to the pillar at the head of the table and saw Simeon's synthesized face. *So, he knows about shellpeople, but he's surprised to find one here.*

"We are grateful for your succor," Amos began formally, bowed his head, touching forehead and heart with one hand.

"I am Amos ben Sierra Nueva, and my companion is Joseph ben Said." The short man repeated Amos's gesture.

Seeing it, Gusky frowned slightly and moved his fingers. Simeon read the message. *I figure the short one for a hard case.*

The brain accepted that verdict. There were some things that only personal experience could teach. Amos continued speaking, pausing as he sought the appropriate words but gradually becoming more fluent and his blue eyes began to warm with sincerity.

"We are of the colony on Bethel. I am loathe to tell you, in the face of your generosity, of a terrible scourge, a bright evil that flies upon us even now."

"A . . . bright evil?" Channa asked uncertainly.

Scourge? Evil? Sheesh! Simeon wondered. The archaic syntax made the man sound as salted as a historical holoplay. *What's he talking about? Devils? So he can blame the whole disaster on the supernatural?* There was a rustle as the others around the table leaned forward. They had expected to hear about something safely in the past, not a new threat to the station. Yesterday's had been more than enough for a long while.

"Indeed, lady, you are in grave danger." He caught the blank or startled expressions around the table. "Has Guiyon told you nothing?" he asked desperately.

"Guiyon is dead," Simeon said, and saw both men go rigid with shock and grief. He thought better of them for it and paused to let them recover. "The ship's logs are all but unreadable. Why don't you fill us in?" Simeon suggested quietly.

"He is dead?" Amos's drawn face had gone pale under its smooth light-olive coloring. "But, how is that possible? He was a shellperson, an immortal. Ah, perhaps that is why we are not at Rigel Base or some other Central Worlds facility where we thought to seek assistance."

"He brought you here, to SSS-900-C, a space station and many light years from Rigel Base."

"How can an immortal die?" Joseph asked softly, suppliant as he spread his hands wide in his lap.

"The feeder lines to his nutrient sources had sheared off and, as there was no backup . . ." Simeon trailed off and both Bethelites bowed their heads a moment, honoring the dead. "Considering the state of that truly ancient vessel of yours, he did well to get you this far."

Amos glanced at his companion. The other man's hard blocky face was drawn, and he nodded his head slowly twice, as if encouraging.

Amos hesitated, cleared his throat and, throwing his chin up, spoke directly to Simeon.

"This is even worse than I had imagined. Guiyon must have been truly desperate. Can you defend yourselves?"

"Well, we *fended* off your out-of-control ship pretty successfully," Simeon replied. "What did you have in mind?"

Amos leaned forward, supporting himself on the armrests of the chair. His eyes took on a fierce glow.

"I will tell you," he said passionately, sweeping a look at those around the table. "We of Bethel are a peaceful people." His fists met and clenched. "Virtually a defenseless people." His mouth twisted in pain. "We were attacked from the skies above our peaceful planet. I do not know how you count the hours in a day or the days of a week, a month or a year. I do not know how long we were unconscious in the Sleep. We fled our home world for four periods of twenty-five hours before I took the drug. Just before I did, Guiyon told me that he thought we would have a solid five days' lead. So nine days of twenty-five hours—two hundred and twenty-five hours."

"Sixty minutes in yo' hoah, Mr. Sierra Nuevah?" Patsy asked.

Looking over at her expressionlessly, he nodded slowly.

Simeon called up a holo of Bethel, culled and realized from the Survey Service data base.

"That is our world as it appeared before this Exodus," Amos said bleakly, watching the slow rotation on the screen. "Our capital city was there," and pointed to where two large rivers flowed into a bay. "Keriss, we called it. The place where the Pilgrims landed and erected our Temple. The Kolnari . . ." He broke, squeezing his eyes closed, his face a mask of pain.

Reference, Simeon prompted silently, feeling the computer begin its work. Then he felt a mental lurch as he reviewed what Amos had said. The city of Keriss *was* there: past tense. Gus caught it as well, his pupils widening.

"They demanded unconditional surrender," Amos was saying, his face wiped clear of any emotion. "By sneak attack, they disabled our orbital habitats, our communications, everything we might have used to call help."

He folded his shaking hands, clasping them so tightly the knuckles showed white. "The Council of Elders convened," he said. His lips tightened. "They decided this tribulation was punishment for the increasing immorality of the younger generation. Me!"

He stabbed himself in the breast with his fingers, "And those like me, who only wanted a little more freedom, who only wanted to have answers to reasonable questions. They would not *listen* to me—even though I am a male descendent, in the Prophet's own line."

Locked in bitter memory, Amos did not notice the surprise his words generated.

Ah, patrilineal descent system, Simeon thought.

"I thank the All-Knowing for Guiyon, for when I left the council chamber that last time, he called to me. Escape, he said. 'To go where? How?' I asked. He told me then of the colony ship that had brought us to Bethel. For three hundred years we had used it as a weather and relaying station, nothing more. I left to gather those who might follow me."

His hands knotted together. "And the Kolnari . . . when the Elders refused surrender, they destroyed the city with a fusion weapon!"

A shocked murmur ran around the table. No one had used fusion weapons in generations. Certainly not in any sector answerable to the Central Worlds.

"Murderers! Looters! Pirates!" he spat out the words and rubbed his face with his hands.

Another murmur. SSS-900-C was in a very peaceful sector; the only nonhumans were species who did not practice institutionalized violence. The settlers were mostly well-integrated types, if a bit rambunctious, but no more than was expected on a frontier. Piracy was an historical phenomenon or a sporadic occurrence far out on the Arm.

In a steady voice, all the more effective because of its calm, Amos went on. "A tenth of our people died in that moment, and all our leaders. The Kolnari told us that we must capitulate or they would strike again. They broadcast their message from a dark screen. They would strike again and again until we were obliterated to the last man. Just this implacable voice. The cowards! They did not even show us the face of our enemy. They gave us two hours to make up our minds.

"And so we began. It was very hard. We had to determine who we could take." His cheeks grew red with shame as he continued. "First we took Guiyon from his column. We could not open the main bay doors. Ah, but we were so stupid, so innocent, so untrained! We'd managed to get supplies, disconnect Guiyon, gathered our people, fly to the ship without being detected and then," he gave a harsh bark of laughter, "the doors refused to open! Some murmured that the Elders had been right. We were being punished for our sins.

"Then, Joseph here," and Amos laid a light hand on the short man's shoulder, "opened one of the service airlocks. Only it was much too small for Guiyon's shell. He insisted that he didn't have to be inside, that we must strap him to the hull near the bridge, so that his brain synapses could be wired into the command panel. He had to tell us everything that had to be done. We knew so little of such matters." Another bitter snort. "And we were so afraid. None of us knew anything at all about spatial navigation. I had piloted a ship, but only a small one, and never beyond Bethel's moons. Beyond Bethel's moons," and he made a broad sweep of his arm, "was not fit for men of Bethel. Also, we know nothing of the worlds outside our little system. Guiyon handled what outsystem commerce was permitted to us on Bethel."

He paused, swallowing hard, and Chaundra filled a glass with water for him. Amos nodded gratefully and drank before he resumed his story.

"Guiyon dared not risk bringing us to one of the nearer colonies for fear of leading those monsters to an equally defenseless planet. Instead," and he gave a mirthless laugh, "we may have led them to an even more defenseless space station. At least on a planet, one may know of safe hiding places. I do not know why we are here and not at Rigel Base. Guiyon must have changed course again. There were four fiends in our wake when I had to accept the drug. Well-armed warships, or so Guiyon thought. And we have led them here to you who have saved the poor fragment of our people who fled from our once beautiful planet." He bowed his head, his shoulders slumping with his consummate despair.

An appalled silence had broken into a quickly rising babble of "they've brought trouble here," "they led fiends to *us*?" "But we're defenseless." Simeon let out a modulated howl and they all shut up.

"Thank you," Simeon said ironically when silence fell. *When in danger, or in doubt, run in circles, scream and shout,* he added to himself.

"Guiyon brought them here because first, the engines were about to blow, and second, they were dying fast anyway, and third, SSS-900-C is, after all, on the main route in this quadrant of Central Worlds sphere of influence. Now, if we could examine the problem more calmly?"

Claren turned to May Vickers. "As security chief, you're required to defend us!"

Vickers looked at the man. "With stundart pistols?" she asked incredulously. "I'm a police officer with fifty part-time assistants. I lock up drunken miners and see domestic disputes don't get out of hand," she said. "I've never had experience with fiends and I want no part of four warships." She crossed her arms across her solid chest and looked accusingly up at Simeon.

"Is it possible that you might have lost them?" Chaundra asked.

The two Bethelites shook their heads glumly.

"Unlikely," Simeon said, "not when Guiyon was overdriving the engines and leaving an ion trail a blind alien could follow."

Gus nodded. "Any warship could."

"Iffen they couldn't see the trail, thar's all them pieces of the ship rollin' about, saying 'theah heahh!'" Patsy waved her arms like a signalman. "We cain't hardly say they passed on through."

"My information banks give me no information at all about any group, or star system, known as Kolnari," said Simeon. "While I realize that your experience with these people is short-term, had you even *heard* of them on Bethel before they struck?"

Amos shook his head. "Guiyon had heard rumors of a band of marauders in the Arm from the few traders that came to Bethel. He was also forbidden by the Elders to tell any but themselves what news traders brought of the worlds beyond Bethel. On the ship, he did tell me," and Amos furrowed his brow, trying to remember the exact words the shellperson had used, "that they struck so swiftly that no alarm could go forth. That that was how they avoided detection by any force great enough to come against them."

"Central Worlds, for instance," Channa said with a rueful quirk of her lips.

Amos nodded. "The first wave of destruction was aimed at our air and space ports, at communication installations. The strike was as complete as it was unexpected. They chose not to show themselves to us until all our space capacity was destroyed . . . or so they thought. All we know of them was from a very brief time when we fought them. They follow us to destroy the evidence of the destruction of Bethel, the latest of their crimes. They will kill, and quickly. No doubt," he added with scorn, "they feel uneasy being only four instead of three hundred."

"Three hundred?" Simeon asked.

"Three hundred ships. So Guiyon told me. He had seen them coming in but was forbidden by the Elders to speak until they had decided what to do."

Gus whistled. "If that's three hundred *warships,* people, not only do *we* have a problem, this whole *sector* has a problem." The Navy was much larger, but it was scattered.

"Have you had any recent word from Central, Simeon?" Channa asked him.

"Basically no more than an acknowledgement of the ... ah ... incident in the vein of 'Gee, that's too bad, but you're equipped to handle it and when your reports are filed, we'll see what we can do.' But of course that's based on what happened yesterday; *this* may get us action."

At least I hope it will, Simeon thought. *Three hundred ships! Shit!* Simeon opened a tight beam to Central with a mayday flag attached. Hopefully he'd have some hard news before too long.

"What sort of armament did they have?" Gus asked while the rest of the station's leaders sat, trying not to look at each other and especially not at Amos and Joseph. Amos had gone even paler and the blue of his eyes had faded. He just sat there. On the other hand, Joseph was watching each and every one of the station heads with a critical gaze and the slightest of knowing smiles on his full lips.

Simeon could see that the initial numbness his people had felt was giving way to fear. Gus was fighting it with trained reflex, but the others were edging slowly toward panic.

"You must have something to fight with," Joseph said, suddenly leaning his arms on the table and directing a piercing gaze from one face to another. "We fought, and we had much less than you did who turned the vessel from your station yesterday. With what did you blow it into pieces? Do you have more? That is something. It is more than we had who saw our ships withered to slag. Our city . . ." He broke off and struck his fists impotently into the table. "We have brought you warning. We had none!"

Amos caught his friend by the wrists before he could damage his hands. "Peace, my brother," he said softly.

"Oh, youah brothas?" Patsy said in mild surprise, peering closely at both to find some familial resemblance.

"Not of the blood," and Amos touched his temple with his index finger, "of the mind."

"Unh-hunh!" Patsy blushed and tightened her lips into a straight line.

"I've sent a message to Central Worlds," Simeon told them in a brisk voice that he hoped sounded as if he had matters well in hand. "They're consulting with the Space Navy brass—to see what to do. I was hoping they'd tell me what they were *doing,* and or what we can do. I should've anticipated a full fledged diplomatic-bureaucratic-governmental-gun-fight, complete with quarrels over jurisdiction. Everyone with something to say about this has to be tracked down and given an opportunity to give his fardling opinion in triplicate. Amos, believe me, kid, I know just how you feel about elders. The good news is that Navy intends to act fast, only there *aren't* any Navy units close. The nearest is eighteen days away. This is assuming the brass cut movement orders today and not sometime after we've become the subject of mere academic debate, because we don't exist anymore.

"Which means that at *best* we can look forward to thirteen lucky days with our naked butts hanging out waiting for a kick from a booted foot. That nearest Navy unit is a patrol corvette, a warship only by courtesy."

"Then you must flee!" Amos leaned forward urgently. "You cannot hope to defeat them. You must leave this place."

"Great idea," Simeon agreed, "in principle. Only the station can't move. That's why it's a station. It's stationary. Get it?"

"You mock me most unfairly," Amos replied with solemn and offended dignity. "I have no knowledge of space stations or of your capabilities. Further, I am not wrong. If the station itself cannot move, then its people must."

"As far as such advice goes," Gus cut in, "he has a point. We should evacuate as many as we can—children, the sick, nonessential personnel. Whoever we can, or whoever's hot to go."

"By my calculations," Simeon said, finishing them in that instant, "given the number of ships currently in or near me at the moment, we should be able to evacuate over a thousand souls." He liked that touch. "Not counting crews."

There was silence for a moment. A thousand was a fraction of the average ever-shifting population of the station.

Amos broke the silence hesitantly. "How many people will that leave on the station?"

"Fifteen thousand, or so," Channa said grimly. "Our population varies. Simeon, does your estimate include emptying cargo bays and stuffing our people into them in suits?" A desperation procedure and liable to result in some fatalities.

"No, we could evacuate a few hundred more that way."

Although, given the average softperson's reaction to long-term confinement in tight spaces, we probably won't get many volunteers for traveling that way.

"And before you ask," Simeon continued, "no, I haven't even asked the captains their views on such an . . . exodus. That's a best case scenario. We can't prevent those who aren't docked in the station physically from leaving, so the scheme is still just inside this room. I think that before we start bringing anyone else into this, we should have at least one plan to present, preferably more than one."

"Evacuation plans?" Chaundra asked, his brow farrowed.

"Those," Simeon said, "and plans to fight for the station."

There was a certain brightening around the table. Nothing visible, but the lift in attitude was almost palpable.

"That's right up your alley, Simeon," Channa said gently, "even if this isn't a military installation."

"To fight," Joseph said, his dark eyes glinting with revived hope. Or was it vengeance? "Yes, this is what we would like to do, but how? Did you not say that you had no weapons? And surely they will not give you a chance to combat them. Why should they not simply rush in and destroy you? That would be but child's play for them."

"We will employ guile." *Geeze, their lingo is contagious,* he thought. "Remember, you said these people were pirates?"

"Yes," Amos said. "When they made their initial demand for surrender—they mentioned deliveries of materials, machines, labor. Pirates, but they speak as though they were a people, a nation. The High Clan, they sometimes named themselves. At others, the Divine—" his mouth puckered in distaste "—the Divine Seed of Kolnar."

"Right." Simeon spoke briskly. *This is just another exotic scenario,* he told himself firmly. *Games theory experience—don't freeze up now. You've done things like this thousands of times.* "So they're no more than criminals, not a true army, disciplined, strategically trained. More like guerillas. Jump in, grab what they can, jump out. Right now, they're pursuing you, and these four ships aim to destroy you to keep you from spreading any nasty rumors about them. So, what we better do first, is get their minds off killing by distracting them with the material things they wanted from you in the first place. Right?"

Every station officer thought about this. Then Gus nodded slowly.

"If these people are space-based, and from the description I think they must be—what a prize the SSS-900-C would be!" He turned to Amos and Joseph. "What sort of industries does . . . did Bethel have?"

"Very few," Amos said, rubbing a thoughtful hand along his stubbled jaw. "We could maintain equipment and manufacture some components for in-system work. We traded rare foodstuffs and organic molecules for what little else we needed. Traders came perhaps once in a generation. The latest only last—"

Joseph swore antiphonally with Gus, Patsy, and Simeon. Channa snapped her fingers. "They must have been . . . what's the phrase?"

"Casin' the joint," Patsy said for she had a store of such archaic phrases.

"Spies!" Joseph said. Tears welled in his eyes, tears of pure rage.

"Always someone who can be bought," Simeon said, giving his holo image a wise appearance. *Or so info tapes say, but I've never had to use that tactic.*

Joseph nodded jerkily. "I knew several who would sell their mothers and fathers . . . maybe their fathers . . . for the price of two bottles of arrack."

"Back to the here and now, please," Gus said, boulder-solid.

Amos shook his head, sending the long black curls flying. "We have . . . had, very little high technology, and of what there was . . . much was in Keriss."

"So they'll be hurting for equipment, possibly for skilled labor," Simeon said. "They've got to be. Whaddya bet that most of those three hundred ships are transports, factory vessels, that sort of thing. They wouldn't be self-sufficient even if they have a home base or star system."

"There've always been folk who'd rather steal than work," Gus said. He had no arguments on that score from anyone. "And they'll want to steal from us."

SSS-900-C was a maintenance and repair center. It was also heavy with rare materials intended for shipyard and general shipbuilding use. No one argued with that, either.

Simeon addressed the two refugee leaders. "First, we have to get them thinking along those lines. Otherwise they may simply sweep in and put a couple of high-yield missiles into us. My plan calls for a sacrifice on your part that I'm reluctant to ask of you."

"Ask," Amos said quietly. "A drowning man will grab even the point of a sword. I should like to prove worthy of Guiyon's sacrifice. Ask!"

"I want to tempt them with booty too rich to resist and get their acquisitive jukes flowing. We'll commandeer one of the company yachts that salesmen travel in when they show their samples to rich customers, and we'll cram its holds full of things the bastards won't be able to resist. With the promise of much more easily available—here!"

"Such as?" Channa asked suspiciously.

"Technological stuff, upgrades in software, in computers, the latest improvements in fuel efficiency. We'll include luxury fabrics, perfumes, jewelry, exotic delicacies . . ."

"Bribery will only make them hungrier to sack the station," Joseph all but shouted, half-rising from his chair.

"Peace, my brother," Amos soothed him, "remember that sicatooths do not eat grass. One must put out a goat to bait the trap for them."

"See, you don't shoot the cow you're milking," Gus contributed.

"Hell no, you don't eat a pig lahke that all at once," Patsy said.

Simeon almost laughed aloud to see the puzzled expressions on the faces of Amos and Joseph. *Good one, Patsy, remember that "my brother" fake they pulled on ya and don't let 'em think they can be more obscure than we can.*

Chaundra explained the humor and only raised his brows slightly when Joseph asked, "What's a pig?" Channa herself was puzzled. She would have expected the natives of an agricultural world to recognize the name of an important farm animal. Her own protein came out of vats, the way nature intended, as far as she was concerned. If not literally, then she didn't want to think about it.

"Won't they think it's kinda odd, though, one guy sellin' so many different things?" Patsy asked.

"Not if he's a middle-man type, importer-exporter, rather than a manufacturer's rep," Simeon said. "It's not that hard to deceive people once, Patsy."

"But we have none of these things you have mentioned," Amos said, puzzled. "We have no cloth or jewels or software. What is this sacrifice you would ask of us?"

"We need someone to put in the yacht we'll be sending out, and I'm not about to send a living person. I'd like to send one of your people who died in transit from ship to station. Preferably someone who died as a result of the environment failure, since that's why he's going to be out there in this luxury ship, broadcasting an offer for a huge reward to anyone who'll rescue him."

Amos and Joseph looked shocked. They sat unmoving for a minute, then slowly turned to meet each other's eyes.

"Impossible!" Joseph said, his lips tight with fury. "What you ask is base sacrilege!"

Channa glanced at Simeon's column as though appealing for help, then plunged in, knowing no diplomatic way of putting this. "Your funerary customs are ... firmly set?"

"Yess!" Joseph hissed. "We honor our dead, we bury them and revere their resting place."

"Well," Simeon told him, "we have no place to bury our dead here on the station, and it's prohibitively expensive to ship them back to their home planets. You can't simply bury them in space because eventually they constitute a navigation hazard. Here we cremate our dead."

"And the ashes?" Amos asked.

"Unless specifically requested, there are no ashes."

Amos bowed his head. "For our dead, we request ashes, so that one day, hopefully, we might return our friends to Bethel. As to your ... your appeal for the body of one of ours, I think, my brother," and he turned to Joseph, "that we should consider that an honor to serve is being offered one of our dead rather than sacrilege. Surely, whoever we choose, would have been pleased to be of help to those who survived."

"It is wrong!" Joseph said. "And I object!"

"My brother," Amos said through gritted teeth, "if you angle with a straight hook, only those fish which are willing get on it. Be reasonable, or we may all be dead. It is only a hope, a possibility we are offered. If they destroy this decoy, they will then destroy the station and we will join our friends who are dead and we can *all* go unburied forever." He stared at his companion until, after a long moment, Joseph lowered his eyes and nodded. To Simeon, Amos said, "Choose the person most suitable for this ruse from among our dead brothers."

"Thank you," Simeon said simply, and the others around the table murmured their thanks as well.

"Okay," Channa said, bringing them back to more immediate concerns, "these pirates come upon this derelict space-yacht. They hear the message, 'Help, help, my environment system is down, auggh, I'm dying, save me and I'll reward you with umpity-zillion credits.' "

"Right."

"They give him a buzz, no answer, so they bip on over to his craft and board it."

"Right."

"They find—whomever—several days dead due to environment failure."

"Right."

"Why don't they just hold their noses and sail on?"

"Um, well, first, it's the nature of pirates to be greedy. So we'll pile the ship high with cases of samples, clearly marked samples, clearly marked as coming from SSS-900-C. Second, no one likes to go back to their senior officer and say, 'It was a total waste of time, sir,' because it makes *them* look bad in their captain's eyes. So I think we can expect them to make at least a cursory search of the ship. Third, there'll be a curiosity factor, since I plan to choose the most opulent yacht in the area. These guys probably haven't seen anything like it hanging around the out-systems.

"So they'll probably be crawling all over it saying, 'I can't believe it! Look at this! What luxury!' One of these factors will attract their attention to the com screen, which will show a report our salesman was inputting when disaster struck. It will say something to the effect of *O frabjious day, I've just made the biggest sale of my career to the SSS-900-C. I've promised them delivery in fourteen days or less. The home office has confirmed the delivery date. Order manifest follows. Hooray, hooray, bounce bounce!*

"And there will be a listing that would make *me* drool and want to turn pirate."

Gus nodded. "It sounds do-able, though I hate to spare even one ship from the evacuation effort."

"I can understand that, Gus, but balance the dozen or so who could be evacuated on the yacht against the fifteen thousand plus people at risk on the station, and I think the sacrifice is justified," Simeon replied. Seeing that he had his audience listening very carefully, he went on. "Now, to prepare the rest of the station for pirate-fall, I want all irreplaceable equipment disconnected and hidden, or if it can't be moved, I want it disguised or dismantled with no spare parts visible. All menus on all computer terminals will be changed. I intend to make them as confusing and difficult to understand as possible, in order to encourage any outsider using our equipment to make as many horrible and damaging mistakes as possible. We'll need to have the emergency crews on alert at all times."

Twenty glum faces surrounded the table.

"Just a minute," Channa said slowly. "You're suggesting we *let* these . . . these *fiends* occupy the station?"

"We can't stop them," Simeon explained patiently. "We can't stop a single real warship from sinking a missile into the station's equator and blowing all fifteen thousand of us to MC-squared. I don't like it either, Channa. But we have to keep them from doing too much damage until the Navy gets here—and we know the time frame on that. If we can confoozle them long enough so the Navy can catch 'em, that'll solve how to get rid of them.

"Once they make a few disastrous mistakes, they'll prefer to use our people. Why should they break their brains trying to learn how to run a station they'll only be occupying until they can loot it empty? I want *our* people, not theirs, in sensitive positions. No matter how it looks to them, I want real control of the station to remain in our hands. I'm willing to take a few risks to gain that advantage."

"Oh," Channa said carefully. "Sounds reasonable."

"Doctor Chaundra, you're really going to hate this one."

"You want me to make people sick."

"Got it in one. How'd you guess?"

"I assume that you know I didn't become a physician because I enjoy watching people suffer," he said calmly. "I will not kill. Otherwise, who do you want me to do it to and why do you want me to do it?"

"I want to be able to declare a class-two quarantine, make them reluctant to enter the living quarters. We can't keep them out entirely unless we declare that a deadly disease is rampant on the station, in which case, we might as well blow the place ourselves and spare them the missile. I'd like to see the infirmary littered with volunteers groaning in misery, for authenticity's sake. But, most important, I want every one of the pirates who enters the living area to walk out with whatever bug you're using in his or her system doing what it does best. Fairly soon, they'll get the idea they should confine their communications with stationers to holocasts."

Chaundra wore a crooked smile. "Leper, unclean, unclean," he said in a singsong voice. Patsy was the only one at the table who understood his reference, but Simeon did, too. Then Chaundra shook his head. "Too little time to fake that particular disease. So! Agreed, I will search for a suitable virus. We can synthesize readily—but we must hope the . . . Kolnari? have inadequate medics and no equivalent facilities."

"Patsy?" Simeon began.

"Yo, lover."

"As soon as we've got some data of a physical nature on these fiends, I would appreciate it if you could come up with some spore, or pollen or mixture of gases that would make our anticipated visitors *real* unhappy. If you can arrange to afflict their ships only, and not the station, I'll like it even better."

"Oh, Simeon, an opportunity! You do love me, doncha honey?"

"First and always, sweetpea."

"Aw, blush." She consulted her keyboard. "Allergies'd be a good bet. They're pretty dam specific in groups with low genetic divers'ty. Once we get some tissue samples, *yeeehah!*"

"Seriously, we can evacuate people or critical supplies like mining explosives, but not both," Channa said.

"I was just coming to that. We'll have to leave some in the stores or it would look odd. After all, we are a supply center. But I want as much of that particular commodity relabeled, rerouted, or hidden wherever. We should leave, maybe, four percent below the lowest reserves we've ever recorded. Have the records show that we're between shipments, the additional four percent shortage of explodables is because we used some of the stores to blow up the colony ship." Simeon saw no point in giving the Kolnari free weapons. "I'd like to do the same with food and medical supplies as well. Any questions?"

"Yeah," one of the supply officers spoke up, "where are we gonna *put* all this stuff, particularly the explosives?"

"You get it together," Simeon said, "I'll tell you where. Right now, let's work out what supplies the evacuation ships will need and I want you to start pulling together those tasty goods we're going to use to tempt the . . . sicatooth."

"You got it," the woman said.

"We, too, would like to serve," Amos said earnestly, "in any way that we can. Ask and we will aid you to the best of our ability."

A passle of farmboys, ranchers and students from a medium tech planet. I'm sure we'll find lots for you to do, Simeon thought.

Amos continued. "It is to our great shame that we have brought this terror down upon you. Better that we had all died..."

"Shut up!" Channa snapped, the verbal equivalent of a slap to a hysteric. "How *dare* you say that? All lives are precious. Guiyon thought so. He recognized that he must save as many of you as he could and he did. Stop beating your chests. You'll only get more bruises. For all we know, they might have come this way anyhow."

"You have been harbingers, and though such aren't much appreciated, I'd like to say now that I, Simeon, SSS-900-C, am grateful to you, and particularly to... Guiyon. If you'd all died at Bethel, no one in this sector would have known of the Kolnari and how they operate." Simeon paused. "I gather they operate on a scorched earth policy?" When the two Bethelites looked puzzled, he added gently, "They clear away all traces that they've been there? That anyone's been on that planet? Hmm. Thought so. Can't leave clues behind if they want to keep on cutting their swath of destruction."

Simeon caught an odd sound coming from Joseph and did a quick enlargement of the man's face. The Bethelite was actually grinding his teeth. Amos' blue eyes dulled with the pain of his own thoughts on the subject of total annihilation.

By now that concept was dawning on three or four stationers and their expressions reflected their shock. Piracy and looting were bad enough, but these Kolnari had gotten away with implied multiple acts of genocide.

"Central and the Navy are receiving hourly update blips," Simeon went on to provide what reassurance he could that SSS-900 was already ahead of the Kolnari on the dice roll. "Bethel will have retribution, if not blanket reparations when the accounting is rendered. You've saved not only yourselves, but us and what's left of your world."

"'He who fights and...'" Diplomatically Channa edited the old adage slightly "'... escapes away! Lives to fight another day.'" She even made it rhyme. She went on firmly. "Dying would just..." She waved her hands, racking her mind for the right words.

"Would be wasteful suicide," Simeon concluded for her. "And allow the Kolnari to sweep the board." He caught Channa's little grimace over his constant use of war-gaming terminology.

"Exactly, and you can't let those..." Again she fumbled for a dire enough epithet.

"Black-hearted sons of bitches?" Simeon offered. *Nice combination of informality and traditional epithet,* pleased with himself.

"Thank you . . . black-hearted sons of bitches go on killing and stealing. So, if you want to wish somebody dead, wish it on *them*," Channa finished, thumping the table with a fist for emphasis.

Amos smiled in chagrin. "You have burnt away my weakness with your fiery speech, beautiful lady. I shall direct my hatred towards our mutual enemy."

"Fine! Glad that's been settled. Now I'm going to adjourn this meeting," Simeon said. "Channa and I have to address the ships' captains in two hours and you all have plenty to do. I'd like progress reports every six hours from everyone, please. You may contact me at any time with any difficulties encountered. Amos, would you be good enough to accompany Doctor Chaundra to the morgue to choose our decoy. He'll also assist you with *proper* funeral arrangements for the other victims."

Amos nodded solemnly. Chaundra put his hand sympathetically on the younger man's shoulder, powered up the floatchair, and they left the lounge together. Joseph's float, activated by one of the guards, started back to the infirmary. The station officers bustled off, no one of a mind to chat or rehash the meeting. Only Channa remained, staring off, her eyes unfocused.

"I take it back."

"What?"

"At the moment, I'm deeply and utterly grateful that you chose to study war instead of romance."

CHAPTER NINE

"THERE GOES ANOTHER one," Simeon said glumly.

A spot crawled through the plotting tank Simeon was screening on one wall of the lounge, trundling out of SSS-900-C's vicinity and heading for the low-mass zone and its interstellar transit.

"How did they find out?" Channa said.

"That's the *Herod's Dream*. She's an independent. One of those merchant-family ships that kick around the fringes, picking up stuff that's not worth the big outfits' while. They don't have to be *told* about trouble. They can *smell* it."

"I suppose it's understandable. They've sunk their savings in their ships which produce their livelihood." Channa sighed tolerantly. "What about the others?"

"They should be . . ." He broke off. "By Ghu!"

Channa also heard the tramp of boots in the hall and swiveled in her chair as a half-dozen variously dressed figures swung into the meeting room.

They may well head out again faster than they came in, Simeon thought as he watched captains file into the room in pairs, or clumps, or singly. *As motley a crew as ever docked here.* Shipsuits were designed to be comfortable under a pressure outfit. From there on, individuality was often loudly or vulgarly expressed by adjustments to that basic attire. For instance, the woman with the shaved, tattooed skull wore a particularly vile shade of pinkish blue that wasn't the least bit becoming—if highly visible. The two nonhumans didn't need to be

136

anything but themselves to fit in with the other surly faces. *They know something's up, but at least they came to listen, unlike those who scampered.*

What the hell, he thought with a mental sigh, *we'll use what we've got and be glad we've got it to use.*

As the captains began to fill the room, few taking chairs at the table, Channa, looking far too elegant in a light blue suit, had gone to the head of the conference table. When a minute had passed with no new arrivals, she opened her notescreen on the podium and looked out at the assembled captains, waiting for them to settle. Especially after a couple of Vicker's part-time police appeared just beyond the entrance, with breather masks and gas projectors as well as shock rods and dart guns. Channa made a note to remind Vicker that the enemy was not yet here and not to make enemies out of anyone else just now.

"Thank you all for coming," she said.

You're probably wondering why I've called you here today, Simeon thought, anticipating Channa's opening words.

"No doubt you're wondering why we've asked you here," Channa said.

Close, but no cigar.

"Station SSS-900-C is currently involved in an emergency. I am Channa Hap, brawn to Simeon and we are invoking section two, article two of the station's charter." Which she tried to read out so that everyone knew the station had the right to commandeer their vessels.

A roar, surprisingly loud from so few throats though the nonhumans helped a lot, swelled through tie room, drowning her out. An occasional "whereas" or "said captain" were all that could be heard.

Let 'em get it out of their systems, Simeon thought. It was understandable—breaking schedule would be expensive, particularly for the small companies and the independents. Hopefully they'd be more cooperative afterwards. In any case, he had control of them all, either because their ships docked to the station or their skippers were attending this meeting. And *nobody* was going to leave without accepting an assignment. Not a single captain here had an ounce of altruism, but station vouchers would be valid anywhere on their routes. There'd be insurance when the dust settled but, psychologically, neither voucher or insurance-when-it-might-be-paid was as comforting as cash-in-hand.

At last they wound down. Simeon turned his volume up to an almost painful level.

"*Sit down, please.*"

The mechanical roar filled the room. He added subsonics that ought to make the humans feel uncertain and cowed.

"Now that I have your complete attention," he said suavely, adjusting to a more bearable level, "I'd like to remind you that we have duly declared an emergency."

He paused and examined the defiant, angry faces. "The station is expecting to be under attack shortly."

Another roar, this time of fear.

"*SHUT UP.*" A second's pause. "Thank you very much. We're all in this together. Except that you gentlebeings are going to get away safely, which is more than the rest of us can look forward to. Please keep that in mind.

"Now," he went on, "we're going to evacuate everyone we can; children under twelve and pregnant women first, of course. They number eight hundred, give or take a few." Not all that many, but passenger facilities on freighters were generally nonexistent or cramped cubicles. Adding any more bodies would make a voyage of weeks uncomfortable, but would at least keep life in those bodies. "I want to reduce all the edible supplies on the station, so commissary is advised to stock you up to your comtowers." There was a murmur of appreciation. "However, at this moment in time, I *cannot guarantee* full compensation for cargo or non-delivery fines. I'd like to and you'll probably get it, but I can't guarantee it."

"Just a damn minute!" a stocky captain with a bulldog face roared. "Who's attacking the station? We're three month's transit time from any trouble, and *that's* minor."

"Pirates," Simeon said succinctly and that one word was sufficient to cause sturdy captains, and even one nonhuman, to pale. He waited as accusations and counter-accusations bounced about the hall, noticing hands going to belts that were, by station regulation, empty of accustomed defensive implements. This time it was Channa who brought them back to order.

Adjusting the volume on her microphone to the highest notch, she bellowed, "SIT DOWN!"

"As you were," Simeon said sweetly. "Could we consider any further riots as done and noted, and not waste valuable escape time? As I started to explain, a complement of four, heavily armed, pirate ships were in pursuit of the colony ship that . . . ah . . . docked here yesterday. Having ascertained details from the survivors of that vessel, we are reliably informed that these pirates were in hot pursuit. We are given the distinct impression that these pirates will either destroy the station immediately, or strip it of everything valuable and *then* destroy it. We have to evacuate as many as possible, which isn't that many, even if you are generous in your assistance. But you're all we have to save as many as we can. Sorry."

"You're sorry?" the bulldog was on his feet again. "You're sorry! I'm supposed to leave my cargo behind for pirates and you're sorry? Well, *I'm* sorry, too, cause 'sorry' don't pay no bills!"

"Captain . . . Bolist," Channa said smoothly, checking the list on her notescreen, "you're telling me that a cargo of . . . chemical salts is more important to you than saving the lives of forty children, which is the number that can be accommodated on the size of vessel you command?"

The man lowered his head, like a bull considering a charge. "Ms. Hap, me and mine worked for forty years to get the *Gung Ho*. We're still paying off our loans. Losing a major cargo—we'll pay forfeits if we don't get the load to Kobawaslo et Filles—could break us. Then we'll be on the beach. Hell, I like kids s'much as the next guy, but a man's gotta live."

"Well, then, Captain, you'll be pleased to know that children are much lighter than chemical salts. Exchanging one for the other should get you well out of the danger zone in excellent time." Channa gave him a pleasant smile, and held his gaze until the man's eyes dropped. "Yes, you have a question?" And she pointed to the shaven, tattooed captain who had leaped to her feet, waving both hands to be heard.

When the question of how to deal with pregnant women giving birth on her ship was satisfactorily settled by assuring her of a trained medic in her consignment, she subsided.

In the end, all capitulated, but nine begged a few hours' leeway to ditch and buoy-mark such cargoes that a period in space wouldn't damage beyond use.

"Phew," Simeon said as the captains walked out. "That was unpleasant."

"Not by comparison," Channa said grimly.

"Comparison to what?"

"Announcing it to the station," she said.

"Oh."

✧   ✧   ✧

"You are shitting me, Joat," Seld Chaundra said scornfully. "Pirates! What do you think I am? A playschool kid?"

Yes, Joat thought. "I am not lying, shit-for-brains," she said.

They were in Seld's quarters, which were comprised of a bedroom and study, off his father's suite near the main sickbay in North Sphere. The study was crammed with ship models and holoposters, most of them from travel catalogues but a few from adventure serials. Joat particularly liked the one of the bug-eyed man screaming in the jaws of one fanged head of a three-headed monster which waved him above the rubble of a burning building. Curiously enough, the man resembled the captain who had won her from her uncle.

"Gimme another bar," she added. Seld flipped it over from the sofa where he sprawled. Joat caught it out of midair and discarded the wrapper on the floor. Seld winced but said nothing.

"How can you *eat* so many of those things?" he asked as she gobbled it.

"Gotta eat 'em while the getting's good," she replied, chewing with her mouth open. He winced again. *He's a wuss,* she thought. "Anyway, they're supposed to be here soon."

"Suuuuure."

Suddenly Seld was tumbled backward against the back of the sofa. He gave a strangled squawk as Joat's thin strong hands, crossed at the wrist, gripped his jacket below the throat. Her bony knuckles dug painfully into his windpipe. He couldn't breathe at all, as she was also kneeling on his stomach.

"Look, you wuss—"

"I am not a wuss!" he wheezed.

"—and I am not shitting you! *Here.*" She let him up, marched over to his work table and slapped a chip on the receiver plate of his screen. It lit, showing the control lounge and Simeon's pillar, the shouting captains surging around it.

Seld listened open-mouthed. "Pirates," he concurred weakly. "Hey! That's private, you stole that chip!"

"Did not, just jacked the feed and *copied* it."

"Unauthorized copying is stealing, Joat. And eavesdropping on official meetings is . . ." Seld trailed off, unable to identify the offense though he knew it must be one.

Fardling wuss, she thought. *He sounds just like his father when he says things like that.* Yet his father was a lot nicer than hers had been.

Her memories of paternal care were the kind you woke up at night sweating from. Hopefully he was dead from Jeleb nightmare-smoke by now. Her uncle had been worse, after he took her over, but at least she *knew* her uncle was dead. She pushed such thoughts aside as time wasters.

"Okay, I'm a Sendee mud-puppy eavesdropper and data-bandit— so *listen to what they're saying,* will you?"

Seld blinked and did so. "Holy shit," he whispered. "We *are* going to be attacked by pirates." His eyes lit. "Hey, Joat, this is like a holo."

Joat kicked him.

"What did you do that for?" he demanded, outraged.

"Because I like you, fool," she said.

"You do?" he said, straightening up and then wincing. "Hell of a way to show it, fardler."

"Fardler yourself. This *ain't* no holo, Seld. Those pirates, those Kolnari, are for *real.* Half the outies on that ship that nearly clipped the station were *dead,* osco. That's d-e-a-d, dead, finished, off to the big tax-haven in the afterglow, *dead.* This is major criminal we're talking, Seld. Like, we could get seriously fardled up—you, me, Simeon, Channa, your dad."

"Yeah," Seld said, in a small voice, looking totally scared. "But what can we *do?*" That word came wobbling out as Seld tried not to show Joat how frightened he really was.

"Come close and listen to momma," she said. "Simeon has some ideas. I got more."

Rachel bint Damscus sat and shivered on the edge of the bed. There was nothing under it. Not even legs to hold it up, just some sort of field mechanism, yet it did not move. She shivered again, looking down at the pill in her hand. The strange dark man they called Doctor Chaundra had given it to her, saying that it would make her feel better. She didn't want to feel better. She wanted to feel pain, because pain told her she was still alive.

Her eyes flicked around the little cubicle. There was a sink in the corner. She darted to it and threw the pill down the drain, scrabbling at the unfamiliar controls until a gush of water followed it. Then she scrambled back to the bed, humiliatingly conscious of how the thin hospital gown revealed her body. Conscious also of the emotions roiling beneath the surface of her mind, like great boulders grinding and moving in the dark. . . .

I wish I was home, she thought desolately. But home was gone, further than all the light-years between this accursed place and the sun Saffron. Home had been in Keriss . . . Keriss was poisoned dust floating in Bethel's skies. *Mother,* she thought, *father. Little sister Delilah.*

Most of the other Bethelites who escaped had been from the Sierra Nueva lands. Amos' family had been direct descendants of the Prophet, members of the Synod of Patriarchs for twenty generations. They had owned the city of Elkbre outright and tens of thousands of square kilometers around it. And they had always been an enlightened family, as much as any, more than most. Hence, the Second Revelation had spread widely there. Rachel had come to it late. *After I heard Amos speak,* she thought, burying her face in her hands. *He was like the Prophet come again.* A new voice, sweeping away the intolerable stuffy load of convention. *And he is so beautiful. . . .*

The partition door opened. Joseph came through first, one hand tinder the flap of his jacket as was his custom. Amos followed, and Rachel flung herself forward into his arms, gripping him fiercely. It was a moment before she felt the awkwardness with which he patted her back. She withdrew, clutching at the gown. That only emphasized its skimpiness, and she flushed deeply, looking down at the floor.

"Pardon, excellent sir," she said.

He made a dismissive gesture. "No need to be formal, Rachel," he said. "You are well?"

"Relieved," she said. "They would only say that you would return, but not where you had been taken or why. Where have you been?" She raised her eyes anxiously to his face.

He hesitated for a moment. "Joseph and I have been meeting with the station managers. We have arranged a funeral service for those who died on our journey here."

She turned aside to spare his embarrassment. "They are not to be trusted."

"What do you mean, Rachel?" His tone was apprehensive but also stern.

"Nothing, yet," she said sullenly, hanging her head. Then she grasped his wrist painfully tight, meeting his eyes earnestly. "But who knows? They are *mezamerin.*" *Strangers.* In the ancient liturgical language, *infidel.*

"Rachel, do not start parroting the Elders at this late date," Joseph said in exasperation. More gently, he put a hand on her shoulder. "Did you take the medication?"

"Yes," she said brusquely, shrugging off his hand. Then she turned to Amos with a sigh. "I am sorry, Excell . . . Amos."

The memory swept over her again: the crowded chamber and the sickly-sweet taste at the back of her mouth as the coldsleep injection took effect.

"I . . . thought I had died, when I woke here," she said. "My father . . . did I tell you?"

"No," Amos said, taking her hand. His large dark-blue eyes held a sudden compassion. "He cursed you?"

"Yes. When I left home to follow you, he put the Patriarch's curse upon me: hell, and miserable rebirth, and damnation again, forever."

Amos blanched slightly for, though his father had been disappointed in his son, even appalled by his son's apostasy, he had not uttered the curse. Perhaps that would have come about had his father not died during Amos' early teens. *If I had been cursed? Perhaps that was why I, fatherless, could become the leader of the Second Revelation*, he thought. *What courage my followers had, to dare the curse for me!*

"I thought I was damned indeed," she whispered. "Since I awoke . . . I . . . I really do not feel myself, Amos."

"It is to be expected," he said, patting her cheek. "You will feel better soon."

"And did you tell them of what follows us?" she asked, blurting out the words since his touch had given her the courage to speak them. "Have they defenses?"

Joseph had been brooding, facing slightly away. Now he laughed bitterly. "Defenses? These people are as open as a canal-side harlot."

Rachel drew a shocked breath.

"You forget yourself, Joseph," Amos said as Rachel drew closer to his side, an instinctive move toward his protection. "There is a lady present."

The shorter man bowed. "Apologies, Excellent Sir," he replied stiffly. A deeper bow. "My lady."

"I cast your own words back, my brother—do not imitate the Elders," Amos said. Unnoticed, Rachel stiffened.

"Is it true?" she said. "They have no defenses?"

Amos nodded, his mouth drawn into a line. "Yes. These are peaceful people, as we were. Fortunately, they are in communication with the Navy of the Central Worlds. Unfortunately, the Kolnari will be here before that help arrives."

Rachel gasped. "How can we flee from here?"

"We cannot," Amos replied, shrugging away the chance of flight. "There are ships, but they are small and have no facilities for passengers. Children, those with child, and the infirm are to be evacuated. The rest of us must remain here and seek to delay the enemy."

"They will know us!" she said in a trembling voice.

Joseph shook his head. "I think not, Lady bint Damscus," he said formally. "Not in this place, and among such as inhabit it. Already we have seen more races of men than I knew existed outside legend. Some very different customs," he pulled his mouth down in disapproval, "and non-men as well."

Rachel's eyes went wide. The most cogent incentive for the Exodus to Bethel had been the Prophet's determination not to pollute the pure blood by congress with non-humans. Nonhuman intelligence was the creation of Shaithen, whether flesh or machine.

Joseph made a soothing gesture. "They are not rulers here. Still, among so many and so various, our handful will disappear and not be remarked by the Kolnari for what we are. The fiends must believe that they strike without warning, that no help will be called to this station. So they will wait, thinking to feast at their ease. Then the warships will come, to rescue us—and return us to our poor Bethel."

"Yes," she said, thoughtfully. "I had not thought of . . . returning."

"In a sense," Amos began, and her eyes snapped back to him with a fixed attention, "we have won the war. Now we must try to survive it. Please, Rachel my sister, would you go among the other women and children? They are awakening, and will be lost and frightened. Prepare those who are eligible to leave here."

"I obey, Amos." She looked around, realizing that she could not go even among women and children of her own people in what she wore.

Joseph opened one of the closets and handed her a large, shapeless robe. Rachel nodded a distant thanks before she donned it and left, the full folds sweeping behind her.

"We have something we share, she and I," Joseph said bitterly, throwing himself down in his float chair. Even his solid bulk did not make it bob on its supporting field. Amos noted the fact and filed it.

I must make a quick review, he thought. *Find what technologies have arisen during our isolation on Bethel. Whatever supports the chair could be altered to support other heavy weights.*

"What do you share?" he asked the other man.

"We both aspire above our stations, she and I," Joseph replied.

Amos blinked in surprise. "Oh," he said after a moment. "Sits the wind so? I had thought her merely devoted to the cause."

"So she is, but that is not the whole story."

"Even if we followed the old customs, I would not take her even as a second wife," he said with a dismissive shrug. "Since I have not even a first, speculation is useless." Then he raised one eyebrow. "You have not pressed your suit?"

"Was there time?" Joseph asked rhetorically. Then he sighed. "Amos, could you see me going to her father for permission? *Bastard son of a whore and a dockside pimp* he would have called me, whether he had disowned her or no—and it would be no more than the truth."

Amos laughed grimly and thumped his follower on the shoulder. "Joseph, my brother, you are a bold man who has saved my life more than once. But there are times when you allow your birth to blind you as much as any hidebound Elder."

At Joseph's puzzled look, he continued. "Joseph, where did Rachel's father live?"

"Keriss—ah! I see."

"Where did the *Elders* live, for the most part?"

"Keriss—and those that did not, they were in the city for the council meeting," Joseph said. "You *have* had time to think, eh?"

"It is necessary that someone do so," Amos said. "We of the Second Revelation were planning to leave, to escape the bonds of customs gone sterile in their changelessness, Joseph. When—if—we return to Bethel with the Space Navy at our backs, very little will remain unchanged after what the Kolnari have done. God has given us a sharp lesson. If we ignore the universe, the universe will not necessarily ignore *us.* And on Bethel . . . the last shall be first, and the first, last; that at the very least.

"Furthermore," he went on, with a man-to-man grin, "I now stand in her father's place, in law. I hereby formally give you leave to press your suit, and for the marriage portion, I will dower her with the Gazelle Rancho at Twin Springs."

Joseph's laughter matched his leader's. "I may press, but I doubt she notices my existence," he said. "Consent may be as far away as the Rancho." A pause. "Although that is where I would take her to live, if we were wed and our cause victorious. She is stronger than she suspects, I think—but her liking for the new ways you preach is of the head, not here." He touched his heart. "As lady of an estate, there would she be happy. She would not thrive among strangers."

CHAPTER TEN

"DETECTION. SHIP TRACK."

Belazir t'Marid looked up from his crash couch where he had been rerunning a tactical manual on the screen.

"What signature?" he said.

"Ion track, very faint," Baila said. "Could have been weeks ago."

Belazir ran his hand through the long blond mane of his hair and cursed inwardly. *The second in two days,* he thought. They were getting into well-traveled space, despite the fact that their data showed little or no settlement in this area. The centuries-old Grand Survey reports listed no inhabitable planets, although there was a nebula with potentially valuable minerals. There must be a regular traffic now, perhaps habitats or small space colonies. Dangerous, very dangerous.

A time would come when the Kolnari would not have to skulk around the fringes of known space, biding like scavengers. But that time was not yet.

"Reduce speed," he said. "Pulse message to the consort ships. Keep formation on new vector." That form of communication was so short-range that it was undetectable. "Anything more on the subspace monitors?"

"Plenty of nearby traffic, but mostly encrypted," the intelligence officer said. Belazir nodded. Perfect codes were an old phenomenon, available to anyone with decent computers.

"And the prey?" he asked.

Baila shrugged. As she was almost as well-born as Belazir, he

147

decided to let the informality pass unreprimanded. Also, she was daughter to a staff officer of Chalku's.

"The track is firm and hot," the woman said. "We gain, at an increasing rate. Signs of deterioration, as one would expect from old engines heavily stressed—sublimated particles from exterior drive-coils and cooling vanes. She cannot survive much longer."

"Much longer, much longer! You've been saying that for days!" Belazir snarled, starting half-erect. The junior officer's eyes dropped before the captain's lion stare. Belazir sank back, satisfied that deference had been restored.

"Transmit to all vessels," he went on. "Maximum alertness. We strike hard and then we run. Plasma tells no tales."

"Dad, I'm not going," Seld Chaundra flatly told his father.

The head of SSS-900-C's medical department looked up in surprise. For a moment, he tried to fit the words into a context that made sense as his hands continued automatically packing a carry-all for his son's trip. Then he shook his head. He was very tired. Since the announcement was made two days ago, there had been absolute chaos in the station. Literal chaos in some instances, and sickbay was full of injuries, everything from carelessness through flare-ups to attempted suicide.

"Do not make troubles now, son," he said. "There is too much to be doing."

"I'm *not going*, Dad," Seld said again.

Gods, but he looks like his mother, the doctor thought with despair. She had had exactly that set to her jaw when she decided to stand on an issue of principle. *And I could never convince her of her error when she looked like that, either.* Fortunately, he did not need to convince his son, who was still a minor.

"Yes," Chaundra said, "you are going. I *need* for you to go."

"Well, I *need* for me to stay!"

Chaundra grabbed his son by his upper arms and shook him gently. "You're all I've got, Seld. You're the most important thing in my life and I've got to keep you safe." He pulled out his ace. "It's what your mother would have wanted."

Seld's red-headed temper flared and, for the first time in his twelve years, he contradicted his father. "No, she wouldn't! She'd say what I'm gonna say. You're all *I've* got, and if you can't be safe then I've got to be with you!"

He pulled his son to him in a fierce hug to hide the sudden glisten of tears in his eyes. Then he sank into his armchair, covering his eyes with his hand.

"Yes," he said thickly, "that's just what she'd say. But," he pointed a finger at Seld, "she'd be talking about herself, not about you."

"Dad . . ."

"I have packed one change of clothes, two changes of underwear and one," he held up one finger for emphasis, "thing you can't bear to part with. I'll be back in half an hour to walk you to the ship."

"Dad!"

"Half an hour." He stood and left. There are times when a man must weep alone.

"Joat!" Simeon said in exasperation, "Answer me! I'd hate to have to send someone in there to flush you out."

He heard laughter echo softly then, from somewhere in the ductwork. *Damned tunnel rat,* he thought in exasperation. She had rigged the sensor in her room to show her present and he was still trying to figure out how it had been done.

"You know they wouldn't find me."

"C'mon Joat, you've got to go. Channa has packed some of your things. She'll meet you at the lock. You're one of the lucky ones. You don't have to wear a suit and travel in the hold for the whole trip."

"Hunh. Done it before."

"Well, you don't have to do it now. Come on! They're leaving in fifteen minutes."

"I'm not going."

"Perhaps I left something out here? Pirates, heavily armed, almost certain death and destruction? Did I mention any of those?"

"You need me," she said simply.

"Yeah," he said slowly after a moment's pause, "but I think I should do without you for a while."

Joat came into view, grinning. "You are *so* soft," she said and shook her head. "You need me because no adult except you knows this station the way I do." She crossed her arms smugly. "This is my home, too, and I want a crack at defending it. Besides, I'm not about to deliver myself to Dorgan the Gorgon." *If she's still alive. Those demonstrators looked* mean. "So here I stay!"

"Joat, is avoiding Ms. Dorgan and the orphanage worth risking your life for?"

"You better believe it!" That forced an unwilling chuckle out of Simeon.

"Look, Joat, no more kidding. Channa and I are fighting for our lives. If we have to worry about you, too, it might make that last little bit of difference and get us killed. We can't *afford* distractions from a kid."

Joat's lips went white. "You fight dirty," she whispered.

"I fight to win," Simeon replied.

"*Well, so do I!*" Joat shouted. "And I'm *alive*, aren't I?" She paused for a moment, breathing hard. Then the urchin grin came back. "I've got an instinct for this kinda thing. Trust me." She took a step back and disappeared.

I wish I knew how she did that, Simeon thought. *It would come in handy when the Kolnari get here.*

"Channa's expecting you on Boat Deck!" he called after her.

A voice filtered in from nowhere. "Tell her I'll be seeing her."

"Detection . . . *ship detected! Ship detected!* Captain to the bridge!"

Belazir t'Marid had been kneeling between his wife's thighs, with a heel in each hand.

"Demonshit!" he swore, diving off the pallet and toward his clothing. The woman—she was his second wife, and a third cousin—cursed antiphonally, rolling away in the other direction.

"The Divine Seed damn them," she said, hopping on one leg as she stuck the other into her skinsuit.

"Easy for you to say," he snarled and kicked at her, struggling with the humiliating and acutely uncomfortable process of getting into space armor in a state of arousal. Then he raised his voice. "Battle stations, full alert. Brief me."

"One vessel. Approaching on path of our trajectory, in normal space."

"Normal space?" he said. The door hissed away as he trotted out of his quarters which were aft of the bridge and one deck down.

"Confirmed," Serig said as Belazir stalked into the bridge. While the captain slept in hostile space, the executive officer stood the watch. He now rose from the commander's couch; a squat man for a Kolnar, a hand below Belazir's height, and muscled like a troll. "You have the bridge, lord."

"Acknowledged." Belazir felt an obscure comfort as he slid into the crash couch and let his hands fall on the controls. *And that cold plastic catheter has settled my other problem,* he thought with an inward quirk of the lips. "Data."

"Vessel is in the one kiloton mass range." The battle team was on the bridge now, the circular room brightening as consoles came up to ready status. "Neutrino signature indicates merchanter-class engines, presently running on ballistic. There may be energy or kinetic weapons, but I detect no triggers for fusion warheads."

"Interesting," Belazir said calmly. "Serig."

"Command me, lord."

"Indeed. We're going to take a closer look. Prepare for drop into normal space. Notify the flotilla."

"Lord . . ."

"Yes, yes. The primary mission. We are gaining swiftly and have the time. Also, if we detect this ship, it may have detected *us.*" The Kolnari fleet had the best instruments they could steal or copy, but there was no telling how much performance had improved in areas in close contact with regular shipyards. There had been one or two nasty surprises like that before in the Clan's history. "If they have, all the more reason to investigate and make sure they have no tale to tell anyone."

"Prepare for breakthrough." Alarm chimes tinkled and sang. "Thirty seconds, mark."

A twisting at the fabric of the universe; the view on the exterior screens did not change—the computers compensated during FTL running—but a subtle sense of reality returned, something at the corner of the mind.

Serig's voice spoke beside Belazir. "Lord, we have her on electromagnetic detectors. No answer to hailing. Shall we use the kinetics?"

Their relative velocities were in the thousands of kps; solid shot would strike with nuclear force.

"Not yet," Belazir said thoughtfully. "Give me a visual."

The image sprang out before him a few seconds later. There was a noticeable lag now that they were confined to Einstein's universe. A flattened spheroid, quite a small ship. Fairly fast, from the size of the exterior coils; neatly made, nearly new. And totally unarmed, as far as the detectors could determine. Certainly not meant for rapid transit in atmosphere as a Kolnari warship of that size would be.

"They have a small laser," Serig said. "Meteorite-clearing type. Apart from that, nothing."

"Is she dead?"

"The cabin is at sixteen degrees," he replied, and touched a control. The screen's image split. A molded double of the ship appeared, infrared scanning to show temperatures.

"But no reply to our hail," Belazir mused, tugging at his lower lip. "This is too interesting to pass by. All ships, establish zero relative velocity and stand by."

"Great Lord." The communications officer. "The *Age of Darkness* is hailing, imperative code."

"Put her through." Belazir nodded to himself; exactly what he would expect. A face that might have been his brother's flashed into a screen on his couch-arm.

"Aragiz t'Varak," the man said. Equal-to-equal greeting, full personal and subclan-name. Socially correct as the t'Varak were one of the noble gens of the High Clan, but a military solecism. One of the problems of a family business.

"t'Varak," Belazir said, reminding him of it. In a social situation, he would have replied with his own full name.

"Why are we halting?" Belazir waited. "Sir."

"Because there is a potential prize of great value here," Belazir said mildly. "In any case, we must deal with it."

"A missile is quick." *And Father Chalku is impatient:* the unspoken thought was plain enough.

"A missile is wasteful," Belazir said. He grinned for an instant. Aragiz looked slightly alarmed. "But your objection is noted. You will not, therefore, insist on sharing in the prize credit—you or your ship."

Now Aragiz's face was unreadable black iron. *Fool*, the captain of the *Bride* thought. Everyone on the *Age* would be monitoring this, as the *Bride* was broadcasting in ship-to-ship clear. An intact merchantman could be a prize of great worth, particularly a new, fast ship, suitable for conversion to a family transport or an assault carrier. No matter how well-born or ruthless, a captain could not afford to alienate the common crew too badly; not to mention the relatives who would fill most of the command positions.

T'Varak had just sharply reduced his chances of surviving to flag rank. Belazir's hand cut off his protests and the intership screen.

"Serig," he said, allowing himself a slight feral smile of satisfaction. "You will take the assault team. One boat, three fighters. Full monitor at all times."

Serig grinned, white against his ebony face. Being petit-noble, he could afford such open enjoyment at the t'Varak's discomfiture.

"Perhaps there will be a scumvermin woman aboard," he said.

The lock cycled open.

Serig na Marid signed behind himself: *on the count of three.* He felt good, loose and easy and fast, the plasma gun in his hands an extension of his body. Nothing else felt quite as good as the tension just before combat: not sex or wealth or satisfied revenge. The knowledge that his lord would be observing through the helmet pickups was an added bonus. Whatever he accomplished would not be just another small byte in the chaotic melee of large-scale destruction: it would be uniquely his, with commanders and officers on all four ships watching.

"Now!"

Swiftly, smoothly, the three figures in dark combat armor swung into the lock. The deck rang under their boots as they landed in the interior field.

"Still no sign of reaction," Serig said. "Field is point six-three GK." Kolnari gravities, that was. It was 1.0 G Terran, the old human standard. "Pressurizing."

Serig dropped to a three-point stance on the floor, fingers of his left hand, toes of both feet, knees bent. The two ground-fighters were on either side of the airlock. The inner portal was of standard form, circular, with a seam down the middle where the leaves met. Air hissed into the lock, and the light went from vacuum-flat to a warmer, yellow tone. Much like that on some planets he had seen, although the Kolnari fleet still kept the harsh brightness of their vanished homeworld.

"*Go!*"

The leaves snapped back. In the same instant Serig vaulted forward, plasma rifle ready. A single octagonal corridor lay in front, ending five meters ahead in a T-junction. He went to ground just before the intersection and pressed a thumb to the stock of his weapon. A long stiff thread extended out, and Serig keyed the image it carried onto his faceplate. More empty corridor, this time running north-south through the main axis of the ship. Again octagonal, 2.0 meters in diameter, with a synthetic fabric covering on the "down" side and the ceiling; extruded synthetic sides, luminous at regular intervals, and recessed hatchways. Another door was at the north end of the corridor with a keypad, and a duplicate at the south.

A careful one second later the two backups leapt past him,

facing either way. They waited in silence, eyes flickering in trained patterns.

"Nothing," Serig said, coming to his feet and walking into the axial corridor. He glanced down at the readouts on his gauntlet.

"Air is Terran-standard basis." Thinner than Kolnar, but with more oxygen and less sulfuric acid and ozone. Homeworld had much ozone at the surface, little in the stratosphere. "Slightly depleted oxygen levels, high level of necrotic decay products. Wouldn't like to have to breathe it."

"*Proceed*," Belazir's voice said.

"As you command, lord," Serig replied. In the language of Kolnar, that phrase was one word. "Proceeding up axial corridor now."

Almost all human-made ships still had a notional "bow" at the north pole, and that was the most common location for a bridge. Serig directed his subordinates forward with hand signals. They moved from one compartment to another, opening each, checking inside with a vision thread and then going on to the next.

"Sensors detect no live presence," Serig reported. They moved forward again, two covering the one exposed, up to the small ship's control center. "These chambers appear to be staterooms, lord, presently disused."

"Better and better," Belazir's voice said. That implied extensive life-support facilities.

The north-end hatch yielded to the same simple random-number code as the exterior entranceway. The control chamber was a domed hemisphere with three couches, only one occupied. It had half-closed around the pilot's body in a coldsleep cocoon, not fully deployed.

Serig moved to look down at the body.

"You were right; a woman," Belazir said dryly.

"Not one that appeals to me," his second-in-command replied. "Tshakiz, get a tissue sample." He was glad for the filtered, neutral air that flowed through his helmet.

The rotting flesh slid greasily away from the probe. Serig looked elsewhere, touching the controls with slow caution. The shrill accented voice of the Medical Officer broke in. That was a low-status occupation, and the man was the gelded son of a slave mother.

"Subject has been dead approximately four days," he announced. "Scan, please, my great lords."

One of the ground fighters detached a sensor wand from her belt and ran it slowly from head to toe of the corpse. A minute's silence followed.

"Preliminary analysis: death from overdose of coldsleep drugs, combined with oxygen starvation and dehydration when cocoon failed to properly deploy."

Serig nodded. On single-crewed vessels the pilot would often use coldsleep, relying on the AI systems to handle the simple and tedious work of long interstellar transits. Slightly risky, but it saved lifespan.

"Ship systems are live," Serig said. "Cryptography, please." He punched a jack into the receptor and waited while the powerful machines on the *Bride* worked on the guardian programs of the enemy ship. "Worm is through. I have control of the computer." *That was simple,* he thought. Not much computer security at all, and . . .

"Ah! Lord? The coldsleep system was sabotaged."

"How wicked," Belazir said, and they shared a chuckle. "Why?"

"A moment, lord. Yes, by the dugs of the Dreadful Mother! This is a commercial courier. The female was an agent for some merchant house, traveling with samples. She boasts of making the 'sale of a lifetime' at her most recent stop, a nexus-station designated SSS-900-C. Some rival did it."

"It was the sale of *her* lifetime," Belazir said.

This time Serig could hear more laughter in the background. He turned sharply to his assistants. *"Nobody told you to stop working,"* he barked. "Divine Seed of Kolnar! Lord, I have accessed the cargo manifest!"

He could hear Belazir grunt like a man belly-punched as the figures and data scrolled across to the Kolnari warships. Computers and computer parts; engineering software; fabrication systems; drugs; luxury consumer items, wines, silks . . .

"And lord! The cargo compartments have full climatic control!"

Rigged for the carrying of delicate cargo? That made the vessel beyond price to the Clan. With climate-controlled holds, she could be easily and cheaply rerigged to hold families or troops in coldsleep.

Belazir's voice grew sardonic. "Captain t'Varak, I hope you are satisfied." Nothing came over the circuit but the sound of teeth grinding. One of the other captains did venture a comment.

"Does this not seem too much like the answer to a prayer?" he murmured. "I sacrifice much to my joss and the ancestors, vessels of the Divine Seed, but . . ." *The joss help the strongest first,* the saying went.

"Under other circumstances, Zhengir t'Marid," Belazir answered him coolly, "I might agree. But cousin, who could know we forayed in this direction? Only those we pursue, and they press forward in a disintegrating hulk with no communications capability since we blew it away." Command snapped in his voice. "Serig. Secure the ship. Discard the corpse and flush the environmental systems. Are fungibles adequate?"

"More than adequate, Great Lord," Serig said, hammering the glee out of his voice. *My gods! My greed!* he thought. A full percentage point would be his as noble-in-command of the boarding party. *My lord is well pleased with me,* he decided. He must, to give his bastard half-brother such an opportunity. Petit-nobles had been translated to full status for less.

"There is plenty of air," he went on. "Surplus water. The pilot never awoke to renew."

"Good. Await the prize crew—Alyze b'Marid will command it—and then return. Expedite! We will resume superluminal in less than an hour, or skin will be stripped."

Alyze was the commander's new third wife. Serig suspected she might be pregnant, and Belazir anxious to have her out of harm's way before even the slight danger at the end of their chase. He nodded to himself. Such was good noble thinking, for a man's honor was in the diffusion of his portion of the Divine Seed.

"Hearkening and obedience, lord," he said. *And this SSS-900-C will also be in the path of our pursuit,* Serig thought. *I will light ten sticks to my personal joss in apology.*

He had kicked the little idol across his cabin in anger when he learned they were to be sent on a lootless, honorless pursuit mission while their comrades and clanfolk plundered Bethel. It seemed he had been premature.

CHAPTER ELEVEN

"TOLD YA," Joat said.

"Yes," Seld Chaundra said, turning his head aside.

The transit levels of SSS-900-C were still chaotic and barely-suppressed panic was rampant. Squads of weeping children pressed by, herded by an adult with a child in her arms. A caterpillar of toddlers held on to a cord which was tethered to a few protesting sub-adolescents.

Joat and Seld were off to one side in the shadows of an access bay. There were many at the upper globe's north pole, what with the pumping and docking facilities and the multiple feeds needed. The housekeeping programs were laboring overtime, pumping odors of pine, sea-salt and wildflowers into the air. It still smelled of vomit and unchanged diapers and fear, and the baffles only muted the roar of voices. The two teenagers stepped backward as a man wearing the armband of a part-time policeman went by.

"I hate running out on my dad like this," Seld said in a choked voice. "He's gonna kill me, Joat."

"No, the pirates may kill you, but all he can do is slap you around."

Shocked, the boy looked up. "Dad never hits me!"

"Well, then you've got a pretty good dad, and you're not running out on him—you're staying *with* him. 'S what you wanna do, isn't it?"

"Yeah." He turned his face to the wall. "I *can't* go . . . my mom. . . ."

he said in a fierce tone. "I never saw her again . . . I woke up and she was just . . . gone."

Surprised at herself—she generally hated to touch people—Joat put an awkward arm around his shoulders. He clutched at her for a moment, sobbing.

"Sorry about blubbering," he said after a moment. Then he grew conscious of the bearhug grip he was exerting, and broke away.

"'Salright," Joat said. *Somehow it is,* she thought, then flogged her mind back to practical matters. "Need a snot-rag?"

"Thanks." He blew noisily on the one which she offered and then gave it back to her. "What do we do now?"

"We get out of sight. Channa's going to go ballistic, and she's nearly as hard to hide from as Simeon. Worse, 'cause I can't screw up *her* sensors."

"There she is," he said.

Joat's head whipped around. The noise was reaching tidal proportions around the tall lean figure of Channa Hap. Only the escort of Vicker's security personnel kept her from being bowled over in the crowd. She had a canvas carrier bag in one hand. Joat recognized the foot of the stuffed bear sticking out one side.

"That satisfies the letter of it," she said. "Let's go."

Channa stalked into the lounge, opened the door to Joat's room and flung the canvas bag she carried as hard as she could against the room's far wall. It made a solitary spot of disorder in the servo-neat room. Then she shut the door and walked stiffly to her desk, sat down and began keying through her messages, back hunched in rejection.

"It's not my fault," Simeon finally ventured to say.

She turned slowly to glare at his column.

Oooh, I'm glad this is titanium crystal, Simeon thought. *Now, if only there was something similar available for the psyche.*

Just as slowly, just as silently, Channa turned back to her console.

Simeon sent her a message that read. "I'm sorry you had to go through that scene at Disembarkation."

Channa let out an exasperated little hiss and slapped the screen. Simeon's image appeared on it, wincing realistically.

Unwillingly, a smile quirked at her mouth. "Simeon, I would have been there anyway, to speak words of encouragement, to wish well, to shake hands, to show solidarity." She swung a fist in a go-get-'em gesture. "But I would have had a *lot* more credibility if I hadn't been standing there with an overnight bag in my hand. Did you see the suspicious looks I got? Half of the evacuees probably think I'm on one of the other ships. You could have *said* something, a quiet word of warning in my ear, as it were. Then I could have dumped that damned incriminating bag!" She turned to look at his column again. "Why wasn't she there?"

"She wouldn't go," Simeon said weakly. "She *said* she'd see you. I thought she meant there at the Boat Dock."

"You *did*?"

"Well, I *hoped*," Simeon said. "I tried my best to get her there. Pushed every emotional button I could. Manipulated shamelessly, you know the way I can."

"Ol' silver-tongued Simeon slips up again, huh?"

"I can't exactly get out of my shell and chase her down and hog-tie her, Channa. She wouldn't go. She told me that we could never find her in fifteen minutes and she was right. Even *you'd* have to agree with that. Trying to manipulate Joat is like trying to suck liquid hydrogen through a straw."

Channa sighed. "Indeed! But standing there with that bag was hideously embarrassing for me. Besides, I really wanted to get her to safety."

"I know how you feel," he soothed her. "This surrogate parent stuff is pretty intense." *And it was* your *idea*, he reminded himself. Oddly, he felt no impulse to remind her. *I guess I like it*, he decided.

She ground the heels of her hands into red-rimmed eyes. "I apologize."

Well, that's a first. "I accept."

"Announce me," Amos ben Sierra Nueva said to the door.

It hinged softly, and he knew it would be turning to a screen on the interior, showing his image in real-time. Such things still made him a little nervous. Bethel had never used much in the way of sophisticated electronics. Doors there were usually plain honest wood. He smiled slightly in spite of himself. Here, wood was an unthinkably expensive luxury, and the most advanced technology, the stuff of common life. At least he had been able to dress properly, from the baggage somebody threw into the shuttle at the last minute. It was demoralizing to look like some cottonchopper goatherd from the backlands. Loose black trousers tucked into his boots, silver-link belt emphasizing the narrow hips, open robe throwing his broad shoulders into relief. He bowed ceremoniously as he entered, sweeping off his beret to Channa.

"Come in." Channa's voice was flat and tired as the door opened, but her face lit in an inadvertent smile of welcome.

Good, he thought, smiling back. Even in this desperate hour, it was pleasant to have so exotic and attractive a woman smile at him. Then he bowed again, to the column. *To Simeon,* he forced himself to think. And tried not to think of the pale deformed thing in there, among the tubes and neural circuits. Whenever the image came to him, a slight tinge of nausea accompanied it. He was afraid that Simeon could detect his reaction. He could imagine several sensors that would make it difficult or impossible to lie to a shellperson. Guiyon he had never thought of so. Guiyon had always been there in the background, a sympathetic voice from his earliest days. *Guiyon was my friend.*

"I am sorry to disturb you," he began. "Now that the most urgent tasks are done, I wish to reiterate my desire to assist in the coming battle."

"When our plans are more solid, I assure you there will be a place for you in them," Simeon said.

Amos's mouth quirked. *You mean, when you've figured out something we can do,* he thought.

"We are not trained as soldiers," he said with a self-deprecating smile and a shrug. "And we are from a backward world. But," he raised a finger, "I have thought of something which you both, being so close to the matter, may have overlooked." He glanced from Simeon to Channa and back again. "It is something that Guiyon said that makes me think of this.

"He said to me, *I am one of Central Worlds' most valuable resources. The Kolnari do not have any brainships in their fleet and I do not intend to be the first.*"

"Oh," Channa murmured.

"Hell," Simeon said. "I knew it but I didn't think of it. Brains are so rare, out in the backlands."

"Yes." Amos nodded vigorously. "We must hide the fact that Simeon exists. Or the *first* thing that the Kolnari do will be to cut out Simeon's shell and send it back to their fleet. This must not happen."

"Indeed it must not," Simeon said, his voice slow and flat. All three of them knew what followed from that. If the Kolnari *did* get their hands on a brain—one trained in strategy, at that—it would immediately change them from a wandering pack of scavengers to a first-rate menace.

"Simeon would never—" Channa began body, then trailed off.

"Yes." Simeon's voice was now as expressionless as a subroutine robotic. There were dozens of unpleasant ways of forcing a captive brain to capitulate. The most effective was also the worst: simply cut off the exterior sensor feeds which would mean sensory deprivation fugue in days or less. "I tend to forget how . . . helpless I am, most of the time," he went on. "Forget I'm a cripple, so to speak."

"*You are not!*" Channa blazed.

Amos blinked at the sight. She seemed to *bristle*, the widow's peak of her rusty-brown hair rising. *I would not like to have this lady wrathful with me,* the Bethelite thought respectfully.

She forced herself to be calm. "Compared to you, *we* are cripples, Simeon," she said. "You have a hundred abilities we lack."

"Thank you," he said in more normal tones. "Still, what Amos says is true. At all costs, we can't let the Kolnari get their hands on me."

The self-destruct sequence surfaced in the minds of both brawn and brain, like some monster rising from the depths of the ocean, with a wave of cold black water sweeping before it.

Amos coughed. "There is a way, I think. We may fool them. Convince them that there is no brain controller on this station. If indeed," and his lips peeled back over his teeth in a nasty grin, "barbarians such as the Kolnari even know of such persons."

Seeing Channa about to speak, he held up his hand to forestall her. "Do I assume that Simeon's name appears on far too many documents or news holos or whatever, for us to hide his very existence? Also, someone is sure to lapse and mention the name, thus giving rise to questions. So," and he gave his cloak a little flourish, "I have come to offer myself as a false Simeon. To deceive them." He looked from one to the other eagerly. "Is this not a good idea?"

"It's . . ." Channa began, and looked at him with shining eyes. "It's damn brilliant!" She sprang up and hugged him for a moment, then began to pace. "*If* we can get the substitution to work."

"Well, it sure beats suicide," Simeon said, for he had had to consider that as his only option. "One small point pops up, Amos. I've been here for forty years, and you're what, twenty-eight?"

"Ah, a valid point to consider," he said, "but as you have already pointed out, during their stay in this station, they are unlikely to spend time reviewing its history. They would have no reason not to accept me as Channa's assistant. If you feel it is an important concern, we could always tell them that Simeon is a title, I could then be the Simeon-Amos."

"Yes," Channa said enthusiastically, "we could pretend it's a traditional title. A position named after the first person who held it, an honorific! Why would they check if we *say* it is so and has always been? And that ploy would involve jimmying fewer personnel records—that's a major plus. Especially with people who've been here a while. Faking that is like trying to pull one card out of a tower. Every change means more changes and pretty soon it cascades out of control."

"There are the transients," Simeon said meditatively. "Most of them don't bother about who manages what so long as they're not inconvenienced. We've pretty near dispatched so many who *do* know that the ruse might just work." Simon began to enlarge the concept of deception. "Mmm, you know, we could use that old secondary control center that was on-line when the station was being built. Before I was installed here. These quarters don't *look* much like an office. We could say this is a living accommodation."

"Ah! Then you accept my offer as impostor," cried Amos. "Excellent! I shall move here as soon as you require me. Until then, I'd like to remain with my people. If you do not mind a companion in your lovely rooms?" he asked, turning swiftly to Channa, concerned that he also might have offended her with his presumption.

"We'll let you know when," she said, a little dazed.

"Of course," he said. He took her hand and kissed it tenderly, smiled in Simeon's direction, and left.

Channa stared at the closed doors for a moment, then turned to Simeon's shaft. "Excuse me, but did we just accept his offer?"

"Well, not exactly, but we didn't say no."

"I noticed that. Why not, I wonder?"

Simeon was a little amused at the idea of Channa being bowled over by another personality. "Hmm. Maybe because we agree with him?" Slyly: "Or it could be the pheromones, in your case, Happy baby."

Channa bridled and threw a cushion at the column. "Get serious. It *is* a good idea, even if I didn't think of it first. You *have* to be protected from the Kolnari."

"Yes," he said, enduring excruciating embarrassment at that truth.

"Nor can I see any reason not to take him up on his offer. Maybe having an outsider close to our counsels will keep us on our toes, so to speak."

Channa gave a little grunt. "As I said, it's a good idea, but on second thoughts, why *him*? He'd have to learn a lot in very little time to sound as if he knew what he'd been doing all this time. I *still* have trouble finding my way around, and I not only grew up on a station, I had time to study the layout of the SSS-900 before I came here. Why not someone from the station? Someone we know and have confidence in?"

"I think we can have confidence in him, Channa," Simeon said thoughtfully.

"Hunh! Based on what?" she asked challengingly, hands on her hips.

"Authority usually stems from character, Channa. I've been watching him with his people, and there's no doubt that he's the man in charge. They look at him the way that people look at someone they can depend on. Consider the shocks they've all been through, especially him. Don't forget he went with Chaundra down to the morgue. Then he came to us with this . . . viable, I think . . . plan. We could do worse than accepting his offer. Besides, who else is there?"

"Since you ask, I was considering Gus."

"And who's going to be Gus, while Gus is being me?" He watched her cross her arms over her bosom and frankly pout. "We could end up changing every name in the station if we go that route. What with this and that, we could get so snarled up, we wouldn't know our arse ends from our ears."

She laughed, suddenly visualizing the corridors full of people checking their noteboards to see who they were that day.

"Besides," Simeon said, "I like Gus."

"What's that got to do with it?" she replied. "Oh."

Whoever fronted as the station's manager was the most likely to receive the brunt of occupational hazards. She liked Gus, and even on such short acquaintance, she liked Amos. He was undeniably nicer to look at and had already been through several layers of hell. On the other hand, *somebody* had to do it. If she was right there beside him to give judicious guidance—and being beside Amos was not a chore, maybe they'd get through without any really bad gaffes.

"All right," she said, raising her hands in capitulation. "Shuffling people around really could become more difficult than teaching one stranger the ins and outs of station management. At least enough to fool these thugs. But, on your enhanced head be it, my brave brain, if he turns out to be a disaster."

"I accept your challenge, my beautiful brawn. Shall I have him move in tonight?"

For a moment, Channa looked as though she'd inadvertently swallowed something too large and lumpy. "Ah, of course. We'll have to get his training started right away, won't we?"

Amos frowned. As attractively as he smiled, Simeon noted.

Sheesh. When this is over, he could earn megacredits as a vid-star with Singari Entertainments, making historicals.

"But I had wanted to stay with my people," he said.

"I know," Simeon told him, "but we're placing the least injured in their own quarters, effective immediately, and scattering the rest. We can't risk having them identified as a group, you know."

The young man clasped his hands behind his back. "Yes, I see. All will be strange to the Kolnari, in many different ways. Our strangeness will be one more anomaly."

"You're not *that* strange," Simeon felt compelled to say. *Too bloody handsome for my peace of mind. Or maybe being* that *handsome is stranger'n I realize.*

The elevator opened onto the corridor outside Simeon and Channa's quarters. Channa stood in the open door of the lounge to greet Amos. She held out her hand to him, wearing a formal, welcoming smile. He took her hand tenderly in both of his, bowed over it gracefully and kissed it gently, his eyes never leaving hers. Channa raised one brow and smiled crookedly, taking back her hand and gesturing him into the lounge.

"I know you wanted to stay with the others," she said, "but there's a lot you'll have to be briefed on, and we should get started. Also, Simeon may have told you, they'll be moving to their own quarters this evening."

"Yes, so he has told me," Amos said softly.

He looked at her with a warm attention that she found unnervingly intimate. "This will be yours," she said, opening the door farthest from her own.

He entered, looked around, his hands clasped behind his back once more. He nodded judiciously, "It is very nice," he said. He opened a closet, empty but for a few hangers.

"One of the things we'll have to do is fit you out according to your new position," Channa said from the doorway.

He smiled at her. "Yes, I need everything. And Bethel clothing would not be appropriate."

He walked over to stand right beside her. She had noticed that the Bethelites did that; their social distance was close and they were a very *tactile* people.

"I shall enjoy that," he said, "if you will help me choose?"

She lowered her eyes. "Perhaps, if time allows. Though you'll be guided by experts in men's fashions, which I am not." *Down, girl!* she told herself.

The door chimed and Simeon opened it. "I've sent down to the commissary for dinner. I doubt you've found the time to eat, Amos, so I've taken the liberty of ordering for two," he said.

"You do not like to cook?" Amos asked, turning to Channa in surprise.

"Not when I have more important things to do," she answered. "It isn't among my hobbies."

"Ah, well, doubtless your servants are skilled." His voice implied that a chatelaine should still oversee them personally.

Ah, good one, Amos. Simeon thought, feeling more cheerful. He had been reviewing what little was known of Bethelite culture. He did *not* think Channa would find it agreeable. *Why don't you ask her to sit on the floor and rub your tired feet while you're at it, then retire to the rear of the house while the men talk business?*

It was worrying, though. *Much as I hate to admit it, maybe Channa was right. This plan has inherent elements of disaster. I forgot to take into consideration that he's from an insular and probably—I'll be kind, old-fashioned. Nah! Why be kind—backward culture.* All their preparations were a mishmash of improvisations. Would this be one too many?

Amos looked quickly from Simeon's column to Channa and said in mild dismay.

"I have caused offense. Please, forgive me. This was not my intention." He smiled ruefully down at Channa and sighed. "I clearly have more to learn than I had imagined. Even my speech—the more we talk, the more I am conscious of how old-fashioned I must sound to you. And, forgive me, we of Bethel are not used to dealing with people of strange—of different customs. That was one thing I disliked about my home, the insularity."

Hell, Simeon thought. *He's not stupid. Adaptable, in fact.*

With a smooth professional smile, Channa gestured for him to take one of the seats at the table.

"Then let us begin," she said.

To his back she made a small moue of distaste, which quickly turned into a smile as he held out her chair and looked at her expectantly. She grinned and waved him to his seat.

"First," she said, "you must learn that we're much less formal here. We reserve our 'company manners' strictly for company."

"But," he said, smiling as he took his seat, "a beautiful woman should always be treated like a treasured guest."

Channa served herself from a platter and passed it to him, letting go of it almost before he'd gotten a grip on it.

"Flatterer. I'm not ugly, but I'm no great beauty, either."

He almost dropped the hot platter in surprise, its contents tilting alarming close to the edge and burning his thumb. He put it down hastily and sucked the injury for a moment.

"No, truly," he said, flapping his hand to cool it. "I think you are most attractive." There was no doubting the sincerity in his wide, gentian-blue eyes. The lashes, she noticed, were long and curled. His gaze grew playful. "In a strange, foreign, exotic fashion, of course."

"Well, you're very attractive, too, Amos," she said seriously.

"I like attractive women," he said, and his gaze was subtly challenging.

"Mmh, I don't like attractive men," she said positively. *Actually, I don't* approve *of them, which is not exactly the same thing,* she amended to herself. "They tend to be spoiled and self-centered and in general much more trouble than they're worth. Now, let us eat before the food cools. We have a great deal of work to do and not much time and energy to spare." She gave him a direct stare. "I'm sure we're going to have an excellent business relationship, manager to manager."

"Of course," Amos said with a neutral, social smile.

"Shouldn't you start calling Amos Simeon-Amos, Channa?" Simeon broke in, before the atmosphere got any cooler.

"Good idea," Channa said.

Amos, as far as Simeon could tell, was sulking slightly.

Aha, Simeon thought. *With those looks, plus brains and charisma and high position, he's probably used to women succumbing to his every ploy.* And, he noted charitably, the Bethelite was only in his early twenties. All the textbooks said softshells were highly subject to hormonal influences at that stage in their pitifully short development spans.

Nine gets you ten, he told himself, *that there's a worn-down track in the carpet between their doors within a week.* The notion was oddly unpalatable. He put it aside and launched into some of the nineteen million things Amos would have to become familiar with about station management.

CHAPTER TWELVE

AHHHA, GOTCHA! Simeon crooned to himself. "Channa? You awake?"

"You can always tell when I'm awake. Why ask?"

"Because it's *polite,*" he replied.

"What is it?" Her tone noted that the sleep period was three hours gone and, in barely five more, she would have to be awake for more of the interminable meetings and briefings.

"I've found out something about our expected and uninvited guests," he went on.

That brought her alert, sitting up in bed and reaching to key up the lights and switch off the soft fugue she had been playing to court sleep.

"Couldn't sleep anyway," she said. "Let me have it."

"Got a download from Central. Had to burn some butts to get it released. It's not much. Planet named *Kolnar,* settled way, way, *way* back. Quite a ways from here, too, as such things go. About forty times as far as the sun Saffron, further in on the spiral arm."

Channa frowned. "That's really out in the boonies, settled in the second or third waves."

"Uh-uh. It was *first* wave."

She pursed her lips in a silent whistle. "Right at the beginning of interstellar colonization."

He went on. "Involuntary colonization. Translation program running . . . Okay, a whole bunch of bad-hat groups; the *Khimir*

168

Reddish Rice Cosmetic, the *Temil Large Striped Felines,* the *New Council Men,* the *Resurrected Aryan-Germanic Statewide Associationist Employees Party,* the *Sons of Chaka,* the *Luminescent Footway,* the *Darwin-Wilson Society,* the—"

"What's so amusing?" she said as she caught the laughter ripple in his voice.

"You'd have to be a historian to understand, my voluptuous popsie," he said cheerfully. "Anyway, according to the records, they sent out about ten thousand of these oscos, and about three thousand reached their destination."

"Bad voyages?"

"Internal fighting in the holds," Simeon said. "With fists and teeth and soft plastic cups, since they didn't have anything else. Then when they got there, they realized they'd have to interbreed, like it or not."

"What sort of planet *is* Kolnar?"

"Nickname was 'Hell's Orifice.' They picked it because it was easier on tender consciences. Society could pretend the planet killed the convicts, who deserved it, from the records. One-point-six gees, hot sun, enormous heavy-metal concentrations, thick but low-oxygen air, superactive and largely poisonous biosphere. No ozone layer. Vulcanism, unpredictable climatic shifts . . . the whole nine yards! Not much visited since. When the Grand Survey went through a few centuries later, they were fired on. Evidently the locals have a nuclear war about once every forty years or so, and the ship got in the way of one. Their descriptions of the physical type match what Amos and the others say. There's been some contact with them since. That incident with the survey seemed to remind them that the rest of the universe was still there, unfortunately."

"Unfortunately?"

"Well, I've got cross-references under *piracy, brigandage, police actions, war crimes* and *aggression.* Also entries in the anthro files under *genocide, slavery, cultural pathology, xenophobia* and *societal devolution.* There are apparently pockets of the descendants of the original social aberrants scattered through a number of systems in the area nowadays. Little asteroid colonies, freebooter dens, unsurveyed worlds."

"Urk. Characteristics?"

"Apart from not being very nice? Dark skin is a climatic adaptation—all that UV—and the hair and eye color genetic drift you'd expect in a small initial population. They breed like, hmm, rabbits, though. Puberty at eight, all children twins or triplets. Overall, the Kolnari subrace seems to have very efficient immune systems. They're extremely strong and fast. You'd expect good reflexes on a planet like that—those with bad ones didn't survive. They can see in the dark like cats, and they've got an amazing tolerance for ionizing radiation. There's so much fallout and natural background radiation on Kolnar that they've genetically adapted to it. The scientists seem to disagree whether their paranoia is inbred or just cultural."

"Hard to get rid of, I'd expect."

"Like cockroaches," Simeon said, deliberately misunderstanding. "One Space Navy type a few generations back said the only way to solve the Kolnari problem would be to drop antimatter bombs from orbit. Even then, you wouldn't be really sure of destroying them all."

"Very depressing, thank you, and now can I get some rest?"

Later that night, still unable to sleep, Channa called out his name softly.

"You should be sleeping, Channa."

"I know, but I've got to clear my mind first. Will you talk with me?"

A pause hung in the air. She took a breath and went on. "I know I haven't been as good a brawn as—"

"Ancient history," Simeon said. "You've been handling a hellacious emergency better than most anyone could. I can certainly listen. What's on your mind?"

"*He* is," she said, as if the two words covered the problem adequately.

"Ah. Not what you expected, huh?"

She sighed, "No, the opposite. Too much what I expected. He's . . . I'm afraid I won't be able to work with him."

Why am I not surprised? Simeon thought. "Why? What's wrong?"

"Aside from his being a smug, pushy, egotist, you mean? Well, he doesn't have any faith in my competence and I expect to have to fight to keep him from trying to usurp my position. He's very much a take-charge kind of person, you were right about that. And he has no respect for women."

"What makes you think that?" *Let's hear how you came to that difficult conclusion.* Simeon enjoyed the challenge of following the workings of her mind.

"For crying out loud, Simeon, he expected me to *cook* for him!

Oh, yes, he got over that. He's always ready with an apology for 'different customs.' But, deep down, he doesn't really *believe* it. He thinks 'customs' is whether you sit on the floor or on a chair, stuff like that. He doesn't grasp the difference in fundamental cultural views."

"Channa-my-sweet, back on Bethel, there *aren't* any fundamental differences. This quarrel he had with the Elders, it's hard to grasp exactly what it was about . . . but it seems overwhelmingly important to *them*."

"Oh, I *understand* why he's that way," Channa said, striking the pillow with a frustrated fist. "And it's not as if he's stupid. He's intelligent and he notices things, but that makes it more irritating, not less. You could ignore what a stupid person does. What's more, suddenly he's living in my pocket. I'm just a little surprised he didn't ask to see the other rooms in order to choose the one he preferred." Her face suddenly flushed a becoming rose.

Simeon noted that. After all, he could see in the dark, too. "And he came on to you like the colony ship he flew in on, didn't he?"

"Damn right he did," she muttered, half under her breath. "'I *like* attractive women,'" she said in exaggerated imitation of his manner and accent. "What do you suppose he does when he has to deal with an *un*-attractive woman? Carry a bag to put over her head? I hate men like that!" She thumped the bed with both fists for emphasis.

"I thought you were attracted to him," Simeon said in a calm and mildly curious tone.

"I am," she said with exasperation. "I hate that part of it the most."

"I'm a little confused here. How can you be attracted to someone you can't stand?"

"I don't know," she said grimly.

"Pheromones?" Simeon asked slyly.

"Maybe. It happens." She sighed.

The mysterious pheromones strike again, he thought. *There are times I'm extremely glad I'm a shellperson. At least I can adjust my own hormone feeds.* The thought of having his biochemistry unpredictably mucked about by emotional factors was nerve-wracking.

"You mean," he said carefully, "this has happened to you before?"

A look of annoyance crossed her face. "Not just to *me*. It's happened to a great many people."

He waited expectantly and patiently.

With a resigned sigh, she went on. "He was a professor of

economics, of all people! I fell for him like a stone. And the weird thing was, I never liked him. Quite the opposite. He was attractive enough, but he was sarcastic and lazy and snide—ugh! Never to me, but it bothered me to see him doing it to other students. One day I was sitting there and I looked up at him and I said to myself, *I'm in love with him.*" She widened her eyes and held out her hands in a "go figure" gesture and let them flop back onto the bed. "Hmmp."

"So . . . you're in love . . . with Simeon-Amos?"

"No! Of course not! I said I was in love with my professor, not Simeon-Amos. They're two different cases." She started to laugh. "I'm older and wiser now, Simeon-Simple."

"As long as you're not sadder, love."

She chuckled. "No, not sadder."

"Naturally you and Simeon-Amos will have to undergo a bit of a period of adjustment," he said seriously, "but he really wants to help. And he's going to be very busy helping. That'll go a long way in curbing any ardent tendencies he may have. Try to cut him a little slack, Channa; he's the victim of an inbred culture. Besides which, we're all under threat of death."

"Mmm. Tell that to the subconscious—it interprets threats of death as a reason to get *more* interested. I do wish this crisis wasn't so immediate." She sighed again, wearily. "Maybe they're not out there. Maybe they gave up and went back to Saffron, to Bethel. All we'd have to do is file a report, while the fleet floats by us."

"I wouldn't bet on it, babe."

"I must be mellowing," she observed, "I've allowed you to call me 'love' and 'babe' and . . . I actually let you get away with 'luscious popsie,' didn't I?"

"Yeah. I'm counting coup. Maybe you *like* me?"

"I wouldn't count on it," she said grinning. "Goodnight, Simeon."

"'Night, Channa."

"Oh, God, not another meeting," Channa mumbled to herself around the light-pencil clenched in her teeth. In one hand, she held the notescreen she was studying and, in the other, a cup of coffee. Hot as hell, black as death, sweet as love: *not* the way she generally drank her caffeine, but the proper dose to jolt a body into action after inadequate sleep. For something stronger, she would have to go to Doctor Chaundra.

"Why meetings?" she continued to herself as she stumbled into the lift at the end of the corridor. "Why can't I just send memos?"

"Mornin', honeybunch," Patsy's voice said.

Channa started so violently at the presence of two other people on the lift that she almost slopped the hot coffee over her hand. Gus put a steadying grip under her elbow.

"Why meetings?" Gus repeated, "because they're civilians. They're not used to facing a military emergency. They need to be told the information again and again before it'll seem *real* to them."

The lift hissed to a stop. "Fortunately, I don't need to be told so often, so I can get right on with my work," he said. "See you later, ladies."

Channa looked across at Patsy. The older woman was leaning into the padded corner of the lift, eyes closed and a dreamy smile on her lips. "Patsy?"

One eye opened reluctantly and a sweet smile lightened her expression as she stretched languorously. "Yeah?"

"You look almost as exhausted as I am. Aren't you getting enough sleep?"

Patsy's eyes widened, and she worked her eyebrows melodramatically. "Not much," she said with some enthusiasm. "Unless you use 'sleep' in the euphemistic sense."

"Anh hanh. Gus?"

"Con mucho Gusto!" Patsy giggled. "Ah've read about this. People in crisis, they jest get together, y'know? You ask Simeon about it. He'll tell ya."

"I wouldn't presume to ask Simeon about private matters. I suspect he's morbidly fascinated by the subject. Besides, I know what you mean."

"Ohho! Ah heard about yoah pretty li'l roommate," Patsy said with a wink. "Hubba hubba." She nudged Channa with her elbow.

Channa cleared her throat, stuck the light-pencil over one ear and took a sip of her coffee. *Ghastly,* she thought. "Simeon told me that 'hubba hubba' meant 'sexy lady.' "

"Did he? Well, when he says it, it probably does. No, really, it jest means somethin' sexy, anythin' sexy. What, is up to the beholder." Patsy rose onto her toes and clicked her heels together a couple of times. "Ah think Simeon-Amos is sexy," she said teasingly.

"Right now you'd think taffy was sexy," Channa said repressively.

"Oooh, yeah, ya can puulll it . . ."

"Patsy!"

"Loosen *up,* girl! If ya get too tense, all yore hair falls out. Doncha know that?" She grinned and waved as she got off on her floor.

"Damn," Channa said, leaning against the wall. The padding held a faint trace of Patsy's body heat. "It's been entirely too long since I went to work with a smile like that."

"Great Lord, we cannot determine whether the craft we pursue left the area of the station or not," Baila said, tugging at the cupid's bow of her lower lip.

Belazir tapped a meditative thumb against his lower lip. "Why not?" he said mildly.

The technical officer swallowed. "There is too much traffic here, lord. Individual trails fade in the background clutter."

Belazir raised his brows, the only outward sign of an icy stab of concern. According to their best calculations, the way the fugitive ship had been pushing its engines, it should have blown itself to a ball of plasma and fragments long before now. Granted that, in the old days, ships had been built to last, still . . . If, by unforeseeable fortune, they reached a well-traveled zone first, the unthinkable could happen. The Clan would be in danger. *He* would be in even more danger—from the rest of the Clan.

"Computer," he said, the command-voice that slaved its attention to him. "Extrapolation: the vector of the prey, matched against last definite location and possible destinations, as updated from the chartlogs of that captured merchantman."

A spray of possibilities flicked out in the 3-D tank. "Now, eliminate all those that would require more than four days' transit from last known location."

All faded but one. "Ah, that station," he said. It was the most probable search vector in any case. "We must continue the pursuit. Comments?" he asked the other captains' faces. They were present by holo, a ghostly ring of faces on the shadowed command-couches of their respective bridges, similar to the *Bride's.*

Aragiz t'Varak, of the *Age of Darkness;* Zhengir t'Marid, of the *Rumal*—Strangler, in the old tongue—Pol t'Veng, of the *Shark,* old and scarred and the only woman among them, the only one with an independent command in the Clan fleet. Enemies and rivals; his ability to make them move in concert was another test the Clanfathers imposed. *That which does not kill us, makes us stronger,* he reminded himself.

"Captains and kin," Belazir said. "You have the data. We must decide whether to continue the pursuit, or break off. My recommendation is that we continue."

Aragiz's face pushed forward, tensing like an eagle held by jesses to a hostile wrist. "If you had not stopped to loot, we would be closer on the prey's trail," he said sharply.

Pol cut through his words with a snort. "Irrelevant. We must continue the mission."

Belazir nodded at her.

"I do not like it," Pol said in her guttural rumble. She was known to be a canny and prudent commander. "Something is just slightly out of kilter." She made a rocking gesture with the claw-scarred hand.

Belazir considered her remark. What had that contractor—one of the ones the Clan fenced loot to occasionally—said? "There are bold pirates, and old pirates, but there are no old, bold pirates."

"Still," she went on, "the balance of risk is clear. We must know if the prey reached this station. To do that, we must take it in our fist."

"And if it did?" Aragiz said.

"We kill, send a message torpedo to the fleet, and we run," Pol said. "With as little as one week's lead, we can lose the Navy among the stars and dust. Nothing is lost save time."

"And the effort we put into subduing Bethel!" Aragiz snapped. "Stopping for that merchantman—"

"Was irrelevant and consumed no significant expense of time!" Belazir said. "In any case, there is a substantial chance nothing was left alive on the prey-ship by the time it reached this station. If it did reach them. In which case, there is the station itself."

"Ah," Zhengir said. He was a close relative, and a man of few words. "A target of great opportunity."

"Risky," Pol said, rubbing her chin.

"We come in fast at the limits of their sensor capacity and launch hyper-velocity anti-rad missiles to knock out their communications," Belazir said. "We pulse our engines to jam subspace for the time required. It will look natural to those who come to investigate later. A black hole evaporating, or some such."

"Hmmm."

Pol rasped a hand over the horrible keloid scars that furrowed one half of her face. Since cosmetic repair would be easy enough, Belazir suspected she kept them as an affectation. But with those scars, even the most arrogant seldom remembered that Pol was a woman. Those grooves had been made by the claws of an animal which Pol had subsequently strangled with her bare hands. She wore its tanned hide around her shoulders.

"Hmmm," she said again. "That would be minimum-risk strategy. However, we cannot find out if the prey reached the station if we obliterate the station. We must be sure that no warning of us has gone out. On the other hand, a swift raid, catching them unawares, would discover the truth and we can act accordingly."

"Taking with us whatever the station holds," Belazir said, grinning avariciously. Greed was quickly kindled, since everyone knew what the merchant ship had yielded: the merest trifle in comparison to what a full station would render up. "Depending on what we find, we might even have time to call for the Clan's transports to come and haul the loot. Even what we could load on our frigates makes a raid more than worth our while."

Agreement rolled around the circle with the exception of Aragiz. Belazir quirked a brow at him. After criticizing his commander for sloth, he could not be behindhand now.

"Attack, then," Belazir concluded. The others nodded. "Tactical instructions follow. Confirm on receipt."

Several of Simeon-Amos's instructors were female.

Woof, Simeon thought. Thin, plain and severely ascetic in middle-age, Flimma Torkin blossomed visibly as Simeon-Amos bowed over her hand.

Her smile died a few minutes later. He appeared to be hovering attentively, but . . .

"Mr. Sierra Nueva—"

"Simeon-Amos," he said.

"Will you please *listen* to what I'm saying? As station head, you should have *some* knowledge of how our communications system functions."

"I am sorry," he said meekly.

This should be interesting, Simeon mused. The rest of the session went much more smoothly, although several times Amos absently called the communications chief *nama.*

Nonstandard. Simeon thought the computer into action; a few nanos later it came up with a probable derivation, from the languages other than Standard spoken among the first settlers of Bethel, plus observation of the refugees.

nama: aunt, auntie. Probable meanings: female authority figure from childhood, nurse, teacher [primary].

"That didn't go too badly," Amos commented as Flimma left.

"You learn quickly," Simeon said: sufficiently true as well as polite encouragement.

Meanwhile, Simeon had been busily switching assignments. The assistant power chief was really the logical person to brief Amos. The fact that Holene Jagarth was stacked and less than thirty was irrelevant; at least to Simeon and anyone else dealing with her as an expert on plasma containment.

Twenty minutes later she stood, ominously silent for a moment, then turned to the pillar.

"*Talk* to him, Simeon. Or send him around to my place for recreational duty, but in the meantime I have *work* to do!" Holene said in a terse voice, turned on her heel and stalked for the corridor.

Amos blinked in astonishment. "What was the matter with her?" he asked plaintively.

"Ahem," Simeon said, and watched Amos turn back toward the training display they'd been using. "I wonder if you could tell me, what role do women play in Bethel society?"

"Role?" The question seemed almost meaningless to him. "They are mothers, of course; daughters, sisters, wives. They keep the home, raise the children, follow gentle skills such as medicine and painting, the writing of novels and poetry." He looked puzzled. "What do you mean?"

"I was wondering if, perhaps, women played a more subservient role on Bethel."

"Subservient? No, of course not! Bethel has, as yet, a very small population. Therefore, to us, the bearing and raising of children is the highest calling a woman may attain. We revere our mothers, and we feel that women and children are to be protected and nurtured."

He frowned, mildly indignant. "There are exceptional cases, such as Channa. And I have never been one of those who think that women should keep to the inner rooms and stay silent in the presence of men. That is old-fashioned and ridiculous. Why, some of my primary associates in the New Revelation were women! I feel as though you are telling me that respect is disrespectful."

"Not at all," Simeon said soothingly, "but I think you may be confusing respect with condescension." Amos' face took on the set look it had worn through the last half of his dinner with Channa. "A little less patting on the hand, Simeon-Amos. You give them the impression that you claim authority because of your gender."

"No, no," Amos exclaimed, throwing up his hands in rejection. "If I have an aura of authority, it is because of my position on Bethel. Birth aside, I am a junior member of the ruling council. I rule the family estates, of course. I have been an administrator for several years now." He smiled in a confiding manner. "Although, I have found that women react differently to my orders. I do not deny that I find it simpler to work with men." He gave a negligent shrug. "There is no problem of seduction between men."

Well, he's consistent, at least, Simeon thought. *Maybe he needs to cling to whatever ego-confirmation he's got, since he's so displaced.*

"Do you realize," the brain said coldly, "that you've just patronized *me?* Based on your belief that you're such a treat for anyone to deal with? I'm a part of this culture. You're not. I know these people, you don't. I run this station and have been running it since before you existed, and will be running it centuries after you're dead. And I'll be running this station throughout this emergency while you're only pretending to. So listen up! You're treating your women instructors as if they're only adequate until someone *real,* meaning male, arrives to take over. Well, the experts here just happen to be female! We're short of time, so I'm going to pay you the compliment of expecting you to be able to adjust to that alien concept. We need you to be one of us. We need you to forget about Bethel for the time being.

"I know how much we're asking of you, Simeon-Amos," he concluded, his voice less stern and more understanding, "but you're asking us to trust you with our lives."

Amos gasped, his eyes wide with a mixture of embarrassment, puzzlement and astonishment.

Oh, fugle, Simeon thought. *Channa was right. I do have the sensitivity of a demolition charge.* Seventy-seven of Amos' followers had died fleeing Bethel. And, being the conscientious sort of leader Simeon had seen him be, he probably had them marching through his dreams at night, asking, "Why?"

"Sorry," Simeon said, "that was badly phrased. Look, I need to know if you can do this. I need to know *now.* You'll be dealing with Channa, under her authority, daily. I'm not going to waste time. If we have to replace you with someone who doesn't have the same hangups you have, then six hours is all we can afford to waste on a false start. Now, can you or can't you?"

Amos put a hand to his brow. *They depended on me, and they died,* ran through his mind like a prayer response. Followed by: *No. I saved some, who would otherwise have died. And Bethel may yet live, what is left of it.*

"I have never yet failed to accomplish a thing that I have set out to do," he said grimly. He touched head and heart with two fingers as he bowed to Simeon's column. "Would you be so good as to convey my apologies to the lady who has just left?"

"No, but I'll be happy to show you how to call her so that you can tell her yourself." Simeon watched Amos' Adam's apple bob as he swallowed hard.

"Of course," Amos said with a strained smile. "That would probably be best."

CHAPTER THIRTEEN

THIS IS WORSE than the captains' meeting, Simeon thought.

It was absolutely amazing that so little rumor had leaked out. In that alone was an indication that they *might* be able to bring the whole thing off. SSS-900-C personnel had an uncanny instinct for keeping their mouths shut when silence was more than golden.

Not so at this meeting, where everyone was sounding off—barring Channa and Amos—and no one was listening to a word being said.

The meeting was being held in the largest auditorium on the station. *Which, thank Ghu,* Simeon thought with relief, *is not nearly large enough to hold all of the station's population.* The sensible had stayed in their quarters watching the whole spectacle on holo. The skeleton crew now running the station would have their own briefing later. *Just as well I didn't bother to activate sound from the private quarters' screens,* he thought wearily. He was getting a good enough cross section of opinion right here. *For the first time in my life, I think I'd like to be able to sleep through something. I can always turn the audio off . . . No, that's useless.*

He contacted Channa on the implants in her mastoid. "This was a mistake. We should have briefed their counsel-reps, who would have briefed their aides, and so on. This could build panic to critical mass." For some reason the shouting in the auditorium rose to a higher pitch. "Or simply get so loud the noise shakes the station to pieces and saves the damn pirates the trouble."

"Hindsight," she said softly, "is always so clear. Actually, they look more angry than frightened to me. I've gotten more used to the smell of fear than I like, but the ambience here has a different reek. Of course, I can't *hear* what they're saying, they're all yelling so loud."

Simeon picked out phrases from the uproar with directional sensors:

" . . . *those goddamned assholes in that colony ship . . .*"

" . . . yeah, how many ways are they going to try to get us killed . . ."

" . . . where's the damned Navy? That's what I want to know. They cripple us with taxes and . . ."

" . . . this is crazy. They don't even know this is what's gonna happen? Meanwhile, I'm sittin' here losin' money. . . . what do they expect us to do?"

"WHAT DO WE EXPECT YOU TO DO?" Simeon asked in a tone that overrode the babble. He added in a stew of subsonics intended to stun and intimidate. The noise dropped off abruptly, pleasing him.

"For starters, shut up and listen!" he suggested in a reasonable tone. "We expect you to take the emergency seriously, to listen to instructions and to carry them out." He paused for a moment to let that sink in. "This meeting will give you what you need to know on how to handle yourselves during the anticipated emergency. Remember, what you don't know, you can't reveal. From this point on, I remind you that rumor helps the enemy, not you or me, and not this station.

"If you hear something you think is a rumor, report it to your section leader, who's the same person who leads your ordinary emergency evacuation team. If it's true and it concerns your safety, he'll know about it. If he hasn't heard it, he can check with me and I'll confirm or deny it. I *will* tell you the truth. Do *not* spread rumors. Remember that. We fully expect shortly to be occupied by an enemy force which has a very bad reputation for space piracy."

Echel Mckie, station newscaster, waved both arms for attention. Simeon acknowledged him.

"Pirates?" he asked. "Look, is this another one of your damned *games,* Simeon?"

"Absolutely not. This is as real as death. They'll be here in less than three days. We've notified Central and the Navy, who assure us that a rescue mission is already under way. But it won't be here before the pirates are likely to arrive. Therefore this station and its personnel must initiate such delaying tactics as possible. *To stay alive!*" That silenced the last bit of muttering.

"Why weren't we told this earlier? Every ship has left—we're *stuck* here!" Mckie's face was a study in outrage.

Channa moved forward to the front of the dais. "You weren't told because we used the available space to evacuate children and the sick," she said crisply. "Any objections to that, Mr. Mckie?"

"As I said," Simeon went on, "we are not only expecting to be occupied, we are hoping we *will* be." He paused again to see that they had absorbed that distinction. He was proud of his people! They got it in one! Shocked pale faces now accepted what he did not, after all, have to spell out.

"Listen up now. These are your station manager's orders. Don't offer direct resistance. Cooperate whenever necessary but don't volunteer anything. We expect that most of the enemy won't speak Standard, so misunderstand when you can. Make your answers as brief as possible, when you can't be silent. If you don't know, say so, but do not tell them who does know. Stay in your quarters as much as possible. Keep your emergency suits ready to use. Listen to information passed to you by your group leaders rather than anything you may hear over the vid. Remember, we're on your side. They won't be.

"Finally," he said, "this is Simeon-Amos." Amos stood up and bowed politely. "This is the only Simeon on the station. He is co-manager with Channa Hap, the term Simeon means co-manager. We have a longstanding tradition of having the male station managers carrying that name. It's in honor of one of the first station managers. There is no brain or brawn on this station, there never has been. Shell-persons are only used on ships."

He paused to gauge their reaction, studying their grim faces. "If they don't know about me, I'll be able to continue running the station unimpaired—literally behind the scenes. If they disconnect me from the station—and they will, if they find out about me—we're *all* in trouble. So, as of now and for the duration, I don't exist. This is Simeon-Amos, your station co-manager."

Amos smiled and nodded. The audience had that stillness of about-to-boil-over. Faces began to reflect expressions now; mild alarm, disbelief, skepticism.

"This . . . this *backworld mudfoot* is supposed to manage *us* in an emergency?" somebody said, with all the hauteur of the space-born.

Amos' head went back, and he stared down his classical Grecian nose with ten generations of aristocrats behind his eyes.

"To *pretend* to run things," Simeon said. "Furthermore, he *volunteered* to front for me! Not a role you'd get many to take under the circumstances," he added, and got a few snorts of agreement. "So, before anyone frets over Simeon-Amos' leadership qualifications, I'd like to replay the man in action. The tape's authentic. I've checked it." Nobody could do that better than a brain.

What Simeon screened for them then were shots that he had accessed from Guiyon's files. It began when a wall flashed with intolerable brightness, then diminished to show troops in black combat armor trotting down a burning street of brick-and-timber buildings. The sensor was pitched low, looking up from a half-basement window or a hole in the ground. Across the way, a human figure hung out of a window, long black braids trailing in a pool of blood on the sidewalk. A child's body lay there too: its crushed skull suggesting it had been thrown against the wall.

The screen was abruptly blank. Then lit up again with a dimmer scene.

Amos' recorded voice cut through the blurr-roar of flames. "*Now*," he said.

The picture shook as the ground heaved, and the burning walls cascaded across the street, drowning the black figures in a tide of brick and flaming timbers and glass. Other figures darted forward, Bethelites to judge by their rough, improvised uniforms. When the first powersuits began to claw their way out of the rubble, the defenders were ready. Amos was unmistakably leading them, an industrial jetcutter in his hands. He plunged it down on the massive sloped helmet that jerked itself free of the ruins, and helm and head exploded in steam.

The screen jerked, a different scene coming into abrupt focus: a manor-house among formal gardens, only a few scorch-marks on its walls. Invader infantry stood at their ease; the picture had the slightly glassy look of a flatpic extrapolated by a long-distance camera. Armored fighting vehicles rested in leagues on the lawns, their cannon pointing outward in a herringbone pattern, lighter weapons on their upper decks tracking restlessly across the sky. An aircraft slowed overhead. Bulky armored shapes disembarked, one in a suit marked with complex blazons in a script of angles and sharp curves.

The viewpoint zoomed in, as a group of young women in long

robes were pushed out of the front door of the manor, many carrying bundles. They knelt under the alien guns; one opened the chest she carried, filled with miniature crystal vials. She smiled, gesturing to the bottles, opening one and smelling, extending it to the warrior in the decorated suit. From her looks she was about sixteen Standard years and very beautiful, with the classic features similar to Amos'. The pirate raised both gauntlets to his helmet, lifted it free and tucked it under one arm, bending to sniff. The exposed face was scored with age, roughened skin pockmarked by radiation damage, blossoming growths, thinning blond hair startling against dark complexion. It smiled . . .

Leered, Simeon thought, reviewing the scene. *I've heard the word, but never really seen the corresponding expression till now.*

The view of the pirate's face was brief. Even as he bent, a red dot appeared between his brows. Less than a second later, his head exploded into mist.

The body stayed erect in the armored suit, blood pumping in a high arc from the stump of the neck. The girl with the perfume box stood, smiling truly this time as the blood bathed her. Until one of the other warriors stepped forward and, gripping her head in a powered gauntlet, squeezed. Her head burst in a spray of pink bone and gray matter. The other girls joined hands and were singing when the plasma gun scythed them into ash and steam.

Someone in the hall was retching; several sobbed.

"For the death of that Kolnar, I claim only the marksmanship," Amos said, his archaic accent adding gravity to his clear tone. "The bravery was my sister's. Sahrah led the maiden volunteers. I did not know what she had planned. I was trying to reach the manor before the enemy could. We think . . . we think that dead dog was fourth or fifth in rank among the pirates."

All heads turned to him; his was slightly bowed. "Such was Bethel, when the Kolnari came to us," he said. "They have the souls of—" he spoke a nonstandard word.

"Rats," Simeon said.

"—rats that walk like men. They kill for killing's sake, they rape and torture and steal, and what they cannot steal, they foul out of depravity."

Another holo came up. "Keriss," Amos said. There was total silence now. A city by a bay, astride a river, lower-built than the worlds influenced by Central's architectural styles, bright-colored buildings amid broad gardens. A scattering of taller buildings at its center, and one that led the eye up and up in a leap of towers and domes.

"The Temple," Amos said. "This was a remote pickup, a news-service shot, just before the end."

White light flashed. The city dissolved as the bulging doughnut shape of the Shockwave billowed out. The slow scene gave it a terrible grace; trees exploding into flame under the heat-flash and scattering as less than splinters an instant later, the water of the bay beginning to flow and swell into a wave taller than the hills.

"So died Keriss," Amos whispered.

"I'm not calling wolf this time," Simeon said, matching that same tone. "If anyone doubts, speak now."

He let the ensuing silence echo. "Does anyone think they're better equipped to play me than Simeon-Amos is?" No one gainsaid him. "This emergency is all too real. Until help arrives, we're going to have to rely on each other. I believe we can do that," he said confidently. "If you weren't pretty brave and independent sorts of individuals, you wouldn't be on a station anyway. You'd be on a planet somewhere trying to figure out how to get the bugs off your vegetables."

This got more of a chuckle than it deserved, he thought, but they needed the release from tension.

Channa rose, ubiquitous notescreen in hand.

"There will be a meeting for council members at two," she announced, "and there will be a meeting of evacuation group leaders at four. Subsequent to those meetings, evacuation groups themselves will meet at times appointed by the group leaders. We aren't going to take questions because we're now on a need-to-know basis. We thank you for your cooperation. Ladies and gentlemen, this meeting is adjourned."

"Right, listen up, you crap-headed rock hounds," Gus bellowed.

The noise level in the docking chamber fell fairly quickly. *Stands to reason,* he thought. These were working spacers, not data-pushers and entertainers. About fifty of them glared up at him as if he'd thought up this little crisis himself The shapes of the tugs and miners in the interior dock bulked at their backs, huge and shadowy with all but one of the overheads turned off. That cast a puddle of light over the assembled pilots and crew. He had staged the meeting this way at Simeon's suggestion, to make them feel like a group.

"You know what's coming down," he said, making his voice intense without making it loud. "All our shipping with interstellar capacity has been moved out."

"Not all," one of the miners said, running a hand over her luridly tattooed head.

"Can it, Shabla. You can do maybe ten lights, scouting for minerals. That won't get you to the next system."

She shrugged, grinning at those ranged about her.

"What we've got left is the tugs," said Gus, "and some mining scouts. It isn't much, against four frigate-class warships."

"It's fardling nothing," another said. "Unless you want us to ram 'em?" The man didn't think much of that idea even as he voiced it.

Ramming was not completely out of the question; if you cut something heading toward you at high speeds into smaller pieces, you were just multiplying your troubles. You had to blast it into gas, or deflect it, before you were safe. They all understood the principle, and the limitations.

"Ramming's not on," Gus said, shaking his head even as he gave them a sly grin. "Not when we lose to any beam-weapon they care to turn on us. But," and he waited until a schematic of a standard tug came up on the screen behind him, "what *has* a tug got? A *big* normal-space engine and a great big power plant, and a fardlin' humongous grapnel field. Mining scout's about the same, only with a sampling laser. So there isn't much sense in us getting into slugging matches with warships." He caught the universal sigh of relief that wafted about the bay. "But—" and he held up one gnarled finger "—there *are* things we can do."

Then he outlined the changes needed on the screen behind him. Gratified and slightly vulpine grins replaced frowns even when he explained the strategy to be effected by such alterations.

"Hey, wait," Shabla said. "I got a husband—two, actually—on this tin can. You want me to leave 'em here while the place is taken over?"

"Exactly," Gus said, giving her stare for stare. "What the crap could you do for 'em here? Get your head kicked in? Start a firefight in a corridor and blow the pressure hull? Out there, we've got a *chance* to do something worthwhile for all our skins. We've all got someone here, or nearly all of us. This is what we can do for 'em. Who's with me?"

The cheer was more nearly a howl.

✧   ✧   ✧

He's really much more attractive when he isn't trying to be, Channa thought dismally. *And when he's really working.* Which he *was*, now.

"And it's been so *long*," she murmured to herself.

Amos turned to look at her, his brow furrowed in concern. "Something troubles you, Channa?" He grinned. "Besides, that is, our possibly imminent demise?"

She gave him a jaundiced smile. *He would mention that,* she thought, *just when I was getting involved enough not to think about it. Well, since we might all die, why not take the plunge?*

"This is beginning to get to me. I feel so . . . so alone."

His eyes kindled, and a lovely feathery warmth tickled her lower belly. Her smile spread to a grin, and he rose from his place and came to sit beside her, their thighs lightly touching. He took her hand in both of his.

Ooooo, she thought. *If this one were on the holos, there wouldn't be a dry seat in the house.*

"You're not alone! *I'm* here," he said, his voice rich with sympathy.

An hour later, things had progressed to the point where they had drifted into Channa's quarters arm in arm. *And damn Simeon's opinion,* Channa thought. *I'm going to enjoy myself.*

They were both three-quarters undressed and a lot warmer when Simeon imitated the sound of a knock on the door and shouted from the lounge.

"Simeon-Amos, Rachel's here." The voice was flatly neutral, but Channa savagely thought she could detect a suppressed giggle.

"What!" Amos shrieked softly as they both sat bolt upright.

"Here?" Channa demanded. "What do you mean, here?"

"She's in the corridor outside," Simeon said cheerfully. "Should I let her in?"

"Just a moment," Amos said desperately, leaping from the bed and frantically grabbing up clothes.

"That's mine," Channa said, rescuing her shirt from the pile.

Amos bolted from the room, opened the door to his quarters, flung his clothes in and ran to the door. Realizing he was in his underpants, he ran back to his room, grabbed his robe, and struggled to pull it over his head as he staggered back to the lounge. The arms seemed to knot and tangle so deliberately, he wondered if the robe had turned animate and was resisting. Amos made desperate, despairing little sounds.

Channa rolled her eyes, sighed, and headed for the bathroom. "Cold water, pulsed, shower," she told the fixtures. *As if I need one with Rachel at the door,* she thought.

Amos took a deep breath, finally pulling the robe down over his body.

"Why am I agitated?" he asked himself. "I do not have to account for my actions. There is no one in authority over me." On the other hand, Rachel *could* make an unfortunate scene. At least there would be no outraged father, brother, uncle, or cousin likely to break in with a hunting rifle and blow off the offending equipment.

He opened the door. He hopped backward just in time to avoid a blow from Rachel's fist, aimed at the lounge doors. "Rachel!" he snapped.

She stood glaring at him. She was breathing fast, her nostrils flaring, a sheen of sweat across the pale olive of her skin.

"What are you doing here?" she demanded.

He looked at her in astonishment.

"You know perfectly well what I am doing here," he said. He had himself sufficiently under control now to speak with his usual gentle authority, and he could see her purpose falter. "I am living in the manager's quarters because I am to be a co-manager of the station. I'm studying very hard and constantly to be worthy of this honor. I have told you this. I told everyone." He let his eyes widen slightly in unaffected innocence.

She narrowed her eyes. "It is true, Amos, that you told everyone. But, you did not tell *me!*"

"All right," he said soothingly, "all right, come in." He placed his hands delicately on her shoulders and steered her to the couch. "Sit!"

She looked first at him, then at the couch as though she suspected some trap before she cautiously folded herself down to the cushioned surface. Looking up at him, she patted the place beside her.

"You sit down, too," she insisted.

"You will have some refreshment?"

"No. I will have an explanation."

He drew over a straight-backed chair, placed it in front of her and sat down. Her eyes widened and she sat up straighter, looking, if possible, even more affronted than she had been.

"I am sorry," he said, "if I have offended you, but I have been very busy." Unspoken was the inference that she should be also, helping to brief the Bethelites and settle them into their temporary roles. "I told Joseph about our plans, and I assumed that he would explain everything to you."

"Oh!" she said sarcastically, "You told Joseph. Well, then of course there was no need to enlighten me! He could tell me whatever he pleased of your plans and that would have been sufficient. Then I could go to sleep this night, knowing that you had moved in with that blackhearted slut-bitch, with an untroubled heart."

"*Rachel bint Damscus!*" he said sharply. "You forget yourself!"

She raised both fists above her head and shouted, "It is not I who disport with the daughters of the heathen, an act forbidden by every scripture! Nor is it Joseph's place to tell me of what we do. It is yours, yours alone! Are we not to be betrothed?"

He stared at her in shock. "No," he said in blank astonishment. "Whatever gave you that idea?"

She blinked. "No?"

"No," he repeated, shaking his head in the negative.

All of the color drained from her face and he could see the white of her eyes all around the iris. She breathed in and out through her nose with a sound like tearing silk. She trembled. She tried to speak and only a garbled sound came out, then she said in a grating voice, "She has seduced you."

"No," he said and shook his head again, waving both his hands in the same negative gesture, but his eyes slid away from hers.

"Always," she said harshly, "from the time we first met, I knew that you were mine. *Mine!*"

"No," he said. "You are meant for Joseph, who has always loved you. He will make you happy, and he wants you." He forced his voice to gentleness. *She has become unbalanced,* he thought desperately. Of all the times for such a thing to happen! He had thought her only a little more given to hysteria than most of her sex, but something had changed her; perhaps the trauma of the attack, perhaps the massive drug dosages they had been forced to use on the trip.

Her eyes widened still more, until the whites showed all around the iris. He had heard of such things, but never seen them, except once when an ancient hermit had gone into a trance and prophesied.

I should have paid more attention to my first-aid training, he thought ruefully. Perhaps then he would know how to deal with her instability. Whatever her faults, she had sacrificed much to follow him.

She had been invaluable in the chaotic scramble of the last days on Bethel. *My dear friend, I have failed you.*

"*He* wants me," she said in the same low growl. "And you do not?" Her mouth twisted, and she bit her lip as she turned her head from side to side and nodded several times. Abruptly she rose and was out the door before he could rise from his chair.

He grabbed his hair in both of his hands and pulled. "Arrughh! Simeon," he asked, "what have I done?"

"Pissed off Rachel, I'd say."

Amos sighed, then groaned. "No," he said despairingly, "I have done worse than that I allowed myself to be talked out of doing what I knew was right. I knew in my heart that she should be evacuated, but Joseph asked me to let her stay. Perhaps I gave you the wrong answer today, my friend. Perhaps I cannot play this role if I am so easily convinced to go against my better judgement."

"You thought Joseph could keep her in line?"

"Yes. I hoped that, because he would be nearby and considerate of her, she would turn more to him and less toward me."

"Not a bad reasoning," Simeon replied truthfully. "Sending her away might break whatever hold she has on reality."

Amos looked unreassured and more miserable than ever. He might be a good-looking man, but he sure had cornered the supply of gloomy looks.

"Today, you have said quite correctly that you are older than I, and also that in many ways you are wiser. Today I should have been the wiser." He shook his head sorrowfully and shuffled into his room like an old man.

Well, Simeon thought, *what an interesting evening! Looks like the forecast for true love is—not smooth.* Such marvelous material for teasing Channa. So tempting to see how she'd react. No! He had to keep his mind on more important things. Like that Rachel. The girl had shot out of that interview with Amos as if she'd lost her rag. *Better keep an eye on her,* he told himself. *And so should Doctor Chaundra, if he's got the time.* Most acute mental illness was chemical, or could be adjusted with the judicious use of neutralizing chemicals.

With a weary woof, Doctor Chaundra sat at his desk and, setting his coffee cup in the most spill-proof area available in the surface clutter, he keyed up his mail. It had been two days since he'd had an opportunity to look at it. Twenty-five attempted suicides, four of them among the refugee Bethelites who chose gruesomely old-fashioned methods. One had actually *hanged* herself! Good in one respect: easier to revive, although there might be some memory loss from oxygen deprivation, and he'd have to use a nerve-shunt. The *sight* of that bloated, blue-tinged face with the protruding tongue lingered unpleasantly.

He slipped himself a calmer; just one, although the gods alone knew what it would do with all the caffeine he'd been absorbing. He had to get on with this accursed viral project even if he was a doctor, not a gene-sculptor! It disturbed him to deliberately make a virus more harmful: too much like making medicine into a weapon. Chaundra had grown up on a planet where personal violence was fairly common, and done his internship in a trauma ward. His own family came from a pacifist tradition, and the internship had confirmed him in it.

At least Seld is out of this, he thought with relief.

The first message was yet another requisition for calmers. He signed it out; the organosynth machines were going to be running overtime. Would pirates take notice of supernatural calm? The doctor smiled ruefully at that and told the machine to show him the next message. It was flagged *personal,* which was odd. He began to read.

His heart stumbled; he could feel the pain in his chest quite distinctly, but it seemed distant and unimportant. Vision grayed down to a tunnel; it was long minutes before he could speak.

At last he managed to croak "Simeon? Simeon!"

"What is it, Chaundra?"

I don't like the way he looks. The sound of the doctor's voice had been sufficiently worrisome for Simeon to activate visuals. The doctor was visibly tired but, considering the work load he was pushing, fatigue would be normal. Nor unusual for Chaundra who tended to push himself. If Simeon had been capable of experiencing fatigue, he would be knackered right now. The slightly built dark man was gray-faced with sweat beading his forehead. Simeon ran a diagnostic program; not good. Extreme stress, to the point of endangering the man's health. Chaundra was not young anymore, and had endured some very hostile environments in his career. Not to mention the current problem.

"This message . . ." and Chaundra managed to point to his screen.

Dear Dad—Simeon read.

"Why on earth didn't this trip my watchman programs—I'll have Joat's *hide* for this, by God!"

—*I couldn't go, I'm sorry. I hope you can understand and forgive me, but if anything were to happen to you and I wasn't there, I'd never forgive myself. I have to be here, because Mom can't be. I love you. Seld.*

"Oh!" Simeon paused in full comprehension of Chaundra's state of mind. "But didn't you put him on. . . ."

"No," Chaundra said, in a voice drained of affect. "He was in line, almost to the lock. Then I received a bleep message—the most urgent of codes. Seld said I must answer. He understood that. We embraced, said good-bye and I left him there."

Chaundra flopped one hand over weakly, unable for more effort than that. "He was practically *on* the ship. How the *hell* did this happen?"

"I'm sorry. I've too good an idea!" Simeon told him. "I'll try to find out where that wicked young rascal is right now." He didn't mean Seld, but did not qualify his term. After a moment's pause he came up blank. "I'm not finding him, so he's well hidden wherever he is. That should be some consolation, Chaundra," he said in a firmly reassuring tone. "If I can't find him, neither can our expected visitors. I'll keep looking. Count on me for that!

Looking with every eye I own, Simeon said grimly. How *could* the well-mannered, well-brought up Seld have fallen for one of Joat's schemes? And what part would the kid play in it? *And I'm to blame for this situation and Chaundra's heartache.* Joat had been so eager to learn, and he'd seen no reason to restrict her terminal's access to the schematics. She had been bad enough before this emergency sent her to cover; now, he didn't know what she was capable of doing.

I've an idiot-savant running feral in my station, he thought bitterly. *Ten years' precocity in advanced engineering techniques and the morals of a five-year-old.* The selfishness of small children can be charming, when they don't have the power to do much harm. In a near-adult, and a brilliant near-adult at that, the possibilities went out of bounds.

"Well, Seld is here—somewhere!" Chaundra said, recovering himself enough to shout and to be livid with rage. "The clock says this message was entered ten hours after his ship left!"

"I know, I see it. Don't worry, Chaundra. We'll find him."

"I know we'll find him. What worries me is that he should hide! That he is no longer as safe as I thought he would be by now. Do you understand? My son could die. My heart is pounding with the anxiety."

Simeon ran another quick scan of the station, this time including apartments left empty by the evacuation.

"Still searching. There are so many places he could hide and even I couldn't find him," he said by way of reassuring Chaundra. "He's a big strong kid who can handle himself." *As well as any of us,* he thought. The odds for anyone on the station were not good, but there was no point in reminding Chaundra of that now.

"No," the doctor said between clenched teeth, "he isn't a 'big strong kid,' and he *can't* handle himself. He's never going to be strong. The plague that took his mother left him with nerve damage."

"Nerve damage?" Simeon said incredulously. Regeneration of nerve tissue was an old technology, and well understood. Without it, shellpeople would be impossible, for the same technique knitted their nervous systems into the machinery that supported them and that they commanded.

Chaundra shook his head. "I have done what I could to bypass the damage, but if he puts too much strain where the repair exists . . ." His voice trailed off, and when he raised his face to Simeon's visual node, he had turned into an old man.

"It was a little clinic, you understand. Mary, she was the meditech, I the doctor. A new continent on a new colony world. Much to do, we were on research grants. Then people began to die. There was nothing I could do . . . They imposed quarantine—quarantine, in this day and age! When I found what had happened, already it was too late for Mary. The virus . . . was a hybrid. A native virus-analogue combined with a mutant Terran encephalitis strain. The native virus wrapped around the Terran, you understand. So the immune system could not recognize it and had no defense. The Terran element enabled it to parasitize our DNA.

"Seld was damaged, on the point of death. It took three years of therapy for him to be able to walk and talk and move as well as he does."

Chaundra turned, picking things up from his desk and putting them down.

"But he will never be strong. If they seize him, he'll be as helpless as someone half his age. There could be convulsions: stress accelerates the damage. It is cumulative. Why do you think I took this position? He must be near a first-rate facility at all times. He must not suffer extreme stress or the effects could snowball. As it is, he will probably not live much past adulthood."

Chaundra slumped in his chair, anger, even anxiety draining out of him as he buried his head in his hands.

"Then we'll make sure they don't hurt him," Simeon said grimly. "First, let's find him. He's probably with Joat."

"Seld's mentioned her." Chaundra's voice was muffled. "He has many friends, but she sounded . . . different."

"She is. Oh, she's different, all right. And she wouldn't leave, either. So in a way, you and I are in the same boat."

Chaundra rubbed his mouth and chin. Whiskers rasped; unusual, since he was normally a fastidious man. "Yes," he said and laughed sardonically, "and the boat is about to leak."

"Not necessarily," Simeon said firmly enough to make himself believe it. "Seld has something else going for him."

"He has?"

"Yes. Seld has Joat, and she's got such a strong survival instinct that even if the rest of the station blew, she'd find a way to stay alive . . . and keep Seld alive, too. He's actually far safer with her than anywhere else he could be. So I wouldn't worry about his infirmities, or stress. Though I hate like hell to admit it, I can't think of anyone better qualified to mind him than Joat!"

"Seld," Simeon called. "Seld Chaundra, come out where I can see you."

Joat popped into view rubbing her eyes, "What are you yellin' about, Simeon?" she asked, yawning.

"Send him out, Joat. This is the only place he can possibly be."

Joat crossed her arms and looked sleepily defiant.

"Your father is worried, Seld," Simon went on. "He sent you away so that you'd be safe. So you know he's not really going to kill you for staying, even though you deserve it."

Seld appeared beside Joat, who shoved him in the shoulder. "Toldja to stay outta sight!"

He hung his head and said, "I know. But I can't let you take my rap. Mom wouldn't like that in me. At least that's what my dad says she'd say." He shrugged and gave her a feeble grin.

Joat rolled her eyes. "Do what'choo want," she said in a scathing tone, and disappeared.

"Actually," Simeon told them both, "I don't see any need to rough it just yet. Why not sleep comfortably while you can, eat what everyone else is enjoying, because we're certainly not going to leave it to the pirates to gobble up. I'd *prefer* that you hide out when the pirates arrive. Meanwhile, Seld, give your dad the benefit of your company: he needs it. Save your rations, Joat. Eat with us. Food's better. For now."

He picked up her disgusted sigh, and then she walked into view, arms still folded, expression still defiant.

Simeon warmed to her all over again. *I don't think I was ever that young,* he thought, *but, y'know, she makes me wish I could swagger.* "Okay guys, let's go."

CHAPTER FOURTEEN

"VERY LARGE MASS," Baila said, whispering. "Several score megatons, at least."

"You need not lower your voice," Belazir said, amused and more so when several of the bridge crew jumped. "We are proceeding stealthed, but sound waves do not propagate in vacuum."

He turned to the schematic and long-range visual views. *Impressive indeed,* he thought. Far and away the largest free-floating construct he had ever seen. Twin globes, each at least a thousand meters in extent, linked by a broad tube. More tubes at the north and south axis, evidently for docking large ships, although none were there at the moment. Around the station was an incredible clutter of material: loose ore, giant flexible balloons of various substances, radiating networks, fabricators.

Large but soft, he decided. Like a huge lump of well-cooked meat, steaming in its own juices and touched with garlic, waiting to be carved into bite-sized pieces. It was a target so rich that he had trouble convincing himself of its reality. Mentally he accepted it, while his emotions could only kick in every minute or so, as jolts of near-orgasmic pleasure. He stretched like a cat, acutely conscious of the anticipatory tension beneath the quiet ordered activity of the bridge. Everyone in the flotilla would come out of this a hero. He couldn't believe this plum could be snatched away—not from the Kolnari and especially not when he commanded the Kolnari flotilla! And he, Belazir t'Marid Kolaren, would be more than a hero. He would be placed firmly in the logical line of succession to Chalku t'Marid.

"A pity it is so big," he mused. "A shame to have to waste any of the possible plunder." He sighed for, of course, they would have to destroy what they could not take.

The flotilla were warships by specialty, not cargo carriers. Even if they had time enough to bring in the heavy haulers from the Clan fleet, only the merest tithe of the goods to be found in this size station could be transported. On the other hand, the ecstasy of sheer destruction had its own euphoria—the knowledge that so much data and effort could be casually blown to dust.

"A message torpedo to the fleet?" Serig asked.

"You echo my thoughts, Serig," Belazir said. "Ready for instant transmission once we close our fist on our prey."

The message sent back with the captured merchantman would have the Clan fleet on alert. But the transports could not yet have arrived at Bethel, much less landed there. Rigged for deep-space running, sufficient ships could be diverted to assist him without hindering the effort at Bethel. Say, ten days' transit from the Saffron system, to be conservative; two or three days loading, depending on how many Father Chalku decided to send. Then set demolition charges, nice large ones to leave nothing larger than gravel. There might well be prisoners worth taking for skilled labor. The huge rectangular frame of a shipyard was now visible on one side of the station, and that meant that there would be rare and valuable slaves to sell.

With an effort, he restrained himself from rubbing his hands together. "Oh, what a surprise they have in store," he said.

"Indeed," Serig said. His eyes and teeth shone in the dim blue lights of the bridge and his voice was husky, like a man in the grip of lust. Which, Belazir reflected, was exactly what it was. Metaphorically and literally.

"Keep your eagerness in chains, my friend," he said genially. "It is a good slave but a poor master." He turned to Baila. "What traffic inbound?"

"None, Great Lord."

"None?" Belazir raised a brow.

Curious, he thought, *a space station built in an area nearly devoid of traffic. Is it old and due to be abandoned? Or is it new and as yet rarely used?* A small chill diluted the perfection of his pleasure. There were alternatives here; he might be the hero who brought unimaginable wealth, or the immortal villain who revealed the existence of the Clan to an enemy more powerful than they.

He shook his head with a small, *tssk* of disgust. Impossible. The merchantman had been rich with treasure and it had just left the station. "Indications?"

"Great Lord, the background radiation is consistent with large-scale departures over the past five days." Baila paused, hesitant. "Lord, it is difficult to be certain, with the density of the interstellar medium here. Subspace distortion damps out very quickly . . ."

The small chill became fingers of ice stroking the base of his spine. His testicles drew up in reflex.

"I want information, not excuses!" he said in a harsh voice. "Ready the seeker missiles." If the accursed Bethelite cowards *had* warned the station—prompting the normal traffic to flee—they would destroy it and run immediately. He was nearly certain he had crippled the prey's communications apparatus in the pursuit, but "nearly" grilled no meat. But, if it had escaped, where was it? Or had the station done his work for him? A rich station would have cause to be wary of unexpected visitors. "Continue stealthed approach."

That meant running with the powerplants down, off accumulator energy, on a ballistic sublight approach. Slow, they would take years to come near at this speed, but quite safe at a respectable distance. At any moment they could power up and close in swiftly at superluminal speeds. This was a modification of a tactic the Clan sometimes used against merchantmen on the outskirts of a solar system. And they were close enough that lightspeed was not much of a problem for detection purposes. Briefly, he considered running back on FTL for a few parsecs, to see if he could pick up traces of in- or outbound traffic over the past week. Then he shook his head, rejecting that plan. Signal degraded too much over distance, and his own trail would advertise his presence. While the station retained subspace communicator capacity, it presented the Clan with a deadly risk.

Taking time to consider a problem from all angles was no excuse for inaction. Strike the hardest blow you could, then see if another was needed; that was the Kolnari way.

"See if you can pick anything up from their perimeter relay beacons," he said. In dust this thick even local realspace beacons needed amplification.

"Message, Great Lord," said Baila.

"I would hear it."

Immediately a woman's crisp voice filled the control center, "Warning all ships, warning all ships. SSS-900-C is under Class Two quarantine: I repeat, Class Two quarantine. The following species are advised not to make port at these facilities under any circumstances."

A list of alien species followed, most of them unknown to t'Marid.

"Human visitors are restricted to the dock facilities and the entertainment areas immediately adjacent to them. You are advised to continue on to your next port of call. Warning . . ."

The message began to repeat and Baila cut it off. "Further scan, lord: there are two debris fields. Both of them between us and the station. The one nearest the station is largely of natural ferrous compounds, probability ninety-seven percent-plus semi-processed asteroidal material. The other, nearest the *Bride,* is of . . . metal and ship-hull compounds, finely divided. Computer assessment is that the mass represented by the metal debris is equivalent to the mass represented by the prey ship."

She touched several controls, and the multiple screens displayed a scene of tumbling scraps of half-melted metal, no single piece larger than a meter wide or long. Most were a fog of metallic particles.

His eyes narrowed. The quarantine could explain the absence of shipping. Baila's analysis suggested that, either the prey ship, which he knew had been ancient, had disintegrated under the stress of redlining or the station had destroyed it. The former was more likely since no weaponry had been detected on the station. No doubt the truth of the end to the Bethelite refugee ship would be found in the station's records.

"Your appraisal?" Belazir asked his weapons officer.

"Great Lord," the man said, collating a probability run, "the bulk of the fragments are definitely the result of ultra-high temperature breakdown. The profile is completely compatible with sudden energy discharge from the main internal drive coil of a very large ship. Some of the other debris—" he called up relevant views "—show blast fragmentation. That could either have been the result of direct hits with chemical-energy warheads, or secondary propagation effects when the engine blew. The Shockwave through the hull . . ."

"I'm aware of the phenomenon," Belazir said dryly. The weapons officer shrank back. Belazir t'Marid had fought his first space engagement before the younger noble was born. "Continue scan and analysis. Inform me of any anomalies."

"They blew up," Serig said.

"Just as they arrived? How convenient," Belazir said. He gnawed a thumb. "Possibly too convenient?"

"Possibly. However, we were expecting their engines to fail catastrophically at any moment. They were sublimating bits of their cooling vanes for the last thirty light-years."

"True. It is still a coincidence."

"Once is coincidence," Serig said in ritual tone, "twice is happenstance—"

"—and the third time is enemy action, yes," Belazir finished irritably. "But for the station to be plague-ridden at the same time?"

"The scumvermin races are weak of body, lord," he noted.

Belazir signed confirmation. The seed of Kolnar was strong. It had to be, to have survived so long on a planet not suitable for human beings, and further devastated by so many centuries of reckless development and continual war with every nuclear, chemical and biological weapon ingenuity could produce. When the Clan fled a losing struggle, they had kept the tradition of culling any child who showed signs of vulnerability to infection. In fact, it was a stroke of fortune to have the enemy immobilized by a menace that was no menace to the Kolnari.

"Hold position. Call in the consorts."

"Yes, Great Lord."

Belazir glanced at his communications officer. Her face was bright with excitement, too. He smiled. She was young; this was her first term of duty. He remembered well that sharp, eager feeling. He grinned. Ah, but he was feeling now, at the ripe age of thirty, that his life was half over.

"All captains confirming receipt of your orders, Great Lord. Moving into position."

"Excellent," he said, glancing back at the schematic. *You have already given a cry of distress, oh rich and beauteous station,* he thought vindictively. The entire universe was in conspiracy against the Clan— against all of Kolnar and its children. *Soon you will scream.*

Channa turned at her desk. "Hi Joat, welcome home."

A relieved, shy smile greeted her. "Um . . . gonna take a shower."

"You can use it," Channa said, sniffing. "When you're through, I want to introduce you to someone."

"Ah," Simeon said lightly. "We're a family again."

"Shut up, you hunk of tin," Channa said good-naturedly, throwing a wad of scrunched-up tissue in the general direction of the pillar. "How does *this* look?"

She punched a key to feed in the distribution of supply caches.

"Hmmm. Not bad. Okay, how about we seal off the following passageways?" A schematic of several decks sprang up. "If you didn't know about modern fabrication methods, that would look right for structural members."

"Good, good—what does that give us?"

"About a thousand people we can stick away in corners—the 'b' list." Those were the ones that they hadn't had space available to evacuate.

"Nobody essential, I'm afraid," Channa said. They had agreed that they had to let essential staff take the risks, as their absence would elicit questions.

"No, but it'll cut down the number of potential victims quite nicely. Also, it'll give us a chance to scatter around some stuff that'll come in useful later. Ah, Simeon-Amos."

The Bethelite leader's eyes were red-rimmed, but his smile brought a warm lurch to Channa's diaphragm. "I think I have mastered the basic administrative structure," he said. "It is not too strange."

Channa raised a brow. *A 900-series station isn't too strange to a backworlder?* she thought.

The thought must have been obvious, but Amos only spread his hands and tossed his head, setting aswirl the coal-black curls of his shoulder-length mane. The blue eyes twinkled beneath the broad clear brow.

Oooooo, Channa thought, and fought to bring her attention back to his words.

"In any large organization, there will be certain constants," he said. "The central authority; officers in charge of various departments; a structure for meetings to coordinate activities; procedures for routine decision-making, and so forth. This is not too dissimilar to my family's holdings on Bethel. We, too, were essentially coordinators of the activities of many independent entrepreneurs. There are no ranchers or farmers here, of course, but both communities have mining, manufacturing, education, cultural facilities . . ."

"Culture?" Joat ducked back into the lobby, toweling her wet hair. For a wonder, she had on something more formal than the shapeless, patchwork-colorful overalls that were current fashion among SSS-900-C's youth. "Like holos and virtie games and stuff?"

"Ahhh . . ." Amos hesitated. He had been thinking more of choral song and traditional dancing. "The general principle is the same."

The servos had been setting out the evening meal. Simeon had programmed them to meet the basic dietary superstitions of the Bethelite religion, although Amos had turned out to be flexible. Channa shuddered mentally at some of the things she'd screened in that Bethel text. How in God's name, for example, were they supposed to check that none of the materials had ever been touched by a menstruating woman?

They sat down, Amos murmured a prayer, and for another wonder Joat waited a second before grabbing the nearest bowl. She had turned out to be a monumentally unfussy eater, but in sheer capacity she belied the scrawny underdeveloped frame. Between—or sometimes during—mouthfuls, she grilled Amos about Bethel.

"Sounds dull," she said at last.

"I thought so, too," Amos said, pushing a bowl of steamed millet closer to her. She shoveled several helpings onto her plate and heaped them with sour cream and chives.

"Joat," Channa said gently. "That really doesn't go with pineapple slices, you know."

"Why not?" Joat asked, turning to her with a milk mustache on her upper lip. The girl licked it away with satisfaction as Channa searched for a reply, gave up, and turned her attention back to Amos.

"Hiding away all that stuff was smart of Channa," she said thoughtfully. "Always gotta have supplies in your bolt-hole unless you're fardlin' stupid."

"Sound strategy," Amos said seriously.

He certainly seems to be good with children, Channa thought, stirring her food around with her fork. *Girls don't bother him.* Not prepubescent ones, at least.

In her inner ear, Simeon began to croon an ancient song: "*Across a croooowded room . . .*"

"*Shut up,*" she subvocalized.

"This place has got more back-alleys than you'd believe," Joat was saying. "Not like a ship at all, really. You can get anywhere from anywhere and ain't *nobody* can stop you, if you know where you're goin'. Some of the places pinch grudly, but they're in-able if you're sveltsome."

"I would have thought it much like a ship of space," Amos replied courteously. Channa could see his lips move silently for an instant as he puzzled out Joat's slang. That was no wonder. Half of it was her own invention.

"A whole other order of magnitude," Simeon said. "No mass limits on a station—the SSS-900-C wasn't expected to go anywhere. The outer shell was fixed, as well as some of the major facilities, but the rest was intended to allow organic growth up to a couple of hundred thousand people, max. We've found natural expansion is the best way to stabilize a real community, as opposed to a transient community, like a passenger vessel."

"That is good sense," Amos said meditatively. "On my family's estate, planning towns was similar. If you set down every detail, the place has no life. When Uncle Habib decides to put his tobacco store next to Aunti Scala's pastry shop or Brother Falken's saddlery, and that brings an ice-cream parlor, it then follows that the town becomes a living and efficient entity."

"Why do you talk so funny?" Joat asked.

"Why do *you* talk so funny?" Amos parried, and they both laughed. "Because Bethel was cut off for so long. We did not even screen or broadcast data from other worlds, so our people's way of speech changed little, and those changes differed from those in the Central Worlds, which had dealings with many other worlds and cultures."

"Central Worlds?" Joat asked. "Oh, you're fardlin'—'cuse me—way off there. This is the *hikstik,* frontier, you know."

"To you, not me." He paused. "I think, Joat, that someone besides yourself should know of these hidden ways of yours."

"You should see it," she said enthusiastically. "You wouldn't believe what's back there!"

"I would very much like to see it," he told her gravely. "But, I have not much time left for my studies." Her face fell. "Still," he said, "I think that it is important that trusted people, other than just you and Simeon, should know these back ways of yours. Would you be willing to show my friend, Joseph?"

"He's your head honcho, hey?"

"My brother and my right hand," Amos said seriously.

"Okay, if he's nanna grudly."

Amos gave up trying to interpret that remark and glanced over at Simeon's image in the screen.

"Grudly," the brain said in his most professorial. "An all purpose negative. In this context—'not too grudly'—straight-laced, conventional, boring, unimaginative."

"No, no. To tell the truth and shame the devil, Joseph was, in fact, a dockside desperado when I met him," Amos said.

Joat lit up, her urchin smile taking a year or two off the extra time life had dealt her, so that she looked twelve. "Sure! I'll be glad to show Joseph around. Whenever you like."

"Thank you. And now I must return to my studies." He sighed theatrically and rose.

"I know how you feel," Joat said, shaking her head in resignation.

"He's made a conquest there," Channa subvocalized. *"Wonder how he did it?"*

"Joat is no longer a feral child," Simeon pointed out. *"We broke the ground for him. Being glamorous doesn't hurt. And he* listens *to her. He's naturally interested in people, I think, under the weird socio-religious stuff they rammed down his throat."*

"You're right," Channa said aloud, looking dreamily at the now closed door of Amos' quarters.

Well, Simeon-Amos, Simeon *thought, you're a hit with both my girls.* A petty observation, but couldn't he indulge in pettiness in the privacy of his own mind?

"'Course I'm right," Joat said. She was having more of the pineapple slices, fresh from the vats, lavishly dolloped with ice cream. "You flipping the sheets with him yet?"

"Joat!" Channa said warningly, reaching over to flick her on the ear with thumb and forefinger.

"Watch it!" Joat said, rubbing the offended lobe. "I'll report you to Gorgan the Organ." She grinned unrepentantly. "I know all about it, y'know."

"You may have observed—and I wouldn't put that past you for a nanosecond, but you don't *understand* what you've seen. You also have no manners."

"Yeah, that's true," Joat said complacently.

"You needn't act so smug about the lack," Simeon cut in.

"Why not?" Joat asked. "Lots of way-neat stuff you can't do if you've got manners."

My God, Channa thought, looking up from her notescreen.
All of them were looking terrible, but Doctor Chaundra looked

old. And haunted as well. Channa was a little surprised. She would have thought him one of the ones who could handle the fear.

"Here it is," he said bitterly, holding up a small synthetic container.

Channa automatically glanced down at the box, a capsule dispenser, standard model, but looked more closely at him.

"Are you all right, Doctor?" she said anxiously. There were other medicos on the station, but only one Chaundra. Personal factors aside, he was also the only specialist with experience in original viral research.

"Tired is all," he said. The non-Standard accent in his voice was stronger than usual, a trace of liquid singsong. He stood for a moment by her desk looking at the box he carried, then he placed it in front of her. "They're ready," he said, pointing to it.

Channa touched the dispenser slot and it dropped a gelatin capsule filled with clear liquid into her palm.

"The virus," she said.

"Yes," he murmured. "I, who am a healer, have created for you a weapon."

"A *nonlethal* weapon for *self-defense*," she said in gentle correction.

"Hopefully nonlethal. How can I be sure, with a genetically nonstandard target population? I cannot even be *certain* nobody on the station will die of it!"

"The probability—" Simeon began in a firm tone.

"—is vanishingly small, yes, indeed," Chaundra said. Then he sighed. "There is no sense in complaining after the fact. We have made enough so every man and woman on the station gets five. I can't imagine anyone being unlucky enough to need more than that. What you do, is bite down on it. Don't swallow and breathe it all over the Kolnari nearest you. It is contagious even if swallowed, you understand, but more so with direct contact. If the pirate wishes to kiss you, by all means let them."

"Ugh!" Channa said, making a face.

"I've alerted the group leaders to call in at the clinic to collect dispensers for distribution to their people," Simeon said.

"Remind them, will you," Chaundra said, "that anyone who uses a capsule should report as soon as possible to the clinic for the protective shot. They'll get a light dose then, but their . . . um . . . victim will get very sick indeed."

"Symptoms?" asked Channa.

"Headache, nausea, diarrhea, fever, possible delirium." He shivered.

"I must get back to my lab. So much more needs to be done, and there is so little time to do it all in."

"*You* need to sleep," Channa said firmly. "Go to bed for a minimum of six hours."

"That's an order, Chaundra," Simeon told him, "as of now, you're off duty until tomorrow morning."

"Yes, of course." Chaundra nodded abstractedly. "And the volunteers," he continued, "have them in the hospital as *soon* as the pirates appear. We can accelerate the onset—"

"*Go to bed!*" Channa took him by the arms and gave him a little shake, finally getting his startled attention.

"Oh . . ." He smiled. "Good idea. Um . . ." He paused at the door and blinked. "Oh, yes. Joat—I have met young Joat. She is a bit . . . more mature than I thought she was." He frowned, looking concerned. "Do you think it will be all right, their being together so much? Her and Seld, I mean."

Channa blinked. *At least nobody has been unkind enough to mention any grisly tales of Joat's life story,* she thought.

"Uh, I don't think it will matter," Simeon said, slightly amused. "They'll be kept well-occupied, you know, and they are neither of them physically adult."

"You are very off-handed for a proper father of a daughter," Chaundra said owlishly.

"Well, I *am* her father—or will be when the papers are completed. Truly, Chaundra, I think we can depend on Joat to be responsible. I trust her. She may operate on her own code of ethics, but she is more consistent about it than many adults I have encountered. I'm not worried."

Chaundra sighed. "I wish I had a credit for every time someone has told me that they are not worried. They're at a volatile age and they can't even trust themselves. Hell," he said throwing his arms wide, "under all this pressure, the *adults* on this station can't trust themselves. How can we expect these kids to?"

Channa felt her color rise. "We can only anticipate the problem and talk to them and hope for the best. If they're so inclined," to her surprise, she couldn't force herself to be more specific, "they'll find a time and place where we can't interfere. So let's not wear ourselves down worrying about it."

A whole new set of problems, she thought. Correcting the damage done to Joat's psychosexual development was probably going to take many years. Right now the girl needed Seld to be her friend, not her bed partner. He was definitely her friend but . . . Channa remembered what boys were like at that age, too. *There's more of a danger that she'd break his arm. But she* needs *a friend.* Something else to lie sleepless and worry over. Or had anyone told Joat about Seld's medical problems? *Privacy,* she thought. Seld had the right to deal with *that* in his own time.

"Hey!" Simeon said. "Yoohoo! Channa! Chaundra. You're both tired. Everything looks manageable when you've had some sleep. So go sleep. We'll take care of the capsules and we'll organize the volunteers. Don't worry about a thing."

Chaundra sighed again and assumed a wry expression. "Amateurs," he mumbled. "What you're experiencing, Simeon, is denial. You can't avoid such problems by pretending they don't exist." His shoulders fell "I'll have Seld bring her home with him after they're through working today." He waved goodbye and left.

"Denial," Simeon said musingly. Strange, knowing what he did of her past, he *knew* that sex was the last thing Joat would think of as a recreational activity. That was the commonest symptom of the particular form of abuse she had suffered—and still the idea made him uneasy. *Fatherhood.*

"I don't want to talk about it," Channa told him, and marched briskly back to her desk. She sat down and spun the box of capsules around with one finger. "I was thinking," she said, "wouldn't it be great if we could up the ante on these?" She looked at Simeon's column.

"Yeah, it would. But we're already putting our people at risk. I'm not willing to do the enemy's work for them. Y'know?"

"Mmm. True. What if we could make them believe it's worse than it really is?"

"Hard to say without knowing their physiology, tissue samples . . . Oh. You're talking about a con game, aren't you, Happy?"

"It all depends on their psychology, of course. And I'm *not* happy."

"Well," Simeon said dubiously, "the Navy psych reports aren't too detailed. These splinter groups are usually aberrant. Generally speaking, the reports say the Kolnari are extremely aggressive towards those they perceive as weak, treacherous but willing to bargain with their equals in power, and have a flight/submission reflex towards superiors—until the superiors let down their guard, which is a sign of weakness."

"Oh, what a love-feast their culture must be!" Channa said. "Hmmm. They'd be vulnerable to status and power anxieties, then. And lots of internal rivalries."

"You betcha. According to the reports, they're also as superstitious as horses. They know some science, but they're not scientific, if you know what I mean."

"I think I get the picture. So?"

"We could modify some of the holo-projectors beside the security cameras and flash 'hallucinations' for the benefit of those who've had the virus. Auditory hallucinations are no problem. I could project them and no one would be the wiser."

"Oh, really?"

"*Yeah,*" he seemed to be whispering directly into her ear, "*and without using your implant.*"

"Wow," she said, touching her ear, "that's spooky. How did you do that?"

"Just threw my voice—heterodyning waves from multiple sources. It takes practice, but as you saw, the effect is worth it."

She shook her head, wide-eyed. "If you can come up with something visual to go with that, they'll be running for their ships the first day."

"Can't overdo it. It'll be easiest if they're alone when they see these things, otherwise it could be considered suspicious. I'll sound Joat out. That girl's a fountain of ideas."

Channa winced and forbore to ask what kind. Chaundra's comments almost visibly flooded back into her conscious mind.

"Don't let it worry you, she's a good kid," Simeon said emphatically.

"I don't want to think about it."

"You really are concerned about Rachel's sanity, aren't you?"

Amos and Channa were settled comfortably on the settee. Simeon had tactfully withdrawn his image from the pillar screen, leaving a strikingly realistic crackling fire in its place. Somehow he had even manage to replicate the scent of burning cedarwood. Amos had had to tactilely reassure himself that the fire was an image.

"Yes, she is definitely unstable," he said, his shoulders sagging hopelessly. "Among all the other problems, I must worry about this! It is so . . . so *petty.*"

"Humans can be a remarkably petty species," Channa said

philosophically. *Particularly that hysterical bitch Rachel.* "When you get down to cases, lots of 'big issues' have been decided on personal matters. From Harmodias and Aristogetion on down." Amos looked blank. "Two ancient Greeks. Never mind. Briefly, a government was overthrown because of a love-triangle."

Amos sighed again and reached for his snifter of brandy. "I care nothing about her and my best friend would give his life for her," he said, shaking his head. "Channa—"

"Yes?"

"I know here—" he touched his head "—that this . . . delusion of hers has nothing to do with me. But *here*—" he touched his heart "—I cannot help but feel that I *must* somehow be to blame. I was a . . . caller-of-spirit: you would say a preacher. Oh, yes, I knew that half the women in those crowds were in love with me. What of it? I would never touch any of them, for that would be dishonorable and destroy my cause more surely than any other offense. The folk of Bethel are . . . inflexible about such matters. Yet if I knew and accepted love, if it flattered my vanity, am I not in some manner responsible? How desperate she must be, and how lonely. It is sad."

Channa patted his arm and smiled soothingly. "From your description, it was never this bad before. If you're to blame, then so is every charismatic politician and holo star since time began. Her . . . delusion . . . may have been aggravated by those drugs, although she's not responding to medication. Simeon, has anyone talked to Chaundra about this?"

"Not yet," he said, after a tactful pause to suggest he hadn't been listening.

"I have decided to keep her under my eye," Amos said, adding reluctantly, "Mental care, the cure of souls. It is part of our religion that only those consecrated can perform cures of the human soul."

"Mmm." *Your religion sucks wind,* she thought silently. No sense in offending Amos, of course. Humans shouldn't be forced to *take* religion. That should be free choice. "Maybe we'd better let Chaundra know that Rachel isn't responding to treatment. She may need stronger calmers. Let's face it, when the pirates arrive, you're going to have a surfeit of problems to keep under your eyes."

"I can keep my eye on more than one thing at a time, Channa," Simeon cut in abruptly. "Simeon-Amos?"

He nodded. "I agree with Channa. I will speak with the doctor of this. This is my burden, my obligation. I will do it." He rose and disappeared into his room, shoulders bowed.

Channa shook her head, "You'd think he was sending her off to be executed."

"Who knows how his people view psych treatment? Confession seems to be a major element in their religion. To him, treating this as a medical problem could be equivalent to blasphemy."

"Hmph." She turned to squint at his column. "By the way, don't try to tell me that you didn't enjoy that little interruption, Simeon. I know you too well by now."

"Okay." His voice was downright cheery.

She smiled ruefully. "Just don't make a habit of it, okay?"

"There are no guarantees in life, Channa."

"Oh, no? If I ever get the idea that you're engineering any more little disruptions of my love life, *I* guarantee that you'll regret it."

"Hey, be reasonable, Channa! What could I possibly have to do with Rachel going bonkers? I didn't even let her into the lounge. I could have, y'know."

Channa shrugged and grunted.

"I thought about not telling you she was trying to beat the door down, I really did. But then I figured she'd go grab a laser and cut her way in. And, of course, if she had caught you two in flagrante delicto, she wouldn't have stopped at cutting up doors."

"Oh, *thank* you, Simeon, you *are* such a hero, saving me from a fate worse than death and death itself. Consider yourself hugged and slobbered over in an ecstasy of gratitude."

"That's short for 'my attitude's back,' isn't it?"

She got up and started for her room. "Yes, Simeon, my attitude's back."

"Well, why? What did I do?"

She spun on her heel and threw up her hands. "I'm horny, all right? I'm horny and I'm frustrated!" The door snapped shut behind her.

Simeon shut down his pickups in the lounge, escaping the charged atmosphere in the only way he could. *Sheesh,* he thought. Softshells were *strange.*

CHAPTER FIFTEEN

"NOTHING, GREAT LORD. Nothing but rebroadcasts of the same warning message."

"Tsssk. You have had no success in monitoring internal communications?"

"No, Great Lord."

This time Baila's voice held a slight touch of resentment. This was no backwater, no half-barbarian slum that used electro-magnetic signals for internal communication. This was a sophisticated Central Worlds installation they were planning to attack. It had internal optical circuitry. What did the Great Lord expect her to do? Fly over to the station and burn her way through to tap a line?

We are all impatient, Belazir thought. The Clan impulse was to leap upon the prey and take it. Loot it bare, move on. They had been very successful following that course of action for a long time.

"Any other ships?"

"None since that freighter who acknowledged their warning beacon and sheered off," she said.

"Serig."

"Command me, lord." The verbal formula was more than routine in Serig's mouth; he fairly quivered with anticipation.

"We will move in exactly one-point-five hours from next day-cycle termination." This was about three hours Terran Standard time, since Kolnar rotated more slowly than Manhome. "All vessels to launch their seekers simultaneously and then begin subspace jamming pulses.

211

Strangler and *Age of Darkness* will remain on combat over-watch, ready to provide fire support as necessary. *Dreadful Bride* and *Shark* will move in to the upper and lower polar axis respectively and force-dock, then occupy the station. Here are the areas to be secured."

His hands keyed a sequence, and the schematic of the SSS-900-C was overlaid with color-coded plans for movement.

"Move swiftly! Crush any sign of resistance with utmost force. If resistance slows the infantry down, secure those decks and blow them open to space. I will be with the second wave at the north polar axis."

"Lord."

"Captain Lord Pol is *not* to disembark before the target is fully secured. Those are my orders. Repeat them to her in the message."

"I hear and obey, Great Lord," Serig said. He made a few notes to himself. "Tightbeam?"

"Of course."

"I may lead the assault party?"

Belazir and his henchman shared an identical wolf grin. "Of course."

Joseph ben Said nodded gravely. "I am glad that you have shown me these things, Joat."

Joat looked downshaft between her legs—it was the only way to see the Bethelite's face since they were both climbing up—and smiled cockily. They had paused at this intersection with two small feeder ducts so she could give him directions. He had hooked one thick arm around a rung so he could squint down the other shafts.

"You learn pretty quick," she said. "Hey, and you don't get fardled up in a tight spot, neither."

Joseph's square face split in a raptor's smile. "Joat-my-friend, where I grew up one learned quickly, or one died. Also I spent much time in narrow places. Sewers and tunnels, rather than ductwork, but the principle is the same."

"Yeah, I guess we got a lot in common," she said. *You poor bastard,* she added to herself. Not aloud. Evidently these oscos were sensitive about language.

"But I am surprised that you can move with such freedom when any section can be closed off and air-evacuated," Joseph went on. He cracked his thick-fingered hands reflexively, and took out a long curved knife to trim a callus. "And then there are the maintenance servos, also centrally controlled."

"Yeah, well, you gotta look at that sort of thing from the bottom up," Joat said. "Follow me."

They muscled upward, back and legs against opposite side of the passageway, then crawled out into a slightly wider connecting way.

"See? There's the seal," she said, running one finger along the edge of the octagonal opening where the two ducts crossed.

"Ah." Joseph peered more closely. "I see—a thin sheet?"

"Naw, interlocking pointed wedges, 's stronger or some fardling thing. *Don't* get in the way if it's gonna close. They don't have no safety pressure stops here where people aren't supposta be, so they'll cut you right in half."

Joseph nodded, continuing his examination. "And this?" He touched a slight bulge.

"Access panel. Here."

Joat brought up a square piece of electronics from her harness and touched it. The bulge withdrew into the wall. Inside were readouts, a keypad, and a datajack. She squirmed until her backpack was on the floor between her knees, then pulled out a jackline from her Spuglish and clipped it into the socket.

The machine lit. **Hello, Joat,** scrolled across it. **Simeon's gone bye-bye wurf!**

"What is that?" Joseph said, fascinated.

"I usta *think* it was Simeon in a grudly strange comedown," Joat said, her fingers flying in a rapid *taptaptaptiptiptip.* "Only it isn't. 'S just a really neato AI program running on the station main computers. Fools ya, y'know? Real easy to get to thinking it's a real person, but it isn't. Smart piece of junk, but I can get around it. When it thinks you're Simeon, it really comes down as an *animal.*"

Hello, Simeon, the screen printed. **What's up, boss? Huh? Huh?**

Joat's fingers scrambled. *Nothing much,* she keyed. *Updating Shame on Me,* she added.

Don't rightly know that one, pardner, the machine replied. **Uhyip.** The tip of Joat's tongue was clenched between her teeth in a rictus of concentration. At last, she leaned back and sighed, cracking her fingers two-handed.

"Now it thinks I'm Simeon again," she said.

" 'Shame on Me'?" Joseph enquired.

"Fool me once," Joat said, quoting, "shame on you. Fool me twice, shame on me."

Joseph's laugh was quiet and appreciative. Joat felt the quiet glow of satisfaction you only got from another operator. Seld was neat, but he wasn't a . . . Well, he wasn't grown up, in the special way Joseph was grown up. She'd known a lot of people who were grown-up that way, but Joseph was the first one she had ever liked or trusted.

"So you manipulate the system through the central computer?" he said.

"Naw, not most of the time. Too con-spick-cue-us. Finkin' obvious, in fact. There's a distributed node system, fambly *thousands* of little compus, all got backup authority, *if* you can cut in. And nobody cuts in like jack-of-all-trades, my man."

Joseph clapped a hand on her shoulder. She stiffened and stared at it. He took it away, not snatching or lingering, either.

"How did you pick this up?" he said in admiration, pointing at her Spuglish.

"Dad." *Fardling swiney.* "Learned more from the bastard who won me *from* my uncle," she said. "He was smart, really smart, when he wasn't drunk or—well, when he was sober. Knew his way around any system there was. Never got caught, except once."

"Who by?" Joseph asked.

Joat turned her face toward him, and for a moment it was not a child's face at all. "Me," she said softly. "He forgot me. And I cracked *his* system. They think he's still alive. He went thataway out the lock, peeing blood. His ship's computer said everything was fine."

"Well," Joseph said with a cold smile, "if it's good enough for the official records, it's good enough for me. Now, show me how you decouple the local subsystems again."

"Like, it's got to be physical," Joat went on, animated again. "You—"

"I am glad to see you two are friends," Amos said.

Joat and Joseph had walked in the door laughing uproariously, slapping each other on the shoulder.

Joseph smiled at his leader and bowed formally, hand on heart. "My brother, you have done me a great favor by introducing me to this young sorceress," he said. "And our cause."

"You guys are brothers?" Joat asked suddenly.

"No," was the spontaneous answer from Channa, Simeon, and Amos.

"Oh?" Joat looked from one to the other, frowning slightly, then she shook her head dismissing the problem. "Yeah, we had a great time!" she went on. "Joe here picks things up pretty good, for a grown-up."

"For a grown-up?" Amos said, raising a brow.

"You know," Joat explained kindly, "for somebody who's *old*."

Amos pursed his lips. He was a year older than Joseph. "I am glad to see you found him worthy," he said dryly.

"Yeah, I did." Joat frowned. "Can I ask you something?" she said.

"By all means, foster daughter of Channa," Amos said.

"Most grown-ups are funny about kids knowing things," she said. "You aren't. How come?"

Amos blinked. "You are . . . what, twelve?" he said.

"'Bout. Gets hard to tell when you do a lot of FTL 'n some coldsleep."

"At your age, I was running my family's estates," Amos said. "Of course, I would not have been, had my father lived. Sons of poorer folk are apprenticed at twelve, doing a day's work and paying for their own food. Should I be surprised if you can do likewise?"

Joat glowed. "At *last*," she said, turning triumphantly to Channa. "*Told* you I'd learn more doing a real job!"

"What did I say?" Amos asked, flinching at the glare Channa leveled at him.

"Promised I'd go catch Seld," Joat said, wolfing down the last of her breakfast and sticking a few pieces of fruit in the pockets of her shapeless overall. "Ta-ta, all."

"Speaking of the Chaundras," Channa said meaningfully, glancing at Amos. "I have to run. More—ack! pftht!—meetings. Don't forget."

Joseph waited until silence had fallen again, then looked at Amos with concern. "Something is wrong with you, my brother?"

Amos looked at his plate. "No," he said. He gestured Joseph to a seat, but stood himself, his hands clasped behind his back. "There is nothing wrong with me. This concerns Rachel." He held up his hand to forestall Joseph's protest. "Let me finish. She came here the other night, furious, raving. She claimed we were betrothed. Her *eyes*, Joseph! They were wild, and she shook . . . her face was so white." He looked at his friend. "Our Rachel is shaking to pieces before our eyes. I am going to tell Chaundra what I have told you, and if he decides that she needs treatment, then she shall have it."

Joseph nodded jerkily, resting his face in one hand. His shoulders moved convulsively, then he steadied.

"I am grateful that you share your thoughts with me," he said. "Though you now stand as her father."

"We have no Healer of Souls here, Joseph," Amos said with deep remorse.

"So Rachel must lose her soul's privacy before an infidel, an outsider," Joseph replied.

"I had not thought you so pious."

Joseph sighed, shaking his head wearily. "It is strange how ingrained is the training of one's childhood. At the last, I find I, too, am a son of the Temple."

"If you truly are against such procedures, I will not force her," Amos said.

Joseph rose and gave Amos the embrace of brothers. "Thank you," he said, "but, if my heart rebels, my mind tells me you are right . . . damnably right. That is an irritating habit you have, Amos ben Sierra Nueva."

Amos grinned. "So I have been told. *To* myself not least, brother. Do you wish to be with her?"

Joseph hesitated, then shook his head. "No," he said, after a moment. "As she is . . . it would be no kindness. I will continue with my work." His mouth quirked. "Work is truly the mercy of God, as the Prophet said. No?"

"I find more truth in his words every time I return to them," Amos replied seriously, his hand on the other man's shoulder. "Truth too strong for the chains of dogma. Go in peace."

"To make ready for war," Joseph observed.

Amos laughed ruefully. "Another truth the Prophet left us: 'If you would have peace, then prepare for war.' "

"What a pity the Elders thought that meant the spiritual struggle alone," Joseph said.

"The Prophet was a surprisingly practical man," Amos observed. "I strive to emulate him."

"You do so. You do so very well," Joseph replied and bowed formally: a rare gesture between them.

"Let's go get Seld Chaundra," Joat suggested when Joseph caught up to her at the elevator. "We're supposed to go into hiding when the pirates show up, so he'll need to see this stuff, too."

"I have no objection," Joseph said mildly.

"You and Simeon-Amos fighting about something?" she asked bluntly.

"No." Joseph shrugged. "We are angry together, at what is and cannot be changed."

"Yeah, life's like that," Joat observed.

They reached the main corridor and took two people movers down from the wall. Joseph looked a little dubious as he stepped onto the disk. As it silently lifted from the floor, he gripped the handhold tightly with one broad spatulate hand. Joat showed Joseph the address to tap to reach the Chaundras' home. The little floatdisks took off, dodging agilely through traffic and summoning elevators when their route took to the upper decks.

Seld himself opened the door.

"Hi," he said somewhat nervously.

"Hi, this is Joseph ben Said," Joat said indicating the swarthy man beside her. "Simeon-Amos suggested that I take him round, and I thought you might like to come."

"Aw, I'd love to," he said, all eagerness which dissolved the next moment. "I can't. I'm grounded."

"You're what?" Joat asked, puzzled.

Seld blushed to the roots of his auburn hair; the colors clashed horribly. "I'm being disciplined. I can't leave our quarters."

Joat's expression was amused and aghast, *Glad I don't have parents,* she thought. *I won't get stuck someplace I don't want to be.*

"Geeze, Seld, your dad can't seem to get it right. First it's too much 'go,' now it's too much *stay.*" She shook her head in awe. "You can't win playing that way. So come anyhow," she added, cocking her head at him.

"I *can't,*" he repeated, glancing nervously at Joseph. The Bethelite crossed his arms and looked at the ceiling, humming an idle tune.

"He's okay," Joat assured him. "Why not?"

"'Cause Dad's gonna call and check up on me."

Joat rolled her eyes. "So call in to the answering machine ev'ry so often. If he's called, you can call back and say he caught you in the head. He's so worried about your safety, Seld, he should worry more if you don't know this. You gotta know your way around the backside of the station. Hey! If it really bothers you we can ask Simeon to help, or Joseph . . . ?" She turned appealing eyes up to his.

Joseph uncrossed his arms. "I believe it could be put to your father—" He broke off, his eyes focused on some one in the corridor beyond Joat. "Rachel?"

Rachel bint Damscus stopped, looking him coldly up and down. "Well, Joseph ben Said. I wonder, do you have any messages that you are withholding from me?"

He was nonplussed. "Whatever are you talking about, my lady?"

"No lady of yours, peasant," she said, spitting the last word at him, her eyes wide and flashing. "Amos told me that he had delegated you to inform me that he was moving in with that lanky, sallow-faced slut. But you, apparently, chose not to tell me. Why is that?"

"We are at war," he said shortly. "Time is short. Rachel bint Damscus, be known to Joat," he said, gesturing courteously to her, "the foster daughter of Simeon. Be known also to Seld Chaundra."

Rachel looked at the two young people as though he had introduced her to a pair of rodents. "Simeon . . . ?" she said, picking up what was important to her.

"Yes," he hissed in a whisper, moving closer to her. *Not now*, his expression said. *Spare these children.*

"Who is this 'Simeon' that everyone addresses with such respect?"

"He and Channa run the station," Joat told her.

"Ah," Rachel said, looking at her with a false smile, "does that make you the whore's foster-daughter, too?"

Joseph's hand moved very quickly, deflecting Joat's hand, which was halfway to delivering what it held.

"Drop it," he said. "*Now*, Joat."

Struggling against his grip, Joat drew her lips back from her teeth, but she had to comply. The grip on her wrist was not tight enough to hurt, but it had the implacable solidity of a mechanical grab. The Bethelite wrenched the small square box from her with his other hand.

"Weapon?" he said, turning it over briefly. "Do not strike without thinking, Joat. And rarely from anger. That causes problems, always," He handed her back the gadget. "Wait."

Rachel's face had turned an ugly mottled color, partly from fright and partly from being humiliated. Her complexion went brick-red as Joseph grabbed her by the upper arm and began to pull her further down the corridor.

"Take your hands from my arm, peasant," she shouted. Joseph ignored her stolidly, as he did her attempts to halt their movement. "Let go of me!" she shrieked.

Passersby turned at the sound of her voice. Joseph cast a look up and down the corridor. There was little privacy here and none within easy reach. He released her arm and spoke in a firm low voice.

"My lady, you are not yourself. The coldsleep medications have affected your . . . balance. Please, accompany me to the sickbay and—"

"Yes! Back to the infidel doctor, so he can drug me, *poison* me, leave so-wonderful Amos to wallow between the thighs of that *slut*, that *whore*—"

He reached out a hand, a pleading gesture. Rachel struck it away with the contempt she would have dealt a spider.

"Don't touch me, you peasant whore's-get! You make me *sick*. Don't *touch* me!"

She struck again, a hard ringing slap across his face, backhanding him again and again. Joseph's head moved only a little on his thick muscular neck, although a trickle of blood started from his nose and the corner of his mouth. On the fourth slap, he caught her hand. She began to thrash, trying to free herself from that implacable grip. He turned her hand, exposing bleeding cuts where her knuckles had smashed against teeth and bone.

"My lady," he said, cutting through her shrill cries. "Strike me if you will, but you will hurt your hand using it so. Here, take this."

His free right hand made a small flip, and a knife appeared in it: a short leaf-bladed dagger with a plain leather-wrapped hilt, looking sharp enough to cut light. Rachel shrieked and pulled back again, but Joseph's hand made another movement, holding out the hilt. He waited, his eyes on hers. Silence fell broken only by Rachel's rapid, gasping breath. The bystanders were crowding away, their voices sunk to a murmur. Then Rachel pulled loose and ran, blundering into a corner as she scrambled out of sight down a side aisle.

Joseph clicked the knife into its wrist-sheath, his eyes thoughtful. Wiping his face on a kerchief, he returned to the two adolescents.

"I don't think I like her," Joat said laconically.

"I apologize," he said quietly. "Lady Rachel was gently reared. She is suffering from stress and adverse reactions to medication."

"She's bughouse," Joat said bluntly. *He's gone on her,* she thought. *Geh! What a fardlin' waste.* People should reproduce the way bacteria did, splitting cells. That was cleaner. Even ungrudlies like Joe got strange when they had the hots.

Joseph frowned at her. "Negative reaction, as I said."

"Yeah, bughouse, like I said. . . . Okay, forget it. How did you do that thing with the knife?"

"Spring-loaded sheath," Joseph said, obviously relieved to change the subject. He bent back his wrist and showed them.

Joat glanced at Seld, caught his eye. He shook his head in silent agreement. *Adults! They're nuts.*

Channa stumbled into the lounge and fell facefirst into the cushions of the couch. "I *hate* commuting," she said with a theatrical groan.

"Hah!" was Simeon's mocking comment. "Call that commuting? Why, in my grandfathers' day . . ."

"In your grandfathers' day," she said pulling herself into a sitting position, "they probably commuted by ox-cart through subspace and drifts of snow fourteen feet high, and that was in high summer, being dive bombed by stinging insects the size of ore-freighters, just to borrow a cup of sugar from their next-door neighbor three light years away. I," she said, indicating herself with a delicate hand and a raised eyebrow, "am not as hardy. And I hate to commute."

"Not a problem I'm likely to have," he commented.

"No!" she agreed.

"So I should just offer sympathy and understanding," he suggested.

"Absolutely, and I, of course, will accept this with gratitude as the very balm my bruised and battered spirit craves."

"Poor baby."

"Ah," she sighed. "Well! I feel better. What's new on the home front?"

"Apparently Joat's gotten Seld grounded until he turns twenty-one."

"How'd she manage that?"

"Chaundra disciplined him for staying behind and she talked him into exploring the station with her and Joseph."

"Poor Seld. What's Joat's reaction?"

"Oh, it's all her fault, she's got the kiss of death or something—"

"Seld staying behind is her fault?"

"No, no. It's *all* her fault. The minute we decided to adopt her, Bethel was attacked, so that Amos escaped, the pirates chased him and the station is now endangered. You see the logical sequence of events. One of her depressed moods."

Those tended to be temporary but of unpredictable duration.

"I can't deny," she said, fighting a laugh, "that the logic's inescapable when the data is structured in that fashion."

They were still laughing when Amos came in.

"What causes such merriment?" he asked, grinning.

Channa looked at his handsome face, and it seemed to her that for a moment the station stood still.

"Oh," Simeon told him, "the horrors of being twelve."

Amos shuddered. "Indeed," he said, rolling his eyes. "Would that all horrors were both so transient and so amusing in retrospect. I fell in love with the cook. When that was over, I decided I was religiously inspired—and never recovered from *that*."

Channa gave an involuntary snort of laughter, glanced over at him to be sure, then dissolved in whooping gales of laughter.

"At least," she said, wiping her eyes with the back of her hand, "you don't take yourself too seriously."

"I cannot afford to," Amos said, bowing with hand on breast. "Far too many others do. If their prophet cannot laugh at himself now and then, they are lost as well."

"My adolescence was worse," Simeon said. They turned and looked at the pillar. "Imagine my pure, unsullied, young self thrust among hardened asteroid miners."

"It certainly left its mark," Channa said dryly.

"No one escapes without being marked," Amos said wisely.

"And no one gets out alive," they all said together.

"Are you talking about the station?" Joat asked in horror, emerging from her room.

"No, no," Channa said. "Life." *Teenage life, actually, but let's not be specific right now.*

Joat began to rearrange Channa's desk, banging down the implements.

"It's so stupid!" she said, clattering a note organizer screen down.

"What is?" Simeon said, soothingly. Sometimes that tone annoyed Joat so much she forgot what was troubling her. This time she was too focused.

"Seld," she said. "I mean, this could be the last week of our lives and Seld is locked in his room! What a great way to go! Y'know?"

No one answered her. Channa and Amos wouldn't meet her eyes. A look of mild exasperation crossed her features and she tried another tack.

"Look, I *need* him," she said earnestly. "He's really pretty good, in a junior-grudly way, hey? I want to help. Y'know? So, I thought we, Seld and me, could . . ." She stopped, tapped her fingertips together and stared upward, biting her lip. "I thought we could maybe make up some of those signal disrupters I use," she said in a rush.

"You mean the ones that keep me from seeing or hearing you?"

"Yeah," Joat appeared fascinated by her fingernails. "Those."

"Joat, you could do that in the engineering lab. Anyone there will be happy to help you. If we get enough people assembling the elements, we could make quite a few in the time we have left."

"No," Joat said and sat down, looking right at Simeon's column. "I mean, I like the idea of working in the engineering lab, don't get me wrong on that. But the signal disrupter is *my* idea, and I'm not going to just give it away. I know I'm just a kid, but I know you don't do *that*."

"I'm not going to let anybody steal the credit for your invention, Joat. I fully intend to watch out for your interests. I give you my word on that."

"Thank you," she said simply. A silence fell, oddly solemn. After a moment, Joat continued, "Y'know, it's probably not a good idea to have too many of them around. I mean, the more there are, the more likely some jerk will lose one and the pirates will find it and figure it out, then where'll we be?"

"A valid point," Channa said judiciously.

"So," Joat slapped her legs, then rubbed her palms up and down her thighs, "what I thought was, Seld and me could make up enough for you guys," she turned to point at Amos and then at Channa, "and as many of the council reps or team leaders as we can." She looked at the adults' faces, checking their expressions, then turned to Simeon's column. "Whaddaya say?"

"I'd say you're a heartless hard-bargainer, a blackmailer, and a techno-witch. That said, I'll talk to Chaundra, and I think he'll allow Seld to assist on an authorized project. But use more sense next time, Joat. When I adopt you, you're going to have limits, too. Oh, and don't work him too hard. He's just not . . ." Simeon tried to finish the caution diplomatically " . . . the hardy type."

"I know," she said softly, nodding solemnly. "I'll take care of him, I promise." Then she smiled a tight, professional-looking little smile, and rose. "Well, goodnight, everybody."

"Goodnight," they wished her in return.

When the door had closed behind her, Amos looked warmly at Channa, then dropped his eyes. "I, too, am weary, and there is still so much to learn."

"Do what you can," Channa advised, "and play the rest by ear."

"And don't forget," Simeon told him, "all you have to do is ask and I'll try to help. Channa, why don't you give him that contact button now?"

"Yes." From a desk drawer, she took a small box, which she presented to Amos.

"We should probably give one to both Joat and Seld," Simeon suggested.

Channa nodded.

Amos took out the small button curiously.

"That gadget will let me see what you see, hear what you hear, and respond in relative privacy," Simeon told him.

"It is so small," Amos said, examining the tiny device.

"But so effective," Simeon answered through the button.

Startled, Amos dropped it.

"I can see that it could be very useful," he said, laughing as he retrieved it. "Thank you, Simeon."

Channa hesitated. "See you in the morning."

"Yes, altogether too briefly," he replied, giving her a rueful bow.

Channa yawned hugely and looked up at the time display. Evening again already! Almost time for dinner. Hopefully it would be more cheerful than breakfast, which had been subdued in the extreme. "Gods, another day gone? Where *is* everyone?"

"Amos is on his way back home and should be here any second," Simeon said. "Joat is committing illegalities in the engineering lab, chortling madly with Seld, when I can pick them up at all. She'll be back here to eat, or so I believe her plan to be."

Channa stretched. "I need a break." She flopped into an easy chair and said, "Would you put on the 'Hebrides Suite,' please?"

He listened to it for a moment and said, "This is nice."

"One of my favorites. My great-grandmother once told me that this music held the soul of Earth's oceans in its phrases. I've loved it ever since."

"Your great-grandmother was *from* Earth, Channa?"

"No, but she'd been there. Oh, this is my favorite part—a little louder, Sim."

She raised her hand, palm up to show that he should raise the volume again, and again. The door opened on Amos, who stepped backward as though the magnificent swell of sound had washed him out on a wave of music.

Channa laughed at his startled expression and signaled Simeon to lower the sound. "Sorry," she called.

Amos poked his head in cautiously, "Whew!" he said. "Channa, it is dangerous to play music at such volume. Your hearing will be impaired."

She made a face at him. "Don't be a priss, Simeon-Amos. No one ever lost their hearing on classical music."

"Beethoven?" Simeon suggested.

"Hah!" she said. "You men all stick together," and stumbled to the galley for coffee. When she had doctored it with cream liqueur and whipped Jersey floating on the surface, she took an appreciative sip. "Ah! That's good!" *Although when I learned where Jersey originally came from, I nearly lost my lunch,* she added to herself. Simeon had picked up on her tastes quickly.

"Now, *that* is something I feel I've missed out on," Simeon said. "Mmmh?"

"Coffee, food, everyone who sits down to dinner at the Perimeter says, 'Wow! That smells good!' closely followed by 'Mmm! This is delicious!' and I haven't got an analogue for either of those sensations. Smell and taste—you'd think they could have given me one of 'em. Oh, I can *taste* when something's off in the chemo-synthesis plants, and I can *smell* an ion-trail, but it's not the same thing. Sometimes the people at Medic Central are downright inhumanly utilitarian."

"Why don't you put Joat on it?" Channa suggested.

"Put me on what?" Joat asked, arriving at that point.

"I was just saying that I've missed out on tasting coffee, or smelling it even, everyone says it smells so good. I don't even know what that means. I just can't get my mind around the concept. I don't like the feeling that I'm being denied one of life's greatest pleasures. However, the thought of anyone poking about with my neural interfaces is enough to keep the thought merely wistful."

Channa and Amos locked eyes a moment, then flicked away. Not before Simeon had caught the look.

"That's terrible," Joat said sympathetically, "'though, maybe if you gave me your specs . . ."

"Now, sex . . . sex provides a lot of mental pleasure." Simeon continued with relish. "I'd be willing to bet that I get almost as much sexual pleasure out of my own imagination as anyone does actually having it."

Joat made a derisive grimace.

"I'd say in your dreams, Simeon, but that would be redundant," Channa said archly, making her way back to her desk. "What have you got there?" she asked, pointing to the box in Joat's hand.

"Oh, this is something for you guys." Joat opened it to display the two short, gleaming metal rods, perhaps three centimeters long, with crystals at either end. Joat looked at Channa expectantly.

Channa took one out of the box, turning it over. In the center of the rod was a small gap, bridged by a narrow tube which joined its two halves. She touched the crystals experimentally, then looked queryingly at Joat. "It's pretty?" she asked, puzzled at its use.

Joat laughed. "Seld said we should make 'em into jewelry, but I figured we didn't have time to experiment with the effect that might have. I wear mine in a sheath in my boot." She tugged up her pant-leg and pulled down the cuff of her boot to show the top of an identical wand.

"How does this artifact of yours work?" Amos asked her, picking up the other.

"You push the two halves together to make a contact."

Amos did so. There was a click as the two halves came together to form a smooth even surface. He looked at Channa and Joat, then at himself. "Is . . . is it working?"

"Ask him," Joat said, jerking her thumb at Simeon's column.

"Simeon?"

Simeon didn't answer because he hadn't heard the question. He had, however, seen Amos wink out of existence, and he was experiencing some very uncomfortable feelings about that disappearance. Suddenly, he was unsure that he wanted anyone besides Joat to have this ability. Such disappearances definitely gave him the willies.

"Apparently not," Channa said, pleased. She clicked her own rod together and vanished from Simeon's sight and hearing.

Amos leaned close to her. "I can already see much potential for his device." His smiling eyes were warm and full of meaning.

"Seld and me knocked seven of these off today," Joat explained to Simeon. "We'll contrapt more tomorrow, now that we've found the parts we need. What's the matter?" she asked in response to Simeon's groan.

"Sorry, Joat, seven is pretty good really, and there's nothing to say that we can't share these around. Right, Channa? Channa? Ollie-ollie in-free!"

Channa grinned smugly at Amos. "He really can't see us, can he?" Then she pulled gently at the rod.

"How nice of you to drop in," Simeon said in a sour tone. *Damned if I'll let you know how much that bothers me.*

"Sorry," Channa said. *"I know it bothers you,"* she subvocalized. Somehow Sim connected it with being cut off from his sensory input. *Me, now I'm a sensory input?* She turned to Joat. "Um, do you actually have to have it on your person for it to work? Or would it work if, say I had it on the desk beside me?"

"It should keep you disappeared if you stay very close to it. You're not really blanked out. It's more like a local override command to the sensor not to record you, you know? I didn't really measure it very close." Joat gave a self-deprecating twitch of her hands. "I need more theory and stuff, I know."

"Well, I'm impressed, Joat." She clapped her hands together. "Let's celebrate, and send out for dinner." She took the rod out of Amos's hands and unsnapped it.

"You know," Simeon commented as Amos reappeared, "this invention of Joat's could be the biggest boon to burglars since hacking."

Channa froze, then looked over at Joat. The girl managed to look sweet, innocent and furtive at the same moment. It was true. AI-driven surveillance was universal in public places. So were attempts to counteract it. Joat's seemed to work better than most. Of course, once the device was publicized, counter-measures would be initiated. No *wonder* Joat wanted to keep her ace-in-the-hole secret.

Well, of course she steals! Simeon whispered in her ear. *How did you think she survived before you took a hand?*

"Like many swords," Amos agreed, "it is two edged. But, they will be of help, and I shall enjoy testing mine." He smiled at Channa.

Channa looked at Simeon's column. "Just think, we'll be able to keep secrets from you, Sim. How will you stand it?"

Amos tiptoed carefully out of Joat's room. "She never woke," he said in a half-whisper. "I put a blanket over her."

Channa shook her head. Joat's subconscious seemed to know who to trust. This evening was the first time she had noticed the girl sleeping with the limp, irresistible finality of the trusting child. She'd also had a long, hard, if triumphant, day.

"I thought she'd never get enough of your stories about Bethel," she said. *And neither would I.* It didn't have the urban sophistication of Senalgal, but Amos could make his world and his way of life sound . . . *beautiful,* she decided. Of course, he was an eloquent man, and he was describing what he truly loved. He had described what she had always yearned for in a planet-side posting: the hugeness, the variousness, the *aliveness* of a breathing world.

"It was as much for me as for her," Amos said, leaning back on the sofa and raising his face to the ceiling, eyes closed. "I speak, and I see what can never be again."

She put a hand on his. "Bethel will be freed and made beautiful again. The Kolnar only stripped the surface, not the nature of the planet."

"Yes. Yes, I believe—must believe that." His fingers curled around hers; fine long-fingered hands, a little calloused.

From riding horses, she thought. A sport she had only read of before. Simeon had provided holos, and riding looked more dangerous and exciting than piloting mini-shuttles.

"Yet when the enemy are driven off, the wounds . . . and beyond that. We need to change, we *must* change. More than I thought or wished, and I was a rebellious youngster, a radical, a breaker of images, or so they called me." He turned his head to her. "The enormity of the task ahead frightens me, overwhelms me. Yet with help . . ."

Oh, great, she thought. To herself: "Lost prince of beautiful, exotic planet, seeks helpmate/companion/lover to assist in rescue/reconstruction. Requires intelligent, forceful manager with strong sense of duty. Will furnish lifelong love and affection, plus palaces, estates, interesting experiences. Apply Amos ben Sierra Nueva." What was that quotation? Get thee behind me, Satan?

Amos sat quietly beside her and placed Joat's box in her lap. His glance was filled with meaning. Channa opened the box and they each took out a crystal-tipped rod. Then they glanced at Simeon's column with identical scheming smiles and clicked the two parts together.

Amos leaned over. They kissed; she stroked his dark hair and gently cupped the back of his head in her hand.

"It is good to have privacy," he said huskily.

"Yes," she agreed, "it is good." *And it adds spice,* she thought. *Like sneaking out of bounds when you're in school.*

✧   ✧   ✧

Simeon watched Channa's door open and close, though no one appeared to be near it. He suppressed a burst of resentment. He had *told* them he'd turn off the sensors if they requested it. But no, they'd just gone and shut him out without a word . . .

What is the universe coming to? he thought in irritation. *Besides, there's a child present!*

A child who had presented him with a techno-itch he could not scratch. On reflection, he decided the analogy was maddeningly accurate. Try as he might, his attention came looping back to the nagging gaps in his recordings. He was *accustomed* to knowing everything that went on. Joat's earlier white-noise machines and attention-deflectors were minor irritations compared to this newest gadget. Of course, she hadn't had access to the engineering labs before this.

"The child was probably born with a microtool in her hand," he muttered. Now, how *did* the wands function? Joat had, after all, given him a hint. She might be a genius, but Simeon was a shellperson, with all the computer power and experience that implied.

And I'm also constitutionally unable to resist picking up the gauntlet, he thought happily. There were times when the only way to get rid of a temptation was to give in to it. . . .

I can't believe this, he told himself, fifteen minutes later. Equipment made by the best minds in the Central Worlds flummoxed by a preteen! Which confirmed long-held thoughts about the quality of minds attracted to the Central Worlds bureaucracy. Simeon had long thought that it was a private miracle he hadn't come out prosthetized into a camel, since the design teams were committees. Now, *he* must meet this challenge.

Channa arched her back against Amos's weight, her hands caressed the slick, silken skin of his back. He kissed her throat and she sighed happily, ready for—

"Oh, Chaaannaaa, I seee yooou."

"Ack, ckgak!"

Amos raised his head from the crook of her neck to look at her. The mixture of puzzlement and sensuality on his face looked very silly, not to mention slightly nauseated. Simeon laughed.

Oh, this is terrible, Channa thought. Yet it was impossible not to see the moment from Simeon's point of view for a second. She laughed, caught between rage and helpless mirth. Amos bobbed up and down with her laughter. His expression assumed a martyred quality that caused her to lose control completely.

"Channa," he said desperately, rolling off and holding her in his arms. "Channa, my darling—are you all right?"

She struggled to speak, to reassure him that her sanity was intact. "Sim . . . Sim . . . he . . . hehe . . . hehehe," she had to avoid the word *he*. "Sim . . ." she gasped, "my implant . . . he . . . hehe, mmrrmph . . . can see us."

She stopped, panting and watched his look of concern melt. Suddenly she was slightly frightened. This was a man accustomed to redressing insult, and his ego had just received a terribly humiliating one.

"Simeon!" he roared. The door seemed to recoil before his headlong passage, and the cooler wind from the lounge brought goosebumps to her skin.

Amos picked up the first thing his hand encountered, a vase, and threw it against Simeon's column.

"You incest eater!" he bellowed. "*You* filthy pi dog! *Banchut!*"

Channa appeared in her doorway, wrapped in a sheet. *I've never seen a naked, erect man in a fit of rage before,* she thought dazedly. *Oh, I really shouldn't have broken up. Men get so* focused *at that particular moment!*

"How could you do something so vile! Have you no decency?" Amos was demanding.

"What the hell is goin' on?" Joat asked, and stopped, poleaxed at the sight of a naked and raging Amos.

Amos dived for the sheet Channa was wearing and they tussled for it. He settled for dragging a small corner of it over his hips.

He drew himself up. "Go back to bed, Joat, this does not concern you." The pure mad anger had drained out of his voice. Bethel had a nudity taboo, and he was suddenly and acutely conscious of being naked before a twelve-year-old girl.

"Don't take it out on her, Simeon-Amos, I'm the one you're mad at," Simeon said.

Amos spun round, losing his grip on the sheet. "I am unlikely to forget that!" he said between clenched teeth.

"Nice buns," Joat murmured in abstract appreciation.

Channa and Amos turned to stare at her.

"Hey, you guys," she said blushing. "I'm young! I'm not dead."

"What kind of people are you?" Amos murmured in shock. "Your children leer, your shellpeople are voyeurs . . ." His gaze snapped to Channa. "And you, what sort of pervert are you?"

"Me? Oh, now wait just one minute, Simeon-Amos, I'm a victim here, too."

"I do not think so. *You* find this amusing, but I do not!" Turning his back on them all, he strode to his quarters in a fury, the door calmly swishing shut behind him.

"Whoa!" Joat said enthusiastically. "What's a voyeur?"

Channa's mouth firmed grimly. "A voyeur, Joat, is a nasty-minded son of a bitch who keeps poking his nose into private matters."

"Ah. Sorta like Dorgan the Organ from Child Welfare."

Ouch, Simeon winced.

Channa nodded, with crisp malice. "I promise I'll explain tomorrow, but right now I have to talk to Simeon."

"Oboyoboy," Joat said. "Are *you* ever in the deep pucky, Simeon." She slapped his column on the way back to her room. "Naughty, naughty!"

Channa hiked up the sheet and sat herself down in one of the lounge chairs. She clasped her hands in her lap, saying nothing, chewing her lower lip.

"Um," Simeon said. "He's still furious. He's throwing things around in there."

"Stop spying on him!" Channa said irritably.

"I don't have to spy. Just listen."

It was true, even through the door the sound of objects hitting walls could be heard. Then an ominous silence. After a minute, a fully dressed Amos emerged and left the quarters without a backward glance or a further word. Channa rose quickly and took a step in his direction.

"Hey! You can't follow him like that! Besides, where's he gonna go?"

"Well . . . I suppose this show of your vigilance was our own fault," Channa said grimly. "We would challenge you." She smiled, a wintry expression. "I guess you showed us."

Simeon gave a soft groan. "I'd rather end the evening on a positive note. I now know that I can contact you even when their sensors can't find you."

"Yes, there is that application of tonight's experiment," she said tiredly. "I'll be sure to point that out to Simeon-Amos when next I see him. *If* I see him."

"I'm sorry, Channa," Simeon said contritely after an awkward pause. "I was out of line."

"Yes, you were. For that particular activity, an invitation is required."

"And I know that it's difficult for you folks when coitus is interrupted."

She raised a brow. "Are you asking for information?"

"Um, nooo," he said hopefully.

"You *are* a swine, Simeon, an utter filthy pig! If you want to know, look it up, in a medical text, skip the pornography." And then she gave a despairing laugh. "Oh, God, he'll never speak to me again. Where is he?"

"He's still on the move. At a guess, he's going to Joseph's. Best thing for him really, a little male bonding. Maybe they'll get drunk together and complain about how badly the women in their lives treat them."

"*This* woman in his life was treating him just fine until you showed up!"

"Is it my fault he's so parochial?"

"Parochial!" Channa exclaimed. "Simeon, wrong use of that word. A man, any man who is one, will take offense at being spied on while making love. So now you've called him a name, it's all his fault, and none of your own, is that it?"

"No," he said calmly, "I still accept responsibility for what I did. Let's not fight about Simeon-Amos, Channa."

She leaned her head against the back of the chair, "No, let's not fight about Simeon-Amos. We don't have time." She looked at his column from the corner of her eye. "It occurs to me that you were defending him not so long ago."

"Maybe I was wrong."

"No, you weren't. You know it, too. We are putting a lot of pressure on him when he'd arrived already under a crushing weight. He's lost everything, Sim, a whole world, family, friends. He blames himself for bringing the pirates to our door. Now he's working himself into the ground to save us from them. We should try very hard not to subject him to these little power games we play."

"Ah . . . sure."

"Because, Simeon, if you can't, you're not the person I thought you were. And if you aren't, I don't want to have anything to do with you once this is over."

"Channa!"

"Think about it, Simeon. You're sixty-eight years old. *Grow up!*"

✧   ✧   ✧

Amos returned to the lounge for work the following morning, pale, distant, and polite. Simeon found an opportunity to apologize and convinced the Bethelite of his sincerity, vowing never to do such a thing again. Amos accepted the apology with the same detached courtesy that he received Channa's explanation, then closed himself firmly in his room.

Dinner conversation that evening was so stilted that even Joat noticed. It was still early when Channa was left sitting alone next to the titanium pillar.

"Simeon, come talk to me?"

"Ah, she asks now instead of demanding."

"Your charm has humbled me," she said with a grin. "Besides, I'm bored and really crave your company."

"You sure it's my company you crave?"

"Heh. Last night I was horny! Tonight I'm bored. Different things, fella."

"I think that if I were you, I'd rather be horny."

"Then you'd be an idiot," she said scornfully.

"But I wouldn't be bored."

She was silent a while. "Simeon, I'm scared. We may die."

"Yeah," he replied. "I'm scared, too, Happy. Real scared. We don't have much time left." Another pause, and he added more brightly, "That was a hint."

"Nah!" she said, shaking her head. "The moment came, was interrupted, and went. Amos needs someone kinder than a ball-buster like me."

"Channa!" Simeon exclaimed, laughing and appalled. "I wouldn't call you a ball-buster."

"You probably have."

"But that was before I knew you," he admitted. "Rachel is a ball-buster. You're just a bit prickly."

"Prickly?"

"Yeah,"

"Maybe I am horny," she said thoughtfully. "Lordy, all the male generative organs that are creeping into this conversation. But you know I'm right. We have to maintain a certain distance to carry this thing off . . . Simeon, *say something* to make me feel better."

"Um, how about . . .

"Stern daughter of the Voice of God!
O Duty! if that name thou love . . .
When empty terrors overawe;
From vain temptations dost set free . . ."

"Hey!"

"No huh? Wrong mood?"

"You might say that," she answered between clenched teeth. "Right now, the stern voice of duty is overrepresented in my thoughts."

"True. Hmm. Different mood. Okay, how about:

"Sound sleep by night; study and ease
Together mixed; sweet recreation;
And innocence, which most does please
With meditation."

"Sarcasm ill becomes you, Sim. Don't you *want* to help?"

"Sorry, one more try,

"I am the lion, and his lair!
I am the fear that frightens me!
I am the desert of despair!
And the night of agony!
Night or day, whate'er befall,
I must walk that desert land,
Until I dare my fear and call
The lion out to lick my hand."

She was silent for a long time. He could tell by her breathing that she was not angry, and he waited for her to think it through. At last she sighed.

"You know me pretty well on short acquaintance, Sim."

"Channa, he won't refuse you. He needs you as much as you need him right now. I screwed the pooch! I admit it. My only excuse—" she gave him a tired smile "—is that it's an area of life I'm just not equipped to understand very well. Why should you both be miserable alone, when you could be much happier together?"

"After last night? And don't forget, I've already turned him down once, Simeon. He's got one free refusal coming to him."

"What is this? A competitive sport? There are scores and free throws and penalties?"

She laughed. "Sometimes. Depends on who you play with."

"Take up military history, Channa. It's a lot easier on the psyche."

She sighed again. "Not when you're about to *become* military history."

"Oh for Christ's sake, Happy, get your butt off the couch and go knock on his door! You know you want to. C'mon, be honest."

"I'm going to get changed, first, at least," she said glumly, striding into her room. "And don't call me Happy," she called over her shoulder.

Why should I accommodate you on that, Channa, when I've noticed that, whenever I call you "Happy," you do what I tell you. I'm not giving up an advantage like that.

"Ready?" he called.

"What do you think?"

He opened a sensor inside her room. She now had on a simple black skinsuit, but he thought it showed her off to advantage.

"You'll do."

Channa walked glumly to the door. "Here I am, courting rejection. You'd think I learned about *that* back when I was Joat's age."

The door slid aside to reveal Amos on her threshold, his hand raised to knock. They exchanged looks. After a moment, they reached out to one another, and touched. Amos stepped into the room and the door slid firmly closed.

They melted into an embrace that marked the first step in a climb to the heights of passion.

Simeon echoed the thought off the computer. When it came back, it had a fruity announcer's voice. He keyed on Ravel's "Bolero," an insinuating thread of sound that swelled and grew in intensity and volume until its passionate, vibrant climax. On the council table, he projected scenes: palm trees crashed in the wind and waves rolled in to welcoming shores, trains roared into tunnels and out again, wild beasts roared in the forests and people worked wet clay into messy phallic symbols on spinning potters' wheels.

"Perfect," he decided, saving the program to hard storage. It wouldn't be tactful to show it anytime soon, but someday they would be a lot older and more mellow. Providing, of course, they survived the next weeks. Shellpeople had a lot of time to fill in. He listened to the music as it billowed and soared and swooned.

Bless you my children, he thought in the direction of Amos and Channa. *And now I will check in again with the auxiliary bridge.* Soon to be the fake/real command center for SSS-900-C's encounter with the Kolnari.

CHAPTER SIXTEEN

"HEY, SIMEON," the Traffic Control watch said.

"Yeah, Juke?"

"I think I've got something here."

Simeon shunted much of his attention to the sensors. This was part of the reason no computer could ever replace a colloidal brain; apart from the inherent lack of self-consciousness, of course. Computers were wonderful at collecting and collating data, but they could never really *interpret* it the way a human could.

And there's no interface like that between a shellperson and his extensions, Simeon thought smugly.

"Yeah, that *is* something," he said aloud. "But what?"

"No powerplant neutrino signatures," Juke Cielpied said. He was a fresh-faced young man with a thatch of blond hair. "But the mass is there, that's for—*Holy shithouse!*"

Suddenly the sleepy torpor of Communications and Navigation was a blur of activity. "Missile signatures, multiple, homing!"

Simeon made an incoherent prayer. This was *it.* They might have no more than thirty seconds to live.

"Starting mayday call," he said, "jammed! Engines pulsing."

"Oh, boy, I'm getting powerplant signatures *now*," Juke said. "They just kicked online and then steadied. Four. Big mothers. Way overpowered for the masses, even more than a tug."

"Warship engines," Simeon said grimly.

The missiles were streaking in from all sides. He deployed the anti-meteor laser. Seconds later it slagged and exploded in a spectacular burst of vaporized synthetic and metal.

"Neutral-particle beam," Simeon said. "Damage report follows." Thank The Powers That Be that it hadn't hit an inhabited area, at least. "Red alert. All personnel to emergency stations."

This time there would be no fooling around. It was for real.

Ooops.

Simeon activated his sensors in the lounge and listened, hoping that things hadn't gotten too far in the very few moments that had passed since he'd politely turned them off. Unfortunately, judging by the soft sounds emerging from Channa's quarters, that was a vain hope.

She'll never believe I didn't plan this, he thought, and wavered. *It's an hour before they'll be here.* His sensors showed the ships boosting at a very respectable normal-space acceleration. *But if I don't tell her, I'm going to be in the same bad odor, just a different situation.* A more important situation. *Okay, here goes everything.* He knocked.

Channa froze and Amos slowed down. "I'm going to kill him," she said.

Amos chuckled and kissed her; his hips moved and she gasped. "Why don't you ask what he wants first," he advised.

"WHAT IS IT NOW?"

"Uh, the enemy's just come into sensor range, four heavily armed ships, E.T.A. forty-one minutes. Sorry, guys, you needed to know!"

Channa clasped Amos to her with arms and legs. "That's . . . enough time," she gasped. "And if you . . . stop I'm going to *kill* you."

The hull of the station toned like a giant bell as the sprayshot slammed into the subspace antennae. Automatic alarms made their banshee wail. Dutifully waiting with his sensors turned down, Simeon might have mistaken Channa's high shriek, under other circumstances, for a cry of alarm.

"Brief us," she called a few moments later.

Quite brief, Simeon thought, but did not say. He began, using a focused beam to cut through the noise of a very quick shower.

The corridors had been full of rushing people. Now their floatdisks were speeding down empty hallways, banking at the corners in emergency-override maneuvers as the population suited up and huddled in their shelter-sectors. The silence held no calm, only a tension so great that Channa expected sparks to pop from her hair.

She gripped the handhold and looked aside at Amos. His face was set and remote, a carven image framed by the fluttering black curls of his hair.

"I'm sorry," Simeon said to Channa, whispering through her implants for the tenth time. "I wish this hadn't happened."

"Oh, give it a rest, Simeon. I'm hardly going to blame you because the rest of the universe won't organize itself for my convenience."

"Sure! Sorry!"

She grinned. "And for future reference, buddy, I much prefer 'Carmina Burana' to alarm klaxons as background music."

The enemy warships were in plain sight now. Simeon magnified, analyzed, and projected the results on the big screen in the secondary control chamber. The room was the usual shape, a C with a large virtual-screen at the flat section and a bank of positions and consoles. There had been a full crew here for the past few days, to eliminate the slightly fusty air of an unused facility. Now the circulators were working overtime to carry off the ketones of tension-sweat, and there were very convincing coffee-stains and rings by most of the recliner seats.

"That is the enemy," Amos said somberly.

The ships were very different from the usual stubby egg shape: elongated darts, with triangular vanes swelling along most of their lengths, like flight-feathers on an arrow. Designs scrawled across their sides in the spike-and-curve script.

"Yup, Kolnari naval architecture," Simeon said. He set the computer on the names. "Phonetically: *Shuk, Kelyug, Dhriga, Rumal.*"

"Why the odd design?" Patsy said, leaning forward. "Not your most efficient layout."

"It is optimized for rapid atmosphere transit," Simeon said grimly. "Courier Service ships are much like that. I think the Kolnari have different maneuvers in mind for their vessels. For example, swooping down to sack a town planet-side. Note the design's not uniform. They probably build, or rebuild captured hulls, as they get the chance. But it's still a class-type. Roughly equivalent to a Navy frigate, I'd say. Bigger hull, though; they must carry a humongous great crew. A hundred, at least." He studied the armament and whistled. "And, with all those weapons mountings, they must sleep in shifts."

"I'm glad you've finally gotten a chance to indulge your hobby," Channa said tightly.

"I'm not," Simeon said. *Odd,* he thought. *That's true.*

"Closing," Juke said, licking his lips. "Two of them are orbiting the station around our notional equator. The other two are closing at the poles. Closing fast. *Hell!*"

Exterior screens dampened to cut the energy flux of sudden deceleration. Alarms cheeped and burbled as energetic particles sleeted into the exterior shielding fields.

A voice roared through the hull; an induction field, vibrating the substance of the station itself. The words were blurred by the coarseness of the medium and by a thick accent. It sounded like the shouting of an angry god.

"*SCUMVERMIN SUBMIT!*" Then a feedback squeal tore at their eardrums as the broadcaster adjusted. "*SLAVE TO THE SEED OF HIGH-CLAN KOLNAR ARE YOU, PERSON AND NONPERSON THING OUR POSSESSION. CEASE EXTERIOR SCAN AT ONCE!*"

"What—" somebody began.

Then the lights faded for a second. Everyone gasped as pressure fluctuated, and the temperature rose perceptibly. On the heels of the pressure wave came a rising wave of vibration through the hull. Banks of lights flashed from amber to red.

"Hit! We have been hit!" Patsy was shouting from her environmental systems console. "Loss of pressure, N-7 through 11!"

Simeon's hands itched, metaphorically. He had to step back and let the infuriatingly slow responses of softshells handle *his* station, his body. There was one thing he could do. He cut all the active exterior sensors immediately. Except, of course, for the one that had just been converted to vapor along with a section of hull.

"Passive scanners only," Juke said. "Th . . . that was a high-energy particle beam."

"Chaundra here." The doctor's voice had the slightly flat tone of a vacuum suit pickup. "Rescue squads in place. The people here were all suited up. No fatalities so far. There will be radiation problems." From secondary gamma sleeting, where the beam had struck matter.

Channa acknowledged his report. Injuries could have been much higher. Would have been if the warship had come on them with no notice whatever. A screen activated, showing suited forms moving down an interior corridor, but it had the depthless bright look of light in vacuum, no blur at the edges of the shadow.

The huge voice struck again. "*OBEY. GENTLE WARNINGS NONE*

MORE WILL BE FOREVER. STAND BY TO BE TAKEN INTO THE
FIST OF HIGH-CLAN KOLNAR, SCUMVERMIN."

"Eat shit and die, you fardling maniacs," Channa muttered. Amos
cast her a quick look, then nodded and gave a thumbs-up gesture.

"Still closing," Juke whispered. The infrared and other passive
receptors were still working. "Closing on the docking tubes, but
inboard of the docking rings."

"*Quick,*" Simeon said to Channa, like thought in her inner ear. "*Get
anyone there away from the tubes.*"

"All personnel in north and south polar docking tubes, into the
core! Move!" Channa barked. Then, to privately to Simeon: "Why?"

"They're going to force-dock. I've heard of it."

The *Dreadful Bride* floated close to the docking tube. So close, that
of a sudden she seemed small to Belazir, waiting impatiently in the
off-corridor to the boarding tube, with his personal guard around
him. He had an exterior feed, one of the multiple tiny screens around
the lower rim of the helmet's interior. It took long training to assimilate the information without being distracted. His ship seemed like
a tiny fleck of brightness next to the huge bulk of the target.

"Now," he said. *But a knife is smaller than a man, too,* he thought
with hammering glee.

Serig stepped forward and slapped an armored palm on the bulkhead beside the combat lock. The assault party filled the antechamber.
Decking shuddered beneath their feet. From his helmet's exterior view,
Belazir could see the accordion-folds of the boarding tube extending their armored length. Grapnels and cutting-beams protruded from
the forward edge, like the teeth of a hungry monster. A faint *clung*
went through the ship as the tube struck. Then a savage roar of white
noise as the weapons punched an oval hole through hull, conduits
and inner surface, into the enemy vessel, force-sealing it with a sudden
crude weld.

Air whistled past them from the higher pressure of the *Bride* into
the station.

"Go!" shouted Serig. The first team leapt forward, pushing a floating, armored powergun platform before them. "Go, go, go!"

Serig followed them. Belazir bit down on his tongue, suppressing
the impulse to take immediate command. Instead, he froze the joints
of his armor and commanded the faceplate to show Serig's inputs,
seeing what he would see.

✧   ✧   ✧

"Oh, smooth, very smooth," Simeon said in some dismay. Channa made an enquiring sound into the clenched silence of the control room.

"To begin with, they're wearing heavy field armor," he replied, calling up interior shots.

The Kolnari were in powered hardsuits. At once more massive and sleeker than the Central Worlds naval equivalent, the suits were a soft matte black, and moved with the jerky quickness of servo-powered systems. In a closed environment they looked more elephantine than they had in Amos' shots from Bethel, more unstoppable. The deck thundered under their weight, though the pirates moved with fluid precision and the snapping quickness of long practice. Teams of three or more secured corridor junctions; techs moved behind them, tying down control of one facility after another.

"And look at the way they're moving," Simeon went on dolefully. "Look." He brought up a schematic of the station. "Power, atmosphere, communications. They're coming here, too. They've done this before." *And those plasma guns they're carrying like rifles are crew-served weapons in the Navy,* he added to himself.

"Yes," Channa said, "that's how it looks to me. They've done this before. Only where?" *And did that station die? Do I remember ever hearing of a dead station?* She watched in a morbid fascination as the units moved inward, following the direction of the conduits. "Of course, they're heading here now."

"No resistance," Serig reported.

Either they are wise cowards, or simply wise, Belazir thought. "Secure the control center! Pol?"

A miniature of the scarred face of the *Shark's* commander came up on one helmet screen.

"My people are meeting no resistance," she said. "All targets occupied on schedule. We have them in a nutcracker fist."

"Good, clan-kin Captain," he said. He trusted Pol more than most. She had no ambition to climb beyond her present position. Any equal of his own rank and age was a dangerous rival—rival by definition, and dangerous if they had survived to climb so high. "Now we will crush their stones. Serig! Watch and wait when you've secured their command center, I'll join you there."

"I hear and obey, lord," Serig said, slamming through another door with his assault team.

Serig's pickups showed a roomful of suited figures. Plain vacuum suits, some small enough to hold children, and the chamber looked to be an emergency shelter, reinforced and near the core of the station. The people moved away from the armored violence of the Kolnari like grass rippling under wind. To Serig, their cringing was a profoundly satisfying sight.

"Faugh!" he said in sharp disgust. "There are *non-humans* here! Shall I open fire, lord?"

"No, Serig," Belazir said patiently. Of course, nonhuman sentients were worse than scumvermin. They bore none of the Divine Seed that made Kolnar. "We're going to destroy this place and everything in it, Serig. Or had you forgotten? In the meantime, we need it functional."

"I abase myself before you, Great Lord," Serig said formally—another one-word expression in their tongue. "Proceeding with plan."

"Ooof," Channa said.

They were all lying with their feces in the fortunately soft decking with their hands tied behind their backs. The Kolnari had not moved or spoken since they ordered the others down on the floor, except when one of the stationers so much as twitched—in which case they prodded them with the muzzle of a plasma rifle, hard, as one had just done to Channa. None of them spoke Standard, she thought, except perhaps the leader with the gold slashes on his arm. He had the same thick accent as the amplified voice which had hailed the station.

The iron tramp of powered-armor boots sounded in the corridor outside. Another squad of Kolnari entered. All she could see was feet and a glimpse of something heavy carried in by the last two. A voice spoke in the invader's incongruously musical, lilting tongue, and the feet with the load put something over the main communications console. There was a *chung* and then a minute of high-pitched buzzing, followed by silence.

More clanks and clicking sounds. *They're getting out of their armor,* she thought, watching a pair of bare feet step to the deck.

"You may kneel," a voice said in Standard, much less accented than the first. Either an interpreter, or the big boss; from the authority in the tones, the latter. "Let those who once led here, identify themselves."

"*Obey!*" screamed the other voice, the first one, and a foot sank into her side.

Channa grunted and came to her knees, sinking back on her heels. Then she raised her eyes and gasped.

The pirate chieftain was the most beautiful human being she had ever seen. 190 centimeters, but so perfectly proportioned that he looked shorter. His skin was *black*—not the dark-brown usually miscalled as such, but an actual gunmetal black; tightly stretched over long, swelling muscles, and he stood and moved as lightly as a racehorse. Much of this was visible, because what the pirates wore under their armor turned out to be a pair of tight briefs the same color as their skins, and an equipment belt. The chieftain's face had the same inhuman exotic perfection as his body: high cheekbones, slightly aquiline nose, full lips, slanted yellow eyes, and the long mane of white-blond hair was caught at the back with a clip of silver and iridescent feathers.

Channa blinked, shook her head, and forced herself to look at the others. Apart from a pair still in power armor, the rest looked eerily similar. Two of those were women, with the same features and long lean bodies. Even their breasts looked as if they were carved out of ebony . . . and the expressions differed, of course. The pirate beside the chief was paring his nails with a small sharp knife. He looked at her and smiled. Channa glanced down again.

Oh, great, Simeon thought, noting the reaction from the others as well. *We've been boarded by the Ultimately Intimidating Elves from Hell. Ow!* That *hurt.* Something tugged at him, calling.

Behind Channa, one of the armored troopers touched his belt. The unoccupied suits turned and marched like a line of lockstep golems to stand themselves along the walls.

Ow! Pain-signals flooded in from the computer extensions of Simeon's mind. Emergency overrides. He turned his attention inwards.

"*Simeon?*" Channa subvocalized. There was no reply. "*Simeon!*" Silence.

"I am the Lord Captain Belazir t'Marid Kolaren," the pirate chief said softly. "Master here now, by right of conquest. I hold your lives in my fist, to spare or crush as I will. Who led here before we came?"

CHAPTER SEVENTEEN

helpbosshelpbossowowow OW!

Simeon had never told anyone about the AI system. Well, nobody but Tell Radon. He was interfaced with the computers directly, of course; he could "remember" anything in the banks and use their capacities the way he could those of his own human brain. The AI program was something else again. It was as sophisticated as anything this side of Central. He and Tell had spent many a happy hour tweaking it further. Simeon *needed* the best. There were limits to how many tasks even a shellperson could do simultaneously, and many were far too routine for continual supervision. An ordinary human had the hindbrain for running heart, lungs, and other physical basics, a consciousness for thought, and a subconscious for monitoring and mental housecleaning. Simeon had the AI.

help! boss!

Of course, it was impossible to actually *visualize* what was going on in the AI system, any more than you could visualize every neuron firing in your brain. Simeon had chosen to make it something of a playground, with something he had always wanted.

"Here, boy!" Simeon called.

He was standing—he had a softshell body in the virtual world of the AI—on a grassy plain, cut up into pathways by tall hedges with gaps. The sensations were full-tactile; only smell and taste were missing. This part of the landscape was memory-scan and basic access-control programming, all analogued to the physical. Both sense

244

and response, automatically translated into algorithms by a subprogram.

"Here boy!" He whistled sharply. "I'm here, boy!"

A dog bounded into view around a corner. It was the dog of his dreams, big and shaggy-red, with floppy ears and a cold wet nose. It was also the SSS-900-C's primary artificial intelligence program.

Now it was surrounded by a swarm of wasps, huge malevolent things with wingspans a meter across. Their beaks were hollow, and out of them wormed long pink tongues, lashing and rasping with serrated teeth set along their sides. A dozen bleeding wounds marked the dog's sides. One of the wasps clung to its head, with the tongue pulsing out and into the animal's ear.

boss! help!

The dog's barking voice was weakening. Simeon stepped forward, and the ground shook with his anger. Beneath it was fear. The pirates had clamped something to the communications console and now he knew what it was. A specialized battle computer, stocked with worm and subversion programs. If it took over his hardware, he was doomed.

He turned the Jets cap backward on his head and gestured. A glowing green enchanted bat appeared in one hand, a hand that was suddenly gauntleted with steel, part of the armor that covered him. With the other steel glove he grasped the wasp on the dog's head and crushed it, pulling. The long tongue flailed as he pulled it out of the brain, jerking and cutting bone with a tooth-grating sound.

On my own, then, Channa thought. "I am Station Chief Channa Hap," she said. "This is my colleague, Simeon-Amos."

The Kolnari commander remained motionless, like a statue in oiled ebony. His companion reached down and jerked her to her feet by the front of her coverall. Fingers like steel rods slammed into shoulder, ribcage, hip. Pain flowered through her in a wave that snapped her teeth shut with a grinding clack and left her limply boneless when he released her to sprawl facedown on the decking.

For minutes she was too limp to do more than sprawl. Amos had surged halfway to his feet. The Kolnari who had struck Channa turned and gave him a casual buffet across the side of the head: the sound was like a wet board hitting concrete. Amos flew backwards two meters and ploughed into the deck at an awkward angle. One of the others hooked him back to Channa's side with a foot. He lay with glazed eyes, breathing in a harsh rasp that sent bubbles of blood oozing from nose and mouth. She forced down an overwhelming impulse to rush to him, but their lives depended on her wits.

"Scumvermin address the Divine Seed of Kolnar as 'Great Lord,'" the second-in-command said. He put a foot on Channa's neck and ground her face into the coarse fabric that covered the floor. "When the Lord Captain Belazir addresses them, they respond with 'Master and God.'"

Eat shit and die, Master and God, Channa thought.

"Master and God," she managed to choke out, the words muffled by the synthetic fabric.

Belazir nodded benignly, a slight smile on his carven lips. "Let her rise to her knees once more. Ignorance pardons nothing but explains much. Do you understand?" he said to Channa.

"I understand perfectly, Master and God," she said to the Kolnari leader. "You're the Good Pirate and he's the Bad Pirate, eh?"

Belazir frowned a moment, then threw back his head and laughed in delight as he caught the reference.

"No, no," he said, restraining his companion with a slight gesture. The feral aggression in the other man's face was unchecked, but he sank back obediently. "You do not understand my good Serig's role at all." He turned to the other prone figures. "Up on your knees, scumvermin. Announce your functions."

The lights flickered. Belazir looked up sharply. One of the Kolnari spoke from beside the mechanism damped to the communications terminal.

Channa felt her stomach clamp with a fear older and more visceral than the pirates. Something was interfering with basic station functions.

The dog lay panting, healing visibly but more slowly than it should. The wasps lay crushed or buzzing malevolently at a distance. Simeon's great bronze shield prevented their approach. On its surface were concentric rings of figures. Great heros: Armstrong, da Luis, Helva. At last the dog crawled over and licked Simeon's ankles, whimpering.

good better make'emgoaway(!) boss

Simeon checked the dog, who had sustained no permanent damage, although there was some memory loss.

"Get up," he said. "Run."

run!

"Change it as you go," Simeon said. "Game." He added specifications.

game!

The hedges melted and shifted as the dog ran, long ears flopping in the mild afternoon sun. A new sound came from around a long corridor in the memory-maze. A long raw *raaaaaaaaaaaaaaaa* sound, like—what was that ancient holo? Like a chain saw! Then the beast that made the noise surged around the corner.

Wow, Simeon thought. *Worm program, indeed.*

The end of the creature stretched off into the distance, a grayish-pink tentacle covered in rough-edged scales. It was two meters thick, an endless segmented arm of tough fibrous muscle, dripping acid mucous. Where it passed, the bare ground smoked. Each drop of slime turned the dust into a pulsing globule the size of a fist, like a wet cyst. When these popped, a long-tongued wasp crawled out, flexed its wings, and took to the air to join the buzzing cloud around the worm. The head of the thing reared up suddenly, sprang open like a fleshy blossom. Twenty looping pseudopods whirled around it, each one tipped with a lidless eye. At their meeting was a series of circular mouths, one within the other, each ringed with pyramid-shaped teeth of urine-colored diamond. The teeth spun and clenched and gritted over each others' adamantine surfaces in a continuous blurred roar of hostile sound.

"By their programs shall ye know them," Simeon intoned, suddenly wishing that he had not made the construct he inhabited in this virtual reality quite so vividly lifelike. He could definitely do without the dry mouth, pounding heart, and sinking stomach right now, for example. He could change the setting, but that would deprive him of one more slender advantage: his familiarity with it. So long as the matrix remained, the intruder had to fight on his terms.

"These people are *not* going to garner many SUM's," he said resolutely, and stepped forward, raising his shield. Central awarded Social Utility Marks to a number of unlikely people, but this would really be stretching the bounds of possible recipients.

"Come on, you bastard!" he shouted aggressively. "*Nobody* hurts my dog!"

The worm program struck. Simeon groaned, stamped his feet into the ground, and braced his shoulder against the shield. Data/fangs gnawed at it, recoiling with a sound like frying bacon amid choking clouds of green vapor. His bat flailed, knocking aside eye-tentacles and tongue-wasps. For a long subjective time there was only batter and strike, leap and wiggle and dodge. The oozing serrated mouth loomed in constant menace. *It wants to swallow my pattern whole and assimilate it in one gulp!* Tongue-worms flicked alarmingly around his head. *They would subvert the Master Control Programs with their probes.* He continued to flail the wasps out of the air, stamped them underfoot, swung the bat, and an eye exploded in a shower of black syrup like a giant overripe fig. Finally, the worm recoiled for a moment, and Simeon whirled aside and fled, dodging and jinking through the maze.

Got to keep it off-balance, confused, he thought, listening to its triumphant screeching hard on his heels. Every muscle in his "body" already felt bruised. But it was more satisfying that way, too. Knowing you'd disorganized a section of code wasn't nearly as much fun as seeing blood—or ichor, in this case—fly and feeling flesh pulp under a blow. The howl sounded again, closer.

"Talk about your slash-and-burn data collection," he gasped in time with the pounding of his stride. What sort of maniacs would let something like this loose inside an information system? It had to be destroying as much as it gathered.

Got to make it think it's won, eventually. Isolate it in the outer subsystems of the computers, keeping the ultimate control-keys behind barriers the worm thought were the edge of the entire system. Otherwise, it would infest the whole system, like maggots in rotting meat. Including his own mind, unless he committed suicide by severing all connections between his organic brain and the data system.

That was an unfortunate image. He flashed back to the refugee ship and the dead Bethelites, their bodies moving with burrowing life.

I will *pull the plug first,* he thought grimly. Theoretically, it was impossible to self-destruct the station. In practice, he probably could. *Win or die.*

"*Raaaaaaaaaaaaaaaaaaaa!*" the worm screeched.

"As Channa would say, eat shit and die." Simeon panted the words out as he turned a corner and took a stance again. Thorns and leaves flew into the air as the data-worm tried to smash directly through to him. Then there was a huge *splat* sound and a wailing cry of pain as it ploughed into the stone core of the hedge. That persuaded it to come around the corner. It seemed larger; frothy pink blood streamed around the working, palping mouths. Some of the teeth had shattered on stone, but they regenerated as he watched. The worm's approach made the ground shake. Behind him, he could hear the wuffle and growl of the AI, setting new barriers and deceptions.

"Step right up, lay right down!" Simeon bellowed. *Don't worry about the others. This is going to take all your attention for a while.*

"Raaaaaaaaaaaaaa!"

This time the gravity bounced them about as the lights flickered. Belazir turned to the technicians with a well-controlled snarl of impatience.

"What now?"

"Great Lord, there is unexpected resistance. We thought the worm was successfully penetrating the Master Control programs, but they wiggled free. We are making progress, but the AI is exceptionally agile—the parallel—"

Belazir cut them off with a gesture. "I am interested in results, not jargon-laden excuses. Grasp the core in your fist, and quickly."

He turned back to his prisoners. *What naked faces they have,* he thought. In a new conquest, it was often so. Those who survived long learned better, but it could be entertaining.

Reports of the station's assets and supplies were flooding in.

Better than I expected, he thought exultantly. *Far better. Unimaginably rich!* This facility could build *dreadnoughts,* given a little time and the plans which were available in the Clan's computers.

The High Clan's greatest weakness was the lack of large purpose-built warships. They could turn out frigates, more or less, but for larger craft they could only modify captures. No cobbled-together merchanter could rival the performance of real battlecraft. A warship was more than a ship with weapons and defense-systems: it was a single organism, almost living in itself. *Must we abandon the shipyard?* The frustration was as agonizing as the satisfaction of taking the station was euphoric, with its destruction as a second orgasmic "hit." On the other hand, possession of such equipment would cut generations from the great plan, the spreading of the Divine Seed of Kolnar and the power of the Clan.

Even worse was the humiliation the Clan had suffered for too long. The human galaxy *teemed* with such prizes, yet the Clan fleet must skulk about the outworlds, gnawing discarded scraps: border worlds, miserable settlements of poverty-stricken exile, like Bethel. Skulk like

jackals, even as they had been driven from their lands and possessions on their ancient homeworld. Gnawing poor bones, while feasts
like this lay spread before them. Intolerable! It was not to be borne!

His pleasure dissolved. "You have maintained physical separation?"
he asked, his irritation at this check palpable.

The technician ducked his head. "Of course, Great Lord. No data
enters our machines from this system save by hedron. All such
hedrons are first analyzed to the last byte of information. Our
duplicate backups are kept powered down and physically severed while
any captured data is running."

Belazir nodded. "Continue," he said, satisfied that elementary
precautions were being taken. *You will suffer, you will suffer, ahhhh,
how you will suffer,* he thought, barring mental teeth at the universe
that stood between the Clan and its apotheosis. *All* of them would
writhe in the fist, one day. "You have a preliminary report?"

"Affirmative, Great Lord," the technician said.

*Why can technicians never use a simple word where their accursed
slang can be stretched to fit?* Belazir wondered as he heard the technician out.

"We captured the message logs in the first penetration, before the
AI reacted. No nonroutine messages to Central, except the arrival and
spontaneous destruction of a large, mysterious ship. Little evidence
was left. Central said they would search their files."

With a white-toothed grin, Belazir condescended to give a nod in
reply. "Excellent! Order: launch the message torpedo. Summon the
transports, all that can be spared; also personnel for the disassembly."

He looked around at his fighters, smiling. "Well done. We will settle
in, drinking the prey dry and eating it to the bone at our leisure.
Staff, draw up a preliminary plan to strip as much as possible as
quickly as possible and load efficiently when the transport arrives."

Smaller, high-value loot would go to the victorious flotilla, of
course. He would have to arrange priorities: priorities that would give
the *Bride* the first and best pick, and t'Varak's *Age of Darkness* the
last and worst, of course.

Part of his attention had been on Serig's interrogation of the
prisoners. He brought his head up, smiling at the executive officer's
wit.

"He says," he translated for the benefit of the scumvermin Serig
had been taunting, "that he will explore your internal environment,
Environment Systems Officer Coburn."

❖   ❖   ❖

No! Channa thought hard at her. *Don't resist, Patsy!*

The older woman's broad fair face was flushed, red spots on her cheeks showing her rage. The pirate reached a hand down her shirt and squeezed a breast casually.

Patsy spat in his face.

Channa started to rise. Belazir jabbed a precisely calculated toe into her bruised stomach. She collapsed to the deck again. The pirate grabbed her ear in strong, almost prehensile toes and forced her head around.

"Watch, scumvermin," he said pleasantly. "And learn not to defy the High Clan."

Behind her there was a flurry as Amos tried to rise again. A Kolnari pounded her heel into the small of his back over the kidneys and he collapsed with a stifled shriek, thrashing. Nobody else moved.

Simeon, she thought desperately. *Simeon!*

Serig touched his face where the spittle ran and spoke in his own language. The other Kolnari laughed or grinned, watching with bright-eyed interest. Patsy took advantage of his inattention, lashing out in a kick at his groin. A fist snapped down and met the rising foot with a sound like a mallet hitting rock. Patsy gave a sharp gasp of pain. With bound hands, she was thrown off-balance and staggered back against the coffee table. The Kolnari laughed as she almost fell, stripping away his harness and tossing it aside. The briefs came away with it, memory-plastic rolling up into the belt. The stationer's clothes followed, torn away as if they were paper while one hand held her immobilized, clamped to her jaw. He stepped back and stood like a licentious Greek statue, gestured.

"Down," he said in Standard. "Spread."

Yes, Belazir thought, looking down at Channa. *In the end, this one is mine. But not at once. With subtlety.*

As a child, Belazir t'Marid had been the despair of his mothers and nurses. For all their whippings and shock-rod treatments, for all the day-cycles spent locked in the hotbox, they could never break him of the nasty habit of toying with his "food."

CHAPTER EIGHTEEN

SIMEON DROPPED TO the ground, panting. Atop the distant mountain, another wing of the castle crumbled and fell into the gulfs below with an earthquake rumble of rock. The worm screamed triumph and wound itself further around the central tower as flames billowed into the darkening sky. A tiny figure stood on the battlements above the monster, waving a bat that glowed iridescent green. Queasy, Simeon switched viewpoints, just in time to see the open maw engulf his pseudo-construct duplicate. The gnashing teeth ripped it into shreds. The illusion faded and his last sight from it was a rushing universe of light and **onoffonoffonoffonoffonoff** as the code was disassembled and "digested" by the intruder.

Phew, he thought, shakily turning his Jets cap right-side around again. *That ought to hold him.* For a while, at least. The worm would be here, always probing and testing, as long as the Kolnari battle-computer stayed clamped to the SSS-900-C's system. Even if he destroyed the program and purged his system, that would merely ring every alarm the enemy had. They'd only launch another worm immediately, with a different configuration. Despite its self-modifying abilities, he *knew* this one now!

Gently, stepping backward, brushing his footprints out of the sand, he faded from the blasted landscape of cinders, where pustules in the soil spewed line after line of questing wasps.

"The Knight came home from the quest;
    Muddied and sore he came.
    Battered of shield and crest,
    Bannerless, bruised and lame—"

Channa was weeping. That was his first thought, as his "other" awareness flared back. Everything was a little murky, but he could see clearly enough down into the lounge. She was sitting on the sofa next to Amos, head cradled against his shoulder, sobbing with slow misery. Both of them looked battered, as if they'd been thrown from a moving vehicle. Amos winced every time he moved.

"Channa!" Simeon said when a few microseconds of a scan told him the room was safe. A little further adjustment put an innocuous scene on the security system the Kolnari and their computers were monitoring. "Channa, are you all right?"

"*Where were you!*" Channa shouted, springing erect. "Where were you, Simeon?"

"I was—"

Simeon noticed what was playing over the general channel, again and again, locked in from the command circuits. Nearing the end of one loop, Channa was kneeling by Patsy's side, trying to staunch the hemorrhage with the scraps of her clothing.

"Please, Master and God, may I summon the doctor?"

"Of course," the pirate chieftain said. "We are a reasonable people." A broad smile. "As you see, you were wrong. *I* am the 'bad pirate.' Serig is the *worse* pirate."

Simeon blinked back to the present. He felt his automatic feeds cut in, damping down hormonal flows and adrenal glands, filtering his blood. Even so, he came as close to feeling faint as he ever had.

"I . . . oh, God, *God,*" he whispered. "*Shit.*" There were no words adequate in any lexicon.

"Where *were* you, Simeon?"

"Fighting," he said. "Channa, they put a worm program into the station system. I *had* to fight it, it was—is—a monster. If I hadn't, it would have burrowed right into my brain and eaten *me.* I'd also be under their control and telling them everything they wanted to know. I couldn't even self-destruct!"

"I see," Channa said. "Not that there *was* anything you could have done for us. Excuse me." She walked quickly into her quarters: he could hear water splashing.

Amos stood, left hand clenched around right fist. "Though they be thieves from their birth, for this, they shall pay," he said softly, almost to himself. "For Patsy, for Keriss, for my sister and my father's house and for all they have done, by the living soul of God, they shall pay in full, every jot and tittle."

Channa came back, her face set harder than Simeon had ever seen it. She waved Amos back and turned to the pillar.

"What damage did you sustain?" she asked in a professional tone.

"Nothing crucial—yet," Simeon said. "I've got to keep a fair share of my attention and the system's capacity involved in just watching and waiting. That worm program mutates like a retrovirus: the sort that never gives up. I could clean it out—if I dared. Apart from that, I've lost about a third of the memory and computational capacity. That's what could be termed 'occupied territory' at the moment. With luck, their computer will keep thinking that's all there is. It's powerful but specialized. They haven't hooked up their ship computers to the station, yet. Probably afraid of us hacking in to them.

"But," he went on, "I've got to be really careful. Any action I take in what they think is safe territory has to be elaborately screened. I can jimmy the records. However, even I can't make the impossible convincing."

She narrowed her eyes. "Could you take back those functions in a hurry?"

"Somewhere from seconds to minutes. They'd know pretty quick, and that battle-computer they've got jacked in could . . . hmm. Come to think of it, I could probably take that over, too. But they'd know."

"No problem . . . later. Can we conference?"

"Yeah, I've got all of their people under continuous surveillance."

"We'd better get moving as soon as we can," she said.

Simeon made an affirmative sound. "Our people are going to be pretty shook up," he said. *I sure am.* "We've got to get things in hand, before they start lashing out. It'll take *some* time though, for a cycle when they're all available."

"Good. Let's get, hmmm, Chaundra, the section leaders, and—" Amos began.

"Everyone's gone," Seld Chaundra said in a low and careful voice. "You sure we oughta do this, Joat? Joseph said—"

"Joe can wait a minute, 'n so can you, carrot-face," she whispered. "Now keep that thing running, hey?"

He nodded and bent again over the two modules and the jack clipped to the main conduit above them. This way was very narrow— an adult would have to be a dwarf to get through—but it came in conveniently over the sickbay entrance.

"Look," he went on, without glancing up. He was still breathing hard from the effort of crawling up the axial ventway. "Look, maybe Ms. Coburn doesn't need someone else talking to her right now? It's been less than a day, and—"

"Yeah, I saw the broadcast, too," she said. She had. Seld had fainted. His meds weren't doing him as much good as they should. "You stay here."

She crawled forward, pushing the local sensor-override unit ahead of her. To the naked eye, the cover of the duct was a panel just like all the others. The only real difference was that it was selectively permeable and much thinner. It recessed obediently and Joat looked down into a darkened room. One floatbed, the usual furniture, and a figure under the sheet. She curled herself into a ball and somer-saulted slowly through the opening, holding on with her fingertips and then dropping the final meter to the floor.

"You awake?" she said, moving to the bedside. "It's Joat."

Coburn's eyes were open. She lay motionless, but they tracked through the darkness. Joat shone a small light under her own chin. She had procured for herself a very expensive coverall, made of adjustable light-fibers. Simeon had gotten it for her because it was fashionable, but with a little creativity you could rig it to mimic the ambient background color, which was right now a mottled charcoal gray. Her face floated above it in the lightstick's feeble low-setting glow.

"Go 'way, Joat," the woman said in a dull voice. Her face looked old, under the sealant bandages. "I don't need any more sympathy. Leave me alone."

"Great, 'cause sympathy's not what I'm gonna give you," Joat said. She brought her face closer to Patsy's, and her own eyes held the same flat deadness. "Let me tell you something about me." She explained, in a flat, matter-of-fact tone all about her father, her uncle, the captain.

"So I *know*, Ms. Coburn," she went on. "Forget what anyone else's said. They don't know jack shit. But Joat, she knows *exactly* how you feel. And like I said, you don't need sympathy right now. I know what you do need."

Slowly, Patsy raised herself on her elbow. "An' what would that be?"

Silently, Joat reached around and opened her haversack. Her gloved hand came out with Patsy Sue Coburn's gunbelt and arc pistol.

"Payback," Joat whispered steadily. "And here's how it's gonna be—"

The medical-storage room had its own surveillance subloop. That made it a good place for the clandestine meeting. It was also chilly, bare, and crowded. The walls were gray metal bins outlined with fluorescent paint.

Appropriate, given the state of our morale, Channa thought.

"I have two hundred fifty-seven people down with the virus," Chaundra said. "The symptoms are spectacular but not life-threatening, as long as they stay hooked to the machinery. I have also treated sixty-four patients for traumas and wounds of various sorts. No fatalities, so far. One or two are in critical condition, but they should recover. This total includes several of my medical aids who have been assaulted by Kolnari coming to check up on our 'sick.' They seem to find the sight disgusting and . . . exciting at one and the same time. Several of the *patients* have been assaulted."

So *much for scaring them off with the virus,* Channa thought. "Patsy?" she asked aloud. *She's my friend.* Patsy hadn't wanted to talk to her or anyone else, which was understandable. *But I want to know about her.*

"She . . . there were no broken bones, apart from the foot. I internally splinted that—" gluing the bones together in a synthetic sheath stronger than the original material, to give them a matrix to heal "—replaced the lost blood, and plas-sutured all the soft tissue injuries. Ms. Coburn is mobile although in some . . . physical . . . discomfort. With the usual growth stimulators, full recovery should take no more than a week."

He licked his lips nervously. "I cannot answer for her mental state. I fear catatonia. I have administered the usual psychotropics, but the mind is more than the brain and its chemistry."

Channa nodded jerkily. "Anything else?"

"Yes. I now have . . . abundant tissue samples from the Kolnari. There are things we should discuss privately."

Amos looked at the faces in the screen. "Continue as planned," he said. "The enemy are pushing you to work. Be as stupid as you dare.

Make mistakes as often as you dare. Above all, keep as much material half-disassembled as you can."

"When are we going to *fight* them?" somebody burst out. "You and Simeon talked a good fight, about Cochise and the Viet Gong—" *Cong,* Simeon corrected silently "—so far all we're doing is rolling over!"

"There is the virus," Simeon said. "That's working, they're catching it. I've begun psychological operations. Most important, I've deciphered their language." That brought a rustle. "It's not much like the ones in the survey files—both are pidgin Sinhala-Tamil, but . . . anyway, I've got it. They've ordered sixty units here."

"Oh, great!" the man barked. "More of them!"

"Shut up," Channa remarked. "That means they're not just going to strip the station of everything they can carry in their warships and then blow it up. You can't kill a cow and milk it. It'll be at least a week before the transports arrive. There ought to be about sixty of them. You know how long it takes us to load sixty freighters with homogenous ore when we're *trying* to work fast. Imagine what it will take to remove and load fixed equipment, with everyone dragging their feet. And the more of them that are here, the more will be caught when the Fleet arrives."

"And," Amos said, with a feral smile, "that means we can be more direct in the interim. Do not worry, my friends. They, too, will suffer, know fear and pain."

That brought a chorus of satisfaction.

We think revenge is primitive, Simeon thought, *until we need it to satisfy indignity and humiliation.* He was feeling considerable desire in that direction himself.

Amos lifted a hand. "Wait. We want to lure as many of them into the station as possible—as insurance, and so we can wear them down. But we *cannot* risk key people who know a good deal about our plans and our station prisoners being dragged in for interrogation because they thought they could be clever. *No action* is to be taken save on my express orders. The personnel to effect those orders will be fitted with a suicide tooth and have psych profiles which assure its use. Wait until you receive orders. We have a fine general—" he nodded in Simeon's direction "—and we must follow his words."

That brought silence.

"We'll try levering them to cut back on the atrocities," Channa said.

"Say it's reducing working efficiency—that's true enough. Stay tight, endure! We'll see them all fried yet! Out."

One by one the faces vanished from the screen, except for Chaundra's.

"The bad news, Doctor," she said.

This meeting was a fleeting thing, time stolen as they were all supposedly on their way somewhere else. They could fool the sensors for a while, but nobody could explain being in two positions at once, one of them under the real-time eyes of the enemy. Only the fact that there were fifteen-thousand odd of the stationers and less than a tenth that number of Kolnari made it possible at all. That and the invaders' imperfect control of the surveillance computers.

Channa studied Chaundra's grim face. "What is it?" she asked him.

He scrubbed his face with both hands and shrugged, exhaustion in his voice. "It's not working."

"*What* is not working?" Amos asked impatiently.

"The virus," Chaundra said. "They are infected—somewhat—but it hardly bothers them at all."

"Shit!" Channa swore. She had hoped the illness would make the Kolnari shun civilians of their own volition. "Doesn't it have any effect?"

"Mild headache, some nausea, one or two cases of diarrhea for a day or so. All in all, much less than our people have experienced even with the immunization. The afflicted individuals act embarrassed, not frightened, and their companions laugh at them." Chaundra shrugged in despair. "I move that we discontinue this plan. Our people are getting raped, beaten, humiliated *and* catching the flu while the Kolnari just have fun. I tested their tissue samples—the Kolnari immune system is barely human. If some of the rape victims were not pregnant, I would doubt that the *Kolnari* are human. No, I correct that. Of human origin. Their actions certainly are not," he added bitterly.

"Pregnant?" Channa asked, bewildered.

"I terminated," he said, "ectopic pregnancies, in the fallopian tubes. This despite slow-release implant contraceptives." Those made the body's own immune system treat sperm as foreign matter until counteracted.

"Channa, the pirates seem to have metallic-salt and other contaminant levels that should make every one of them stone sterile. Instead, their sperm are a whole order of magnitude more motile than the norm. The rest of their systems are built the same way. Their anti-body response is . . . their bodies use the poisons to kill bacterial or viral invaders. Their DNA is locked into position with redundancy and self-repair mechanisms like nothing I have ever seen, resistant both to radiation and to viral contamination."

"I refuse to believe these animals are supermen," Amos said.

"Oh, they're not that," Chaundra said. "From their DNA, I'd say they have shorter lifespans than ours. I imagine the degeneration past early middle-age is . . . spectacular and swift, as the whole system abruptly fails. Several other disadvantages; for example, they could not live without dioxin and arsenic compounds in their food. An equivalent of scurvy would strike them."

He fell silent.

"There's something else you're hiding, Doctor," Channa said quietly. Amos sat more erect, glancing narrowly from the woman to the screen. "Tell us!"

Bingo, Simeon thought, narrowing in on Chaundra's pupil dilation and breathing.

"There is a possibility," Chaundra said, looking aside from the pickup. "Another virus." A long pause. "The one that killed Mary. It is of unparalleled virulence. Possibly the worst natural . . . unnatural disease ever to be discovered."

Amos' head jutted forward. "Why did you not mention this before?" he asked harshly.

"Because it killed my wife!" Chaundra shouted suddenly; the more startling coming from so mild a man. "Because it is killing my son!" More softly, more rationally: "Because I swore that the filthy disease should never kill another human being. I no longer classify the Kolnari under that heading."

"Still," Channa said, "the virus is a good plan. The enemy don't have much medical capability at all. And Chaundra has lucidly explained why they don't need it. For our purposes they are medically ignorant. Little expertise beyond treating wounds and broken bones, really. I get the impression they just sort of . . . junk anyone who's sicker than that."

Chaundra looked thoughtful, professional competence taking over despite himself. "I do not have the live virus, you understand. But I have the information on a minihedron. The protein is nothing, the replicator can produce it immediately. But modifications . . . yes. What sort of disease did you have in mind?"

"Something scary," she said.

"Something fatal," Amos added.

"If possible," she agreed. "But at the least, spectacularly incapacitating, disgusting, horrifying. Something with mental deterioration? We want them terrified, and what's more terrifying than madness?"

"Whoa now, I dunno," Simeon said. "Do you really want a stationload of crazy Kolnari? Crazier than they already are, I mean."

They looked thoughtful and slightly sick.

"No, no, wait a moment," Chaundra said, and paused. "As Channa suggested, we could target only those who've had the virus. They *catch* it. It's just not capable of getting much beyond the first few cells. Antibody response is very quick. That's a manageable part of the Kolnari force, enough to hurt and rattle them without driving them into a killing frenzy. It would be cumulative, spread among themselves. Close contact is needed, and I could increase that. Immunize our people stealthily, under the guise of normal treatment. It can be done. I'm sure of it."

"Get on it, then," Channa said. When the doctor's image had faded: "That takes care of that!"

Simeon's image nodded. It was less mobile than usual, with so much capacity tied up. "This is a war of morale. Guerilla war always is. We have to demoralize them, and much more important, maintain our own morale."

Or our people will crack and someone will go to the Kolnari, went unspoken among them.

"Speaking of which," Amos said, rising.

"Must you?" Channa said quietly.

"Yes, I must," he replied, walking over to her and lifting a hand to his lips. The gesture seemed far more natural than it had at first, less staged.

"This isn't going to work for long," Channa said to the air, after he had left.

"It doesn't have to," Simeon replied. "Only long enough."

"Get ready, Seld," Joat breathed.

"I'm ready," he whispered back. He was pale and sweating heavily.

Her hand rested on the diaphragm that separated the vent from the corridor. Her other hand gripped the spring-loaded device, adjusting it so the red dot on the notescreen image beside her lay precisely over a spot in the corridor. Below, Patsy waited at the junction of the passageways, one hand behind the concealing wall. That hand held the arc pistol, but if all went well they would not need it.

If all did not go well, they were probably going to die in the next twenty seconds or so. Die quickly if they were lucky.

"One of them," Seld said. "Still only one." He was peering into the miniscreen jacked into the security cameras from their local lead. "Still coming."

Bare feet scuffed lightly below. The Kolnari came swiftly, not running: they seemed to walk on the balls of their feet in a light half-trot most of the time. He checked slightly at the sight of Patsy.

"Who goes?" he called.

Stationers not on essential duties were supposed to be in their cabins. Then he recognized her and smiled. One taken by the na Marid was a prestigious victim and here she was, walking alone. He started towards her, speeding up as she dodged around the corner.

The warrior was stopping and turning even as Joat keyed the diaphragm open. His speed was awesome, but she had triggered the hand-cobbled device at the same instant the panel came down. Behind her there was a click that meant Seld had cut in the damper. For the next few minutes, security records would show an empty corridor. Safe, unless a human observer were looking. Even checking the files would show recording errors, normal enough considering the havoc the Kolnari had caused the station computers.

The darts struck the Kolnari as his finger was tightening on the trigger of his own weapon. A hundred thousand volts flowed through the thread-thin superconductor wires behind them. He convulsed.

K-tash. Hot air blossomed away from the plasma rifle around a rod of sun-hot violence. Literally sun-hot; it was an ultra-miniaturized, laser-triggered deuterium fusion pellet focused by magnetic fields. Normally the pirate's muscle and reflex would have been enough to hold it steady on his aiming point. Now the superheated gas slewed his lifeless body around and the substance of the walls sublimed away, the beam chopping through synthetics and conduits and the empty chambers beyond. There was a hiss and *cherp-cherp-cherp* of pressure alarms as the outer hull was punctured.

Joat winced. That was *not* part of the plan. "Quick," she said in soft urgency. Dropping down into the corridor and grasping the pirate's weapon, she heaved it up.

"*Here,*" she gasped, wobbling under the burden of the clumsy thing.

Between them, Seld and Joat got it up into the duct. Then she bent and grabbed one of the Kolnari's arms. She heaved and her heels skidded. The juddering, twitching body was *heavy,* far heavier than a man dressed only in a belt and briefs ought to be. Patsy darted back.

"It's not *him*," she said.

"It'll do for starters," Joat said with a grunt. "C'mon!"

Together they dragged the body to the airlock around the corner and cycled it through.

"Meet you at N-7a x L," Joat panted, trotting back to the open diaphragm. "Need that stuff on the list."

"I'll be there," Patsy said.

"It will work," Joseph said reassuringly. "At least once," he amended. "Joat is an odd child, but any contraption she claims will function, will function."

Amos nodded dubiously. *I have never found reason to doubt you in matters of violence,* he thought. That was comforting. On the other hand, no man was infallible, and even Joseph was an amateur at war.

They were in the lower-equatorial park, near the central core of the station's upper globe. For a wonder, there *were* no surveillance cameras here. By Central World law, there had to be such places in any substantial habitat. Most of the inhabitants being law-abiding types, SSS-900-C's was in the park. It was fairly large, several hundred hectares, with part of the station water-reserves deployed as lakes and ponds. Currently it was in night-cycle, and the Kolnari seemed to find that fascinating. Amos could understand that. He had found it heartbreakingly like, and yet unlike, Bethel. The scents were strange, greener, and fresher than the arid hills of the Sierra Nueva estates, milder than the irrigated lowlands. Strange birds—or was it small animals?—chirred and rustled in the undergrowth. He was an outdoorsman, but these were not the fields he knew.

"They come," Joseph said. "To stay," he added.

He moved off into the shadows of the bushes, bent low, moving with a skill he had learned in the alleys of his childhood and the hunting grounds of his leader's properties in later years.

God was not entirely unfair. The Kolnari hearing was not quite as good as human norm; it need not be in the thicker air of their homeworld. Amos crouched with hunter's patience, waiting as if for sicatooth.

God of our fathers, be with me now, he prayed with utter sincerity. *Strengthen my arm against the children of Hellmouth.*

"Hai, dog-turds, what brings you out this fair night?" Joseph's voice rang clear. "Tired of banging your mothers or looking for sheep?"

Amos felt a lurch of fear. They were counting on the enemy's inexperience with guerilla tactics, their arrogance. That was perilously close to counting on the Kolnari being stupid, and *that* was dangerous.

Pounding feet came closer: Joseph's heavier tread, and the lighter, faster sound of the folk the hell-planet bred. Joseph flashed between the trees with his head down, arms and legs pumping. The pursuers seemed to float by contrast, loping effortlessly like men on a low-gravity moon. Their eyes and trailing manes glowed lambent in the simulated starlight, and their movements had the aching gracefulness of swans taking flight. They were beautiful, and horrible beyond belief, and he feared them in a way that had nothing to do with the long knives in their hands.

He stepped out. They stopped with a plunging abruptness. Their heads turned to scan him with the smooth accuracy of gun-turrets tracking under computer control. Joat had counted on that in designing her gadget. A scanner detected the alignment of their eyes.

The *thing* he carried strapped to his chest yawped. Then it was red-hot, and he was scrabbling to rip it loose and toss it away. The pirates stumbled as if they had run into a wall of iron. They screamed as if that iron were white hot and dropped their knives to tear at their feces in a frenzy of pain.

Scream, dogs, Amos thought, gratified. *Scream as Bethel screamed, as Patsy screamed,* scumvermin *filth.*

Cries of pain were not going to attract attention on the SSS-900-C: not while it was held in the Fist of High-Clan Kolnar.

A dozen men and women edged out of the shadows. Cutting bars and lengths of dull-gleaming synth tubing were in their hands. Amos reached over his back and drew a long curved sword from its sheath with the slender sound of steel on steel: the motion so long practiced from blade-dance training that it was as unconscious as breathing. The heads of the Kolnari turned toward the sounds he made; their ruined eyes were circles of blood-red now, and tears of blood dribbled down their cheeks. They moaned in their agony, but they moved toward him, teeth bared in a rictus of pain and savagery.

"Quickly, but carefully," Amos said to the others closing in on their victims.

Afterwards they must throw their clothes into disposal and go through full decontamination cleansing.

Joseph was behind the blinded pirates, a half-dozen stationers at his back. Two knives glinted in his hands.

"Now!" Amos said.

CHAPTER NINETEEN

"SHALL I PERFORM an autopsy, Great Lord?" the eunuch medico asked in its shrill whine.

Belazir t'Marid looked down at the bodies in their separate bags. Separate bags, but who knew what went where? One bag might be a few parts short or extra, for all he could tell.

"Creature," he said to the eunuchs, cuffing one aside, "when men have their skulls crushed by heavy blows—as these have—and their eyes gouged out—as these have—and their throats cut to the neckbone—as these have—and their bodies cut to pieces, as *these have*, then generally speaking, as a rule, they *die*. An autopsy seems somewhat superfluous."

The noble's voice was even and pleasant, as it usually was, but the slave medico sank deeper and deeper into a crouch of abasement with every word, as if they were blows from the powered whip normally used on such. At the last, all the eunuch could do was whimper.

"Cease," Belazir said. "Now, this other; in that, I have interest."

The medico sealed the bags containing the body-parts of the two dead Kolnari and hastened to the intact casualty. Relatively intact. He stroked a hand down the opaque material, and the stuff turned utterly transparent.

"Whatever killed him, he was not pleased with it," Belazir remarked to Serig, looking at the dead man's bulging, staring eyes. Shifting to the interrogative tense: "Creature?"

"It is uncertain, Great Lord. Either the electrocution or the explosive decompression would be fatal, of course. Here, the dart struck. See, a burned patch, high on the shoulder, towards the angle of the jaw. As he was turning to confront that which killed him, it struck from the rear."

"Blindingly obvious," Belazir said facetiously. "Go. Preserve the bodies."

"And what do you propose to *do*, t'Marid?" the third Kolnari noble present said.

"Do, lord Captain t'Varak?" Belazir said, turning with an expression of perfect courtesy.

T'Varak's presence provided a welcome distraction. A kin-enemy was always more entertaining than outsiders, if more predictable. He waved a languid hand about them, at the dew-cool grass, at the holos far overhead that mimicked the blue cloud-scattered sky of Earth. The temperature was far below what Kolnari preferred, but they could endure anything down to and below freezing without undue discomfort. None of them needed to wear more than briefs and shipbelt for utility. For status, the nobles wore long open-necked robes of watered silk, jewelry of fretted silver, and homeworld fire opals. Their hair was brushed to shining shoulder-length waterfalls, pinned back with combs of sea-ivory and precious metal, and the knife-sharp feathers of Kolnari birds.

Belazir stretched. His robe was severely plain, dazzling white with gold and indigo trim.

"I shall enjoy the beauty of this place. So fair, and so tragic because soon it will perish as if it had never been." He added a classical quotation on transience and death in the three-tonal scale.

Anger glowed from the other man, lambent as hot metal. He might have been Belazir's twin, except for a hair-clip of gold rather than silver and the petulance of his expression. Belazir t'Marid never showed an enemy his frustrations.

"Three of my men are *dead*, t'Marid," he said.

"Dead!" agreed Belazir in a mild tone. "One slain from ambush, another two destroyed *hand-to-hand, by scumvermin*. Of course, to be caught so carelessly, they became little better than scumvermin themselves. Far better for the Clan that they were cut off before they could breed." Or breed much; Kolnari became fertile early. "Culling by the universe, not so? They will leave no sons of disgrace to propagate lines of weakness amid the Divine Seed."

For a moment, he thought Aragiz would attack him here, while

Belazir was in clear command, with Serig at his side and armored crewfolk from the *Dreadful Bride* at his back. If he did, he *was* better culled out of the Divine Seed. That was the point of the delicate insult, of course. Back on Bethel, old Azlek t'Varak had taken off his helmet a moment too soon and lost his head by such precipitousness. That had been a scandal of some note, shadowing the prestige and honor of all his sons—Aragiz t'Varak not least. *The t'Varak were always hotheads,* Belazir thought, amused at his own pun. Azlek had been all of fifty, though; time enough to be slow and senile. Aragiz should know better.

He did, though barely. "You should bring the scumvermin here under better control," Aragiz said in a bland tone which matched Belazir's. "Kill a few hundred. A hundred for one."

"T'Varak, t'Varak," Belazir murmured. He bent and plucked a flower, sniffed deeply of it. "There are fifteen thousand or so scumvermin on this great fat-dripping morsel that the Clan—and Father Chalku, by the latest message—yearns to pop into its ever-hungry mouth. And, if the scumvermin suspect that almost all of them will die when we are done, some one of them will sabotage this station and rob the Clan of that feasting, for all that we can do. Despair makes even scumvermin brave. Hope brings forth their cowardice, each one hoping for himself."

A songbird swooped by. Belazir's band snapped out like a trout rising to a fly and caught the tiny creature within the cave of his hand. He brought it up under Aragiz's nose as the soft feathers brushed his skin, in rhythm with its heartbeat.

"I have them in my fist, cousin," he went on. "Shall I open it—" he suited words to action "—and let them go?" The bird flew away.

"Blood calls for blood," Aragiz said. "Avenge our blood, or you are no Clan leader."

"Blood-call can wait a few days," Belazir said, his voice flint-hard as the two men stared face-to-face. "Until the transports arrive," he added negligently. "Eight days to load and leave, and watch this station vanish in a spark of fire as we go. Because Father Chalku's message giving me mandate over all the High Clan in this action has already come, *has it not?*"

"It has," Aragiz said. "Be glad, O cousin, be very glad of that!"

"Be assured I am," Belazir said ambiguously. "And now, Lord Captain, load your ship with choice loot. Let you and your fighters enjoy themselves as they will among the scumvermin, so long as they do not reduce the slave work-output." He dropped his voice to a whisper. "Do not obstruct me, t'Varak. Not until you can bring the Clan a prize like this."

"No. Not yet."

Belazir watched him go. "Serig," he said, "behold. Never underestimate an enemy."

"*Aragiz*, lord?" Serig said incredulously.

Belazir threw back his head and laughed merrily. "No, no. I should have specified; never underestimate even a *scumvermin* enemy. As that dolt does. This station's two leaders, they have between them a three hundred percent increment upon poor Aragiz's sum total of wits. He has the technique of a *tunglor*."

That was a metaphor for the younger Kolnari, who had never seen homeworld. In Kolnar's seas, there was an animal—more or less an animal—that concentrated the abundant transuranics from seawater in a specialized section of its gut. It sucked in water and sprayed it on the heated chamber that resulted, expelling it behind as steam for propulsion. Tunglor massed in at about the same as the *Dreadful Bride,* and they attacked by rising from depth at fifty or sixty knots and ramming with their metal-sapphire-fiber prows, never deviating from the shortest course. Belazir's ancestors had made themselves nobles by hunting tunglor, hunting them to gain plutonium for weapons and powerplants.

"As you do when you take your pleasure," Belazir went on, slapping his companion on the back of the neck in mock reproof.

Serig grinned slyly. "It's not as if they were *women*." He omitted the "lord" in this brief instance, speaking man to man. "And how will you take this Channa creature?"

"With slow care, fool, as all true pleasures should be savored: wine, a woman, revenge. And on the *Dreadful Bride,* when we have left," Belazir said.

Serig raised brows in surprise. "You think her worthy of bearing slaves, lord?" he said.

"Many." The male offspring would be castrated—that was how such as the medico were made—and the females bred back to the Divine Seed. In four or five generations, with careful testing, they could become Kolnari of the lowest caste.

"I will need some pleasure to relax me after our labors," Belazir added.

Serig nodded, needing no further explanation. They would have to destroy and leave for Bethel immediately. The Central Worlds Navy would be all over these stars as soon as they learned of the destruction of SSS-900-C. The Clan would run a long, long way, to wait among unpeopled, unsurveyed systems while they assimilated this treasure and bred the strength to use it. Empty systems held raw materials and energy in plenty, if you had the tools, and the universe was unimaginably vast. That voyage would be a giant step nearer the good day when it was the Central Worlds' scumvermin who were the scattering of fugitives, and the Divine Seed the power that bred and covered world upon world upon world. A long, if necessary, flight would be tedious.

"So, leave me," Belazir said. "See to the preparations for the transports. Now I will speak with the two scumvermin."

Their Kolnari guards seemed incapable of letting them just walk through a doorway. The prisoners were always propelled over the threshold with a hearty shove. Thus far Channa and Amos had managed to keep their feet, which seemed to inspire ever more energetic pushing. Channa wondered if the two guards bet money on which of them would stumble first. Such treatment irritated her and it must infuriate Amos beyond endurance, since he was born noble among a ceremonious people.

The last door gave onto the nature deck, one of the jewels of the SSS-900-C. Amos straightened then, almost smiling. The deck covered several hundred hectares; lakes, several small wooded areas, and meadows. A stream wandered from savannah to a miniature rain forest, through prairie and into the softly informal confines of a classic country-house garden, here by the entrance. Herons stalked through the reeds by the river, alert for the fish that leaped after dragonflies. The smell was overwhelmingly green. Off in the middle distance, a herd of small deer browsed. The air was full of birdsong. Normally there were parties of picnickers and the shouts of children. Now a plasma gun swung down before them.

"Wait the Great Lord's pleasure, scumvermin," the amplified voice of the Kolnar said.

Oh-oh, Channa thought, with a sinking stomach. *That sounds bad.* She and Amos had discussed what to do under interrogation, but she had doubts about his ability to keep control of his temper.

As for me, I'll live through what I have to. And I'll dance on their graves, she thought grimly. She had been one of the first to take the new virus.

"Buck up, kid," Simeon's voice whispered in her inner ear. It had the odd gravelly tone he adopted in tense moments. "Remember, I've got no fixed sensors in there, so the implants will have to do. I'm with you, and I'll give a running translation of anything the pirates say in their jabber. Okay? And from the structure of their language, the phrase they just used means something like 'front and center.'"

"*Got it,*" she subvocalized.

They jumped back against the wall smartly when a Kolnari bossman came through, looking as if he would rather walk over them. For a moment, Channa thought it was Belazir, and then caught the few subtle differences which told her he was not. Simeon's voice confirmed it. Serig followed, a minute later. They both cast their eyes down, to avoid showing the raw desire to kill they shared.

"Now, scumvermin," the guard said.

"*Ohhhhh, am I getting sick of hearing that word,*" Channa subspoke.

"You and me and Simeon-Amos both," Simeon agreed. The Bethelite had the button in his ear, but he hadn't been able to train a sub vocal level that was inaudible. The Kolnari didn't hear all that well at the margins of audibility and had no reason to use sensitive hearing devices.

Belazir had set up his command post beneath a huge oak tree. He lolled at his ease on a reclining chair, a wreath of fresh wildflowers adorned his hair, dappled shade moving on his sleek skin and the priceless silks of his clothing. On one side of him was a mobile console and a table scattered with notescreens, printouts, small pieces of equipment. Also some artwork which Simeon recognized, garnered from galleries and the museum.

One piece Channa did not remember and the brain could not name, a flamboyant carving in some bone or ivory of a . . . *submarine with fangs? jet-propelled spearfish?* Whatever, it had the same air of ruthless speed that a striking hawk might.

"Ah, your eyes light on the tunglor," Belazir said affably. As always, the sheer physical *presence* of the man struck her like a blow. "From homeworld . . . Kolnar."

The guard behind them reached out an arm to force them down.

"No, to one knee will do," Belazir said easily. His Standard was better, even in these few days. "Do you wish refreshment?"

He waved to his other side to the table where food and bottles of wine rested, patently supplied by the Perimeter Restaurant. The young waitress was from the Perimeter, too, although there she had worn clothes.

"No, Master and God," Amos and Channa said in meek unison.

Belazir smiled and held out his hand. The waitress put a waterglass tumbler of Mart'an's famous apricot-brandy liqueur into it. He drank it off in ten long swallows and Channa knew a moment's wild hope.

Simeon's voice was sour. "No joy," he sent. "I checked with Chaundra. They metabolize ethanol so fast he'll only be mildly buzzed."

"Well," the pirate said in that voice like a bronze bell that purred. "There is business. The matter of the attack on the Divine Seed of Kolnar."

"He's not too upset, I think," Simeon told them. "Heartbeat absolutely Kolnar-normal, no pupil dilation. Got an idea the victims may have been from one of the other ships. Play it polite-firm."

"Lord and God," Channa said. "The criminals will be found and punished."

Subvocal from Simeon: "*You hit his funnybone with that, Happy. He's killing himself laughing inside.*"

Channa went on. "I've made several general broadcasts calling for obedience, Master and God."

"So you have. I notice, too, that it is always you and not your companion . . . colleague?"

"Simeon-Amos is—" Channa fell silent as the Kolnari's hand indicated that Simeon-Amos should answer.

"I am the junior, Master and God," Amos said, eyes fixed on the ground.

"Look at me, Simeon-Amos." The stares met for long seconds. Then Belazir gestured again, turning his attention back to Channa. "Well and good. As we expect to hold the station in our fist for some time, these acts of stupidity must cease."

"*Lying through his teeth, babe.*"

"You sent messages desiring audience, Channahap," Belazir went on. He rose, like a black fountain tipped with white gold, the loose sleeves floating back from his arms like wings. He looked down from his near two meters of height. "Continue."

"Master and God," she said, in a tone as empty of any but the formal semantic content as she could make it, "your troops fornicate like—" she paused to search for a word "—rottweilers."

"*Big chuckle at that one, Channie.*" Simeon was furious.

Belazir crossed his arms. "Why does this not seem complimentary?"

Channa looked up at him. "They bite," she said emotionlessly, covering her disgust, "all the time."

"Then the sc—the chosen ones should not resist their fate," Belazir said. "It is our custom when we meet resistance."

"They don't resist!" Channa said sharply, then managed a taut smile. "Should we bite back?"

A rustle went through the line of armored troops behind Belazir and the cluster of officers with feathers and jewels in their hair. The noble silenced them with a toss of his head.

"I would not recommend it," he said sardonically. "The custom to which I refer is that of enjoying the fruits of victory. A most ancient custom, surely, even you must know of it? Make another of your speeches. Outline their duties. A hard, sincere effort to please. Then they shall be caressed as they labor, not savaged."

"Master and God, when you bruise the fruit too much, it goes bad! The problem is that I have a hundred people in sickbay being sewn back together and under medication due to human bites and various other wounds. Initially, there were three hundred sick to begin with, not counting the ones who've been flogged."

"Are they injured?"

No, apart from shaking and crying and waking up with nightmares, she thought. The Kolnari had a whip that did something to the nervous system. "Master and God—" however she tried, she couldn't quite keep the sarcasm out of *that.* "—the problem involves vital work positions which are left empty. This isn't a planet. It doesn't run itself. Everything has to be done without error. Fatigue leads to error, error leads to failure, and failure can lead to death. I cannot do the impossible, order me however you want."

"Now that," he said, "is the wrong tone." Suddenly he was much closer, and took her chin between thumb and forefinger. "Entirely. Do you understand, Channahap?"

"Yes," she murmured, "yes, I understand." Time seemed to slow.

He smiled. "Excellent. However, your remarks, if not the manner in which they were delivered, are reasonable. I shall give orders that my troops be . . . gentler with their slaves. After you have emphasized the proper attitude toward their duties."

Channa's eyes widened.

He actually laughed this time. "Yes," he assured her, "that, too, is our custom. Those of you that please us or are useful will leave this place on our ships." He watched her absorb this privilege.

"Walk with me," he said, putting a hand under her arm. She jerked slightly at the contact, like the touch of a live conductor.

Amos started to follow. A servo-powered gauntlet closed down on his skull, so gently that it would not have cracked an egg. A duplicate of the one that had crushed his sister's skull. Wind blew through the trees above them, making the leaves move in a dance that contrasted to the stillness of the humans below.

"A strange way to spend so much effort," Belazir said, as he nodded to the landscape around them. A chuckle passed his lips. "Preferable to expend effort and strength on this than on weapons."

"*Who does he think built his ships and the weapons they're carrying?*" Simeon whispered in her ear.

Channa shrugged in answer to both.

"Still, it is beautiful," he said. His hand traced the back of her neck, lightly enough that the pads of his fingers just touched the hairs. She shivered involuntarily.

"I am not Serig," he added, stroking the fingers down her spine and away. "This is like Earth, is it not?"

"Mostly," Channa said. Unconsciously she tilted her head to one side away from Belazir as Simeon gave her the relevant information. "A few of the plants and organisms are from Rigel 4, but they're compatible."

"Like looking back into the past," he said. They stopped, out of sight of the tables. He looked up into the sky. "Computer," he said. "Night."

The constellations of Earth's northern hemisphere blazed out, as they had not in reality since men learned to bend electricity to light.

"Yes," t'Marid said, looking upward at the false sky. "Very beautiful, but it seems too much openness. As if a body might fall upward and be sucked out into limitless space."

Well, a weakness, she thought. Many spaceborn were slightly agoraphobic. That could be useful, if Belazir had been spaceborn.

She thought a smile appropriate. "The sensation is called vertigo. I've occasionally experienced it myself when planet-side. I was born and raised on a space station, so I feel more comfortable under a ceiling."

"Something of that," he admitted. "But also . . . Computer. Night on Kolnar. From Maridapore."

Channa gasped in shock at the change. The dark sky overhead vanished. In its place was a glowing moon-colored cloud full of colored lights from horizon to horizon. She blinked, then realized the light was not that much more brilliant than the Terran sky. Yet this phenomenon was not a sky: it was a *ceiling* across heaven.

"*A dozen times full Luna brightness,*" Simeon supplied.

Off to the north, auroras circled and moved, scrolls vaster than worlds, electric blue and white and pearl. Beneath them, on the horizon, a volcano was a glowing firestorm spout, powered by its own natural fission reactor. Something gigantic and winged slid across the alien constellations. Smaller things pursued it, diving and tearing as it fluted an intricate song of grief.

"I have never seen this sky," he said thoughtfully. "Not really. Not even a simulation as good as this." He issued a second command and the Earth night returned. "This is more restful."

"Ah . . . The birds won't like it if you change day to night like this," Channa said. "You'd better set it back when you leave. Master and God," she added absently.

He looked at her in astonished amusement. "The birds won't like it?" he said. "Channahap, you are a wonder. The birds won't like it, the insects will be disturbed . . . does this matter?"

"We brought them here, to a totally unnatural environment. If we expect them to thrive, then it's our responsibility to provide them with whatever they need. They're a part of all this," she said gesturing widely. "Without the birds and the insects, this would be sterile, a lifeless tableau. So we have to be mindful of their needs."

He nodded. "I shall leave it on night setting and dawn shall be in twelve hours. Things have changed here. Even the birds must realize it."

Channa had no reply for that bit of arrogance.

"That is the supreme law, of course," he went on, "for Earth, for Kolnar, for the universe."

She made an interrogative sound.

"Adapt! Master changing circumstance, or die unbred. The Seed—the genes, you would say—are the reality that underlies all this. Taking energy from the Dead World, growing in complexity and adaptation. All this," and, with a swift movement of his hand, he caught a dragonfly by its legs for a second, then released it, "is waves on the surface. Beneath is the Seed, seeking to replicate itself. All beings, all mind, all war and trade and art and science, mere waves on the changeless sea." He smiled kindly. "And fittest of all, of course, is the Divine Seed of Kolnar. Of that Seed, fittest is the High Clan. Which is why you long for union with it, for such immortality."

"I disagree. Lord and God."

"No, you do not. Your mind may, but that is merely the vehicle of the . . . gene. Watch, when we return. Your Simeon-Amos will be enraged. Naturally enough, for he suspects the immortality you offer is to be taken from his seed." He sighed and turned back towards the tables, hidden behind a line of trees. She trotted to keep pace, although he did not seem to hurry. "Enough of pleasant idleness and philosophizing. To work!"

"Simeon, why do all my Prince Charmings turn out to be toads?" Channa subvocalized. Amos stood stiff and withdrawn beside her on the people mover as it slid down the corridor. *"Is he really jealous? Under these circumstances, that's ridiculous!"*

"It's also maybe involuntary. Your girl goes walking in the woods with Lucifer, chatting it up . . ."

"Absurd!"

"Beats me, Channa. But I'll never, ribbit, turn on ya. Ribbit!"

"Or turn me on, either. It's nice to know someone is still safe to be with."

Whoa! Kick me again, Channa, I think some of my ego is still unbruised.

"That is the scariest son of a bitch I've ever had the misfortune to meet," she said. Amos nodded silently.

"Simeon-Amos?"

"Yes, Channa?"

"Hold me, would you?" His arm went around her, and she melted into the firm supportive warmth of his side. "Thank you," she said.

"For what?" His tone was light.

"For not really being green and warty or eating flies."

"Ah, guys?" This time Simeon's voice came to both of them. "I just figured something out."

"What?" Amos said.

"Bad news about Bethel."

The Bethelite stiffened again, his face drawing in lines that showed what he might look like on his deathbed, in the currently unlikely event that he would live to die of old age.

"What?" Amos repeated, this time as a command.

"These scumbags—I'm not going to use *scumvermin*, even in reverse—they're planning to loot me bare and then blow me up."

Simeon was understandably upset if he was referring to the SSS-900-C as "me."

"That is bad news for you," Amos said, steeling himself for how that would also be bad news for Bethel.

"But if they do that, the Central Worlds Navy will find out—would find out, even if the Kolnari had pulled this hijack off the way we fooled them into thinking they had. Central Worlds'd send flotillas all through this sector and look behind every space rock. For sure, they'd inspect any inhabited system. While the Saffron system may be fardlin' remote, it's still on the maps. *And the Kolnari know that, hey?* So they're sacrificing their chance of stripping Bethel in exchange for the station. Means they gotta leave *both, fast.* So what odds they plan on doing Bethel the same way they do me, when they go? Blow it, too, and cover any traces they hadn't time to sweep under the carpet. These guys are pigs, but they're not stupid."

"Yes, I see," Amos said, barely moving his lips. "Sound strategic analysis. Thank you, Simeon."

Thanks for nothing, the brain thought dismally. Amos had had the comfort of knowing the Navy would at least rescue the survivors on his homeworld, win or lose here on SSS-900-C.

"Anything we can do about *that*?" Channa asked as they entered the lounge.

"Not much more than what we're doing now," Simeon said. "But it's going to be a very close run at the end. We've got to be *ready,* at all costs. Minutes may make the difference."

Keri Holen tried to read, but she'd been on the same page for some time now and still had no idea of its content. *Trivia,* she thought. Before her life was put in danger, all her friends and family's lives, she hadn't known what triviality was. It was anything that didn't have to do with keeping you alive; anything that didn't have to do with *winning.*

"On the other hand, fretting doesn't do me any good, either," she said. *Why did I volunteer?* she asked herself. *Well, the risk was there anyway, and we need to get the second virus working,* she thought. Not everyone was a gymnast and martial artist, either.

Frustrated, she threw the reader onto the cushion beside her and rose to pace the room. There was a soft chime and Simeon's public face bloomed on the wall screen.

"The Kolnari are in your area," he said, warning all those in the threatened sector. "Get your virus capsules in position. Don't panic. Don't argue or they *will* harm you. Remember, place the capsule in your mouth, bite down, try not to swallow. Good luck," he added fervently.

Keri rushed to the cabinet where she had stored her supply among other pharmaceuticals. Her hands were shaking so much the capsules flew out of the bottle like confetti when she at last got it open. Moaning, she rushed to gather them up and put them away before the Kolnari arrived. She put one in her mouth, holding it between cheek and gum.

She returned to the living area and stood watching the door, fingers twining with the tabs of her robe. She could feel her pulse beat in her lips and fingertips, she felt as though she'd been running.

The door opened.

God, she thought as she bit down on the capsule. *There are four of them!* The capsule dissolved with a rush of coolness. Keri smiled broadly and let the robe drop.

"Welcome to my parlor." *Said the spider to the fly.*

CHAPTER TWENTY

MAZKIRA ENTERED THE elevator and selected her destination. The mining components fabricator was a treasure of immense value to the Clan. With it, they could scavenge several crucial materials from uninhabited asteroids at need. Besides that, the scumvermin operator was a pleasure to torment, in several different ways. She grinned. Then the expression faded. She could *smell* him, the scent was heavy in the cage—far more than it should have been when he merely passed through several times daily.

She looked up . . . into the barrel of a rock-cutter and above it the grinning face of Kevin Duane.

"Eat this, bitch!" he snarled and powered up the cutter. He cut the Kolnari woman in half lengthwise and smiled as he watched the two sibling halves crumple to the floor.

The elevator arrived at his level and he replaced the hatch cover. There was the access tunnel, just where Joat had told him it would be.

He handed Joat the rock-cutter and she raised an inquiring brow. He gave her a grin and a thumbs-up sign. Suddenly the elevator dropped out from underneath him and he was holding on by his elbows, feet scrabbling against the slick shaft walls. He inched his way in, his broad shoulders making it difficult to maneuver. Far below he could hear the elevator coming up again.

"Hurry up!" Joat said, sliding the rock-cutter down the access tunnel and turning back to pull him in by his shirt.

All she succeeded in doing was pulling it up over his head; his arms were almost immobilized by the tough fabric.

"Stop," he said. "Stop it."

"Hurry up!" she cried and slid backwards to give him room. "Or that elevator will smear your carcass all the way to the top of the station."

He was most of the way in now, but couldn't seem to get his feet in. He began to panic, barking his knees on the side walls of the tunnel, the space too narrow to allow him to turn or pull up his legs. In a panic, he caught at Joat's legs and yanked. Her palms squealed on the slick metal as she struggled futilely to keep her place.

The drag was just enough to get him all the way in, the side of the elevator lifted the soles of his feet gently as it passed.

Kevin dropped his head into his arms and giggled with mild hysteria.

Joat glared at him for a moment, then grinned and whispered, "Hooray! Another one for our side."

"Yes?" Belazir said, looking up from his notescreen.

It was the medico again. The Kolnari repressed an impulse to kick it. If you hit messengers, messages ceased coming. On the other hand, his time was valuable. Especially now, with the transports here and loading round the cycle.

The thought restored his good humor. Sixty ships, a fifth part of the Clan's fleet, under *his* command. Not only transports, but a fighting platform and a couple of the factory ships. It was as good as having Chalku proclaim him successor. Better, since his chances of living long enough to claim it were much higher. A formal announcement might drive some brick-skull like Aragiz t'Varak to desperation.

"Great Lord, there is . . . a problem."

"Mine or yours, creature?" he said, slightly impatient. The loading was going so *slowly*.

"Great Lord, we have disabling sickness."

"*What?*" Suddenly he was looming over the eunuch.

"No, please! Don't hurt me. It's only old Veskis, the bonesetter. *Please,* my Great Lord?"

Belazir's aquiline nostrils flared. "Speak."

"Over sixty ill warriors have sought medical aid, Great Lord. We have never seen the like." It swallowed. "Great Lord, we do not know how to cure the illness!"

Belazir had just finished a large meal. Now it lay like curdled hot lead in his gut. *Impossible.* He tapped at the notescreen, accessing recent files. Yes, over thirty warriors put down or suicided for infection. Not completely unprecedented, but among the heaviest numerically of instances on record. If another threescore had reported sick, there must be many who had not.

"How does the illness run?" Belazir asked.

"Swiftly in some, Great Lord. Fever, loss of nervous control, debility, nausea. Others more mildly. Still others recover quickly and are whole. From the blood of those I may produce a vaccine, in time."

"Do so," Belazir ordered. "Swiftly." *In time to avoid spotting my triumph here,* he thought. "Wait."

He tapped his notescreen again. Most sickness occurred among those on no fixed duty. Of those, t'Varak's ship suffered the most casualties. Belazir racked his brain for what he knew of diseases. Not much, since Kolnari were rarely bothered by disease: accident, yes. He reflected on this problem, queried the info-banks, thought again.

"Orders," he said. "Isolate those infected." Those whom they could, that is. A noble could be killed but not placed under restraint. "This may . . ." He hesitated. "*May* be related to the disease troubling the scumvermin." Hideous, that a disease would strike the Divine Seed more strongly than mere scumvermin. "The infected scumvermin are to be avoided. Go, post the orders."

That such a scourge should arise *now*, he thought, looking back at the notescreen. Loading was moving far too slowly. Chalku had given him a deadline; past that, they were to abandon anything remaining, kill and leave. If there was much less than he had promised, he would go from hero to goat. Even if the total he did manage was more than any other Kolnari had amassed, performance and prestige would be measured against expectation.

"Time," he muttered. Time was wasting, and the margin for error with it. He stood. "Computer. Kolnar, noon at Maridapore."

White-blue light flashed across the parkland, hurtful even to him in the instant before his pupils shrank to pinhead size.

Jekit nor Varak prowled the corridors. He was not in powered armor. There were not enough suits to go around and their maintenance requirements were fierce. The patrol was to enforce curfew and prevent sabotage, which was becoming a problem. He was in a flexible suit, with a comlink and a plasma rifle. The corridors in this section were darkened, which gave his IR-sensitive eyes the advantage over any scumvermin.

As if I needed it, he thought. His main enemy was tedium. The corridors were changeless and identical. Ten paces left, take a turn at random. Trot down a long length, checking that the seals on the doors were unbroken. Flatten to a wall and wait. He did isometrics then, muscle pulling on muscle against the strong flexible bones of his body. Nothing much else to do; except that he tired too soon, probably because of the damnable light gravity he had been living in on this station. It would be a relief to get back to Kolnar-standard on the ship.

Although there were compensations. Keriholen, for example. Jekit's teeth clicked together as he remembered how they had taken her, he and his brothers. Many times since the first occasion.

Worth the trouble, *he thought. Limber as an eel and tireless as a real woman.* Women were scarce for commoners. The nobles took so many. He and his four brothers—they were born at one birthing—had only two wives between them, held in common, and a mere eight children.

Jekit was sweating. He wiped his face on a sleeve and resumed the pacing, trying to push such thoughts out of his mind. Not until after his watch. It was *hot,* whatever the gauge said. His stomach felt odd. Maybe the plundered food was bad, although the Divine Seed could eat pretty well anything organic.

Simeon watched the pirate. This Jekit was a perfect choice. Definitely had the Mark-II virus, too pig-ignorant to know it and he was almost asleep from boredom anyway. A little surprise would be good for his circulation.

He checked the progress of the relief party, ten soldiers and a squad leader. Plenty of witnesses, also perfect. Timing was the key. They had only two guards to relieve before they reached Jekit.

Hurt my people, will you, Jekit? he thought. *Okay, now let's see how you like being on the other end of the stick.*

He began whispering. The words were loud enough to be audible, but not loud enough to be understood. Just nonsense syllables pronounced in inflections similar to the Kolnari language, minute after minute, not steadily but rising and falling and stopping altogether for random intervals. Then an increase in the volume until the nonsense was a tease, tantalizingly on the edge of audibility. Add subsonics guaranteed to have the hair standing up along the spine, although Kolnari didn't have body hair.

Goosebumps, then, he decided. Jekit paced, stopped, shook his head and brought the plasma rifle to port, thumbing off the safety.

Doesn't this snardly have any nerves? Simeon asked himself in frustration. Then he added the refinement; *things* flickering at the edge of vision. The pirate was probably seeing things without Simeon's visual aids since the sensors said his temperature was five percent over normal and rising. Sweat poured down his face. That was rare since the Kolnari metabolism didn't waste moisture.

Simeon constructed a less transparent image. *Ah, that made him jump,* Simeon thought. "Rahkest!" he whispered, just loud enough to be understood.

Die, in Kolnari.

"Who's there?" Jekit called out, swinging his weapon around. "Who goes? *Answer me!*"

Simeon had a conversation going now, male and female voices whispering vehemently. He moved the whisperers down the corridors, through chambers and halls and galleries. Now they were around the corner, now they were overhead, now right behind him.

Jekit spun, his weapon leveled. "Scumvermin!" he shouted. The warning indicator flicked as his forefinger took up the slack on the trigger key.

The squad had exited the elevator on Jekit's level and were marching towards his station. Trotting like a wolf-pack, rather; the leader was in armor, moving at the same pace. *Slam-slam-slam,* half a tonne pounding down at every step.

The Kolnari had his back pressed to the wall. Simeon overlaid the powersuit's footfalls, turning them into drumbeats in time with the fevered warrior's own heart. His head was snapping back and forth wildly, rims of white showing around the amber of his eyes.

Off to the right, around the corner from which his replacement would come, a voice called.

"Jekit!" His officer called. "Turn to, idler, fool! Report."

Jekit almost moaned with relief opening his mouth to call back. When he did he found the words matched, overlaid, neutralized *by something.* Shout, scream, nothing but the same blurred yammer.

"Painrod for you, seedless slothman," came the warning from his officer.

Jekit crouched and began making his way along the wall towards the voice. Halfway down the long wall, he jerked and vomited convulsively, bewildered. It had never happened to him before, that he lost his food.

Footsteps sounded from around the corner as the replacement squad advanced smartly towards him. He heard a soft hiss behind him and turned. He screamed as he looked into a shape out of homeworld legend, a twenty-eyed worm with gnashing concentric mouths, thicker through the body than a man was high.

"*Ancha!*" he screamed and fired. *Grinder.* There was nothing wrong with his reflexes yet, and the spear of nuclear fire lanced through the monster.

Gotcha, Simeon thought again. He'd been pretty sure that worm program was modeled on something native to Kolnar. So its name was "grinder"! Appropriate enough.

"Grinder" vanished. Behind it was a figure in power armor, slowly toppling over backwards with the whole upper part of the torso gone. The squad behind had already gone to earth and returned fire. A line of light touched Jekit's right shoulder, and the plasma gun fell away. The blurring, blanking wall of un-sound fell away from his ears so suddenly that he could hear the slight whine as the weapon automatically cycled another deuterium pellet into the chamber. A plasma beam licked out at Jekit and his legs vanished from the knees down.

And he was still *hot.* His wounds did not hurt yet, insulated by shock, although he could smell the heavy fried meat odor. But his *head* hurt, it hurt . . . The others were rushing forward to secure him for interrogation. It would go very badly for them if he died first.

Awright! Simeon thought. Still, it should be fun listening to Jekit, the mighty warrior, explaining why he freaked like that. *Now, who's next?*

Belazir and Aragiz knelt together before Pol t'Veng. She was wearing the black robe and hood of an adjudicator and, in the dim light, that left only the yellow glow of her eyes visible. Belazir knelt with grace. The t'Veng was inferior by rank and birth, but she was efficient. Also a woman, of course, but that meant less these days than it had on Kolnar. Everything in space was a protected environment, like the fortress-holds. You either lived or died, generally. Aragiz knelt in quivering tension and the smell of his rage was musky, irritating to Belazir.

"I find," she said at last, "that Jerik nor Varak, free common-fighter of subclan t'Varak, opened fire on clan-kin while in hostile ground, without prior attack." That was the only excuse, and motivations or reasons mattered nothing, by Kolnari law.

"He killed: one petit-noble officer of subclan t'Marid. He destroyed: one suit of powered armor. Here is the judgment of the High Clan.

"At the next rendezvous of all units, t'Varak gens shall render to Belazir t'Marid forty hundred units of Clan credit or goods to the same value, neutrally appraised. They shall also render five breeding-age but unbred females of petit-noble or higher rank, fully educated. In addition, Belazir t'Marid may go among the concubines and wives of Aragiz t'Varak for one cycle and sow there as he wills. Aragiz t'Varak shall do likewise among Belazir t'Marid's. Judgement is rendered."

As one, they bowed low enough to touch their foreheads to the deck. *A good judgement,* Belazir thought. Fair, wise, and most of all, expedient. Part of the longstanding trouble was that the t'Varak gens were not as closely linked by seed as the rest of the High Clan families. They had been landless mercenaries on homeworld, and had had the bad luck to sign on with the High Clan just before a war that ripped up half a continent and ended in headlong flight for the survivors. Technically mercenaries were not subject to the extermination-proscription of the vanquished nobility. Like peasants and commoners, they could switch allegiance to the winning side. Technicalities did tend to get lost in the fine glow of victory, though. . . .

Of course, Aragiz t'Varak would be unlikely to look at it in quite that way. Still, in the long term, knowing the closer relationship would reduce hostility. Hopefully.

Without word or gesture, Aragiz rose and stalked out. *No style at all,* Belazir thought. The fine was a trifle compared to what the station was bringing in, and they both had sixty or seventy children already. He merely hoped the t'Varak intellect was training and not a taint.

The lights came up, and Pol removed the hood. That changed her from adjudicator to ordinary noble once more. "Fool," she said, with no need to say exactly who.

"Dolt," he agreed, and snapped his fingers.

Serig entered. They settled in comfortably.

"Loading is going too slowly," Belazir said.

"Truth, lord," Serig answered.

"Okay," Simeon whispered in Channa's ear. *"He's in position."*

The loading bay at the south-polar docking tube was more crowded than it had ever before been in the station's seventy-odd years, mostly cluttered with disassembled equipment from the electronics fabricators two levels below, broken down just enough to let them be moved through the freight elevators. It would be more efficient to strip them down further and box the components, but that made them too easy to sabotage. There had been executions of stationers after Kolnari inspections showed *how* easy. Delicate electronics . . .

Weird, Channa thought, ostentatiously looking down at her notescreen. There had been no reprisals at all for the *deaths* and there had been a fair number. The Kolnari had just increased their patrols, as if taunting the stationers.

Channa turned to the pirate technician. *Even weirder.* You didn't think of pirates as having technicians. They looked much the same as the sleekly dangerous warriors and flamboyant nobles, but brisker.

Then again, they've kept thousands of people and hundreds of ships going for three generations—seven of theirs.

"Lord," she said in the appropriate meek tone, "here's the next load. Do you accept?"

The Kolnari looked at the fabricator. It was a spindle-shaped synth-and-metal machine about three meters long and one through at the widest point; half tubing and molecular shape chambers, half modules. Both points of the spindle ended in tapped burls that fitted into a bearing race. Underneath it was a floater cradle with—apparently—six arms and a twenty-centimeter base.

The Kolnari said something in her own language to her team—women were more common among their technical class, evidently—and they went to work, plugging in their own info-systems and a portable power-feed to bring the fabricator up to standby.

"All order is," the pirate said to her, waving her back. "Scumvermin, next bring."

The loading bay was one hundred meters by two hundred by three. Two Clan transports were docked at the outer hatches. Two-thirds of the way down the deck, the enemy had drawn a red line. On either side was a squad in power armor. Floating over *them* were pods of small servo-guns, antipersonnel weapons, heavy needlers that could be fired without endangering the fabric of the station. The weapons were highly dangerous to anyone not in combat armor, of course. Stationside of the line were civilians, working mostly in their own teams with a few Kolnari for supervision. Dockside of the line were only the Clan crews. There were three checks from the initial position to the line: once while the equipment was being stripped down, a second when the stationer stevedores took charge, and a third when it was ready to go over the line itself.

If any of the checks showed damage, the stationers in charge were flogged to death with a powered whip. Falling below quota earned ten strokes, which reduced the team's efficiency drastically but was a *very* potent motivator.

It was ingenious, and working far too well.

Simeon murmured again, "*Yeah, they're locked in.*"

Channa forced herself not to look at the eyes of the Kolnari. However Simeon was doing it, it was not simple holographic projection. Maybe tightbeam on the retina. . . .

Amos was whistling cheerfully as he swung the lifter around. *God, he's even gutsier than he is pretty,* Channa thought. They'd volunteered for this. Too many nerves had been shattered by the holocast record of the floggings. Someone had to restore confidence. To the Kolnari, it looked like the leaders were giving an example of enthusiastic obedience. Joseph bowed low as he handed over the controller pad for the cradle. Across the back of his overall was printed *Scumvermin Rule OK*. One of Simeon's suggestions to build morale.

The cradle followed obediently over the red line, behind the Kolnari technicians and toward the waiting cargo bay of the transport. The line divided the gravity fields; one Standard gravity at the line itself, running quickly up to 1.6 at the lowered ramp-entrance. The work party moved through the crowds and the waiting chains of lifters. There was a howl as the four light arms—suddenly there were only four—of the cradle gave way. The Kolnari team leapt in fearlessly, but the lifter failed in a burst of sparks and boomed hollowly to the deck plates. The fabricator slewed out of the broken cradle and onto the bent legs of the crew chief as she heaved back at the weight ten times her own.

The pirate alarms rang like angry windchimes. Channa and the others froze. So did the damaged tech. The other Kolnari lifted the damaged fabricator and set it down on a pad of packing-fiber nearby; lifting with unison grunt of effort and walking six steps with a low-voiced chant. They set the machine down with a mother's tender care. The tech lay with the broken bones projecting through the dark skin of her kneecaps, blood welling around them and the whites showing all around her honey-colored eyes. The flying guns swooped in. Channa found herself looking down the business end of one, and so did each of the group that had brought the ruined machine to the edge of the Kolnari line.

Warriors followed; not the armored specialists, but crew on rotation duty. One was pulling a powered whip from his belt as he came. Channa closed her eyes, but the first stroke never landed. She heard his voice murmur the Kolnari equivalent of, "Yes, sir."

She opened her eyes again. Amos and Joseph were rocking back on their heels as if they'd been ready to spring.

"*He queried the big boss,*" Simeon ghost-spoke through her implant. "*Belazir's telling him to check the inspection records.*"

The Kolnari did, snapping away her notescreen, then going over to check the injured technician. Nobody had attended to her. Despite her being an enemy, Channa felt a little squeamish looking at the white splinters and the quivers of pain that ran across the fine-boned oval face.

"*She's saying it was a regulation medium-heavy lifter, when she looked it over,*" he said. "*He's checking. Belazir says it's not your fault.*"

Sweat was running down Channa's back. She began to relax, then swore under her breath as the warrior drew a knife. The technician closed her eyes and tilted her head; a quick stab in the back of the neck and she was still.

"*Well, that worked,*" she said to Simeon.

"*What do you mean?*"

"*I'm not quite sure.*"

The fabricator would have to go back to the machine-shop, two levels up, to be repaired. The machines required to produce replacements for the damaged parts could not be disassembled until the work was done.

Belazir moved a squadron of light cruisers to a new quadrant and sat back. *So,* he thought.

Amazing. Channahap was fighting him to a standstill in this strategy game. She had actually *won* one of the earlier rounds. A very, very good player; few Kolnari senior officers could have done better, and war-game tournaments were one of the main ways they filled their leisure.

"The Channahap does well?" Serig said. He looked over his commander's shoulder into the *Bride's* display tank, then reran the opening moves on a smaller screen nearby. "Well, indeed."

Belazir nodded. *What a woman!* he thought enthusiastically. He had stopped referring to her as scumvermin to himself some time ago. The battle of delay and lies she had waged against him was just as skillful and tricky as the war games. It was a true pity she was not of the Divine Seed; an even greater pity that she would not live very many years in the environment of the Clan's ships. Outsiders rarely found the air, food, and water of Kolnar life-supporting. Certainly the Kolnari's own ancestors had not, until they adapted.

But I will enjoy her greatly while she lives.

"Now, these reports," he went on to Serig. "They read like the ravings of the insane. What do they mean?"

"An excellent question, my lord. One that I should like to ask some of these scumvermin."

"You consider this to be the result of enemy action?"

"It seems reasonable to me, my lord. Drugs to the troops affected. Or, they may know something about these phenomena."

Belazir considered his second. "Or they may know nothing. It could even be some sabotage scheme of Aragiz, difficult though that is to believe. Or a side-effect of this . . . illness."

"Bad for morale either way, my lord. And the illness itself may be a weapon."

He nodded. "Very well. Take five slaves, chosen at random, none critical to the station's function, and torture them."

"Only five, my lord?" Serig's soft voice expressed astonishment.

"These are an unusually soft and sensitive people," Belazir answered. "Five will be quite sufficient. More would cause panic. For now, let the scumvermin as a whole remain calm and complacent and cooperative. Let them panic later at a time of our choosing. Hmm? Torture the five for the information we need on this—phenomenon. If they know nothing, take others."

"Shall I broadcast that?"

"No, no, Serig. If we broadcast our ignorance, we make plain that there is something our warriors fear. If it is enemy action, they will know what we seek—or the next five."

Serig bowed from the waist. "Very good, my lord."

Belazir returned his attention to the game.

"Why?" Channa asked.

"You will take your hands from my desk and you will stand straight," Belazir told her calmly, pointing a slender dagger at her. He stared at Channa until she complied.

"Two of those people are probably going to die," she whispered, breathing hard. "Lord and God. They were tortured."

"Of course they were. I ordered it so."

"But *why*?"

He stood and walked slowly around the desk to stand close behind her, then spoke softly into her ear. "We are conquerors. We do *not* *explain* our actions. This is not a game such as we play in your quarters, lovely Channa, this is reality."

She carefully folded her hands before her and lowered her eyes.

"I apologize for my impetuousness," she said humbly. "I was trained to take my duties seriously, and sometimes this makes me rash. It's why I must ask about this terrible matter. I can't believe that you enjoy doing such things." She looked at him appealingly over her shoulder. "Please don't hurt my people."

"And you lie so badly," he said. He studied her face for a moment. "My troops," he went on thoughtfully, "spoke of 'things' flickering at the corners of their eyes, of 'voices' murmuring things not quite heard."

"What has that got to do with *us*?"

He walked around her and sat on a corner of his desk. "Perhaps nothing, perhaps everything. That is what we wanted to know."

"And it never occurred to you that perhaps something in the mixture of gases that we breathe might cause this effect in your people? Or that these 'things' flickering just out of sight might be an infestation of insects . . ."

"Oh no, they were, according to the reports, much too large to be mere insects."

"Some other vermin, then."

"Doubtful."

"Well, what about my first suggestion, perhaps our atmosphere requires adjustment?"

"Possible."

"Then perhaps you could send some volunteers to our medical center for tests."

Belazir laughed. "No. We know that a virus is loose. However, we have no interest in a cure for it. If it causes troops to become non-functional, we will kill them ourselves. Unless it endangers this mission, we will take no countermeasures."

Channa gaped for a moment.

"We did not become the Divine Seed," he continued, "by pampering weakness. After investing so much capital and time in training, it is, however, inconvenient to have adults die. When we return, we will spread the virus ourselves, quite deliberately, among the children of the High Clan. If this sickness is your doing, you do us a service—as do those who ambush our troops in the corridors. It reduces the ranks of imperfect Seeds."

"Ah, she is magnificent," he quoted softly to himself in his own language. "Her stride is the lightning striking. In her right hand is a sword of flame, in her left the goad of pain. Her voice is the shriek of the north wind. In her eyes flash comets, portents of wonder, and her hair is a storm at midnight. Between her thighs is the road to Paradise. I look upon her and my strength rises, yet I rage without fulfillment." He leaned closer and Channa could feel his breath on her lips.

Well, Simeon thought, *that last bit rather neatly sums up my relationship with Channa.* He relayed a running translation.

"You've made a real conquest, Happy."

"*That*—is—*not*—*funny,*" Channa subvocalized.

The Kolnari touched her lightly with the point of the dagger, then returned to his chair, leaving her shivering where she stood. He touched his tongue to the bead of blood on the steel.

"Perhaps," Belazir said, his voice amused, "I should take you with me when we go. I would give you something to fight besides boredom. You deserve the challenge." Then he smiled. "You may go."

Channa turned and walked away on shaking legs. When she was in the elevator, she vented her frustration in a savage tone.

"I really want to kill him, Simeon. I can see myself doing it, just what I would do, and I think I would enjoy it." She paused. "See how bad company corrupts my morals?"

"What did you think of that poem?"

"I wasn't listening."

"I think he was trying to flatter you."

"'Her voice is like the shrieking of the north wind'?"

"I thought you weren't listening?"

"Well, I caught *that.*" She laughed weakly. "Never tell a woman her voice reminds you of something shrieking. It won't win you any points."

"Important dating tip, Channa, thank you."

"Oh . . . I love you, Simeon. You keep me sane. And the Prince of Darkness can—"

"—eat shit and die." *I love you too, Channa, and you drive me crazy.*

CHAPTER TWENTY-ONE

ANOTHER POINT OF light flared in the holo tank.

"You have destroyed my dreadnought," Belazir said, surprise and amusement in his voice. He looked up at Channa. She was sweating heavily, strings of black hair plastered to her forehead. The Kolnari was calm as ever as he took another draught of the sparkling water flavored with metal salts.

"That makes . . ." He paused to recollect. "Seventy-five wins for me and three for you. Ah, well." He dapped his hands, and attendants brought his equipment. "Enough pleasure; there is work to be done."

"Okay, people," Simeon said. The voices died down. "We've got a little time. You-know-who's sleeping the sleep of the wicked."

The screens went silent, and so did the little clutch of men and women seated around the lounge table.

"They're going to be more or less finished in one more day-cycle," he went on.

"One?" Amos said. "They have more items marked for shipping than they could handle in one day."

"Trust me. I've been eavesdropping. They're doing that to fool us. Nearly fooled me! Only their top people know."

"How long has it been?" Patsy whispered.

"Sixteen days," Simeon said.

Doctor Chaundra swallowed. "A hundred dead. Many times that are . . . injured, in various ways. We cannot endure more of this."

"We won't have to. One more day, and we're saved or we're all dead."

"The Navy?" Joseph said.

"They dropped a scout into the system today," Simeon replied. His image raised a hand to stem the babble. "It's heavily stealthed. I have the recognition codes, or I'd never have detected it. Yes, the flotilla is coming.

"They *should* be here, and soon. However, we've got to have a plan for the worst case." He paused before he could go on. "The worst case is the Navy *doesn't* get here quite in time. We've got to give it our best shot. The Kolnari've got a lot of their people spread out, and their ships docked. They're planning on keeping it that way until the last minute. I've figured out a few indicators that'll tell me right down to the minute."

Channa swallowed and nodded. One of them would be Belazir coming to take her off to the *Dreadful Bride*.

"The battle platform will undock first. When they start that, we've got to begin our uprising! If we can cut enough of them off from their ships and keep the ships from undocking—I've got some plans on that tactic—then they *can't* blow the station."

Amos nodded somberly. "The cost . . . the cost in lives will be very high. But there is no alternative."

"We cannot fight for long," Joseph said. "A delaying action at best. They have the weapons, armor, organization. And they need not fear damage to the station. They will use their onwatch ships to force-dock through the hull, outflank us. We have no real weapons."

"How many times have we gamed the uprising?" Amos said, rubbing his hand across his face. "Forty, fifty? Not once have we won, no matter if you or I command."

Simeon nodded. "Better to die on your feet than die on your knees," he said. Grim smiles greeted the sally. Most of them had seen his tapes of the Warsaw Ghetto. "I can disorganize them a lot more than they expect," he went on. "We've got some weapons, too."

They all looked at the column.

"Mikesun?" he said.

The section rep was haggard and drawn, as you would expect from someone who had been working in cramped quarters for more than two weeks.

"I've got them unpacked and ready," he said. His hands moved into the light. "'Bout a thousand. Plus the explosives you told us to get ready."

Suddenly he had a needler in his hands. A huge chunky-looking thing, of no make any of them recognized.

"Where on . . . where did you get *those*, Simeon?" Channa asked.

"Ah, um." Simeon sounded slightly embarrassed, she thought. "Well, you know how I like to collect stuff. They were cheap—a ship needed some fuel bad and didn't have credit. And I just liked the thought of having my own arsenal. 'Someday we might need this kind of stuff.' I was right, wasn't I?"

"Yes, bless you," she said simply, because the relief she felt at seeing honest-to-God weapons was so intense.

Somebody swore. "Why haven't we had those before now? I've had my people attacking Kolnari patrols with their bare *hands*—"

"Because we couldn't let them take us seriously too soon!" Channa said sharply. "Any sort of formal weaponry would have alerted them. We had to do as much damage as we could without such assists, until the last moment. They won't be expecting us to have needlers. We'll have surprise *and* shock on our side."

Amos leaned forward, more warmth in his tone than was usual when he spoke to the brain. "How are they to be distributed?"

"Remember when I said I'd put some other stuff that might be useful in the sealed-off sections? And Patsy and Joat've been mixing stuff around, too, through the passageways."

"With a thousand needlers—" Amos began, and then shrugged, oddly hopeless. Joseph nodded.

"Hmm. What make are those?" Patsy said, with a spark of her old interest.

"Ursinar manufacture," Simeon said. "Obscure race, big and hairy, always insisted that it was their right to arm bears."

"This may only prolong the agony and delay the inevitable," Amos said. "So little against so much." Then he shook himself. "Still, it is better to die fighting."

"Hell, better to win and live," Simeon said.

"In the meantime," Amos said, standing and sweeping his eyes from screen to screen, "push them hard. They are incapable of resisting a territorial challenge from a weaker opponent—even when it would be logical to pull back. Take more risks."

Well, he takes as many as the rest of us do, Channa thought. *Quite the little commander all the same.* Wry amusement colored her exhaustion.

"Security monitor's locked," Joat said. "Now, your bit."

Seld went to the electronics access panel and began fiddling with its innards. Then he inserted the hedron he had prepared. The resulting picture would be distorted in the way the security computers had been since the pirate worm program went in. But they *would* distort the images of Joat and Seld in selective ways. Making them appear taller, much darker . . .

Joat went in the opposite direction, placing herself at the end of the corridor in the lookout's position.

When he had finished he joined her and tapped her shoulder. "Time," he whispered.

"Just a sec." She opened her pack and withdrew a monocrystal filament dispenser. The thread was a molecule in diameter but incredibly strong. Dangerous to handle, too. Thinner than the thinnest knife-blade could ever be.

"What are you gonna do with that?" he asked puzzled. "I thought you were planting something."

"Stick around and you'll see," she said, waggling her eyebrows.

She knelt beside the wall and attached an end of the beryllium monocrystal filament to the corridor panel at about knee height. Using the tiny laser that was part of the dispenser, the end was soldered into place, leaving a slight stickiness when she touched the wall. She reeled out the invisible fiber and tacked the other end to the opposite wall, keeping a careful mental image of where it was.

Seld turned pale. "You can't . . . you know what that stuff does!"

"Sure do," she said smugly. "Ol' Jack-of-All-Trades is gonna give new meaning to 'cut off at the knees.'"

"You *can't*," he said, and grabbed her arm. "They're bastards, but they're . . . they're *sentients.* You can't be maiming them like that." His voice had taken on a tinge of his father's accent again, but he was shaking with tension. Drops of sweat broke out at the edge of his reddish-brown hair. "It's evil! What are you thinking about?"

She snatched her arm from his grip. "I'm thinking about what *they* did. Tortured people. What they did to Patsy, and your friend Juke. I'm thinking about *payback.*"

He licked his lips. "Not like this, I won't have anything to do with it. Couldn't you just . . . kill them clean? C'mon, Joat?"

She pushed him back with her shoulder and tacked another line through at about waist height for a tall adult.

"Sim says," she went on, drawing three more lines about shin-height, "that cutting the enemy up is better than killin' 'em. Shakes them up more, and they gotta take care of them."

"If we do stuff like this, how are we different from them?"

She turned on him, snarling. "'Cause we *live here* and we're not doing this for *fun*! Or to make a nardy *credit* off it!"

Seld sat down abruptly against the corridor wall.

"Seld?" she said, her face smoothing out abruptly and her voice changing. "Seld, you okay? You need your meds?"

"I'm okay. I just . . . I just don't like you as much when you're like this, Joat. And I really like you. You know?"

Sometimes I don't like me much, Joat thought. She turned away and blew out her lips in exasperation. "Don't go buckawbuckaw on me now, Seld, 'cause it's gonna get worse around here before it gets better. *If* it gets better." *Everything always gets worse.*

He raised his head from his knees. "If I'm going to die soon I want to die clean," he said. "Gimme your V-pills."

"Why?"

"Lost mine."

"Okay." They were supposed to take the pill if they came into *contact* with a Kolnari. Joat didn't intend to, or to live if she did. Seld pocketed the pills and stalked off toward his own escape route.

She pursed her lips and tacked a new line to the wall at the opening of the connecting corridor, at what she estimated as head-height for a Kolnari.

Then she ducked under it by a wide margin, tip-toed back toward the first line. She stopped well short of it and listened.

Come on, you gruntfudders, she thought. *Fardling move.* They should be amazed that it was taking the first patrol so long to respond. She went to stand by the sabotaged panel and listened, hearing only the pounding of her own heart, which felt as if it wanted to tear free of her thin chest. Then at last, her quick ears caught the sound of movement. She counted to five and began to retreat toward the second line. She entered the corridor just as she heard a shouted "Halt!" in Kolnari.

Perfect, she thought, *all they saw was the coverall!* They hadn't said *halt, scumvermin,* either.

A couple of shots were fired; light weapons, needles spanging off metal. The squad leader barked an order for cease fire and pursuit. Feet tapped the mesh covering of the corridor, in the distinctive long strides of the pirates.

Screams rang down the corridor, clanging and echoing in the close space. Joat leaned forward from where she crouched and looked out around the corner. There was a malicious grin on her face, but it died at what she saw. Two of the Kolnari soldiers lay on the floor in a small pond of blood, hanging over the ultrastrong invisible wire that had sawn through their legs and opened them up from navel to backbone like a butterflied shrimp. As she watched, a body fell to the ground in two pieces, and there was so *much*, so much blood and guts and all the colors, and a pink-purple lung . . .

One Kolnari trooper reached toward her severed legs and cut her hand in half to the wrist. Two fingers flopped uselessly as she clutched her arm and screamed and screamed, not in pain or fear but sheer terror of the invisible *something* that had killed her.

"Oh, multi grudly," Joat whispered to herself. The sound of the words against what she saw was so out of place that she felt hysterical giggles bubbling up. Something warned her that that sort of giggling would be very difficult to stop once it started, so she backed away. Her eyes were huge saucers in her thin pale face.

At the other end of Joat's corridor was one of Simeon's hidden elevators. She tossed the wire spool out into the corridor before she entered it. Behind her there were shouts: the next enemy squad. From the ringing sounds, they tested to find the wires with the barrels of their weapons. There was a double thud as one unwary Kolnari turned too fast into the corridor and decapitated himself on the final trap.

Moving briskly, Joat exited the elevator three levels up and entered an access corridor meant for electrical repairs. She transferred to one of the small ventilation shafts and dragged herself quickly and efficiently to a larger open area where an array of the shafts met. She was safe here: it was one of her bases, with a pallet and some ration boxes as well as tools pilfered from Engineering, if you could call it pilfering when they handed them to you willingly. They were calling Joat the "Spirit of SSS-900-C," or Simeon's Gremlin.

Then she was violently sick to her stomach. Servos arrived, clicking and cheeping to themselves, and cleaned up the mess.

Joat lay down, cradling her face on her arms, and wept bitterly. Long wracking sobs, like nothing she could remember.

"Joat . . . honey, have you been hurt?" Simeon's voice was soft and warm, like a vaguely remembered something that once held her.

She lifted a face flushed with weeping, but her lips were white.

"I'm not as tough as I thought," she said through her sobs. "I didn't think . . . Shit, no! I've gotta heart like a rock. That's me, Joat the killer! Did you hear me snancing Seld for a wuss?" A cough racked her, and she wiped her eyes on the back of her hands. "He'll hate me! I hate myself! It was so—" And she threw herself down and bit the mattress. An eerie crooning wail echoed through the corridor.

"Shhh, it's all right, it's all right."

"I wanna go home!"

"Joat. Joat, honey. I'm with you. You are home. You'll always have a home with me. *I* don't hate you, Joat. You're not bad, honey. But sometimes things get through to the good part of you that doesn't like the tough part of you, and that's what just happened."

The servos rolled forward and tucked a blanket around her. Simeon began to croon, directing it at her ears where she hugged the blanket about her head and only tufts of hair escaped.

"I want Channa."

I can't hold her, Simeon thought. *But I can sing. . . .*

"Do you call me liar to my face, Aragiz?" Belazir said.

"My people were killed," Aragiz t'Varak replied. "Security recorded Kolnari setting the trap, perhaps thinking to throw the blame on scumvermin. I *knew* scumvermin could not—"

"Do you give me the lie, t'Varak?"

The other captain stopped, torn between unwillingness to retract and inability to attack. Belazir was under no such constraints.

"Did it never occur to you, oh so straightforward cousin, that it might be scumvermin posing as Clan? That they are as capable of playing on our divisions as we are on theirs?"

"You call me dupe of scumvermin?"

"I say that you *bore* me, Lord Captain Aragiz t'Varak. You bore me beyond words, beyond bearing. Your existence makes the universe a place of tedium beyond belief!"

Aragiz's face relaxed, into a soft, welcoming smile. "When?"

"When Lord Captain Pol t'Veng's judgement is fulfilled. To the fist." A death-duel in the old manner, with spiked steel gloves.

"And now," Belazir went on, "get your household and all else to your ship." Quick suspicion marked the other captain's face. "Yes, I know you were massing your groundfighters. There is no time for feud here, t'Varak. Believe me."

The screen blanked. Serig took a step forward, an eyebrow raised.

"Lord, he *is* the dolt you named him. There is nothing wrong with his reflexes, though."

"As it may be," Belazir said. "I spoke the truth. It drives me to fury to have to call that one cousin, it truly does." He shook his head. "Today, we triumph, Serig. By running, yes: but triumph nonetheless. So, we—"

The dockside guards' chimes rang through the bridge. "Great Lord, we have a scumvermin female, claiming to have information for you."

Serig chuckled. There had been a fair number of scumvermin females coming to the dock and asking for Belazir. Some few he had taken himself, and passed the others on to Serig or the crew.

"No, wait," Belazir said. "Information of what?"

"A conspiracy, involving the scumvermin leaders-that-were and the prey-ship, lord."

"Send her up." Belazir looked at Serig and shrugged. "Why not?"

Waiting was swift. "I would speak with you alone, Master," the woman said, looking meaningfully at Serig.

"I am generous to women," Belazir declared. Quite true, or she would never have reached him. "So generous I did not hear you, scumvermin."

She blinked and swallowed hard, looking from one to the other.

"Why have you come?"

"The . . . they held me prisoner, Master and Gggg—" Even then, she could not quite bring herself to utter the blasphemy. Then Belazir looked up at her, and she felt herself huddle down behind the barrier of her skull, knowing it was not enough. So a sicatooth looked at a lamb.

"—God," she completed, uncertain if it was the obscene honorific they demanded or a prayer. "I . . . I have information." She stammered, put a hand to her face. *I escaped,* she thought. They must be really conspiring against her—against Amos, as well. Holding her from him. She whimpered slightly. She could remember his words of love, the promises—and nightmares of rejection, of failure. The brass-colored eyes were waiting.

"I am Rachel bint Damscus. I am from Bethel. I was on the ship that you were chasing. Forty of us survived the journey and took refuge on this station."

Neither of the Kolnari moved or spoke.

"So . . . you are from Bethel?" Belazir leaned his head on his fist. One finger caressed his lower lip. "Turn your head. Stand. Bend. Sit once more."

Belazir turned to Serig. "Possible," he said meditatively. "Similar scumvermin race, but there are many varieties here."

"Unlikely, lord."

Belazir nodded. And in any case academic. They were nearly ready to go. *If they have deceived us, what matter?* The memory of his slap in the face of the *Bride's* joss came back to him. Perhaps the old customs had some real strength after all. . . .

She stared at him. There was something odd about her eyes, Belazir decided. Her lips trembled, and her fingers, but not in terror; he could always identify *that*. Some nerve disorder, perhaps? He leaned forward and snuffed. Not a healthy scent.

"Yes." She nodded once, sharply. "Master and God."

"Why do you tell me this? Surely you know that it is dangerous?"

The woman began to tremble with rage, and tears filled her eyes.

"She . . . that black-haired, black-hearted whore seduced my betrothed! She promised him power! But she lied. He plays the fool for her, does what she tells him, sleeps in her bed . . ." Her voice broke and she stopped, swallowed a few times before she could speak again. "The one you have been told is Simeon-Amos is truly Amos, the leader who brought us here from Bethel. The real Simeon is a shellperson, a thing they call a brain, and he is still running this station."

"A . . . shellperson?" Belazir t'Marid closed his eyes for a moment. "Ah! We have heard, but never seen."

Serig leaned down to him. "Lord, a sort of protein computer, no? But our worm subverted their system and holds it in our fist. Would we not have known?"

"It would explain anomalies," Belazir said, chasing the elements that made him believe the impossible "And—ah! I am as great a fool as Aragiz t'Varak!"

"Surely not, lord," Serig said, surprised. "Not on your worst day. Not on my worst day. Not on the worst day of this scumvermin womb here."

"I was about to dismiss this, time being short. Dismiss potentially the richest single piece of loot on the station!"

"A shellperson is so much?"

"A strategic asset," Belazir said. "Come, we will look into this. It is time, in any case."

He turned his eyes back to the scumvermin. From all he could see, she was manic-depressive, swinging from healthy, normal terror to an exalted state where she had complete confidence in his interest, in his support. As if he were a player in her play . . .

"Mad," he said. "Yet . . . My vanity, perhaps, but little Channahap plays the war game far too well. An encysted brain, tied to great computers and their data banks, though?" He cocked an eyebrow at Rachel.

"I can only tell you what I have heard," the woman said, babbling in her desire to be believed. "I have been told that they are people who have been put into a casing as infants and that they then become like a computer." She wrung her hands and looked desperately from one to the other. "I'm telling you the truth. They are plotting against you, Master and God!"

Belazir smiled in polite agreement. "Of course they are." On that, at least, they were agreed. He rose. "Come, we will go and talk to them." He turned to Serig. "Have Baila tell Channahap that I will see her in her office. Tell her to have Simeon-Amos there as well."

Simeon spoke, interrupting Channa at her work station. "Channa, Belazir t'Bastard is heading this way with Rachel in tow. I don't know what's up, but he's looking both grim and pleased."

Before Channa could speak, the comm chimed and Baila's face appeared.

"Channahap," she said. "The Lord Captain t'Marid is on his way to your office. You will await him there. He commands the presence of Simeon-Amos. Obey." The screen went dark.

"*Shit*," Channa said, and tapped her fingers thoughtfully. "You're right, Simeon, this does not look good. I am so sick of that girl. She's driving me . . . crazy. Simeon?"

"You're right on the button about her state of mind, Channa. Our Rachel's crazy, not just going crazy but absolutely nuts, gonzo, a sandwich shy of a picnic, packin' a short seabag . . ."

"Sim!"

"Right, I'll have Chaundra draw up a case history about some kind of dementia. You brief Simeon-Amos, I'll spread the word."

"You got it. Simeon-Amos," she said over the intercom, "get in here."

"And Channa?"

"Yes?"

"I think this is it. The battle platform just started severing its stationside power leads. We've got a real opportunity to hurt them hard if we can get Belazir out of comm with his people. It could make the difference."

Channa nodded. She had been prepared to try an assassination on the *Bride*, but that, at best, was unlikely. Fear was remote: no time for it.

"Simeon-Amos," she began, when he entered the lounge. "Belazir's coming, with Rachel." His face froze. "Here's what we're going to do— no time for an argument."

The crates made gentle plopping noises as they slid out of the meter-deep green water of the algae pools and stood dripping on the slotted metal of the walkways. Ships had a closed system of tubing and enclosed tanks, but this arrangement—open metal rectangles stacked like trays—was more efficient for a station. The environment systems workers moved quickly, without wasted effort or much talking. This had not been a cheerful section since their chief returned to them, but there was a stolid satisfaction as the vac-covers were peeled back and the weapons went from hand to hand among the hundred or so technicians, office workers, and laborers.

Patsy Sue Coburn watched the needlers emerge, brutal and compact. She slung one over her shoulder. Ursinid weapons were submachinegun size for humans. Then she reached into the pool and retrieved her arc pistol, stripping off the plastic film.

"Wait for it," she whispered. If the Kolnari made one last swing through on their usual routes, they'd be by in half an hour or so.

The crew were crowding around the supervisors, getting a quick lesson on how to use a needler to best effect. Luckily, the weapons had simple controls: set the dial on the side to the full clockwise position and take up the trigger slack. Look down the barrel at the target and pull the trigger. Line of sight weapons with little recoil at short ranges, they should do well enough.

And they're all we've got, she reminded herself. She felt completely calm. In a way, she had been calm since she woke and saw Joat's face floating before her, like a ghost's in its pool of light. There was a feeling under that, a feeling that when she wasn't calm anymore, it was going to be very, very bad.

"Reckon I kin wait fer it," she told herself.

The others were looking at her.

"Just wait 'n till they come around," she said patiently for the hundredth time. "Simeon'll keep us all in touch." *I hope, I purely do.* "Now, when they git here, you burn 'em down. Then go down axial G-8 an' hit the bunch of 'em there. Amos'll be by about then. If not him, then me."

She nodded curtly and slung the needler further around to her back, freeing her hands for the climb up the interval ladder. The entrance to the venting system was where she would rendezvous with Joat. Not a difficult climb at first, since these were the biggest vents on the station. The circle of faces fell away below her, growing tiny amid the rectangular Escher shapes of the ponds and the huge color-coded maze of pipes for nutrient and water and waste.

Amos stood impassively behind Channa, hands clasped at his back. They dropped to a knee as Belazir entered. He took the seat before her desk, gestured to Channa to sit. The squad of soldiers began to crowd into the small office. The t'Marid snapped out an order in his own language and all but two of them withdrew.

Rachel stood beside his chair. She glared at Channa and then turned away, her fists clenched by her sides. To Amos she smiled tremulously.

Definitely, as Sim would say, a few cans short of a sixpack, Channa decided. *She looks as if she's* rescuing *him.*

Channa folded her hands in her lap. "Master and God, to what do I owe the honor of this visit?"

Belazir smiled and indicated Rachel with his hand. "I have been given some interesting information."

"I have told him everything!" Rachel said spitefully.

Channa and Amos regarded her blankly, then shook their heads and turned to Belazir.

"Everything?" Channa asked.

"She has told me that she and forty others survived the trip from Bethel, and that this man," he flicked his chin at Amos, "is her betrothed. She tells me that he is pretending to be Simeon and that the real Simeon is in fact a brain in a container or some such thing, who is running this station and the resistance to the High Clan."

He folded his hands and regarded her calmly. "This truth would solve certain difficulties."

Channa fought not to smile, making her eyes wide with disbelief. Belazir studied her closely. Amusement was not what he had anticipated.

"Simeon-Amos," she said at last, "please inform Doctor Chaundra that Rachel has been found and ask him to come and fetch her. Advise him that he may need some form of chemical restraint."

Belazir raised an eyebrow.

Channa looked to the t'Marid for permission for Amos to comply. Belazir flicked his fingers. Amos nodded and went into his own office to make the call.

"She lies yet again, lord," Rachel said, but she fell silent at a second flick of Belazir's hand.

Channa assumed an understanding expression. "This young woman is deranged. We don't restrain her because usually she is harmless and so are her fantasies. A tragic case, very resistant to psychotherapy."

"Foul whore—" Rachel began, urgently stepping forward.

Belazir made a chopping motion with his hand. A guard stepped forward and Rachel shut her mouth with an audible snap.

"Who is she, then?" he asked.

"We don't actually know," Channa said. "She was abandoned here, apparently by some transient merchanter. She had no I.D. No one came forward with any information about her. The doctor isn't sure if her insanity is the result of drugs or trauma. He says the only way to be one hundred percent sure is to do an autopsy, which obviously is out of the question. She's usually very sweet, at worst a mild nuisance. Perhaps the conditions . . ." and Channa made a vague motion with her hand to suggest that the occupation might have added to her instability. Channa made herself lean back casually in her chair, appearing at ease. "Perhaps it's a sign of progress that she is this aware of, ah, current events, Master and God. She must have concocted this fantasy about Bethel from the newstapes, for example."

Rachel exploded. "She lies!" She lunged for Channa, coming up with a jerk when the guard pulled her back by her long hair. Her gorgon's mask of rage did not even register the pain. She struggled briefly and then subsided as Amos came back into the room. "Amos," she pleaded, weeping, "help me!"

He looked at her with sympathy.

"Of course, I will help you, Rachel," he said. His mellow voice rang with sincerity. "We *all* wish to help you." He leaned close to Channa. "The doctor is on his way, Ms. Hap."

"No!" Rachel screamed. "No! How can you do this to me? She is using you, my love! Do not betray me! Please . . ." Tears began to leak down her long nose. "Please . . . please."

Channa's stomach twisted. *She is crazy.* Probably curably crazy—most were. Irritation faded before pity, and pity faded before the threat of the Kolnari putting any weight into Rachel's tale.

Amos' sympathy was achingly real.

"There, there," he said soothingly. "You are ill, Rachel. Daddy will call the doctor to make it right." He offered the rag doll he was carrying. "You can have Siminta with you." He pressed it into her hands.

For a moment Rachel's sobs stopped and she stared at him in confusion. "What?" she said. "You are my betrothed, not my *father!*" She looked down at the doll, then dashed it to the floor and stamped her foot. "Stop *mocking* me!"

Amos shifted uneasily. "I cannot keep up with this. May I be excused until Doctor Chaundra comes?"

"It might be best," Channa said, addressing Belazir.

The t'Marid's eyes flicked over the three of them. "Daddy?" he said dubiously, then quirked an involuntary smile.

Channa sighed. "Last week, she thought she was five years old and Simeon-Amos was her father. She would start to cry if he left the room. For some reason, she's totally fixated on him. Chaundra supposes that he resembles whoever dropped her on us. We don't know."

"Lies!" Rachel shrieked. "lies."

"The doctor should be here by now," Amos said, clearly uncomfortable. He picked up the doll and placed it carefully on a chair. "Ah . . . she will grieve later if it isn't there."

"You may go," Belazir said to him. His eyes never left Channa's.

Chaundra strode in. He walked over to the weeping girl and touched her shoulder gently. "Poor Rachel," he said soothingly, "poor little girl."

"Doctor," t'Marid said sharply. Chaundra turned and stood very straight, looking down. "This is your patient?"

"Yes, Master and God."

"I do not appreciate having my time wasted on the daydreams of this madwoman. If she is so much as seen again—no, no point. You may go. Wait. You have records of her illness? I want to see them."

"Yes, Master and God, but I can't access them from this computer. Medical records are on a closed system to protect the privacy of the patient."

Belazir made an impatient, dismissive gesture. "Serig," he said. "See to it, then back to the *Bride*, continue on the matter we were planning. I will join you shortly." Serig bowed deeply.

"At your command, lord," he said, his teeth showing slightly in cold amusement. "The doll, too?"

Belazir snorted. "Go, insolence."

Rachel took a deep breath and seemed to fight for dignity; the twitching lessened in her face. "They *are* lying, Master and God, you will see. I am telling the truth."

That ended in a squawk as Serig turned her about and pushed between her shoulderblades. She ran to avoid falling, and the door hissed open before her.

"Now," Belazir snarled. Chaundra followed.

In the strained silence that followed, Belazir and Channa studied each other.

At last Belazir spoke. "Have your man return."

Channa pressed the intercom button, "Simeon-Amos, would you come in here, please?"

"This Rachel is in love with you," t'Marid observed, a hint of laughter in the yellow eyes.

"I confess," Amos said bitterly, "that I am beginning to despise the very sight of her."

The Kolnari raised an eyebrow.

"One day," Channa informed him, "she became convinced that Simeon-Amos was God and went around the station trying to convert people to worshipping him. She's been a very difficult experience for all of us, but she's been a particular strain on Simeon-Amos."

"Simeon-Amos," Belazir said, "is rather obviously the victim of a similar fixation on you, Channahap. A strong reason to believe your tale."

"Yes, Master and God," Channa said. She closed her eyes. *Simeon?* she asked.

"*He's halfway convinced, but still wondering. Impatient. Channa, it's starting. No more than twenty minutes until the pirates' sound alarm.*"

She opened her eyes again. "Simeon-Amos," she said. "Why don't you go see to the primary warehousing?"

He hesitated for a long second. "As you wish."

Now, Simeon commanded.

The worm raised its head from the ruins of the castle, looking out across a plain of volcanic fumaroles and blue-glowing lava. Flights of tongue-wasps patrolled there and arcs of lightning jagged over crater and canyon in patterned displays.

Thunder rumbled. A barking broke loose, louder than the thunder, and the vault of heaven split. The worm reared up, endless, longer than time, glutted with its feeding.

Simeon burst through and new skies sprang above the blasted landscape. The light changed from a pitiless white to the softer yellow of sunshine. The wasps fell, twitched, died. Three-headed and elephant-sized, the dog paced beside him. He raised the bat, struck.

The Grinder lunged and the concentric mouths damped on the end of the weapon. Then it recoiled, as the wood turned to a hoop and expanded, thrusting the rows of teeth back. It tried to shake loose, but the dog's three heads pinned its body to the earth. Wider and wider the glowing green circle swelled, until the mouths were a doorway.

A scalpel and icepick appeared in Simeon's hands. He walked into the worm's mouths and raised the tools.

"Heeeeeeere's Sim!" he shouted. "Open *wide*."

On the auxiliary command deck of the SSS-900-C, the Kolnari tech was reaching for the rear casing of the battle computer when he noticed the telltales.

"Lord!" he cried. "The—"

At that instant, the self-destruct charge built into the base of the computer detonated. It was not much in the way of an explosion, but much more than was required to destroy the sensitive inner workings. The designer had intended that to foil tampering. However, the flattened disk of jagged housing was more than enough to decapitate the pirate.

His companion reacted with tiger precision, scooping up his weapon and leaping for the doors. They clashed shut with a snap, and the warrior rebounded into the control chamber. It was empty save for him and there was no other exit. He pivoted, holding down the trigger of his plasma rifle and firing from the hip into the consoles.

"Naughty," a voice from the air said. The vents began to hiss. The Kolnari staggered at the first touch of the gas. His last act was to strip a grenade from his belt and trigger it, carefully held next to his own head.

"Damn," Simeon muttered. The mess was considerable and the

equipment wasn't going to be much use for a while. Then he took the equivalent of a deep breath and *concentrated*. Several dozen things must be done at once.

"Let me up," Channa said, stroking Belazir's back.

"Not for a while yet," Belazir said lazily. "I have hastened as it is. There is another five minutes available." His body was dry against her sweat-slick one, but much warmer, with the higher metabolism of his breed.

"Are we staying, then?" she breathed against his ear.

"No," he replied. "You suspected?"

"That you'd take me with you, or that today would be the day to go? Both." She wiggled. "Now, *please*. I have to get some stuff."

"I shall keep you well," Belazir said, then rolled away off her. "Be swift."

He lay idly on the sofa, watching her disappear into the bedroom. *Memorable,* he decided. Starting with her skinning out of her clothes the moment they were alone. *Anticipation is the best garnish.* The Kolnari consulted his interior timesense: twenty minutes, unusually swift. Well within the day's schedule, too. He grinned to himself, stretching and tossing back strands of white-blond hair. Tomorrow stretched out before him in a road of fire and blood and gold.

"We are close to Channa's quarters?" Joseph asked.

They were leopard-crawling down the ductway; an action that was hard for one of his shoulder-breadth. Behind them Patsy was having less of a problem, since much of her volume was compressible.

"Yeah . . ." Joat paused. "I haven't actually been this way, y'know. I was trying to *hide* from Simeon." A pause. "We're right over the main corridor to the elevator shaft. I think."

"I think I had better check," Joseph said, with a tight smile. "Are you all right, Joat-my-friend?"

"Yeah." She threw a smile back at him. "Just . . . I got a little shook, is all. I'm fine."

She touched the junction node and her jacker. The membrane beneath them turned transparent. Chaundra did not look up. Instead, he glanced behind him, shook his head, moved on.

Joat crawled past, then froze as two more figures came beneath. Rachel was running, but Serig caught her easily in one hand, pushed her against the corridor wall. She screamed, breathy and catching in her throat, like someone awakening from one nightmare into another.

"Don't do it, Joe, he'll kill you!" Joat cried sotto voce, lunging for the Bethelite's belt. She missed and knew it would have done no good. Her hand could never have deflected the solid charging weight of the man. He was through the space and dropping to the deck before she could finish the sentence. His knives were in his hands: one long and thin, the other short and curved.

The Kolnari had his hand back to cuff Rachel again as she screamed a second time, hopelessly.

"Pirate," a voice behind them said.

The warrior threw her aside as easily as he might a sack of wool, and she thudded into the corridor wall. The same motion turned into a whirling slash with one bladed palm, a blow that would have cracked solid teakwood. Joseph was not in its path, but the long knife in his right hand was. The yellow eyes slitted in pain and a broad streak of blood arched out to spatter against the cream of the sidewall and flow sluggishly down. The Clan fighter leaped back half a dozen paces, out of reach of the blades, but also farther from the discarded equipment belt. He was naked and unarmed, and the slash in his forearm was bone-deep. He dared not even squeeze it shut with his other hand. The raw salt-copper smell of blood was strong as the wound began to ooze more sluggishly. Superfast clotting would save him . . . if he did not exert himself

"Come to me, pirate," Joseph said softly. "Come, see how we fought in Keriss, on the docks."

The Kolnari snarled and leaped to one side, flipped in midair and bounced off the upper wall. He was a hundred-kilo blur of muscle and bone snapping at Joseph behind a clenched fist. Huddled against the wall, Rachel gave a whimper of despair, but Joseph was not there anymore. Anticipating such a tactic, he had thrown himself down on his back. Both knives were up. The pirate jackknifed in midair, but when he rolled erect, there were two more long slashes across his chest.

His grin was a snarl of pain as he slid forward. The long wounds were orange, the runneling blood a shocking deep umber against his raven-black skin. He held his arms up: one in a knuckled fist, the other open in a stiffened blade.

"Come," Joseph whispered. Rachel blinked back to full consciousness and the sight of his face chilled her. "Come to me, yes, come."

The knives glinted in either hand, splashed orangey-red now, the edges glinting in the soft glowlight as they moved in small, precise circles.

What followed was a whirling blur. It ended with one knife flying loose and Joseph crumpling back, curled around his side. The other knife still shone in defiance. The Kolnari warrior staggered and shivered for a moment, then drew back his foot for the final blow. Rachel flung herself forward, grasping blindly. Her arms closed around the poised leg. It was like gripping a tree, no, a piece of steel machinery that hammered her aside like some giant piston-rod. But blood loss and the unexpected weight threw the pirate off-balance. He staggered forward into Joseph. For a moment they stood chest-to-chest, like embracing brothers. Long-fingered black hands damped down on Joseph's shoulders, ready to tear the muscles of his bull-neck free by main force.

Then she saw the Bethelite's left arm moving. The right hung limp, but the left was pressed against the Kolnari's side. There was something in it. A knife-hilt, and the blade was buried up to the guard; the curved blade of the *sica,* whose density-enhanced edge would carve steel. It slid through ribs as the pirate's killing grip turned to a frantic push that arched him like a bow.

The two men had fought in silence, save for the panting rasp of their breath. Now the Kolnari screamed, as much in frustration as in final agony. The cry dissolved in a spray of blood as the diamond-hard *sica's* edge sawed open his ribcage and ground to a halt half-way through his breastbone. He flopped to the ground, voided, and died. Joseph wrenched his knife free and stooped. He forced his right hand to action, gripped the dead pirate's genitals, severed them with a slash. Then he stuffed them into the gaping mouth of the corpse and spat in the dead eyes, still open like fading amber jewels.

Blood. Rachel wiped at her mouth, suddenly conscious of the blood: in her mouth, her hair, over her body, spattered on corridor walls and ceiling, dimming the glowstrips, more blood than she had ever imagined could be. Joseph was coated with it, his eyes staring out of a mask of blood, his teeth red.

She stared at the mutilated corpse. "Serig," she said. "His name was Serig."

"A dead dog's name dies on the dungheap," Joseph said in a snarl. Then he turned to her and his eyes were alive once more. He bowed, checked himself with a sharp gasp, then completed the gesture. "My lady, are you hurt?" he inquired solicitously.

His face, for once, was naked. Rachel gasped and swayed, looking down at the body and then at the man she had despised.

"Joseph!" she cried, clutching at his arm. "I . . ." Reality whirled, splintered, as if a glass surface between her and her thoughts had shattered. "Joseph," she said more softly, wonderingly. "Something has happened to me. I . . . I remember things that cannot be. I—" she blushed "—I remember being so cruel to you, so vicious. And, and I—" she looked up at him, shaking her head in denial even as she whispered in growing horror "—betrayed Amos to the Kolnari?"

He touched her cheek, a feather soft caress. "Lady, you have been ill. You were poisoned by the coldsleep drugs that we took. It is not your fault."

"Oh," she said, "oh," and threw herself into his arms, weeping. "Please forgive me," she pleaded, "I am unworthy, I am foul, but I beg you, Joseph, do not despise me. Do not leave me."

"I could never despise my lady," he said simply. He extended a hand which she grasped, though the fingers were slippery with death.

"Come, we have little time," he said. "We must get you to a place of safety, and I have much work to do this day."

"Then let us hasten, Joseph," she replied.

Joat and Patsy dropped down, halting at the sight of the body. They scanned the hall tensely, then edged nearer. Joat looked at it out of the corner of her eyes, but the older woman stared hungrily.

The arc pistol rose, then fell helplessly.

"It's him," she whispered. "It's him. And it's been done!" Her tone was aggrieved, indignant.

Joat moved up beside her. *Boy, is he* ever *done*, she thought with her newfound squeamishness, and tried to ignore the smell. *This skudgesucker worked up an awful lot of mad against himself.* It was not that she regretted his death, just . . .

"Sorry it wasn't you?" she said, looking up at her companion.

For the first time since her rape, Patsy Sue Coburn was weeping.

"No," she said, her voice thick. "No, I'm not sorry. Not sorry he's dead, not sorry it wasn't me. Jist glad this dawg will never hurt nobody agin. I . . . won't have to remember doing it, now."

"Yeah, that's right," Joat said desolately, slamming the doors of memory firmly shut. "C'mon, we got work to do."

They turned to Joseph and Rachel. "Let's boost her up," Joat continued. "Axial up one ought to be safe enough to stash her. Then we can get on with it."

"Simeon?" Channa said softly. "You back?"

"Part of me." His voice sounded dim, although the implant's volume was always the same. "I'm dancing on a sawblade, keeping their communications down and fighting off their ships' computers. Can't keep them out of touch forever." More sharply. "You all right?"

"You want to know?" she said, dressing with calm haste.

"Yeah."

"It was annoying as hell . . . and sort of strenuous." A moment's urchin grin. "And to tell the truth, I'd have been forever curious if I hadn't. What I'd *like*," she said as she finished sealing her overall to the neck, "is to see his face when he realizes I'm not coming back through that door."

"I'll record it."

"And don't tell Amos."

A section of the ceiling paneling turned translucent and slid back. Joat's face showed through and then her body somersaulted down.

"There's a crawlspace we c'n get into now that leads to a bunch of air-ducts and electric-conduits. Come *on*."

Channa examined the hatch in the ceiling and smiled wryly. "Just like in a holovid," she murmured.

Joat grinned. "Yeah, only a *lot* smaller." She looked anxiously at Channa's lean length. "You may find it a squeeze. Had to leave the others back a ways. Do you nurdly when you're cramped?"

"Is there a choice?" Channa said.

"Then you don't. Push yourself along with your hands and toes. Don't try to use your knees or you'll eventually black out from the pain."

"Do you speak as one who knows?"

"Uh-huh, I've seen it happen. Give me a boost?"

Channa braced, cupped her hands, lifted Joat towards the ceiling hatch.

"Ready." Joat's voice came down, sounding a little hollow.

"Stand back." Channa crouched down and sprang upwards, catching the sides of the hole and pulling herself straight up, arms trembling with the strain.

The crawlspace was narrow and cramped and confining. She had to breathe and move in different motions. It was wonderful.

CHAPTER TWENTY-TWO

"OKAY," FLORIAN GUSKY croaked. "Go." He coughed, his lungs and throat a mass of pain and fire. The air system had not been designed to be occupied for two-week stays. "Go, you bastards."

Eight tugs and the mining scout *In Your Dreams* brought up their systems. There had been ten tugs, but Lowbau and Wong hadn't been answering on tightbeam for four days. If something had gone wrong with their life-support, neither of them had made a sound while it happened, accepting death in the silence of their powered-down ships, alone in the dark.

"Comin' home," Gus whispered.

The tugs had drifted with the other debris that cluttered the vicinity of the station. He gave silent thanks for the fact that Simeon had never been a neat housekeeper. More that Channa hadn't had time to reform him before the trouble struck. Now the energies of their drives painted half of heaven. Acceleration pushed him back into the padding, beyond what the compensators could handle. The screen ahead of him was a holo-driven schematic, with his target and approach vector marked off as a box, and the tug a blip that had to be kept inside it. Easy work for a military craft, but these tugs were designed for hard slow pulls, not whipping around. Nothing else mattered but the vector, and the load of scrap and ore trailing behind him. Through his body the drives hummed, pushed past all prudence and all hope.

His mind found time to note the bright spark that was a tug going

312

up, a pulse from the engine detonation and then the brighter flash of the destabilized powerplant.

"Well, that ought to let 'em know we're here," he muttered. Whiskers rasped against the feeding nozzle and the mike as his head moved in the helmet. He knew his face must look neither sane nor pleasant. The tug surged as he corrected. The station filled a sidescreen, and the bristling saucer shape of the Kolnari battle platform docked to its north polar tube, like some monstrous tick swelling with blood.

"You're *mine*," Gus shouted past cracked lips. "*All mine!*"

Simeon stood in the passageway. Rock rumbled around him, the bomb exploded away from a spot above, chips stinging his eyes and going *spang* off his armor. The long head that battered through was scaled in sapphire and had eyes set all about it, in a bone rill that turned to spikes. The muzzle split four ways, and each segment was lined with fangs. The tongue between was a metal-tipped spear ready to strike.

He struck first, grabbing it in an armored gauntlet and hauling back before the quadruple jaws could slam shut. When they did, it was on their own tongue. A high whine of pain drove needles into Simeon's ears. He kept his grip on the lashing end, whipped it three times around the muzzle and tied a quick slip-knot. Then he stood back and took a double-handed grip on his glowing baseball bat. *Tkwak.* The guardian program shivered, slumped, dissolved into metallic fragments that scurried back and forth disorganized, then decayed instantly into floating bytes.

"Next," he said, walking forward toward the iron-strapped door, which was *probably* the entrance to the CPU. "Geeze, I've got to patent this AI interface," he said, taking stance again. "It's—"

Boom. Oak splintered, wrought iron bent and shrieked.

"—fardlin'—"

Boom.

"—fun."

"Lord, *lord!*"

The commander of the High Clan battle platform *Skull Crusher* pivoted on one heel. The big circular room was half-empty; the liberty parties were only now returning.

"What?" he barked at the info-systems watch-officer. *Not now.* He was scheduled to undock and begin transit first, to be there when the transports came in for rendezvous with the rest of the High Clan. Just in case, but the weight of the responsibility was heavy, and this was his first independent command.

"Lord, our system is under attack!"

"The worm program?" Chindik t'Marid was a specialist in those. He had designed the standard Clan attack worm himself. He was also a game designer of note, although that was merely a hobby.

"No," the tech said. His fingers were dancing over his board. "Something's just *smashing* its way in."

"Aside." Chindik called up a graphic. He whistled silently. Something with *enormous* computational power was battering at the defenses with tremendous force, trying *all* the solutions. There was no indication of realspace location. His computers were spending all their capacity just keeping the enemy out. But since there was only one enemy installation in sight—

"Cut the cable feeds to the station," he said. "Battle alert to all other vessels."

"I *can't* cut the feeds," the tech said. "The retractors won't answer. Neither do the landline comms to the rest of the flotilla."

"Well, then—" Chindik began. Another cry stopped him.

"Detection," the sensor operator said. "Multiple detection. Power-plant signatures. Close, lord, close. Approaching."

"Attack vectors," the tactical computer announced. "Vessel is under attack."

"Those aren't warships," Chindik said in astonished dismay as he read the screen. His head whipped back and forth, reflex in a creature attacked from all sides. Then he straightened, strode back to the commander's station, and sank into the couch.

"Combat alert," he said. The chimes began to sound, wild and sweet. "Battlestations. Deploy short-range energy weapons. Fire on any of those . . . gnats as the weapons bear. Gantry?"

"Lord?" The dockside guards were looking away from the pickup. "Lord, we hear—"

"Silence! Send parties through the sidelock and blow the feeds connecting us to the scumvermin hulk."

"Lord?"

"Obey!"

The guards scattered like mercury struck with a hammer.

"Blast-broadcast," Chindik said. "Five-minute signal, all crew rally to the *Crusher*. Then undock."

"Lord, I've been trying to activate the decoupling procedure." The bridge was filling as the standby crew ran in and slid into their stations. "My telltales say it is working, but the visual scanner shows no activity."

"Send a party from engineering to dog it manually. Engines, prepare to maneuver."

"Lord, we're still physically linked."

"I know. We'll rip loose, and take the damage. Estimate."

"Six minutes to readiness, lord."

The weapons team were working in a blur of trained unison. "Enemy closing. Velocities follow. Preparing to engage . . . Lord, we need maneuvering room! They are too *close* for interceptor missiles."

"Make it three minutes, Engines." He turned back to the communications console. "*Get me the commander!*"

"Down two decks, use the emergency shaft. Down two decks, use the emergency shaft."

Simeon's voice rang through the corridor. All up and down it, the doors of the residential apartments were opening. Stationers came out, first singly, then in groups, in scores. They ran past the working party at the corridor junction, grabbed whatever shapes were thrust into their hands: needlers, industrial torches, bundles of blasting explosive with fuses cobbled together out of calculators, handlights and spare consumer-goods chips. Their faces were set and tight, or grinning, or snarling wordlessly.

Simeon broke off another fragment of attention as Amos came up.

"Channa?" the Bethelite asked. Then, as she moved into sight from behind Joseph, he cried in relief. "*Channa!*" They had time for a single swift hug.

His eye widened slightly as he saw Joseph's body splashed with drying blood from knees to neck.

"Mostly not my own, Brother," Joseph said grinning.

"You are hurt."

"Cracked rib. It is nothing."

Amos nodded briskly. "So far, they are surprised," he said to Channa. "But that will not last." The fabric of the station quivered beneath their feet.

Belazir t'Marid stepped back from the door. The frame of the chair was bent in his hands, but only gouges showed on the surface.

He dropped the shattered mass and looked around, his eyes narrowed.

Fool, he thought, and suppressed anger. There would be time for recriminations later. Perhaps . . . He retrieved his equipment belt and extracted the universal microtool. There *had* to be a connecting line *somewhere* around the entranceway. He cast a glance over his shoulder at the titanium pillar that had been beneath the tapestries.

"You will pay for this, my friend," he said. "For a very long time."

"Eat shit and die, Master and God," Simeon replied. *God, that felt good. I've been* waiting *to say that.* "You screwed the pooch. You did the doo-doo, big. You've got a place in the next edition of *From the Jaws of Victory.*"

Belazir turned away with a smile and a shrug, going to work on the exterior access panel.

"Can you feel pain?" he said as he began slicing it open with the short-range cutting laser in the tool "I hope so. Very much." He deployed the hair-thin probe.

"*And* I was playing below my level on the war games," Simeon added.

"Barricade at the next junction, lord."

The groundfighter's voice sounded in her headphones. Pol t'Veng filed it with the other voices filling her helmet, squeezing at them with the force of her will until they began to assume some pattern.

"Takiz," she said to her second. He looked around from the six power-armored figures at the junction. Just ahead the corridor had been wrecked by a satchel-charge; the tangle of walls, tubing and the remains of the floating gun was still white-hot. Two of the suited Kolnari forced their way into the narrow place and began to straighten. Metal screamed as it was deformed again. Hot gases pooled around them and the remains of the gun-crew.

"Takiz, when we're through here, take four and make another attempt at Lord Belazir's last location. Maximum effort."

That translated as "Bring him or don't come back."

"I hear and obey, Lord Pol."

"Lord Pol, we have a cleared line to the main axial corridor."

"Good," she said. Good news, the first since this started. "Reports."

"Fighting on all the docking levels, Lord. Data follows."

It did; also pickup views. One for only a second; the view from a powersuit as its wearer backed into the open port of a Clan transport. Stationers were firing from behind barricades of machinery and crates in the open space beyond. The lights were out and the view had the glassy look of light-enhancement. Softsuited crewfolk ran past the groundfighter. His plasma rifle snapped again and a makeshift breastwork exploded along with the bodies of the scumvermin behind it. Then all the telltales that ran below the visual flashed red. Not good news for the occupant of that suit, since the internal temperature was now over two hundred degrees. The scene began to fog just as she could make out a bundle of plastic bricks wired together arcing toward the airlock. Then it cut out abruptly.

Bad. That was one vessel that would be undocking with extreme difficulty. She projected a schematic on the corridor wall and studied it as the information flowed in. More bad news, but at least she had a picture.

"General transmission," she said. "Lord Pol t'Veng, assuming command in the absence of Lord Belazir. Crews, report to nearest vessel. Those near the exterior, blow your way out of the pressure hull and EVA to the nearest vessel."

Many of them would be suited, and emergency clingmasks—films that protected the face somewhat, with a miniaturized recycler—were standard issue. For that matter, Kolnari could endure about four minutes of vacuum if trained and prepared.

"We retreat?" someone asked, shocked.

"No, fool!" she said. The speaker was an officer with an intact company ranged behind him. It was worth the time to answer as she might herself fall, in which case he would need the information. "Look!" She downloaded her appraisal. "They fight to keep us here. We fight for fighting room. We have *completed* our mission."

"I hear and obey, lord."

"You had better," she muttered to herself. Now that the blockage had been cleared, more Kolnari were gathering in the cross-corridors.

"We fight our way through to the axial corridor," she said. "You, Dittrek. Is that barricade still holding?"

"Yes, lord. I do not have enough men to rush it again."

"Blow through the access walls to either side of your position," she said. "Then blow through the connecting partitions and flank them. Quickly."

"Lord."

She turned to the others. "To the docks—follow me!"

✧   ✧   ✧

"Now!" Gus muttered to himself. The computer did the actual release. The tug released its grapnel field and applied lateral thrust, just enough to swing him wide of the station itself.

He removed his hands from the controls and slapped the main power switch; the safest thing to do, now. There was a lot of high-velocity debris around . . . including the wrecks of the other tugs. He felt a curious peace, almost as if he could sleep.

"Lord, we boost," the engine comm of *Heart Crusher* said. At the same moment, the weapons console gave a cry of fury.

"Kinetic slugs inbound. Prepare for impact. Inner defense batteries on auto."

"Full maneuver power. Boosting."

Chindik t'Marid prayed silently to the platform joss, making reckless promises. The big vessel lurched and rending sounds echoed through the fabric of its hull as the jammed connectors tore out, like roots parting in the earth. The most effective weapons were on the underside, and *that* was still pointed towards the SSS-900-C. There was nothing he could do, anyone could do, except the AI systems handling the close-in defense—something beyond even Kolnari reflexes.

Sprays of trajectory crossed on the screens. Absently he noted the second to last attacking vessel taking a beam. An irrelevancy now, after the huge scatter of high-velocity projectiles had been loosed against his command. The slew of dots diminished, as the beams swept, more and more with each second as the stubby disk turned its teeth toward the sky.

Tinnggggg. Tinnggggg. He waited, tense. No more contact. The rest of the incoming flotsam had been stopped, or missed, or struck the station instead.

"Damage control!"

A few lights were strobing from green to amber to red. The engines screen came on.

"Lord . . . the exciter coils for the FTL were hit."

"How long?"

"A week, lord. It is a dockyard job." The Kolnari on the bridge exchanged looks. They had just heard news of their deaths.

"You," Chindik snapped to a backup crewman. "Take that—" he indicated the joss "—and *space* it."

"We have Lord Pol, lord."

✧   ✧   ✧

The doors hissed open. Belazir jumped back with a yell as the plasma rifle leveled.

"Lord!" The man seemed ready to weep with relief Belazir ignored him, diving for the empty suit that followed behind the warrior. For a wonder, it was his own.

"Where is Serig?" Belazir barked. He had expected him to be here, or taking command. Matters should not have gotten so far out of hand.

With the door open, the smells and sounds of combat were obvious: deep toning sounds as explosions tore at the fabric of the station, far off chuddering of beam weapons, the stink of hot metal and ozone. Belazir folded the suit around him, leaving the catheters for later. *If I have to piss down my leg, so be it.* It came alive with a jerk, and he flexed the servo-powered limbs and gauntlets with exultation.

"Lord Serig is dead, Great Lord. Lord Pol commands. We have a link."

The news staggered Belazir for a moment. *Serig dead?* Then he damped the helmet. "Lord Pol?"

"Here! Report follows." Mostly disaster. "They came at us out of the walls, must have been hiding there since the occupation began."

Belazir nodded jerkily.

"We hold the ships," Pol said crisply. "Except for one transport that has, incredibly, been overrun. They attack the docks and encircle pockets of our troops."

"Continue consolidating the pockets and punch through to the ships," he said. "Status?"

"*Heart Crusher* is free but her FTL is down," Pol said. "My *Shark* is also disengaged and I am not bringing her back. Half the transports are moving, but some with heavy damage. *Dreadful Bride* has nearly full crew, plus personnel from others, and is in control of her docking area and ready to boost."

"*Age of Darkness?*"

"Still not even answering her comm," Pol said, her voice taking on emotion for the first time. "My youngest daughter against a used wiperag. Her outer info was penetrated and they did not even," she spat the word, "*notice.*"

"No wager," Belazir said. He reached back over his shoulder and swung the punchgun rack down. It clicked into its rest along his right arm. The aiming bars lit on his faceplate as he turned and cycled for sonic and IR scan on the pillar that held the brain. *Ahhh, yes. There is the interior structure, and the access hatchway.* "You may assume tactical command from the *Age of Darkness*, Lord Pol, once you reach it. I will follow to the *Bride*. There is a matter to attend to here."

"Through there," Amos said. He pointed to two broken access doors across the circular open space. Most of it had been covered with kiosks, stores, restaurants and other structures until an hour ago. Now those were smoldering ruins, scattered among that were the bodies and the wreckage of the servomechs the stationers had used as their first wave. "They are back from the entrance on the second to the right."

"We'll go through subaxial E-9 and punch across," Keri Holen replied. "That's one of the hidden sections."

She turned to her squad, a mix of station repair people with their working tools and ordinary civilians armed with whatever.

"C'mon, scumvermin," she said. "Let's go show the lords what we think of 'em. Follow me."

"How are we doing?" Channa said beside Amos, bobbing up and loosing a burst with her needler. Covering fire from all the stationers lashed out at the exit shafts as the assault team dodged forward. The barricade ahead of them was corycium, brought in by the handler servos, and plasma rounds had splashed off the front, or welded the ingots together and made the barrier stronger. They still had to expose themselves to shoot, if only in a crevice between two ingots.

Amos ducked down with her as another series of bolts hit the metal. They could feel the barricade shudder and tone. The inner layer was barely warm, but the temperature above flash-heated enough to make their skins tingle. The stink of hot corycium made them cough, and Channa thought how worried she would have been in ordinary times; the fumes were not healthy. Then the whole station shuddered, and the gravity fluxed sufficiently to be noticeable.

Nothing like a plasma bolt to give you a sense of perspective, she thought.

"Not doing too well, my darling," Amos said absently. A team from the Perimeter Restaurant was crawling from person to person with bags of sandwiches and juice. More of the restaurant's people were back two junctions, running a triage station under the direction of one of Chaundra's meditechs. "They are using the battle platform and the warship for fire support from outside, and we cannot stop them uniting their scattered groups. The groups that survived, that is." He sighed and smiled at her through the black smudges of powdered metal. "I cannot think of finer company than yours to travel to God with, Channa Hap," he said.

"I'm glad, too," she said. "Sorry it was this way, but glad."

He reached out to touch her shoulder. Then her face went glacial. For a moment he feared she had been hit, before he recognized the expression. She was communing with Simeon. Her throat worked. "Amos!" she burst out. *"They're taking Simeon out of his column!"*

The Bethelite paled. Without their all-seeing commander and chief of general staff, the station *was* doomed, and quickly. Channa turned and began to leopard-crawl backward. He grabbed for her ankle.

"There is nothing you can do," he hissed

"I'm his brawn! I *have* to!" she cried, and kicked free. Amos looked after her and cursed.

"Joseph!" he said. "We have to retake main axial, at least for a moment—along the path to the central command. Take—"

The final lead connecting Simeon to the station came free. *No!* Simeon cried into the darkness. The self-destruct had been left too late. The Navy had not come, and the enemy were breaking free. When they had him on board, the station would die.

He had nothing now, nothing but the single pickup and audio circuit that were part of his inner shell, life support was on the backups. It would keep his nutrient feeds going for days . . . but a single hand could switch him into total darkness, utter isolation. Madness, death without the mercy of oblivion. *No!*

Belazir was still visible, leaning over the shell. He lifted off his helmet with both hands, looming over the pickup to smile whitely. The shell surged as the powersuited warriors bent carefully and lifted, the huge weight coming up slowly as their armor whined in protest. There was a slight klinking sound as the helmet rested on the upper face of the shell itself.

"So that you should have my face for your last sight," the Kolnari chieftain said, reaching for the keypad on the shell exterior. "When you see again, you will call me Master and God . . . and you will *mean* it." He touched a finger to the control. "Beg, Simeon."

"Eat shit and die!"

The Kolnari chuckled. "Not good enough," he said, and pressed the stud.

The doors to Channa's room slapped open. Channa stepped through, needler at the ready. Belazir could feel the aimpoint on his forehead.

"You wanted me again, Belazir?" she said. "Better late than never. Here I am." A slight movement waggled the muzzle. "This is set on spray. It's quite fatal. Now, away from the shell, please."

Belazir smiled at her. *What a woman!* he thought. *I will beat her, but not too badly.* "There are three of us," he said, shifting slightly. *Although unfortunately I have my helmet off and these two are immobilized by the load they carry,* he added to himself. "We are in armor. You can scarcely expect to frighten us with that toy alone."

Patsy Sue Coburn followed her friend out of the quarters, leveling her arc pistol. A red burn-mark welted one cheek, bleeding knees and elbows showed through the holes worn in her coverall, but there was real pleasure in her smile.

"Life's full a' surprises, ain't it?" she said as Belazir snarled silently. "Real bitch sometimes, too."

Channa tossed her head in a vain attempt to get the sweat-soaked hair out of her eyes.

"Yes," she said evenly, "I do expect to frighten you. Now, replace the shell in the main column cradle and reconnect it. Then, all of you, throw your helmets aside and move over there." She gestured towards the door to Amos' quarters. "I expect your pirates will trade a good deal for you."

"And keep your hands up," snapped a voice from above.

Kolnari heads turned to the opening in the ceiling. A head and arms protruded, far too small for an adult of their bigboned race, but the muzzle of the plasma rifle was held steadily in those slight arms. The weapon looked absurdly large for the person who controlled it, but it was braced against the interior wall and the lip of the hole, and he *could* see the aimpoint, a red dot that wavered over the three pirates.

"Up," the child repeated, lifting the muzzle of the weapon for emphasis.

Belazir's mind computed the angles. *Good. My left hand is not visible,* he thought.

"You leave us little choice," he said aloud. Which was true; honor aside, he had no choice at all. Pol t'Veng or any other Kolnari noble would cheerfully let Father Chalku or their own sires be flayed alive rather than disgrace them by paying ransom, much less do so for *him*. He would rather be flayed than live on those terms himself.

"Move the shell," he said to the two troopers. "It's only *three* paces."

He raised his gauntleted hands, closing his eyes and flagging positions. The deck boomed like a drum as the pirate groundfighters moved a pace in lockstep unison, the ton weights of their suits added to triple that of titanium and machinery . . . and the few kilos of a body that had never seen the light of day.

Three, he counted and dropped the flash grenade. Before it hit the shell, he was leaping backwards, and so were the two other Clan warriors. He squeezed his eyes tight and willed his pupils shut, but even so the flash was dazzling. He hit the doorframe going out, went flat, scrabbled the helmet he had snatched onto his head. The plasma rifle had crashed simultaneous with the grenade. A brief scream and the smell from inside told him it had still been on target.

He blinked open his eyes as the locking ring of the helmet clicked. The combat medsystem sprayed a mist into his eyes, but his vision was severely degraded in any case. He activated the sonic sensor, to cheep the location of things at him.

"Takiz!" he called.

"Fully functional, lord," the warrior answered. "Kintir is dead."

I will beat her very *severely,* Belazir amended. Even with the dazzles before his eyes, he could see several arc-pistol shots snap out through the doorway, and his machine-augmented hearing picked up the telltale click of an arming plasma rifle. The walls were reinforced here, as well. It would be tricky, and he had not much time. Now he did not put it past these *extraordinary* scumvermin to blow the station themselves.

The comm chimed and Baila's face filled one of the chinscreens, a vague dark blur. Her voice was scratchy with interference but audible. "Great Lord," she said calmly. "Ships detected, incoming."

No! he shouted inwardly. *No!*

"Lord," another voice spoke. The senior ground-fighter officer. "We're holding a counterattack on the main axial, but I cannot guarantee your withdrawal. Not for any period beyond *now.*"

For perhaps ten seconds Belazir panted sharply.

"I will be there in five minutes, or not at all," he said. "Out. Takiz, follow me. We head for the docks." *Thank the joss,* he thought with savage irony, *the north polar docking tube is so close to here.*

✧   ✧   ✧

I'm blind, Channa thought. Her skin crinkled, waiting for the clamp of powered gauntlets. Beside her Patsy was shooting.

"Careful, Pats," Channa gasped. The blackness was starred with red, now, and she felt needles of pain in her forehead. Her free hand felt upward, touched her eyes. Wetness . . . tears, only tears. The eyes *felt* normal to her fingertips. For a long moment, she had feared it was something like that horrible popper Joat had made.

"I'm careful, all raht," Patsy said. "Got my shootin' iron right on the doorway. They cain't move quiet in those tin suits."

"Joat?"

"I'm all right," the girl's voice said. Her voice had a saw-edged note that denied the words. "Hurts and I can't see, though. I'm coming down."

"Don't get between me an' the door!" Patsy said sharply.

Channa dropped to her knees and shuffled forward, hand outstretched. That touched something hot, which brought a sharp gasp of pain; next a warm wetness. She wiped her hand on the carpet and tried again. The smooth titanium-matrix surface of the shell was like a benediction. When she moved to the keypad, a smaller hand touched hers. They gripped for a moment, then pressed the key.

"*Nnooooooooooooo—*" The scream was piercing, but Simeon's backup speakers on his inner shell had limited volume. He stuttered, babbled, then organized his voice.

"Thhh . . . *ank* you," he said. "Channa? Joat?" Patsy came into the field of his vision. "What's happened?"

"He dropped something," Channa said. "There was a white light and we can't see."

"Flash grenade," Simeon answered. "Don't worry! It isn't permanent!"

Channa gave a sobbing sigh of relief and heard it echoed. "How long?"

"Well . . . how close were you?"

"Two meters to six, and looking right at it."

"Oh." A pause. "About a day, with medication, I'm afraid," he said. *At least for the person who was six meters away. About the others I'm worried.* Long-term reaction was variable.

"Oh, *great.* They may come back in the door—"

"No, they won't. I can hear their armor moving away toward the docking tube. Lots of fighting. Look, it's the answer to my prayers to have three beautiful women hugging my shell, but could you get me reconnected? Please? *It's important.*"

"We can't lift you back, that's for sure," Joat said.

He frowned inwardly at the shakiness in her tone, but he had no instant remedy for her.

"There's plenty of spare play in the cables," Channa said. "How did they?" Her voice trailed off tactfully.

Simeon felt himself cringing again.

"No, it's all right." *Sure it is.* "They cut the cable guards and then just pulled the jacks," he said. *Cutting away my strength, my sight, my feeling, cutting away me.* "Problem is . . . they're color-coded. And the receptors may be damaged."

"I'll get them sorted out," she said as she moved out of his severely limited range of vision.

How do softshells stand *only one pair of vision sensors?* he wondered. Even for a few minutes, his control had been strained to the breaking point.

She returned with the cables, a double armful even with ultra-high-data-density opticals. The jacks for the leads were like a spray of fine hairs.

"Oh, oh," Simeon said.

"What do you mean, 'oh-oh,'" Channa replied.

"Everyone knows what 'oh-oh' means," Simeon said. "It means, 'I screwed the pooch.' Your hands . . ."

" . . . are too big," she answered. "*Damn.*"

"I can do it," Joat said.

"You can't see, Joat."

"Neither can Channa. I've worked in the dark lots of times. Had to. Got that toolbelt with the micros from Engineering, too."

"They gave you one?" Simeon said, momentarily startled.

"No."

"Don't tell me," he said. "All right. Someone should stand guard. I can hear if anyone's coming and give you a bearing. Patsy?"

"Surely will," Patsy said. She felt her way to the doorframe.

"You keep the slack on the cables, Channa."

"I've wanted to yank your cord for a long time anyway, Simeon," she said with an attempt at a gallows humor. Simeon felt his heart turn over as she smiled down at him.

"Okay, feel your way up the face of the shell, Jack-of-All-Trades and master of some." Her small hands slid upward over the smooth surface to the rounded top. "Stop," he said to prevent her fingers from tangling the hair fine wires protruding from the receptor couplings.

"You be my hands, kid, I'll be your eyes, 'kay?"

She took a deep breath. "Okay, what do I do?"

"Walk the fingers of your right hand two paces forward, one pace to the left. Feel that wire?"

"Yeah."

"Follow it to the lead. Now, with your left hand . . ."

A minute later Simeon yelled again, this time a long high screech that sounded something like Patsy as she had at game-time rooting for the home team.

"Sorry, I'm *sorry* Simeon, I didn't mean to hurtcha, honest!"

"You didn't." A bugle fanfare blew through the lounge, and segued into a Souza march, then the Ganymede Harp Variations.

"You've bollixed his oxygen feeds," Channa said frantically, groping forwards.

"It's the *cavalry*! Ta-ta-tata-ta*ra* tat-teraaaa!"

"Simeon!"

"Has he gon' an' lost it?"

Aragiz t'Varak lolled, half-dreaming. A very pleasant daydream. He was back on homeworld, a territorial lord like the old recordings, and somehow Belazir t'Marid was there. Aragiz had just defeated him the old way, spectacular battles amid spouting radioactive geysers. Blasting into the stronghold with primitive fission weapons, hand-shaped plutonium triggered by black powder. Belazir groveled, begging mercy for his line, but they were led out and slaughtered before his eyes. Aragiz was just getting into the interesting post-victory part when the communications officer interrupted him.

"Detection . . . Outer ring satellites. Ship signatures, inbound."

The bridge of the *Age of Darkness* came alert. Everyone had been waiting, nothing more to do until they undocked next cycle and escorted the transports back to rendezvous. He had brought everyone in, ready for departure. Now—

"Another pullet for the plucking," Aragiz said lazily. He felt tired. Perhaps from that scumvermin boy, what was his name, Juke. A nice active squealer, not like that unpleasant one who'd gone into fits after a single kiss, back in the corridors. He'd kicked that one aside with a shudder. Not for a moment did he think that *he* would catch any disease, but it had been an unpleasant sight.

"Action stations." The soft chimes rang, eerie and ironic in their gentle harmony. "Give me a reading, and relay to flotilla command and station-side."

The sensor officer consulted the machine. "Very large mass, Great Lord. Seventy to eighty kilotons."

"Probably an ore carrier," the captain said. "Useful, if not dramatic." The Clan could always use—

"Link is down," Communications said.

"*Again?*" Aragiz barked. He couldn't decouple from the station without clearance. That Bad Seed *chugrut* Belazir had been fairly dear about that. Also, running an intercept on an incoming freighter could be tricky. And his head hurt, as if he'd been knocked unconscious and recovered . . .

"Check climate control," he said. It was *hot*. He was sweating, and he rarely did, even in combat practice at Kolnar-noon temperature.

"Yes, Great—*we have lost comm with the station-side watch.*"

"*What?*" Aragiz sat bolt upright. "When?"

"Some time ago. We have been getting repeats of the last routine hailings."

That made his stomach lurch, and suddenly he bent over the arm and spewed.

"Fool!" he screamed. "Alarm—" He choked on bile. *What is happening to me?* He tried to rise, fell back, thrashed, and slipped over the arm of the commander's couch into the spilled vomit.

Shouts of alarm rose from the crew. The groundlink screens flickered. One cleared to show a Kolnari face being pounded against the pickup.

The executive officer looked down at the jerking form of the captain, and took command.

"Remaining crew, prepare for boarding action. Suit up and—"

"Cancel that," a gravelly voice said.

The officer blinked, and almost shouted in gratitude. Pol t'Veng trotted in, her combat armor scored and still smoking in places, like that of the others behind her. Still, she was t'Veng—

"Lord Captain," he began. There was a careful protocol about subclan ship territories.

She cut him off. "Uprising. Couldn't make the *Shark*. Stationer electronics scrambled, hostile-controlled. Emergency. Dump your system and call up the backup."

Pol glared at him, sparing the time until he submitted and saluted.

Then she sank into the command couch. Inwardly, she sighed. Every time the joss seemed to throw the Clan a little luck, they were knocked back to a handful of homeless fugitives again. Every system on the ship dipped, then firmed, as the duplicate backup computers came on-line. A glance at the captain's readouts gave her the situation.

"Monitor the incoming," she said.

"Lord captain, it is a freighter. Should we not be assisting in getting the station back in the fist?"

"Shut up. You *assumed* it was a freighter. Check that reading again. Now!" Her voice was a bellow, its natural volume increased by the suit's system to an ear shattering volume.

"Reading . . . Anomalous readings, lord."

"Let me see." He keyed over to her the feeds, unfiltered data. "Young fool, that's not anomalous—that's *Fleet!*"

She paused a second to free a sidearm and pump a pulse of energy into Aragiz's thrashing body. His squealing was distracting.

"Emergency decouple," she said. Besides, she had wanted to kill him for years. This one should have been culled before he walked.

"We are loading fuel!"

"*Move.*"

He did. His hand swept the controls, and the *Age of Darkness* shuddered as explosive charges blasted it loose from the SSS-900-C's north docking tube. Fire blossomed out of the dockway after them, along with steam and pieces of cargo and humans. Kolnari as well as scumvermin, she supposed.

"Broadcast, override, *High Clan seek Refuge, High Clan seek Refuge,*" she snapped. "Put it on loop, open Clan frequency."

The officer's eyes flared wide. That was the command to break, run and scatter, to approach the preset rendezvous points only years later and with maximum caution. Those points were in no file, no hedron, only in living brains and only a few of those. The final desperation measure to protect the Divine Seed, that it might grow again.

"*Heart Crusher.* Chindik t'Marid."

"Put it through."

"Lord Pol, you are receiving what I do?"

"Yes."

"Data coming in," the sensor chief said.

Pol t'Veng looked down again. The Fleet warships were coming up out of subspace like tunglor broaching in the seas of Kolnar; huge masses, neutrino signatures of enormous powerplants, ripping through into the fabric of reality.

"Command frequency broadcast! Identifying following," she said. "Fleet units emerging coordinates follow, probables: destroyers, six—correction, six destroyers plus three light, one heavy cruiser and possible . . . Confirmed, three assault carriers. All Clan ships, report status. Lord t'Marid, report status."

"We coordinate?" Chindick asked.

"No. You have not the insystem boost. Use the station for cover as long as you can. They will not endanger it."

"Repeat?"

"Scumvermin psychology. Go. *Lord t'Marid, status.*"

"T'Marid here," the familiar voice said, harsher than she could remember. "*Bride* decoupling. We can cover."

"No, with respect. Yours is the more valuable Seed." *Especially since this ship has t'Varak's sweepings as crew.* "*Bride, Shark* and *Strangler* should cover the transports."

A pause. "Agreed. Wait for us with the Ancestors, Pol t'Veng."

"Guard our Seed and Clan, Belazir t'Marid," she replied.

Then her attention went back to the work at hand. A Central Worlds Space Navy medium attack group bore down on them, with a dozen times the firepower the High Clan had available here and now, given the general pathetic botchup. About equal to the whole current Clan armada, give or take a dozen factors. Pol had fought the Fleet before and had a healthy respect for their capabilities. They were dangerous scumvermin.

"Helm," she went on. "Set course. Coordinates follow." She had plugged the suit's leads into the couch. "Maximum boost."

"Lord Captain," the executive officer said. "That is a course *for* the enemy fleet. What are we to *do* there?" With one undercrewed frigate, went without saying.

"Do?" Pol t'Veng roared out a single bark of laughter. "We *die*, fool!"

The commander's couch reclined, locking into combat position. "We will attempt to break through to the transports," she said. "The warships will maneuver to protect them. We fight for maximum delay. Any questions?"

"Command us, lord!"

"Prepare to engage."

❖   ❖   ❖

"They are smashing us like eggs," Joseph said.

Amos nodded. Without Simeon, the stationers lost their advantage of superior coordination. Against professionals, he had been the only one they had had, once the Kolnari recovered their balance.

"Simeon was a . . . a brave man," Amos said. *And if he were really a man, a dangerous rival,* he added to himself. "And very skillful. I honor his memory." Joseph nodded; they clasped hand to forearm. "Farewell, my brother."

"Fardlin' touching, really," a voice said in his ear.

Amos leaped upright, then ducked again frantically as a bolt spattered metal near his face.

"Simeon?" he gasped.

"No, the Ghost of Christmas Past," the brain replied. "I'm back. So," he went on, glee bubbling through his voice, "are some other people."

A holo formed behind the barricade: a figure in green power armor of a chunkier, more compact design than the Kolnari suits Amos was used to. In the background was the bridge of a large vessel, battle-clad figures moving about. A woman, with a man in like equipment but different insignia beside her.

"Admiral Questar-Benn," the woman said. Remarkably, she appeared to be in late middle age but undeniably healthy and close-knit. "Commodore Tellin-Makie, of the battlecruiser *Santayana.*"

"Oh, God is great, God is Merciful, God is One," Amos murmured through numb lips. "Bethel?"

"Don't worry. It's a big navy. We hit them as they were getting ready to leave. Reports show not much damage to the planet since you left, if you're Benisur Ben Sierra Nueva."

"Keep firing!" Joseph barked to the others at the barricade. "You can die just as dead winning as losing."

The commodore laughed shortly. "Profoundly true," he said. "Simeon, Ms. Hap, all of you, you've done a very good job. Heroic, in fact. We didn't expect to find anything but bodies and wreckage."

"It was a close-run thing," Simeon said feelingly. "A damned close-run thing." Both the officers seemed to find that amusing.

"Here's my record of the whole thing, start to finish," said Channa and the Navy officers' eyes turned. Evidently they had video of her. Amos hissed a low complaint, and three more holos joined the image of the *Santayana*'s deck.

"We've still got a lot of the pirates in station," Channa said. "Should we back off?" She swallowed. "A lot of our people have been hurt."

"Negative," the admiral said, shaking her head. "Give them time to think, and sure as death and fate, one of them will find a way to blow the station. I've got a Marine regimental combat team in the transports. We'll forcedock as soon as I swat the Kolnari warships. That battle platform could be tricky."

The commodore leaned out of the sight picture and spoke to someone else. "Well, then, get the destroyers to *englobe* it, then!"

"It's not over until it's over," Questar-Benn said.

"Er . . . not *the* Questar-Benn?" Simeon asked, awed.

"Not if you mean Micaya," she said dryly. "I'm the dull sister, the straight-leg." She glanced down at the data flowing in from SSS-900-C. "Bastards. Murdering sub-human mutant *swine*. Maybe *now* the inbred penny-pinching High Families incompetent corruptionists back at Central will get their thumbs out of their backsides and let us *do* something about Kolnar and all its little offshoots."

"Ma'am," Tellin-Makie said warningly.

"I'm not bucking for another star, Eddin," she said. "I can afford to tell the truth without a bucket of syrup on it." She looked up and out at the stationers. "Here's what we want you to do," she went on crisply.

God, Amos thought. *Thank you.* For victory, and for someone else to tell him what to do for a change. Leadership could get very tiring. He suspected Fate was going to send more of it his way. The prospect did not seem as attractive as it once had.

CHAPTER TWENTY-THREE

"I NEVER UNDERSTOOD what he meant before," Simeon said, looking out at the huge docking chamber which held only the dead, now in covered silent rows. "I thought I did, but I didn't."

The medics and their patients were gone, to station sickbays or to the trauma stations of the warships. Equally silent were the motionless Marine sentries who stood with weapons reversed by the Navy dead. The squad at the docking airlock snapped to attention as each shrouded body went by. The civilians looking among the stationer dead were nearly as quiet, only a few sobbing faintly.

"Understood what who meant?" Channa said, blinking behind the dark glasses that hid her bandages. She appeared detached, almost aloof, just like the two Navy commanders who stood with her and the little group of stationers.

"Wellington," Simeon said. " '*I don't know what it is to lose a battle; but certainly nothing can be more painful than to gain one with the loss of so many friends.*' He said that after Waterloo."

The admiral nodded. "I remember when I found that out," she said very softly. "If you've got a grain of sense, you never forget it."

"Ain't that the truth!" Patsy Sue Coburn said. Beside her, Florian Gusky put his synth-splinted arm companionably around her shoulders. She stiffened, then forced herself to put up a hand and pat it gently. "You don't forget anything. But you learn to live with it. C'mon, Gus. I do believe you owe me a drink."

Channa turned her head toward their footsteps. "Yes," she said, with a bitter smile. "We learn to live with it. If this is heroism, why do I feel like such crap?"

"Because you're here," Questar-Benn said. "Heroism is something somebody else does somewhere far away. In person, it's tragedy." Her voice sharpened. "And it could be worse, much worse, and would have been but for you. We *did* win. You *are* here. And," she went on more lightly, "you're heroes in the media, at least. Which means, by the way, you can write your own tickets."

"Tickets?" Simeon asked.

"You always wanted a warship posting, didn't you?" she said. "With this on your record . . ."

Simeon hesitated. Joat had been standing by Channa's side, quiet and drawn. Now the old coldness settled over her face, and she began to edge away.

Everyone's always left her, or cheated her, or hurt her, he thought.

"I'm not so sure," he said aloud, "that I *want* a military career any more."

Admiral Questar-Benn nodded vigorously. "That makes you *more* qualified. They shovel glory hounds out of the Academy by the job-lot and we have to spend years breaking them of such fatuous nonsense."

"Besides, I have a daughter," and his instant and totally gratifying reward was the dawning of hope on Joat's face. "Thanks, though. Maybe, someday." *Some dreams don't transfer well into reality,* he told himself. He could see Joat's chest lifting with the deeper breaths of self-confidence and she didn't look about to disappear on him.

"And have you soured on Senalgal?" the commodore said, turning to Channa.

"It's still a beautiful world," she said, shaking her head slowly. "But it's not my home." She reached down to Joat beside her and, touching the girl's face with her fingertips, felt the slightest of resistance to such fondling. Learning to trust, and to be a human being, was not something that came quickly or easily. But you had to *begin* somewhere or you never arrived. "Besides, Joat's my daughter, too. And I've friends here, the best there are."

Questar-Benn threw up her hands. "Simeon, you're going to be around a *very* long time. The offer still stands. I'll leave it on record."

"Hey, Pops," Joat said, her voice a little unsteady despite the cocky tone. "I mean *you*, Simeon."

"Great Ghu! Can *you*, of all people, not think a more suitable title than 'Pops' to call me?" Simeon demanded in a semi-indignant tone, but he would have settled for anything of a familial nature from Joat.

"Sure, but I don't think you'd like to know 'em!" She smiled her urchin grin in his image. "Any rate, I'm gonna be sixteen standard in a few years. Enlistment age. And I don't want you blaming me for screwing up your career plans. I . . . I'd sort of like to keep this from happening to somebody else, you know?" She turned to the admiral. "Think these brass-a . . . um, general-type people might have a use for me?"

Questar-Benn shuddered. "I'm probably perpetrating horrors on some unsuspecting commander left to deal with you in the future, young lady, but yes. I'd be very surprised if we couldn't find a use for *all* of you." She swept the present company with her piercing gaze.

"Then we may take you up on that offer," Simeon said. Although he was too enervated to enjoy thoughts of revenge, no amount of emotional exhaustion could remove the need to do something about the Kolnari: next week, maybe. "But right now, I'd rather call in the gratitude as a favor, if you don't mind, Admiral," Simeon said.

"Favor? For who?"

"A friend," he said. A holo grew, of a boy about Joat's age.

Joat started violently. "Seld! They wouldn't let me see ya, said you were sick!"

The figure nodded. "You knew that. You know I've been sick a long while, Joat," he said with the incredible patience of the chronic invalid. "Only it went off the screen. I can see this," and he looked down at his frail, limp body, strapped in an upright position on the bed, "but I can't feel anything or move it, or do anything, really."

"Oh, damn!" Joat moved a hand through the holo as if she could reverse the damage somehow.

"The navy medicos have got me hooked up to a nervesplice monitor, to keep my heart going and stuff. Simeon himself," and now he managed a proud grin, "is hacking into it."

Joat blinked. "I'm sorry," she said in a small voice. "I shouldn't've called you a wuss. I heaved my cookies afterwards, too. I guess it's my fault, hey? Expecting you to do more'n you could, should!"

"Nah," Seld on the holo said. "I was stupid, you know. You could do all those things I couldn't, and I was . . . hell, Joat, I was gonna end up like this anyway, sooner'r later. Grudly, but I knew it. Dad knew it, but he sort of didn't at the same time. I've had a lot of time to think about it."

Joat nodded, then narrowed her eyes. "Those caps were the final push, weren't they? Why'd you *use* one?"

"'Cause I was so scared of seeing you get killed, Joat. You're my best friend. Besides," he went on, "that Kolnari Lord'd just belted me real hard. Then . . . I tell you, the ultimo grudly," and Seld rolled his eyes in disgust, "when he *kissed* me, so I wanted some of my own back."

"Yeah," and Joat nodded in approval, "you would at that!"

"That's when I had a fit. Would have happened eventually, really it would, Jo. Dad says another ten years, max."

Joat looked around at the Navy officers. "I don't think that's good enough. Can't you guys better the odds for 'm? Doesn't he *deserve* more than ten years?" Her hard voice cracked a little.

Questar-Benn winced and the commodore focused his eyes on something else.

"I never get used to this," the commodore under his breath. "What's the favor, Simeon?

Channa's head came up sharply. "Simeon? You've a suggestion?"

"I do," Simeon said in such a positive, you-should-have-known-I-would tone of voice that he commanded everyone's attention. "I've been checking around and the AlexHypatia-1033 told me about new tricks that Dr. Kennet Uhua-Sorg's been working on. No one—yet—is able to regenerate the spinal nerve sheaths. Kenny Sorg developed a prosthesis—for himself, incidentally, but it'll suit Seld's particular requirements, too. Kid, you're too old to be a shellperson: you'd never psychologically adjust. Kenny Sorg's condition is about the same as yours and he gets around just fine," and Simeon projected a holo of a man, moving down a corridor but too smoothly to be "walking." He "walked" upright, true, but his body was framed by an slender exo-skeleton which held him erect, with his feet on a platform, similar but much thicker than the station float disks. The base ingeniously held the power supply and monitoring equipment. "I'm told, Seld, that you'll have use of your arms and the base is sophisticated enough to do as much for your body as my shell does for me. Long as you don't try slipping through ventilation ducts or falling headfirst out of services hatches, you should last as long as most softshells, skeleton man!"

In this instance, Simeon's rewards were many: Joat jumping up and down, gurgling with laughter while tears streamed down her face, as well as Channa's, and Seld crowed like he'd turned rooster. There were expressions of intense relief on the faces of admiral and the commodore.

"I do like to see alternative solutions," Questar-Benn said, "and we'll put a naval courier B & B ship at the disposal of Seld and his father for transfer to the Central Worlds Medstation where Dr. Sorg is currently practicing. Is that the favor you wanted, Simeon?"

"The very one," the station replied.

"Frabjus, Skelly Seld," Joat was saying to Seld, "I'll be right down and we can celebrate together," and she waved a jaunty farewell behind her as she left.

Exhausted as much by this unexpectedly felicitous outcome as the weight of problems still to be resolved, Channa sank back into her float chair.

"One more on the up side," she murmured to reassure herself. "Simeon, I'm sort of tired. Could you . . . ?"

The others murmured apologies and moved aside while Simeon guided her chair away.

"A moment then, Amos ben Sierra Nuevo," Questar-Benn. Amos turned in surprise, shot one anxious look at Channa's disappearing figure but had no choice but to give the Admiral his attention. "If you'd be good enough to accompany the Commodore and me to our quarters . . ."

He was as glad as they appeared to be to leave the sad ambience of the cargo bay, though only one more of his shrinking band of Bethelites lay there.

The Admiral and Commodore noted his interest in the interior of their flagship and explained as they walked through the maze, absently accepting salutes or nods as they passed details of men and women hurrying about their tasks.

None of the Central Worlds' ships had taken much damage though the battle with the desperate Kolnari warships had been fierce, if brief. The guided tour was enough to make Amos wonder anew how Guiyon had managed to get the old *Exodus* anywhere, much less reach SSS-900-C.

He was sighing in semi-despair for all the problems he now faced in giving his poor plundered planet even a semblance of the efficiency and expertise Central Worlds took for granted.

"Ah, yes, here we are, Benisur . . ." the commodore said and Amos with suitable humility corrected him to "a simple Amos, sir." "We've been receiving updates of affairs on Bethel and have need of your assistance."

Five men and women were seated about the lounge, the two youngest—a man and a women in their early twenties, jumping to their feet at the entrance of Admiral, Commodore and their guest.

"Here he is, gentlefolk," Questar-Benn, "Benisur ben Sierra Nuevos, aka Simeon-Amos and the putative leader of the Bethelites."

"No, no," Amos said, shaking head and hand to deny that title. He didn't want that mantle laid on his shoulders. Not now.

"As you will, young man," Questar-Benn said curdly, "but you *were* the leader of the dissidents as well as the defender of Bethel and we need your input." Then while Amos continued to demur, she over-rode him by introducing the group. "Senior Counsellor Agrum of SPRIM, Representative Fusto of MM, Observer Nilsdotter, PA's Ferryman for SPRIM and Losh Lentel for MM. Simeon, are you here?"

"I am," Simeon said, his voice issuing from the comunit.

He might have warned me, Amos thought sourly. *But perhaps swiftly done is best done.* He gave them a dignified greeting, hand to heart and mind. The young woman, the Observer, was both startled and charmed.

Suddenly he was seated and stewards were passing among the group with drinks and finger foods.

Perhaps I'm merely light-headed with hunger, Amos thought, feeling the better after a sip of a sustaining hot drink and a sample from the plate of delicacies offered.

"Quite simply, ben Sierra Nuevo . . . all right then, Amos," the senior counsellor began with no more to-do, "we need your help to reassure those elements of your people who managed to hide away from the Kolnari. They are terrified and not about to take the word of any strangers even when we holo-ed every surface with 'casts of the Navy taking Kolnari prisoners."

"And making them unload all the loot they'd stored," said the beetlebrowed Representative Fusto. He looked as if he had personally overseen that operation and enjoyed it. He had a narrow face and close-set eyes in a narrow head set on shoulders much too muscular in contrast.

"Some of my people survived?" Amos tried not to wince for this only reinforced the inevitability of his return.

"Specific figures number the survivors as 15,000 . . ."

The population—the former population—of this station, he thought, unable to suppress a groan.

The Observer misinterpreted it with a smile of great sadness and understanding. "Your people have been very brave and suffered terribly. We of SPRIM and MM," and she pointed to the other four, "are empowered to assist the reconstruction of your world. . . ."

Amos groaned again. So much to be done. And his people would resent the intrusion of infidels, no matter how well intentioned.

"We cannot, of course, interfere with the government of any planet," Agrum said, clearing his throat and giving the woman an admonishing glance, "but humanitarian aid certainly falls in our jurisdiction and we are able to provide whatever supplies and materials are needed on an interim basis."

Beetle-brows Fusto gave his opposite number in SPRIM a dark look. "MM requires you to survive on your own efforts but we prevent exploitation of minority groups for any reason whatever. We prefer to establish contact with a senior government official, preferably elected by the minority in question, but you qualify—according to Simeon—as the logical and most accessible representative."

For this I thank you, Simeon, Amos said, hoping that no one, especially the Observer, would hear him grind his teeth.

"Your planet got pretty well razed to subsoil," the commodore said. "'S going to take *help* to restart," and he, in turn, gave the MM official a quelling look, smiling at Amos as if to say "they mean well but they're heavy-handed." "We had to put up a transmitter," and he shrugged as if such a facility was a mere nothing, "and the engineers put up a temp at the space field—which is littered with a lot of hulls, some of which could well be refitted for whatever lunar mining would put you back on-line there."

A transmitter and space facility? Re-usable hulls for the craft the Kolnari had fused. Amos began to feel less despondent, though half of him resisted.

"Humanitarian aid will be sufficient to see your people through the on-coming winter," Agrum went on, "using whatever shelters your culture prefers . . ."

"We cannot *land* alter-culturals on Bethel, of course," Fusto half-interrupted, "but orbital staff is not considered by Central Worlds Authority to compromise indigenous integrity . . ."

"If you wish, you may request additional colonials of your own persuasion . . ." from Nilsdotter.

Amos turned from one speaker to the other, half dazed.

"Give the kid a break," Simeon said suddenly. "Why don't you let him read the reports so he knows what you're talking about, huh?"

"Of course," said SPRIM.

"Our intention, I assure you, Station Simeon," MM said defensively.

"Then let it be so," Admiral Questar-Benn said, smiling encouragingly at Amos as she handed him several disk files and led him to another room where he could digest the information in private.

"Not over until it's over," the Admiral remarked to the commodore as they watched the sometimes contentious delegation leave their quarters.

"And it's never over," Tellin-Makie replied, pouring them both snifters of brandy in the flag quarters. "I didn't have the heart to remind them that those aren't the only bunch of Kolnari running around loose."

"And if you leave a pair, they breed up again," she said wearily. "They know that. Which is the reason I suspect we'll have Simeon and the others on the rolls in a couple of years. The Kolnari will be a menace as long as two of them are left alive."

"The Psych people swear they can be rehabilitated."

"Rehabilitated to E equals M and C squared," she said, taking a sip. "Dam' cockroaches." Another sigh. "Maybe this little atrocity *will* get us some resources."

"For a while, until the general public become inured to these particular atrocities," Tellin-Makie said, "then we can go back to peeing on bonfires. It's not as if they were the only serious problem, either."

"Would that it were so. Would that it were so, my friend."

She looked at the screen, which showed an exterior view of SSS-900-C. Repair servos and suited figures were already working on some of the more urgent damage, though it would be a generation before the devastation was fully repaired. She made a mental note to have Engineering help out while the task force was on station here.

"All in all, though, I'm glad we don't have *their* problems, poor heroic sods," she said.

"Amen."

"Yes, yes," Joseph said eagerly when Amos finished telling him of the help promised by SPRIM and MM, up to and including a Brain

Planetary manager to replace Guiyon. "We must return as quickly as possible."

"Yes, you and Rachel must."

"Rachel and I?" Joseph repeated, staring in sudden alarm at Amos.

"Yes, because there is much to organize on the ground before we may accept the beneficence . . ."

"But it is you, Amos ben Sierra Nuevo, who *must* return!" Joseph's face was stricken. "It is *your* duty. Our world is but a lake of mourning. They need *you*. They need a hero—and their Prophet."

Amos paced, hands behind his back, clenching and unclenching, up and down the floor of his room in Simeon's quarters.

"They need a hero, granted, Joseph," he said, stopping in front of his friend, "but if I am a hero, then so are you!"

"Me?" Joseph laughed. "I am your henchman. Your right hand, and proud to be so. Your friend, and prouder still of that. But you are the prophet, the hero, the one the people follow."

Amos took him by the shoulders. "You are my brother, as truly as if the same mother bore us."

Joseph blinked as Amos drew him into the double cheek-touch of close kin to emphasize his words. "And it is *you* who will return while I deal with these infidels and make certain that what charity they would foist on us will not weaken our people but allow them to become strong in such ways that no other scavenger can ever catch us unawares." *Who saves the saved from the savior?* he thought.

"And I . . . I wonder," Amos went on aloud. "I wonder if it is good, that the new leader is of the old Prophet's line—may God smile on him! Too many generations have the people followed the old families." He winced. "And followed them to ruin."

"You would lead us to greatness!" Joseph said forcefully. *The more so if you doubted yourself less,* he added to himself. "You have shown your strengths as a self-thinker, a defender of his planet, a guileful strategist . . ."

"History does not show many *battle-leaders* who had the same talent for being *peace-leaders*!"

"But you are of a peaceful nature until roused to defend what you hold dear," Joseph said, "even as you have seen your duty now to protect us against those who *wish* to protect us!" Joseph turned sternly grim now. "It is the blind face of Channa that hides your way."

Amos looked so fiercely at him that Joseph turned his face away, his shoulders sagging in acknowledgement.

"I also cannot abandon these here to whom *we*, for our very lives, owe a debt of gratitude. If, in this one instance, duty and honor are both served, let me serve it." Amos sighed deeply, torn between love and duty. "Are Simeon, Joat and Channa to be merely a chapter of my life because fourteen generations ago the Prophet fathered my many-times great grandfather? We saw on Bethel what comes of that."

"Yes, Amos, in all truth we did. And you are right to wish to be indebted to *all*," and Joseph laid a subtle emphasis on the word, "the stationers even though the need for *your* special role is now over."

"Yes, that is over. In its place, I must assume several roles and do each well in all honor." Then he gave the younger man a sudden smile, the son that had always drawn the required response from any recipient. "And I give Rachel the chance to restore honor to her name."

Joseph gave him a sudden stare as fierce as the one Amos had given him. "What do you mean?"

"She was, after all, trained as an infosystems administrator. It is *her* duty to assist *you* in calling our people from their hiding places, to organize the reports that I must receive to know what is most needed. With you two side by side—that is what you wish, is it not, Joseph? Rachel by your side?"

The younger man laughed and blushed, which seemed to embarrass him more.

"You know it is what I wish but, Amos, do not blame her for what she did."

"I do not," Amos lied stoutly, "but she will need to redeem herself in her own eyes!"

"Ah, yes," said Joseph with a sigh. "She is anxious to do that. She talks to me about it," he went on in a softer voice. "She talks of you but she also talks of you to me."

"Then go to her, Joseph my brother, my friend. If you insist on making me wear the mantle of a leader, then I have issued an order to you. But think also of what I have told you, brother hero. You return to Bethel as my brother and my equal, not my retainer—not even first among my retainers. The time for those petty protocols is past."

"I go," Joseph said. He turned on the threshold. "And you, too, have earned a little happiness, I think. God willing, may you find it!"

Channa had insisted on returning to her brawn's quarters, pointing out that there was nothing else Chaundra or his staff could do for her in sickbay.

"I'll be much better off there," she told him, "because I know my way around. Simeon can remind me where I put things so I can find what I need. Only time will make a difference now."

Once Simeon had angled the chair float beside her satin-draped bed, she lay down, not seeing, not speaking, absorbing the most recent events. Not that she wasn't overwhelmingly relieved that Seld had been granted a reprieve. But there were so many decisions to be made, hanging in the air, over her head, where she could feel them, even if she couldn't see them. She could feel a trickle down her cheek and, with a gesture she hoped masked the real reason, she blotted the cheek on the gray satin cover.

"Penny for your thoughts?"

Because Simeon had picked exactly the appropriate light tone, she gave him a wan smile though she wondered how he had noticed such a small thing as a tear.

"I've none to sell," she said, "just bits and pieces floating around. Like, *Happy endings suck the galactic muffin.* It's enough to give you a headache."

"D'you have one?" Instant concern colored his voice.

"No, no," she said, shaking her head on the pillow.

"Look, Channa, you *will* be all right," he said in the firm tone one uses when one is hoping against hope one's statement is correct.

She nodded once sharply, minding her temper and her manners. "Yes, I'm sure I will." Her voice was tight.

"I've scanned every report I could find on this kind of temporary blindness, Channa," he went, infusing his voice with confidence. *I'd give anything to be able to hold you in arms and comfort you but all I've got is voice contact. Talk to me, Channa.* "Worse scenario and you'll still see—through my sensors. Remember that, Channa. And I see real good and wherever I need to!"

She had stiffened and cut through his opening words in a rather shrill voice. "Simeon, spare me the . . . *Could* you do that for me?"

"Sure," he said, both surprised and testy. "But surely you *knew* that. You've been using my senses for the last two weeks!"

Her jaw dropped and then a tremulous smile crossed her lips. "So I have, haven't I?" she said in a broken voice. After a moment's silence, she added in a contrite voice, "I owe you, and everyone else an apology, for acting like a self-pitying wuss!"

"Well, after all, you've had quite an adjustment to make."

"But I didn't have to snarl at you."

"Oh, that? I wouldn't know how to answer smartly if you didn't. Don't break that habit, Channa-mine."

Her smile was stronger. "Then I certainly won't."

"Because you like the challenge, don't you? And, by and large, I'm good company."

"And so modest."

"So witty and intelligent," he reminded her.

"And so handsome."

"Do you really think so?"

"Oh yes," she said, "I especially like your dueling scar, that's a nice touch."

"Thank you," he said, gratified. "You're the first person who's ever mentioned it. I've been waiting for years for someone to ask about it. Sometimes people think it's dirt on the projector lens."

She grinned. "It goes well with the baseball cap."

He paused a moment, unsure, "Um . . ."

"No, really," she assured him, "That projection's a perfect portrait of your personality. It's not based on a chromosomal extrapolation, is it?"

"Naw," he said, putting a grin in his voice. "It's me as I want to be. I'd have hated it if an extrap of me came out with a receding chin and a big nose, so I never tried to find out. I'm Simeon, the self-created!"

"Wise," she agreed, "very wise."

The door opened and Amos stood on the threshold. "Channa!" he cried out in a passionate voice.

She sat bolt upright on the bed, her lips parted in surprise. "I thought you'd left."

He rushed to her side and drew her into his arms. "How can I leave you like this?" he said, stroking her hair.

Simeon cursed under his breath. Leave it to Amos to undo all his hard work. *Just when I've got her cheered up and back to something near her normal—for her—frame of mind.*

Channa put up a hand, found Amos' face and leaned forward to kiss him, smiling because she had caught the corner of his mouth and was working her way into a position that satisfied her.

When the long kiss ended, Amos said with a sigh, "You want me!"

No, you ass! She wants a double malt and a ticket to "Death in the Twenty-first." Would that I had hands, Oh Amos ben Sierra Nueva, to clout you up alongside the head with.

Channa didn't answer but held her head as though looking at Amos through her bandages. Amos smiled at her, the smile of a man who believes he can accomplish anything, a smile that proclaimed the bearer to be the recipient of a miracle.

"I came to ask you to come with me," he said, laughing.

"You did?" she said in a dreamy tone. They kissed again, more deeply. Channa burrowed deeper into his embrace, sighing like someone relieved of a pain they did not know they suffered.

"I love you, Channa," he said.

"I love you, Simeon," she murmured,

Amos stiffened. Channa raised her blind face to his and whispered huskily again. "I love you."

He released her and moved back. She hesitated and turned her head from side to side. "Amos? What is it? Is someone here?"

"Yes," he said stiffly, "someone who comes between us."

Puzzled, Channa reached out blindly with one hand, the other resting on Amos's chest. "There's no one here but us. What are you talking about?"

"Simeon," he said the name with a hiss. "For whom you have just declared your love."

Her face altered abruptly from joy to chagrin. "I . . . I . . ." she began in confusion.

"A gentleman of the Sierra Nueva does not intrude. I am in the way," Amos said, flinging off her hands and jumping to his feet. "I will leave you alone together." And he was gone.

Channa swung her legs from the bed and lunged after him. She moved with unexpected speed and before Simeon could warn her, she crashed into the wall, just beside the door. Weeping, she stepped to the right point and the door opened for her.

"Amos! Wait!" she shouted and this time Simeon opened the outside door but she paused on the threshold to get her bearings and heard, all too clearly, the elevator's closing.

"Amos! Don't go!" she cried, and heard it engage. She stood leaning her head against the metal, sobbing gently, tears soaking the adhesive synthetic of her bandages.

Inside the descending lift, Amos leaned his head against the wall, Channa's desperate voice echoing in his mind. Almost, but not quite louder than her whisper—"I love you, Simeon."

"Where do think you're going?" Simeon asked him.

He straightened and gritted his teeth. "To the docks," he said crisply. "I must return to Bethel!"

Simeon gave a dramatic sigh. "And who's to go between Bethel and SPRIM and MM? Who saves the saved from the savior?"

Amos was aghast at hearing his own thoughts come back at him from Simeon.

"Someone has to handle them," Simeon continued.

"Rachel can. She's a trained infosystems spe . . ."

"Rachel!" Simeon roared in surprise. "She wouldn't know how to handle them. They'd twist her up into little knots. Not that she isn't twisted right now."

"They say they cannot interfere . . ."

"They say, they say," Simeon chanted back at him. "Use your wits, Amos, and don't suggest Joseph. He's the guy you need on the planet, coaxing your people out of whatever lairs they've hidden in. No, you're the only one who can be johnny-on-the-spot here!"

"What I do now is my business," Amos said in a snarling tone. "You have no right to interfere either . . ." Only then did Amos notice that the elevator had stopped moving. He crossed his arms. "So, do you mean to hold me prisoner here until Joseph, Rachel and the others have left?"

"Emotionally you've been a prisoner since you got here. Why do think I went to so much trouble to get SPRIM and MM involved with Bethel?"

"*You* did. But the Admiral and the Commodore . . ."

"Listened to what I had to tell them, which is more than you ever do. You've got to be here . . ."

Outrage, indignation, disgust and fury raced unchecked across Amos' face. "So? You admit it."

"Huh?"

"You admit that you only wish to make of me a sex toy," Amos cried passionately, "a surrogate for yourself with Channa!"

"I what?" Simeon's voice reverberated in the confines of the small chamber. "You *are* bughouse! Which is probably why it's such an interesting idea," he added in a reasonable, half-amused tone, "but you said it, I didn't. However, it's not on *my* behalf you've got to be here. It's Channa's. She really is in love with you, Amos. Can't you get that through your arrogant to-the-manor-born head?"

"Loves me? Loves me? Then why does she embrace me and say, *I love you, Simeon?*"

"And, of course, she hasn't been calling you Simeon-Amos for the past intense two weeks, has she?"

"Banchut!" Amos smacked his forehead with the flat of his palm, his expression one of utter dismay.

"It sure wasn't me, or my holo, or even the shell of me she was kissing just now! Cut her a little slack. She's been *blinded,* dammit! She's scared, she's exhausted, she's under pressure. Don't cut the heart out of her for a slip of the lip!"

"A slip?"

"A slip! You ego-centric rag-head selfish bastard!"

"But you love her, too!" Amos brandished his fist, glaring about him to find a target for his frustration and wrath.

"Yes, I love her. Just as much as you do. No, probably a lot more. And yes, she's in love with me a little, and I treasure that. But I can't touch her, Amos. I can't hold her no matter how much I would like to. What are you worrying about?"

"That she dreams of you and wonders what it would be like to be in *your* arms." In the confines of the elevator, Amos heard the sound of his angry jealous words echo back at him. "I think that she would like to close her eyes and hear your voice whisper to her as I make love to her. I will not be that fantasy for her, nor for you."

"Well, I'll tell you what *I* think. I think that you are a dirty-minded, fat-headed, parochial, small-minded, jealous hunk of pig fat. Just let me give you a taste of what she's going through and you stalking off and leaving her alone with it."

Simeon turned off the lights in the elevator. Amos was plunged into pitch blackness; just long enough to reach the stage of imagining lights and colors to console himself. The human eye is not meant for complete darkness. Even on an overcast night with eyes closed there is *some* ambient light.

The darkness and motion were disorienting.

And frightening, the Bethelite admitted to himself.

"Stop it." Amos said calmly, but firmly. Simeon didn't answer. "Stop it, I said," a trace of unease creeping into his voice. *An accident, who would doubt his word?*

Simeon brought the elevator to a halt.

"It's unpleasant, isn't it?" Simeon asked quietly.

"Yes," Amos said shortly, sullenly. "Please, would you turn on the lights?"

"Channa can't," Simeon observed. "It's possible they won't come back on and she'll have to get a prostheses, one of those devices they set into your face. Yup, things could look like this to her forever."

"What do you want me to do?" Amos demanded. "I would give her my sight if I could."

"That's a safe offer," Simeon observed contemptuously, "she wouldn't accept such a sacrifice even if it was needed."

"Then what would you have me do?" Amos was nearly shouting now, flapping his arms hard against his sides.

"Something a lot easier. Hold her. Just put your arms around her and hold her close. You softshells need that. I never had it so I don't miss it."

Amos shifted position, silent.

"I would hock my shell if I could *physically* comfort her. But I can't. I *can* make sure she gets what she needs from the one person she'll accept it from. And let me tell you something, lordling, *even to comfort Channa, I wouldn't want to* stay *a softshell.* You're *cripples* next to us! You realize that? We have senses, abilities, that you can't even begin to imagine. But yes, in this one area, I am jealous of you. Despite that, I arranged . . . yes, *noble* being that *I* am . . . arranged for you to have to stay on this station to handle all the details the Bethelite leader will have. So that you could also comfort the woman we both love. There I've said it aloud!"

"I've done all I can, Amos," and now Simeon's voice was tinged with a helpless note. "I've been with her since she was brought to the hospital. I haven't left her. When she wakes up, I wish her good morning and mine is the last voice she hears at night. I'm the one who guides her safely across a room. I'm the one who tells her that what she's looking for is a little to the right. I'm the one who makes sure she gets her meals. I've put up with her bouts of temper and self-pity and I've talked her through her moments of panic. I'm with her constantly. But you walk into the room—at long last I might add—and it's like I've never existed. Did you see her? She lit up like a star going nova. And *you* have the gall to walk out on her!"

Simeon turned the lights back on and Amos squinted briefly as his vision adjusted.

The door opened and Channa raised her head, half-disbelieving she heard the sound of *his* step, the eagerness with which he approached her.

"Oh, Amos!" She reached out her arms tentatively toward him.

"Ah, Channa," and Amos took her hands and pulled her into the circle of his arms. *This only I may do,* he thought possessively, proudly

348 Anne McCaffrey & S.M. Stirling

and yet, because of that brief darkness, sadly, too, because Simeon would never *have this.*

"I'm sorry. Forgive me," he whispered, stroking her hair.

Channa sobbed once and tried to apologize, the words stumbling over his, but he stopped her with a kiss.

Simeon watched them enter the lounge, but decided not to follow them. *This is going to be tough enough,* he thought, *I think I'll work up to it gradually. But wasn't it a great game I played?*

"Before . . . I came to tell you that I must stay longer on the station than we had thought," Amos said. "When I must return to Bethel . . ."

"Stay?" and the gladness in her face and voice reassured Amos as no argument from Simeon ever would, how much Channa did indeed love him.

"Stay . . . for now," he said, trailing caressing fingers around her lovely face. *This, too, I may do that he cannot.*

"For now?" Then a return of her deep and genuine fear caught at his heart.

"I *must* return to Bethel," he said slowly. "I have obligations there."

"I have them here. I can't leave Simeon or Joat," Channa said piteously.

And Amos knew that she also meant these quarters which she knew even in her blindness, and this station which was surely now as much her heart's home as Bethel was his.

"Neither can I leave my people, my planet. Nor do I ask such sacrifice of you," he said, using the force of his personality to reassure her. He smiled down at her, thumbs caressing the velvety skin of her temples. She searched his face with her fingertips and smiled in response.

"But several times in every year, I must return to this station on the business of my people and my world," he went on. "That, I may in all conscience do." A wry shrug. "If my people cannot do without their prophet now and then, then I will not have taught them well. Perhaps the day will come when they need no man to stand between them and God, and I will be free to raise my horses and roses in peace."

Her face lit. "And I could visit sometimes, couldn't I?" she murmured.

"With Joat," Amos said, and then in a far more persuasive and loving tone, "although it is not well for a child to be alone, without brothers and sisters . . ."

"Yes," she laughed as she sensed the change in his stance, falling formally to one knee but before he would speak. She held him upright with her hands.

"In a matter such as this, I should ask permission of your father," Amos said, rising and drawing her close. "But Simeon will do."

She fisted him lightly under the short ribs. "I'll speak to Simeon on my own behalf."

"We will then both address Simeon the Father. But," Amos said in her ear, after a time. "There is one condition."

"What?"

"You must never call me Simeon again." She drew her head back and nodded solemnly. He touched her chin gently. "You may, however," he went on, wishing for once that Simeon *was* listening, "call me Persephone."

EPILOGUE

THE CHILLS WERE less now, and the survivors recovering, although a quarter of the crew had died of the fever and more gone mad.

Belazir t'Marid clenched his rattling teeth against a paroxysm as he lay in the darkened bridge, while the Dreadful Bride fled outward all alone.

"Someday," he whispered.

~ THE END ~

THE SHIP AVENGED

S. M. Stirling

PROLOGUE

BELAZIR T'MARID, War Lord of the Kolnar, Clan Father after Chalku, gazed at the row of crystal vials in their rack, admiring the amber liquid within them. With a lover's tenderness he stroked one jet-black finger across them, reveling in their cool, smooth surfaces.

"Perfect," he murmured, holding the rack up to the light.

His face was no longer an ancient Greek's vision of masculine beauty colored the depthless onyx of a starless night. The quick aging of Kolnar had seamed and scored it, until the starved hunger of the soul within showed through the flesh. The brass-yellow eyes looked down on the vials with a benevolent affection he showed no human being.

Then he smiled, teeth even and white and hard, and laughed. His fist squeezed shut, as if it held a throat.

His son fought not to shiver at the sound of that laugh. There was hatred in it, and an overtone of madness. It made the narrow confines of the bio-storage chamber seem constricting—an odd sensation to one born and raised in the strait confines of spaceships and vacuum habitats. Life-support kept the air pure and varied only enough to simulate Kolnar's usual range of temperatures, from freezing to just below the boiling point of water. Yet now it felt clammy and oppressive . . .

"Not perfect," Karak's voice rasped across his father's reverie. "This disease does not kill. I call that far from perfect. Clan Father," he added, when Belazir turned to glare at his oldest living son.

The elder Kolnar allowed himself an exasperated hiss; it was entirely natural for a boy to plot his fathers death, but also for his father to strike first if it became too obvious. And the boys resentment and dislike were, if anything, obvious.

At times, he wondered about Karak's paternity, for the boy had no subtlety. But the face that looked defiantly back at him might have been his own, some years ago. Once, he too had that youthful swagger, the crackling vitality that sparkled though the lean, panther-muscled body and the vanity that showed in silver ornaments woven into waist-length silver-white hair.

"Child," he said with deceptive gentleness. Karak stiffened. Belazir enjoyed the reaction, and the reaction to reaction. Let the heir realize the old eagle still had claws.

"It pleases me to enlighten you as to why this is a punishment that most admirably fits the crime. Central Worlds, and the damnable Bethelite scum, created The Great Plague to eradicate the Divine Seed of Kolnar." He paused and raised one eyebrow, as if to inquire, *Is this not so?* Karak nodded once, resentfully. "And we shall repay that evil by inflicting upon them a disease that will not simply destroy, but will terrify and humiliate them."

Reluctantly he placed the rack of vials back on its shelf and closed the cooler door. Then he turned to his son:

"Is it enough for you that they should merely die?" he asked in mild astonishment. Karak frowned, but did not answer. "True, it does not kill. What it does is far worse, and the Bethelites shall appreciate that, where you cannot." Belazir laughed, a low chuckle full of gloating pleasure. "It will be a living nightmare to those few not afflicted.

"As you lack imagination, Karak, let me tell you what will happen." Belazir made a sweeping motion with his arm, as though activating a holo-display. "Once the scumvermin realize the magnitude of the threat they face, first, they will call upon their god, as they did when we took Bethel in our fist. And when he does not answer them, some will say that they deserve their fate; a view that we, of course, share. But not all of them will lie down and wait to rot. No."

Belazir ground his teeth, remembering one Bethelite in particular who had refused to he down.

"So. They will next call upon their allies, the mighty Central Worlds, for aid." He spread his hands. "But there is no cure! Oh, a few paltry doses of one," he jerked his head dismissively, "but they are in our possession. Their champions will have no choice but to quarantine their miserable little planet. The all-powerful Fleet of would-be saviors from Central Worlds will watch helplessly from orbit while the pleas for help from below slowly fade away, as thousands starve and the so-moral Bethelites turn to preying upon each other to survive. They will watch until Bethel's civilization falls and the last of them dies—and no human foot will ever walk upon that accursed planet again!"

Belazir wiped the spittle from his lips and studied his son's impassive face with growing impatience.

"Think, my son! Our revenge shall have symmetry." Belazir made a fluid gesture with his hand, "subtlety."

"Your love of *subtlety*," Karak said bitterly, "has already cost the clan dear."

True. After their disastrous rout from the Space Station Simeon-900-C, what the Central Worlds Navy hadn't destroyed, the Great Plague did. From the Navy they could run or hide, but they brought The Plague with them to every gathering of Kolnar-in-space, to all of the exiles from homeworld.

Also, as was their custom, for the strengthening of their seed, they had exposed the children to it. Virtually an entire generation, with their caretakers, died. The adult population had been reduced by three quarters. Only now was their natural fecundity increasing their numbers once more.

The Plague had been created by minions of the beauteous Channa Hap, station master of the SSS-900-C and by the "brain," Simeon, the station's true ruler, whom she served.

And by the Bethelites. The damnable should-have-been-crushed Bethelites who had lured them to the Central Worlds station and their doom.

Belazir's hubris had allowed him to believe he held their hearts in his fist. He was so sure he'd terrorized them into believing their safety was guaranteed—*if* they followed every Kolnari order to the letter.

He should have broken Channa Hap's spirit, broken all of their spirits, he knew. But he'd so enjoyed the cat and mouse game they were playing.

Belazir sighed. This was hindsight. He couldn't have known about The Plague. Even his Sire, Chalku, would not have anticipated a sickness that could afflict the mighty Kolnar. Had not the Divine Seed shrugged off diseases that annihilated whole populations of scum-vermin? *All that does not kill us, makes us stronger,* Belazir told himself. But this had come close to killing them all, very close. Almost as close as homeworld had come to killing all the exiled Terrans who were the first ancestors of the Divine Seed.

Yet some survived to breed, he reminded himself. Survived, to become the superior race and made a home of a planet their per-secutors had thought would kill them all. The Clan had escaped Kolnar too; escaped into space for endless revenge and conquest.

He glanced at his scowling son. Belazir understood the boy's bit-terness. *Do I not feel it myself, ten-fold?*

"My mistake was not in being subtle," he said to Karak. "It was in not being subtle enough."

CHAPTER ONE

THE BENISUR AMOS ben Sierra Nueva sat before the viewscreen in his cabin, watching the beloved shape of Bethel grow smaller, until it was merely a bright spark, another star in the star-shot blackness of space. An exterior view was a luxury he allowed himself, even as he insisted on this simple cabin in a hired merchantman. Bethel had always been a poor world, poor and remote; their ancestors had chosen it to preserve their faith in isolation. It was even poorer since the Kolnari raid, if less solitary; the Central Worlds had sent much aid, and the people had toiled without cease, but so much had been destroyed.

Alarms rang. He braced himself, as he did before every transition; it was futile, but not something you could help. Nausea flashed through him as the engines wrenched the ship out of contact with the sidereal universe. He swallowed bile. Some men could take the transition without feeling so, but he was not one of them. *But I can bear it.* Life taught you that, how to bear things.

Still Amos watched. The screen was a simulation now, a view of how the stars would appear if the outside universe were there. He watched until he could no longer distinguish Bethel's star, Saffron, from the others. Then he switched off the viewscreen and rose wearily. It was always a wrench to leave his home, his people.

Think of what is to come. A week or so to Station SSS-900-C. He removed his robe and lay down on the narrow bed, yawning. The drugs that helped one make an easier transition always left him sleepy.

Channa, he thought, and her image rose to delight his mind's eye. Her long, high-cheekboned face framed by curling black hair, teeth white in a smile of welcome.

He'd never imagined, at the beginning, that this makeshift arrangement would last ten years. They'd agreed then to steal twelve weeks from their lives each year so that they could be together. Half of that time he visited Channa, the other half she was with him on Bethel; allowing for travel time, that gave them four weeks together in either place.

He closed his eyes in pain. Four weeks. Just time enough to make each parting agony.

I was so sure she would stay, once she saw my home. Bethel rose before him. The stinging salty wind from the desert marshes, dawn rising thunderous over the sands. The warm sweet smell of cut grass in the river meadows . . . *And she always wanted to live planetside.*

Amos's mouth quirked. They had too much in common—both were prisoners to their sense of duty. Being reliable made one susceptible to the demands of others. He could not leave Bethel, not while they struggled to rebuild from the devastation the Kolnari had left. And Channa's commitment to her Station was equally strong; as was her friendship with Simeon, the Brain whose body the Station was. So much of her identity was tied up in being a Brawn, a calling to which many aspired but for which few were qualified. And from among those few, she had worked her way up to an unusually high and responsible position. She was respected in Central Worlds. She wielded power and influence.

But among his people, her profession was not understood, her strength and capability, her ambition had been disparaged. She was considered mannish, and his love for her was considered unnatural by many. Not a few of his worried followers had told him so.

He sighed and turned over, thumping at the pillow.

Ten years. He'd thought that if she did not come with him, that perhaps their attraction would gradually grow less. But that had not been the case. The attraction between them was as powerful, the parting as painful, the reunions as rapturous as ever.

Just as her dedication to the Space Station Simeon remained as strong as ever.

Simeon. There was the spur that galled his spirit; that one whom he esteemed as a brother should be his rival for the woman he loved.

Unfair, unreasonable, he knew. Simeon's twisted, non-viable body had been encased in a titanium womb at birth. A life-sustaining shell fitted with neural implants that would allow him to be connected to various housings—to the space station that became his body and his home. Channa was his Brawn, the mobile half of the team of which Simeon was the "brain."

Amos twisted around in the bed again.

His jealousy was baseless, but still, it tormented him. Simeon's love for Channa and hers for Simeon was, perforce, chaste. Simeon could never hold her, as Amos could, nor run hand in hand with her along a beach, nor . . . other things. And yet, Simeon had the greater share of her time, her company, the sight and sound of her that Amos himself yearned for.

In five years her contract will be finished. Then she would have to choose to renew it—or not. Amos smiled as sleep drifted in, as gentle as weightlessness. *She is too full of life to choose more years among metal and machines.*

"Is it true, my Lord, that when you return to Bethel you will at last choose a bride?"

Amos—Prophet of the Second Revelation, Hero of the war against the Kolnar and Leader of Bethel's Council of Elders—suppressed a violent start.

Not again! The Council must have been at her. He put his book aside reluctantly—Simeon had tracked down an original Delany— and turned his recliner to face her.

Soamosa bint Sierra Nueva, for her part, sat silently, dressed in a very proper, long-sleeved gray dress which covered her from throat to ankles. Her hair, amazingly blond for a Bethelite, was completely hidden now in a matching gray bag that framed her small face unbecomingly. Amos ran a list of the usual suspects through his mind. *One reason I have lived so long is that I do not have an heir.* There were many traditionalists on Bethel who loved the thought of a regency—with themselves pulling the strings from behind a minor's chair.

Amos considered his cousin, trying to see her as a stranger might. *She is no longer the tomboy I once knew,* he admitted reluctantly. *She is a woman, a terribly proper one.* He suppressed a sigh. *I should have brought her with me earlier.*

Bethel had become considerably less isolated since the Kolnari attack. Before that he'd been viewed as a heretic for wanting to open their planet to the universe—and he hadn't been heir, either. The Kolnari fusion bomb that destroyed the city of Keriss and the then-Council and Prophet had driven home his point about the dangers of isolationism quite thoroughly.

Soamosa licked her lips nervously.

"I do not wish to overstep, my Lor . . . cousin," she looked up at him with soft blue eyes and smiled shyly. "But it is true that the people wonder when you will take a wife. For ten years, they say, you have left us to go to this woman who is married to an abomination and still she has given you no heir. The people say it is a judgment and they are troubled, cousin."

Soamosa lowered her eyes and her head when she'd finished speaking. Her slender back was straight, her slim feet pressed together in their thick, homely shoes, her hands were folded modestly in her lap. She was the perfect picture of traditional Bethelite womanhood.

Perhaps a perfect candidate for the Prophet's wife. Amos wondered who had been in charge of her education these past few years, regretting his lack of involvement. *There was too much to do,* he protested to his creeping guilt, *too many documents and summaries and reports . . .*

Amos breathed a quiet, frustrated sigh. *Ah, Channa,* he thought, *how you've changed me. Once, not so very long ago, I would have approved of such overwhelming self-negation. I would have been pleased at the way she distanced herself from her own opinions so as not to seem overbold. What would you advise me to tell her, my love?*

He realized now, far too late, that choosing to bring Soamosa had been something of an error. Insensitive at best. No doubt his young cousin's mother had visions of an elaborate wedding ceremony with thousands of guests upon their return; her daughter would be the radiant bride, himself, the blushing groom.

He sat up straighter and spoke to her firmly.

"Soamosa, look at me."

Her lips trembled and her eyes were huge and shining when she looked up.

"I have told you that Simeon is neither an abomination, nor Channa's husband. He is my dear friend, and Channa, who is completely unbound, is the woman that I love. Do you understand this?"

A frown struggled to manifest itself and then her face smoothed.

Ah, Amos thought, *such control. For one so apparently timid she's actually quite strong.*

"No," she said firmly, "I do not."

"I do not owe you an explanation, little one."

She bit her lip and lowered her eyes, then looked up at him again, abashed, but hopeful.

Amos sighed.

"We will begin with Simeon," he said patiently. "What is your objection to him?"

"He isn't human, cousin. He is a thing that mocks the perfection of man as God created him."

"And is our uncle, Grigory, an abomination because his heart is made of plastic mesh?"

She frowned. "No, of course not."

"Simeon simply requires more mechanical aid than does our uncle. He is still a man, just as Grigory is a man. And he is good man, one of the truest friends that I have ever had. If you will but open your heart to him, he will be your friend too, Soamosa."

Predictably, she looked both doubtful and queasy.

"As to my relationship with Channa Hap . . ."

Her interest sharpened to a sword's point.

"Frankly, it is none of your business." He watched her blush a deep scarlet. "This I will say, Channa and I do not need a marriage ceremony to sanctify what is already a very real and pure love. Nor is it necessary for me to produce an heir."

Soamosa actually gasped and clutched at her heart in horror.

"Let the family divide my estates and wealth among themselves when I am dead. Our world and people will not falter because I am gone. Let them find another to head the state."

"But your holiness will also be gone. We would be so comforted if you left sons behind to guide us," she said passionately.

Amos smiled at her. "Sweet cousin, when God touches a man's heart and urges him to speak as a prophet to the people, that man is not chosen because of who his father was. Only think what it would be like if the people turned to you, expecting you to fill my shoes."

"But they wouldn't!" she said in horror. "I'm only a woman."

Amos tried to imagine Channa's reaction to *that* remark. He gave a complex inward shudder. Channa Hap in full fury was enough to make a strong man blanch and cringe; like a thunderstorm on the sands, or a driven ocean crashing on high cliffs.

"Ah, but they might think that my taking you on this trip had some deeper meaning." She blushed at that and quickly lowered her eyes.

"And if I were to offer you such special attentions for the rest of my life, then they would surely think it significant. After all, there have been prophetesses before."

"But . . . but . . . I have no calling," she protested, both horrified and confused. "I know that I have not."

"So, why should I create an heir, who might have no calling either, but of whom the people would expect such? Imagine the life my son or daughter could look forward to. Should I be so unfair? Should I arouse such expectations?"

"No," she said almost sullenly. "But, then why . . . ?"

"Have I invited you to accompany me? I have invited you because I like you, cousin. Because you are young and I thought that you might enjoy seeing one of the greatest space stations in the universe."

Because I didn't want to see you living your life in a gray sack, with your mind pinched off like a plant being deliberately stunted.

He had changed Bethel, the Kolnari war had changed it more, but there were limits to what could be done in a single generation.

"I thought you might like an adventure."

He was pleased to see a sudden gleam come into her eyes. It reminded him of the girl who'd put a desert *gurrek* under his pillow. His heart grew content when she grinned back. Perhaps, after all, those horrible clothes and the mealy-mouthed behavior were the result of an ambitious mother's determined schooling. With time and care she might return to her own true self.

A sudden twisting wrench made both of them cry out involuntarily. Soamosa fell to her knees, hands over her mouth to hold back the retching. Amos turned his chair and lunged for his console, knowledge driving out the merely physical misery.

They'd been ripped out of hyperspace.

Dangerous, exceedingly so. Without drugs, or preparation, susceptible and unlucky passengers had been known to slip into a psychotic state.

Amos gripped the arms of his chair and closed his eyes waiting for his body to readjust. Soamosa gave up the unequal struggle and ran for the washroom. Amos swallowed hard as the sounds she made urged his body to sympathetic action.

He activated the com and snapped, "Captain Sung!"

Before he had finished speaking a voice came booming through the ship:

"Attention merchanter ship *Sunwise*. Stand by to be boarded.

Resistance is futile and will be punished. Repeat. Prepare to be boarded."

The skin at the base of Amos's neck clenched as though stabbed with a jagged piece of ice. *Kolnari.* The accent was different, but the arrogance the same.

The captain hadn't answered his call. Amos made an impatient sound deep in his throat and headed for the bridge, calling out to Soamosa to remain in the cabin. The two guards standing watch outside the door turned smartly and followed him.

I have waited too long. I thought . . . The Kolnari never forgot an injury; but they never attacked a foe they thought too strong, either. They had already found the SSS-900-C a mouthful large enough to choke on. Bethel had a space navy of its own, these days—small, but enough to defend the system until a Central Worlds squadron arrived.

In the merchant ship *Sunwise,* Belazir t'Marid had found a target easy enough to take, which also meant he felt strong enough to survive the inevitable retaliation. The Kolnari leader had the cunning of Shaithen his master. He might be right. . . .

"Ship is in the five kiloton range," the communications tech was saying. "Warship, from the neutrino signature. Corvette class, but not a standard model."

Amos nodded to himself, standing at the rear of the horseshoe-shaped command bridge. *Panic, but well-controlled panic,* he decided. Captain Sung was snapping out orders; hard, almond-shaped green eyes glittering in a stern middle-aged face. Young Guard-Caladin Samuel stood behind him, one hand on the captain's chair, one resting on the console. Occasionally he leaned close and spoke urgently to the distracted Sung.

On the forward screen, to Amos's vast relief, was a somewhat worse-for-wear ex-courier ship. An ordinary pirate vessel, nothing like the augmented ships the Kolnari favored.

Mere pirates, he thought. *I am relieved that it is* merely *pirates.*

"Have they indicated what they want, Captain Sung?"

"They want to board," the Captain snarled. "Beyond that, Benisur, I don't know." He rubbed his chin. "But this is no happy accident on their part. There's no trace of recent drive energies; they had to've been waiting for us."

Sung glanced at the controls. "With a grapple already engaged and waiting to trip us out of hyperspace. Timing like that . . ." he let the thought trail off.

Amos's finely chiseled mouth thinned to a grim line. Yes, timing like that meant a traitor, a spy high enough in the Bethelite Security Forces to have access to privileged information. *Traitors or Kolnari agents, or both,* he decided. *Joseph, I should have listened to you.*

Complacency. Letting the wish be father to the thought. *I thought you paranoid.* Mind you, a Chief of Security was *supposed* to be paranoid. *I should have listened.* Of late years he'd even given up the simple precaution of booking passage on several different ships, leaving at different times.

"That spawn of Shaithen would know where I was," he'd argued with certainty. "It would take more than a simple trick to escape his grasp."

Joseph would have preferred an escort of destroyers, and a company of Guards. Amos had argued that Central Worlds would, at the least, see that as an insulting lack of trust, and at worst as a provocation—the Bethelites were thought barbaric enough as it was.

Amos glanced at his escort. Four of them; all were young. *And untried,* he thought, realizing for the first time that they might well die today. Regret and anger washed through him. He'd chosen youngsters because he wanted to expose as many of the young as he could to Central Worlds culture, because that was their future. Just as these vibrant young men were meant to be Bethel's.

Joseph, my brother, if I ever see you again I shall allow you to scold me for as long as pleases you about my foolishness; and in future I will bow to your will. He would let Joseph boot his Prophetic arse, for that matter, if he lived past this day.

"Benisur, I'm afraid they may be after you. There's nothing else on the ship that would be worth their trouble."

Nothing, unless the pirates were after a cargo of sun-dried tomatoes, dates, goat cheese, leather handicrafts, and preserved meats. Valuable enough on SSS-900-C, with its rich manufactories and well-paid, highly-trained inhabitants. Not the sort of thing which pirates selected for their raids.

Amos nodded. "My thinking exactly, Captain."

He paused. Pirates would squeeze Bethel for a ransom it could ill afford.

"I am reluctant to place your people or your ship in any greater danger, Captain, but I believe we must consider resisting. After all, if I am the object of this exercise, then they cannot risk firing on the ship and possibly killing me. So that is one danger we need not fear. And as they are in a small ship, how many of them could there be? Ten perhaps? Fifteen?"

The Captain shrugged. "Fifteen tops, more would overtax life support."

"So we outnumber them as well. Let them come aboard, lure them in and when they are in far enough, strike, and take hostage any survivors. What do you say?" Amos glanced at his young Caladin, courteously including him in their council.

"I had not even considered surrendering you to them, Benisur." Samuel's brown eyes held an innocent bravery.

"I'm no soldier, Benisur," Sung said, and pulled on his lower lip. "But I like your plan a whole lot better than just letting these animals grab my ship and take you off it." He nodded decisively: "We'll do it."

There was a slight quaver in Sung's voice as he issued orders to break out the arms. He glanced at Amos to see if it had been noticed. But Amos was studying the monitor showing the lock through which the pirates would enter.

An echoing clang resounded through the ship as the pirates extended a caterpillar lock to connect them to the *Sunwise.*

Amos looked up from the screen to watch the crewmen depart for their ambush site and murmured a blessing over them, knowing that most of them would neither understand nor thank him for it. But the eyes of the four Bethelites showed gratitude as they ceremoniously touched forehead, lips, and heart.

Then he watched as the Captain keyed the monitors that covered his crew's progress under the direction of the Bethelite soldiers.

The camera trained on the main lock showed the hatch recessing. Air hissed as pressures equalized; Bethel's was well below the Earth-derived standard the Central Worlds used.

A long second's pause. Two men in black space armor swung out from the airlock, crouching, plasma rifles up. After a moment one of them signaled and five more swept out. Three split off and moved carefully towards engineering, the other four, hugging the walls and moving with extreme caution, headed for the bridge.

Amos's stomach knotted. Their armor was too much like the Kolnari's—though a stripped down version of it—and their movements were too professional, too disciplined, for mere criminals. If the Kolnari were so reduced as to use outsiders . . . mercenaries . . . But no, surely they would despise and avoid such creatures.

Yet these men behaved like the product of intensive Kolnari training—that was an inhumanly businesslike civilization.

He opened his mouth to advise the Captain to call off the ambush, when a final invader left the airlock and entered the ship.

A foot, clad in massive black battle armor, hit the *Sunwise*'s deck with a crash that seemed to move the ship. Slowly—majestic as an eclipse—the Kolnari entered, turned, and marched towards the bridge.

Amos could not speak. For a moment his throat was paralyzed, he couldn't breathe, he couldn't move. It was unexpected, to be so overwhelmed by horror at seeing one of them again, for he was no coward. But an evil that had almost destroyed his people had returned; the nightmare was marching again—coming to collect him personally.

"Captain!" Amos managed to choke out. "Call off the ambush, call it off or they'll kill you all!"

The Captain stared for a moment as though he hadn't understood, then activated the com and spoke, just as Samuel, the Bethelite Caladin, fired on the invaders.

"Stand down! Stand down! Lay down your weapons and fall back!"

Some of the crew heard him, reacting with confusion at first, looking around to see if anyone else had heard the order, lowering their rifles, backing off. But Amos's guards engaged the enemy—too intent on battle to listen—certain that if the Benisur Amos wished them to hold their fire *his* voice would have told them so.

One crewman stood up, his hands lifted in surrender and died for it, a steaming hole blasted in his chest by a plasma rifle.

The doubtful broke then and fled, while the others fought and retreated, and died, one by one. Retreat turned to slaughter.

Amos was thrown with bruising force at the feet of Belazir t'Marid and lay face down, unmoving, on a rough carpet made from the scaly hide of a great beast. Behind him, he heard the gentle whir of servos as the battle-armored Kolnari lowered the arm that had flung him here. He heard soft grunts as his companions, Captain Sung and Soamosa were tossed to the floor beside him.

Soamosa, her blond hair freed from confinement and her gown much torn, clung to Amos's arm, burying her face against him and trembling.

"Look at me, Benisur," purred a voice silky with satisfaction.

Amos raised himself onto his elbows and slowly lifted his head. Belazir grinned down at him, white teeth gleaming in a predator's snarl from a face as black as a starless night. *He has aged*, Amos thought, shocked.

The hawklike nose was more prominent and the flesh hung on his face like slightly melted tallow. But the golden eyes were as bright and cruel as they had ever been; though now they held the glint of sheer mad glee, where before there had only been a lazy amusement.

"So good to see you," Belazir continued, almost whispering.

The control room was centered on his chair, like a massive throne set among control consoles and display screens. The Kolnari lord wore only a white silk loincloth and jeweled belt, besides his ornaments; he lolled like a resting tiger between guards in powered armor, his own suit standing empty and waiting. Behind him a holograph showed a nighted landscape where armored plants grew and moved and fought slow vegetable battles with spikes of organic steel. In the distance a nuclear volcano spat fire that red-lighted the undersides of acid clouds. A giant beast with sapphire scales trumpeted its agony at the sky as six-legged wolves leaped and clung and tore at its adamantine sides. Thick purple blood rilled towards the ground, and the very grass writhed to drink of it.

Kolnar, Amos knew with a shudder. *Antechamber of hell.* Belazir had never seen the planet that bred his kind, but it lived in his genes.

"So *good* to see you like this," Belazir said. He slowly clenched his hand. "You are in my fist," he explained, as though Amos might not know it. "You and your companions." He grinned at them and indicated the Captain. "And who have we here? Captain Sung, I presume?"

A vicious kick from a mercenary prompted a response.

"Yessir," Sung grunted.

A flurry of kicks caused Sung to roll into a ball, covering his head, drawing his feet up to protect his privates. The kicks concentrated on his kidneys until he sobbed.

"Beg," the Kolnari said.

"*Please!*"

Belazir raised one finger. The mercenary stepped back, grinning. He had a particolored beard and a brass hoop in one ear.

"You must tell the Captain the rules, Benisur. We would not want a repeat of this lesson, not at his age."

"We must address the Divine Seed of Kolnar as 'Great Lord,'" Amos said, his voice flat and distant, his eyes fixed on the space below the Kolnari's feet, "and when the Lord Captain Belazir addresses us we must respond with 'Master and God.'"

"And what are you, Simeon-Amos?" Belazir asked with delicate sarcasm.

"Scumvermin," Amos ground out. Belazir laughed with delight.

"Ah, there are times—like this one, Benisur—when a despised enemy can be more welcome than a beautiful bride." He smiled benignly at Amos, then indicated the cowering girl at his side. "Is this *your* bride?"

"No! Lord and God," Amos said with such obvious sincerity that Belazir raised an eyebrow.

"Do not tell me you are still saving your seed for the delectable Channahap?"

Amos tried to school his features to immobility. He knew the slight shifts in his expression conveyed his outrage to the Kolnari like a shout.

Belazir smiled a cream-eating smile.

"A most . . . satisfying woman, truly. I can understand your obsession." He indicated Soamosa again. "Then no doubt this little one is a virgin; your people have an inexplicable admiration for such. Do not fear, girl, I can cure you of it."

Soamosa's body jerked as though she'd been struck. She muffled a cry with the sleeve of her robe.

"She is only a child, Master and God," Amos pleaded "Her family will pay a ransom for her safe return."

Belazir shrugged, "I had eight children by her age, and all of my wives were the same age as I. If I return her to her family in . . . *almost* one piece, I doubt they will complain. Much." He grinned. "And certainly not to me."

He flicked a hand at the guards, "Take them away." To Amos: "We will talk again later, scumvermin. I shall look forward to it."

CHAPTER TWO

JOSEPH BEN SAID paced restlessly through his office. It was on the top, the third story of a building well up on the slopes overlooking New Keriss. He stopped and looked down from the open window; mild salt air caressed his face, smelling of the gardens outside and faintly of the city of low, scattered buildings that stretched down to the waters edge.

How different, he thought—as always.

How different from the days before the Kolnari came. Old Keriss had occupied the same site; the airburst hadn't dug much of a crater when the city died in a moment of thermonuclear fire. But the old city had been bigger, more densely built, narrow streets as well as fine avenues. Thickest of all along the old docks, with their shrilling tenements and slums. The New Kerris was cleaner, more modern now that Bethel was in touch with the rest of the galaxy once more. Cleaner, safer, more prosperous . . . although perhaps less happy than the old city had been.

Or perhaps I was happier then. His lips quirked as he remembered a lord's son down slumming, and how he'd saved that young noble from the knives of a rival gang. Then turned and found a hand extended; taken it in his own, astonished. Met Amos ben Sierra Nueva's eyes, and been lost to his old life.

That brought him back to the present; his face clenched like a fist, eyes narrowing. He sat behind the desk and keyed the screen.

"Home," he said.

It cleared, and his wife Rachel looked up in surprise from her own keyboard as his image replaced whatever she'd been working on. In the background he could hear children playing. His children . . . *No. They are safe, and my duty is clear.*

"Joseph!" she said, concern in her dark eyes. "Is there any news of the Prophet?"

He shook his head. "Nothing from SSS-900-C," he said. "Simeon reports no word. No trace of the Benisur's ship has been found; it is as if they had vanished from space-time."

He took a deep breath, and saw her face change. Rachel had come to know him too well, in the years of their marriage. Joseph held up a hand.

"Please," he said softly. "My heart, do not tear at me; this is hard enough to do. But Amos is more than my Prophet; he is the friend of my soul, my brother."

"There are younger men to do this work!"

Joseph smiled ruefully. "Are there any better trained to seek him offplanet?" he asked.

Rachel met his eyes for a moment, then glanced aside. Hers shone with unshed tears.

"Where will you go?"

"I cannot say," he said. *Must not,* they both knew. There was a leak in Planetary Security. "But it must be soon." He willed strength into his voice. "Do not fear, my love. We have friends beyond Bethel, as well as enemies."

"Why the fardling void can't they just say *give me a bribe*?" Joat Simeon-Hap demanded.

New Destinies hung in space four thousand kilometers away; much closer in the main bridge screen, of course. It wasn't very large as independent stations went, merely a cylinder ten kilometers long by one in diameter, spinning contentedly—*smugly,* her mind prompted—in orbit around an undistinguished orange-brown gas giant, which orbited a run-of-the-mill F-class star. That was a pinprick of violent light in the distance; closer in were a few barren rocks, none of them larger than Mars, and some asteroids.

Junk system. Junk station. Barely worth visiting because it intersected a few transit routes. There weren't many fabricators in space nearby, either. One long latticework, a graving dock that looked capable of repairing fair-sized ships or building small ones. A couple of zero-g algae farms, huge soft-looking bubbles. Some in-system traffic, miners and passenger craft and wide-mouthed scoopships to skim and harvest the gas giant's outer atmosphere. Probably they didn't pick up the litter on the station, and charged you extra for the gravity.

Joat chuckled sourly at the thought; it appealed to her sense of the ridiculous. It didn't make her less impatient. New Destinies had a reputation as one of those places that looked the other way. A fair number of the ships who docked here were in the smuggling trade, which, frankly, was what kept the station going. But a couple of generations of *not noticing* had an effect. Here, bribery and graft were just the way things were done. So Joat couldn't understand why none of her hints had been picked up on, or no overtures had been made in that direction.

She loved the *Wyal,* and not just because the ship was hers. But there were times when you had to get off the ship or run starkers, raving and frothing.

The jerk's on a power trip. She combed a hand through shoulder-length blond hair and spoke, altering her tone slightly:

"Find out who this fardling bureaucratic nightmare is, wouldja Rand?"

"You mean Dilton Tolof in Health and Immigration?"

"Yeah."

There was a confused pause.

"Joat, he's Dilton Tolof in Health and Immigration."

She rolled her eyes. "Do you have to be so *literal*?"

"That's the way I'm made, Joat."

"I mean find out about him."

"Why?"

"Just do it!"

"You're upset," Rand sounded surprised. "Is it me, have I caused offense?"

"No, but he has. I'd like to tailor-make a little lesson in the etiquette of negotiation for him."

"You want to benefit him?" Rand sounded mildly astonished.

She smiled slowly.

"In a sense."

"It's been my observation, Joat, that you're not inclined to return good for bad. Nor has there been any solicitation of bribery. Yet, you seem to believe that Mr. Tolof is somehow asking for one. I admit to being puzzled."

"Logic, buddy. It isn't as though this little station is the most sought-after destination in Central Worlds' space, Rand, so sheer volume of work can't be the reason for this kind of delay."

Joat frowned. Two things about her tended to make the overbearing and officious think they could push her around. One was her age. At twenty-three, Joat was extremely young to be the captain and owner-aboard of a starfaring freighter. The other was that she was the adopted daughter of Space Station Simeon-900-C and Channa Hap; the first child to be adopted by a Brain-Brawn pair. For some reason that Joat couldn't fathom, these facts were supposed to make her malleable and stupid. Or, worse, naive, which she couldn't even remember being.

"It's just the way these little, out-of-the-way places operate. Now, I don't object to baksheesh, within reason," she said in a tone that would have alarmed anyone who knew her well. *If you lay on the sweet talk thick as honey, make no demands, don't insult me and you sure as blazes don't throw obstacles in my path.* Maybe then, she'd pay. Maybe.

Joat spun her gimbaled pilot's chair around and fondly regarded the winking lights of her friend's "face." Technically it wasn't a person—perhaps even not really a personality, if you wanted to get philosophical—but definitely a friend.

The rows of lights that formed its countenance served no purpose but to give Rand expression and to satisfy her low taste for ancient popular entertainments. Just now, they were predominantly yellow, signaling puzzlement.

"Civil servants are like rugs—you have to whack them now and then to get the dirt out. I just want to give him a little goose to teach him not to mess with me," Joat told it.

All the lights flickered yellow.

"You want to give him a barnyard fowl?" Now Rand *did* sound astonished.

Joat laughed. "In this instance, Rand, a goose means a pinch on the butt to get him going." *No sense in shocking a machine.* Sometimes she wondered who did the component blocks she'd bought for the basis of the AI.

"Ah!" The lights flickered blue, signaling pleasure in this new understanding; then back to yellow. "But, the references I found to that use of the term referred to it as an expression of erotic interest."

"Not in this case, I assure you," she said dryly.

"Well that's why I thought you wanted to give him the bird."
Joat choked back a laugh.

"I've said something amusing," it accused.

"No, it's me. I took it wrong."

After a moment it said, "Joat, really! If I'm to avoid these verbal
pitfalls it would save time if you'd simply tell me why you're laughing.
Just because the information is in my files somewhere doesn't justify wasting my energy searching for it."

"So you know why I laughed?"

"You had a misspent youth."

"And a largely misspent adulthood."

"Not really. You've actually accomplished quite a lot for such a
young woman. You've only been an adult legally for two years."

Joat squirmed. Praise made her feel as if she was being set up;
not least because she'd used it so often and so effectively that way
herself.

"Y'know, you sounded kinda exasperated there for a minute," she
said lightly.

"I was. And a particularly stupid reaction it is, if I may say so."

"Hey," she shrugged, "you're the one who wanted to understand
emotions."

"*Understand* them, not *have* them."

Joat raised an admonishing finger. "Knowledge is never wasted."

"While time and energy too often are. Specifically by forcing me
to apply this program."

"Well, in general, emotional responses aren't voluntary," she
said.

It wasn't really fair to force emotion-analogues on the AI. *On the
one hand I feel guilty. On the other, it's fun. Such a grubby little emotion,
guilt.*

"If you don't experience an unexpected reaction once in awhile,
then how can you understand emotions? Or put up with 'em for that
matter. Remember, understanding makes all things tolerable."

"I had fewer problems with tolerance before I was capable of
exasperation! Knowledge or lack of it isn't the problem; this *program*
is the problem."

Uh oh. Clearly Rand wanted that program gone, and was perfectly
capable of erasing it.

"Oh no you don't," she said. "I didn't sweat blood creating that program just so you could erase it the first time it runs. You leave it alone. Y'hear me?"

A neatly clipped "Yes." Then: "I suppose I should be grateful that you haven't found a way to irritate me."

"I'm getting close," Joat threatened with a grin. "Frustration and irritation are in the same family, so be prepared. After all, if you want to understand someone you have to walk a kilometer in their . . ."

"Would you can the quotes, please? If I want to drown in cliches I have access to all four volumes of *The Wit and Wisdom of the Known Universe*. The unabridged version."

Joat pursed her lips. "Sorry. Uh, have you got anything on Dilton yet?" she prompted.

"According to station records Tolof has had numerous citations for unauthorized power-grabbing. He's exceeded his allotted limit of power seventeen times, but was fined for only the first three."

"Interesting. And what's the name of the individual who waived his penalty charges?"

"Graf Dyson. I'm searching for references to that name."

After a full minute Joat raised a brow and prompted, "Anything?"

"No. Nothing significant, anyway. He lives here and is employed by the Bureau of Fines and Levies, but he has never been recorded as being guilty of the most minor infractions. He leads an exceptionally ordered and modest life, and his credit balance reflects that. Puzzling."

"For a citizen of New Destinies it's unbelievable." Another effect of catering to smugglers; their awareness of what constituted bad behavior was deeply impaired. "Do any of our friends or acquaintances show his name on any of their documents?'

"Yes," Rand replied promptly. "Captain Yandit has received several citations for disturbing the peace, but was never fined. Records show that the fine was waived by Graf Dyson."

"Well then, as Graf Dyson is a friend of a friend, I think we can safely claim acquaintance. Don't you?"

"No."

Joat linked her fingers and cracked her knuckles with a flourish. "Put me through to that mudpuppy in the health office, buddy, and watch me finesse this."

Dilton Tolof's pinched face appeared on the screen.

"New Destinies, Health and Immigration." Then he realized to whom he was speaking and smiled, a thin and somehow sour expression that fitted his pinched face. "Ms. Simeon, if you continue to pester me like this, I'm never going to be able to process your records."

"Well, I was talking to Graf, Graf Dyson? He asked me what was taking me so long. I've got a little present for him, and you know how impatient he gets. We're *real* good friends." She simpered at the man on the screen in her best fluff-head imitation. "Anyway, he said mentioning his name might serve to, you know, expedite things. Like, as a favor to a friend?"

Tolof's narrow face flushed and he glanced nervously around. "You know . . . G. D.?"

"Sure do. Captain Yandit, you may have dealt with him, huge, Ursinoid fellow with a temper? He introduced us at a party one time, and we hit it off right away." Joat snapped her fingers, indicating the speed with which she and Dyson had become fast friends. "Graf said you guys were real close, mentioned that you'd done some deals?" She raised an inquiring brow and smiled knowingly.

Dilton's sour smile turned slowly into the expression of a man who'd just opened a box of chocolates and found maggots.

"Well," he said, "heh heh, your documentation appears to be in order, no need to be, uh, nitpicky."

He punched a few keys and her comp received the "cleared" signal that would allow Joat and her crew the freedom of the station and permit docking robots to begin unloading the *Wyal's* cargo.

"*Thank* you so much," she gushed and gave him a wink. "I'll be sure and tell *G.D.* what a pal you were."

Joat punched off the connection and sneered, "No need to be nitpicky." She shivered. "Ghu, but I hate bureaucrats."

The ship rumbled and there was a slight swaying sensation. *Docking tractors attached* blinked across the screen, and a grid swelled to fill the view. She kept her hands poised over the controls, but the AI and Stationside kept the *Wyal* steady as she slid towards the non-rotating docking ring at the north pole of New Destinies. About the running of the station and their docking procedures, the New Destinites were consummate professionals.

"Especially you, Dilton," she added in the same tone. "You worm." "Whozzat?"

The air scrubbers whirred into overdrive as a sudden, overwhelmingly sweet and spicy aroma invaded the control cabin, followed by Alvec Dia, one of her crew. In fact, he was her crew, with an Admiralty

Grade artificial intelligence, a three thousand kiloton freighter didn't need more than two.

"Gak!" Joat wheezed, waving her hand in front of her face. "Alvec, what is that stench?"

"Stench, Boss?" Alvec seemed genuinely puzzled. "That's Senalgal Spice, the favorite cologne of the Rose of New Destinies."

He put his hands on his hips and raised a brow, archly. Or as archly as a middle-aged man with scar tissue across the knuckles of both hands and a build like a freight carboy could. Joat couldn't help grinning at him, and an answering smile split the rough, lived-in face.

"You have a lady-friend here?" she asked, trying to breathe shallowly. He had friends of that sort on a number of stations, all answering to the name of Rose.

"Not yet." He winked. "But I aim to."

"Do me a favor, Al, air out a little before you go a-hunting. I wouldn't want you arrested for assault this early in the day. I'd have to bail you out."

"I'll be careful, Mother. We cleared?" He jerked a thumb dockside.

At Joat's nod he waggled his fingers farewell and left with a jaunty step.

She watched him leave. The monitors showed him dodging cargo robots trundling forward across the open space just inside the hull of the docking ring. Then, taking an experienced spacer's leap across to the entrance of the spindle, he grabbed the handholds, did a neat turn and went feet-first through the hatchway, ready for the transition to spin gravity in the core.

There was a clanking through the hull as the robots boarded; she watched on screens slaved to the interior monitors as one busily rushed up to grab a pallet, loaded it onto the flatbed of its body, then hustled off to dockside to unload it onto a stack already piling up on a larger float that would take the shipment to a warehouse.

Joat watched them idly for a few moments, then her interest was caught by their human supervisor.

He was tall, with a soldier's posture but a soft gut. His eyes... they never stopped tracking. Back, forth, back; the eyes of someone expecting trouble, someone who'd been expecting it so long they couldn't stop. Scarred face, with the distinctive red splotch on one cheek. At some time in the not-too-distant past he'd been caught in an explosive decompression. Not an uncommon industrial accident off-planet, but... His uniform was just a little too...

something. It fit him, it wasn't new, but somehow, it wasn't right.

He wore it as though it wasn't completely familiar, Joat realized. It had been his hand fumbling for a pocket that wasn't there that had caught her eye. Joat sat up straight.

Who? Nobody she could think of was gunning for her right now— angry with her, yes; ready to do her the dirty in any underhanded way they could, yes. But not killing mad, not enough to hire muscle to go after her. And this man was obviously muscle of some sort. His whole body screamed *retired mercenary.* But why would a retired mercenary accept a pick-up job on New Destinies?

Not a merc, then. So, he was a cop. And he was watching the *Wyal.*

But why were they watching her? Dilton hadn't had time to sic this guy on her, even if he'd the guts to do it. Neither had Dyson, whoever he was, because he couldn't possibly have reacted this fast to the little scam she'd just pulled on his buddy. He probably didn't even know about it, at least not yet.

Her mind went to the small mysterious package she was carrying for Central Worlds Security. Did New Destinies know about it? Were they after it? Was it something that would incriminate her?

Joat frowned. She wasn't about to risk her ship for some CenSec song and dance. The package was supposed to be dropped with the local operative at The Anvil, one of the bars around the rim of the station. She glanced at the time, she was due there in one and a half Earth standard hours.

Joat gritted her teeth. So *I owe them. That doesn't mean they own me.* More to the point, it didn't mean they could endanger her *ship.* She'd drop it all right, and then she'd tell them what they could do with their special courier packages.

"Rand, I gotta go."

"Now? Before unloading is completed?"

"You see that osco on monitor four?"

"The unloading supervisor?"

"Yeah. He's a cop."

"He can't be, Joat, he's wearing a supervisor's uniform. The police uniform for this port is very different, I assure you."

Rand put a holo snap of a local policeman on screen for her edification.

"I know what a cop looks like, Rand, in or out of uniform. And that's a cop, and he's watching us."

"I'm impressed by your prescience, Joat. Why is he watching us?"

"I don't know and I don't intend to find out. I'm going out the side door."

"The . . . ? Joat, we don't have a side door."

"I'm going out the service hatch and into the station via one of theirs," she said, briskly closing out the file she'd been idly working on while waiting for clearance.

"That's illegal . . ."

"I know that, but . . ."

"And dangerous!"

"I'm relying on you to help me avoid getting caught," she explained. Joat wondered how Rand would choose to respond, for she'd given it almost complete autonomy. It might decide to have nothing to do with this scheme, which would complicate things tremendously.

"Could we talk deal?" Rand asked smoothly.

Joat's eyebrows went up and she cocked her head.

"Excuse me?"

"That exasperation program . . . ?"

Joat frowned and folded her arms thoughtfully. Then she sighed. "Okay, deal, you can erase the program. Now will you help me?"

"I'll do my best." Rand's voice conveyed pride in self combined with disapproval of her plans.

Joat suppressed a smile. Sometimes Rand was downright prissy. She wondered if she'd unintentionally programmed it that way—it couldn't have caught it from *her* behavior, that was sure.

"Don't worry Rand."

"When you say not to worry, worry becomes imperative."

"Where's the station's nearest service hatch to *Wyal?*" she asked.

Rand threw a schematic on the screen, replacing the smiling policeman. Wyal was represented by a bunking yellow dot, the nearest service hatch blinked red.

"Now, show me the surveillance cameras."

A pause, then Rand indicated them on the schematic in blue.

"Whew," Joat sighed. "They have pretty good coverage. Any chance you can hack into the surveillance network and simply run a tape of empty space while I'm out there?"

"Doubtful. With so many suspect elements sharing the station's amenities, New Destinies has a fairly sophisticated security system. Something of that complexity would probably activate an alarm."

"Fardles." She drummed her fingers on the console. "What can you tell me about the lock?"

Rand threw up another schematic. "It's a standard design. Nothing complicated, with the usual tell-tales in place." As it spoke small arrows blinked on indicating the areas spoken of. "There are cameras in the corridor outside the service hatch."

Joat brushed her hair back. *Time for another trim,* she thought inconsequentially. She went to a locker at the rear of the bridge compartment and palmed the sensor. It opened, and she began to take out various useful items and slot them into pockets and less obvious hiding places in her taupe overall; also in her belt, in the heels of her boots, and one or two in special cavities in her molars.

"Is there any time when the route I'll have to traverse and the lock itself isn't under observation?"

That came out as a mumble, since her fingers were in the back of her mouth, but Rand had excellent voiceprint filters.

"For approximately ten seconds the route and the lock are clear. As it won't alter their function, I may be able to slow the sweep of the cameras so that you have forty seconds," Rand told her. "I can do nothing about the telltales, though, and the cameras inside are stationary."

She considered the diagram before her.

"It'll take me twelve seconds to get from *Wyal* to the lock," she murmured.

"Optimistically."

"Twelve seconds." She grinned. "And if I can't silence a tell-tale in twenty-eight seconds I deserve whatever happens to me. Can you take out the camera in the corridor?"

"I believe so. But it will surely be considered suspicious."

"Feh!" Joat made a contemptuous face and a dismissive gesture. "It probably happens all the time."

Then she rose and laced her fingers together, cracking her knuckles briskly. "Let's do it. You're in charge of the *Wyal* until I return. *Don't accumulate too much time* on the station's virtual reality net—we can't afford it."

"It's research," Rand said indignantly. "My interactions with humans increase my versatility."

"You can research Alvec and me for free," Joat said firmly, running a mental checklist of the devices she was carrying. *A few more?* No, the only really useful item would be a laser welder—you could

do really astonishing things with a laser welder, if you knew how—
but it was a bit conspicuous.

Useful, though. It was a pity. She and a couple of other students
at Vega Central Institute—Simeon had sent her there for six months—
had cut down a bronze statue of the Founder, cut it in half, and
rewelded it around a shower fixture in the quarters of the Dean of
Cybernetics. And she hadn't had to use anything but a hand-cutter
and a floater platform to do it, either.

Actually Simeon had sent her to Vega Central for a year. They'd
sent her *back* after six months.

Bureaucrats, she thought. *No sense of humor at all.*

Joat tied her hair back in a ponytail and paused to study herself
in the screen set to mirror beside the airlock; large, gray-blue eyes
stared solemnly back, examining delicate features in a sharp-boned
face. Not much trace of the feral child she'd been when Simeon and
Channa found her hiding in the ventilation ducts of SSS-900-C; she'd
been living in a nest of stolen blankets and cobbled-together computer parts. Good training to be a high-tech guerrilla during the
Kolnari occupation of the Station, but not so hot as a preparation
for life.

She pursed her lips and looked at the package she was to deliver.
I must have grown up. I haven't opened it.

CenSec would have all sorts of cyberdog guardians built in, but
that just increased the itch. Her fingers twitched as if they held
micromanipulators and a datacode bar. She sighed and shook her
head. No, it wasn't worth the hassle. She'd made up her mind to that
the first time she'd agreed to take on a CenSec shipment at Simeon's
request.

The less she knew, she'd told herself, the better. Because CenSec
was the kind of organization that considered you were in their debt
if *you* did *them* a favor. They started out owing you and ended up
owning you. That might appeal to straight-arrow types brought up
in boring rectitude, who fell down on their knees in thanks at getting to play Galactic Spy.

Not me, Joat thought defiantly. *Nobody's gonna get a piece of my
soul.* She'd gotten far more adventure than she wanted by the age
of twelve. And she knew that, for preference, adventure was somebody *else* in deep doodly, far, far away.

She gave herself one last appraising look, then picked up the

CenSec package and zipped it into one of her pockets before heading for the suit-storage locker.

Joat suited up quickly. It was a process she'd always handled well, winning a fair number of credits in Brawn school betting on just how fast she could do it.

No gruddy sense of humor there either, she thought. Her knack for separating her fellow students from their disposable income was just one of many reasons she'd finally been asked to leave. By the time they finally got around to asking her, though, she was already half packed. *I don't understand how Channa ever got through without freezing into an icicle.* Then again, a lot of people thought she had.

The fact was she and her teachers and fellow students were fundamentally incompatible. She regarded them as too stiff-necked, they saw her as *far* too flexible.

Her only concern in leaving Brawn training had been the possibility that she might be disappointing her adoptive parents. She grinned reminiscently, remembering their words as she stepped out of the Station airlock—Simeon had waited, "standing" beside Channa in his favorite vid persona, a big blond bruiser with a dueling scar and a Centauri Jets cap turned backwards.

"Toldja," he'd said blithely.

"I knew they'd never hammer you into a straight arrow," Channa said with a warm smile. "You were born to be independent."

"Or to hang," Simeon added.

Joat tapped the lock controls. Air bled out; the telltales in the rim of the helmet below her chin showed hard vac. She crouched in the open door of the lock, studying the surface of the station, pronged and spiked with various sensors and antennae. This close even a modest station loomed immense, a metallic god-sized lathe twirling forever against the orange glow of its planet. It turned with a slow ponderous inevitability; at this range your gut refused to see it as an artifact. She turned her head, looking for the flashing red light that indicated the location of the service hatch.

Joat sighed. This little excursion would be so much easier if she'd never revealed the secret of the device that had rendered her invisible to virtually all sensors and recording devices. Simeon had *insisted* on letting everyone know how to counter it. Of course the patent had accounted for a big part of the down-payment on her ship. *Create the problem, solve the problem, collect the money,* she thought.

Ah, well, New Destinies was one of the few windowless stations. They'd spun it up from the nickel-iron of a single asteroid, and nobody had bothered putting in luxuries. So at least she didn't have to worry about some tourist catching her in the act with their holo camera and immortalizing this exploit for the delight of station security.

Light strobed across her target. She estimated the angle and aimed the magnetic grapple built into the sleeve of her suit, leaning forward, arm extended.

"Ready," she said into her suit com. "Say when, Rand."

"Standing by, Joat." Rand paused a moment. "Now."

There was a slight twitch that pushed her arm gently backwards as she fired the grapple. The contact plate spun out on its near-invisible line and clung to the station's skin about a meter from the small service hatch. Joat activated the mechanism in her sleeve that would reel her towards the station, then gave a jerk on the line that propelled her outward.

Joat pulled her feet forward and her knees up against the suit's resistance, rolling herself head over heels in a controlled somersault; timing it so that the stickfield on the soles of her boots would strike first, and her bent legs absorb the impact.

When she left *Wyal's* gravity field the blood in her veins leapt within her, rushing to her head in a dizzying surge. The weightlessness made every part of her feel strange, as though she'd been bounced upward, never coming down, only climbing, soaring. *Swimming in the universal sea,* a friend at Brawn school had called it. *No lie.* The few moments of queasiness until she adjusted was worth it; then gravity returned as centrifugal force spun her outward. The stationary docking ring fell behind, and suddenly *up* was towards the rotating bulk of New Destinies. It was the docking ring that seemed to move, with the *Wyal* embedded in it like a pencil in a sharpener.

She felt closest to Simeon, her adopted father, when she moved through space in her suit. Encased, as he was, in a machine that kept her alive in a murderous environment, yet personally in contact with the infinite.

Joat watched the universe flick by, ship, stars, station, three times before she reached her target.

The stickfield on her boots held her to the station against the surge of recoil and Joat clasped an extended hand around a utility handle jutting out from the station's skin. Her inertia surged, balanced and stabilized by the grip and the automatic flex of leg and thigh. The anchor cord finished reeling itself back into the sleeve of her suit with a small definite *click*, de-energizing the disk and whipping it back into the slot. Her eyes were telling her that she stood upright on a huge metal plain. Weight said that she was hanging from her feet with a great metal plain *above* her. Both were wrong, and she had no time to waste.

"Now," she muttered. "Down the rabbit hole, or I'll be *very* late."

Her suited fingers traced the exterior of the airlock. Standard model, a fiber-steel oval with memory putty sealant around the edges and a mechanical doglock wheel in the center for emergencies. No use trying that, it would be safetied. Instead she took out a multitool and began opening the access cover of the lock control, whistling soundlessly between her teeth.

Well, and aren't you clever, she thought, as the first choice undid the couplers that held it closed. You found some of the weirdest nonstandard components on these out-of-the-way Stations.

Her suit had some nonstandard components, too. She unclipped an extension datalink from her belt and clicked the connector into the link on the control card. Then she closed her eyes and sub-vocalized a series of code words.

A chittering voice sounded in her inner ear. *"Whhhaaat's up, boss?"*

"Got a little job for you, Speedy."

She opened her eyes again. Playing across the thin-film crystal of her suit visor was a holo of a ferret. Not a *real* ferret; this one was vaguely anthropomorphic and wore a beret. One hand clutched a smokestick in a long ivory holder. *Stylish*, she thought. There was no point in being mechanical when you designed an AI, even the fairly simple specialized type.

This one, for example, was a specialist in locks.

"Cycle this airlock, but don't let anyone know about it."

"Rrrright, boss."

The holo image vanished. It was replaced by a schematic of the circuitry and the control program for the access. The picklock program slunk through the commercial programming with sinuous ease, then struck. Red slivers appeared on the green circuitry, marking the spots where false data was being fed back into the systems central monitor. That severed the controls from the Station's computers, at least for a while.

Of course, there was always the chance that some interfering type would be actually *looking* at the inside door of the airlock when she came through. Harder to fool the ol' Eyeball Mark I.

"Rand, is there any way for you to tie into the vid monitor covering this accessway and let me know if anybody's out there?"

"No, Joat, there isn't. I've already knocked it out. But this access is located in a maintenance area that's not very thickly populated. It's a chance you'll have to take. You have seven seconds."

"Fardles!"

Joat imagined some passerby attracted to the mysteriously cycling lock, watching in puzzlement the flashing of the warning light that showed the lock was in use.

What if there's a klaxon or a bell? she wondered. She sighed mentally. *Then I get arrested, I guess. Bad planning, Joat. If the worst happens it'll serve you right for being so impulsive.*

She gripped the handholds on either side, disdaining the steps set into the doorway, and popped herself feet-first through the hatch with a grunt. That left her straddling the entranceway, now a hole between her feet. Reaching back, she pulled the hatch closed behind her and glanced at the chrono display down at the chinbar of her helmet. Well within the time limit.

Jack Of All Trades strikes again, she thought, slightly smug. Breaking-and-entering was one of those pleasant hobbies you didn't have much opportunity for when you'd gone legitimate. A pleasure to indulge the skill on good, legal—well, quasi-legal—Central Worlds business.

Air hissed into the narrow airlock, quickly growing thick enough to hear through the exterior pickups. A faint *ping* told her when the pressure was near-enough ambient. Immediately she popped the seal on her helmet and began stripping off the suit, wrinkling her nose slightly at the metallic smell. No excuse for that, in a station—even a small one.

Snaps, locks, and seals parted before her fingers with the easy grace of a lifetime's practice; she had the full measure of finicky neatness common to the vacuum-born. She folded the suit tightly, tucked the gauntlets into the helmet and pulled a small black rectangle from a pocket. It clung when she tapped it onto the inner airlock door over her head, and she snapped a thin cord into a jack on its side. The other end of the cord was pressed against the bone behind one ear. She scanned the sounds from the other side of the metal.

Nothing, she thought cheerfully. Nothing but mechanical noise, none of the irregular thumps and gurgles that indicated an organic sapient. Carbon-based life-forms had messy sonic signatures.

"Rand, can you give me the name of an outfitter? I might as well have my suit seals checked as carry it around with me."

"There are sixteen outfitters licensed to maintain suits. The nearest specialty store is Stondat's EnviroSystems Emporium, Spin Level 3"— that would be counting inward from the outermost deck, standard throughout human space—"Stack 14b, corridor 9. The camera block is running." Rand's passionless voice took on a faint overtone of contempt. "Very bad security."

Joat smiled. Her attitudes towards sloppy workmanship *had* rubbed off on the AI. She used a small extensible probe to key the interior door of the airlock and trotted up the ladder into an access corridor running both ways until it lost itself in the curve of the Station's outer hull.

"External cameras are back online, no detection," Rand said.

"Grudly. Out for now." Broadcasts were a needless risk.

The corridor was bare except for the color-coded conduits and pipes that snaked in orderly rectilinear patterns over walls and ceilings. An occasional small maintenance machine trundled by, usually following a pipe rather than the floor.

And footfalls rang. Joat felt herself relax, vision growing bright with the sudden clarity of extreme concentration. The young man who walked in from a side-corridor was wearing the same Stationside police uniform as the one in Rand's holosnap, but his face had the pleasant formlessness of youth. Sheltered youth.

"Oh hey, am I glad to see you!" Joat caroled, an expression of surprised relief on her face. "We just got in, and I'm looking for Stondat's. The suit outfitter? I've obviously gone wrong," she hoisted the suit up a bit with a little grunt, "and this thing is getting heavier by the meter. Where am I?"

She let a trace of wail into the last words, making her eyes go wide in an expression she knew knocked six standard years off her apparent age.

"Let me show you, ma'am. These corridors are for Stationside Maintenance only."

He led the way to a lift, reaching past her to palm the entry. Her hand brushed across his arm.

"There, that's set for Spin Level 3. You can't miss it."

Joat's smile turned broader and more sardonic as the door irised shut. Insect-tiny in her ear, she could hear the young policeman's report via the sticktight she'd brushed across his uniform to blend with the fabric. It was a carbon-chain type, too, almost impossible to scan and biodegradable.

"*Just someone who got lost,*" he said. "*Some vapor-brain from a miner family-ship, probably, can't find her way around anything bigger than a thousand cubic meters. Proceeding.*"

CHAPTER THREE

BROS SPERIN SAT quietly at his table, a drink in his hand, and watched the patrons of The Anvil enjoying themselves. *Extremely respectable place,* he thought. Perfect for a dropshop. Criminals and spies only haunted known dens of vice in bad fiction, or in places much farther from the right side of the law than New Destinies.

"No, thank you, gentlebeing," he said for the seventh time that night.

The tall—possibly human, probably female, but you couldn't tell sometimes without a xenology program—bobbed her/its/his crest and swayed gracefully off to the sunken dance floor that hung in the center of The Anvil's main room. It was surrounded by tables of spectators, diners, and tourists. Bros Sperin himself wasn't out of place, a man a little above medium height and densely athletic of build, brown of skin and eye, with short black hair cut to resemble a sable cap. His jacket was brown as well, loosely woven raw silk, belted with silver above black tights and low boots. A soft hat lay on the table beside his long-fingered hands, covering a belt data-unit.

He looked relaxed, which was as much a lie as the appearance of a well-to-do merchant out for a peaceful night on the town in this costly, pleasant nightclub.

Given the number of serious deals that went down here it was in the regular patrons' best interests to see to it that no one got too rowdy, and the management was very solicitous of their guests' interests. Those who insisted on getting out of hand mysteriously and permanently lost their taste for dancing at The Anvil. So did people who annoyed the regular patrons.

If they only knew who I really *was, they'd probably be* very *annoyed indeed,* the Central Worlds agent thought. Annoyed enough that he'd disappear with a quiet finality.

Bros raised his glass to his lips and checked his watch. Then glanced at the door. There she was, right on time. Odd, how she looked so little like the scarred, scared child he'd met when he was a lieutenant in Naval Intelligence, assigned to SSS-900-C in the aftermath of the Kolnari raid. And yet what she was now was what he'd seen *in potentia* then, hidden beneath the claws-and-teeth defensiveness her short life had left.

Those straight women who noticed her looked askance at her drab spacer overalls, the gay women observed her over their glasses with mild curiosity. Various aliens had reactions less comprehensible, but they shared a certain caution. The men never looked at her at all.

Their loss, Bros thought. She was beautiful, though she played it down and attitude did the rest.

Joat reached the bar and fixed her gaze on the busy bartender. He'd already noticed her and had caught Bros Sperin's eye. Sperin gave him the high sign to give her a drink as arranged, and to tell her it was from him.

When the bartender placed the drink in front of her, Joat looked at it as if it were a Sondee mudpuppy. The bartender pointed and said a few words to her and Joat turned to look at Bros.

Their eyes met and she raised one brow, suspicious and unsmiling. He grinned and waved her over. After a moment she nodded, picked up the drink and sauntered to his table. He rose to meet her and she smiled and lifted the brow again over his courtesy.

She raised the drink in a little salute.

"Thank you," she said and looked him over, then frowned slightly. "We've never met before, have we?"

"No, I've seen you at a distance, but we've never met."

"Then . . . how do you know what I like to drink?" she asked, curious, suspicious.

Bros grinned down at her.

"It's a game I play, matching drinks to faces. I usually guess right. So . . . do I have you pegged?"

She nodded with a little smile. *At least that far,* Joat thought.

"Please, sit down." He indicated a seat.

"Thanks," she said, and looked around. "But I can't. I'm here to meet someone."

"I know. Me."

Oh, Ghu, Joat thought. *I may lose my lunch.* How could such a neat looking guy have such a macho-maniacal attitude. *Pity.*

To Bros she looked both weary and disappointed at the apparent pick-up line; but smiled as she turned to go. *I don't blame her. That one was probably a cliche when bearskins were the latest fashion.*

"The names Sperin. Bros Sperin."

Her eyes went wide. *The spy?*

"I thought you were dead!" she blurted.

He laughed. "A rumor I've carefully spread. It's useful. Actually, I only *felt* like I was dead. They put me back together looking different, and they've had me behind a desk the last few years."

They looked at each other for a few moments.

"Shall we sit down or," he indicated the dance floor, "shall we dance?"

Joat sat. *I don't think so. I don't want to get any closer to you than arm's length, thanks.* Something about him made her wary on a personal level. She wondered what the heck was going on.

"I usually deal with Sal," she said uneasily. *And I wish I were now.* Not that Sal was such a great guy or anything. *But something's up, my antennae are tingling.*

"He's around somewhere. I understand you have an unbirthday present for him."

She nodded, frowning again. *An unbirthday present.* She sneered mentally. *That's cute.* "Actually, it's more of a parting gift. Something that might go well with a broken arm."

"In that case he'll be sorry to have missed you. I'll be sure to pass along your good wishes." Bros picked up his glass and looked at her over the rim. "But I needed to talk to you."

"About what?" Joat kept her face and voice as carefully neutral as his.

Bros felt the package placed in his lap; she'd done it so smoothly he hadn't noticed her hand going under the table. *Whoa!* he thought, startled. *What am I doing out by myself if I can't even keep an eye on the girl's hands?*

He didn't show his surprise and dismay however. His face was dead calm when he said, "There's something we need you to do, someone we want you to talk to. We thought the *Wyal* would make a good place for a meeting."

Joat put her untasted drink on the table and gave it a little shove away from herself. *Glad I didn't touch that,* she thought. *Who knows what kind of go-along syrup they put in it.* She didn't like the way this meeting was going. *Of course the drink could be intended as a bribe. CenSec's cheap enough, Ghu knows.* But there was a heavy-duty hook in here somewhere and one lousy drink was insufficient bait to hide it.

"I've been told before—with heavy regret—that I'd be terrible at your kind of work. As if I'd asked. Y'know? As if I'd want it." She crossed her legs. *That stuff's for adrenaline addicted university students. Me, I've got a life.* "Now, all of a sudden, I get this clammy feeling that I'm being recruited. I mean, *Bros Sperin* comes out from behind his desk to meet little *me.* And reels off quite an interesting wish list, by the way; something needs doing, someone needs talking to and how about my place for a meeting. Oooh! It's so exciting." Joat began a slow burn. *This is just a little presumptuous. Don't you think, Bros?* "What makes you think I'd be interested?"

"You've done things for us before."

"An occasional passenger, or a package delivery, that's it." Her voice was sharper than she'd intended, and she saw that he was taken aback. But then, she'd come here with the intention of cutting her ties to CenSec, not strengthening them. *And in any case* Wyal *is off-limits to these people. I can't just let them get away with deciding to use my ship like it's their property.*

"And got cash on the barrel head," he reminded her grimly. Her attitude was a surprise and it was beginning to annoy him.

"Of course."

"So what's your problem?"

From long practice, Joat froze her reaction, which was to flare up and twist his nose for him. "Well," she said sweetly, "so far as a meeting goes, my ship is under surveillance. Not very clandestine, wouldn't you agree?"

Bros grinned.

"That was Sal's idea. He thought it would confer status on me." He cocked his head at her. "Pretty obvious, was it?"

"He might as well have been in uniform. I thought he might be after . . . Sal's present." She glared at him. *I don't believe this!* she thought, outraged. *I could have been arrested and fined, just for trying*

to keep this package a secret. Meanwhile he's *hiring the cops as escorts!*
"You couldn't have advised me, of course."

He shrugged.

"Need to know. Sal thought it would make things easier. I don't
see why it's a problem."

"It makes me look like trouble. My reputation is for doing things
well and discreetly; it's how I make my living. This does not help."

He rubbed his upper lip to hide his smile. She was going to love
this.

"I didn't request a guard for your ship in my CenSec capacity. In
fact, they'd be quite startled to learn I was with CenSec, here. Bros
Sperin is an extremely respectable smuggler, with an hilariously
inappropriate name. At least as far as New Destinies is concerned—
I deal in arms, mostly, and fencing loot—and the local police give
excellent value for money."

Her eyes narrowed. "Oh. Lovely. Do you realize how much higher
on the bribe schedule my ship will be, now that they think I'm
running with the big boys? What are you trying to do to me?"

"It's S.O.P., Joat. To be frank, my cover is more important than
your budget." He shrugged. "It's all part of building the right picture in the minds of certain people. I assure you, when you learn
exactly who this meeting is with, you'll take a *personal* interest." He
smiled. "Trust me."

She snorted an unspoken *not likely,* but he was sure he'd caught
a sparkle of curiosity in her eyes.

Good, he thought. Aloud he said, "I'll call off the cop, since he
was ineffective anyway. Will that help?"

"Sure." She rose and left.

I may have overplayed that a little, he thought dryly as he watched
her walk away. He rubbed his face vigorously. *I'm badly out of practice.
I used to know better than to make assumptions about the players.* Still,
they were reasonable assumptions based on knowledge she didn't have
at the moment. She'd probably come around.

Joat Simeon-Hap was a righteous woman.

In her way.

Joat grinned with a cold anger. *Master Spy isn't as subtle as he
thinks.* Five years ago she might have jumped at the chance to get
on the CenSec payroll. Not now. *Wyal* was hers; yes, Simeon and
Channa—and Joseph—had helped bankroll her, but she'd paid them

all off. The ship was hers, and she was meeting payroll and running expenses and putting something by. Meanwhile she was seeing the universe. On *her* terms, and nobody else's. *Which is just the way I like things, thank you very much, Bros Sperin!*

A passerby jumped back in alarm from the glare she gave as she shouldered by him.

She hoped Alvec was back from sniffing the Roses, or rather, letting them sniff him. Joat grinned at the thought of Bros Sperin's dark face when he walked up to an empty berth.

The docking area was nearly deserted as she pulled herself into the zero-g section and walked towards her berth, skimming her feet along the deck to keep their sticktights on the metal. Nobody was around except a couple of Ursinoids, crewfolk off one of their lumbering freighters, hairy creatures with blunt muzzles standing nearly two meters tall and strapped around with various knives, energy weapons and slug-throwers. She chatted with them for a few minutes, using their shaggy bulks to disguise her slow scan of the area. That was no strain; she *liked* Ursinoids, even if they did always try to sell you a collection of lethal ironmongery. They were good types on the whole, extremely independent, but not very subtle.

Bros had been as good as his word. The cop was gone. She wondered if she was under more covert surveillance.

Well, how would she know? Electronics she might detect, but Sperin should be able to call upon better talent than the local security forces.

As she passed a row of containers stacked head high, a hand flashed out and grabbed her arm.

Joat spun into the direction of the grip, stripping her arm out with leverage against the thumb. The same motion flung her backwards half a dozen paces and flipped the vibroknife into her right hand, held low with the keening drone of the slender rod-blade wailing a warning of how easily it would slide through flesh and bone. She filled her lungs to shout—the Ursinoids would be at her side in seconds, loaded for . . . well, loaded *like* bears. Heavily armed bears.

Joseph ben Said held up both hands palms out and grinned at her. The sleeves of his loose robe fell away from thick, corded forearms where the scars lay white against the olive skin. He raised one blond eyebrow.

"So fierce, little one? Perhaps I should not have taught you so well, eh?"

"Joe!" she said, moving forward to slap his arm lightly. "If I was still on your training protocols, you'd be dead right now."

She looked him up and down. The Bethelite never seemed to change; still as fit and muscular as when she'd met him ten years ago, his blue eyes mild and calm between the squint-wrinkles of a man who spent much time in the desert. Perhaps a few strands of silver hair among the gold. He had been born in Keriss before the Kolnari came, a child of the dock-side slums, and right-hand man to Amos ben Sierra Nueva when the future Prophet had been a radical and half an outcast.

Now he was Deacon of the Right Hand—head of the Bethelite police and counter-espionage forces.

"What are you doing here? Is Amos here too?"

He shook his head.

"No, I am here alone." He cast a meaningful glance back and forth. "Look, I have a gift."

He reached into the hand-luggage at his feet and tossed a heavy bottle of green ceramic in her direction. Joat caught it with a yelp of protest at the risk; she recognized the brand. The surface was pebbled and cool, the fastener held in with twisted copper wire and sealed with wax. Despite herself she felt her eyes mist a little. *Joe was always a good osco,* she thought. And he'd taught her a great deal, some of it things that Simeon and Channa never suspected.

"Bethel-brewed Arrack," he said and kissed the tips of his ringers, dropping into the singsong of a *bazari* merchant for a moment. "From the Prophet's private store. Blessed with the heat of Saffron's golden sun."

She grinned.

"C'mon aboard, I've got someone I want you to meet."

Joat led the way up into *Wyal*'s berth and spoke:

"Knock, knock?"

"Who's there?" The cybernetic voice sounded as if it would wince if it could.

"Jo."

"Jo who?"

"Jo'at the door."

Joseph did wince, in sympathy. "Among Simeon's many crimes, not the least was teaching you his depraved sense of humor."

"Tell me the news from Bethel, tell me about Rachel," Joat said.

She cycled the lock closed and stood while the sensor field swept them for unauthorized sticktights. "And tell me what's wrong."

"Rachel is well, the children are well . . . and what should be wrong, my young friend?" The blue eyes blinked guilelessly at her.

"Joe, unlike Amos, you're no great traveler. If you've left Bethel and Rachel and it wasn't with Amos, there's a reason. What is it?"

"All in good time," he said.

Joat smiled wryly, restraining an impulse to grind her teeth. From Joseph she could take the odd mystery.

"Joat, I am most impressed by the quality of this AI, but it is a machine, nothing more." He looked at her with a frown of worry. "You know the difference, between a person and a machine?"

Joat sipped her Arrack. The liquid slid down her throat like a living fire with velvet fur, leaving a ghost-taste of ripe dates.

"Joe, I'm a programming expert. If I don't know the difference, who does? And if you say, *Joat you are alone too much,* I'll punch you in the nose, I swear I will."

"I taught you better than that," he said, mock-offended. "*If you are naked and your feet are nailed to the floor, you may hit an enemy in the face with your fist. Short of that, use something more effective,*" Joat quoted in a sing-song voice. "I remember."

She leaned forward: "Look, if Simeon can turn his AI into his dog—to be precise, an Irish Setter—why can't I go a step further and turn mine into a friend?" She lowered her voice confidentially. "We're not romantically involved if that's your worry."

He laughed and shook his head at her.

"You, little rebel, should be married, with a husband to fix your wayward thoughts upon. Look at how my Rachel has prospered by my side."

Joat pulled a judicious expression and nodded solemnly.

"You're right, Joe, she's quite a gal."

Yup, she's not a demented, murderous, traitorous bitch any more.

Now she was Joseph's executive assistant in the Bethelite Security Forces, handling the technical end of things. She also ran their rancho, a sun drenched spread at Twin Springs, and was a devoted mother to their two children, Simeon Amos and Channa Joat.

"Marriage would make a new woman of you, you should try it. I know!" He flung his hands up as if struck by inspiration—but did not, she noted, spill a single drop of the Arrack.

"Marry me, Joat! Become my second wife and you can live on the rancho and ride to your heart's content. You can take care of the children. Think how restful your life would be! And I swear that I would be as faithful to you as to my beloved Rachel."

"Joe! How can you claim to be faithful to Rachel while you're asking another woman to marry you?"

"Because I *am* asking you to marry me. If I were asking you to be my mistress, *then* I would be unfaithful. There is a tremendous difference, you must agree."

Joat blinked. He *was* joking—but to a Bethelite, that made perfect sense. There were times when she forgot Joseph was from the deep backwoods of the universe.

"Hunh! If I ever do hitch up with someone, I'm not gonna be anyone's second anything." She took a sip of Arrack. "I want a virgin, myself."

A discreet cough from behind brought her to her feet, spinning around, knife in her hand again, ready for throwing.

Her eyes widened at the sight of Bros Sperin, arms crossed over his broad chest, leaning casually against the hatchway.

"How did you get in here?" *Wait a minute. Not only was the hatch locked and dogged, but Rand should have warned me—and the motion sensors should have gone off—and . . .*

He shrugged.

"The lock was open, I knew you were expecting me, so I came in. Is that a problem?"

"It was not open. I *do* take some rudimentary precautions."

"It wasn't locked down. Not," he added with an annoying smile, "locked down very securely, that is."

"Yes, it was," she said through clenched teeth.

He shrugged again, and spread his hands. He *was* there. Joat felt an overwhelming urge to kick him.

"Joat," Joseph said before she could speak. "You asked me what had happened to bring me here. Now is the time to discuss the matter."

"Maybe I should make sure my hatch is locked," she said sullenly.

"No problem," Bros said, walking around her to swing his lean body into the pilot's chair with authoritative ease. "I took care of it." It was the first time he'd gotten a spontaneous reaction from her and he was feeling a bit smug about it. Then he glanced at the Bethelite seated beside him and grew serious again. To Joseph he said,

"You asked for my presence here, excellent sir. I'm most anxious to hear why."

Joseph took a deep breath; Joat saw that his fingers were white from the pressure of his clasp. Joe was not a man who put his feelings on display like this. Her irritation fell away—not forgotten, but filed.

"Our prophet, Amos ben Sierra Nueva, left Bethel ten days ago aboard a merchanter ship bound for the SSS-900-C. He did not arrive and the ship has not been heard from or found." Joseph rubbed his chin and looked at Bros. "I think you know why I asked to see you."

Joat shaped a silent whistle. No *wonder* Joe had seemed tense under his usual banter.

Bros nodded. "The Kolnari," he said.

"You are CenSec's resident expert on . . . them. And this will be an offworld affair. We . . . I am desperate for any help that you can offer. This is our prophet; and he is my brother-of-the-spirit, a bond closer than blood. They have taken him, I am sure. I must find him."

After a moment Bros leaned forward. "My superiors think I'm paranoid about the Kolnari. You understand me? They think that my information is unreliable, that every time a bandit hijacks a ship I see the Divine Seed. You take my advice, you're taking the risk that evaluation will rub off on you."

Joseph gave a bitter laugh and shook his head.

"Your superiors have not met the Kolnari. I have. To be paranoid about them is to be sane. I will trust your advice, Bros Sperin, for I know these devils. Advise me."

Cautiously, as though probing an open wound, Bros said, "There will be no ransom demand."

"I know it. If they have him, they will not so easily release him."

"I was aware of the kidnapping before you asked to see me, excellent sir," Bros said. "Simeon and Channa Hap reported that he hadn't arrived on the day he was overdue." Bros paused for a moment, gazing steadily at Joseph. "Just before I came over here a report reached me that the black box from the *Sunwise* had been recovered from a field of space debris. The box hasn't been evaluated yet, but the ship that found it reported signs indicating that the engines blew."

"I have no doubt that they did," Joseph said quietly.

"But I'd be surprised if that's all the box shows," Bros continued. "Even if there's not a Kolnari in sight, I believe that the Benisur was taken off that vessel either by them or for them. No question."

"We are agreed then," Joseph said, studying this legendary stranger. "Can you offer any advice? Anything at all."

"I hope so, excellent sir." Sperin paused. "I'm ashamed to admit it," he continued, "but we haven't caught up with all that many Kolnari since we routed them at the SSS-900-C and at Bethel. They went into hiding, and very effectively too. For quite a while we," he glanced at Joseph, "all of us, thought that perhaps Dr. Chaundra had wrought better than we had any right to hope and that they'd been exterminated by the disease he'd created.

"Then, gradually, but more and more over the last few years, pirate actions that fit the Kolnari m.o. began to crop up. Objects recorded as being taken in those specific raids suddenly were being offered for sale and we began to trace them back through a trail of legitimate dealers with flexible ethics to downright fences. Most of the time the trail led back to a Station called Rohan and a man named Nomik Ciety."

He turned to Joat. "This is where you come in," he said and smiled.

Oh really, she thought, *gosh, wow, I feel so privileged. Get out of my chair, blast you!* She nodded instead of speaking.

"Ciety is a notorious fence, a smuggler, a weapons broker. But we've never been able to touch him. Because Rohan, his base of operations, is a free-port, only nominally associated with Central Worlds, we have neither jurisdiction nor power there. In other words, as long as he keeps his nose clean on Rohan and makes his tax payments on time he can do anything, and I mean *anything*, that he wants to, there.

"We've sent people to Rohan to check him out, to look for Kolnari activity, to look for loot that we think the Kolnari might have taken. They've disappeared. Every one of them."

"And this is where *I* come in?" Joat asked, eyebrows raised.

Bros rubbed his hand across his upper lip.

"Exactly. I want you to go to Rohan and look around. I trust your capabilities and you're not known to be connected with Central Worlds Security so you should be in minimal danger. I repeat, I want you to look. Don't confront Ciety, don't troll for loot, don't try to find any Kolnari, just see what's there. You've been around, you'll know what to look for, what stories to listen to. If you see anything suspicious, that is, of a nature to help us with this problem, note it. Do nothing else. Note it and get back to us."

"Sounds exciting." she said dryly.

Bros turned the pilot's chair until he was facing Joseph.

"Excellent sir, this man Ciety is also an information broker. It is possible that, for the right price, he might be willing to supply you with information about this kidnapping. All that I can guarantee you about him is treachery, so if you do approach him, watch your back and don't make payment final until you're well away from Rohan. The man is completely mercenary and if he discovers who you are he would willingly sell you to the Kolnari. It would be wise to make your approach through a third party; the place is rife with professional go-betweens, so finding someone shouldn't be a problem. Of course a major concern in that case would be that you're so obviously a Bethelite that, knowing your desperation for any information, they might inflate their prices at the sight of you and give you next to nothing at all. Or they may decide to mention your curiosity to Ciety, or someone else you don't want to take an interest in you.

"As Joat is already bound there . . ."

"I am?" Joat said in mock surprise and earned an arch look from the CenSec agent.

"I urge you, most strongly, excellent sir, to commission her to act for you while you stay clear of the place altogether." He looked over at Joat, his eyes narrowed. "Amending her mission to accommodate your needs might even improve her chances of finding out what CenSec wants to know. I think she's both clever and discreet enough to be able to handle such a commission. And if she arranges it through a go-between, or better yet, through several of them she might succeed in remaining completely anonymous. That's where I'd advise you to start. Joat can send your information back with her first report to CenSec and I'll relay it to you."

"Are you aware that I'm in the same *room* with you, Sperin?" Joat asked.

Bros gave her an exasperated look, then turned to Joseph and spread his hands. "That's all we can offer at the moment, excellent sir. I'm sorry." Bros dug into his pocket, pulled out a datahedron and handed it to Joat.

"This is Ciety's dossier. Read it when you can concentrate on it because it will erase itself as it's being read."

"Well that's useful," Joat muttered.

"We don't want him to know what we know about him, Joat. And since your security is barely worth mentioning you could hardly expect me to give you a permanent record." He stood. "Are there any questions?"

"Yup. One, when did I agree to do all this stuff? And two, how much are you offering to pay me for this?" Joat asked.

"Seventy-four hundred, plus reasonable expenses," Sperin said, ignoring her first question entirely,

"And to think I passed up a career in CenSec," Joat murmured sarcastically.

"Seventy-four hundred is considerably more than my salary for this year," Bros said. "Don't you want to help find the Benisur Amos? He is an old friend of your parents."

"You forgot to appeal to my patriotism," Joat said dryly.

"I may be a scoundrel, but I'm not down to my last resort quite yet."

"I was just hoping you could do a little better than that. After all, a trader who goes to Rohan is a little like a virgin taking tea in a whorehouse. It taints your reputation even if you haven't done any business." She smiled sweetly at him. "Expenses to include all fuel and repairs."

And Flegal, but I am going to repair the dickens out of this ship.

"All right," he said. "Point taken. On my authority, CenSec will pick up for any expenses and repairs this mission gives rise to." He held out his hand to her.

She raised her hand, but held it back.

"I wonder if you might be willing to offer some kind of a bonus, considering that this *could* be a dangerous mission and that I am, after all, a civilian. Nothing outrageous," she assured him, holding up a denying hand. "You might arrange some trading concessions, for example. There's many a place I'd love to ship to but I can't afford the docking fees. What do you say, Bros? Think we can work something out?"

Bros put his hands on his hips and studied her through narrowed eyes.

"Where did you have in mind?"

"Senalgal?"

"Get real, Captain."

"The SSS-900-C?"

He raised his brows. "I would have thought Simeon . . ."

"I like to earn my way," she said sharply.

He nodded slowly. "I can fix it."

Joat held out her hand and he shook it, surprised at the strength of her grip.

"You can contact me at The Anvil," he said, "my cover name is Clal va Riguez." He nodded to Joseph, gave a half smile to Joat and was gone.

Joat turned on a monitor and they watched Sperin leave the *Wyal* and walk away without a backward glance.

"He told me he was known at The Anvil as Bros Sperin," she said resentfully.

"Wheels within wheels," Joseph murmured.

"Rand," she asked, "did he leave anything behind?"

"Yes, Joat. On the left arm of your chair, just where the seam is on the front of the arm."

Joat examined the area Rand had described. Nothing. She pulled out a scanner and flicked it; a framework extended, and she fitted it over her head. Joseph came to her side and pulled a huge, clumsy-looking optical from a pocket in his robe.

"Got it," she said.

"Here," Joseph grunted, his words crossing over hers. They smiled at each other.

He rose from his knees, bowing. "All yours, child."

"Child, hell." She pulled a toolkit from another pocket and opened it, twiddling her fingers. "Ta-*dum*."

It was about the width of a human hair and no longer than the thickness of a fingernail; one end was razor-sharp, to make it easier to implant. Probably it was this large only to allow it to be manipulated easily.

"Hel*lo*, Bros!" Joat said brightly, smiling a toothy smile with the sticktight held at eye level. "Why do I get this feeling that not everything is As It Seems? Anyway, you seem to have forgotten something. I couldn't allow you to waste the taxpayers money like that. Tsk, tsk upon you."

She opened an envelope and dropped the sticktight into it. "Addressed to Clal va Riguez, The Anvil," she said. The envelope obligingly showed the name on its exterior, and she confirmed it with a pinch that sealed the container. "Deliver." She dropped it into a slot on the console.

"Oooh," Joat went on to Joseph. "Spy stuff. I wonder how much that little thingie is worth. I wonder how many more there are."

Joseph still had the optical to his eye; looking at the recording of the sticktight. Bethelite technology wasn't subtle, but it got the job done.

"Interesting. Passive sensor, I think—burst transmission when keyed."

"Confirmed," Rand said. "I was only aware of it because I saw Mr. Sperin install it. As for the rest of the ship, nothing seems abnormal, but I can make no guarantees. Mr. Sperin seems a devious man, and we've no idea how long he was actually aboard before he chose to make his presence known."

"About that," Joat interrupted. "Why didn't you tell me he was onboard?"

"The first I knew of it was when he appeared on the bridge, Joat."

"But how could he *do* that?" she demanded.

"I suppose that CenSec has been extrapolating from your design," Rand said, "and they've come up with a superior version."

Joat bristled and her eyes sparked with fury. "Not for long, they haven't," she growled.

"In any event," Rand continued, "if he's left something behind I can't find it until it's contacted by an external signal."

"Don't worry about it, Rand. It's not your fault." *If anything,* she thought, *it's mine for becoming so complacent.* Or so honest. Joat shrugged. "I think it's safe to assume he'd leave his best stuff on the bridge. That's where we'll be most of the time, after all."

She picked up the bottle of Arrack and freshened both of their drinks.

"Disappointed?" she asked.

Joseph grimaced slightly.

"I am more annoyed than disappointed. Why I do not know. I certainly did not expect Central Worlds to charge to the rescue with banners flying. But I expected . . ."

"More than to be told to go home and wait for word from us big important people?"

"Yes!" he said firmly.

"You expected to be treated as a professional equal who doesn't need obvious instructions on how to behave in a hostile port?"

"Yes!"

"More importantly, you were hoping to receive some offer of backup from Central Worlds if you do find out who has Amos and where they've taken him."

Joseph tossed back the rest of the Arrack in his glass and looked at her.

"Without the aid of the Central Worlds Navy there would be little that we could do. If they are unwilling to help us, or if they delay, then my brother will die." He laughed in self mockery and rubbed a hand across his eyes. "Ah, Joat, I had hoped for hope."

Joat grinned at him. "All that regular living has made you soft, Joe. You don't need hope, you need luck . . ."

" . . . and you make your own luck!" they recited together, they clicked glasses and laughed.

She folded her arms and leaned her hip against her main console. Her eyes went over the readouts, registering automatically without interrupting the flow of thought

"We're fueled, we're set for supplies; as soon as my crew gets back we can cast off. So if you've got gear you'd better go and fetch it now."

Joseph grinned wickedly at her and indicated the small bag at his feet. "That is all that I have, Joat. But I must say that I do not think Mr. Sperin would approve of this invitation. I do not believe that he wished me to go to Rohan."

"Hunh, by the time he was finished talking I wasn't sure he wanted *me* to go! Pushy osco, ain't he?"

"Perhaps he wanted to go himself," offered Rand. "He had the overtones, if I may say so, of a man stretching his instructions to the limit."

Joat and Joseph exchanged glances.

"Y'know Rand, I believe you've hit the nail on the head," Joat murmured.

With a soft hiss of breath Amos completed the final movement of the seven hundred and fifty separate steps of the Sword Dance of Natham. He stood upright, panting slightly, sweat running freely down his bare, muscled sides.

The dance helped to center him, to stave off rage and panic, as well as wearing him out so that he could sleep. He had just repeated it twice in succession, once slowly, once very fast.

Now he wished that he could be clean. But the Kolnari brig did not include such amenities as a shower. There was a small sink, however and he went over to it intending to do the best he could.

The cell was small, perhaps two meters by three with double-decker bunks that folded down from the wall, the sink and a commode for furnishings. The walls, ceiling, and floor were of cold, white enameled metal and the light never went out.

The food was neither good nor bad, but bland, soldier's rations, in reasonable quantity, delivered at unpredictable intervals.

Were he a man who could find no comfort in his God, Amos knew that he would be howling and beating on the door by now. He smiled grimly. The Kolnari couldn't know that a severe religious retreat could be very like this. There would be better facilities for cleaning one-self, and books, and the light would be under his control, but otherwise there were strong similarities. With the obvious exception, of course, that he could end a religious retreat at will. Assuming that God willed it so.

He sighed and turned on the faucet. No water came.

How petty, he thought, *Belazir must be finding me boring.*

He sat on his bunk and turned his palms upward to begin meditating on the devotions of the prophets. That would fill his time both pleasantly and well, since there were over eight thousand of them.

The hatch swung open and two figures in black space armor violently flung Captain Sung into the room. Amos leapt to his feet and caught the older man before he could crash to the floor. By the time he had the Captain righted on his feet the cell was sealed once more.

"Captain," Amos said in astonishment. "What of Soamosa? Have you seen her, have they told you anything?"

The Captain's face was badly bruised and he was shaking with reaction.

"I thought they were gonna space me," he said and shuddered. "I knew they couldn't get a ransom for me, they already took every-thing I ever had. I thought they were going to vent me with the rest of the garbage."

Amos put an arm around the older man and guided him to the bunk.

"I would give you water if I could," he said, "but they have turned it off." He paused for a moment. "Captain," he said softly and waited until the other man looked at him. "Soamosa, do you know anything about her?'

The Captain shook his head regretfully. "No, nothing. I haven't seen her since we were split up, and they don't talk to me." He raised a shaking hand to brush back his short hair. "I'm sorry."

"I did not expect that you would know, I only hoped that they might have become careless and allowed you to see something. It is no matter."

"How long have we been here?" Sung asked.

"I do not know. I have slept four times, and I have been fed eight. But what relation that might have to real time I could not begin to guess. What is your estimation?"

Sung shook his head, his face looking infinitely sad.

"I don't know," he said, "I just don't know."

"Rest," Amos said gently and placed his hand against the Captain's shoulder, urging him to lie down. He grinned ruefully. "We shall have a wealth of time to talk later. Put your head down for a while."

Sung nodded tiredly and lay flat, his eyes closed before his head touched the pillow.

Amos sat on the floor in a lotus position. Before resuming his meditations he offered a brief prayer of thanks for the gift of a companion to relieve the silence of his imprisonment.

Several hours later Sung stirred and woke. He turned to Amos and stared at him in puzzlement.

"Who the hell are you?" he asked.

"What?"

"Who the hell are you? What are you doing in here?"

"Captain, what are you talking about?" Amos studied the Captain's irate face with astonishment. "I am Amos ben Sierra Nueva, a passenger of yours . . ."

"Passengers aren't allowed in the captains quarters! What are you doing here?"

Amos licked his dry lips, uncertain how one answered a man apparently losing his mind and growing more angry by the minute.

"Captain Sung," he held out a placating hand, "we are not on your ship, we have been thrown into the brig of a Kolnari pirate. Don't you remember?"

The Captain's eyes widened, a look of fear shuddered across his face to be replaced by confusion.

"What did you say my name was?"

"You are Captain Josiah Sung, of the merchanter ship *Sunwise*."

"The *Sunwise*," Sung reached out and gripped Amos's hand desperately, "I remember her. She's my ship, the *Sunwise*. I know her. You see? I'm all right."

"Yes, of course you are, Captain. It was only a moment's confusion. You woke from a deep sleep to find yourself in a new place, it is not uncommon to be disoriented under such conditions. All is well." Amos gave the Captain's hand a squeeze and smiled encouragingly at him.

Sung raised his tear-slicked face to glare at Amos.

"Let go of my hand you bastard! How the hell did you get in here?"

Amos felt his heart pounding in the cage of his ribs, more strongly than it had when he pushed his body to its limits.

"I'm the Captain dammit! I don't *entertain* the passengers. You got that? Get out of here!" Sung pointed to the hatch and then blinked. With a gasp he turned to look at Amos. "What's happening to me? What have they done?"

Amos shook his head, equally horrified. The bruise on the Captain's face was proof of a head wound, but would such a wound have an effect like this? Had the Captain been poisoned? Was he being shown the effects before they did the same to him? It would be like Belazir to torture him so, the Kolnari idea of subtlety.

Suddenly Belazir stood before them. The edges of his image bore a soft white fuzz for a moment, then the holo snapped into clear focus.

A white silken robe emphasized the inhuman blackness of his still-magnificent body. A feathered clip held back his brittle white hair.

"Good morning Simeon Amos, or good evening, whichever you have decided it must be. How are you getting on down here?"

"Not well, Master and God. The Captain is not himself." Amos's eyes dared to demand answers, but he would not give Belazir the pleasure of hearing him ask for them.

"Is he not?" Belazir said with amusement. "Then who is he? Captain Sung, who do you think you are?"

"What . . . what do you mean?"

"Who are you?" Belazir asked.

A look of blank astonishment crossed Sung's face and he raised his hands helplessly.

"I don't know," he said, his voice tight with horror. "I don't remember." Tears gathered in his eyes and he struggled visibly not to blink and send them rolling down his cheeks. "I don't remember."

Amos glared at the Kolnari, letting his face show contempt. He spat at the feet of the image.

Belazir quirked a smile at him. "You offer little sport, scumvermin; you tell me everything that I want to know without my even asking. Why should I tell you anything?"

"You knew before you did this that I would despise you for it, Master and God. Why you even bothered to show up I cannot imagine."

"Is this wise, scumvermin, to bait a man who holds your lives in his fist? I am sure that your friend Channahap would advise you otherwise." He folded his massive arms across his chest and regarded Amos with amusement. "It may be that I have information that you might wish to have. If you ask me very politely, I might unbend sufficiently to enlighten you."

Amos's lips quivered with rage, but his need to know the fate of his young cousin won out over his pride and his hatred.

"I beg your pardon," he said formally. "Master and God."

Belazir raised an eyebrow. "I will assume that was a request for knowledge. I know that you wish for information about your young cousin. But I will instead unfold a larger plan before you. One that touches the fate of all your people." He paused, smiling, to observe the effect this pronouncement was having on Amos. "You can see that the Captain here is not behaving normally, can you not?"

"Of course I can," Amos said through gritted teeth. "Master and God."

"You are thinking that we have beaten him into this condition, or that we have poisoned him."

Amos nodded.

Belazir's face suddenly seemed weary. He shrugged and half-turned away.

"In fact he has been overcome by a contagious, progressive disease that attacks the memory center of the brain. You are a carrier of this disease, Simeon Amos, but we have made sure that you are completely immune to it. You have seen how rapidly it works, how devastating it is."

Belazir's golden eyes narrowed. "We Kolnari have gained great respect for such weapons. You and the rest of the scumvermin on that accursed station taught us a singular lesson about biological weaponry. Now we of Kolnar shall return the favor.

"You will be given a drug that will prevent you from moving or speaking and then you will be returned to your people."

Amos rose from the bunk, to confront Belazir on his feet.

"We are not stupid, Belazir. My people will know that something is wrong. Why else would you return me?"

"Oh, but they will have to fight to recover you. It will all be very convincing, I assure you. A raging chase through the skies of Bethel. But they will win, for yours is a valiant people. And their reward shall be to become like the Captain. We will leave him here with you so that you can fully appreciate what your return to the bosom of your people will mean to them."

As Amos rushed forward the grinning image of Belazir blinked out and he crashed into the wall instead. He slid down until he was sitting on the floor, and then he looked up to meet Captain Sung's gaze.

"Who are you?" the man asked. "Who . . ."

CHAPTER FOUR

JOAT STARED MOODILY at the screen. It listed the latest Standard
Commercial Report listing of cargoes in demand at Rohan Station,
together with charter listings and container requests from New Destinies. *Item: thruster units.* Officially, Rohan didn't have shipyards. *Item:
power plant spares.* From the specs, there were some *awfully* fast merchantmen operating out of Rohan—merchantmen who were prof-
ligate enough to burn out their overpowered drive units with some
regularity. The sort of maneuver you needed to transit an atmosphere
at high speed, or wrench another ship out of FTL transit.

"There are some things I just won't do," she muttered.

Running that sort of cargo into a pesthole like Rohan was one of
those things. Fuel, maybe. Foodstuffs, medical supplies, sure—if they
went into a pirate's sickbay or galley, that wasn't her affair. But no
fardling *way* was she going to run drive coils or fire-control electronics. Not to Rohan.

"Joat, will you be advised by me?"

*Lessee. I could offer to take those fifteen containers of pharmaceu-
ticals at, say, three percent, then—*

Joat glanced up from the cargo manifest she was studying to look
at Joseph. His face was solemn and his manner formal. She raised
her brows.

"I'm always willing to listen to advice from people I respect, Joe.
What's on your mind?"

"I keep thinking of something you said to Bros Sperin. That going

408

to Rohan was to a trader the equivalent of a virgin entering a whorehouse. It is a good analogy, Joat, and it troubles me."

Joat leaned back in her chair, eyes narrowed thoughtfully.

"Go on," she said.

"It is not simply your reputation with Central Worlds that concerns me. You are known as a captain who keeps her hands clean. Will they not wonder why you have come to them? As well, your association with the SSS-900-C is widely known. As the adopted daughter of a shell-person you became quite famous for a while. To those guilty of aiding the Kolnari your name will surely set off a train of associations which could result in considerable danger for you."

She folded her hands on her stomach and nodded slowly.

"You're right. I will need a reason for going there that's completely dissociated from Amos or the Kolnari. You know, I have this sneaking suspicion that Mr. Sperin *wanted* me to be under suspicion. So that it would be easier for someone else—say, Bros Sperin—to slip in himself while everyone worried about me. Hmmm."

"Perhaps if you were to take on smuggled goods," Joseph suggested tentatively. "New Destinies has a reputation for looking the other way in such matters, so having this as your last port of call would lend credibility."

"I'd need to justify that," Joat said thoughtfully. "I'm the first to admit that I bend the rules till they scream for mercy, but seriously criminal behavior is something I've managed to avoid so far."

She tapped her fingertips together and stared into space for a moment. Then she smiled.

"Rand," she asked, "do we have a recording of that little walk I took earlier?"

"Yes Joat. I saw no reason not to make one."

"Can you adjust it to make it look as though it had been recorded by someone else?"

"I can."

"Do it. Then transmit it anonymously to Station Security." She winked at Joseph. "I took an unauthorized space walk and entered the station illegally. They'll hit us with a wonking great fine and I can use that as an excuse for needing fast and dirty credits." She grimaced. "It may take us there round about, but I think the added safety margin should be worth a small delay."

"But Joat, the fine will be real," Joseph objected. Frowning he asked, "What if you cannot pay it?"

"No problem." Joat grinned at him. "CenSec will pay—at least, I think I can thumbscrew any reasonable amount out of them. We'll just put it under expenses. Might come to four, five thousand credits; even ten thousand. Enough to make the treasurer wince. Can't be much more than that."

Joseph laughed. Bethelites tended to be straightlaced, but Joseph ben Said had the wholehearted love of a well-thought-out swindle natural to a Keriss wharf rat. This would not only make CenSec cough up the money, but a certain Bros Sperin would have to justify the expense.

"You are wicked! You have always been wicked. Why did I think you had outgrown it?"

"Wishful thinking?" Joat asked, blinking innocent blue eyes.

A good notion, Sperin thought as he watched the clip of Joat breaking into the station. *Getting herself into trouble with station security should give her greater credibility.*

He'd wondered how she managed to avoid the man they'd had waiting for her. *He's not the best that ever was, but he's not blind either.* Bros shook his head and smiled slightly.

Now how can I benefit from this situation? Sperin rubbed his upper lip thoughtfully. The little captain had been talking about ditching her career as a courier, not something CenSec would like to happen. *She's smart and she's reliable.* It was amazing how rare those qualities were.

Joat hadn't been invited to join CenSec because she was too independent, too unpredictable. But it had turned out that in every way that it counted she was a gem. *Be nice to have her beholden to us,* Sperin mused. *She's the type that pays her debts.*

He'd been given a name in the Bureau of Fines and Levies to contact if need arose. Bros rubbed his palms together. *I believe I feel a need.*

> *"Roses sweet and tender she has twined in her hair,*
> *and the scent of spring and roses is with her everywhere."*

Joat yawned and half-groaned as the baritone voice boomed through the sound system.

"I take it Alvec is back," she said.

"Yes, Joat," Rand said.

She dumped a packet of sweetener into the coffee—she could afford real sugar now, but preferred the more familiar taste—and said: "On display."

The viewscreen over the galleys preserver unit came live, showing a holo of the deck outside the *Wyal*'s berth. Alvec Dia was there, engaged in an enthusiastic good-bye kiss with a woman of about his own age and poundage; she had a spectacular head of red hair, and was clutching a dozen long-stemmed roses in her free hand. Or grinding them into Alvec's back, at times.

"Alvec?" Joseph asked from the other side of the galley.

He slid several eggs off the frictionless surface of the heater and onto a plate.

"Ahhh, Brunoki sausage. Almost as good at the morning meal as toasted sand rats. Alvec is the crewman of whom you spoke?"

Joat broke a yoke with a strip of toast. "Yup. And this happens at every dock. Well, nearly every dock. You don't *really* like sand rats, do you?"

"They are a traditional delicacy."

"Screen off. This is depressing."

"Only because you are lonely," Joseph said slyly. "As my second wife, you—"

"Do you really want to die, Joe?"

Alvec checked for a moment as he came through the galley door.

"You remember Joe?"

"Sure," he said easily, nodding at the Bethelite. They had met once before, briefly.

His expression showed that he also remembered Joseph's allergy to questions. The craggy-faced spacers expression went carefully bland as he pulled a container of coffee out of the cupboard, broke the seal and settled across the tiny table from Joat.

"Ah, she's beautiful, boss," he told them. "Sweetest gal you'd ever want to meet."

Joat and Joseph exchanged a look.

"He's always like this after he's been on leave," Joat explained.

Joseph nodded, "Of course, quite understandable."

Joat cocked her head at her crew, her brows raised.

"Um, Al. Would you like to pursue your acquaintance with this lady while Joe and I take a brief jaunt elsewhere?"

Alvec looked from Joat to Joseph suspiciously.

"Not especially. I mean, yeah, I want to pursue her acquaintance, she's beautiful, but not at the expense of my job."

"Your job is safe, Al. Joe's just visiting, he's got a wife and kids dirtside on Bethel. We've just got this thing we've got to do. And you deserve a vacation, you haven't had one in ages."

Alvec studied his employer, her little half smile, the raised brows, the wide innocent eyes.

"Now you've got me worried, Captain," he complained. "When you look this reasonable, you're usually up to something. I'll think about it." Alvec allowed his manner to convey his deep suspicion.

The com chimed. "Merchant Ship *Wyal*, Captain Joat Simeon speaking," Joat answered.

"Good morning, Captain Simeon. My name is Graf Dyson." The man smiled grimly. "Although I understand you know my name."

Oh-oh. Graf Dyson. I claimed to be a very good friend of Graf Dyson. Influential people tended to disapprove when you took their names in vain. She'd intended to be far away by the time Mr. Dyson got wind of how she'd used his influence without his permission. *Oh, well, I never expected to* want *to get fined.*

The man on the screen was dark haired, middle-aged and heavy featured. *Looks honest,* Joat thought. That was a bad sign. Conmen and sharps usually did.

"I am employed by the Bureau of Fines and Levies, as I believe you already know." He paused to let that sink in before continuing: "And I'm contacting you in regard to a matter that has been brought to the attention of Station Security and through them to my bureau."

"Mmmm?" Joat murmured cautiously, setting her coffee aside.

"A recording was anonymously sent to Security of an unauthorized space walk and illegal entry into the station through an emergency repair hatch by someone from the *Wyal*. We have reason to believe that the person shown on the recording might be you."

There was something about the tone of his voice and the look in his eyes that unnerved her. *Me and my bright ideas.* Using Dyson's name had been a good idea. Making the illegal entry had been a good idea. Tricking the New Destinies into giving her a cover story by fining her had been a good idea.

But when you added them all up, they didn't come to a good idea. *This is what Channa used to mean by keeping the big picture in mind,* Joat thought. For a moment she wished poignantly that Channa was there with her, someone older and wiser to lean on. . . .

Fardling void with that, she thought stubbornly. *I'm twenty-three. And even when I was twelve, I could look after myself.*

"That's completely ridiculous!" she said briskly. "What possible reason could I have for doing such a thing?"

Joat stared back at Dyson with an expression of injured disbelief that had baffled even experienced child-welfare workers in its time.

"Your ship was under observation yesterday by Station Security. It's assumed that you became aware of being under surveillance and chose to avoid it by taking this round-about method of entering the station."

"Wait a minute," she said, hunching forward in her seat. "*I* was under surveillance? What for?"

"Why you were being watched is irrelevant, Ms. Simeon. What you chose to do about it is."

Oh it's Ms. now is it, you clabber-faced oaf! What happened to Captain *Simeon?*

"I think it's very relevant," she said aloud. "I demand to know why you were spying on me!"

"I'll have Station Security send you a report," Dyson said through bared teeth. "However, in regard to the matter in hand . . ."

"I did not take any unauthorized space walk!"

"Then how do you explain that you were not seen leaving your ship, but were observed returning?"

"Maybe I can walk through walls."

"Heh, heh. How very clever. And how do you explain being found outside the very lock shown in the recording, with your suit in your arms?"

"I was taking my suit to get the seals checked."

"And being in the corridor outside the lock?"

"I got lost."

"The Bureau finds it reasonable to fine you for this incident. And as you aren't a station resident, I have plenary authority. Unauthorized breaches of hull security are a serious matter."

They were. Spacers took pressure integrity even more seriously than Bethelites took fresh water. Joat felt a small twinge of guilt; she hadn't *really* endangered the Station's atmosphere . . . but if it ever got to a jury, they wouldn't be amused. At all.

Joat smacked both palms on the sides of the console and leaned forward menacingly.

"I protest!"

Dyson regarded her coolly. "That is certainly your right, Ms. Simeon. New Destinies is well supplied with lawyers who are specialists in dealing with the Bureau. I suggest that you avail yourself of their services, if you feel you can afford it—after paying the fine, that is. In the meantime, the fine will be registered against your ship and will be due in forty days."

Joat glared. "What's the fine?" she growled.

"Thirty thousand credits."

Joat's eyes snapped wide. Alvec gasped, and Joseph grunted in the background like a man belly-punched.

"You're crazy! No way can you justify a fine like that!"

"Shall we double it?" The man's features grinned like a shark for an instant, then went friendly-bland again.

She gave a shaky little laugh.

"What is this? Some kind of shake-down? You can't possibly hope to get away with this."

"Double it again. It's you that's trying to get away with something, Ms. Simeon. I'm simply doing my job and I'm fairly confident that I can get away with that. You now owe New Destinies one hundred and twenty thousand credits. I think you should stop talking before you owe us the value of the station itself. Don't you?"

Joat closed her mouth with an effort. This had gotten way out of hand. She sat still for a moment, feeling pale and shaky. What if CenSec refused to answer for this debt? She could lose her ship. They *would* refuse to pay it. Ten thousand she could have gotten out of them via Bros, and enjoyed him squirming on the Treasury's pin. A hundred and twenty thousand they'd refuse out of hand.

What can I do? Sue Central Worlds Security?

"Now you mentioned protesting the fine, didn't you?" Dyson asked pleasantry.

Joat nodded vigorously.

"Well, unfortunately the only date we have open for a hearing is sixty days from now. Also in that case we'd have to impound your ship. And since the fine is due in forty days, well, that would mean that your ship would probably already have been auctioned off by the time your case came up. Do you want to think about it? You have five days to protest the fine." He gazed at her blandly.

"Yes," she said. She found it hard to talk. "I ... I could lose my ship?"

"Yesss, you certainly could. In fact, I'd be extremely surprised if you didn't." Dyson stared out of the screen at her, his hands folded neatly before him. He smiled again, the same friendly, honest-looking smile.

She thought of her remaining mortgage.

I'll be ruined, she thought desperately. *I'll be a slave to the bank, working off a debt on something I don't even own.* She pictured years of work under someone else's command with nothing to show for it but a slowly diminishing debt.

"You should have thought of that before you went out your hatch, Ms. Simeon," Dyson said, as he disconnected the automatic recording device.

"And before you opened your big mouth. *And claimed an acquaintance you didn't have!*" He cut the transmission with a decisive snap.

Dyson sat back, a satisfied sneer on his face. *I enjoyed that!* he thought. It wasn't every day that you got your own back with the blessings of Central Worlds Security.

He grinned as he recalled the look of sick horror on her pretty face. *It's moments like these that make life worthwhile*, Dyson mused.

The fine wouldn't stick, of course. In fact he wasn't even supposed to register more than a minimal fine. *Ah, but what if the good Captain checks?* he wondered as he entered the astronomical fine. *I can always erase it later.* He sat back again. *If they tell me to.*

He chuckled. *Life is good!*

Joat just stared at the blank screen for a moment, frozen in shock. "Ooops," she said.

Alvec cleared his throat. "I know what *ooops* means," he said. "It means, *I screwed the pooch.* Boss, you got something you wanna tell me?"

Joat opened her mouth, and then looked over at Joseph. He lifted his brows, and she nodded.

"Captain Simeon-Hap has arranged to visit Station Rohan," he began. "On urgent business."

Alvec choked on a mouthful of coffee. "That jackal's nest?"

Joseph nodded. "Exactly, my friend. A normal trading and freight-charter trip would appear suspicious; honest traders try to avoid Rohan. So, she—we—needed a plausible reason to take high-freight but, shall we say, questionable cargo on a run to a . . . questionable location."

"Jeeeze, Boss, how do you get into these things?" He shook his head in wonder. "I've never heard of a fine like that for such a piddly little infraction."

"Some piddly little bureaucrat in Health and Immigration named Dilton tried to shake me down when we came in, and I dropped Graf Dyson's name, pretended that I was a friend of his. Evidently Dilton checked up on it and now Dyson's leaning on me."

"How can this guy get away with that?"

"In this case, Alvec, it's timing," Rand said. "Before a hearing there is no opportunity to work off the debt, after the ship is taken, Joat will have neither the leisure nor the credits to file suit."

"And," Joseph put in, "our business is too urgent to delay. We cannot afford to tie ourselves up in a bureaucratic . . . process," he finished for want of a better word. He had one actually, but he would not utter it in front of Joat.

"I didn't think that it would be wise to claim acquaintance with him, Joat," Rand scolded. "Why did you risk it?"

"At the time," she said tiredly, "I never expected a petty crook to be so smart . . . or so efficiently vindictive."

"You didn't study the matter. You acted impulsively."

"Rand," she said, "shut up or I'll punch your lights out."

"I don't like the smuggling thing, Boss," Alvec said. "It's like a drug for some people. They get started for the profit and they get hooked on the excitement." He shook his head.

"I think I've got enough excitement right now to supply me for a lifetime, Al. And now I actually *need* the damn credits. No way CenSec is gonna spring for a hundred and twenty thousand. You could buy a corvette for that, used."

She brushed her hair back off her face and then flung herself back in her chair, gripping the armrests until her fingers turned white. "I'm gonna need something good," she said grimly.

"Joat, my friend, calm yourself," Joseph said. "Certainly the outrageous size of this fine will ensure that your troubles become known quickly. We will hardly need to exert ourselves to make our desperation convincing. Indeed, rather than having to seek someone out, they may approach you. And," he held up one finger, "Central Worlds has enough influence and authority to get this cruel fine reduced to something reasonable. Send a message to Mr. Sperin, and doubtless he will see to it."

"You're probably right, Joe." She gave him a weak smile and turned to Alvec: "Feel up to a pub crawl? Best way I know of making yourself available for an approach."

"Let me ask Rose where would be a good place to start," Alvec offered. "She might know some places."

"Where did *you* meet her?" Joat asked.

"Ah . . ." Alvec flushed. "The Station personals column."

"Rimrunners," Rose said. "Rimrunners would be a good place, up near the North Quadrant. But any bar in the same general neighborhood will probably do. They're all crooked as a Phelobite's elbow up there."

Joat studied the bed-sitting room behind Rose. It was fairly large for a Stationer; Rose was evidently a mid-level tech in a gas-refining outfit, and spent a fair amount of time out-of-habitat. The wall behind her was a slightly blurry holo taken over the flared bows of a scoopship, with the gas-giant filling the entire forward quadrant; Looking at it made Joat's piloting reflexes scream *vector up!* until she had to glance away.

"You need some help on this, honey?" Rose asked Alvec.

He shook his head. "Ship's business, darlin'. But thanks." He blew her a kiss and turned off the view-screen.

Maybe we should take her up on that, Joat thought. *From the look of her, she'd be a good friend to have behind you in a fight.*

No. That wouldn't be fair. Rose hadn't gotten them into this mess. Speaking of fair . . .

"Maybe you should take Rose out to dinner while Joe and I scope out Rimrunners," she said hopefully. "It's not like anything grudly is going to come down."

Alvec stood, stretched on to his toes and came down in a posture of relaxed alertness.

"You don't know nothin' about this stuff, Boss."

"And you do?"

Alvec looked down at his feet. "Yeah, some."

Joat studied him. Alvec had a mysterious past. He didn't talk about it and she paid him the courtesy of not asking, appreciating the fact that he returned the favor.

So *we both have things we're happier not talking about,* she thought. That might be a bit of a handicap now; they were probably both assuming a degree of naiveté in the other that wasn't justified. *I'd better take him at his word.*

She'd always had the feeling that at one time he might have been master of his own ship. His competence, his knowledge and the high rank of many of his friends argued for the idea. But whatever happened had left him quite content to be Joat's crew.

She shrugged.

"Yeah, well, I'm not doing so well on my own, so maybe you'd better come along. Between you, you and Joe should be able to keep me from making things worse."

"Your faith alarms me, my friend," Joseph said with a laugh. "But I shall do my best to earn it."

Alvec gave Joseph a long, considering look.

Joat laughed. The two men looked at her. "We're all of us bundles of surprises, aren't we?" she said, and linked her arms through theirs. "Let's get going."

How did they do it? Joat wondered. *How did they manage to make a place that was built at the same time as everything else on this station look this dilapidated?*

North Quarter was reasonable enough on its outskirts, comfortable low- to middle-income housing and the modest shops that catered to that group. It was the people that signaled the change as much as anything else. As you got closer to the unspun docking sections the clothes got plainer and grubbier, or more spectacularly flashy. Joat found her fingers curling instinctively around the hilt of her vibroknife where it was tucked into its charging sheath in the right sleeve of her overalls. It was a small movement, nearly undetectable . . . but half the people on the corridor moved a little farther aside when she did it. Which said something about their perceptions, even now in night-cycle, when the overhead ambients were turned down to let the shopfront glowers and holes shine by contrast.

This is the sort of place Uncle used to stop. Before he'd lost her in a card game when she was about seven. She felt her shoulders hunch, her face tighten. Her body remembered those years; the feral child was still there, hiding inside the skin of the civilized young woman.

The professionals were out, too. Down here they didn't just saunter; you got detailed propositions. Complete with anatomical details so lurid that she blinked.

"What you said about my succumbing to soft living would seem to be true, Joat," Joseph whispered in her ear. "I, who grew up on the docks of Keriss, find myself embarrassed!"

Joat grinned at him. "At least you don't smell of cop."

The Bethelite nodded. "In Keriss too we could always smell a thief-taker," he said. "Still, I remember a little more discretion from the Daughters of Joy."

"Don't be embarrassed," she said. "This bunch're way saltier than average. They're beginning to get to me too."

Alvec leered. "Y'oughta be storing this stuff up for use on Rohan. New Destinies is a deacon's convention next to that."

"Do you speak as one who knows?" Joseph asked, his voice cool. Alvec bristled.

"Tell me something," Joat said. "Why is it that men—even smart ones—are dumb as iridium ingots while they're settling who's big bull baboon?"

Alvec snorted. Joseph raised his eyebrows—a habit he'd picked up from Amos—and chuckled. "Women are more subtle about it," he admitted. "I will try not to leap, gibber, or scratch my armpits too often in your presence, *saiyda.*"

The Rimrunner was an Earth-style bar with furniture that only accommodated the humanoid form. The windows were one-way, opaque on the outside, with colorful advertisements for liquor flashing across the dirty black surface. Inside they gave a clear, if not clean, view of the street.

They made their way to an empty table, covertly studying the other patrons, who studied them in turn. Some of the men and women sitting at the tables or standing at the bar were sleazy-gaudy like most of the crowd outside; there were a few in conservative business jumpsuits, a few *too* well dressed, and a number in spacers coveralls. Those looked neater. You couldn't be messy on a vehicle with boost, not really. Not if you wanted to live.

A bored and blowzy waitress slouched over and took their order. When she'd returned with their drinks and departed with an air of never planning to return, they sat quietly and sipped grimly for awhile. Conversation had died when they walked in, and was slow to revive. Most eyes were on the holo over the bar—an act showing surprising gymnastic skill, among other things—with occasional darts in their direction.

Finally, Joat leaned towards her crew and murmured: "So, Al, is there something we do? Talk to the bartender, put a note on the bulletin board, walk around shouting *we want to smuggle,* or what?"

"Someone'll come over," he murmured. "They're just checkin' us out."

They sat a little longer and Joat began to drum her fingers on the table. Two of them had sticky ends from a film of something on the surface.

"That's it," she said finally, putting her hands flat on the tabletop to push herself to her feet "I don't really want to do this anyway—"

A pale, thin-faced man with dark hair and a neatly trimmed beard was suddenly at her elbow. He wore a black jumpsuit with flared sleeves, which might be hiding anything.

"You're, uh, Captain Simeon-Hap, aren't you?" he asked quietly.

Three pairs of eyes bored into the stranger as he reversed the empty chair at their table and laid an open messager on the surface, sitting with his arms resting on the chairback.

"Mind if I join you?" he asked.

Joat shook her head. "You already have," she pointed out.

"Word is you've fallen on interesting times," he said, and smiled. Like the rest of him, the smile was thin and vicious-looking. "As in the curse."

She raised her brows. "Word gets around fast."

"Is it true?"

She sighed. "Yeah. It's true." She smiled in her turn, tight and controlled and dangerous. "We're gonna drink the money we have left."

Something invisible relaxed in the thin man's posture. "No need. Let me buy you a round." He looked pointedly at Joseph and Alvec. "Would you guys mind placing the order? Lisha will bring ours over to us, but you'll probably prefer to drink yours at the bar."

They looked at Joat, and rose at her nod. Joat could sense their reluctance, but they were both too experienced to queer her pitch. Nobody would want to book space with a captain who couldn't command her crew; particularly not people who wanted to be sure that their cargo got to its destination without inspection.

When Al and Joseph reached the bar they leaned against it, putting their weight on their elbows as if they were completing a journey of a thousand miles and their feet hurt.

"What'll it be, gents?"

"Arrack?" Joseph asked hopefully.

The bartender shook his head. "We got gin, we got whisky, we got beer . . ."

"Earth beer?" Alvec asked straightening.

"Four kinds," the bartender named them.

Alvec slapped Joseph's arm with the back of his hand

"Ya gotta try this stuff," he said. "You're gonna love it!"

Joseph looked skeptical but nodded.

"Two," he said. He looked briefly in Joat's direction.

"Don't worry," Alvec said. "It's nothin' she can't handle."

Joseph sighed. "Yes, no doubt you are right. Still . . ." He shook his head. Then he looked around, as though really noticing the bar for the first time.

"It is amazing," he said, "Except for the signs, this tavern could be on Bethel. It is like any number of places on the docks where I grew up."

"Yeah," Alvec sighed nostalgically. "Me too. I think they invented a place like this back on Earth, and they've been shippin' them out wholesale from the same factory ever since."

"C.O.D.?" Joat asked in disbelief. "You expect me to ship this cash on delivery?"

"Captain, smuggling is like any other business. There has to be an element of trust or nothing can happen." He smiled his thin smile again, showing a sliver of teeth. "For example, we're trusting you not to fly off somewhere and sell the cargo."

You're trusting that I know what happens to people who try to stiff the Organization, she thought. The criminal equivalent of the Better Business Bureau wasn't a formal league, but it did have a strong, working joint policy on welchers.

"Nobody ships interstellar C.O.D.," she said firmly. "At the very least I'll need credits up front that will pay the expense of the trip. I'm not interested in getting to Schwartztarr and finding out that this has been a joke."

He pursed his lips. "So, what would that come to?"

"Two thousand," she said firmly.

He raised his brows and laughed faintly.

"You'd better check your engines, Captain. Your fuel consumption is *way* off the mark."

"I'm going to have to bribe my way off this station. I consider that a legitimate," she smiled briefly, "expense of the trip."

"They're supposed to let you continue to operate your business so you can pay your fine."

"Yeah, and they're not supposed to fine me the value of my ship for a misdemeanor, too. Two thousand up front, my man; twenty-five thousand on delivery. I won't even consider it without."

Joseph raised his brimming stein to his nose and sniffed dubiously.

"It smells like meat," he said.

"Meat!" Alvec sniffed his. "Mine's okay. Whaddaya mean, it smells like meat?"

"To me," Joseph explained, "this 'beer' smells like raw meat."

Alvec looked at him.

"Yeah, well," he grinned, "I can't wait to have a steak on your world."

Joseph took a tentative sip and smiled.

"You shall have one of the best when you visit my rancho," he promised, "*if* you will bring the beer."

He was raising his still brimming stein to touch glasses with Alvec when a shabby fellow in a once-yellow ship suit elbowed him aside; beer slopped over Joseph's sleeve and down the front of his robe. He set the remainder down and wiped the fabric with a napkin. The spacer ignored him . . . until he poked a rigid finger into the man's shoulder.

"That," he said, "was clumsy."

The spacer turned to him; when he spoke it was with a strong accent, wheezing and sharp. "Donchu touch me you bastard son of a whore!"

Ooops. Alvec thought. Joat had told him a little about Bethel, and he'd accessed more from the *Wyal's* database. That was *not* a good thing to say to a Bethelite; especially in Joseph's case, because it might well be literally true.

The bearded man handed Joat a credit chip and a blue datahedron.

"The information is protected by a very nasty virus, so I warn you, don't try to access it or you may find yourself drifting in hyper-space until you become a ghost story."

She smiled. "Smuggling is like any other business, there has to be an element of trust or nothing can happen."

He leaned his head to one side in acknowledgment, then looked over sharply to the bar.

Thwack.

She had never seen Joseph look quite like *that*. His face was pale, with paler circles around his wide blue eyes. He was holding a spacer in a yellow suit with one arm twisted up behind his back. Blood ran down the man's face from a broken nose.

"Apologize, you furrower of pigs," the Bethelite said quietly, in a voice that carried. "For the insult you gave my mother."

"Fardle you *and* your mother, like your pig daddy!"

"That was unwise."

Joseph's other hand gripped the spacer by the back of the neck and slammed his face into the glassteel surface of the bar again. *Thwuck.* This time something else broke.

Joat started to rise; that was *not* like Joseph. She also started to shout a warning, as another spacer in a yellow shipsuit rose with a chair in her hands. Alvec moved before she could speak, a quick snatch for the chair and a short chopping punch to the stomach— much less hard than he could have dealt, because the spacer simply staggered back clutching her gut rather than collapsing. The bartender had ducked down; he rose again, with a short bell-mouthed weapon in his hands.

Sonic riot gun, Joat thought, as she prudently dropped flat. That didn't block her view of a beer stein sailing through the air and thunking with solid authority between the barkeeper's eyes. He fell backward, and this time stayed down.

Her new business acquaintance had vanished silently. *Good idea,* Joat thought, crawling towards the bar. *Good idea, prudent idea.* The tables were bolted to the floor, providing reasonably safe passage to the thick of things; bodies and pieces of furniture sailed through the air above, and grappling pairs dropped down to her level but couldn't roll past the table legs.

Joat encountered the waitress under one of them, just lighting up the stub of a dream-smoke stick and looking mildly entertained.

"I like the little blond one," she said to Joat, blowing a stream of smoke towards Joseph.

The Bethelite had just kicked a tall humanoid in the crotch, seized his head under one elbow as he bent over—evidently a vulnerable spot in that species, too—and was energetically punching him in the face.

"I got a thing for guys with muscles," the waitress went on. Alvec picked up another yellow-suited spacer and threw him in the direction of the door, clearing a pathway.

"He's married," Joat told her.

"So?"

"Uh," Joat shrugged, "whatever. Have you called Station Security?"

"Oh sure. We got a button under the bar, they'll be here in a couple a minutes." She drew deeply on her dream-smoke stick and offered it to Joat.

Joat shook her head. "No, thanks. I'd better be going."

She crawled under the next table and found herself beside Joseph and Alvec. Joat leaned out and grabbed their sleeves to get their attention.

"We're leaving. Now. Out the back."

"Aw, Joat—" Alvec began.

Another spacer was struggling with a stationer just behind him; the stationer staggered away, clutching at an arm. The spacer waved a long blade and shouted something blurred, lunging wild-eyed for Alvec's back. Joat and Joseph moved with the perfect coordination of dancers; Joat grabbed handfuls of cloth at wrist and shoulder and pulled the attacker forward, redirecting his force and hip-checking him into a sideways stagger. Joseph whirled aside like a matador as the lunge was thrown his way, stepping inside the curve of the out-stretched arm and driving the stiffened fingers of one hand up under the spacer's ribs.

The figure in yellow collapsed, wheezing, and curled into a ball. Joseph toed the knife up against the brass rail and broke it with a quick stamp of his heel.

"Yeah, I see what you mean," Alvec said. "Fun's fun, but knives are cheating. Let's go, Cap'n."

Joat picked up a pseudosilver tray; Alvec picked up a chair and pulled it apart, like tearing the wings off a chicken. That left him with two lengths of gleaming alloy. Joseph walked between them; a knife of his own appeared in one hand, curved and looking sharp enough to cut light. They put their backs together and moved in a rotating circle towards the doors at the rear of the bar, through a kitchen that made Joat glad she hadn't ordered any food, and then through a hatch marked *danger* into an access corridor.

The lights blinked. "*Station Security,*" a voice said, vibrating through the metal of the circular corridor. "*All wrongdoers will cease disturbing the peace and submit to arrest. Station Security—*"

"This way," she gasped.

The access door three spaces down was dogged shut, and she fumbled in her jumpsuit for the picklock. It hung beeping for a nerve-wracking twelve seconds, and then the hatchway hissed open and they tumbled through into a dark and narrow corridor smelling of greasy food and dirty rest rooms. A weedy youth pushing a floater full of dirty plates and glasses stopped and gaped at them, his eyes going wide, and paled at the sight of the weapons.

Joat tossed her tray onto the floater. Behind her she heard a clank as Alvec dropped his chair-legs; Joseph's knife had never made any noise, coming out of the hidden sheath or going back in.

"You never saw us," she said, tucking a half-credit piece into the pocket of a stained white apron.

The chinless face smirked. "Saw who?" he said, and pushed the floater on through a door whose lying stencil read *sanitation*.

"You two go clean up," she snapped, looking at their grazed, bloody faces. "I'll get us a table, and we'll make innocent. *Just* what I needed, arrest on a breaking-the-peace charge with stolen goods on me!"

She pushed through an opaque forcefield door; it was maladjusted, and the harmonics set her teeth on edge. There was a corner table by the wall-window free; it gave an excellent view of Rimrunner's patrons being dragged out of the premises next door by helmeted Station Security police in light-impact armor. Shock-rods snapped amid shrieks and curses; brawlers were lifted and tossed bodily onto the flat-body back of the Black Mariah, where a tanglefield held them in uncomfortable stasis, just as they fell. One of the police was sitting on the pavement with a compress on his flattened nose.

"Hid deb one for be!" he called. A comrade boosted his captive onto the flatbed with an enthusiastic boot.

Joat looked up as the two men returned, and jerked a tight-lipped nod towards the scene.

"I—" Joseph began. Then he looked down at his hands, opening them and closing them once. "He should not have insulted my mother . . ." He looked up. "And there has been no news of the Benisur Amos for more than three weeks. He is my Prophet, my brother, my friend . . . and I have failed him."

Joat sighed and let her shoulders relax. "Okay."

It was Joseph who'd taught her to keep her emotions out of business, though. *Nobody's perfect. I guess learning that's part of growing up.* Even Simeon lost it sometimes, and he *could* control his emotions, literally, by regulating the endocrine feeds to the body inside his Shell.

"You are right, Joat," Joseph admitted. "It was foolish of me and it will not happen again, you have my word."

"Mine too, Boss."

She sighed. "Thank you. And you're right, no harm came of it. Except for your bruises." *And I hope they hurt!* she thought.

She reached over and gripped Joseph's hand. "I realize you're under pressure, Joe. Sorry I snapped at you."

"Hey, Boss, what about me?"

Joat looked at Alvec out of the corner of her eyes and growled softly.

"Yeah," he said, "that's kinda what I figured."

She stood. "Let's go, I want to hustle up a cargo if I can. It won't look good if we leave with an empty hold."

"D'ya mind if Joe and me stick around here and have a few, get acquainted?" Alvec asked. "We're going to be on the same small ship for a long time." He shrugged: "Unless you need us for something?"

"No," Joat said, a little surprised. "Go ahead. Just remember . . ."

"You have my word, Joat," Joseph said firmly, but with a smile.

"Well, see you later then," she said, uneasy.

I trust them not to get into another fight, she realized as she left. It was what the heck *else* they might get up to that worried her. Alvec had a positive gift for trouble, and Joseph was half-crazy with worry over Amos. Rightly so, if Amos was in the hands of the Kolnari.

She didn't believe in the Bethelite hell, but being in the Fist of High-Clan Kolnar was a pretty good approximation.

CHAPTER FIVE

"CLAN LORD," Karak called.

Belazir paused on the threshold of his quarters and turned his head to look coldly at his approaching son.

"May I speak?" Karak asked him.

Belazir considered the request, wondering what aggravation his eldest son had in store for him. Then he surrendered to curiosity, gave a short nod.

"The scumvermin female languishes in her cell, Great Lord, ignored and lonely."

Belazir sighed and turned towards his son, contempt visible on his face.

"When I was your age, child, I too was excited by the terror of the prey. But I am older now and have known the pleasures of conquest often. I refuse to feel *obliged* to take every screaming, worm-colored girl I come across simply because it is expected of me."

Karak's face was expressionless, but the stiffness of his posture told Belazir that he was humiliated by his father's response.

Had his son asked for the girl outright Belazir might well have given her to him. But this behind-the-back way of asking annoyed him. He had never been easy to manipulate and this exceedingly clumsy effort was an insult.

"Leave her to my pleasure, Karak. See to her health and well-being, but do not touch her."

Let the young hot-head chew his spleen over that, Belazir thought

427

in amusement. With a nod to his son he turned and entered his quarters.

Soamosa paced her small cell, seven paces one way, five the other. She counted her steps. She had walked nine thousand one hundred and fifty four steps since waking. The cell was featureless save for its minimal furnishings, a neutral-gray box of ship metal. *Doubtless intended to weaken prisoners by sensory deprivation.*

The thought came to her that she should be praying. That she should find solace on her knees instead of on her feet. But she had tried that and it didn't work. Soamosa found herself praying for things that reminded her of the terrible fate that she and the Benisur Amos and the Captain shared.

At first, the prayers had been for deliverance, and for the safety of the Benisur, and then she had prayed that she not be raped, or locked in and left to starve. With every prayer Soamosa had brought herself closer to mindless panic. And so she paced and counted her steps, to keep her mind cleared and calm. And that worked.

Her back was to the hatch when it opened and she froze. Soamosa had made it her habit since being imprisoned in this cell not to look at the Kolnari who brought her food.

She had found them disturbingly beautiful, uniformly tall and blond, with shapely figures and stern features. Her mother had warned her not to be fooled by their appearance.

"You can tell that they are not human by the way that they despise all that is. If ever you should be so unfortunate as to meet them do not let their beauty blind you. They are devils in the world of flesh, inhumanly cruel and selfish. You dare not look upon them lest you should be lost."

Their leers and gloating remarks had made her all too aware of her torn dress and unbound hair and she had been unable to keep the tears of shame out of her eyes. Her only means of preserving her modesty and her dignity was to keep her back to them when they came.

Besides, she did not want to see their faces as they attacked her; which she knew they might do at any time. She had resolved to keep her eyes closed if it came to that. And she would sing a hymn, the one about smashing the enemies of God like pottery. That would show them what Bethelites were made of.

"Turn around, scumvermin," a stern voice commanded.

Soamosa stiffened, and after a moment complied.

"Look at me, scumvermin."

She bit her lips to keep them from trembling.

"No," she said coolly and clasped her hands before her.

Karak was astounded. It had never occurred to him that this tiny female would defy him. He was honestly puzzled and completely put off his stride by her refusal. What would his father do? And how did he make her obey without touching her? Coercion he knew all too well, of persuasion he was ignorant.

She turned her head away from him and looked up at the ceiling before lowering her eyes again.

"What do you want?" she asked haughtily.

Karak frowned. He'd lost the initiative and must wrest it back from her. *This is not like the simulations.* One did not allow prisoners to ask questions. He felt a spurt of anger. It wasn't as if she was a person.

He stepped close and began to circle her, allowing her to become aware of his bulk and to feel him looming over her.

Soamosa fought her trembling, fought to keep her eyes lowered and her feet firmly in place while her heart hammered and mind demanded run, flee, hide! She could feel the floor vibrate under his heavy tread and the heat from his near-naked body was extraordinary. He felt like a dark sun orbiting her.

The girl wasn't intimidated in the least that Karak could see. She kept her place, her face a mask of cool disdain.

His own face warmed in shame. All of his life he'd been laughed at and called soft because he lacked ambition in the arts of war. "The Poet" his agemates had named him and made his life a hell of mockery. Only his elder brother had befriended him:

"You will be a perfect second to me, brother. We will be a team," so you said. But you died, and I must stand in your place.

A place that everyone, from his father on down, knew he could never fill.

He came to a halt before her, looking down on her and quivering with rage. *Lucky for you I have been forbidden to touch you. Because I would rip you limb from limb.*

He said softly, in a deep uneven voice, "Your dress is very torn."

Soamosa clutched at the worst of the rents in her gown without thinking and she felt the color rise in her face. She was very ashamed.

"Yes," she forced herself to say, "it is."

"Perhaps I should find you something better to wear," he taunted.

"Thank you, that would be very kind," she replied automatically, while her mind screamed in panic, *Be silent! Don't provoke him!*

Karak blinked. She was either very brave or very stupid. Within him curiosity began to bloom and feelings of amusement and admiration mixed. It pleased him to be generous, he decided.

"I shall see to it then," he said and left her without a backwards glance.

Soamosa looked up when she heard the hatch close behind him. She stood staring at it for a long minute with her hands pressed hard against her rib cage, as though to hold in her frantically beating heart.

Then she turned and stumbled to her cot, falling back on it to gaze at the ceiling.

I did it! she thought. *I faced down the enemy without flinching!*

And then she burst into tears.

Belazir laughed until tears ran down his cheeks and he began to choke. At last the spasm passed and the laughter slowed to sighing chuckles until he could once again get his breath. Then he sat smiling before the surveillance screen.

"Perverse," he said to himself, chuckling again. "Utterly perverse. Yet oh so amusing." He knew he should be mortally offended, furious almost beyond his own iron control.

But he had never been close to this particular child of his loins, nor to the wife who had bred him. And the girl had shown incredible spunk, given the circumstances.

He wondered if he was going to kill Karak the next time he saw him.

Belazir knew that, for his honor's sake, he should. *But,* he thought with a sigh, *since The Great Plague ravaged the people we have bred but slowly. Our numbers are as nothing and worse, the children are puny. And Karak has four healthy brats.* He concluded that satisfying his honor with Karak's blood was a luxury the people couldn't afford. *Yet.*

Would that Karak's brother had lived instead. Belazir's lips curled in a wry expression. He had better use for a decent second-in-command than he did for comic relief. On the other hand, the boy's brother would have been a threat.

But he also wanted to see how this foolishness with the scumvermin female played out. He smiled again. His sense of curiosity had always been one of his besetting sins. He decided to indulge it in this case as he could not see any way in which it could become too costly to do so.

He'd intended to amuse himself by experimenting on the girl with the other new drugs he had bought and taunting Simeon-Amos with holos of her reactions. Well, obviously he couldn't use her so and also have her available for amusing episodes with his son.

No matter, he'd have a technician cobble together some sort of holo, extrapolating from the predicted responses that had been described to him.

That would be better, in fact! He wouldn't be distracted and could truly enjoy the Benisur scumvermin's reactions. No doubt opportunities for live experimentation would arise in the course of events; and it would add a certain frisson to known that Amos's despair and anguish were for nothing at all . . .

"Yes," he murmured. "Let him think the scumvermin girl destroyed—and then I shall show her to him, whole and well. And destroy her again!"

Belazir sighed contentedly. *Surely anticipation is one of life's true pleasures.*

I hate my father, Karak son of Belazir thought, as he paced through the corridors of the *Kali*—the Dreadful Bride, his sire's old warship.

A pack of Kolnari children went by, in the wake of something bulge-eyed and long-clawed that squealed and snarled as it ran. They dashed after it with high shrieks of excitement, long razor-sharp knives in their hands. The sight distracted him for an instant; how long had it been since he was an innocent child, with nothing more to concern him than lessons and running down a *drgudak* with his friends? All of five years, now; since he turned eight and came to manhood. The infancy of Kolnar was brief.

I hate my father. What child of the Divine Seed didn't? *But it's worse than that. I hate them all.* He shivered. He was weak, too weak, hiding in his quarters and watching the tapes of the scumvermin female. He told himself it was honest lust, but it was not. *She is weak. Yet she does not despair.* The strangers were like that. His father had thought them weak, when the High Clan took Bethel, when it took SSS-900-C . . . and found that its meal was eating its way back out.

Decision crystallized as he fingered the injector in a pouch. He slapped palm against a communicator.

"Duty officer," he said. "I shall be unavailable for the next hour."

✧   ✧   ✧

"No," Soamosa pleaded, "please don't." Her blue eyes were full of tears and terror.

She was held by two Kolnari, her slender form dwarfed by their muscular height. One of them held out her arm with the inside of her elbow uppermost. Despite her increasingly frantic struggles the arm didn't move. So that when the nozzle of the injector was placed on her arm it was right against a vein.

"Don't, please don't," she was weeping helplessly now. "No! No, NO!"

She tore herself free and huddled in the comer of the room; there were streaks of blood on her arms.

Belazir leaned down and grasped her chin in his huge hand.

"In only a moment, Benisur, it will begin," he said and turned to smile at Amos.

"No!" Soamosa insisted, holding her hands up defensively.

Karak smiled at the gesture, it was completely absurd. Seated beside him she looked like a creature made of gossamer and air, frail as a candle flame. And yet, he knew that she was the one in control. At all of their meetings it was she who had set the tone. Deep within himself, Karak sighed.

"You have nothing to fear from me," he said aloud. "I will not harm you."

Soamosa looked suspiciously at the earnest young Kolnari. Even in the midst of her fear his beauty struck her; and the lost look in the yellow eagle eyes.

"I do not trust you," she said severely.

Karak brushed back his long silver-blond hair distractedly.

"I am concerned for you," he said. "It is terribly dangerous for me to even offer you this protection. If my father knew," his lips tightened, "death would come to me as a friend."

Soamosa narrowed her eyes.

"I do not believe you," she said. "It is some Kolnari trick. My mother told me all about the Kolnari sense of humor."

"Lady," he said and the expression in his eyes firmed. "It is my intention to save you, not to harm you. I will set you free." Karak blinked rapidly and swallowed hard. "And your companions if that is possible. I swear it."

By the sound of his voice, the oath might have been flayed from him. She raised her arm, the inside of her elbow uppermost and he placed the nozzle of the injector unerringly over the vein.

"Now that I've submitted to your injection, you must tell me what it does," Soamosa demanded, radiating poise and dignity and the mysterious power she held over him.

"It will keep you safe from a most dreadful disease," Karak told her. "My father means to use it against your people."

Suddenly, like a splash of cold water, Karak realized that with those words he was forever cast adrift from the Kolnar. He had betrayed them. Even if he failed to save Soamosa and her companions, if it ended here with his leaving her and never returning, he was a traitor. And he was glad. He felt freer than he ever had in his life, liberated from impossible expectations and deeds that he was not proud of. He was free. And the unnameable feeling he bore for this tiny young woman was the cause of it.

Karak leaned forward and Soamosa gasped in alarm. He closed his eyes and very tenderly kissed her forehead in gratitude.

Amos stiffened as the image of Soamosa screamed. Screamed until her mouth sprayed blood, as though she had burst a vein in her throat. And still she screamed, writhing in agony, until at last she lay still, gasping, her eyes rolling back in her head.

Tears ran down Amos's face unchecked. His arms held the weeping Captain Sung who clutched him in terror. The Captain had soiled himself in his fear, not understanding the screaming, nor Amos's soothing words.

"You are evil," Amos murmured, "and you shall be destroyed by your own evil. He shall break you with a rod of iron."

Belazir appeared before him.

"We shall let her rest for a bit," Belazir said in a conversational tone. "Then, if you like, I have some other drugs whose effects might interest you."

Sung whimpered and screwed his head tighter against Amos's ribcage, trying to hide from Belazir.

Amos glared at the Kolnari Lord. "She is only an innocent young girl, Master and God. Why do you torture her so? Is there no pity in you at all?"

Belazir crossed his arms on his chest.

"How can you ask that, scumvermin? Have I not given the Captain there to the only person on this ship who would care for him? It would be more convenient to space him than to feed him."

Amos tightened his grip on the Captain's quivering shoulders.

"Captain Sung has been injured in my service, Master and God," he said humbly. "It is my duty to care for him as best I can."

Belazir's lip curled. "How touching. And he stinks so." Then the Kolnari smiled, he glanced at Soamosa where she lay at his feet. "Why, you have touched me," he said as though in surprise. "I believe that we shall give her a more relaxing injection this time." He looked back at Amos. "It will intensify feelings of pleasure and give her an overwhelming desire to please." He grinned evilly. "So you should enjoy watching this."

Belazir burst out laughing as the image of Amos and the brain-scrubbed spacer faded, to be replaced by his son in the cell of the Bethelite woman. He'd seen sleazy adventure holos created for scum-vermin fools that were more believable than what he was watching.

Belazir pounded the arm of his control couch and shouted laughter. *Ah, the rock-jawed righteousness of that Amos*, he thought. *And Karak, mooning over a piece of walking meat barely fit to serve a moment's pleasure and breed slaves.*

It was pleasant that Amos was totally convinced by the holos his technicians had prepared from a pirated Central Worlds program. There were flaws, but Amos appeared to have missed them. Due, no doubt, to the harrowing content of the recording. And it was exactly the sort of thing Belazir *would* do. Always easier to believe what one expected.

He really would have to think of something suitable as a punishment for Karak. And yet, he wanted to see just how far this . . . romance, for want of a better word, would go.

He sat shaking his head in amazement as he watched Soamosa looking in wide-eyed wonder at Karak's stoic face. Then, tentatively, she placed her small hand on his and smiled.

Belazir began to laugh again as he started the next holo for the Benisur Amos's edification. His youngest wife called from the chamber within:

"How I yearn for you, lord of my life!" There was a waspish note to her voice.

"Anticipation heightens pleasure," he called back, "And silence averts beatings."

Yes. This compendium of erotic fantasies. Tame to Kolnari eyes, but it would torment Amos unceasingly, playing on the insides of his eyelids when he squeezed them closed to shut it out. Run a modification program *here*—

CHAPTER SIX

Mr. va Riguez:

I need to speak to you immediately on a matter of extreme urgency. *Wyal* is scheduled for departure at 03:00. Please contact me before then.

Sincerely,

Captain Simeon-Hap

She should have signed it desperately instead of sincerely, Bros thought, a wry smile playing at the corners of his mouth. He leaned back in the big, faux-leather chair in The Anvil's office. *Still, I'm surprised she said please.* That lonely plea didn't seem to go with the imperious tone of the rest of her note. *Dyson must have taken me at my word.* He'd known the little weasel would.

Sperin had authorized the clerk to fine Joat up to twenty thousand credits. Or at least to *tell* her he was fining her that much. In reality the fine shouldn't be more than five or six thousand. Even that amount would be tough for Joat to scrape together. But *twenty thousand . . .* That was an absolutely staggering fine for any ship, let alone a struggling independent freighter like hers.

Bros grinned. *Ridding her of a fine that size ought to engender a lot of gratitude,* he thought comfortably. Then his pleasure slowly faded. Joat Simeon-Hap wasn't someone he'd like to see broken to the plow, jumping when he snapped his fingers, dancing when he pulled her strings.

He didn't want CenSec to lose her. *But I don't want them to own her soul either.*

Them? he asked himself in mild surprise. He frowned. It had been many years since he'd thought of CenSec as other than *we*, or *I. Some of that girl's independence is rubbing off on me,* he thought ruefully.

"Sal," he said. Getting up he went to the heavy-shouldered man seated at an overburdened desk and dropped Joat's note in front of him. "Take care of this for me, would you? Joat Simeon-Hap's ship, the *Wyal*, has been fined by the station. Pay it out of my special account."

"Sure, Mr. va Riguez, no problem," Sal said. He had a voice like stones grinding together.

Bros picked up his jacket and swung it over his shoulder. "And if Captain Simeon-Hap should call looking for me, you don't know where I am."

"I never do, sir," Sal agreed with a gap-toothed grin.

"But you might ask her if she'd like to leave a message."

Sal's sandy eyebrows went up. "I'm not sure I'm old enough to listen to the kind of language she's liable to use, sir."

Bros chuckled. "You tell her that," he advised.

Sal stared at the door after it had closed behind Sperin, then he glanced at the note again. *I'll take care of it tomorrow,* he thought. *It's not like they charge interest.* He put the note aside and went back to work.

CHAPTER SEVEN

"RAND, I WANT YOU to record this as it plays, all right?"

"Certainly, Joat. I had intended to anyway," Rand said. There was a faintly injured tone to the AI's voice.

"All right, people, got your note screens ready?" Joseph and Alvec nodded. "Well, okay, it's showtime!"

Joat entered the datahedron Bros Sperin had given her and keyed it up. For a few moments, as a fluid computer voice relayed the facts of Nomik Ciety's life, the only sound was the click of styli as they took notes. But with the first holo snap, Joat looked up, and froze.

Her heartbeat speeded up until all she could hear was the sound of her own blood rushing. Pounding through her, beating against her fingertips, pulsing in her temples. Her sight narrowed to a tunnel sparked with black and white.

When at last she took another breath it roared in her ears like a cyclone.

Nomik Ciety, Nomik . . . Ciety. The face on the screen shifted from the scrawny, mad-eyed youth with a number across his chest to a grown man's, well dressed and smooth. A respectable businessman to all appearances, with a friendly smile and a twinkle in his eye. Her own blond hair, face a little angular. Cheekbones like those that greeted her every morning in the screen.

Uncle Nom, she thought. *You're not dead! I was so sure you were dead.* She felt numb now, and her heart rate was returning to normal.

It was in the nature of humankind, to believe in what they most deeply wished to be true.

Joat closed her eyes and took a slow, quiet deep breath. *Amos comes first,* she thought desperately.

But memory bubbled up, eating away at the failing barrier of her will. She tightened her fist around the stylus, gripping it like a life-line.

The part of her he'd betrayed screamed in frustrated rage: *You were only seven! You were just a baby and he sold you to that sick bastard!*

She was looking back at Uncle Nom as a big, smelly, shambling man led her away, his grip like a clamp on her skinny arm. Uncle Nom was waving and smiling.

"Bye-bye," he called.

"Uncanom," she heard her own thin, little girl's voice call out, "Uncle *Nom!*" Tears blurred her vision.

She blinked, her jaw was clenched so hard the muscles jumped and she felt sweat begin to bead her upper lip. Joat took a deep breath, trying to keep control. Trying to deny what she felt, because it was joy. Sheer, undiluted joy; a savage intensity of feeling that nothing in her life had ever rivaled.

How nice that you're not dead, Uncle Nom, she thought, fighting back a giggle. Knowing that she wouldn't be able to stop if she started. *And then they'd ask questions. I don't want any questions.*

Uncle Nom was hers. All hers. *My toy to break,* she thought with gleeful viciousness.

But she didn't have to hurry. Now she knew about him. There was no way he could hide from her, no place in all the worlds.

Don't look back, she warned herself. *There's nothing back there that isn't going to cut you.*

The reminder didn't work . . .

It was dark and she was huddled in a tiny space, a space that soon would be too small for her to hide in. She starved herself so that she could still fit, because he couldn't reach her here. There was a crash of metal on metal.

"Come on out you little wharf-rat! You're only makin' it worse!" His voice rose to a hoarse shout at the end that promised broken bones.

There was a rattle then, and with a clatter the cover over the air duct fell away to reveal the captain's fleshy, red face. He glared down at her, teeth gritted, breathing in a harsh rasp. Then he pulled back, thrusting his arm in to make a grab at her. Joat plastered herself against the duct, breathing in to make a hollow of her stomach. The blunt fingertips just brushed her clothing.

He pulled his arm out with a cry of rage and smashed his fist against the wall. Then his face appeared again.

"You'd better come out, little girl," he sang softly, with the purr of madness underneath. It was very bad when he stopped shouting and went quiet. "Or you're gonna be sooorryyy."

And she knew that she had to leave her shelter and let him have her. Or he'd seal her in. He'd done that once before and . . .

A hot hand touched her and she started with an angry hiss, turning to glare into Joseph's puzzled eyes.

"Jeeeezzz, Joe! Don't *do* that!"

"I am sorry," he said. "I spoke and you did not answer. I did not mean to startle you."

"Sorry," she said curtly. "What did you want?"

"I said that this man is more dangerous than I had expected. I am uneasy allowing you to take all of the risk in this matter."

"I'm not helpless, Joe! And I'm not Rachel, so don't even try to treat me like I am! I don't appreciate it."

She saw surprise in the way his eyebrows quivered, then settled down. *For Joe that marked a profound change of expression.*

Joat sighed, a little ashamed of her outburst. "I see nothing in this recording that gives us a reason to change our plans at this late date. Especially since our plans were to play it by ear and see what happens. You can't *be* more flexible than that, Joe."

"As you say, Joat," he murmured.

Joseph caught Alvec's eye over Joat's head. An imperceptible nod confirmed his judgment. He had never seen Joat afraid, in all the years he had known her—not even when the Kolnari occupiers had walked the corridors of SSS-900-C. *Or could she fear for her ship?* That was more than danger, it was a threat to her dream.

"Joat," he began tentatively, "if you cannot pay the fine to New Destinies what will you do?"

"Lose the ship," she said succinctly, and shrugged. "My fault entirely. The fine thing really wasn't such a good idea."

"Whatsisname, that guy?" Alvec said. "He'll take care of it, right?"

"Sperin?" she asked. Joat made a moue. "I'd feel better about that if he'd bothered to get back to me. But if I'm lucky he's already dealt with it." *And if he hasn't I'm beached.*

"Can you not simply change *Wyal's* name and your name and begin again in another quadrant of space? Surely you need not meekly surrender to them? If worst comes to worst, you can return to Bethel with me and we will shelter you." He saw her look aside and blink.

"Thanks," she said quietly, in his language. Then she took a deep breath and went on: "First, I'm not ducking out on Amos, whatever it costs. Second, I *can't* welch—not without losing my reputation; and this'll have gone out on the unofficial net too; they'd be after me like a sicatooth after a goat if I don't pay up, not to mention the bounty hunters." She paused reflectively. "You know how it is."

They nodded, and Alvec grunted agreement. You might get away with cheating the above-ground companies, but not the underworld. They had a primitive, straightforward approach to those who tried to cheat them.

"You don't seriously think I'd risk visiting your wife and children with bounty hunters on my tail, do you?"

"No," Joseph said and smiled.

"Besides, if I ran, then I'd never see Simeon or Channa again. It's not worth it." She stood and looked around the control cabin. "And," she went on, her hands closing into fists behind her back, "they're not even close to getting *Wyal* yet. We're going to Schwartztarr, and then on to Rohan."

Bros Sperin leaned back from the screen. *So, she's gone.* According to her itinerary Schwartztarr was her destination. *And she's carrying a really weird cargo, going by the manifest.* Most likely she was also carrying something Central Worlds would rather she wasn't. Little Ms. Simeon-Hap was nothing if not enterprising.

Uncertainty tickled his mind like a cat playing with a piece of string. *She can take care of herself,* Bros told himself. *Don't try second guessing yourself at this late date. She's capable.*

Capable of unraveling his carefully made plans. She was like chaos on two feet when she put her mind to it. He knew felinoid species who thought more before they leaped. *Of course,* he had to admit, *like them, she tends to land on her feet.*

But if she wanted to live long in this business, she was going to have to learn some caution. *And some tact.* He grinned, Sal had told him a few stories.

Bros liked Joat enough to want her to live a very long time indeed. He'd especially liked the Joat he'd met on the bridge of her ship; she'd been more spontaneous, more natural.

The universe would be a far less interesting place without that young woman in it.

He shook his head. The idea had been to lock up a loose cannon while he did the real work. Joat was supposed to merely observe. *But having gotten a look at her style up close and personal, I wonder if she's even capable of doing something so passive as simply looking.*

Nomik Ciety *was* involved with the Kolnari. To what degree Sperin had no idea. *I suspect that he's up to his neck in them,* he thought disgustedly. But Bros had long ago trained himself not to treat his suspicions as evidence. *And if he is working with them he's being very discreet.*

It was a calculated risk, sending her after a man like Ciety. Still, given his relatively exalted status on Rohan, he should be a perfect choice for Joat to investigate; a personage all but inaccessible to a lowly freighter captain on her first smuggling run.

And yet . . .

"Enough," Sperin said aloud. *While she leaves a streak across the troposphere, I'll do my entry . . . nice and slow and inconspicuous.*

CHAPTER EIGHT

"WHAT WAS IN those cargo modules?" Alvec asked.

Joat smiled and touched a control. A chime rang through the *Wyal's* bridge.

"Beyond gravity well limits," Rand's impersonal voice said. "Prepare for transition. Three minutes and counting."

"That's for me to know, and you to guess," she said smugly. "Got the destination data ready?"

"Schwartztarr system," Alvec said, tossing a datahedron in one hand. "Why do you want to stop there?"

"It's on the way . . . and I think it might be useful," she said.

"Ten seconds."

"You're the boss."

"Damned right. Prepare to cheat Einstein . . . *now*."

The *Wyal* twisted itself out of congruence with the sidereal universe.

Schwartztarr was the fourth planet of a G6 sun, a little brighter than Sol-standard. *I've never seen Earth's sun,* Joat thought idly as they dropped into normal space. Schwartztarr's star was pinpoint bright in the screens; the schematics showed the nine planets of the system and a running list of in-system traffic, interstellar ships, habitats and space-based fabricators.

Not very much, for a system that had been settled as long as this one. Surprisingly sparse, in fact, for a place with a settled planet bearing a breathable atmosphere. She called up data on the main screen.

Well, that explains it. Sort of large planet, gravity 1.2 standard, with a single large continent in the northern polar-to-temperate zone. Rather far out, so it was cold despite the active sun, and with a fairly steep axial tilt. Long cold winters, and the rest of the system was middling-average. The file showed a few scenes from those winters, and Joat shivered slightly, the reflex of someone who'd spent almost all of her life in the climate-controlled environment of ships and Stations. The people in the vid were wrapped up like bundles, with powered heaters underneath. Another shot showed something with eight short clawed legs, long white fur, red eyes and a head that was mostly mouth filled with long pointed teeth. Whatever-it-was was resting its front pair of legs on something much larger and dead, ripping chunks off and bolting them. Then it looked up at the camera and gave an amazing snarl, with its jaws open at least ninety degrees.

Joat shuddered again. "Remind me never to go outside on Schwartztarr," she said.

Joseph had come onto the bridge, toweling down his bare torso after a spell in the exerciser. Muscle rippled under the smooth olive skin of his chest as he stopped beside her command couch. *Not bad,* she thought. Joe was an uncle, so the thought was pretty theoretical—but Alvec caught her eye and winked.

"That beast looks like it would make interesting hunting," the Bethelite said, nodding to the screen.

Joat hid a grimace of distaste. Bethel *was* the boondocks, and they had some pretty grody customs there.

"But what," he went on, "is that fluffy white material all over the ground?"

"Snow," Alvec said, from the assistant/engineer's couch. At Joseph's raised eyebrow: "Flakes of frozen water that fall from the sky."

"Ah!" Joseph leaned further forward. "But why doesn't it melt?"

"Because the temperature is below the freezing point of water."

"The God preserve us!" he said. "I had heard of such things on high mountains, but . . ."

Joat glanced at him. The furrow of hard concern faded for a moment from between his eyes; he looked like a boy, smiling at wonders. It was only an instant, but it made the pain and worry more obvious when they returned.

"Hey, Boss," Alvec said. "What landing vector do y'want to cut?"

"Standard—Capriana Spaceport. There's not much else here, here. Rand's taking us in, it needs the practice."

"Rand?" Alvec's face went carefully blank.

"*I fixed* the program," she said defensively.

"We've worked on it together," Rand assured him, "I'm certain we've worked the bugs out of it. And I've studied several hundred landings by you and by Joat; I've also exchanged information with several other AIs of my acquaintance. I'm confident that all will be well this time."

"It's different from docking at a station," Alvec said nervously. "You do a real good station docking."

"Thank you," Rand said, its lights flickering blue.

"But I think one of us should co-pilot you until you get the landing stuff perfect. No offense."

"None taken." The AI's tones were always neutral, but that sounded a little flatter than usual.

"It'll be perfect, Al," Joat said through gritted teeth. "It wasn't even Rand's fault the last time, it was the way my program interfaced with that fardling, wonky . . ."

"Just in case . . ." he insisted.

"If you would not mind, Joat," Joseph put in delicately. "You understand . . . I travel by spaceship so seldom . . . the conversation has made me a little, ah . . ."

Joat shrugged. "Sure. OK."

"Why not use a commercial program?" Alvec grumbled, settling into his crash-couch and fastening the restraint harness. "There's dozens of 'em available. Cheap too!"

"Rand is unique," Joat said stiffly. "And I want it to stay that way."

"When it's my butt, I sort of like *standard* and *tried and tested* as opposed to *unique*. You know what I mean, Boss?"

"You trust me," she countered.

Alvec sighed. "You may be unique, Boss, but you've also got a license."

"Point taken," she said quietly. "And since I've already agreed to let you co-pilot, can we drop the subject?"

"So . . ." Alvec said into the silence that followed. "You managed to scare up a cargo after all, eh, Boss?"

"Yup."

After a long pause he asked, "So . . . what are we shippin'?"

There was a longer pause, then Joat answered: "Laser tube guides."

"Lasers?"

"Yup."

"You're shipping laser tubes to Schwartztarr?"

"Yup."

"You're kidding?"

"What is it?" Joseph asked. "What is wrong?"

"Lasers're all they make here. It's their main industry," Alvec said. "I can't believe . . ."

"They were cheap, and it's my money, okay?"

"You *bought* them?"

"Al," she said warningly.

"You're right," Alvec soothed, "someone'll want 'em."

"Attention Central Worlds freighter, this is Schwartztarr traffic control, please identify yourself."

Alvec leapt for the com like a drowning man after a lifeline. His stubby fingers touched the controls with an odd, butterfly delicacy.

"Cleared," traffic control said. *"Planetary approach, Tarrstown spaceport. Welcome to the Schwartztarr system."*

"Yes, welcome," Joseph murmured. He had slid into the vacant navigator's couch. "Joat, observe."

Joat slaved a screen to the scanners the Bethelite was using. "A ship . . . oh."

Alvec leaned over. "Got a neutrino signature like a cathouse billboard," he observed. "Either they're leaking, or . . ."

"Corvette-class engines," Joseph said. "Very similar to the ones the Prophet bought for our in-system patrol craft."

Joat grinned. "I think we've left respectability behind."

The *Wyal* buffeted as they slid down their vector towards the outer fringes of the atmosphere. Screens began to fog as the hull compressed gas into a cloud of ionized particles. Joat's fingers itched to touch the controls; she wrapped them around the arms of her crash-couch instead. Alvec was kneading a fisted right hand into the palm of his left.

"Cloud cover," the AI's metallic-smooth voice said. "We're down to suborbital velocity. Hull temperatures within parameters." It paused. "Ground is at minus twenty, wind seventy kilometers per hour." Another pause. "Down to suborbital speeds. Exterior view on."

Alvec gave an exaggerated shiver as the largest screen cleared to show a swirling mass of storm cloud. The hull toned again as they plunged into it, a different note from the stress of high-altitude reentry.

"*Brrr.*"

A moment later he yelped and reached for the controls. Joat stretched out her own arm and touched him on the shoulder. The *Wyal* rang as if a thousand medium-sized mad gods were pounding on it with their fists.

"Let Rand handle it. Rand, what is that?"

"Frozen water," the computer said. "Nodes of from millimetric to centimetric size, at high velocity."

Joseph's brows rose. "Hail?"

"Yes, hail."

The exterior screens showed darkness shot with lightning and massive winds. Joat felt the skin along her spine creep. The hazards of space were orderly, compared to this; *Wyal* had the capacity for atmosphere transit, but it seemed unnatural, somehow.

They broke through the cloud cover at three thousand meters above their destination. The spaceport was a cleared space of a few square kilometers, set in a sea of green broken only by white-rimmed inlets— the scene twisted mentally, and she realized that it was a forest, fretted by fjords of the sea. Tarrstown lay along several of those arms, its street-patterns bright against the darkening landscape. Snow blew by, nearly horizontal in the gale. A spot on the concrete of the landing field began to strobe.

"Don't believe in luxuries like gantries or tiedowns here," Alvec grumbled. "We'll have to keep the drive hot or get blown over."

"Nope, there's a mobile unit coming out," Joat said, tapping the screen. "Guess they don't have enough traffic to justify the cost of fixed installations. Lots of worlds don't—"

She broke off with an oath that put Joseph's eyebrows up again. Something had slammed into the hull, not enough mass to feel but enough to make the plating ring. Several more somethings followed.

"What *is* that?"

The exterior screen split. A central panel showed something dirty-white and about ten meters from wingtip to wingtip closing fast on the pickup. That went black as it was covered, and then showed flashes of teeth and slaver as whatever-it-was tried to gnaw its way through the metal.

"Not too bright," she said, forcing herself to relax—her arms had been trying to push her body back through the couch in instinctive reflex.

"But hungry," Joseph observed thoughtfully.

"Very hungry," Alvec concurred.

The winds were slower below the clouds; the ship slid downwards as if it were following an invisible string in the sky. Snow blasted away from the landing site, and there was a rumble and clank as the seldom-used leg-jacks extended from their pods in the stern.

"*Adjusting to planetary gravity.*" Weight came down on them, a sluggish feeling. "There," Rand said, "I told you that we'd perfected the program."

"Yeah, well, conditions were pretty smooth," Alvec said grudgingly. "But I guess you did okay."

"Thank you," Rand and Joat said simultaneously.

Smooth? Joat thought wryly. *Conditions were pretty smooth? I hope I never find out what you'd consider rough, buddy.*

"It's nice to know you still have *some* faith in me," she said aloud.

"What do we do now?" Joseph asked.

"Well, you guys can go play," Joat told them. "Rand and I will wait for our contact." She put her feet up on the console and leaned back in her chair, arms behind her head: "To contact us."

"What about selling our cargo?" Alvec asked.

"Don't be silly, Al. Who ever heard of shipping laser tubes to Schwartztarr?"

Joat watched the ground-crawler take the two men towards the buildings at the edge of the spaceport. It was a long low flatbed, born on a dozen man-high wheels, with an armored cab at both ends; a heavy laser was mounted on a scarf-ring above each of the cabs. As she watched the crawler fade into the blowing snow one of the gunners swiveled his weapon and fired into the brawling whiteness. The beam itself was invisible, but it cut a tunnel of exploding steam through the snow. At the far end something unseen gave a screaming bellow that faded into a series of snarls.

"Nice planet," Joat said.

"Low salubrity rating," Rand replied seriously. "Nice compared to Kolnar, maybe. There is a man requesting entrance."

"Let him in," she said.

✧   ✧   ✧

"What do you mean, five thousand?"

The man sitting across from Joat was almost a clone of the man who'd first contacted her; pale, thin, with a beard. The bulky furs and the snow melting on them were different, as was the heavy explosive-bullet slug-thrower he cradled in one arm.

He shrugged his narrow shoulders and said with a sneer: "That's what my principals have authorized me to pay you. Take it or leave it. But, uh, you're goin' to owe me something if you leave it."

"Oh?"

"Yeah, you were given an advance to cover shipping expenses. Remember."

"I agreed to do this for twenty-five thousand, plus shipping expenses. If you've decided to shortchange me on this you're the one breaking the contract, not me." Joat glared at him and added mentally, *You oily little weasel.*

"Contract!" He laughed explosively, leaning back in his chair. "What, somebody signed a contract for this? You think I'm stupid?"

"It's implied," she said evenly. "A verbal contract is still a valid contract."

"So take us to court! You got a case, right? So sue us. Just tell the judge that you agreed to ship stolen information for a ridiculous amount of credits and we only want to pay you a part of it. You can't lose!"

Joat schooled her face to cold disdain, an expression Channa had taught her. The courier seemed to find it excruciatingly funny. At last he looked away, waving a pleading hand.

"Ooh, ooh this has gotta stop, ooh wow!" He shook his head and grinned. "Look," he said reasonably. "If you decide not to take the five thousand and to keep the datahedron, all you got is something you can't use and you can't sell and you're out five thousand. Plus, you owe me two thousand." He stopped and glared at her through narrowed eyes. "And lady, you *will* pay me that two thousand. So where does that leave you? Broke on Schwartztarr with a cargo load of laser tubes. Nobody here is going to buy laser crystals! I'm not stupid, y'know."

"I *know* that nobody on Schwartztarr is going to buy the fardling laser crystals. I'm not stupid either. If the authorities want to think I'm a moron, fine, let 'em. But you *know* why I'm here, so what's your excuse?"

"Okay," he said in astonishment holding his hands up palms out.

"C'mon, you had to know that twenty-five thousand was way too high for a low-risk job like this, huh? You're not stupid, right? Look, you can only lose here. Just take the credits and maybe I can find you somethin' else to do for us. Huh?"

Joat glared at him, her lips a tight line. Then she nodded.

"But I want payment now."

"Okay," he said sullenly.

She called up the branch of her bank that did business on Schwartztarr and spoke the keying phrase that opened up an account, then hit a key that transmitted her account number and the location of the home branch along with her account's most recent update in a single rapid burst. Withdrawals, of course, were much more complex.

Her contact slid over to her terminal and entered a credit chip, transmitting authorization to delete five thousand from it and transfer it to her account.

She handed him the datahedron.

"I don't like being cheated," she told him.

"No, well, life's a lesson, y'know. Separates the smart from the stupid," he said. His grin disappeared behind goggles and face-mask as he fastened his parka.

Joat stood and followed him down through the corridors.

"Sayonara, stupidissimo," she muttered as the hatch closed behind him. "Think he bought it?" she asked Rand.

"He gave every indication of doing so. What will his reaction be when he discovers what we've done?"

"Violent, I expect," Joat said. "Why do you think I locked the hatch?"

She picked up a note screen and stylus and sat down facing her largest screen. "Play the recording of that Nomik Ciety hedron, would you, Rand?"

Rand began playing back the recording and Joat sat quietly, scribbling a note now and then on her belt unit. The hedron described Ciety's lifestyle and career, noting that very little was known of his past; presently he seemed to be living up to the Middle-Level Organized Crime stereotype. There was a long section on his known associates and henchmen which also lacked significant background information.

As the information rolled by, augmented by numerous holos of Ciety and his people, Joat struggled to concentrate. Now that the

BJ's

T.P.
Cranberries
Lady Soap
Hot Choc
Inst Bfst
Auto Dish Soap
Crackers
Pace

syrup
coffee

Knee
___

cat food
litter

ret DVD

shock of rediscovering him was past, she was able, to a degree, to achieve an emotional distance from the man on the screen.

When it was over she sat for a while, her face expressionless, and stared into space, struggling to keep the memories out.

Amos first! she told herself fiercely over and over. *Amos must come first!*

"They've obviously spent a great deal to erase their early histories," Rand observed.

Joat blinked and nodded.

"Yes," she agreed leadenly.

"You were most inattentive the first time we played this, Joat. That's quite unlike you," it observed.

She turned her chair to look at it. Its lights were a flickering mix of colors—Rand's "neutral" face.

"You noticed that?" she murmured.

"I don't think the others did," Rand hastened to reassure her. "But you became quite pale for a moment, and when Joseph touched you, your reaction was uncharacteristically violent. Just now your heartbeat is elevated. Is there something we should know?"

"Maybe," she said thoughtfully. "I'll have to think about it."

"You're a good cook, Joe," Joat yawned.

"It is a manly skill," Joseph answered seriously, sliding the sausages onto her plate.

"Alvec?"

"He will return later." Joseph waved the frying pan under the cleaner, then racked the utensil. "Joat . . . he went away with this woman that he met. She was an amazon, Joat, truly. As tall as Amos and as muscular as I am. She had an expression on her face that had me stammering an apology the instant that I saw it."

"What'd you do?" Joat asked, interested.

"Nothing. I *knew* that I had done nothing to offend her, but still, *I'm sorry* came dribbling out of my mouth before I could stop myself. And then Alvec introduced her as his Rose and she melted. She giggled and covered her mouth with her hand like a shy maiden, and she blushed bright pink! If you saw her, Joat, you would imagine that such a woman would have to think hard for a good five minutes to even remember *how* to blush." He paused for a moment. "Do you know, she could have been the sister of the Rose he met on New Destinies."

Smiling fondly, Joat nodded.

"Yeah, they're a lot alike, every Rose in his 'bouquet'—that's Al's term for the bunch of them—is just like the next one. Y'know, he's stayed friends with all of 'em, and there must be scores of them by now." She shook her head. "You're right, it's remarkable."

"Has he ever failed in his wooing?" Joseph asked.

"Not that I'm aware of. See, he's completely sincere, he really adores his Roses." She grinned. "That's very seductive."

"Ah, yes, I do see." He pursed his lips thoughtfully. "I do not think that I would be so easily seduced though."

Joat suppressed a smile, thinking, *How the heck would you know? After the dance Rachel led you, would you even recognize a seduction that didn't include a slap in the face?*

"Are you susceptible to romance, my friend?" Joseph prodded.

She folded her hands on her stomach and stared at the ceiling thoughtfully.

"Oh, I suppose I enjoy a nice episode of boot-licking flattery as much as the next person. But I'm not inclined to let it turn my head like Al's Roses do. I'm no kind of flower when you come right down to it."

"I think of my Rachel as an althea," Joseph murmured, his face dreamy. "A flower of very subtle beauty."

Joat blinked. Joseph as a romantic was always a revelation to her. And to be honest, Rachel's beauty was of a very subtle order indeed, for Joat herself had never seen it.

"All women resemble some flower," he insisted. "Even you, my friend."

"Yeah, well, maybe one of those flesh eating ones," Joat conceded, grinning. She shook her head ruefully. "You know, I think you're all incredibly brave."

Joseph looked at her questioningly.

"Channa and Amos," she clarified. "And you. I can't see how you do it, no matter how much it hurts, you just keep coming back for more. It amazes me."

He still looked puzzled.

"Amos and Channa's love does bring them pain," he agreed. "But it also blesses them with much joy. As to myself, you puzzle me, my friend. I am very happily married. Why do you include me in your number of the brave?"

"I was thinking of the early days of your relationship with Rachel.

Everything is great now, but I haven't forgotten the sight of her hitting you in the face 'till her hand bled."

He cocked his head at her.

"I must ask you to be fair, Joat. My Rachel was not at her best at the time."

Joat spluttered into her coffee.

"You have a gift for understatement, Joe. I think you're brave because no matter what she did, no matter what she said, no matter how much it hurt you, you were there for her and you never stopped loving her." Her eyes revealed the puzzled amazement that she always felt when she thought about this. "I can't imagine leaving myself open like that. I can't help but think, what's the *matter* with these people, do they like pain and misery? Oh, and let's not forget the humiliation."

Joseph smiled at her warmly.

"It is just that you have never been in love, my friend. When you are in love even pain can seem sweet if it allows you a glimpse of your beloved. I will pray that you may know it soon."

"Gee, thanks Joe," she said dryly. "I'll pray for your mental health too. Wha . . . !"

Alvec had suddenly leapt into the galley where they were sitting, arms open wide he began to sing:

"Her skin is soft and tender as the petals of a rose
and her eyes are as bright as the dew.
Come into my arms, O my Rose of the stars
and I swear I will always love you."

Joat raised an eyebrow.

"Had a good time did you?"

Alvec put his hand over his heart, closed his eyes and sighed.

"I did," he shook his head, smiling, "I really did."

As Joat muttered, "Nuts . . . , you're all nuts!" he bounded over to a cupboard and pulled out a coffee, peeled back the heat seal and inhaled as steam rose in a fragrant puff.

"Mmm mm," he said and took a sip. "So! How'd it go, Captain?"

She grimaced. "About as we expected. We were royally cheated. He only paid me five thousand credits and told me it was a life lesson. Can you believe it?"

Alvec scowled and shook his head sadly.

"The nerve'a some people. What's the universe comin' to, when even smugglers and gunrunners can't be relied on?"

"I am a little surprised that we have not heard back from them by now," Joseph said. "In my experience, such people are not inclined to merely shrug philosophically and go on to the next thing."

Joat grimaced and shrugged.

"It was either going to be an immediate reaction," Rand said. "Or not. For all we know he took it off-planet."

Alvec rolled his eyes.

"Bite your tongue! If you had one," he said. "If that's the case we might not hear from them for months. And we sure can't afford to wait around here for someone to get around to getting mad at us."

"No," Joat said looking a little lost, "we can't. I hadn't really thought of no one coming after us at all."

"Oh, do not worry, Joat, Alvec," Joseph said sympathetically, "I am certain that very soon a heavily armed and angry band of smugglers will be beating upon your hatch crying out for your blood. You mustn't lose faith."

Joat laughed, but before she could speak, Rand broke in.

"In fact, there is a party approaching *Wyal* now, Joat. I have them onscreen on the bridge. Come and have a look at them."

The day had dawned with the aching clarity of deep cold; the sky was a pale blue-green arch above, with both moons full and looking like translucent globes on the horizon. On the main screen was a view of a very expensive landcar just pulling to a stop at the base of the *Wyal,* crisp snow squeaking under its wheels. Both front doors opened and from each a man with the squat, square build of a heavy-worlder emerged. They advanced with the economic efficiency of battle cruisers and their heads swung like gun turrets, ceaselessly examining their surroundings for any threat.

One stumped over to the rear door of the glossy landcar and opened it. A woman emerged.

Alvec gave a long whistle. "Not my type," he said. "But that's *something.*"

"It is hard to believe she is of the same species as her guards," Joseph said seriously.

"All of that party are *homo sapiens,*" Rand said.

Alvec snorted. "You wouldn't understand."

Her long black hair lay in a thick, glassy braid on her shoulder, its color stark against the pale green of her exquisitely cut thermal suit. She moved towards the *Wyal* with the grace of flowing water.

All three of them wore wraparound eye protection against Schwartz-tarr's harsh sun. As one, they raised their heads to study *Wyal*'s height.

"A living cliché," Joat said, feeling an odd mixture of awe and amusement. "You fellas reel in your tongues, now."

She knew the woman. Her name was Silken—no known last name—she was Ciety's second in command, his lover, according to CenSec. A gangster's "moll" and her "torpedoes" in ancient Earth parlance.

"She's a nice lookin' girl," Alvec said judiciously.

Joat grinned over her shoulder at him. "But she's no Rose, am I right?"

"No, ma'am."

"She is no althea, either," Joseph said with a grim smile.

"Permission to board," the woman said, as though repeating a formula rather than making a request. Her voice was soft and pleasant. Her companions waited with a boulder patience that somehow had an edge of spring-steel readiness.

"This is Captain Simeon-Hap. May I ask your business?"

Silken took off her glasses and stared into the pickup. "I'm sure you know who I am, as well as why I'm here. I'd prefer to discuss our business in private—you know why, as well."

Well, Joat thought. *Right to the point.*

"And I'm sure that you'll understand Ms. . . ." Joat paused to allow the woman to introduce herself. After a moment of silence she continued: "Uh, that your companions make me nervous."

The beautiful face smiled. "If we were here to hijack you, Captain, I assure you, you wouldn't be aware of us until we were on your bridge. However, there *is* a limit to how much openness I'd consider healthy for both of us. I repeat, we need to talk."

"I'm unwilling to allow either of your companions to board."

"Don't be ridiculous. I'm not going up there alone!"

"We're not about to kidnap you, lady, not so . . . openly," Joat said sarcastically.

"You have two crewmen aboard," the woman said, her eyes flashing. "I'm not willing to be alone under those circumstances."

"My crew are trained to stand a watch, distribute cargo, fill out manifests and keep the ship functioning. Your friends appear to have benefited from . . . another kind of training altogether." *Like how to turn people's heads around so they can look down between their shoulder blades.* Aloud she said, "May I suggest a compromise?"

"Please. Do."

"One of your people stays with your landcar, one stays by the lock with my crewmen, and you join me on the bridge for a private talk."

The woman considered it. Joat thought she was going to refuse, then she put her glasses back on decisively and nodded.

"All right. That's acceptable."

Joat keyed the lift, raising her other hand to still the protests. "With you masters of self-defense on hand, what do I have to worry about?"

"Energy weapons, capture, torture, death," Joseph suggested.

"Masters!" Alvev said. "Oh, good. I would've been *worried* if I didn't know that."

"Go on and meet them," Joat said. She put a hand on each rocklike shoulder and shoved gently. "I'm a big girl now."

She should have been in the vids, Joat thought. *That entrance was a masterpiece.* As if Silken entering a room automatically made her the most important thing in it.

"Yes?" the Captain of the *Wyal* said after a moment's silence.

Silken simply stood in the center of the room and held up the blue datahedron that Joat had transported. Her gaze stayed unfocused, only the tapping of one slim booted foot demanding attention.

It's times like this I'm really *glad I'm a woman,* Joat thought complacently.

Joat reclined in the pilot's crash-couch, her legs crossed, hands loosely clasped on her stomach. She raised a brow and spoke again, with just a shade more emphasis:

"Yes?"

After a moment Silken sighed in irritation. She put one hand on her hip and flicked the datahedron with one manicured nail.

"This," she said, "is garbage."

"No," Joat assured her, "it's good."

Silken turned slowly towards her, between clenched teeth she asked, "Then why can't I read it?"

"You can't read it because it scrambles every time you try to access it." Joat blinked at her and beamed an innocent smile. "It can be fixed very easily."

"Then I suggest that you do so." Silken held the hedron out to her and walked towards the pilot's station.

Hey, nice slink, Joat thought. *Pity it's wasted on me—I wonder if I could learn to walk like that?*

"There is a problem," Joat said regretfully, ignoring Silken's out-stretched hand. "Your agents shortchanged me."

"I don't see how that's my concern," Silken told her, simply opening her fingers and dropping the datahedron into Joat's lap. Raising one exquisite brow she asked: "You're not trying to shake me down for more credits, are you?" Then she leaned towards Joat until their faces were mere inches apart. "You couldn't possibly be that stupid." Her green eyes narrowed dangerously. "Could you?"

Joat looked back at her. "Would you please get out of my face?" she asked politely.

Silken straightened in surprise. Then she laughed. "You *must* be crazy! Don't you know who I am?"

Joat felt an almost pleasant rush of nostalgia. *Stationer kids on the docks used to act that way.* Expecting you to know and genuflect to their little play hierarchy; and they didn't know squat about the really important shipside ones.

"Actually, no, I don't know who you are, since you haven't both-ered to introduce yourself." Joat waved that aside. "Not that it mat-ters. What matters is, I negotiated my fee for delivery of this little treasure right at the outset. When I arrived here I was due twenty-five thousand credits."

Silken's face reflected her disbelief.

"You can't be serious," she said scornfully. "The job wasn't worth that! No one would agree to that figure."

"Look." Joat held up her hands. "I put my ship and my reputa-tion on the line when I took your shipment; and I deliver on time and in good condition—it's all in my record. If reliability like that is too expensive, then no, you *shouldn't* be doing business with me. I fulfilled my side of the bargain. I am now owed twenty thousand credits. Upon receipt of the outstanding amount, you will receive your shipment. Unscathed. That's it."

Silken must have realized that her mouth was open because she closed it with an audible *clop.*

"You're . . . serious," she whispered, and shook her head in won-der. "Well," she said and looked around for someplace to sit down, "this is refreshing."

Joat looked at her sympathetically. "Honest dealing saves so much time!" she said earnestly. "Had I been paid, you wouldn't be here; you'd be accessing that hedron." She placed a hand on her chest. "But you must see that I can't allow myself to be cheated, it sets a bad precedent. And think about it, if he cheated me, he's cheating you."

"Of course he's cheating me," Silken said with a condescending little moue. She settled herself with catlike delicacy onto the navigator's chair. "Everyone cheats in this business."

"Not me," Joat said. "That's a fool's game and I don't have time for it. You can accomplish a lot more if you're not dividing your energy that way." She looked the other woman in the eye. "Pay me and I can clear that data in a few seconds. I'd like to do that for you."

Silken narrowed her green eyes. "Do you know what I can do to you?" she asked.

Now, that was a mistake. You *should do* menace *cold,* You *don't have the facial bones for direct threats.* In fact, she looked a little like an angry kitten.

Joat shrugged. "That's kind of irrelevant, isn't it? What really matters to you is that you'll lose any advantage that datahedron offers *and* everything you've invested in it up to this point. Although to be perfectly fair, if we can't come to an agreement on this I really should refund you the five thousand that your agent paid me yesterday."

Joat blinked in astonishment as Silken laughed and lay back in the navigator's recliner.

"Surreal," the other woman said. This conversation is . . . *surreal.* Call up your account and I'll give you the damned credits."

When they'd completed the transaction, Silken studied Joat slyly for a moment and then shook her head.

"So, you're an honest woman, are you?"

"I hope so," Joat said. "It's what I aim for."

Silken chuckled.

"Would you consider starting fresh with me?" she asked. "I'd hate to leave you with the impression that I'm not. Honest, that is." With a mischievous smile, Silken cocked her head, inviting Joat to share her amusement.

"What did you have in mind?" Joat asked cautiously.

"Something difficult. Something for which we need that someone who *couldn't* be cheated and *can* be trusted." She stretched. "Shall we send your man for it? The short, blond, yummy one, not the gorilla."

✧   ✧   ✧

The box that Joseph brought to the bridge had a simple elegance. Made of some dark wood, polished to a satin smoothness, it was the size and shape of an ordinary jewelry box, the type that women had kept on their dressers for centuries.

Silken keyed open its lock with a series of deft touches, her hand hiding the combination. Then she turned the box around to face Joat before she opened it. Her eyes sparkled teasingly.

As the lid slowly came up, Joat gasped. It was full almost to overflowing with Sainian crown rubies. The jewels glowed blood red and deep within each of them flared the glint of gold that marked them of first quality. Irregular and flat sided, each one was as large as Silken's small fist.

Sainian crown rubies came from nowhere near the crown of the Sainians who produced them. Originally they'd been called *mouth-rubies,* a more honest appellation—and one that jewelry makers felt might interfere with sales.

Crown rubies were an organic jewel produced as a result of what was, to a Sainian, a socially embarrassing gastric disorder. The gentle, sophisticated Sainians were both amused and repelled that humans could so prize what was essentially . . . drool. Solidified spittle. Absolutely nothing would induce them to produce the rubies if it could be avoided and of course, they were almost always of modest size.

The ones in Silken's box were enormous compared to the general run.

"Wow!" Joat whispered hoarsely. She looked up. "Are they real?"

Silken raised a brow, "Of course." She took one and held it up to the light. "Look at it, see the gold flashes deep within? They can't duplicate that yet. And smell." She held the stone out to Joat, who sniffed. Responsive to the heat of Silken's skin it smelled delicately musky. "They can't even begin to duplicate that."

"It's just . . . they're so *big,*" Joat said with wonder.

Silken smiled and the muscles in Joat's back seized up at the sight.

"Everything has its price," Silken purred.

Joat refused to let herself wonder what would cause a Sainian to produce such stones. But she knew at that moment that she should never turn her back on this woman. This kitten had a tiger's claws.

"I need these beauties shipped to Rohan." Silken replaced the stone reluctantly, as if she hated to give up the feeling of the jewel beneath her fingers. "Ever heard of it?"

"It's a moon," Joat said. "With a freeport Station, over a gas-giant named Eglund. I've never been there, but I've heard about it."

"I'm sure you have," Silken said smugly. "It's *the* destination for most of the quality stuff we . . . freetraders ship. Consider yourself lucky to have won this consignment. Especially under the circumstances." She held up the now descrambled datahedron. "Once you're on Rohan, and it becomes known that you've worked for me you'll have no difficulty finding lucrative cargo, I promise you. Consider it a bonus for the inconvenience my agents have caused you."

Joat chuckled appreciatively. "Sounds great," she said. "Now, let's discuss price."

"What we need to discuss," Silken said emphatically, all trace of good humor gone, "is what will happen if you get too enterprising with my jewels."

"I've already told you my thoughts about dishonest dealing," Joat said, her eyes unflinching. "I don't have anything to add. Now. What are you paying me to ship these?"

A short, sharp exchange of offer and counteroffer ensued. Joat achieved a price slightly higher than what she'd have settled for, with half to be paid immediately. Best of all she knew that she had achieved a degree of respect in Silken's tiger green eyes.

Joat offered a celebratory cup of coffee from her stores and Silken accepted.

"I'd prefer, say, a nice Chablis," Silken remarked.

Joat grinned and tossed her a sealed container she plucked from a storage cabinet.

"Sorry," she said. "But this is Mocha Java. You'll like it, I promise. Now, is there anything else I should know?" Joat asked, sipping the hot, fragrant brew.

Silken raised a brow. "Such as?"

"Is Central Worlds after your box of goodies?"

"Mmmm," Silken murmured. "Good question. They don't know about it, no. But . . . I'm always watched and they like to . . . discuss me with anyone I've spent time with." She sipped delicately. "You may be sure they'll talk to you. Where, when and in what fashion I really couldn't say. But I'd advise you to hide my beauties carefully. I shouldn't like to have them fall into Central Worlds' hands."

Gah! Joat thought, *this woman could say "I love you," and make it sound ominous. I wonder if she could go ten minutes without making a dire threat.* It was all done very elegantly, but she suspected that after a couple of days in Silken's company the impulse to smack her one would become overwhelming.

"This consignment is to be delivered to Nomik Ciety," Silken was saying. "His is a very important name on Rohan, so you should have no trouble finding him. I must insist that delivery be made within the next eight days. That *is* possible?"

"No problem," Joat assured her.

"Then I'll leave you to your preparations," Silken said and rose. She held out her hand and Joat rose to take it. "It's been a pleasure, and most interesting, doing business with you," she said, her sweet mouth lifted in a genuine smile. "I'll look forward to seeing you on Rohan."

"In the deserts west of the Deathangel Mountains," Joseph said thoughtfully, looking at the hatch, "there are serpents of great beauty. The patterns of their scales are like living jewels. They also have," he went on, "venom of surpassing deadliness—a man they bite will be dead before his body strikes the ground."

Alvec nodded. "Yup. And if one of 'em bit her, the *snake* would die."

"The combination is as follows," Rand broke in.

Joat put the box down on the mess table and touched the sensitized plate in the order the AI indicated.

Nothing. "You *sure* you got that?"

"I have a sensor directly behind the position Ms. Silken occupied," Rand said.

Did I write a subroutine with sulky *in it?* Joat wondered. She tried the combination again.

"Subtle," Joseph said.

"It must be a bio-lock," Rand explained. "Responding only to her touch." It paused for a moment. "Some of the more sophisticated models will record whether anyone has attempted to open them."

"Oh, well," Joat said. "There's subtle, and then there's whatever works."

She stood, braced the box down on the table with her left hand, and twitched her right. The vibroknife keened, then screeched in a high electronic wail as she jammed it into the lock. Fire and sparks spurted out of the box, mixed with the scents of scorched metal, synthetic, and wood. Joat twitched her hand again, and the handle of the knife slid back into the sleeve of her overall.

"*There,*" she said.

Joseph whispered softly in his own language. Alvec swore.

"Why would she trust you with this? Especially after what happened with the datahedron. It don't make sense." He rubbed his jaw and thick stubble grated. "Smugglers, excuse me, *freetraders* are cautious to the point of paranoia. And she gives you this."

"The thing is," Joat said, shaking out a piece of cloth and carefully placing the rubies on it, "I don't think Silken, Ciery and Co. think of us as regular smugglers. We're not in that network, we don't know people who are, and we don't have any friends among 'em." She took out an optical intensifier from her kit and clenched it in one eye, holding up a ruby and studying it.

Joseph leaned back and made his joined hands disappear inside the sleeves of his robe, a Bethelite gesture. "Joat, you describe to perfection someone who may be killed with impunity."

"Yup, once their brief usefulness is past."

"Cleared for takeoff."

"Launch," Joat said.

"Execute," Rand replied.

"And so as our ship sinks slowly in the west and the sun pulls away from the dock, we bid farewell to Schwartztarr, exotic land of smugglers, fences, weapons factories, and big furry animals with long, sharp teeth," Joat intoned.

The *Wyal* flung itself at the sky. Alvec leaned back and cracked his knuckles; Joat winced. *He knows I hate it when he does that.*

"Boss," he said after a moment. "How the *hell* did you manage to sell laser tubes on Schwartztarr?"

Joat grinned. "Well, to a laser manufacturer who'd just gotten a big export order. Spared him the time it would take subcontractors to deliver the components, and it was a pre-tested shipment. Then I bought some electronic components and laser crystals."

Joseph frowned and worked out what he was going to say carefully. "Are laser crystals better than laser tubes?" he said slowly.

"Trust me," Joat said smugly. "In fact—"

"I'm detecting an approaching ship," Rand said. "Its just entered *Wyal*'s sensor range."

"Any special reason you mention it?" Joat asked.

"It's a Central Worlds Navy ship," Rand said apologetically. "A customs corvette."

"Oh no," Alvec said and covered his eyes with one square hand. "Just what we needed. We've got a cargo of knocked-down weapons and we're heading for *Rohan* and a customs gunboat stops us."

"Don't be so guilty, Al," Joat said with a confident smile. She suppressed an impulse to rub her stomach, where lunch had turned to a cold, congealing lump. *Schwartztarr food,* she told herself. It tended to the heavy, meat and potatoes and dumplings.

Joseph came in looking sleepy.

"Rand woke me," he explained. "It says we are being approached by a customs corvette."

"Which hasn't even hailed us, for cryin' out loud!" Joat snapped, "Rand!" in exasperation.

"Attention Merchanter *Wyal,* registry number 776445X. This is Central Worlds Customs ship *Charger.* Commander Chang-Yarimizu speaking. Please stand by to be boarded."

"Until now," she said, and sighed. "Oh, well, I guess I should be thankful it's not a brainship anyway. Can you imagine what Simeon would say?"

CHAPTER NINE

BROS SPERIN SAT hunched over his screen in the hidden security office of The Anvil.

"Police archive," he said to the machine. "Crossref, *Ciety, Nomik,* crossref, alias—"

There was always a hope of finding something useful on his quarry. He had a fairly complete dossier on Nomik Ciety, including the supposedly sealed files on his dreamdust detox with its sensitive psych counseling.

"Amazing how everything just happened to get wiped when Ciety was released," he muttered to himself.

The psych file really *had* been sealed; physically disconnected from the system. Even the best worm program would have problems with that—although there was something still lurking in the far reaches of the net, waiting to pounce on any mention of Ciety's name.

Sperin smiled. He liked an agile opponent; it made the game more interesting. Ciety seemed to be agile enough to fool a prison shrink, certainly. He might have kicked the dust, but that just made him more efficient at his sociopathic games.

Outstanding warrants:

The screen blinked live and began scrolling. Sperin's eyebrows stretched skyward. This was just the *new* stuff, the offenses since his release, supposedly "reformed." It was his first concentrated effort to gain a true picture of Nomik Ciety, the man and his methods, not just the haphazard files of those trying to catch the man.

From behind him one of the agents manning a security terminal made a strangled sound.

"Good grief!"

Bros turned: "What is it?"

The man gestured at the screen, speechless. Bros walked to the agent's station and leaned over his shoulder to look into the monitor.

An extremely elderly Sondee had entered the bar.

To other species male and female Sondee looked exactly alike, so it was impossible to guess the oldster's gender. Though in the ultraviolet range the sex difference between male and female Sondee was glaringly obvious.

The fact that most other species couldn't appreciate this was unfortunate, the Sondee agreed, but they still found it appalling, embarrassing, and gauche that anyone would ask such a personal and irrelevant question as *What gender are you?* Which they interpreted as being asked—essentially—*What is the shape, color, and texture of your genitals?*

To accommodate their androgynous appearance linguistically, individual Sondee were "et," the term having been coined because "it" was deemed derogatory. The problem with that was that in most Sondee languages *not* specifying an addressee's gender was a gross insult.

Fortunately for everyone else's peace of mind Sondee who dealt with other species on a regular basis were gracious enough to make an admission of gender part of their introduction.

The ancient Sondee standing just inside the doorway of The Anvil cupped ets withered hands protectively over the delicate whorled ridges that served as ears, and looked slowly around as though seeking someone. Ets two main eyes, though bright and golden, seemed sunken in pale, loose flesh. The upper eyes, which saw into the ultraviolet ranges, were actually closed, as though their owner was too weary to deal with the extra layer of information they would provide. The small, suckerlike mouth was pinched closed, as though in disapproval. It would suddenly expand to gasp in air, then pinch closed again.

The Sondee slowly blinked. Then, with tottering steps, et began to struggle across the club towards the bar.

Clearly, no one in The Anvil had ever seen a Sondee of such antiquity. Conversations stopped and even the band faltered for a beat as everyone watched et pass.

Using the backs of chairs and the edges of tables to keep etself upright on the journey, the old Sondee nodded politely to the owner of the occasional shoulder et leaned on.

When at last et reached ets destination, the bartender was waiting to take the Sondee's order. An unusual event in itself.

"Sakurian," the Sondee ordered in a voice like a creaking hinge. Jaws dropped all around.

The Sondee were held to have the most beautiful voices in Central Worlds. Every one of them might have been a professional opera singer if it pleased them, and musically they'd easily overshadow most humans, however talented.

I don't believe it, Sperin thought. *I don't believe that sound came from a Sondee throat-sac.* Nobody who saw this was *ever* likely to forget it.

"You were . . . expecting a Sondee?" the security op asked Bros tentatively. "Right?"

"Yes," Bros growled. "A male. But I thought they were sending a live one."

When the Sondee at last tottered in on the arm of the young woman Bros had sent to fetch et, et instantly reverted to bouncing youth. And before their fascinated eyes began peeling off wattles, warts, and ridges until, with a dramatic gesture, et stood before them, glue-splotched but handsome.

For a Sondee . . .

"Seg !T'sel," et announced in a rich and vibrant voice. "Male, of the Clenst Defense Group. At your service!"

Bros stood looking at Seg with his arms crossed, hands clutching his arms. *I will not try to strangle him,* he thought, mastering his emotions with a wrenching effort. *I will not.*

"Mr. !T'sel," he said. "This was supposed to be a *confidential* meeting. Would you care to explain yourself?"

"Ah. Well," somewhat crestfallen, the young Sondee shrugged. "My, ah, my hobby . . ." He colored gently: first the ear whorls and then, slowly, the rest of his face flushed a delicate blue. "My hobby is disguise," Seg murmured. "I couldn't resist the opportunity."

"Well," Bros said with a bright, toothy smile. "As long as no one happens to be looking for a Sondee behaving in an unusual manner, there shouldn't be a problem."

Bros indicated a conference room and with a gesture invited Seg to precede him into it.

"But now that you've removed your makeup," he said, "how are we going to explain your present appearance? I'll tell you this, Mr. !T'sel, if I were sitting out there and watched you come in old and go out young, I'd be beating down the door, demanding some of whatever we gave you."

Seg chuckled nervously and sat down, folding his long, four-fingered hands before him on the table.

"Shall we proceed to the purpose of this meeting?" the young Sondee asked, somewhat desperately.

"One moment," Bros murmured, settling his long muscular form in the chair opposite. He reached into his belt pouch and withdrew a small oval antieavesdropping device. He pushed a red button to activate it and placed it on the table before him. "Proceed," he said.

In his element, !T'sel launched into lecture mode and seemed immediately older and more confident.

"As you know, Mr. Sperin, The Clenst Defense Group works closely with the Central Worlds Navy research divisions. Recently, the Navy presented us with a range of biological weapons developed by a rogue group of Phelobites for the illegal arms market."

"Rogue Phelobite is a little redundant, isn't it Mr. !T'sel?" Bros murmured.

"Ah . . . ," Seg shrugged and looked uncomfortable.

The Clenst Defense Group by its very nature was called upon to work closely with weapons manufacturers. Phelobites were unquestionably the premier arms manufacturers for Central Worlds. Officially, they adhered to all of the regulations and accords that being a member of Central Worlds called for, including those that banned the manufacture and sale of certain classes of armament. Unofficially, they would make and sell anything to anybody for the right price if they thought there was a good chance of getting away with it.

In most Phelobite languages, the word for *altruism* translated roughly as "sucker."

It was an open secret that did little to endear them to most of Central Worlds, including the Clenst Defense Group. Who nonetheless felt compelled to maintain a diplomatic silence regarding the Phelobites' less socially acceptable business practices.

Seg stretched his fingers and then folded his hands again.

"There are several bio-weapons that are particularly dangerous that we've been working intensively to find counteragents for."

"Why not just buy 'em from the Phelobites?" Bros asked reasonably.

"Apparently," Seg said nervously, "they never got around to developing them."

Bros sat up straight and folded his hands before him on the conference table, mirroring Seg !T'sel's posture.

"Go on," he said.

"All of these diseases attack the brain or nervous system on some level. Their premiere creation, and the one we're most concerned with, has the effect of destroying the memory center of the brain. Fairly rapidly and with, unfortunately, permanent results. It's highly contagious, primarily airborne, but can also be transmitted through handling things that have recently been touched by an infected person. We estimate that perhaps twenty humans in a hundred will have a natural immunity to it. Actually, we believe that's part of the design, predicated on the idea that one person afflicted will need two or more to take care of them. Obviously," Seg spread his hands in a gesture of appeal, "if this disease were released on a planet the results would be . . . catastrophic."

"To put it mildly," Bros agreed. He wasn't ready to ask questions yet, though he sensed where this lecture was leading.

"Yes. Well," Seg continued. "Three others that we received samples of, from a package of brain or nervous system influencing agents this pirate company has been marketing, are not diseases, exactly. But we've found that a subject can be immunized against them as though they were. However, they're not something we would wish to fall into the wrong hands." He glanced nervously at Bros. "They seem to have been developed with the dual aim of acting as methods of discipline and interrogation. The first creates intense pain, the second intense fear, the third produces euphoria and an overwhelming desire to please."

Here the scientist in him took over, and he said enthusiastically: "The degree of control is exquisite! The timespan and extremity of effect are determined at the time the dose is made up. And the effects may last only seconds or permanently; in other words, at the discretion of the user."

Bros caught his eye at this point and Seg dampened his enthusiasm. "Um, physical side effects will vary depending on how long the dosage lasts. The pain bug can cause neurological damage in very high doses, the fear instigator is likely to produce psychological problems in most people, which the pleasure bug may, depending upon what the victim has been required to do. You see they act by exciting certain glands or in the case of the pain drug by exciting the synapses . . ."

Bros was holding up his hand.

"Before we get too involved in the actual workings of this stuff, why are you here?" he asked. He thought he knew, and he was impatient to hear it said, to have his worst fears made real. *Anxiety is worse than pain. Pain does not hurt; the* fear *of pain hurts.*

The Sondee studied his folded hands for a moment, then looked directly across at Sperin.

"We succeeded in developing a serum for the memory wiping disease. A simple injection will immunize a subject. It cannot reverse damage already done, unfortunately, but it can halt the progress of the disease. The counteragents we've developed to the others are, unfortunately, less effective and require a stepped series of injections. But then, we'd really only begun research on them. I'm sure we would have come up with something more effective if given time."

Bros waved his hand in a rotary motion, "And the reason you're telling me all this is . . ."

Seg looked down/sideways—a disconcerting sight in itself—and remained quiet for a time, as though gathering his thoughts. At last he raised his eyes and looked at Bros again.

"We were due to give a full report to a Navy representative and had gathered everything together, samples, both of the diseases and the antidotes and serum, research, everything we had. It was stolen. Worse, we subsequently discovered that our information about the serums had been corrupted. Meaning that mass production will have to be delayed while crucial research and testing are duplicated. What we fear is that someone intends to use these weapons and soon, while we have no ready supply of counteragents."

Bros sat back slowly, his gaze thoughtful.

"Have you found your spy?" he asked calmly.

"No," Seg told him. "To be honest we consider that the least of our worries. Our primary interest is to find where the information went. There are three arms dealers in particular that Navy intelligence feels are the most likely candidates for handling this product. Agics LLege, the Yoered Family and Nomik Ciety.

"I've been assigned to your team because I have a full understanding of this weapon and clearance to make any necessary decisions regarding it, or the stolen information. I also have a full range of shots to immunize you and your agents. Fortunately we still had a minute amount of the working samples left in the lab."

Bros studied the young Sondee scientist. A horrible suspicion nibbled at the edges of his mind.

"My team? Mr. !T'sel, I can understand the need to send word of this by courier, and of course the need for these shots is obvious. What I don't understand is why CenSec and Clenst are both willing to put someone of your skills in a position of risk. Do they seriously expect me to take you into the field with me? Is that what you're trying to tell me?"

"This discussion has already taken place at a fairly high level, Mr. Sperin," !T'sel informed him haughtily. He reached into his suit jacket and withdrew a datahedron. "This is a recording of the meeting at which it was decided that whatever happened to the stolen materials was my responsibility. It goes without saving that if that necessitates being called into the field, then I will go."

!T'sel wore the most heroic expression Bros had ever seen on a Sondee outside of an opera. The suspicion hardened into certainty. !T'sel was no doubt as good a scientist as his documentation claimed, but he was a romantic. Specifically, a romantic aficionado of espionage.

Bros restrained an impulse to beat his head against the table. What did CenSec expect him to do? Work miracles? Find the Benisur Amos, find the stolen bio-weapons, put the notorious Ciety out of business and shepherd a glory hungry kid-scientist through it all without letting him get scratched?

Sometimes, he thought, *I regret my oath to Central Worlds Security.* He could have been an aquaculture specialist. He could have written dramas for the feelie market. He could . . .

He rose and gestured towards the door. "I'll review this immediately, Mr. !T'sel . . ."

"It's Doctor, actually. But please, sir, call me Seg."

"If you'll promise not to call me sir."

Seg laughed nervously, "Whatever you'd like, Mr. Sperin. I realize calling you *sir* wouldn't be good tradecraft."

The Sondee dropped the term as if it were a magic talisman. *He'd probably like to have a union card with* SPY *written on it.*

"Bros, call me Bros. But not in front of the people here. Here you'll have to call me Clal." He winced mentally. "That's my cover name. Okay?" Seg nodded eagerly. "Uh, I'll assign someone to help you get settled and tomorrow we'll see if we can come up with a plan." He slapped Seg on the shoulder and guided him out the door. "Don't trust anybody here, Seg. And don't tell them anything."

Bros sent the young Sondee off with one of the younger of Sal's operatives via the back door of the club. His last sight of !T'sel was of the young Sondee looking eagerly back with an expression of abject hero-worship in all four eyes.

With a weary sigh he sank back into his chair, burying his face in his hands.

This was wonderful! Seg's blood bubbled like champagne. He couldn't believe that he had actually met *Bros Sperin*. Had shaken his hand, had *briefed* him, for the love of !Gretz.

He tried to hold his features to a properly cool expression as he followed the young operative Bros had assigned to him. It was hard. *Cool,* he reminded himself. *An experienced agent displays no emotion.* Certainly no *genuine* emotion. He'd practiced fake ones often enough.

Sperin was a legend in the lore of Central Security, and Seg had hunted each and every story about him to the source, confirming every unbelievable tale. *Such panache, such wit, such daring!* he thought. Somehow, Seg had imagined that Mr. Bros Sperin must be dead. Heroes simply didn't live in the same world as industrial scientists.

Not Mister *Bros Sperin,* Seg reminded himself, *but Bros, by !Gretz! He shook my hand and told me to call him Bros.*

Now Seg had only to hope that his supervisor would confirm the alleged field appointment he was supposedly reporting for. Once, the recording—which Bros was probably viewing even now—had merely authorized Sperin to call upon Dr. Seg !T'sel for any advice he needed pertaining to the stolen diseases and their antidotes. But Seg had made a few artistic adjustments to the original, lending a whole new aspect to the tape.

The Directors are a conservative lot, he thought. Lost in credentialism. Convinced that merely because his *formal* training was in analysis, he couldn't be an effective field operative as well.

Seg was aware from his research into Bros's exploits that he was careful about details. There was no doubt that in this case one of those details would be to check the contents of the recording Seg had given him with Clenst.

Seg had arranged for any calls regarding himself to be referred to his immediate supervisor. A human—about whom Seg had assembled an intimidating dossier that seemed to confirm his guilt in the theft of the missing diseases.

Actually, Seg had no idea whether his boss was guilty or not, but the appearance was so damning that the man had gone along with his plan.

Hoping, no doubt, that I'd get myself killed, Seg thought happily. Little did he know.

Seg was going to be an agent, and he was going to *shine*.

"Oh, great unborn planets," Bros whispered. The documents looked solid. They *were* solid. What on earth were they thinking of, to saddle him with this amateur?

"Run this through for confirmation," he said wearily, and his comp immediately began working.

He sighed. Well, the work he'd already been engaged in was just as pertinent to the new investigation as to the old. His instincts told him that the Kolnari were involved. The symmetry of the whole thing was too perfect; fitting so well with the shape of their defeat and the Kolnari need for revenge. And if the Kolnar were involved then so was Nomik Ciety.

He sat at his computer and began reviewing the latest batch of outstanding warrants he'd been sent.

Words scrolled up the screen, mostly unheeded except for an occasional term or name that Bros registered. His mind was mostly on Joat Simeon. And Joseph ben Said, who had apparently disappeared.

Right into Joat's ship, and for all I know, into her bed, he thought sourly. He hadn't liked the idea of the older man proposing marriage to her. But the memory of her response brought a smile to his lips.

His eye caught a familiar name on a warrant scrolling by and he stopped it, pulled it back down for inspection.

The complaint was ten years old, but might as well have been centuries old for all the effect it'd had. It had been filed by Channa Hap and Simeon, the Brain and Brawn of the SSS-900-C on behalf of their adopted daughter, Joat Simeon-Hap.

Bros sat up and leaned forward. The warrant had been signed out against a Nom Selkirk, Joat's uncle. It seemed the man had lost his seven-year-old niece in a poker game with the captain of a tramp freighter. The child had subsequently been viciously abused and then abandoned on the SSS-900-C. Both Channa and Simeon had demanded some sort of action. They'd gone so far as to post a reward for information.

Nom Selkirk was one of Nomik Ciety's aliases, one of his oldest, perhaps even his real name. *If he has any real name other than vermin, or something of that kind.*

The hair crawled on Bros's neck. *And I sent her after him,* he thought with horror. An image of Joat's smile rose in his mind; and the memory of holos taken during the Kolnari occupation of SSS-900-C. Most of which Joat had spent in the ventilation system, planning and executing—literally—her ambushes. During which she'd used a monofilament dispenser to give a whole new layer of meaning to the ancient saying "Cut them off at the knees."

If Ciety *was* her uncle, his life wasn't worth spit from the moment Joat landed on the same surface. Not that Ciety would be any loss, but the consequences to the mission . . .

"Outsmarted yourself again," Sperin muttered to himself. "Tell me I'm not as stupid as a vid-series spy. *Please!*"

The customs corvette was a slender needle next to the *Wyal's* torpedo, built to transit atmosphere and fast in space as well. An unpleasant beeping sound echoed over the bridge as the merchantman's sensors picked up the lock-on of the gunboat's particle beam weapons and single torp tube. The corvette came around sharply to match vectors, reached zero-relative velocity, and extended a docking tube.

Joat's eyebrows rose when the airlock door swung open to show the corvette's commander; of course, the crew was only six people, but she'd expected a junior officer.

Commander Chang-Yarimizu stared, nonplused, at Captain Simeon, who stood with her arms outstretched to block his entrance to her hold.

"This device is perfectly safe," he insisted. "Stories of its destructiveness are mere superstitious nonsense."

"Nevertheless," she insisted, "I've got a hold full of extremely delicate electronics. I *can't* afford to take the risk. I'm within my rights Commander, and you know it. I'm not denying you the right of inspection, I'm merely refusing to let you use that instrument."

"But if we do the inspection by hand, Captain, it could take all day, or longer!"

"I'd rather arrive late with a clean cargo than on time with a hold full of trash. This is a freighter, not a garbage scow dumping radioactives! If it takes time, it takes time. I've got nothing to hide, so we'll go through the whole shipment, one item at a time. But I'll tell you this, Commander," Joat waved a stiff forefinger under his nose, "I'm going to protest this! Nothing in my record or reputation could give you reason for this. Nothing!"

"You're going to Rohan, ma'am . . ."

"Captain!"

"Captain. After a conference with a woman who has a reputation a lot less pristine than yours. You're known to have a crushing debt to New Destinies. All in all, it's really not unreasonable to assume that you might have been tempted off the straight and narrow."

"Well, Commander," Joat said, crossing her arms over her chest, "put down that gadget and we'll go discover the truth about that. Shall we?"

Several hours later, Joat and the two luckless sailors assigned to inspect her cargo had finished examining the electronics, now twice reopened and sealed, and were beginning on the laser crystals.

"Lasers?" the Commander said.

"Mining laser crystals. As you'll note, they aren't milspec."

If I have trouble selling those electronics, can I make a claim against customs for making me open up the containers? Joat wondered.

"My fingers hurt," one sailor complained.

"Yeah," Joat agreed, "my cuticles are beginning to peel back." She sighed. "I'm really sorry to put you through this, guys. But what could I do? I don't care what he says about that instrument, too many people have warned me against it."

"I don't think it really causes problems, ma'am. But I can see where you wouldn't want to take a chance," the other sailor said.

They'd gone through several hundred boxes and were beginning to close in on the hidden cache of crown rubies.

Fardles! she thought, *Doesn't that nardy Commander have anything better to do? We've been at this for hours! Surely someone, somewhere is committing a vicious crime that these guys should be trying to stop!*

She reached out and grabbed a box that she knew contained one of the doctored Crown rubies. She could feel the difference in weight.

The two sailors reached for two more ruby filled boxes. Her heart began to pound as she readied the lie she'd been preparing.

"What the hell is this?" one of the men asked.

"It's slag," Joat told him taking it out of his hand. "It's what's left over when they've cut the crystals from the matrix they're grown from." *Please,* she thought, *be ignorant about laser crystals. Be dumb, please!*

"Here's another one," said his companion.

Joat opened her box and dumped out the disguised ruby.

"Fardles! I'll bet the rest of the shipment is like this! I should have known better! There's no such thing as a bargain, just deals you regret. I bet I end up paying top dollar for every good crystal I've got." She slammed the ruby back into the box in disgust and tossed the box contemptuously over her shoulder.

"Pereira, Benavides, heads up! We're moving out."

The two sailors put down their boxes with sighs of relief and rose. Stretching to get the kinks out, they smiled at Joat.

"Sorry about the mess," one said.

"Don't worry about it," Joat told them, grinning. "Perils of passage," she assured them.

She rose too and escorted them to the lock that connected her ship to theirs.

The Commander was there and he and Joat gave each other a fish-eyed stare.

"Sorry for the inconvenience," he said stiffly.

"Not at all," she said, smiling. The hatch clanged shut. "You meddling, officious twit!" she added with a snarl, kicking the hatch-cover.

Joseph and Alvec had stayed carefully on the bridge, on the general principle that absent faces generated no awkward questions. Joseph handed her one of the glasses of Arrack he held and Joat took it solemnly. The three of them clicked glasses and drank.

Joat smacked her lips. "I never thought I'd live to say this, but I needed that."

"We better clean up this mess," Alvec said, "and get underway before we attract any more attention."

"Attention," Joseph mused. "True, I am from a backward planet, but still . . . in my trade—" he made a gesture of apology "—which for the moment is yours, Joat . . . drawing attention to oneself is not a good thing."

"Yeah," Alvec said. "And the way we've been going, we've got a great big holo sign reading *Hurrah, We're Here!* welded to the bow of the ship."

Joseph sighed. "I am haunted by the feeling that we have just refused to grasp a lifeline that fate has thrown us. Whatever happens now, my friends, I pray that the God is watching over us, for I fear we are utterly outside of human help. And too many depend on us for failure to be tolerable."

Joat nodded. If Joseph was right, Amos and his party were in the hands of the Kolnari. She shuddered. *A fate that makes death seem like a fun alternative.*

CHAPTER TEN

"DON'T TELL ME!" Seg said, his long multijointed fingers dancing over the control console. "You set the customs corvette onto them!"

"Yes," Bros sighed.

Remember, he's a romantic, but not necessarily a complete idiot. Not intellectually; emotionally yes, but he could still figure things out. He probably even had a gifted amateur's grasp of the profession— just enough to make inspired guesses about thirty percent of the time, including some occasions when a professional wouldn't see the unlikely. The rest of the time he'd be dead wrong and unwilling to admit it.

"Why? Ahhhh . . . to convince their next contact that they're on the wrong side of the law! That they have no choice but to descend deeper and deeper into the depths of crime. And meanwhile, you'll be closing in! Fiendish!"

Bros frowned. *That* is *my plan, stripped of the adjectives.* And put like that, it sounded pretty lame, particularly now that he knew about Nomik Ciety's link to Joat. Or did it just sound bad because the Sondee was saying it, with mezzo-soprano warbles of excitement on the vowels?

Too late to do anything about it now. "Let's go," he said. The next move would be up to Ciety. Just enough of his shipping capacity had disappeared for one reason or another to make him pretty desperate; in his line of work, clients didn't really deal well with delays. On the other hand, there hadn't been enough to make him suspect Intelligence was onto him. Bros hoped.

❖   ❖   ❖

Silken lay back with a delighted little purr and Nomik laid his head on her bosom. She reached down and stroked his dark blond hair, damp from his exertions.

"You missed me," she said in a pleased little growl.

"You bet I did." He snatched her hand and kissed it. "You're one of a kind, Silky. And there's no substitute for the best."

She laughed and wiggled playfully. He looked up at her and smiled, scooting himself higher in the bed to kiss her. She turned again, sliding out of the bed and padding across the polished black basalt and stark-white Schwartztarr fur rugs to the autobar. She returned with a bottle of champagne and two tall flute cones of carved glass, smoking with chill. He admired the grace of her arm as it curved to pour the priceless Terran wine.

"We *are* good together, aren't we?" she said, slipping back into the satin tangle.

"Especially at times like these," he murmured, winding his arms around her.

The bed rotated and tilted to face the wall that was a single sheet of crystal, giving a view of stark airless white mountains and the banded blue and aquamarine of the gas-giant beyond.

Eventually they leaned companionably against the head of the bed and each other, quietly sipping chilled champagne, filling each other in on their doings.

"I think I may have found a new agent for the organization," Silken confided.

"Oh?"

"I met the most amazing young woman on Schwartztarr. She's about my age and owns her own ship. Well, she and her bank. Her reputation is crystal clean, she's considered a fair dealer and she gets her cargo to destination on time and in good condition. She's discreet, she's smart," she glanced over at Nomik, "she's got guts. Would you believe it, she went eye to eye with me over something and didn't blink."

"And you did?"

She laughed. "Yes, I did. I couldn't help it, the woman was right."

"You gave in to her, just because she was right?" Nomik had turned to look at Silken, amazement written all over his face. "I don't believe it. What is this woman . . . a witch?"

"Mmmm, no." She chuckled, "Maybe a kindred spirit. And she *did* have the whip hand." Silken shrugged and he kissed her shoulder. "The thing is," she tapped his nose lightly with one slender finger, "she's got a massive debt to New Destinies. They've fined her a hundred and twenty thousand credits."

He frowned. "What did she do, poison the water, blow a hole in the station, ram a passenger liner?"

"According to my source, she took an unauthorized space-walk and entered the station through an emergency repair hatch."

"That's it?'

"That's it," Silken shrugged, grinning delightedly. "Now, here's my idea. What you could do, is, buy up her debt to New Destinies and offer her the opportunity to work it off."

"You think this paragon will go for that?" Nomik raised an eyebrow. "What about that pristine reputation?'

"I think she'll go for it. She's sure to lose her ship if she doesn't and then what good will her reputation do her? Believe me Mik, she'll repay that debt almost double before she's free. Just keep it light until she's in too deep to turn back. After that, who else is going to ship with her but you?"

"You're always thinking of me aren't you, Silky?" He kissed her and gave her a squeeze.

"Mmm hmm. She'll be with us in a day or so and you can check her out for yourself."

"Why don't I check you out just one more time?" he asked. "Make sure you got home in one piece."

Silken giggled as he rose over her.

The *Wyal* dropped into normal space. Joat blinked at the scanners. For a moment she thought that transition stress had finally gotten to her after all these years.

"There's nothing here!" she said.

"Correction: interstellar gas and micrometeorites," Rand's voice said. "And an F-class star three-point-seven parsecs to the galactic northwest."

"*Identify yourself.*"

Alvec pointed silently to the screens. A ship had been waiting, stealthed, engines on minimal standby to reduce the neutrino signatures of the powerplant. Now it was coming online. Joat glanced at the data. Nothing standard, not a Central Worlds signature, but the emissions were enough for a very large merchantman . . . or a light cruiser.

Kolnari? she thought. The tiny hairs along her spine crinkled erect in atavistic reflex.

"I have visual," Joseph said from the navigator's seat. His voice relaxed from tightly controlled fear to mere tension. "Not Kolnari, I think."

"Guardship," Alvec said.

The image on the screen was the conventional cylinder-and-globe of interstellar ships not meant to transit atmosphere, but with a hacked and haggled look.

Rand spoke. "A modified fast freight carrier," it said. "Mass reduced to increase delta-v. Shield generators, lasers, particle beam weapons, and missile launchers here—" a dot appeared on the image "—here, here. A more precise estimation of capabilities is impossible without information on the craft's computer installations."

Joat pursed her lips. "Highly illegal setup," she said. "And why didn't Silken—" *that lying bitch* "—give me the right coordinates?"

Alvec cleared his throat. "They always do this, Rohan does. Gives 'em a chance to make sure you're not a ringer for the Fleet."

"*You* knew about this arrangement?" she accused, unmollified.

"Yeah, well . . . yuh. Been around here, oh, a while back . . ."

Joat glared at him. Al was their pilot just now, and he didn't look up from his screens. *Ask no awkward questions, get no fibs.* "So, you know anything about Rohan itself?"

"It's a big moon," he said. "Big enough to hold atmosphere if it had one. Be a nice, livable planet if they terraformed it. Cold, though, a long way from the primary."

"Why have they not done so?" Joseph asked.

Alvec laughed. "They're pirates, folks. Building things isn't their strong suit; besides, keeping habitation restricted makes it easier to control traffic. That's why Yoered Family picked a moon in the first place."

"Wait a minute," Joat said. "The Yoered Family runs Rohan?"

"Yup."

"Then why would they give Ciety a base there? He's their competition."

"They've gotten a little fat and lazy, from what I hear. They let the freelancers do the scut work, and rake a percentage off the top—plus selling information, repairs and stuff, all at fantastic markups." He looked over at Joat. "You can probably fool around with Nomik

Ciety, Boss, but whatever you do, don't mess with the Family. They're way too powerful and they have zero patience."

Joat grinned, a wolfish expression. "And I bet they have no sense of humor."

"I wish I could say yes to that," Al said with a sigh.

"*Attention* Wyal. *Stand by for transition, microjump—slave your control system to ours for approach.*"

Rand maintained an injured silence. "Do it," Joat ordered. "It's only for a couple of minutes."

"How would you like to turn over control of your legs and arms for a few minutes?" the AI asked.

"Gruddy. I managed to write a program that can be sarcastic."

Eglund was visible in the viewscreen and she keyed it to a higher magnification. A bright disk sprang into view, blazing against the velvet-black of space with the gem-clear blue of an aquamarine.

"There's a thick haze of hydrogen-methane atmosphere," Rand said. "That accounts for the blue coloration."

"A lovely color," Joseph added.

"How many moons?" Joat said.

"Seven that I can detect, not counting planitesimals," Rand said. "Several are water-ice, one is mostly sulfur compounds. The others are rocky; the largest is approximately Mars-sized."

Odd, Joat thought. None of them had ever been to Terra, but humanity still used the original system for comparisons.

Rohan swung into view. A yellow-gray dust speck against the great jeweled surface below, trailing swiftly above clouds and storms vaster than worlds. Closer, it became the size of a tennis ball, tiny and sharp-edged. Dendritic patterns of craters, paler flatlands—no significant atmosphere, then.

Joat swallowed and rubbed her palms against the legs of her coverall. *Nomik.* The knowledge lay in her mind the way a stodgy dinner did in the stomach, making her thoughts feel logy and slow. Too much conflict, too many warring fears, hatreds, needs . . . memories.

And I'm holding things back, she thought, glancing at her friends. *It's not fair to them, I should tell them everything.* She knew that, but her mind refused to process the data; her mouth could not speak the words.

This is a lousy time to suddenly need psychotherapy, Joat thought sourly.

"*Attention.*" The voice of the escort vessel broke in. "*Relinquishing control. Enjoy your stay.*"

"Sarcastic nuddling," Joat muttered. She locked the restraints around herself and lowered her hands to the controls. "I'm taking her in."

She ignored Alvec's surprise and Rand's silence. This was something she *could* control.

The main dome of Rohan roofed over a crater a kilometer and a half in diameter; she could see through the transparent cover, down to the surface. Most of it was open space, vaguely seen greenery and trees, small lakes—sensible, not to waste open breathable space on buildings. Those would be under the crater's surface, or burrowed into the mountains on either side. The cruel peaks slid upward on either side as the *Wyal* descended, jagged against Eglund's brightness. Banded patterns of shadow and colored light slid across the empty wastes of rock, down into the pulsing strobes of the landing field. The ship slid into its cradle like a hand into a glove, only the faintest ringing *tock* of sound as contact was made. Almost immediately it began to move, trundling them to a docking ring in the side of the great dome.

Nowhere else did they have this system of hauling ships to and from the landing/launch pad. Only the Family would have felt it worth the enormous expense. By crowding ships together around the station's rim, they made it too dangerous to launch independently; insuring total Family control of arrivals and departures.

"Gravs off," Joat said. They all felt a buoyant lightness as they switched over to planetary gravity, about four-tenths standard. "Connections on."

There was a slight subliminal difference as the ship plugged into stationside power and life-support. Joat took a deep breath. "Time to hit dirtside," she said.

Time to find Uncle Nom.

The representative of Yoered Security looked bored as he lectured. He was a slight dark man with a small clipped mustache that looked as if it had been painted on his upper lip, dressed in a utilitarian dark-brown coverall. A few assistants stood behind him, one in a suit of powered armor; the visible ones looked as if they were close relatives—which they were. Yoered Family had started off as a crime "family" planetside, and moved out of the Central Worlds sphere several generations ago. They married in-clan . . . a standoffish bunch.

"Right, you've probably heard this before, but listen carefully anyway," the enforcer said. "This is *Rohan*. Yoered Family owns Rohan and everything on it. We have rules; you obey those rules, and you can get what you want here. First rule: nobody offers offense or violence to a member of our Family. Punishment—death."

He made a gesture. Behind him the wall flashed to holo; it showed an iron cage hanging by a chain from a massive oak tree in the underdome. Inside it was a human figure, incredibly emaciated, like a skeleton held together by strips of dried gristle. It moved . . .

Joat swallowed as the image disappeared. The enforcer went on:

"Second rule: no stealing, no destruction of clan property, no unauthorized assault, no welching on debts. Punishment—penal servitude." He smiled, a neat, contained little expression. "You may have noticed how clean we keep things?"

The three from *Wyal* looked around. The waiting room *was* extremely tidy, with an almost painfully scrubbed look. The only messy things in its broad expanse were some of the other spacers.

The security operative gestured again. This time the holo showed a man operating a vibroscrubber machine along a walkway. He was naked except for a brief pair of shorts, and a thick pain-compliance collar around his neck. Haunted eyes turned towards the pickup for a second, and then the man's body jerked, muscles crawling under the skin. He gave a thin scream and turned his attention back to the task. Joat had never seen anyone working with such concentrated attention.

"That was a thief." The security man smiled more broadly. "Now, don't get me wrong. This isn't a tight-butt sort of place. You can get anything you want here, if you can pay—or anyone. You want to cut someone, just challenge them to a duel—the Family puts it on the holovid and takes a cut on bets. Want someone dead? You buy a license and hire a Family assassin; standard rate, one hundred fifty thousand credits, with extras depending on the target."

The smile never touched his eyes. "You can even get privacy, within the doors of your lodgings. Standard rate, one hundred and fifty thousand credits down and twenty thousand per standard month. *Everything* else is under constant surveillance—every corridor, every cargo line, every bar, every bathroom, every closet. *Nothing* gets by us. And yeah, by the way, we don't go in for all that evidentiary stuff.

We arrest on suspicion, narcoquiz, and sentence the same day. No appeals." More teeth showed. "So enjoy yourselves, ladies, gentlemen, beings. Do a profitable business. But watch it."

"All functional," Rand confirmed.

"Good equipment," Joseph said judiciously, slipping the tiny button into his ear. "As good as the Naval Intelligence material we got from the military aid package."

"Sure it's not readable?" Alvec murmured. The other two heard him twice, a chorus-of-angels effect from the air and from the little transmitters tucked into their ears.

"I'm modulating it through the internal power lines," Rand said. "The encryption code is jiggered to look like the sort of random fluctuations you get there."

"Excellent," Joat murmured. "I know the virtual reality net here is legendary, Rand, but I need you to spend *some* time trying to crack Ciety's computer."

"I have a sense of responsibility, Joat," Rand said testily. "You programmed it into me. But you can make good contacts in V.R., so I intend to start there. I should have some news for you on your return."

"Just remember the expense," Alvec warned.

"Our expenses are being covered by CenSec," Rand reminded them. "I intend to take full advantage of that. Even if they will not pay the fine, they can be billed for ordinary outgoings."

Alvec's face went thoughtful, then lit up. *Like a kid in a bakery told he can have* six *of anything he wants,* Joat thought.

"Fardles," Joat said in awe. "I forgot!" She hoisted a travel case containing the Crown rubies, still disguised in their laser crystal boxes.

"Rand is right," Joseph said. "We must not become distracted. Amos's life is in the balance, and with it the well-being of my people."

"Yeah, sure, of course," Alvec said to his departing back. "But that doesn't mean we can't go to *dinner*. It wouldn't be right not to take advantage of CenSec's generosity just a little."

"They'll expect it," Joat assured him.

"They do things in person here, the old-fashioned way," Joseph said, slightly surprised. On Bethel, virtual presence was all the rage— newly risen from stagnation and backwardness, the Bethelites put a premium on modernity.

"Would *you* trust the public net, here?" Joat asked.

Joseph grinned, although his eyes remained wary. "You have a point."

That was logical, given that a moderately talented tech could produce a holo of anyone doing or saying *anything* and no one could tell the difference between an actual recording and one that had been faked. Therefore all transactions were real time, face to face, with multiple witnesses. Offices might be obsolete elsewhere, but not here.

Ciety's was located in a quiet neighborhood; just off the underdome surface, which was the prestige area on Rohan. They walked through eerily elongated groves of trees, past flowerbeds and greenswards, beneath the clear dome and the blue sky that was the great banded jewel of the gas-giant. Despite the growing tension that knotted her stomach, Joat was still struck by the beauty of it, and the air of quiet and peace. Nursemaids and children were the commonest strollers; she saw a dog make a long dolphinlike low-gravity leap after a ball and pinwheel off through the air . . .

"The Family do themselves proud," Alvec said sourly. "Who says crime wouldn't pay if the government ran it?"

Joseph looked about. "I am surprised the Central Worlds tolerate this," he said.

"They won't forever," Joat said absently. "But it's a big galaxy. If they mopped up the Yoered Family now, they'd just be replaced by someone younger and hungrier and cruder. Eventually the frontier will move out past this area, and the Family will go legitimate or move again to get outside the sphere of settled law.

"This is it," she said.

They walked through a tall archway carved into the rock of the crater wall; the blast doors that would seal it in an emergency were hidden behind the glowing mass of bougainvillea that carpeted the walls of the corridor behind. It was wide enough to be a street, but only slow floater platforms passed them, and a scattering of well-dressed pedestrians. No bars or sex shows were advertised here. Every office presented an inscrutable face of one-way glass adorned with a discreet sign announcing the name, but not the purpose, of the business within. No doubt that explained the sense of being somewhere very expensive.

If you have to ask, you can't afford it, Joat thought, and read aloud: "N. Ciety, Research and Development." She made a little moue. "I'd say he's a cynical man."

"I would say he is scum," Joseph said quietly. "He deals with the Kolnari."

Joat glanced at him in concern and then at Alvec. He met her eyes with the same concern she felt over Joseph's intensity. She grimaced. *I'm one to talk.*

"Joe," she said quietly. "Maybe you should wait outside."

He turned to glare at her. "You insult me, Joat. The fact that this criminal offends me does not mean that I am unable to deal with him. I would kiss the soles of his feet if it would give me the information I need to find Amos. Look to yourself, girl, and leave my behavior to me!"

Joat choked down the urge to apologize and opened the office door. *Whoa! Is this the Uncle Joe who was always telling me to control my emotions?* But then again, she was grown up now. He didn't need to put on the mask of infallibility with her anymore . . . which was both flattering and disturbing, when you thought about it.

The reception area was a very soothing room. The visible color scheme had been carefully chosen to please all of the species known to the Central Worlds. No doubt those who saw in the ultraviolet spectrum had been considered too, judging from the telltale signs in the paintings and fabrics in the room. In place of background music there was the sound of ocean surf. Again, a choice calculated not to offend any species, whether their oceans were methane or water. The furnishings looked expensive and inviting, if you liked the minimalist style—Joat herself had always thought desks and chair-seats looked better with legs beneath them, rather than floating in suspension-fields.

The human receptionist who greeted them was as polished as the decoration.

"Good morning," he said pleasantly. "How may I help you?"

"I'm Captain Joat Simeon-Hap, and we're here to deliver a consignment," Joat said. "For Silken."

"Ah." The young man raised a golden brow. "Please take a seat while I inform Ms. Silken that you've arrived. Would you care for some refreshment?"

"No thank you," Joat said.

Behind her Alvec and Joseph shook their heads. The three then retired to a furniture grouping for humanoids and sat down to wait silently. After a few carefully calculated moments the receptionist looked up with the distracted air of someone listening to an earphone.

"Captain Simeon-Hap, Mr. Ciety would like to meet you personally and has asked me to bring you and your party up to his suite. If you would follow me, please?"

He turned and started off towards an apparently blank wall, obviously confident that he would be followed.

Joat clenched her hands into fists to hide the fact that they were shaking as badly as her knees.

Get ahold of yourself! she thought fiercely. *This is what had to happen. This is what you hoped would happen.* Blood pounded in her ears.

The wall parted to reveal a lift and the golden-haired receptionist entered and turned to smile invitingly at them. Joat wondered if he was some especially pretty species of bodyguard. The lift accelerated smoothly; from the weight and time Joat guessed that they were several thousand meters up, into the living rock of the mountains that ringed the crater. When the doors opened, across from them was an ornate double door of some highly polished, satiny wood, each side featuring a plate-sized brass doorknob embossed with a single initial, N and C.

Tacky, Joat thought. *But impressive.* She had to admit that. The wood itself was expensive, that was obvious, but shipping it here must have cost a fortune, and not a small one. Uncle Nom had come up in the world, since he was a tramp-freighter skipper and fringe-world grifter.

Their guide crossed the corridor and knocked discreetly on the enormous doors. From within a resonant male voice called out "Come."

Joat licked her lips surreptitiously and wiped her palms on the legs of her shipsuit. Al and Joe were behind her, and the knowledge of their solid backing gave her strength.

The doors swept open. Joat gave a small incredulous gasp before she could stop herself. The walls were sheathed in a geometric design of polychrome marble; texture matched subtly with color, from craggy red to smoothly polished alabaster-white. The furnishings were rich beefleather and pale wood, austerely simple so as not to distract from the impact of the room itself.

Directly across from the door where they stood was an enormous fireplace, complete with blazing fire; cedar logs filled the air with their fragrance. *Burning!* she thought. *Burning* wood *to generate heat!* You'd expect that on a live planet—a barbarian planet. Here, it was barbaric in a completely different way.

Above it a display film in proportion to the fireplace offered a complex work of randomized holo art, swirling ceaselessly into almost recognizable patterns. The mantle was held up by carvings of humanoid figures.

Then, one of them moved.

Joat flinched, recognizing them then as low life bioconstructs, zombielike things also known as realities. *Banned on every planet in Central Worlds,* she thought in disgust. *We're a long way from civilized space.*

A man had risen from the couch before the fireplace to smile pleasantly at them. He gestured, urging them to enter. An attractive man, slender and of middling height. His longish, ash-blond hair was expensively cut in a style that knocked ten years off his age. His appraising eyes were a cool blue, set deep in a narrow, fine-boned face.

But his eyes passed over her briefly and on to her companions. He gestured again, perhaps with a touch of impatience and said:

"Come in! Don't be shy, I won't bite."

Obscurely disappointed, Joat looked down, carefully watching her feet descend the three shining marble stairs that led to the living area.

So *much for "the ties that bind,"* she thought grimly. No recognition at all. Of course, she'd been a child. *When he sold me.*

Ciety reached out a hand for her to shake and she steeled herself to take it. Alvec accepted it too, but Joseph, bowing, kept his in the sleeves of his tunic:

"It is not our custom," he said smoothly.

Ciety continued smiling and bowed politely back, but something reptilian showed in his eyes.

Silken lay upon the white couch, dressed in an emerald satin dressing gown, sipping from a cut crystal goblet which she raised in salute to Joat.

"You've made it in good time, Captain," she said.

"No thanks to Central Worlds Customs," Joat answered. "They went through almost every minor treasure in my hold. I thought we'd never get rid of them."

Silken's gaze sharpened and she sat up abruptly.

"You *have* my jewels," she demanded, combining statement and threat.

Joat placed the travel bag on the low table; Silken ripped open the fastener and tumbled the laser component boxes onto the intaglio surface.

"Where's . . . ?"

Then she opened one of the boxes.

"What the hell is this?" she snapped as she pulled out a dull red, irregularly shaped crystal.

"Dye from a red cargo marker," Joat explained calmly. "It'll wash off with a little elbow grease. The inspectors found three of these before their commander called them off."

Silken laughed in relief and caught Ciety's eye proudly, as though it had been her own idea.

"Why, you clever girl," she purred. "There, Mik, didn't I tell you she was sharp?"

"Yes you did," he agreed and stroked Silken's cheek with one finger. She rubbed her face against his hand like a cat.

Nomik took the jewel out of her hand and weighed it in his own. His eyes met Joat's.

"You *are* clever," he said. "I can use that kind of initiative in my organization. Silken vouched for you," he turned slightly in her direction to indicate her, and Silken smiled pleasantly at Joat. "And of course that's good enough for me. But this," he tossed the stone and caught it, "this is good. I'm impressed. So . . . would you be willing to discuss taking a place with us? You wouldn't regret it, I can promise you that."

I can't believe he's trying to offer me a job, Joat thought desperately. Conflicting emotions tore through her, disgust, amusement, rage, and a vague pleasure. *This is too much. I've got to rethink my strategy. I've gotta get out of here. Right now!*

What most horrified her was that she was reacting to his unexpected charm. That she felt herself wanting to please this sleazy crook—who just happened to be the uncle who had sold her into untold misery—added to her confusion unbearably. The moment stretched.

"I . . . we . . ." she could almost feel Alvec's concerned puzzlement, Joseph's unquestioning support. "We're an independent outfit," she said at last. "We're happy with that for now." She paused to put a polite interval between her refusal and the next order of business. "There's an outstanding balance due on this shipment. If you could just give us a credit chip, we'll be on our way."

Nomik and Silken stared at her. She felt a little relief at the sight of Nomik staring at her like an animal who'd been hit between the eyes with a sledgehammer. Doubtless it had been years since anyone had flatly turned them down. Particularly not a ragtailed freighter captain like Joat.

Ciety's eyes narrowed.

"About that," he said coolly, "Silken told me about your problems with New Destinies. That little debt you incurred there, remember that?" Joat nodded slowly. "Well, it probably won't surprise you to learn that I have good friends there and they were amenable to coming to an arrangement with me. It'll relieve you, I'm sure, to know that instead of forty Earth standard days, you have an unlimited length of time to pay up." Joat blinked, and Ciety nodded smugly. "To me. I've bought your debt." He folded his arms and regarded her with a narrow-eyed smile.

Joat drew in a long shocked breath and felt her body go numb. Beside her, she was vaguely aware of Alvec and Joseph stirring uneasily.

"So what we'll do," Ciety continued, "is put the amount outstanding for this shipment against *your* debt. Leaving you one hundred and fourteen thousand credits in the red." He grinned. "Don't worry, this'll go faster than you're expecting. I'll take care of your expenses, food and fuel and docking fees and I pay well. Anyone'll tell you that. You'll be clear in no time." He held out his hand to her. "So. Welcome aboard."

Joat stared at his offered hand and then at him and her vision narrowed, focusing like a laser beam on his smirking face. "You don't remember me at all," she said in wonder, finding it absurdly difficult to speak.

He studied her for a moment and then shook his head indifferently. "No," he said with a shrug. "Can't say that I do."

Joat slapped his hand aside violently, overwhelmed by an anger so hot that for a moment she didn't feel at all. She watched her own fist fly out to strike her uncle on the point of his chin and he went down with a ridiculously surprised expression on his face.

She lunged for him and Joseph caught her, holding her back.

Alvec moved between them and the golden-haired receptionist, who now held a weapon trained on the three of them, waiting for orders from Ciety.

"I'm your niece!" she screamed in fury, struggling to climb out of Joseph's unyielding arms. She *had* to. Crush that face, see it crumble, stamp it under her heel and feel the bone crack . . .

"Stop it, Joat," Joseph whispered calmingly. "Joat, contain yourself!"

After a few moments his voice penetrated the hot fog in her head. Color began to return to her white face and sanity to her eyes. She was breathing in little panting grunts.

"I'm your brother's daughter," she said, taking control of herself. "You were a dreamdust addict." She gave a loud mocking sniff. "You just had to have it. I remember going hungry all the time so you could have your little fix. Then you lost me in a poker game to a tramp-freighter captain."

She shook herself free of Joseph's grip as it relaxed in horror. "And you can't imagine the nightmare living with that soulless scum was. But *you* don't remember. Lucky you. *I* can't forget!" She spat on him where he lay on the floor. "I have no debt to you," she said in a voice rich with loathing. "I owe you *nothing.*"

Joat turned and stalked out. Even the receptionist/bodyguard was too frozen in shock to stop her.

CHAPTER ELEVEN

IT WAS SILENT in the room after her departure, as though someone had switched off an erupting volcano. The silence seemed to ring.

"Is it true?" Joseph asked, his voice gone husky and quiet. Nomik Ciety's face was still fluid with shock for a moment, then hardened again. "I swear that I never saw that woman before in my life!" he said.

He cleared his throat, looking at the Bethelite with wide, innocent eyes. *That is a dangerous man,* he thought. The evaluation was automatic. In this business you had to be able to size someone up quickly. *That crazy bitch's lover or something?* No way to tell that; there were some who'd kill anyone who'd done what she said he'd done.

Had he? Behind his frown of concern, he searched his memory. It was excellent since he'd been through the treatment. Back when he was dusting, there were holes you could fly a naval assault carrier through. He'd done some crazy things back then, no doubt about it.

Nowadays, he would have sold her, not lost her in a game.

He sat up and Silken went to his aid, helping him to rise from the floor. "I had a brother," he said in confusion. "But whether he had children or not . . ."

Ciety brushed his hair back and tenderly touched his chin.

"She's wrong about one thing, though. And about this I am dead certain. She owes me a hundred and fourteen thousand credits. So you, my friends, had better go after her, calm her down and put her in a better frame of mind. Or I'll take her ship just as happily and just as legally as New Destinies would." He glared at them both. "You got that?"

Both men nodded.

"But if it *is* true," Joseph said in a quiet, deadly voice, "then the matter must be dealt with. You understand this?"

"Look, stranger," Ciety barked, his patience at an end, "I have no living relatives and I don't want any. So if your little friend has some wild idea of running a con on me, you better straighten her out. I'm one of the powers around this place. You are nothing."

He made a chopping motion with his hand and looked into Joseph's eyes. Blue met blue, equally cold. "Now get out."

"You're both crazy," Alvec said after the door of N. Ciety, Research and Development, had closed gently, but firmly behind them. "The Captain is this guy's niece? And you, what was that? You were calling him out in a duel, or what? And what about . . ." He caught himself and leaned close to Joseph " . . . you know? We didn't find out jack."

Joseph sighed and stopped walking. He looked around at the sylvan beauty of the dome, inhaled the odors of cut grass and flowers and running water, folded his arms and stared at nothing.

"To state the obvious," he said, "this has gone badly. The last thing we wanted to do was incur this man's hostility. But we have. Joat should have accepted his offer of employment; it was a perfect opportunity to find out what we *must* learn. She did not."

Alvec brushed a hand distractedly over his hair. "Yeah." he muttered. "Isn't like the Captain at all."

Joseph shrugged. "Exactly. *You* know Joat. *I* know Joat. Was that—" he jerked his chin back at the tunnel mouth "—in the least like the Joat we know?"

"What'll we do?"

"We must play the dice as they fall from the hand of the God," he said. "To begin, let us find Joat. I have," he went on, and a slight chill settled in Alvec's stomach, "some questions for her."

Joat threw herself into the Captain's couch.

"Rand!" she barked. "If you're in V.R. pull yourself out. I need your help here and it's going to take all your attention." Her hands flew over her comp, pulling up Rohan's computer address system.

"What is it, Joat? I was engaged in a most diverting—"

"We've got to break into Nomik Ciety's data system. I want to know who he's been talking to for the last two months. I don't much care about content just now, but I want to know who and where from. And if there's anything specially encrypted . . ."

"All of his incoming messages are encrypted. All of *everybody's* messages are encrypted on Rohan. I wouldn't be terribly surprised to discover that they *think* in encryption here." Rand paused. "Your instructions are the same as when you left, Joat. But your attitude is decidedly more urgent. What happened?"

Joat lifted her hands from the comp and looked at her fingers; they were long and graceful, with the slightly used look of someone who worked with her hands on delicate—but sometimes hot or sparking—instrumentation. She folded the hands into fists and leaned back into her chair, closed her eyes, took two deep breaths.

Then she spoke, without opening them.

"I just lost my mind, Rand," she explained. Her voice had a weary tone. "I almost got us all killed and at the time," she shook her head slowly, "I didn't care." She pushed her hair off her face with both hands. "I don't believe I did that," she said.

"Where are Alvec and Joseph?" Rand asked.

"Looking for me, most likely," she said "Tell them . . . Tell them I need time to regain my composure, that's true enough. Tell them I'll be in touch shortly. Tell them to relax and take advantage of CenSec's generosity. But don't tell them where I am!" She turned to glare at it "You got that?"

"It's done, Joat. Joseph says to tell you that you and he need to talk."

"Did he ask where I was?"

"Yes, I told him that you hadn't said," Rand's voice sounded strained. "I don't understand how you humans can do that so casually. I find it very disorienting to make statements that are contrary to the facts."

Joat smiled gently at it. "Thank you for lying for me, Rand. I know you don't like it. What did Al say?"

"Alvec says he'll bring you home some take-out."

Joat smiled wanly at that.

"I belted Nomik Ciety in the chops," she said. Then she smiled faintly in satisfaction. "I knocked him right on his ass."

After a moment, Rand asked, "Was that wise?"

She sighed, "Certainly not. But I really needed to do it."

Rand's lights glowed yellow in puzzlement.

"I believe I have insufficient information," it concluded. "Because based on what you've just told me, I would be forced to agree that you have, indeed, lost your mind."

"Oh, I did," she assured it. "But it's back now and we have work to do. What have you found out so far?"

"The Kolnari have apparently never actually visited Rohan," it told her.

Joat waved a hand dismissively.

"Not surprising, they're uncomfortable off their ships, they like to have a ceiling over their heads and walls around them. Looking up through that dome would just about drive them crazy. Besides, they don't exactly enjoy socializing with other races." She shook her head "They'd use go-betweens or tight beam communications. My bet is the latter. See if you can find anything unusual in ship to port messages. Meanwhile, I'll try'n get into Ciety's cyber-house through a back door."

The two worked intently for a while and the quiet soothed Joat's jangled nerves. *There's nothing like working out a technical problem to get yourself centered,* she thought.

"I'm in!" Joat called.

"Congratulations," Rand said. Then, "Or perhaps not."

Her head snapped up.

"What?"

"Something's wrong. Something's gotten in."

"What is it?" she demanded.

"I don't know. But it's eating me."

CHAPTER TWELVE

"SAL?"

"Yeah?" he looked up from The Anvil's accounts at his secretary.

"That fine that Mr. va Riguez wanted paid?"

"Yeah?" he said again, with exaggerated patience. This particular employee seemed incapable of just saying what was on his mind.

"Can't do it. Mr. va Riguez's account says insufficient funds."

Sal grunted and reached for the note-screen in his secretary's hand. He skimmed through the bankers' jargon until he reached the amount of the fine.

"Oi vey!" he exclaimed. "That can't be right."

"I double checked it, Sal. That's the right amount."

"A hundred and twenty thousand credits! You gotta be kiddin' me. What the hell did Simeon-Hap do for a fine that size?"

"I couldn't find out." The secretary shrugged. "It's confidential." Sal just looked at him from under lowered brows.

"Get me Dyson," he said at last. "Now."

Graf Dyson shrugged. "She had to be fined, Sal. She entered the station illegally."

Sal gave him a look. "A hundred and twenty thousand?" he said.

Dyson threw up his hands and leaned forward. "Look," he said, "Clal va Riguez says to me, make it a big fine. Use your discretion. And she ticked me off." He leaned back and shrugged. "So I did what he said."

Sal rubbed his chin thoughtfully. "Well, he told me to pay it. But his account says insufficient funds. I don't think he expected it to be this much." He gave Dyson a hard look. "He didn't set a ceiling?"

Graf didn't like Sal's attitude. This wasn't even his affair and he was getting really pushy. Besides, Graf's dealings were supposed to be confidential. And this conversation was lasting way too long.

"Look, maybe you're right, maybe there's been a misunderstanding. Have va Riguez call me. We'll straighten it out."

"He's not here," Sal grumbled, still looking like he was waiting for a concession.

"What is this?" Dyson snapped, suddenly angry. People were supposed to come to him hat in hand and to say thanks when they left. He'd had dealings with Sal before and hadn't gotten the respect he thought he deserved. "I don't discuss your business with other people. I won't discuss va Riguez's business with you. He has a problem, have him get back to me. I don't hear from him, I figure he wants this fine to stick. You," he snapped a finger towards Sal, "I don't wanta hear from." And he disconnected.

He leaned back thoughtfully. *Maybe I should reduce it,* he thought. Mr. va Riguez had told him no more than twenty thousand. *Yeah, but if I lower it now, Sal will think he's scored one off me.* Dyson grimaced.

Then again, if va Riguez has gone missing then maybe he never intended to take care of this. And Dyson was experienced enough to know that to an operation like Joat's twenty thousand might as well be a hundred and twenty thousand. *So. I'll leave it. If he contacts me, I'll say I misunderstood. If he doesn't, New Destinies gets a little richer.* He grinned. *And Sal gets a message. Don't mess with Graf Dyson.*

Sal leaned back in his chair. He wasn't happy about not being able to follow va Riguez's orders. The man was a good customer, and he represented another, more shadowy, good customer that Sal had been doing business with for years.

Besides, he'd learned early in life who was safe to cross and who wasn't. Dyson, it depended on the circumstances, but basically he was a lightweight. But Clal va Riguez . . . that was a dangerous man.

I better put a message in the pipe, he thought unhappily. *That way I'm covered.* If it was important, Clal, or one of his associates would get back to him. If he heard nothing, *Then I'll assume no action is called for.*

✧   ✧   ✧

The *Chadragupta Rao*'s hull gave a shudder as the dockside connectors went home and Rohan's gravity took over. Metal and com-
posites crackled and sighed in reaction as weight and pressure altered.
Fresher air poured in; the *Rao* had problems with life-support, redline
maintenance no Company ship or chartered freelancer would tolerate.

Bros Sperin stood easily on her command deck, adjusting to the
lighter gravity with automatic ease, equally easy with the hostile glare
of the *Rao*'s Captain. For that matter, the only eyes on the wedge-
shaped deck that *weren't* hostile were the four Sondee orbs right
behind him. They were probably bright and shiny . . .

"Far as I'm concerned, Sperin, you cease to exist when you walk
off my deck. You got that?"

The spacer was a pale, flaccid little man. He smelled like a locker
full of sweaty clothes. But then, so did his whole ship. The bridge
went darker as screens powered-down, only the monitors and standby
readouts still active.

Bros nodded, his eyes cool. The little needler in his cuff was ready,
but he didn't think he'd need it.

"All debts are paid," he said evenly. "And in the event that you find
it necessary to alert the Family to my presence . . ."

The little man stiffened.

"You can tell them I'm here to find a friend in trouble. It's a
personal thing."

The spacer's pale brow furrowed in confusion.

"But of course," Bros said gently, "I'd be very disappointed if you
did tell them I'm here."

The spacer jerked his head in a negative. "All debts are paid," he
said sourly.

They were in the shadowy reaches where organized crime brushed
and merged with the fringes of Intelligence work. It was the only
way to keep things functioning at all—the old *lex talonis,* eye for an
eye.

"Thanks," Bros said with a smile and a slap on the back that
staggered the little spacer. "I knew I could count on you."

He hefted his duffel to his shoulder and walked out, deck grat-
ings ringing under his magnetic boots, each stride a little sticky. Seg
!T'sel trotted after him.

"I still say we should be disguised," he whispered.

Bros smiled for the monitors and put an arm around the alien's bony shoulders; they felt warm under his hand, hotter than a human metabolism, and the pattern of bones was more like a lattice than a framework.

"Think of it this way, Seg," he said, between clenched teeth—natural, and it also activated his scrambler. That was a system sophisticated enough to feed a false conversation to the audio pickups. "How many Sondee do you see around here?"

They were out of the docking bay and into a concourse, full of crowds skipping on and off slideways or calling for little robotic shuttlecars, heavy with the scent of ozone. Most of the crowd were humans of various types, the odd Ursinoid, a scattering of other species . . .

"One or two," Seg said.

"And how many of them are wearing eyepatches, or wigs, or walking with canes?"

Seg opened his mouth, then shut it with a snap. The bony plates within went *tok*.

"Nine humans out of ten can't tell one Sondee from another, unless there's something *unusual* about the Sondee. On your homeworld, you get seen as *you*. Here you get seen as a *Sondee*. Grasp the principle?"

A wordless grunt. "But *you* should be wearing a disguise."

Damned if I'm going to wear a rubber nose, either, Bros thought. He shrugged. "Disguises are more trouble than they're worth unless you absolutely need one."

"But they'll recognize you."

"Who is they?" Bros asked.

"Well," Seg temporized, "who are we looking for?"

"At the moment, Joat Simeon-Hap. Ultimately, the Kolnari. Joat's on our side . . . mostly, so we want her to recognize me. The Kolnari will kill you whoever you look like. But the Family will want to know what you're trying to hide. So they'll take you aside and ask you questions until *they're* satisfied. And Seg . . . they're very hard to satisfy. So our best disguise is to look like ordinary spacers."

Seg nodded solemnly, and then nearly fell flat as they stepped onto a slideway. Bros clenched his teeth again and put a hand under the Sondee's not-quite-an-elbow.

They'd left the docking area behind. The tunnels and arcades beneath the crater floor engulfed them, two more anonymous spacers in worn coveralls, carrying the record of their lives in their duffels through the jostling crowds. They passed innumerable cheap hostels burrowed back into the rock, CHEAP ROOMS and CLEAN BEDS blinking in holographic colors outside their barred doors. The drab hostels gave way to chandlers' offices, advertising electronics, software, graving docks, power systems.

"It's not quite what I imagined a pirate haven would be like," Seg whispered.

"Piracy's a business," Bros said. "Ships are ships. They need fuel and parts and maintenance. A lot of other business goes through here, too—some of it even legitimate."

"But I thought it would be something more like—"

The slideway divided around a dropshaft. Bros took them off and into the open darkness. They drifted downward, and images played before their eyes.

"—*any species, any combination for*—"

It was hard for a member of another species to be shocked by human tastes in erotic entertainment, but Seg managed it. All four eyes bulged slightly, then blinked in unison, a disconcerting sight.

"—*come one, come all, contestants welcome*—"

This time the naked shapes were muscular and lithe, sheened with sweat and blood, long curved knives in their hands.

"—*nothing too exotic at the Torture Pit*—"

Bros closed his own eyes, wincing slightly. "This is the entertainment level," he said. "Want to stop and see the sights?"

"Ah . . . no."

"Good. Let's get some business done, then."

Seg cocked his ears at a cacophony of voices, human and alien, clashing music from various bars and an assortment of street sounds from air-scrubbers to ground cars.

"Still, what energy there is in that sound!" Seg exclaimed as they stepped out of the shaft into a more placid level. He turned to Bros his eyes shining. "I'm working on an opera in my spare time," he confessed.

What Sondee isn't? Sperin wondered.

"One day I will work *this*—" he gestured with both hands towards the street before them "—into my overture."

Sperin smiled and nodded. *Not bad kid, Seg. And how I wish he wasn't here.*

"We better get moving," he murmured in Seg's ear whorl. "We look like a couple of rubes standing here."

"I thought you said Rohan was fairly safe?" Seg protested.

"Safe is a relative term," Bros said. "If we were in a Sondee swamp, for example, we'd probably be safe from wild animals, since they're generally shy around people. But even there, smearing yourself all over with beef gravy might be considered putting too much temptation in their way. If you get my drift?"

Seg's ear whorls colored slightly and he nodded.

"Which way?" he asked.

"We'll check the bars along here," Bros said. "I've no idea where Joat might be, but my information is that her crew has a fondness for dockside bars."

"These entertainments do not seem *too* raucous," Seg said.

Well, the one with the two girls and the Nuruzian lizard was a little much, Bros thought, scanning the crowd. On the other hand, the really unpleasant places were unlikely to attract Joat's crewfolk, which was a relief. You had to wade through sewage often enough in this business . . .

Seg made a grand gesture. "Garçon!" he called. "Madder music and stronger wine!" He blinked diagonally when Bros looked sharply at him. "Classical reference," the Sondee said.

"I read Dobson too," Sperin said dryly, and Seg's ear whorls flushed a deeper blue.

The waiter brought a bottle of surprisingly good port from Ceres—the planet, not the asteroid—and Bros gave a realistic wince as the display on the tray showed the deduction from his account. In actuality, the expense account was one of the few real perks of the trade; he sipped at the smooth nutty flavor. The best of everything ended up in Rohan—at a price. A bowl of raisins, pecans, and dried *gunung* went down beside it.

"This tastes much better. Sweeter." Seg threw back his glass and poured another.

Great fardling voids, as Joat is wont to say, Bros thought; this time his wince was genuine. For one thing, that was a lousy way to treat a fine wine; for another . . . Sondee metabolized alcohol faster than humans, but not *that* fast.

For a moment he thought that Seg had burst into song, but the voice was deeper and more gravelly. A human voice, one he recognized, singing *La vie en Rose* . . .

Alvec had his head together with a brawny blond wearing a shy, enraptured smile as he crooned.

Things can't be too *bad if Alvec's out picking roses,* Bros thought. He motioned Seg to remain seated and moved up behind Joat's crew.

"Al!" he said and slapped the man on the shoulder.

Al looked up questioningly, his eyes blank.

"Alvec Dia," Bros insisted.

"Yeah," Alvec agreed slowly. "Who're you?"

"I'm Joat's friend from New Destinies. I'm the guy who told her to check this place out. Hey, listen buddy," Bros pulled out a chair and sat down, leaning towards Alvec confidentially, "I'm looking for a berth. You think maybe Joat can help me out?"

The woman was looking at him and scowling. Bros saw recognition flicker in the other man's eyes, but the face remained mildly friendly, if you could say that about something that looked like it had been pounded out of rough wrought iron.

"I dunno," Alvec said. "We're kinda full up right now."

Bros kept smiling, and ground his foot into the reinforced toe of one of Alvec's boots under the table. *Come on, you imbecile, there's no time for let-the-spook-twist-in-the-wind games here!*

"Well, why don't we let the Captain decide?" Bros asked reasonably. "I'm good at what I do. You can always use a good hand, right? What's the *Wyal's* berth number? I'll go ask her."

Alvec's smile grew wider, and he let his hand drop to the blond woman's.

"Why doncha tell me where you're stayin'?" he asked. "I'll have her get in touch . . . later. I'm sort of busy. Not that you're not welcome or anything, old pal, but . . ."

"Aw, c'mon, buddy. I can get the number from central registry. I just wanted to save the credits." *And keep the Family watchprograms from getting tripped.*

The blond shifted nervously, aware of the undercurrents and not sure she wanted to be around them. Bros thought that decided Alvec.

"SJ 467-Y," he said. "But the Captain isn't there right now."

Bros grinned.

"I'll take my chances. Maybe she'll be back by the time I get there. Thanks buddy." And he slapped Alvec's shoulder one more time.

Alvec watched him leave, his eyes speculative.

"Who's that?" Rose asked.

"Oh, friend of the Captain's," Alvec said and gently took her hand. "You were telling me something about yourself," he said and kissed her fingertips. "I think that's much more interesting."

✧   ✧   ✧

Bros withdrew his credit chip from the meter and dragged Seg out of the ground-car by his sleeve. Then he leaned the young Sondee up against the docking mechanism while he activated the *Wyal*'s com to announce their presence.

Seg began to sing snatches of his opera-in-progress in a light and very pleasant baritone; much to the amusement of passing spacers.

Wonderful, Bros thought in exasperation. *Nothing obvious about you is there, Mr. Wannabe?* On the other had, it could be worse— he could be in disguise. Nobody was really surprised when a drunk started singing, and a Sondee just couldn't sing badly.

There'd been no answer to their hail. Not even from Joat's elaborate AI. That had to mean something was wrong. After all, it wasn't as if the thing could go on shore leave.

He moved to the lock, and shielding his movements as best he could with his body, placed a small and very illegal device above the lock mechanism. In seconds he was able to enter the *Wyal,* drawing Seg in after him.

Joat cut off the connection with Nomik Ciety's data link and turned to Rand.

"Did that . . . ?" Before she could finish asking if the cutoff had helped, they were reconnected with a sharp *plink.* She turned and cut the link again, again it reinstated itself.

As far as she could tell something was flooding rapidly into her comp, but nothing was going out. At least not yet.

And there was only one way to do anything at all. No human brain reading code could deal with this in the sort of time-frame necessary. But the alternative was hideously dangerous; if you linked yourself directly, *your* software was vulnerable.

Her hands danced across the console.

Cutting the link only delayed the worm program's progress for seconds at a time, but she continued to do it. Yet it continuously broke through everything she could throw at it. *Subtle stuff. Whoever thought this up knew their hand from a hacksaw.*

Cold sweat flowed down her forehead into her eyes and beaded her upper lip, tasting of salt and despair. Her hands grew tired and clumsy at the controls, and her fear for Rand distracted her. More than once she'd regretted being human, never more so than now. She wasn't fast enough, she wasn't calm enough, she was losing Rand! *Here I had to go and* design *an AI that was my friend.* It wasn't even a real person, just a very good imitation . . .

"Fardle." Her hands picked up the interfacer unit and snapped home the connector. It settled over her head, blocking vision and hearing. She was alone in a world of darkness.

"Execute."

. . . standing on a featureless plain that stretched to infinity in every direction.

The air smelled dead, with a sterile metallic tinge. The ground underfoot was some gray metal, grooved in endless parallel lines. Scattered about were boulders, each a geometric shape, squares, polyhedrons, eye-hurting things like angular Möbius strips.

Overhead the sky opened its eye. Threads dropped from it towards her, writhing, sentient eyelashes like velvet serpents. They wound around her wrists and pulled her upward. Behind her the metal plain suddenly collapsed, turning sandy and friable, then melting into a smooth bath of liquid that smelled sickly-sweet beneath her. The thick sugary surface moved, sluggish and smooth, as things squirmed beneath it.

exterior interface compromised, off/on circuitry compromised.

The eye blinked closed around her. Within was a garden, green and yellow and purple, in bright primary colors that looked too artificial to be tangible; yet she could feel the grass beneath her bare feet, smell the cinnamon scent of the flowers. A figure walked towards her with jerky quickness, a figure shaped like a man sculpted out of living water.

help . . . meeee . . . it said, in a breathy whisper. Something stirred in the middle of its forehead, between blank silver eyes.

Joat reached in and grasped the tendril, pulling it out into the light. It came easily, and then slid through her fingers. The end of it split and split and split again, into hair-thin threads that reached for her eyes and ears and mouth.

A knife appeared in her hand; where the edge moved, the stuff of space split and bled chaotic patterns of moving light. She used the knife to section the onrushing tentacle, then again, so that there were four ends. Those she wrapped around her wrists, moving hands and arms in an intricate pattern that tied the tentacle into a huge knot whose convolutions led the eye down and away along a path with no ending. More and more of it flowed out of the water-sculpture figure, turning it clear and transparent. The silvery fingers came up and began to knot and twist at the body of the tentacle themselves, and . . .

. . . she fell forward into the figure's open mouth.

Stone jarred beneath her feet. She was in a library, an ancient library of leather-bound books in shelves that reached towards the dark coffered wood of the ceiling. Gilt flaked from their spines, shining in the light of the burning logs in the big stone fireplace that occupied one wall. A stranger in a plush smoking robe was sitting in an overstuffed leather armchair beside the fire, eating books. His mouth stretched as each folio-sized volume was pushed home; then he belched slightly and took a sip from the snifter of brandy in his other hand, before reaching for a new volume. Gaps stood on the shelves, like raw wounds, bleeding sorrow.

There was another chair and table on the other side of the fire. Joat sat in it, and opened the book lying closed. The page was blank, but columns of figures and letters appeared as she ran her finger across it. Pages flipped forward, and then she was standing with the book held open before her.

"Perhaps you'd like to eat this?" she said.

There was no mind behind the eyes that looked up a her, only hunger. The figure's hands snapped out and dragged the book near; she braced her feet and hauled backwards, but the strength in the fetch's arms was beyond her. The book plastered itself across the avid face of the eater.

His lips parted in a vast dolorous gape to take it in, but the book grew faster. Joat could feel it sucking at the skin of her fingertips as she released it; the leaves closed around the eater's face, and now his hands were scrambling to pull it free, but the book wriggled forward, growing, licking hungrily at his skin. The head began to squeeze forward into the jaws of the book, and the figure rose and staggered off across the library. As its substance flowed forward into the pages it dissolved, matter breaking up into a whirlpool of *off/on/off/on/off,* databits streaming into their new matrix.

The walls of the building shook as the book finished its task and fell to the floor.

Joat stooped to pick it up, and—

✧   ✧   ✧

Bros stood, watching the figure slumped in the chair. He could see the sweat running down from below the padded rim of the interfacer unit; figures scrolled by on the screen before her, blurring in their speed.

His teeth clicked together in shock. Direct interfacing like that was *illegal,* outside carefully-supervised research settings. There was no *telling* what could happen when you linked your brain's own operating code with a comp system like that!

And there was nothing he could do; interrupting would be more dangerous than leaving her be. He felt an enormous upwelling anger, and wondered at it even as the muscles of his neck and shoulders tensed in rage.

What's it to me if the idiot kills herself? A waste of potential, yes, but—

Joat started convulsively and threw the interfacer helmet aside. Sweat darkened her flax-colored hair and plastered it to her skull; dark circles stood out like bruises beneath her eyes. Bros opened his mouth to speak, or bellow.

"Get out of here," she growled, turning back to her work with obsessive intensity. Her fingers blurred across the keyboard.

"Gotta be sure, gotta be sure," she muttered to herself. "*Got* it."

Bros craned his neck, trying to make out the flying stream of data. Joat did something and its progress slowed enough that the individual characters could be made out. They were some sort of encryption, vaguely familiar. He leaned forward for a better look and thoughtlessly placed his hand on her shoulder.

The punch was so unexpected that it almost connected. His hand snapped up to catch her fist, moving automatically to clench and stab at a nerve junction. Joat sprang to her feet then, putting the coiled strength of her body behind a head-butt aimed at his jaw and strong enough to shatter bone. Bros yanked her off balance and spun her around, twisting her captured hand up behind her back.

But gently, he didn't want to hurt her and he sure didn't need to add to her hostility. That nearly cost him a broken pubic bone as her heel drove backward. He staggered away, curling around the pain in his lower gut, and Joat writhed free like an eel.

Is she on drugs? he thought, breath wheezing out behind clenched teeth. Blank ferocity met his eyes, and he forced himself into the ready position.

❖   ❖   ❖

Seg watched in astonishment as the two Terrans wrestled. *Why are they fighting?*

Bros had assured him that Joat was on their side: He glanced at the screen where she'd been sitting and his attention was caught by a familiar symbol. Ah, yes, he knew this one.

Flexing his fingers to loosen them up, Seg took Joat's seat and began to work.

query; identity.

He entered it and continued, all twelve fingertips hitting the board microseconds apart. Yes, it was the program—and very neatly tied up in mid-operation, if in an unorthodox way. But it was all there, ready to come out the minute the AI's own defense program relaxed. Better to deactivate it completely . . .

"Thank you."

Seg looked up, blinking each pair of eyes in sequence. A voice-program too; very good, perhaps a little flat on the intonations.

"You're welcome," he said. "That ought to do it. And *this* will set it to eating itself. You can let it go, now."

Joat froze. The cable-strong arms that pinioned her relaxed.

"*Will* you stop trying to kill me, please?" Bros said in her ear.

"When you stop trying to break my arm."

They rolled free and stared at each other warily. "Spook," Joat muttered, disgust in her tone.

"Maniac," Bros Sperin replied, then smiled at her. The grin caught her unawares, and she found herself smiling back. It was crooked, but genuine.

"Is that another spook?" she said, moving towards her control couch. "And what the fardling void is et doing with my AI?"

"Yes, I am a spook," the Sondee said. "Seg !T'sel, male, weapons development specialist. I'm clearing up this infiltration program. I helped design it, it was stolen—it's all on a need to know basis."

Bros smothered a snort at the sound of the phrase.

"I do, really, really, need to know," Joat began dangerously.

"Yes, I think we do," another voice said from the entranceway.

Joat and Bros turned. Joseph stood there, arms crossed; in his right hand was a compact, chunky-looking weapon. Bros recognized it; chemical-energy sliver gun. Messy, but very effective; the length of duramet tubing Alvec was holding in one hand and tapping into the palm of the other probably would be, too.

"How long have you been there?" Joat asked.

"A few minutes."

"And you just stood there?" she demanded in disbelief.

"Watching you, as long as you were winning," Joseph said. "Mr. Sperin is, in a sense, our employer . . . and has valuable information. About a man who may well have dealings with the Kolnari."

"Right," Joat said. "You can tell—"

The com chimed and the three of them looked up in quick surprise at the forward screen. The *respond yes/no* blinked on for a second, then the screen went to two-way in a manner supposedly impossible.

A thickset man in late middle age was staring back at them. *I've seen corpses with more expression,* she thought.

"Good evening Mr. Sperin," the stranger said in a mellow, cultured tone. The small hairs bristled on the back of her neck.

"Good evening," Bros said pleasantly. "Joat, this is Chief Family Enforcer Vand Yoered."

Vand nodded, his heavy face wearing a neutral expression.

"Captain," he said quietly. "And Mr. !T'sel. I'm a great admirer of your work, sir," he told the young Sondee. "It's a pleasure to have you as our guest."

Seg turned to Bros and whispered, "See! I told you I'd be recognized."

Vand stared at him for just a moment, as though put off his stride by that simple statement, then he turned to Bros and Joat.

"You're all friends, I take it?" he asked with a raised eyebrow and a sardonic glance at Alvec's club and Joseph's sliver gun.

Joat blushed and shrugged, moving herself out of Bros's vicinity.

"I've never met Mr. !T'sel before," she said, "but Bros and I are well acquainted and any friend of his, as they say."

"Mr. Sperin broke into your ship, Captain. With a device so illegal that I believe CenSec is the sole owner of the remaining few. We don't allow that on Rohan."

"That's a sort of challenge we've made to each other," Joat said, laughing nervously. "He, uh, breaks into my place, I break into his and we try to keep our security arrangements ahead of our creativity."

She couldn't seem to figure out what to do with her hands when she was through speaking. She wanted to cross her arms, but was afraid that would look too defensive. She dropped them to her hips, then settled for clasping them behind her back.

Oh, Ghu, a Family Enforcer. No, make that the *Chief* Family

Enforcer. Sperin had been back in her life under ten minutes and already she was looking death in the face and lying like a trooper on his behalf.

CenSec Intelligence was building up a heavy account of favors owing.

"That's fascinating," Vand said slowly. "My information reports that you two had no contact prior to a meeting on New Destinies."

"Actually," Bros said, "we've known each other for some time. I first met Joat on SSS-900-C, just after we drove off the Kolnari."

The Enforcer's eyes lit. "Ah!" he said, "how very interesting. The Kolnari."

That was a clear request for information, one to be denied at Bros's peril. He decided to take a chance and ignore it, offering only part of the truth.

"I'm here on a personal mission," he said. "I heard about Joat's trouble on New Destinies and came to offer her my assistance. I'm hoping she'll go back there with me so that we can get this thing straightened out."

"And . . . the presence of Joseph ben Said on her ship . . . ? This is an accident? The Bethelite head of security comes to Rohan, visits Nomik Ciety, this is unrelated to you in any way."

"That is between Joat and Mr. ben Said," Bros said grimly. "I assumed he'd returned to Bethel as I had strongly urged him to do."

"What about this evening's attempt to break into Nomik Ciety's comp?" Vand asked, his face closed now.

"That *is* personal," Joat declared vehemently. "Very. A *family* matter." She stressed the word "family," and the Enforcer raised a brow.

"I'm inclined to believe *that* at least," he said smoothly. "Only family can provoke that degree of bitterness." He paused and sat considering them for a time. "All right," he said at last. "I'll let the matter drop. For now. But I warn you, do not interfere with our respected citizens."

Only a slight pause drew a line of irony under the phrase. "Nomik Ciety enjoys the Family's protection while he is our guest on Rohan. None of you will in any way interfere with his business here."

He looked directly at Joat. "There will be no further attempts to break into his comp. Is that understood?"

The three of them nodded. *And be good children,* Joat thought to herself sarcastically. It was a while since she'd been scolded; she'd forgotten how unpleasant the sensation could be.

"Excellent, then this interview is at an end. Don't stay on Rohan too long, Mr. Sperin. You're liable to prove too great a temptation to some of our more impulsive guests. And frankly, as my staff is somewhat overextended at the moment, we might not be able to adequately protect you." He reached out and cut the contact.

The three of them drooped as though someone had cut their strings. Breath went out in a communal sigh.

"Rand!" Joat called.

"Sssshhhhh!" Seg whispered, waving his hands, palms out, at her and Bros. "Ssshh, ssshhh, ssshh!" Then for good measure he placed one upraised finger against his suckerlike mouth and turned to the com. His fingers flew over the controls and then, following a graceful whirl of his wrist, he pressed his forefinger with dramatic finality on the cutoff switch.

"Now," he said, "we may talk."

Joat stared at him for a moment, then turned to Bros.

Bros was staring at Seg with a speculative glint in his eye. "You're sure he's gone?" he asked.

"Oh, absolutely," Seg said comfortably. "And locked out too. That is until the next time we access the com . . . or someone calls in. But then, we can just lock 'em out again." He folded his arms across his chest and looked smug. "Can't we?"

"Rand?" Joat called, her voice tight with anxiety.

"Present." Its voice was flat and abstracted.

Joat frowned. "Are you all right? You sound different."

"Regrettably, I am different. Several sections of my memory were infected by the worm program and partially destroyed. I decided to simply erase those sections and reboot them from storage. I've lost a great deal of my personality and a small amount of vocal inflection. On the plus side, I was able to erase the infected sections without tripping any eggs. A worm program this aggressively vicious often leaves a small bundle of encryption that can start the whole business over again."

"I took care of that," Seg volunteered, raising his hand.

"Thank you," Rand said. "Joat, I was able to find and hold onto a transmission from Ciety's files before the worm's attack became too overwhelming. If you like, I can concentrate on decoding it before repairing my other programs."

"Yes," she said fervently, "please." Then Joat turned to Seg, where he still sat at the com. She took his hand in both of hers and looked him in the eyes, two of them anyway. "I'm in your debt," she said softly. "If there is ever any way that I can be of service to you, you have only to ask."

Seg's face and ear whorls suffused with color and he began to stammer in embarrassment.

"You-yer-you're p-perfectly welcome, Captain. I'm a uh, a weapons specialist and as an adjunct to m-my usual interests, I-I-I sometimes develop worm programs like this one. That one rather, since it's gone." He laughed inanely and hurried on. "I helped to develop it, in fact. That's how I recognized it so fast and knew how to neutralize it."

Joat blinked, a little taken aback by that revelation.

"Yes," Rand said, "I thought it had a certain Sondee subtlety to it. Almost a rhythm."

"Precisely!" Seg exclaimed and began an earnest conversation with Rand.

Joat turned to Bros. He stood with his feet apart, arms folded across his chest, watching her with an unfathomable expression in his dark eyes.

"Thank you for bringing him," she said, indicating Seg.

Bros smiled. "You'll have to excuse him, he's not at his best. We did a pub crawl halfway across the docks looking for you or your crew and my young friend imbibed pretty heavily."

"If I can forgive him for writing the fardling worm in the first place, I can forgive him for anything, I suppose." She turned to smile fondly at the young Sondee. Then she glanced at Bros from the comers of her eyes. "So, what are you doing here?"

One of the things I like about you is that you don't beat around the bush, Joat. He fought the urge to smile, knowing she'd think he was being condescending.

"I've come to call you back," he said. "Your part in this mission is canceled."

"Oh?" she raised her brows. "Perhaps I'd better bring you up to date."

"As I've already indicated, I know about your debt to New Destinies. Twenty thousand credits, Joat! How in blazes did you manage that?"

Joat studied him. His face expressed annoyance, but his eyes were amused. She wondered if he'd found out about her relationship to

Ciety or if he was recalling her because of the debt. Though he'd gotten the amount wrong. Sperin was really gonna squeak when he found out it was *one hundred* twenty thousand. She suppressed a wistful sigh. *Irrelevant now,* she thought.

"I'm afraid the situation has grown just a liiitttle more complicated," she said. Holding up her hand with the thumb and forefinger almost joined to indicate a tiny amount. "Nomik Ciety bought my debt from New Destinies. I can't leave until I work it off."

Bros felt his jaw start to drop and clenched his teeth so tightly that tendons danced in his face and neck.

"And . . ." she flinched from admitting it, but forced herself to continue. "I lost my temper and knocked him on his ass."

Bros closed his eyes and sighed. "Oh, well, it could be worse. You might have killed him."

Joat began to shift her weight from foot to foot, not sure if she was embarrassed or annoyed.

"So I can't just leave," she said with a shrug.

"No," he agreed in a voice gone leaden. It went without saying that CenSec could hardly buy her debt from Ciety without blowing the operation completely.

Damn. It wasn't the first time he'd thrown an agent in much deeper than he intended. These things happened; but they always bothered him, and this time more than most. Meanwhile, the Benisur Amos remained lost and the Kolnari were still at large, and it was going from a probability to a certainty that they had the Sondee bioweapons. There were larger issues at stake than his highly personal concern for one woman.

Whoa, boy! Bros thought, startled. *No more complications. Admiration, that's all. Avuncular admiration, that's all you feel.*

Rand broke in: "How will we answer Nomik Ciety when he asks us why we were trying to break into his comp?"

Joat shrugged and, with some relief, broke eye contact with Sperin. "I'll tell him that I was looking for the debt contract to erase it."

"And what about why you were looking for coded transmissions particularly?" Bros asked, dubiously.

"I'll just tell him that I didn't think New Destinies would want it known that they're selling honest merchant captains into virtual slavery to criminals these days. So I figured it would be in a coded transmission."

"How diplomatic," Bros remarked, brows raised.

"Blow it out your ears, Sperin," Joat suggested through clenched teeth.

The com chimed. Joat threw herself into the couch that Seg hurriedly vacated; at her wave they all moved back out of pickup range. Silken appeared, looking crisp in a jade-green blouse, her hair pulled severely back, her expression remote.

"I need to speak to you in private," she said. "I've sent some of our security people to escort you here. They'll be there shortly."

"It's a little inconvenient," Joat said.

Something flickered like lightning in Silken's eyes, anger or amusement or perhaps both.

"I'm sure it is," she said. "That's not my problem. We need to talk. Don't keep me waiting or you'll experience whole new levels of . . . inconvenience."

She cut off the transmission and Seg once again locked down the com before anyone spoke.

"Well," Joat said, "looks like I'm going visiting. If we ever want to see Amos again, or find those Kolnari."

Joseph opened his mouth and then closed it again; he made a quick complex motion and the weapon in his hand disappeared.

Bros tried to ignore the leaden feeling in his gut. "Do you think it's wise?" he said.

"I think it's necessary, or the mission's gone," Joat said. She looked back at him. "And that's what's important, isn't it?"

I hate this job, Bros Sperin thought. *I really do.*

CHAPTER THIRTEEN

WELL, WELL, AS the boring machine said, Joat thought. *No Uncle Nom chewing the carpet and frothing.*

Instead, Silken rose from the couch and welcomed her in, gesturing at an elaborate antique tea service laid out on the low table before her.

"Come join me," she said affably. Silken was wearing a forest-green suit—silk, of course—with a silver belt and several ornaments that Joat thought were probably control devices.

She pressed a cup of tea on Joat, handing her a cup and saucer as delicate as a fond memory.

"Its Darjeeling," Silken said gaily. "You'll like it, I'm sure."

It was good. *At least one of my last memories will be pleasant.* Joat decided to follow Silken's lead and relaxed as best she could while she waited.

"Do you follow the theater?" the other woman asked.

Joat blinked. "I'm more of an opera buff," she said. *Courtesy of Channa Hap.*

Fifteen minutes of idle chat later, Silken put down her cup and saucer and leaned forward earnestly.

"You must know why I've asked you here," she said.

Joat looked at her and waited. "I was under the impression you were going to order me killed," she said at last. "I assume you didn't simply want to get my opinions on classic tenors first."

Silken sighed and smiled. "Perhaps you didn't notice it, but you

514

perpetrated a security breach on Nomik's comp. An accident, no doubt."

"Not at all," Joat replied. "I never attack anyone by accident, real or virtual. I was trying to find my contract of indenture to destroy it."

"Oh, don't be so dramatic," Silken said, waving a dismissive hand. "If you play your cards right, you'll come out of this way ahead of the game." She raised her brows and leaned back. "Actually, I think Mik's kind of . . ." She made a little moue and rolled her eyes as she searched for the proper word. "Charmed by the idea that he has family left. All you have to do is be nice," Silken coaxed.

Joat put down her tea cup.

"You don't know what you're asking," she said.

Silken leaned forward eagerly.

"That's where you're wrong," she said. "You'd be surprised. You've had a hard life, Joat. I *do* understand that. I was adopted too. Only my adoptive parents were religious fanatics. You wouldn't believe the way they dressed me." Silken shuddered prettily. "They made me practically shave my head, and my shoes were so heavy they'd have held me in place in zero-g." Her eyes took on a remote look, as though she was searching her memories. "They were strict about everything. Meaningless things. There were endless rules and every breach was punished. Especially by my foster father. When he wasn't beating me, he starved me. I got skinny from being so defiant; many a night I cried myself to sleep from hunger." She looked up at Joat. "So, yes, I do understand."

"Did you find it in yourself to forgive your adoptive father for beating you?" Joat asked.

"Well, after I accused him of raping me and he got convicted and hanged himself in prison, yes, I did. After all, who needs to carry all that emotional baggage through their life?" She smiled at Joat. "You and I are survivors." She touched Joat's knee lightly. "We know how to travel light."

Joat considered her, then she said, "You have had a hard time. And I'm sorry that you have. But there's a difference between your story and mine that seems insurmountable to me."

Silken cocked her head curiously.

"Your adoptive father is dead. When Ciety is dead, maybe I'll be able to forgive him too. But I think that's what it's going to take."

Silken sighed regretfully, then she frowned.

"I can't allow you to kill Nomik, he means too much to me. I mean to marry him one day."

"You're going to change your name to Silken Ciety? It sounds like naughty underwear."

Silken's green eyes narrowed thoughtfully and she stood.

"Joat, I would very much regret having you killed. But I will, if you endanger my—"

Meal ticket, Joat thought.

"—associate. On that note, let us part," she said. "You'd be happier if you could forgive and forget. Because you are legally indebted to your uncle and the past has no bearing on that fact."

"It ought to," Joat said grimly. "Thanks for the tea."

"Oh," Silken called out when Joat had reached the door. "We'll have an assignment for you soon. Don't leave your ship until you've heard from us."

Joat nodded crisply and left.

Nomik entered the room frowning and Silken reached out to him from where she sat on the couch. "I'm so sorry, Mik."

He hastened to take her hand and gave her a reassuring smile. "It's not your fault, Silky. You did your best."

"I know, but I brought her here."

"Well," he sat beside her and cuddled her against him, "you couldn't know she was my niece. And you had no way of knowing how unreasonable she'd be. Did you? Hmmm?"

Silken laid her head on Nomik's shoulder.

"No. But I'm also sorry because I know you must be disappointed."

He shrugged, then smiled.

"I guess it's a good thing I didn't buy her debt after all," he said.

Silken spluttered laughter. "Oh, that's wicked!" she said. "And I was so sure you had."

"After the way she acted yesterday, I thought maybe I'd better feel her out before I did anything drastic." He grinned. "Even you do not fathom the full depths of my duplicity, my sweet. Your natural innocence, no doubt."

"You're sooo smart." Silken pinched his cheek and kissed him. Then she grew serious. "It might be best to consider her entirely disposable," she said. "In fact, I recommend it. It's a pity, but some people just don't take to teamwork."

"I agree." Nomik looked thoughtful. "She's a lot like my brother, and I remember well the time I decided *he* had to go."

His mouth tightened to a thin line. "I've got a little job she can do for me. I was asked specifically for someone expendable." He smiled puckishly. "And I think she'll be perfect; eager, even, if I offer to write off the whole debt. The danger will make that credible. And since I'll also send along one of those *please execute bearer* messages, well . . ."

They looked at one another in affected shock. "Ooooo, that's baaaad," they said in unison and then embraced each other, laughing.

Joat put down the micromanipulator and sighed listlessly. The plasma shield was an intriguing concept, but she couldn't generate any real enthusiasm. Mechanically, her fingers picked up scattered parts from the table and slotted them into the pockets of the holdall. The galley/lounge of the *Wyal* was crowded, with all of them—and the Sondee kept *humming*. She felt too apathetic to work, but not enough to avoid irritation at the minor-key melody. Joseph looked up from the chess he was playing against one of the AI's subroutines.

"I believe I've found something useful," Rand said.

"What've you got?" she asked wearily.

"The transmission I obtained from Ciety's comp said nothing more than 'Goods received. Balance deposited.' *But,* it came from a ship that transmitted from a different quadrant of space each time it sent a message to Ciety."

"Hey, that's helpful," Joat said sarcastically.

"However," Rand continued. "Within a few days of sending their messages, never more than two weeks Earth standard, its passage was recorded by the same buoy. Indicating that somewhere in the vicinity of that buoy is its point of origin."

"Well that only leaves us a few billion parsecs to worry about," Bros said.

"This is a very good beginning," Rand insisted. "We can leave a drone there with instructions to follow this ship sending the messages. Even if it's not Kolnari, it could lead us to them."

"Not a bad plan," Joat said perking up. "Congratulations, buddy. How did you find these connections so fast without raiding Ciety's comp?"

"They were a matter of public record," Rand said. "And I *am* a computer; humans do not notice patterns of that sort. I simply searched Rohan's routine reports from their marker buoys and matched the call signs against the message we stole from Ciety."

It paused a moment, then continued, "Which I couldn't have done very effectively if I hadn't erased that frustration subroutine you gave me."

"You erased that? After all the time it took me to write it?" Joat was a little hurt; that program had taken real ingenuity. And she'd written it at his request, so that he could learn why it was that humans became so easily bored by repetitive tasks.

"Why not? I believe that I very quickly got the point . . . and I now really understand *why* humans invented computers to do this kind of work. I even understand why they practice slavery—I too would not suffer so unless compelled. That accomplished, I saw no reason for my efficiency to be degraded further."

"You're starting to sound like your old self," Joat said, relieved.

"I am reconfiguring from ROM backup," Rand said. "With a few alterations."

The com chimed. "Can you filter that?"

"Yes."

Joat nodded; now the pickup would show only what Rand wanted it too. In this case, herself.

Nomek Ciety's face filled the screen. Silken was curled on a settee behind him; she supposed it was their private quarters, from the hangings and rugs.

"I'm relaying instructions regarding your first assignment," he said.

A light on the com lit up indicating that her comp was processing incoming information.

"Wait a minute," Joat said. "I intend to protest the sale of my debt to you. I'm not going anywhere until I've heard back from New Destinies."

Nomik folded his hands before him with an exaggerated calm. "I have all the rights in this case. You make a stink, you try to leave, you give me one more minute of aggravation and I will have the Family's enforcers remove you and your crew from that ship and dump you on the dock with just a change of underwear and the clothes you stand up in. And if one of you gets hurt in the process you'd better believe that no one on Rohan will shed any tears over you." He stared at her for a moment before continuing. "Are we clear on that?"

Joat chewed her lower lip. Her hands opened and closed and her breathing deepened.

"I'm waiting," Nomik said.

"Clear," she said at last, near choking on her humiliation. She tried to remind herself that the whole point of this exercise had been to get Ciery to use her like this.

"It's a fairly difficult mission. If you'd been more cooperative, I'd have given it to someone else. As it is, do this and we're quits. I don't think we'd work well together."

Joat nodded jerkily.

"Good. Now get your crew on board and get out of here. Oh," he leaned forward, one finger raised. "If you don't show up to meet my clients—say you decide to go plead your case on New Destinies—I won't kill you, but you'll wish I had." As Ciery leaned back, the screen cleared.

After a moment, Rand spoke. "It's safe to talk now."

"I regret getting you into this," Bros said with genuine sympathy. "I can see that it's hard on you."

She turned to him, one eyebrow raised, lips pursed, and studied him a moment. Then she turned back to her station and moved her hands rapidly over the controls.

"Damn!" she said after a moment, her voice sharp with disbelief. "I'm locked out. I can't access the orders he just transmitted."

"It's time encrypted, Joat. Right now, all it has released to the navigation terminal is a point in space," Rand said. "I believe we can assume that when we reach that point we'll receive more information."

"This is incredible. That scumsucker expects me to fly out of here blind!" She turned to face the others.

"Ready to leave?"

They nodded. So did Bros and Seg.

"Why are you really here?" Joseph asked Sperin, after a moment.

Bros drew himself up to his full height and put his hands on his hips.

"I came to call Joat off of this mission," he said wearily. "It wasn't until long after you'd gone that I discovered an important piece of information."

Joseph looked sidelong at Joat.

"You are referring to Nomik Ciety's relationship to my young friend?" he asked wryly.

"Uh huh."

Joat felt a flash of temper.

"I don't especially like being discussed on my own bridge as though I were a runaway child," she said sharply. "I didn't know about Ciety myself until I saw what was on that datahedron. And by then I *had* to go through with this thing. So okay, I didn't cover myself with glory. I could have done better. I admit it. Now can we discuss how we're going to handle this situation without casting knowing glances back and forth?"

"Your behavior endangered my mission," Joseph snapped. "And my mission is the safety of the Benisur Amos. If you suffer a raised eyebrow or a knowing smile as punishment for the offense, Joat, I think that you are getting off very lightly."

"Joat," Rand said.

"What?"

"Rohan Control has informed me that we have a window in twelve minutes."

Joat stared at Rand's blinking face.

"What are they talking about, twelve minutes?"

The *Wyal* trembled as it was released from the docking mechanism and a station tug began pulling them into launch position.

"Apparently Ciety has enough influence to clear our departure before schedule," Rand said.

"Outta my way," Joat barked at Seg as she took the Captain's chair, nearly knocking him off his feet. She keyed up Rohan Control.

"This is Joat Simeon-Hap of the *Wyal*," she said crisply. "We haven't asked for clearance and we are not prepared for take-off."

The controller frowned, and consulted another screen.

"We were told to give you clearance on an emergency basis," he said. "You're fully fueled and have loaded consumables. I'm afraid you're committed to a launch in ten minutes."

"We cannot be ready in ten minutes. I repeat we can *not* be ready for departure in that time. No such request came from the *Wyal*."

The controller stared at her for a moment.

"The request came from Nomik Ciety, Captain. And your options are to lift-off in," he consulted the time, "nine minutes, thirty-nine seconds, or to stay and explain exactly why you didn't." He offered her a superior little smile. "I know which I'd choose." Then he was gone.

"Damn the man!" Joat said and began to work frantically at pre-launch tasks that hadn't been attended to.

Alvec stepped to his station and began working.

Bros and Seg watched their concentrated activity for a few moments.

"Is there anything I can do?" Bros asked.

"No," Joat said shortly. "Joe, could you find these guys a berth, please?"

"Yes, Captain."

Damn, Joat thought. *He usually doesn't call me that.*

Joseph was *really* angry.

CHAPTER FOURTEEN

DANA SHERMAN FROWNED at the message she'd just been sent by CenSec's contact on New Destinies.

What the hell is Sal trying to pull? she'd thought at first. And had sent for confirmation. A quick check through some eyes-only files had revealed that the Clal va Riguez Sal was referring to was, in fact, one of the old cover names for Bros Sperin. And a return message from New Destinies confirmed that he really had ordered Sal to pay this exorbitant fine for a ship named *Wyal*.

Bros Sperin is retired from field work, she thought, puzzled and annoyed. *So what's he doing on New Destinies playing Lord Bountiful with his department's budget?* This didn't seem right. *In fact I think it stinks to high heaven.*

If Sperin was in the field, then he should have a controller, someone who was overseeing his endeavors. *And who else would that be but Bros's superior?* she asked herself cheerfully. With the click of a few keys she rid herself of a potentially loaded situation.

Joat groaned and began to beat her head against the edge of her console. Then she leaned back and covered her face. When she took her hands away she was smiling dazedly.

"This is unbelievable," she said.

"Are you all right, Joat?" Rand's voice tones indicated concern; its lights flickered yellow.

"Yes," she said, shaking her head. "Get the spy master up here, would you, Rand. I've got some questions for him."

Rand hesitated. "Do you mean Joseph, Bros, or Seg?" it asked.

"Seg?" Her voice deepened with amazement.

"He's very knowledgeable on the subject."

"I meant Sperin," she said. "He's the one who got us into this."

"To be fair, Joat, I'm sure that your commitment to Joseph and the Benisur Amos is what motivated our participation in Mr. Sperin's scheme."

She shrugged. "Who wants to be fair?" She keyed up Ciety's instructions and read them again. Then sighed, again. She didn't want to be fair to Sperin; he made her uneasy. And that irritated her. It also irritated her that she was taking pains to avoid him, not an easy thing to do on a ship this size.

She'd finally banned him from the bridge to give herself some space. *Which I needed.* There was a limit to the number of times you could watch a face with that "I know something you don't know" look. At least, without rearranging the face with a multitool set to "weld."

"Captain?"

Sperin was leaning both hands against the hatch, his head thrust through the hatchway.

"Permission to enter the bridge?" he said.

"Oh don't be an ass! I sent for you didn't I?"

He smiled and came to where she sat.

"Not that it isn't nice to be asked, for a change," she snapped. *This man has the patent on smug,* she decided, watching his cool half-bow.

"What did you want?" he asked, leaning against the console.

"Ciety's orders just became available, and surprise! You remember the marker buoy we were discussing just before liftoff? The one Ciety's mysterious contact kept passing?"

He nodded.

"Well, guess what? That's our destination. But wait! It gets better. Our assignment is to pick up a cargo and deliver it to a third party in a place to be named by the shipper." She cocked her head at him. "How does that sound to you?"

He shrugged. "You're the captain. You tell me."

She made an exasperated noise.

"It sounds to me as though we're about to meet the Kolnari," she said.

"Or possibly their minions," he agreed.

"So? What do you want to do about it? Are you going to inform Central Worlds or what?"

He grimaced. "What do you want me to say, Joat? I can hardly call out the Navy on this. I don't actually have any hard information. For all we know this is a minor drug deal or some smuggling job." He held his hands out helplessly. "It could be the Kolnar, it could be a loyalty test. Like you said at the beginning, we're flying blind here."

"Then why would Ciety offer to wipe the debt?"

"Obviously, it's either worth it to him, or he has no intention of paying . . . or both."

"Isn't there something we should be doing? Don't you have someone waiting to hear from you?"

"Yes, to both questions. To the first, we're doing it. We're heading for that rendezvous, and we'll have to wait till we get there to decide what to do next. To the second, yes, I have someone waiting to hear from me. But I'm not about to blow my cover and tell the universe where I am for no reason, I have nothing worth reporting, Joat. Until I do I'm just going to keep my mouth shut."

She sighed. "So I guess I should too."

"I didn't say that!"

"I didn't say you did. Sheesh! All I meant was that I wouldn't pester you about it."

"Very well." He stood up.

"All right."

"If that answers all your questions?" he asked, very politely.

"Yes, thanks."

"How long before we reach that buoy?"

"Not long," she said, "a few hours. Tell the others for me, would you?"

He nodded sharply and left. Joat turned her chair to watch him go.

"Fardles, he's testy," she muttered.

"So are you," Rand told her.

"Maybe it's those shots Seg gave us," Joat suggested. She'd been uneasy about taking them. *Experimental drugs have their place. That place is not in Joat Simeon-Hap's veins.*

"I don't believe so," Rand told her. "No one else has these particular symptoms. You and Mr. Sperin seem to strike sparks off each other." It paused thoughtfully. "Why is that?"

Joat frowned. "It's cause he's a pushy osco and he doesn't like being called on it," she snarled. *And he's too damned attractive and too damned cocky and on my mind too damn much.* "I shouldn't have equipped you with a metaphor function."

"The same could be said of Joseph, but you've never reacted to him this way."

"Well, I trust Joe," she said unhappily. "I'd trust him with my life."

Rand was silent for a moment. Then it said, "He doesn't trust you though, does he?"

Joat blushed and her mouth twisted ruefully. She schooled herself to be patient with Rand who didn't understand how much the rift between herself and Joseph hurt her.

"That's very perceptive," she said quietly. "It'll take a while to win back his confidence. If I ever do."

"He is fair, Joat. Though harsh in his judgments. Eventually, I believe he must concede that if you were on good terms with Mr. Ciety you probably wouldn't have pulled this assignment."

Joat smiled slowly. "You know, you're right. Ciety didn't exactly wave us off with a fond farewell, did he?"

"That's very perceptive," Rand murmured, and Joat began to chuckle.

"Although that doesn't mean that giving him the finger was the right thing to do," she said.

"But it worked. And Joseph attaches high value to that quality."

Bros moved down the corridor quickly, his brow furrowed. "I just can't seem to find the right tone with her," he muttered to himself as he swung into the tiny cubicle. On *Wyal* it was normally used for stores, but a little work had made it habitable—just. He automatically tested the sticktights and monitors; no, Rand and Joat hadn't managed to bug it, yet. That he was aware of; he had the best tools CenSec could produce, but she was a wild card as far as technics went.

"As far as anything goes," he snarled.

He'd worked hard to maintain an attitude of aloof friendliness; watching his words to avoid any hint of being judgmental, keeping his expression a polite half-smile intended to show confidence in her.

I never know what *she's going to say or do.*

It was too long since he'd been a field agent full-time, too much time as a controller. He was used to being in control, manipulating things from a distance.

"Am I losing it?" There was a time when he wouldn't have bucked the Middle Command this hard over the Kolnari matter. Sure, he was right—but he also didn't have the strategic information the Command did. Central Worlds ran a *big* operation; maybe he was being a loose cannon and nothing more. Yet he couldn't stop himself . . .

The enemy appeared to control the game and he felt like one of the little, powerless pieces; the kind that are given up with a good-natured shrug. Meanwhile, virtually every player on his team was annoyed, to one degree or another, with everyone else. The only real asset he had was that Nomik Ciety didn't know he was involved.

He smiled wryly. Even Seg had deserted him to follow Joseph around like an eager puppy. Much to the Bethelite's chagrin.

Joseph's people were uneasy with aliens, to put it mildly. There was no place for nonhumans in the rather conservative religion that permeated every moment of life on Bethel. So finding one of them worshipping at his feet was making Joseph very queasy.

Bros stepped through the hatchway into the galley to hear Seg asking: "But why would you rescue the Lady Rachel when she had just betrayed all of you?"

This was too much for Joseph who burst from his chair and strode to the hatch. Bros leapt out of his way. Then Joseph spun 'round and snarled.

"I am not at the end of my life, boy! I cannot look back and see a pattern. Because there *is* no pattern. Sometimes you react to life as it happens! Just as we are reacting to this situation we find ourselves in. Or are you perhaps planning everything you will be called upon to do in the next few days?" He glared at Seg for a moment. "No? I thought not. I will ask you to stop your annoying habit of questioning every decision I have made in my life, before I compel you to do so." He turned and stormed off.

Seg sat at the table, looking crestfallen. His large, fine eyes were tragic, the smaller ones were closed. His little suckerlike mouth was sphinctered shut, but trembled querulously, and his ear whorls were quite pale.

The young scientist might not be *quite* as upset as he looked— Sondee just weren't equipped by nature to show a poker face—but Bros felt moved to offer some comfort.

"You've got to remember, Seg, that what one person perceives as a moment of glory, another might see as just a really bad day they'd like to forget. That question is probably a sore spot with Joseph because he married the Lady Rachel." Seg slumped down farther in his chair. "I don't know if you were aware of that."

"No," Seg sighed, "I didn't know. The thwarting of the Kolnari raid on SSS-900-C is so *famous*, though. An adventure that will live forever!"

"Adventure is somebody else in deep koka, far, far away and a long time ago," Bros said. "Wishing for adventure is like praying for bad luck."

The Sondee looked shocked. "But . . . but *this* is adventure," he protested.

"No, it'll be adventure if somebody makes a vid play about it after we survive," Bros said. "Joseph's been there and done that. So cut him some slack."

Silence fell for a moment. "Still," Seg looked up at Bros, "you'd like to treat me like that. Wouldn't you?"

Bros raised his brows.

"What makes you say that?"

Seg looked condescending.

"I'm not stupid, Bros. Far from it, in fact. I'm a brilliant scientist. I know that because I know who my competition are and they're so smart it takes my breath away. I'm a better than average musician, and coming from a Sondee that's saying something. And I probably pull in more credits in a year than the whole bunch of you put together could in two. So where do you people get off looking down on me?" He was sitting up straight now, his eyes bright, his ear whorls flushed with color.

"Hey," Bros said, holding up his hands, palms out, "calm down. Why are you yelling at me?"

"Because you're here and you're guilty." He scowled, at least, Bros assumed he was scowling. "So I'm socially tone-deaf, so what? I'm young. And I'm not human—I'm not as bad as this with Sondee." He paused. "Not usually. If it's that important I'm sure I can learn what I need to know. In the meantime, I just thought I'd point out that you haven't got all that much to be smug about."

Bros sat down beside him and studied his young charge, one finger stroking his upper lip.

"I didn't realize I was being smug," he said quietly.

Seg slumped in his chair again.

"You don't want me here."

Bros nodded. "You're right, I don't. But not because I look down on you. It's because I'm fully aware of what a valuable citizen you really are, Seg." His eyes narrowed "Even though I checked it myself, I still can't believe Clenst would put you in the line of fire like this."

"I insisted," Seg said quickly. "I felt responsible for the loss of our work. I made them see that I should go."

"I still don't like it," Bros said. "It divides my attention. You may be brilliant . . . no, I'll be honest, you *are* brilliant, but this isn't your line of work. How would you feel if somebody forced themselves on you as an assistant during a crucial experiment, without training?"

Seg wilted with guilt.

"You've been useful so far," Bros conceded. "But I don't believe in tempting the gods of luck. We've had too much good luck so far, and I'm afraid you may be the straw that broke the camel's back."

Seg looked interested.

"What camel?" he asked. "Like the ones with silver bells?"

CHAPTER FIFTEEN

"CLAN-LORD?"

"Speak," Belazir didn't raise his eyes from the screen he studied.

"Your contact on Rohan has confirmed that he has found shipping for us and has given us an ETA for a vessel named *Wyal*."

Belazir nodded thoughtfully. "How long?" he asked.

"Two hours, Clan-Lord," the young Kolnari hesitated.

Belazir noted it and said again, "Speak."

"The . . . captains name . . . is Joat Simeon-Hap."

Belazir's blazing eyes rose from the screen like some merciless sun. The crewman's pupils expanded in fear and he visibly shuddered, but held his place. Belazir bared his teeth in a parody of a grin. His body began to quiver slightly in arousal.

No. *It is a joke. That scumvermin dares!* Ciety had been arrogant from the first, confident that he was irreplaceable. Even the Yoered Family would draw the line at the sort of dealings Ciety had agreed to, and he thought that made him the master. He dared to taunt Belazir with unsatisfiable desires.

"Simeon?" he breathed. "Ciety dares to taunt me with that name?"

"Get him," he said, glaring into the other's eyes. "Ciety and his doxy, and bring them to me."

The young crewman stared at him like a bird fascinated by a snake.

"Go!" Belazir roared, and the crewman fled with a clatter of boots.

Belazir sat down slowly, his golden eyes wide, staring at scenes that never had taken place. Scenes that soothed and pleasured him. In his mind he saw Channa Hap kneeling, her spirit broken, offering up to him the male child she'd borne him. He sat in a thronelike chair looking coldly down upon her bent head and gently informed her that as a male it must be castrated and made a slave. Licking his lips, he imagined Channa flat on her belly, clasping his ankle and kissing his feet, her tears leaving streaks on the polished ebony of his skin as she begged for mercy for her child.

Next, he imagined Simeon's voice, begging to be allowed to serve the Kolnar, pleading with him not to be left in the dark. And then there was Amos.

He grinned. Yes. There was Amos.

"Zerach, take some troops and prepare our guest, the Benisur, for departure."

Behind him a brawny scarred woman smiled and rose, beckoning to two troopers in powered armor to follow her. They genuflected to the ship's joss behind the command seat and left with a tread that shook the deck.

Karak cleared his throat and his father's eyes fell on him like an accusation.

"You wish to speak, my son?"

"What of the Benisur's scumvermin companions?" Karak asked.

Belazir made a little moue and shrugged, his eyes wandered back to his screen. He gestured idly with two fingers.

"See to them," he said.

Karak rose and bowed to his father, then forced himself to leave the bridge calmly.

Belazir smiled like a man suppressing laughter. Then he too rose.

"Kiriss."

"Clan-Lord?"

"You have the bridge. I will be in my quarters if I am needed."

"Yes, Clan-Lord."

As soon as he was clear of the bridge Karak lengthened his stride. By the time he was near Soamosa's prison he was running. He stopped just before the turning to the brig to calm his breathing. Then he approached the guards outside her door at a measured walk.

"I am to take the scumvermin girl to the Clan-Lord," he said coldly. "She will not be coming back, so you are to report to your unit commander for reassignment."

"No one has informed us of this, Petite-Heir." The woman guard stared at him, obliquely contemptuous.

He gritted his teeth at the title; officially he should be Magna-Heir, as his fathers only living son, although Belazir had never found the "time" for the ceremony. *Enough, I renounce him.*

"*I* am informing you. Just as *I* shall inform your unit commander that you are desperately in need of a punishment drill." He paused long enough to watch her struggle through her resentment.

"Does the Petite-Heir require an escort?" the other guard asked.

Karak narrowed his eyes as he studied the man, not certain whether the trooper was sincere or joking.

"Fearsome as she is," he drawled sarcastically, "I doubt the prisoner will try to overwhelm me. We have her beloved Benisur in our clutches, you must remember, to insure her good behavior." He looked at the door and waved his hand in one of his father's casual, dismissive gestures. "Go," he said, bored with them.

They saluted and moved crisply off, contempt and resentment leaving an almost visible wake behind them.

Karak watched them until they disappeared around the corner, and waited until he could no longer hear their footsteps. Then he keyed open the lock on Soamosa's door and entered her cell.

She rose with a startled gasp, then frowned when she saw it was him.

"You frightened me," she said a bit crossly. Then she rushed to him and threw her arms around his massive chest. "But I am glad to see you." She smiled up at him, waiting for his kiss.

He looked down at her, tenderly cradling her blond head in his big hand, and sighed for sheer delight in her sweet innocence; leaning down to award the kiss she expected. Then he held her against him, gently stroking her bright, soft hair.

"I have come to take you away," he said.

With a sharp intake of breath Soamosa pulled away from him, looking up into his face excitedly.

"We are going to rescue the Benisur Amos?" Her blue eyes shone with a fierce joy.

Karak closed his eyes and swallowed hard.

"That is impossible," he said in a toneless voice. "My father has ordered him to be taken to the technicians who will prepare him for his journey."

He watched her brow darken and her eyes begin to sparkle with outrage. Grasping her upper arms, he gave her a little shake.

"He will be safe, little one. It is your people that are in danger, and they are in danger from him. We must get away to warn them."

He watched, and saw her face harden with resolve. His back relaxed in relief; this arguing was more trying than just giving orders.

"You are right," she said reluctantly. "It is what the Benisur himself would say to me." Then another idea took hold and she started as though struck. "The Captain! If we cannot bring the Benisur Amos away with us, then we *must* save Captain Sung."

"The Captain is . . ." he trailed off. He felt a queasy sensation in his stomach, something unfamiliar, that grew worse when he thought of what had been done to the man.

"You told me that he was still alive!" Soamosa protested. Her face showed her puzzlement and her eyes regarded him uncertainly. As though she had just realized that this could easily be one of the famous cruel jokes the Kolnari loved to play.

"He *is* alive. But not in any way that he would wish to be. It would be a mercy to leave him to be killed, Soamosa. No one should have to live as he is now."

She backed away from him, frightened and furious.

"What have you done to him?"

"*I* have done nothing to him. This I swear by my love for you. My father put him in with the Benisur to be sure that his plan would work. In just a few hours, the Captain took infection through simple contact with the Benisur, and now he is mindless. He is incontinent, Soamosa, he drools and weeps like a baby. And he is terrified of the Kolnar. If I go near him he will scream and howl and run away."

Karak threw up his hands in exasperation at the mulish look on her face. "How are we to escape while we are hauling around a man who is screaming and trying to escape?"

She bit her lower lip and looked down, her brow furrowed in thought. Then she sighed shortly and looked at him with confidence.

"You can knock him out and we will carry him," she said.

The unfamiliar sensation in his gut turned to one he recognized easily: fear. Not quite the same sort of fear that his father's whip or a siblings knife would cause, but similar. *Because I am going to do it for her.* It would be much easier to knock Soamosa out and carry her off to Bethel. But she would never forgive him and he couldn't bear that.

In all of his life no one had befriended him but his brother, and even he had never understood Karak.

"In all my life," he said, looking into her blue eyes with his brass-yellow eyes, "only with you have I felt at home. Therefore I will do this thing for you, even though it is dangerous and makes no sense."

Losing her was inconceivable, death far preferable. He closed his eyes.

"All right," he said. "We will take Captain Sung with us."

"Oh!" She threw her arms around him and hugged him tightly enough to surprise an "Oof!" from him. "Let us go," she said brightly.

Belazir took a sip of the zirse he'd prepared for himself and sat down before the screens in his quarters. He stretched out with a contented sigh; his strength and speed had not fallen off—not much, or he would be dead at a rival's hands—but his bones ached. He dug his hand into a bowl of raw meat chunks and threw one to a plant. Spined leaves gripped home around the morsel and a thin humming filled the air. Tendrils groped towards him, and he threw another piece; it was doubly satisfying, a remembrance of lost Kolnar and a fitting end for the man who'd annoyed him so; the fingerbones were in a necklace around the shoulders of his personal joss, over in the corner.

His eyes stayed on the screen. From here as on the bridge he could view any place on the ship, and a few selected places on the other ships as well. Hoping that he hadn't missed any good comedy, Belazir called up Soamosa's cell.

And found it empty.

A little thrill of something like alarm flashed through his middle. He gave an irritated grunt. He'd missed a great deal obviously. Where were the young lovers?

He instructed the monitors to show random scenes throughout the brig area and waited impatiently as he watched various Kolnari at their daily tasks. Then he came upon a scene from a farce.

Captain Sung ran around the small cell he'd shared with Amos with incredible speed and agility; hopping from bunk to commode to the floor, screaming all the while like a lost soul.

Or like a pig in torment, Belazir thought. He had seen pigs on several of the planets the High Clan had sacked, back before the attack on Bethel.

After him, looking eager to do murder, came Karak, muscular arms outstretched, long-fingered hands curled to grab. Following him came Soamosa, her bright hair flowing in the wind of her own passage, speaking breathlessly, but softly, urging gentleness and restraint. Her little hands reached for Karak, ready to restrain him.

Belazir laughed out loud. *The damned pursued by a devil, pursued by an angel,* he thought. *It just keeps getting better.*

At last, with a desperate lunge, Karak got hold of the Captain. The man tried to fight him off, batting ineffectually at Karak's hands and keening in a high-pitched wail.

"Be gentle!" Soamosa insisted.

Through gritted teeth Karak told her, "Little one, it is impossible to knock someone out gently."

"Captain," Soamosa said, "Captain listen to me."

"He no longer knows what a captain is, Soa; call him by his name." He just wanted to hit the man, but Soamosa obviously wanted to calm him down first. Though what purpose that would serve he couldn't see.

"His name? Uh . . . , James, no no, J-J-J, Joe, no, Joshua? *Josiah!* Is that your name, Josiah?" she looked hopefully at the Captain. The man calmed slightly at the sound of her voice, stopping his futile jerking at the iron grip. "You must be very brave, Josiah. We will take care of you, but you must help us."

Sung watched her fascinated, he reached out and took a lock of her hair. Then he tried to put it in his mouth. That's when Karak punched him, and Sung dropped like a rock.

"Oh!" Soamosa said. "You did not have to do that! He would have come quietly."

"Perhaps. But he would not have stayed that way. Think of him as an infant, Soa; he will react emotionally and loudly to whatever frightens him. I frighten him. We can not take the risk that he will suddenly decide to mention that at the top of his lungs." He hoisted Sung over his shoulder

"Stay by my side," he told her, "act frightened, pretend to weep."

Soamosa glared at him and opened her mouth to speak.

"My people will expect it," he said through gritted teeth. "If you walk by my side like a queen consenting to be escorted they will wonder what is going on. And we do not want them to start thinking. *I* know how brave you are, surely that is all that matters." He leaned over to kiss her lightly on the lips. "And after all, we have Bethel to consider. Do we not?"

She managed to look both chagrined and flattered.

"Yes," she muttered resentfully. "But I do not like it."

That said, she opened the door of the cell and allowed Karak to grasp her slender wrist in his great hand; her head drooped, and her shoulders shook with muffled sobs.

Belazir watched the scene unfold in vast amusement. At some point, however, he realized that his son was facing the highly infectious Captain Sung without any protective gear. He'd seen him immunize the girl, but not himself. *No doubt he never even thought to protect himself,* Belazir thought. *Despite the deaths from The Great Plague that left us so weak, he never even thought that he might become infected.* Belazir wondered if all the Kolnar still dared to be so arrogant.

Then with an almost regretful sigh, Belazir decided that fate had given him a backup plan, and at the same time had punished his son's treason.

He glanced suspiciously at his joss in its niche.

Or perhaps it is some punishment for the disaster of the SSS-900-C. Karak was, after all, the last of his children still living. And it was custom to cull the children of traitors.

No, he shook his head. *Not this time. I will not sacrifice all of my seed. Especially given their precious immunity to the Great Plague.*

However, Karak could bravely serve the Kolnar as a sacrifice to expediency. Belazir smiled. *Yes, I rather like that.* He called up Kiriss at the command post on the bridge.

"Great Lord," Kiriss said, bowing his head respectfully.

"Clear and seal all corridors between the brig and the hangar until further notice. And be prepared to sterilize those areas."

"Yes, Great Lord."

"Karak will be taking a fighter and our two prisoners; let them go unmolested."

"Yes, Great Lord."

Belazir could almost feel Kiriss's curiosity, well hidden behind an impassive face. Kiriss waited for further orders.

"That is all," Belazir said and cut contact.

It wasn't quite all; Karak would contract the mind-wasting disease as surely as the Captain had, though not as quickly. That would leave the girl to pilot them to Bethel, assuming she could pilot a spacecraft. Whether she managed to get to Bethel or was lost in space to be picked up by the Central Worlds Navy or some hapless freighter, his own goal would be accomplished. The mind-wasting disease would be unleashed on the enemies of his people, revenge accomplished, and honor sustained. And it cost them very little, one fighter and a traitor already on his way to a form of living death.

It had a certain symmetry that pleased him. Then an idea struck him. *It is something I can tell the scumvermin Amos.* He smiled wickedly, golden eyes bright with mirth. After all, he had plentiful deposits of Karak's seed, frozen. There were Kolnari girls enough who would be eager for the prestige of bearing it.

"Your Captain Sung and the young lady have fled in one of our small craft," he said aloud, liking the sound of the words. *Surely it will give him hope.*

Belazir showed his teeth and threw another gobbet of meat at the plants. Their tendrils waved in the air, clicking in rhythm with his deep chuckle.

Amos lay stiffly upon a cold metal table. He struggled to move, to open his eyes, and could not. There was no light, not even the swirling patterns behind closed lids.

Anything, he thought frantically. *A finger, a toe, an eyelid,* something *move dammit! I call upon the God!*

But nothing did. His body was utterly indifferent to his commands. He could feel. The technician had proved that by plunging a needle into various sensitive areas and had seemed quite pleased by Amos's lack of response.

"Excellent, excellent," he kept murmuring, continuing his probing long after there was any possible necessity of doing so.

Amos wished that he could at least glare at the man. But he was helpless even to do that. *There is no dignity in helplessness,* he thought.

Now, there is a useful thought, he told himself bitterly, *what a pity I can not write it down.* He railed at himself for allowing things to come to this. *Why did I not kill myself and take this weapon from their hands? How could I let myself live to be used like this?*

He thought of heroes he had read about that chewed through their own tongues rather than betray their people. *Why did I not do so, when they brought me here, when I* knew *what they meant to do?*

Too late for such thoughts. Too late to do any good at all. Amos began to pray. *That, at least, they can not take from me.* The God was a loving, forgiving God.

There was a sound by his side. A rustling like that of the technicians sterile suit. He remembered the man's smooth dark face through the face-plate of the headgear, sweating slightly, his dark bronze eyes fearful. Fearful of the threat Amos represented if the suit should in any way be punctured.

If I had that probe, you pirate swine, I would puncture more than your suit!

The sound came again, closer now. Then Amos sensed something huge looming over him and cold sweat broke out on his forehead; he tried desperately to open his eyes. Feeling, at last, only the barest quiver, so slight it might have been imaginary.

After a terribly long wait that scraped away at the last remaining shreds of Amos's self-control, a cold voice said quietly:

"I have news, scumvermin."

The sweat beading his brow slid down his face and into his hair.

Belazir watched the evidence of his enemy's distress disappear slowly into Amos's thick dark hair.

He smiled, sighing sensuously. *Of such little pleasures are the best memories made,* he thought.

He glanced around the sterile box of a room, his eyes resting for a moment on the kneeling, shivering medtech. He wondered if it would be best to have the creature spaced after handling the scumvermin Amos.

No, he thought, *that would express doubts about the efficacy of these suits. And here am I, wearing one.* It was unwise to put such ideas into the heads of ambitious subordinates.

"Leave us," he said to the medtech, and waited till the creature had scurried from the room.

"Once," he said, leaning over Amos's unmoving form, "We had no need of such rooms as these. It does not please me that I am responsible for making them necessary. Or perhaps I should say *we.* Such rooms as these are common among the scumvermin races," Belazir continued. "But they are probably rare on Bethel."

He watched Amos with a downward quirk of his lips. For all his enemy's responsiveness, the Benisur could have been asleep. This grew tedious. Still, there was no reason to discard his plan.

He leaned close and whispered in Amos's ear.

"The little blond girl, she has rescued the Captain and has fled the ship. I knew you would wish to be informed," he said in mock sympathy. "There is no telling what might befall her, a young woman all alone with only the pathetic remnant of Captain Sung. Tsk, tsk, tsk." He watched Amos, hoping for some sign that he heard, but there was no response. Save . . . yes, the scumvermin's heart was accelerating slightly. "I considered pursuit, of course, but then I realized that it would be unconscionably rude to force hospitality on an unwilling guest. I do hope she will be all right."

Belazir straightened and began to walk heavily around the table, one hand trailing lightly along its edge.

"In any event, we must discuss our immediate plans for you. Soon, you will be placed in an escape pod—I thought that a particularly nice touch," Belazir said with satisfaction. "Then you will be taken aboard a ship that we have arranged to take you home. By the way, interestingly, the captain of this ship is named Joat Simeon-Hap. Ironic, is it not?"

This was useless. Belazir contemplated the paralyzed body of his enemy in disgust. *Why did I not think of this before I had him prepared?* He sighed. It would have been good to watch his enemy try to hide his feelings. These untrained scumvermin were so blatant in their emotions. Ah, well, it would have to be enough that he *knew* the Benisur had heard him, and that every word had left teeth-marks in the scumvermin's heart.

"Enjoy your journey," Belazir said softly, "I have been pleased to be your host."

Soamosa's escaped! Amos's heart leapt, for a moment. Then, *But with the Captain, she'll be infected.* He visualized her vibrant young face slack and drooling. The effort of will needed to control the tears was as terrible as anything he had ever done.

And Joat is here. If I needed proof that this is a nightmare and not truly happening that would be it. For how could things possibly go so smoothly for this devil outside of his own mad dreams?

Amos felt his body being lifted and dropped unceremoniously into what felt like a coffin. It was cold, and his flesh wanted to shrink from the clammy surface, but could not.

Yet this is no nightmare, he thought, his mouth dry with fear. *It is happening. And I must find a way to warn my people.*

Mustering all of his concentration, he began to work at getting his eyes to open.

The *Wyal* dropped into the sidereal universe. Alarms began to ping.

"Detection," Rand's voice said. It was a little louder than usual. "Multiple power-plant neutrino signatures. Details follow."

Joat stared at the readouts and shut her mouth with a *click*. She gasped, fighting against the steel band that seemed clamped around her chest, feeling the clammy trickle of sweat down her flanks.

"What am I seeing?" she whispered.

"Between ninety-five and one hundred ships, depending on your definition of that term," Rand said. "Classes—"

Schematics came up on the screen. One of the ships was enormous, in the two-fifty kiloton range, a bulk carrier or possibly one of the seed-ships used to found planetary colonies back in the old days. The others were a wild mixture, but far too many for comfort had the neutrino-signatures of huge power-plants and drives, and the sleek build of warships designed to transit atmosphere. Constructs and habitats floated among the ships, and the com channels were buzzing with activity.

"Trouble," Bros said leaning over her shoulder. "That's what you're seeing." He pointed to one ship's image on the screen. "You recognize her?"

"I do," Joseph said grimly. "By its outline, it is the *Dreadful Bride*. Belazir's ship."

Joat nodded with a quirk of her lips.

"Well, good," she said firmly.

Both men straightened and looked at her.

"That *is* what we wanted," she explained. "No sense in complaining that our plans worked out just the way we expected them to." Her hands danced over the panel before her, broadcasting her identity.

"They're coming into visual range," Rand said. "Shall I put them on screen?"

"By all means," Joat said. "Let's be thoroughly intimidated."

"Ah, Boss." Alvec's voice came over the auditory system from the engineering spaces. "I can squeeze maybe three, four more lights out of this rustbucket, if you need 'em."

The *Dreadful Bride*, Belazir's own ship, sprang into view, heading the vast armada of smaller warships. The ship boasted new weapons pods, and showed signs of having used them, often. Long star-shaped ripple patterns—damage from beamers firing at extreme range—slashed the hull, and irregular patches laid over the worst damage marred its sleek length from stem to stern.

The marks only added to the *Bride's* menace, like battle scars on a human face.

Several of the warships were slovenly-looking. Probably freelancers-cum-pirates. Behind them loomed the vast bulk of the freighter, its great round belly blocking from view any other ships in Belazir's fleet.

"I can understand they'd need freighters," Seg muttered, "but that thing *has* to be a liability. It's completely vulnerable and look how slow it is." He shook his head. "I don't get it."

"That's the mothership," Bros explained. "Where the Kolnar keep their children and their pregnant wives. They breed like rabbits. That's not a joke, they're incredibly fertile and they never stop reproducing— twins, triplets, and the gestation period is only four months. They start breeding at ten standard years. So if that thing isn't full of baby pirates yet, it soon will be."

Seg looked mildly disappointed.

"Well, if they've got their children with them, they obviously don't want to make trouble."

The others stared at him.

"I mean, they wouldn't put their children at risk . . ." Everyone turned away, gazing studiously at the boards before them, into the forward screen, anywhere but at Seg.

"Well, we could be dangerous!" he snapped in exasperation.

"And what are we going to use to hurt them?" Joat asked sweetly. "Cutting remarks?" She smiled at his mulish expression. "We're barely armed, kid, which is more than most freighters can boast. But if you look out there," she indicated the forward screen, "you'll see the latest and best weaponry available on the black market."

"In other words," Bros said, "they don't have to make trouble, they *are* trouble."

"They're hailing," Rand told them.

"Forward screen," Joat said tensely, bracing herself in expectation of confronting a Kolnari.

The face on the view-screen was human-standard. A woman's face, bony, sallow, with the eyes of a dead fish, but human, Joat realized. *More or less human.* Not only a pirate, but willing to work for the High Clan of Kolnar.

"Captain Joat Simeon-Hap, cargo ship *Wyal,* we're here to pick up cargo for Nomik Ciety," she said as calmly as she could.

"Stand by for cargo transfer," the woman said, her voice as expressionless as her eyes. "And traveling instructions."

"Al," Joat asked, "will you and Rand take care of receiving those? I'm going down to supervise the loading."

"Will do," Alvec said crisply.

"Bros, Joe," she said, "will you come with me, please." Her heart was hammering in her chest, but her voice was flat calm. They were being treated like just another underworld courier. But they weren't "just another" anything and Joat was scared. Her name alone would be ringing up flags onboard the *Dreadful Bride*. Belazir t'Marid would be *glad* to see her, if not quite as glad as Channa or Simeon would make him.

She was in the hatchway, Bros and Joseph bunched up behind her when an all too familiar voice filled the bridge.

"One moment, Captain."

Joat could feel the blood draining from her face, vision dimming, her tongue thick enough to choke her. She turned to the screen.

"This is a most valuable cargo," Belazir said, with a gentle smile.

Joat leaned against the hatchway casually and raised an eyebrow. It was better than falling down, and she hadn't the strength to speak. When she'd known him before she'd had places to hide. Here there was nowhere to run.

He looked much older than she would have expected. Dangerous still, but much changed. *Yeah. They age quickly, too.* The face had lost its fallen-angel beauty, but none of the strength. And the golden lion's eyes were utterly mad.

"I've never damaged a cargo yet," she said at last.

"Still," Belazir said, steepling his hands before him, "I must ask that you leave one of your crew here as hostage. To insure that you will effect delivery with all care and speed."

Joat crossed her arms and walked forward, towards the smiling face in the screen.

"No," she said, calmly. "That's unacceptable. I need all of my crew. If that's unsatisfactory, I'm sure Mr. Ciety can find you a shipper more to your liking." She took her seat and looked up at the screen with her arms crossed, face a mask. *But I'm glad he can't smell me.*

His yellow eyes rested briefly on Joseph, then passed over him to linger on Bros.

"That one," he said, as though she hadn't already refused. "The dark one. We'll take him on when the cargo is brought to you."

"No," Joat said firmly.

"Yes," Belazir said, equally firmly. His eyes widened slightly and his lips lifted from his teeth in a snarl. "Captain *Simeon-Hap*."

He knows, Joat thought and her heart sped again and her mouth went dry.

"You will do as you are told. Or you will not be leaving this place. Do you understand?"

"Yes." *Master and God,* her mind supplied treacherously.

She gripped the console, resolved to tell him that she understood, she just wasn't going to do it, when Bros's hand came down on her shoulder, making her jump.

She glared up at him and he surprised her by the regretful tenderness of his smile.

"I'd better go," he said softly.

"But . . . !"

He was out the hatch before she could continue.

"Most wise," Belazir murmured approvingly, "very wise indeed."

The screen went blank, and Joat was on her feet, rushing after Bros.

CHAPTER SIXTEEN

THIS ISN'T RIGHT," Joat insisted. She'd caught up with him at the cargo bay hatch; he stood looking back at her, hand on the dogging wheel. "I don't want you to go."

Bros smiled down at her.

"Would it surprise you to know that I agree with you? I don't want me to go either."

"Then don't!"

He cocked his head and looked at her affectionately, reaching out to brush her cheek with the back of his hand. Joat started and flinched away from his touch, then scowled at him.

"Is that a look to send a man out to battle with?"

"You're not going to battle," she snapped, "you're going to commit suicide. I can talk him out of this, Bros, you don't have to go."

"He'll kill us all, Joat. He knows who you are and he wants you dead." Bros leaned close, trying to catch her eyes. "Seg and Amos are too important to Central Worlds to risk. And I got you into this."

There was the sound of the caterpillar lock grappling on and filling with air. Bros snapped forward and kissed her lightly before she could protest. He straightened and glanced at the lock, then back down at Joat.

"And you're too important to me," he said as the lock opened with a hiss and a pair of black-clad mercenaries stepped out. "It's a far, far better thing I do . . ." he murmured as they led him away.

Joat watched him go; he never looked back as he was hustled along between his guards, and his step was firm and springy. She could still feel the soft warmth of his lips, and it was as though his kiss had sealed hers shut, for she couldn't speak. She could only watch with wide eyes as more mercenaries dragged an escape pod down the tunnel that linked their ships.

Joseph's touch made her gasp and she spun 'round in shocked surprise.

"Don't *do* that!" she snarled. "Why is everyone sneaking up on me today?"

Joseph suppressed a smile.

"Sometimes, Joat, you are more like my Rachel than you would care to admit."

"How shall we stow this, Captain?" Alvec asked.

Joat closed her eyes for a moment, grateful for Al's understanding. She led him into cargo hold C.

"Here," she said and indicated a rack which would accommodate the rescue pod's awkward shape.

They were busy for several minutes securing it to the mercenaries' satisfaction; the noncom in charge checked with finicky care.

"See them out, would you Joe?" she asked. "I want a few words with their Captain."

"Get me Belazir," Joat said to the dead-faced woman on the screen.

"Who?" the woman asked.

"*Belazir,* you bitch! Do it or I'll open fire on the mother ship."

Belazir's face appeared on the screen, his golden eyes laughing, though his face was stem.

"You wished to speak to me, Captain?"

"I'll be back for my crewman," Joat said tersely.

"Will you?" Belazir asked with a raised brow. "How very nice. You may be sure I shall look forward to seeing you again, Captain Simeon-Hap." He paused, considering. "So much do I wish for such a meeting that I will caution you most strongly, do not open the rescue pod. On pain of death," he said, his voice firm with sincere warning.

Then he was gone and by default the screen returned to the view of Belazir's fleet.

"Only a Kolnari could or would say *on pain of death,*" Joseph said with disgust. "Even then, only Belazir could say it and not sound ridiculous. Come with me, Seg. Let us see what the Kolnar have entrusted to us."

"Wait," Joat said. "Let's get a little distance between us. They might have some kind of tell-tale attached to it."

Joseph sighed impatiently, but nodded and took his seat, while Joat checked out the flight plan the Kolnari had given them.

"It's what we expected," she said, her throat dry and tight. "Our course is set for Bethel."

"I am sorry, Joat," Joseph murmured. "I would rather he had chosen me."

"Don't be sorry and don't be stupid," she snapped. "This isn't finished."

But it was, she told herself. Finished before it was begun. A freighter with a single laser cannon and a few illegal sidearms was no match for the Kolnari-mercenary fleet they were leaving behind. And while they ran like cowards Belazir was taking apart the first and only man she'd ever felt something for.

The fighter was designed to do one thing, fight, and it offered few amenities and little comfort. Karak was at the apex of a three-seat triangle, overseeing the other two. None of the seats were moveable; they were designed to put the occupants within touching range of everything essential, and Kolnari ship designers made even fewer concessions to comfort than the Central Worlds Fleet.

It had been part nightmare and part comedy getting everyone suited and out. He'd handily connected the unconscious Sung to the various catheters and waste tubes built into the space armor. But Soamosa had refused to let him help her, even though she obviously had no idea how to proceed.

Karak eyed her worriedly. From time to time she shifted in a way that spoke of discomfort. But she didn't complain and he felt a little glow of pride towards her for that.

"I have laid in a course for Bethel," he told her. "We can expect to arrive in four days."

Soamosa started.

"So close!" she said. And she asked herself what the Kolnari were going to do that required their fleet to lie so close to her home. *Fool!* she told herself. *The disease of course! They will want to come and gloat.* She wondered if they would be content with what they saw, or would they amuse themselves by bombing the helpless people of Bethel. The way they had before.

"At the end of four days, my love, it will not seem close, I promise you." His voice was tinged with amusement.

Captain Sung began to stir and in moments a thin, heart-broken wailing filled the small cabin they shared. Soamosa leaned towards him and began to murmur soothingly, reaching out for his shoulder.

The Captain batted ill-temperedly at her and increased the volume of his weeping.

Four days! Karak thought in despair. *It will be an eternity.*

"Seg," Joat said, "put on an EVA suit, grab your bag of tricks and report to cargo hold C. We're going to lock you in and put the air in there on a sealed cycle."

!T'sel looked surprised. "How is it you can do that?"

"That hold's designed to ship live cargo. Why else d'you think it's got a double lock?"

"For sterilization procedures, of course," Seg murmured approvingly.

"And Seg, take everything you can think of. Once you're sealed in I don't want to keep opening that outer hatch any more than necessary."

!T'sel nodded solemnly.

"I understand and approve, Captain."

"I will accompany you," Joseph said.

Didn't ask my permission, this time. He'd always been careful of such courtesies before.

"You will also wear a suit, Joe."

He glanced at her in mild surprise and then nodded once. *Meaning, it's still my ship.*

"Yes, Captain," he said and followed Seg.

"Rand? Give me a multiple close-up on the pod."

"Yes, Joat."

Rand flashed four different views of the Kolnari escape pod. Then he brought each view to maximum magnification. The surface was some pebbled synthetic.

"Good," Joat said. "Polarized?"

"Most probably, from the composition—single-molecule silicon and carbon composite," Rand said.

"So far, we're in the clear," Alvec said, watching the Kolnari fleet on his screen. "No one's following, no weapons firing. Looks like we're safe." His voice had a flat, low-affect deadness to it.

"We're not leaving him there," Joat said. "We got Amos out, we'll get Sperin out."

He turned his chair around, his face like a lugubrious hound's.

"Boss, they wanted us to take Amos," he said gently.

"I know that." It was moments like this that you realized Alvec was a very dangerous man.

Joat turned to watch the pod. Behind her, Alvec smiled slowly as he studied the set of her face and the way she held her shoulders. He could almost feel sorry for the Kolnari fleet.

Bros was escorted down long, narrow corridors smelling of dry, recycled air and the metallic-spicy Kolnari body scent. The light was harsh enough to make him squint and the gravity was tangibly heavier than Earth standard. The temperature varied wildly, from chilly to a more common dry baking heat. He was uneasily aware that things he *couldn't* sense might well be killing him slowly; heavy-metal salts, strong UV, radiation . . . the Kolnari's ancestors had adapted to them, on their hell-planet. But that had taken generations, and they were still a short-lived race.

By the time they locked him into a spartan cell he was panting slightly and a fine sheen of sweat slicked his brow. He turned to take in his surroundings. Two bunks that folded down from the wall, a sink, and a toilet. The light was recessed into the ceiling, well out of his reach, even if he tried for it from the upper bunk. Clever. He assumed it would never go out.

Bros examined the bare walls, looking for the surveillance equipment. It was there, he knew, but it certainly wasn't obvious.

"Clever," he murmured to himself, running his fingers over the slick metal-fiber composite. *Not quite state-of-the-art, but they're good engineers in their way.* Probably spy-eyes and holo-projectors combined. He went to the tap and drank deeply, ignoring the unpleasant chemical smell and taste of the water, and the high salt content. The latter at least would be beneficial; he could feel the dry heat wicking moisture out of his skin.

Hands on his hips, he turned and looked at the closed hatch. Then, with a wry twist of his lips, he went over and tried it. Locked. *Ah, well, it was too much to hope for,* he thought. *The Kolnari are big, but they're not dumb.*

Not that he could easily escape anyway. They'd made him strip down to his underwear, even taking his socks. Weirdly enough, though, they'd let him keep his boots.

He went over and pulled down the lower bunk, sat and leaned his bare back against the cool white wall.

With a harsh *sssnnnaaapp!,* a jolt of electricity sent him leaping from the bunk.

As he reached for the burn on his back a woman's voice said calmly: "Sitting or lying on the bunk is forbidden until lights out."

"Yyyouu *bitch!*" Bros muttered, gently touching a rising blister.

There would be no lights out. Of that he was absolutely certain. Clearly Belazir had long-term plans for him.

He wondered if he dared to sit on the floor. Then he sighed. *No, I'll wait until I'm tired. No sense in getting a burnt butt before I have to.* He glanced at the commode. *Oh no, not unless I'm desperate.* There was no reason to start that phase of his torment before he absolutely had to.

Bros stood in the center of his cell, breathing deeply, his eyes closed, attempting to put himself into a trance state to make the time pass more quickly.

A little corner of himself wondered how long it would take for him to want to die.

Seg leaned closer to the life pod and read the bio-display on the capsule's external screen. It showed that the being within was alive, conscious and in good health. Naturally the computer couldn't show if Amos, assuming it *was* Amos, was infected with an unknown disease. But, encouragingly, the brain scan showed no anomalies.

Joseph swore softly, unused to reading through the restricted view of an EVA helmet and not certain he fully understood what he was reading anyway.

"It looks good," Seg told him. "His brain scan appears normal."

"Let us open the capsule then," Joseph insisted. "I must know that it is the Benisur Amos."

"Joe," Joat's voice halted him, "check the capsule for booby traps first. They might have rigged it with explosives. Perhaps that's how they intended to spread the disease."

"And what harm to us could that be in this chamber, in these suits?"

"Amos might get hurt," she said reasonably.

He cooled down instantly. Joat was right. He must not let his emotions destroy his caution. He would proceed slowly, Amos's life was in the balance.

Joseph examined every inch of the outside of the capsule; Seg worked with him, using a sonic scan and circuit-tracer. A cable snaked out of the wall and put Rand in control of the internal circuits.

"Nonstandard design," the AI said. "But simple and straightforward. The controls are exactly what they seem to be."

Unless they contain a trap so subtle . . . Joseph thought, then forced his mind away from the infinite-reduction series.

Seg was having better luck with the bio-readouts than Joseph was with his devices. Life-pods were constructed to be impervious to virtually everything an unfriendly universe could throw at them, including probes, some of which could be deadly to living tissue.

By connecting his own diagnostic devices to those contained in the pod Seg was able to determine that Amos was in very good health. Whatever indignities he'd suffered at Belazir's hands, gross physical torture hadn't been among them.

"No damage to the myelin sheaths," Seg said. "His nervous system has not been overloaded."

"I have done all that I can," Joseph announced at last. "I can find no evidence of trickery here." He ran his hand over the top of his helmet in a nervous gesture, as though stroking his blond mane. "Surely it would make no sense for them to do something violent. If they had planned for the disease to spread by stealth they would want people to rush in to see Amos, to touch him . . . and each other." His lips thinned. "Let us open this and see what they have done."

"I agree," Joat said, smiling wryly as Joseph gave a little start at the sound of her voice. *Poor Joe,* she thought, *he's freaked. This is so hard for him.*

Seg nodded and stepped aside, allowing Joseph to open the pod.

The seals released with a hiss of air and the unit snapped open along its length.

Within, Amos lay still, eyes closed, breathing peacefully.

Amos heard the seals release and sensed the lid rising. Light pressed against his eyelids with an almost tangible weight, and he expected his eyes to open of their own accord in response to it. A sense of free space surrounded him; he could hear air pumps and the sound of a ship's engines. The need to open his eyes was an overwhelming frustration, like an unscratchable itch.

"Elevated heartbeat," an unfamiliar voice said—unfamiliar and inhuman, like words produced by some beautifully-made musical instrument.

Inside himself Amos cringed away from the hand that suddenly touched him. The brief sound of movement he'd heard, a strange crunching sound, hadn't prepared him for the cold, hard touch of the gloved hand.

"Amos," Joseph said, in a voice high and tight with tension. "Benisur?" he attempted when Amos lay still and unresponsive.

Joseph? Amos went alert, tensed within himself to the point of pain. *My brother!* he thought joyfully, then horror filled him. *I am death, my brother, do not touch me! Leave me, leave me!* He thought the words with all his might, with all his soul, as though he could force them into his friend's mind.

Joseph reached out and grabbed Seg, flinging him hard against the open life-pod.

"Do something!" he snarled.

Amos felt the life-pod rock as Seg's body struck its side. *Another?* he thought. *How many?* he wondered desperately, imagining a room filled with victims, and Kolnari laughter.

"I'm a bio-engineer, not a doctor, dammit!" Seg snapped.

"You said he was conscious," Joseph said, his eyes narrowing menacingly. "Does he look conscious to you?"

"The bio-readings on the pod said he was conscious," Seg objected. "Just back off so I can attach my diagnostic equipment to him directly and maybe we'll see what's going on."

"Could he be drugged?' Joat asked.

"Of course. There are dozens of drugs they could have used that would leave him conscious but immobile. Or they could have pithed him," Seg chattered on, unaware of the thunder in Joseph's eyes. "They wouldn't be needing him after this. And there are ways of doing it that are so subtle they wouldn't show up on these scans."

"Pithed him," Joseph repeated, shaken.

No, only drugs, Amos silently reassured him.

"There's a certain strategic value in essentially destroying your planet's religious leader," Seg pointed out. "Though catastrophe-wise it's lame for the Kolnari."

Who is this fool? Amos wondered indignantly. Reflecting that it was no surprise that Joseph threw him around like an ill-mannered cur. The creature actually *was* an ill-mannered cur.

"It's drugs," Joat said positively. "Look, Joe, there's no need to glare at Seg that way. If there's one thing I'm sure of when it comes to the Kolnari, it's that they don't do subtle quietly. Whenever one of them actually manages to be subtle they throw a party and boast about it."

"But why do *this?*" Joseph asked wildly.

"So that he couldn't warn anybody," Seg assured him grimly, tapping the screen on his diagnostic unit. "Because he's definitely a carrier. He's unaffected, so he must be immune, but he's positive. They paralyzed him so that he could only lie there knowing that simply by breathing he was destroying his people. Then when the drug wore off, he'd be one of the few able to help."

Seg was unusually solemn, as though he'd just discovered the real meaning of what he was involved in. He looked up into one of the cameras. "I'd say there's a great deal of subtlety in that," he said.

"Well," Joat agreed, "they know all about cruelty."

Joseph leaned close to Amos and quietly said, "Benisur . . ." He paused, his mouth tight, his eyes suspiciously bright and once again he grasped Amos's arm.

I am here my friend, Amos thought. *Be at peace, I am with you.*

Joseph took a deep breath and tried again.

"My brother, we know the Kolnari plan and we are prepared. We are immunized and cannot get the disease you carry. Even so we are in EVA suits. You need not fear for us."

Amos felt tears of joy roll down his cheeks. They were safe! His people were safe. *Ah, bless the God that gave me allies like Joseph, my thanks! My most heartfelt thanks.*

Belazir sighed contentedly as he watched Bros Sperin standing in his cell and drank deeply from the glass of cane spirit in his hand. Then he frowned and reached over to add a pinch of salts of mercury and a dash of copperas and lead oxide.

Ah, better.

The scumvermin spy had been standing for approximately eighteen hours now and still stood rock solid. But a sheen of perspiration glistened on his hard-muscled body and darkened the waistband of his shorts.

Belazir hoped that he'd be watching when the Central Worlds Security operative eventually fell over. He grinned. How he loved to watch them hop around when the electrical charges hit them. Perhaps if he lowered the temperature . . . shivering would wear him out faster. *No, it will be more informative to see just how long he can last.*

Besides even in one's pleasures one should exercise a modicum of discipline, his eyes sparkled with amusement. *It builds character.*

"No Central Worlds Fleet," he said aloud. "Fool." He'd been prepared to run again, to scatter the painfully accumulated strength amid the dead stars. The High Clan did not need living planets, not since their exile from Kolnar.

But eighteen hours after he'd captured Sperin the mercenary escort he'd sent after Joat Simeon-Hap reported that the *Wyal* maintained its silence and its course for Bethel.

Belazir raised white-blond brows.

Perhaps her crew did not know his identity, he mused. Somehow he doubted that. *Ciety has a lot to answer for.* Belazir's brows snapped down. *First, the insult of Simeon's "daughter" thrown in my face, next a professional spy is among her crew.* He was pleased that he'd sent for Ciety. Never mind that his reasons had been less than rational at the time. *He and his wench are either traitorous or stupid. If the former, I shall kill them.* He smiled as imaginative images swept through his mind. *If the latter, I will punish them. That should give them an incentive to be more alert in future.* Even the most minor members of the crew had to maintain discipline. Without it, all was chaos.

"Rand, I want you to tight-beam this message to the nearest Central Worlds Naval facility," Joat began entering the *Wyal's* coordinates and a Mayday. They were now far enough away from the Kolnar fleet that such a message should be safe to send.

"That's probably not a good idea, Joat. We're being followed. If we alert the Kolnari, they'll be gone by the time a task force can get here."

There was no way to track a ship on interstellar drive from more than half a light-year away. Once the pirate fleet had scattered, only sheer chance would let the Fleet intercept even the slowest. No doubt they had a rendezvous arranged for just that eventuality.

"Followed?" Her head snapped up. "Show me."

"Indicating."

Rand opened a screen onto the rear view of the *Wyal.* The view showed a corrected view of the sidereal universe as it would have appeared to an object with the ship's pseudospeed. Even at FTL, only the nearer stars showed any apparent movement; space was *big.* A point of light strobed, and a line of figures ran down the screen beside it.

"Less than a hundred tonnes mass," the AI said. "But high-powered. Fighter equivalent, nonstandard."

"How long has it been there?"

"I first noticed it four hours after we left the Kolnari fleet," Rand said. "I didn't know just what it was at first. I thought it might be just a probe. The pilot has been careful, and for the most part was able to stay just far enough away to be unidentifiable. But occasionally, like now, it's strayed just this side of the line of scanning range and over time I've been able to determine that it's a small fighter."

Rand showed her a composite picture of a fighter, small and fast, and exceedingly well armed. "I'd suppose it's probably crewed by a mercenary."

"Yeah," Joat murmured, nibbling on her thumb. "They're not likely to risk one of their own on what could turn out to be a suicide mission. From the size of their fleet it doesn't look like they've got any Kolnari to spare . . . that thing looks just barely large enough to go interstellar."

She raised one brow and smirked with satisfaction. Channa would tell her that she shouldn't feel so pleased about it. But Channa was too soft-hearted for her own good. When you came across a killer disease you eradicated it. You didn't let it live out of pity.

"I'm going to guess," she said, "that his job it to make sure we go where we've been sent."

"The pilot has been sending periodic communications in the direction of the Kolnar fleet. But they were tight-beamed and I couldn't catch anything."

"Don't sound so embarrassed Rand. We're not a spy ship." *We're really not,* she thought with amusement, *even though we've been spying.*

"Hmmm. He's there to insure that Amos is delivered to Bethel. Maybe Belazir is afraid we'll grab the life-pod and go running off to the nearest Central Worlds outpost screaming for help. But I think his real fear is that we'll open it and be wiped out by the disease before his revenge plan has a chance to happen." She tapped the screen. "And this poor fool is to board us and take over the piloting if we show signs of going out of our minds."

"That was my assessment too," Rand said.

"So let's get him over here," Joat said. "Let's ask Seg for a complete list of symptoms."

✧   ✧   ✧

Skating along on the narrow edge of his scanner's capacity, Kraig Rendino du Pare followed the *Wyal*'s trail.

He was bored. To the point of pain.

He reckoned that fighters were made to be uncomfortable so you couldn't go to sleep on duty. And you had to stay in your suit, which cut down on your options for personal fun. You couldn't even open the helmet in vacuum, so you couldn't get at yourself. For good or ill. *Merde!*

This particular assignment was *agony.* The ship ahead of him did nothing but proceed quietly on its way.

Damned Kolnari paranoia, he thought sullenly.

When he'd become a mercenary ten years ago he'd done it in hopes of excitement, adventure, loot. Usually, though, it was as dull as regular duty in the Navy had been. With the added drawback that the pay was irregular. Not to mention the bad maintenance, so you had to check everything yourself if you wanted to live.

It's still hurry up and wait, he thought. *Still do what you're told, no matter how stupid it is.* He was going to quit. The pay was okay, but it wasn't high enough to counter Kolnari arrogance. *Or missions to nowhere that last forever.* And they were weird, even if they spared you the lectures on mental hygiene. *Come to think of it, they seem to like it better if you're crazy.*

Yeah. The Kolnari'd hired more head-cases than he'd ever even seen before. Another good reason to quit.

Uh oh. They were broadcasting on an emergency band. He risked scooting closer to pick it up.

"Mayday, Mayday, Mayday, Mayday, Mayday," a clipped male voice recited calmly, over and over.

Alright with the Maydays, Kraig thought impatiently, *get to the message.*

"Mayday."

Oh, Jeeesh!

"Um . . . Mayday."

The speaker seemed to have run out of steam. Almost a minute went by in perfect silence, except for the crisp sound of an open com.

"Mayday?"

Kraig started to laugh. On the other hand, there were compensations. The Fleet would have expected him to charge in and rescue these idiots.

"Tell them we're in trouble," a woman's voice prompted.

"We are?"

Silence.

"I . . ." the woman's voice, sounding uncertain. "Yes, I'm sure we are."

"What's wrong? Are we in trouble?"

"Mayday," she said. "Keep saying . . . May-something."

Merde! Kraig thought in disgust.

This was what he'd been told to watch for. If the crew of the *Wyal* showed signs of disorientation he was to go over and check it out. If necessary he was to carry out their mission to drop a life-pod into Bethel's atmosphere.

Merde!

"Attaboy," Joat said with a grin as the distant fighter began to close with them. She felt a tingling alertness, far more agreeable than the sour taste of fear. "Come to mama. How long before he gets here, Rand?"

"About ten minutes." Rand had long since discovered that humans didn't really want to know *exactly* how long until an event occurred. They were more interested in generalities. He'd often wondered how they'd accomplished all that they had, including his own invention, given their evident distaste for precision.

"Has he sent anything to Belazir yet?"

"No. Perhaps he's waiting until he has concrete information."

"*Verrrryy* good," she said, eyes bright with satisfaction. "Can you intercept any messages he sends once he's in range?"

"I assume you mean stop rather than intercept. If so, no, I can't."

"But," Alvec said. "Even a tight-beamed message can be interrupted so that it's garbage when its received. I'll show ya how, Rand."

"Thank you, Alvec," Rand said. "I'd appreciate that."

"You're a wonder, Al. I don't know what I'd do without you," Joat said, smiling at him over her shoulder. "The things you know . . ."

"I had an unfortunate adolescence," Alvec said piously.

Didn't we all. Joat keyed internal communications. "Seg, how are you doing with that antidote for whatever they gave Amos?"

"Not too badly, given the circumstances," he said, gesturing towards a looming Joseph with a none-too-subtle jerk of his head.

Joat pursed her lips.

"Will Amos come out of it on his own?" she asked.

"Eventually," !T'sel said slowly. "Why?"

"Because I'm going to have to ask you to stop what you're doing and come up here to administer some of those interrogation drugs you brought with you."

Joseph drew himself up indignantly, but Joat spoke before he could voice his outrage.

"Belazir put a tail on us," she said, "we're luring him in now. And somehow I don't think he's going to volunteer information."

Alvec barked a laugh in the background, making Joseph smile.

"Use your most effective drugs," he suggested to Seg, "so that you may return quickly. I loathe seeing the Benisur in this condition. And I assure you, neither the Kolnari, nor those they are likely to use as tools, are deserving of mercy. If your drugs fail, call me. My knife will not."

"I'll . . . take that under advisement," Seg muttered.

He swallowed at Joseph's expression. Usually human faces were a little hard to read, immobile . . . but he suspected that a good number of sentient beings had seen *that* expression the very last time they saw anything at all.

Perhaps Bros wasn't completely wrong about adventure. Suddenly, his quiet, boring laboratory seemed much more attractive.

CHAPTER SEVENTEEN

"EASY DOES IT," Kraig said to himself. "*Pas de problème.*" The High Clan certainly wasn't paying him enough to be a hero.

Nothing but nonsense on the com. He touched the sensitive pads under his gloved fingers, adjusting the fighter's trajectory. The ship itself continued on its way, apparently on autopilot, for neither speed nor course had changed.

He dreaded tight-beaming this information to the Kolnari. It made him feel as though *he* had failed. His mouth twisted wryly. It was definitely time to quit if he really gave a damn what the employer thought. *And they scare me.* He didn't like that sensation, either.

"Calling merchanter ship *Wyal*," he said, and waited for reply. He could hear sounds of consternation from her crew as his voice came through their speakers. *Merde, merde, merde!* he thought. *I don't wanna do this!* Every instinct that had kept him alive for the last fifteen years told him to stay off that ship. And the same instincts told him that if he left now the Kolnari would track him down and make him regret it.

"Kraig to command," he said; the machine intelligence of the fighter would relay and encrypt it automatically. "Crew incapacitated. Am approaching *Wyal*."

It was near enough for visual scan now, an elongated spindle, more streamlined than most freighters—built for landing on planetary surfaces. He was mildly surprised that the Kolnari had let it go; it would be perfect as a fleet auxiliary for surface raids.

This mission must be important, at least to whatever passed for brains inside those silver-blond heads.

Delicately, he established zero relative velocity and nudged his fighter towards the airlock, marked out by its square of strobing lights.

"So, Al, how're we going to handle this?" Joat asked, crossing her arms behind her head and stretching. The black Kolnar fighter approached delicately on the screen, like a cat advancing on a suspicious bit of string. She could think about this and *stop* thinking about Sperin.

Alvec's brow went up.

"I thought Joe was our resident warrior," he said.

"He is," Joat grinned. "But Joe's not likely to leave Amos's side now he's got him under his eye." She glanced over at her crew. "Besides, he knows we can handle this."

"He'll be wearin' space armor," Alvec said gruffly. He frowned and made a clicking sound with his tongue. "Can't charge a guy in space armor."

"Figure he's a merc," Joat mused, "so he won't be wearing Kolnari armor. That's a plus." She folded her hands on her middle and stared into space. "Ninety per cent of the space armor manufactured has lousy surge protection," she said at last. "Give 'em a sustained charge and," she snapped her fingers, "they're fried."

Alvec chuckled. "Set a trap?"

"Either side of the entry hatch," Joat agreed.

"Easily done," Rand said, and displayed schematics of the areas involved. "These segments—" bars of yellow flashed on the screen to indicate the spots he referred to "—are underlaid with support grids constructed of conductive materials. Actually I'm a little surprised at that," it added disapprovingly. "Anyway, they're . . ."

"I see it," Joat said quickly. "Just cut the power there to give us a chance to work. Then when our visitor steps onto those grids . . ."

"You can make him dance," Alvec finished, rising to follow a grinning Joat out the door.

"Actually," Rand said, mildly puzzled, "if this works properly he shouldn't be able to move."

Kraig's attempts to communicate with the *Wyal* had been met with half-hysterical nonsense and unending repetitions of "Mayday."

I'm going to kill that son-of-a-bitch who keeps sayin' that, Kraig thought. *Quick too, just to shut 'im up.* In the twenty minutes it had taken him to catch up with the merchant ship and align the locks he'd conceived a serious hatred for the prattling lunatic on the com. *Aw, Ghu, he's crying now. I'll be doing the jerk a favor.* Weight left him as he switched off his fighter's internal field.

He'd have done the woman a favor, too, if he could only get out of this damned suit. The mercenary shuddered. No chance of that, not with some bug loose on the ship. He disconnected his suit from the fighter's feeds and drifted out of his seat. Gripping hand-holds built into the minuscule cabin he pulled himself over to the hatch. Pausing there for a moment he ran a weapons and systems check on his suit.

All green, he thought, relieved. Even knowing he was unlikely to run into any opposition, Kraig was nervous. "Stage fright," one of his friends called it. *Yeah, stage fright. Well, curtain up.* He hit the control for opening the hatch.

Grapple fields held the two craft less than arm's length apart; the hard flat light of vacuum shone on every irregularity of hull and plating, and the undiffused glow of the airlock lights made the controls of the *Wyal's* entryway stand out.

e-n-t-r-y, he punched into the pad.

The *Wyal's* hatch opened after a second's pause to purge atmosphere. He crouched down and waited a full minute, alarm bells going off in his mind. It was always this way for him when things were too easy. He flipped across, catching the handbars by the merchanter's lock and orienting himself so that the internal gravity field would pull him down on his feet. Vibration shivered beneath him as he stood and swung the exterior door closed. Air hissed in automatically; the readouts below his chin showed it breathable.

He wished he had some of the fancy equipment the Kolnari had access to. Getting a nice, safe view of that corridor out there would suit him fine. As it was he'd have to rely on his eyes, and the few enhancements from his face-plate. Sonic and electromag monitor showed no weapons profiles from the access corridor. He readied the needler built into his cuff and stepped out into the ship.

Carefully, exposing as little of himself as he could, Kraig angled himself to look out the hatch in either direction. Nothing. That didn't mean they weren't there, it just meant they weren't *obviously* there. The suit's sensors would tell him more once he was actually in the corridor.

He pitched himself out of the lock and flattened himself against the wall opposite, his heart hammering.

Nothing. The sensors confirmed it.

He took a deep breath and let it out in a soft whistle. Then he grinned. *'Cause sometimes when it's easy, it's just . . . easy.* Kraig set off for the bridge with a jaunty walk.

"Now," Joat said.

The mottled armor froze in a spectacular shower of fat blue sparks. Ozone drifted through the *Wyal*'s corridors, and the life-support system whined in overload to carry it off. The suit toppled forward slowly in midstride, left leg frozen half-raised. The three hundred kilos of mass struck the decking with a clamor that echoed through the hull.

Help! Kraig thought as the power-armor toppled and he crashed helplessly to the floor, a prisoner inside it. Inertia flung him against the padded restraints inside, hard enough to bruise. His jaw struck the readout panel and blood filled his mouth with a taste of iron and salt. *I've fallen,* he thought in disbelief. *And I can't get up!*

A blond woman sauntered into sight, wearing a coverall with an amazing number of pockets for microtools Kraig didn't recognize. He *did* recognize the arc-pistol in the hand of the bruiser walking beside her. She squatted down beside the fallen mercenary and went to work with one of the tools. A minute later the faceplate came free; Kraig rolled his eyes at the whining head of the tool. Her thumb stroked the control, setting the tiny Phillips' head up and down the scale from a low burr to a tooth-grating whine.

"*Tsk.* Now, that's the downside of cut-rate equipment," she said sweetly. "When it breaks down it's worse than useless. Doncha hate it when that happens? I'm Captain Joat Simeon-Hap, by the way. This is my engineer, Alvec Dia. He doesn't like pirates."

"I'm . . . I'm just a freelancer!" Kraig wheezed. He was lying face-down, his limbs clamped in midstride position as firmly as a tangler-field could have done.

The arc-pistol came closer; he turned his eyes until they ached in their sockets, enough to see the four pointed prongs of the guide-field projector at the end of the weapon. They were pitted with use.

"I don't like mercenaries who work for pirates, either," he said in a voice like a gravel crusher.

"Rand," Joat went on. "Lower the corridor gravity for a second, would you?"

The mercenary felt himself lighten; not that it made any difference, since he still couldn't move anything but the muscles of his face. The face-plate began to swing shut again.

"No!" he shouted. "My air's off!"

"I know," Joat said.

They shoved him onto a cargo sled and brought him to the bridge; a Sondee awaited them, with a medical kit resting beside him.

"I don't want to do this," Seg said.

"Neither do I," Joat said, digging in her toolbox for something to manually open the mercenary's space armor. "But we need information and we need it now."

"No we don't! Amos will be all right whether I come up with an antidote or not. It's just a matter of time."

"Oh yeah? This guy is supposed to signal Belazir that we've accomplished our mission. I need to know what that signal is. What's more, he knows things that'll get me into Belazir's ship," she said grimly. "You may have forgotten Bros, but I haven't."

"Jeeez boss, you can't go back there." Alvec came away from the bulkhead with a startled lurch. "You'll get yourself killed. Let Central Worlds handle it, they've got the manpower."

"Thank you, Al, that reminds me. Rand, send that tight-beam message to the nearest Central Worlds facility."

She turned to Alvec while she continued to manually trip the helmet's locking system. "I guarantee you, I'll bet this ship on it, that they can't get anybody here for two weeks or so."

"Well?" She looked Alvec in the eye. "You want to take that bet?" She turned to Seg. "You?"

They both shook their heads.

"The Kolnari can be beaten," she said positively. "I've seen it happen."

The helmet popped off in her hands.

"Well, hello there," Joat said sweetly to the gasping mercenary. "Welcome aboard."

Kraig looked frantically around him, surprisingly fine dark eyes filled with panic. He was about thirty, balding, with dark hair and a narrow face.

"I won't talk," he said.

"Really?" Alvec said, sounding pleased.

The mercenary laughed. "You're worse than the Kolnari? I don't think so. And if you aren't, I'm not going to risk getting on their bad side. You know what I mean?"

"You're already on their bad side," Joat purred from behind him. Leaning close she continued, "And they're in no position to hurt you right now." She grabbed his sparse hair and yanked his head back. "But we are," she said, smiling pleasantly.

He went white to the lips.

"My name's Kraig . . ."

"I don't care," she interrupted him cheerfully, shaking his head.

"There are laws, lady!"

"You're working for the Kolnari and you're talkin' about laws?" Alvec said with disgust.

"What's civilization coming to?" Joat coolly asked the room in general. "Seg," she said, glancing at the young Sondee. "Prepare Kraig here a shot of one of those wonder drugs you've been telling us about."

Seg's mouth was sphinctered tightly shut and his golden eyes were half-closed, his face gray with tension, the ear whorls nearly white. But he set down his bag and opened it, slowly.

"Joat," Rand said, "I'm receiving a distress call."

"You're joking," she said.

Instead of answering, Rand opened the com for all to hear.

"Mayday," an obviously distraught young woman was saying. "Mayday! Our pilot is ill, he's unconscious, if you can hear me please help us. We must get to Bethel, it's a matter of life or death! Mayday! Please, someone, answer me. Mayday." Her voice disintegrated into helpless sobbing.

Belazir steepled his hands beneath his chin and settled himself more comfortably on his thronelike chair, gazing placidly at Nomik Ciety.

I think this one has some trouble with his internal mapping of reality, the Kolnari warlord thought.

He lounged back, resting his chin on the fingers of one hand. Behind him a holographic night-scene showed a plutonium volcano on Kolnar. Down either wall stood Kolnari warriors, naked except for briefs and their weapons, armored in their leopard deadliness.

Nomik bristled. "How *dare* you kidnap me and my associate?" he shouted. He ignored the subtle stirrings of the warriors, their bronze eyes riveted on Belazir. "Do you have any idea the trouble you've just bought yourself? Do you realize that I'm under the protection of Yoered Family?'

The woman beside him had been glancing about. She looked at the collection of plants in their netted cages, and at the shape of the gnawed bones beneath them.

"Mik . . ." she whispered urgently. The man shook off her hand.

"Answer me, you mutant goon! What do you want?"

He paused, panting and glaring at Belazir's mildly interested face.

Fascinating, Belazir thought, bemused, *the creature seems to think I should be frightened of him. Apparently I am supposed to be intimidated.* If this was an example of intimidating behavior it was no wonder the scumvermin races were so easily conquered.

"*You* are dead meat!" Ciety snarled.

At Belazir's almost imperceptible gesture, two of the Kolnari picked Nomik up and flung him down on the floor hard enough to knock the wind out of him.

The moment they'd moved Silken had flung herself at Belazir's throat, one hand stiffened into a blade. He watched her approach with astonishment and flicked her aside like a butterfly. She crashed to the floor and rolled to a stop not far from Ciety, and the two of them writhed, breathless at the Kolnari's feet.

"She is brave," Belazir said to Nomik. "I shall speak with her first as she is so eager to approach me." He smiled into Ciety's furious and frightened face. "But I shall try not to keep you waiting long."

Well, that was disappointing, Belazir thought as the guards dragged Silken's half conscious body from his quarters. He'd expected more fire from a woman who'd thrown herself at him unarmed. Ah well, some of them considered it properly stoic to affect total disinterest. Though he hadn't made that easy for her.

Who to speak to now? He sat down before his bank of screens, running a quick check on the day-to-day affairs of his people. Then he called up Bros Sperin and Nomik Ciety's cells.

Sperin was on his feet again, his body bearing yet more burns on his legs and sides. He swayed precariously, his jaw slack, eyes bruised-looking and swollen from lack of sleep.

Nomik was pacing energetically. He turned suddenly as the hatch opened. Two guards thrust Silken into the cell, where she collapsed in a boneless heap before Ciety could reach her.

Nomik knelt beside her and gathered her slender form into his arms, rocking her tenderly and whispering her name over and over as he stroked her matted black hair.

Bleh, Belazir thought. *That is enough of that; Karak was bad enough. It is time I interviewed Sperin, anyway.*

And the houseplants were hungry. It was time to cultivate a new crop, in any case. What the spores did to living flesh was *very* amusing.

Bros Sperin wavered. When he closed his eyes it felt as though his body was moving in a circle around the anchor of his feet. He tried not to close his eyes for too long; that meant he kept falling asleep and then over. The crisp white sheets of the bunk mocked him with taunting cruelty. Soft music was playing through the com system, soft soothing music—

He screamed as his knees struck the flooring and current arched through them. Still screaming he touched his hands to the floor to push himself up, then nearly staggered into the wall. Blisters burst on his kneecaps and palms, drooling liquid.

He was very thirsty. He'd promised himself that if he counted to a thousand one more time he could go to the sink and get some water. But he seemed to be stuck on eight hundred sixty-seven. For the life of him he couldn't remember what came next. Or before, for that matter. Eight hundred sixty-seven kept intruding itself into his efforts, offering itself every time he sought the next number.

The bottoms of his feet were numb, but his ankles ached and his calves burned. Inside as well as out.

The thought struck him as funny and he began to laugh. *Wonderful,* some distant, still sane part of him thought, *I'm getting hysterical. That should move things along nicely.*

That same part of him was waiting for Belazir to make an appearance. It unnerved him that the Kolnari hadn't come to gloat. It signaled unexpected new depths of self-discipline in the volatile pirate.

"Wake up, scumvermin," a gentle voice urged.

Painfully, Bros opened his eyes. Slowly, they focused on the face before him, and the wide yellow eyes blazing into his. He gasped and staggered back, almost losing his balance on his numbed and clumsy feet. Bros pinwheeled his arms and regained his balance barely in time to prevent himself from crashing into the wall.

Then he stood there panting, head down, heart beating rapidly, glaring at Belazir from under his brows.

Belazir chuckled delightedly and crossed his arms over his chest. He was pleased that he'd taken the time to dress for this interview in a long, open-necked robe of watered green silk accented by fretted silver jewelry glittering with fire-opals. It nicely emphasized the difference in their status. A refinement Sperin was definitely intelligent enough to recognize, on some level, semiconscious as he was.

"Are your accommodations to your liking?" he asked politely.

"I was more comfortable on the *Wyal*." Bros straightened slowly and found himself equal to Belazir's imposing height. Which pleased him a great deal more than it did the Kolnari, he was sure. "You look older than I'd expected," he said conversationally.

A tiny seed of fury burst into existence in Belazir's heart. His mortality gazed back at him from his mirror with every new wrinkle and hair gone from silver-golden to white. Leaving him ever more aware of the hot breath of ambitious underlings on his neck, well-honed blades clutched in their sweaty young hands.

To be so casually insulted by a man he was torturing was intolerable. Lightning flickered at the edges of his vision. If they were truly in the same room he would teach the scumvermin how little his age mattered.

But wait! Profound surprise flickered across his mind. *Could Sperin be attempting to provoke me? To manipulate me?* He raised one white-blond brow. *Clever, foolish spy.* How interesting that he was so eager to die. It promised useful information as well as excellent entertainment.

"Do you think," he asked casually, "that it is wise to make me hate you, Bros Sperin?"

"I don't particularly care how you feel about me," Bros said.

Belazir smiled serenely.

"Ah, but you will," he said with utter confidence. "And in a very short time, too."

He decided to begin with the drug that caused pain. As yet he'd had no one to experiment on and Sperin should make a fine test case.

Three Kolnari entered the cell, one of them smaller and pudgier than the other two and tremblingly subservient; a half-caste castrato slave, the usual type assigned the low-status occupation of medicine. He bowed to Belazir's image over the small satchel he carried.

The two guards took hold of Bros, one on either arm and he slumped between them, making them stagger as he let them take his full weight. It felt almost good, not having to hold himself up anymore.

"The drug that causes pain," Belazir said to the cowering medical technician. He turned to Bros. "An invention from the Phelobites, some of Central Worlds most clever allies. It ignites the nervous system, I am told, causing exquisite suffering."

Bros looked up at him, tired, but contemptuous.

"You make it sound almost sexy, Belazir. Is this how you people have fun when you get old?"

Again the creature taunted him, and he didn't care to have the issue of his age mentioned before his crew. Rage snapped through him like a power whip and was quickly suppressed. He coiled it in, to be used later. Rage always had a use if turned to the right purpose.

"We are a disciplined people," Belazir observed with a calm smile. "We seldom allow ourselves to have 'fun.' However," the smile became wolfish, "I anticipate that you will provide us with some occasion for merriment in the near future." He gestured for the medtech to administer the dose of pain-inducer and watched Sperin's eyes as it was done.

Bros looked back at him as calmly as though they sat across a table in The Anvil.

The dose went in with no more sensation than the touch of the injector to his skin. But inside, almost instantly, a vile sensation— like worms writhing beneath his skin—began to spread through his body.

Belazir watched eagerly as Sperin stood upright, taking his weight on his own feet and his face wrinkled into a mask of profound . . . distaste.

"Eeyaaahh, that's disgusting!" Bros said, shaking his hands and rotating his shoulders. All the while praising Seg !T'sel within his heart. *What would this have been like without the antidote?* he wondered.

Belazir showed no sign of his shock or disappointment beyond a tightening of his jaw. It wasn't working. Perhaps the drug was unstable and had begun to lose its power.

"Try the drug for fear," he ordered harshly.

The med-tech licked his lips and his dark flesh turned pale gray with terror.

"Great Lord," he said in a voice that shook, "there is a possibility that combining the two drugs could poison the prisoner."

"Do it," Belazir snapped. *Or I will have you gutted where you stand,* he thought viciously, but did not say. It would show too much of what he was feeling.

"Yes, Great Lord."

The second injection acted as quickly as the first, complicating the unpleasant sensation below Bros's skin with a sense of anxiety. His heart speeded up and sweat broke out on his brow. He found himself panting slightly and licked dry lips with a dry tongue. It was very unpleasant.

Almost as much of a strain as the effort not to laugh. The combined effect was about as bad as going three days without a bath or shave; and it was making him less sleepy, too.

Seg, you are a genius. Whatever they're paying you at Clenst it's not enough. If the little Sondee had been before him, Bros would have kissed him passionately.

Fortunately he was still too tired to smile.

Belazir's apparent calm hid a rage that almost frightened the Kolnari. He stood with his back stubbornly turned to his fury; a ravening beast that would overwhelm and devour him if he gave it one moment's attention.

"Leave him," he said coldly to his men, and watched them march impassively from the cell. Then he studied Bros for a moment longer, hating his victim's lack of reaction, hating his men for witnessing this humiliating incident.

"I see we shall have to think of some other means of helping you pass the time," he said to Sperin. "I shall return quite soon."

"Get some rest," Bros said, "at your age this land of excitement isn't good for you."

"I am going to take you to pieces," Belazir promised him, "One millimeter at a time."

Belazir flung himself into his chair before the bank of screens. Breathing heavily . . . he forced himself to be still, his fury as hot as the core of a sun within him. He held up a hand before his face, and the fingers trembled. There was a time when they had been rock-steady, however hard the pulse of rage drummed in his ears.

He would personally kill that medtech. *How dare the creature care for the drugs entrusted to him so poorly they have gone off!* He would tear the little eunuch apart! Belazir's mind filled with images of blood that soothed him somewhat.

He reached for the com, intending to have the creature sent to one of the rooms where discipline was administered, when his eye caught a movement in one of the screens before him.

Nomik sat beside his aide, Silken, on her bunk, holding her hand and talking. He'd reached up to brush her hair aside and that movement had earned him Belazir's attention.

Belazir watched him coax the shadow of a smile from Silken. *My other prisoners,* he mused.

Yes, his other prisoners.

Civilians.

Sperin was a trained spy, perhaps he'd been instructed in methods of resisting drugs, or he might have a natural immunity. Or there might be an antidote of some sort.

Belazir considered that. Those who had sold him the drugs had assured him that no counter-agents or immunizers for them existed. But he'd been dealing with thieves, and salesmen, who were also notorious liars. Anyone who trusted a Phelobite would ask a Kolnari for an insurance appraisal.

He slid down comfortably in his chair and steepled his hands before him, gently tapping the fingertips together. Yes, he would try the drugs on Ciety. Let Silken watch. The female had demonstrated her loyalty already. His lips twisted in a wry smile. *Let us see what her loyalty will bring me,* he thought, anticipating a pleasant interlude.

"Where is she, Rand?" Joat asked.

"Less than an hour away, and on our heading."

"Well we can't do anything tied to that fighter."

"I can pilot that," Al said. "Or did you just want t' let it go?"

"No, we're keeping it. Like I said, that ship, and this fellow's call signs are going to help us rescue Bros." She jerked her head downship, indicating that Al should go, cutting off his inevitable protest.

"You're crazy!" Kraig yelled. "You're fardling crazy!"

Joat ignored him. "Respond to that call, Rand. Tell her help's on the way." Then she stood with her fingers tapping her lips, staring off into space while Seg nervously watched her.

"Joat," he said quietly. "You're serious about rescuing Bros, aren't you?"

She looked at him from the corner of her eye and nodded once.

"It's suicide," Seg whispered in a pleading tone.

"You're fardling right it is!" Kraig snarled. "And not the easiest way to do it either. Do you have any idea what those people are like, lady?"

She nodded.

"I was on a space station they took over."

He went still. "The SSS-900-C?"

She nodded again, her lip curling slightly. "You may have heard of some of the tricks we played on them there." She leaned in close, filling his field of vision and whispered, "So you have some idea of what *I'm* like. Don't you?" He nodded and she nodded with him. Joat leaned still closer, resting her elbow on the shoulder of his frozen suit "Think about this," she said confidentially. "If you help us out, we'll send you to Bethel a hero. You were sent to destroy us, but sickened by the Kolnari, you decided to help us instead. How does that sound? Hmmm?"

He stared at her uncertainly.

"You'd do that?"

"Um hmm." She nodded.

For a moment he almost smiled, then the frown was back.

"It sounds great, but it wouldn't sound so good when the Kolnari catch up with me."

Joat looked at Seg's disapproving face, then moved to block Kraig's view of him.

"Well, you know what, Kraig? You're not with the Kolnari, you're with us now. And now is all you should be thinking about." She smiled sweetly. "Given that I am one nnaaaaasty, dangerous woman.

"But if you're so *hot* to get back to the Kolnari, here's what we could do. After we torture the information I need out of you, I can fix your air pump, put that helmet back on and take you with me when I go." She smiled encouragingly into his horrified face. "Now, how would that suit you, hmmm?"

He went so pale that even his lips faded to white.

"Jeeeeezzz," he breathed. "You *are* crazy."

"You can't do that, Joat," Seg said raggedly.

"Oh, yes I caaaan," she said, playfully tweaking Kraig's nose.

"But they'll kill me," Kraig pleaded.

"I know. It's good to see that you understand your options." She straightened and stood before him with her hands on her hips. "You can either be a hero or a statistic. Your choice. I'll give you a few minutes to think about it."

Without another word, she turned her back on him and sat in the gimbaled pilot's couch.

"Rand, any word from Central Worlds?"

"No, but . . ."

" . . . I wouldn't expect any, as yet," she finished with him.

Rand paused, as though nonplused by her knowing what he was going to say.

"Even if we hear from them in the next instant, Joat, that doesn't mean they will be here anytime soon."

"Tell me about it," she sneered. "Even *Simeon* couldn't get them to move their butts. It was two weeks before the station got help." She was silent a moment, remembering all too well the horror and anxiety of those slowly passing days.

There was a shudder through the ship as Alvec disconnected the fighter's caterpillar lock from theirs.

"So, any word from the Mayday Ms.?" she asked flippantly.

"I've had her stop her ship. She said that it is also a fighter. That she is a Bethelite and her companions are the former Captain of the Sunrise and a Kolnari."

"What?" Seg and Joat shouted together.

"Her name is Soamosa bint Sierra Nueva and the Captain's name is Sung."

"She captured a *Kolnari?*" Joat asked.

"She said he was one of her companions," Rand said carefully. "She made no boast of capturing one."

"Hmmmph! Interesting. The *Sunwise* was Amos's ship," Joat said. She keyed up cargo hold C. "Joe, Amos, does the name Soamosa bint Sierra Nueva mean anything to you?"

Joseph's head had lifted with a start at the sudden sound of her voice, Amos simply lay there, as unresponsive as ever.

"She is the Benisur's young cousin," Joseph said. "She was traveling with him when the Kolnari captured him." He straightened. "Why do you ask this?"

"Because we just picked up a Mayday call from her. She's in a ship ahead of us, en route for Bethel. Rand says we'll catch up with them in about forty minutes. Joat out."

She lives! Amos thought exultantly. *And she is sane. Oh, dearest God, my thanks. Your kindness is as sweet as honey, a balm to my heart and spirit. How astounding that Belazir told me the truth!*

He felt Joseph's hand take his and extended his will to respond.

Joseph felt the merest quiver in Amos's fingers, but he knew it was deliberate, that the Benisur *was* conscious and would, indeed, recover.

"My Lord," he said in a voice harsh with relief.

Soamosa had wakened to the sound of tears. A soft, strained, high-pitched whining, followed by a series of sobs. A sound of heart-breaking loss and confusion.

She blinked her eyes free of sleep and turned to Captain Sung, wondering if this time he would accept the comfort she offered him. *I think Karak may have been a little rough with that catheter,* she thought uncomfortably. Just the idea of a catheter made her squirm. She was certain she had installed her own incorrectly. Resolutely she turned her mind from that path.

There is nothing to be done about it now except to think of something else. It is not as though I lacked distraction, she thought wryly.

That was when she noticed that Captain Sung was quite still, his eyes closed, his face calm. He was snoring gently, she realized.

Then what is it that I hear?

Slowly, her eyes widened with horror and the hair on the back of her neck rose in a ripple that made her shudder. That awful weeping, the sound of a lost and wounded child, was coming from Karak.

Slowly she turned, her heart thudding like a horse's hooves and her mouth dry. *He is having a nightmare,* she thought desperately. *My poor love.* But instinctively she knew that the sound she was hearing never came from a sleeping man.

He was leaning over his console, the helmet almost resting on the boards before him. Then he flung himself back in his couch and flailed his head from side to side as if trying to fling off his helmet.

His face was gray and slicked with sweat. When his eyes opened it was like looking through two golden hued windows into the heart of a furnace. As she watched, tears spilled over and rolled heavily down his cheeks.

Karak touched gloved hands to his head, to be stopped by the face-plate. He groaned and threw his head forward again.

"Karak!" Soamosa freed herself from her couch and pulled herself rapidly over to him. "Speak to me, Karak. My love, can you hear me?"

She placed her trembling hands on either side of his helmet and gently lifted his head. "Karak, you must answer me. Can you hear me?"

She was terrified. He could be dying and there was nothing she could do to help him. Locked into their suits hike this she couldn't even touch him.

He opened his eyes and after a long moment, he seemed to recognize her. He smiled and moved a hand, as though to caress her, then stopped, as though the effort, even in zero-g, was too great.

"My sweet," Soamosa pleaded desperately, "if you can hear me you must give me some sign. Can you speak?"

He looked puzzled for a moment, then shook his head.

"Are you in pain?"

He nodded and his face crumpled like a child's, great fat tears falling unchecked down his sweat-slick face.

"Take a sip of water," she advised him.

He looked at her blankly through the plastic that separated them. Then he looked around, as though expecting a glass to materialize from nowhere. When it didn't, he looked accusingly at her and licked his lips; thirsty now that she had mentioned water.

"Sip on that," she said, pointing at a small flexible tube near his mouth.

He complied and his eyes widened with pleasure when the water came in response to his sucking.

Soamosa smiled reassuringly at him and then turned to the array of tell-tales built into the front of his suit.

Each suit of space-armor had a very basic auto-doc built in, to offer pain-killers and antibiotics, to apply pressure in order to control bleeding, and to administer up to two pints of plasma. Soamosa directed the suit to administer pain-killers. She noted that his fever was one hundred and four and reduced the interior temperature of his suit, hoping to combat the heat in his blood.

"Sweetheart," she pleaded, "why is this happening? Kolnari are never sick. Their bodies are too strong, they fight off everything. Why is this happening to you?"

He smiled bravely at her through his tears and mouthed the words: "I fight." Then his eyes crossed and rolled back in his head and he lay quiet beneath her.

She had panicked then, rushing back to her seat and activating the com, putting out a frantic Mayday call, hoping desperately that it would not be the Kolnari who answered it.

"Answering Mayday," a voice said in her ears. "This is free merchanter *Wyal*. Report your position and status."

Wyal, she thought. *That is . . . that is Joat's ship.* Every child on Bethel knew about the Jack Of All Trades and what she'd done against the Kolnari on SSS-900-C—girls especially knew. *She is the abomination's daughter.*

That thought brought her up short, like a mild slap to the face. She had thought, "abomination's daughter," without the slightest bit of rancor. It was merely an identifying tag, like the security director's wife . . . or the Benisur's Lady. She blushed to remember how she had yearned for that title.

Well, she thought wryly, *I suppose that if I have been impetuous enough to fall in love with a Kolnari, I have no business tossing epithets about. Nor aspiring to be the Benisur's wife, for that matter.*

"I am aboard a Kolnari three-crew fighter craft," she said, her voice a little hoarse. "With me are Captain Sung of the Benisur Amos's ship *Sunwise*. And . . . ah, and a Kolnari. Captain Sung and the Kolnari are ill, very ill—some sort of tailored disease which affects the memory functions. Help us, please!"

The waiting was almost harder than the fear had been. Captain Sung slept on, for which she was grateful. She considered authorizing the suit to give him a sleeping dose, but fought the urge. It would be selfish of her, and might harm him. Who knew how this awful disease had marred the functioning of his brain?

Releasing herself from her couch, she once again floated over to Karak. His eyes were closed and his temperature remained high, but at least had risen no higher.

"Oh, be well, my dear one," she whispered fervently. "I could not bear it if you became like the Captain." Her breath caught on a sob.

For that must be what afflicted him. And his body, in typical Kolnar fashion, was just different enough to cause this violent battle for supremacy over the disease that had broken the Captain's mind. She prayed that his body would be different enough to win.

An eternity later, the *Wyal* slid out of the night.

"Stand by for force-docking." A distant part of her was surprised that a merchanter was equipped for that . . . but this was *Joat's* ship, after all. The smaller vessel shuddered violently as the freighter's lock clamped on to it.

A small explosion of air, part sob, part laugh, entirely relieved, escaped Soamosa's lips.

She heard someone thumping awkwardly through the narrow tube connecting their ships when a thought struck her.

"Wait!" she cried frantically, just as she heard someone's gloves clack against the lock-face.

"What is it?" Rand asked.

The thumper had either heard or been warned to stop, for suddenly there was no sound back there.

"I should have thought of this," Soamosa apologized raggedly. "There is sickness aboard our craft. A very dangerous illness; we dare not expose you to it." She could feel the blood drain from her face as she spoke.

Ancient tales she had once enjoyed, describing noble heroines buried alive for their principles, slipped into her mind. *We're going to die out here*, she thought numbly. *This ship will be my tomb.* Her heart picked up its pace, as though her oxygen were already running out and she gasped for air in sympathy with the thought.

There was a pause, then a woman's voice broke the silence.

"This is Joat Simeon-Hap, Soamosa, captain of the *Wyal*. I assume the disease you're referring to is the one that destroys a part of the brain, leaving its victims like very young children?"

"Yes," the younger woman choked. Soamosa pressed her fist uselessly to her face-plate and then snatched it away with an annoyed sound.

"We're immunized and we have a controlled environment on the ship where we can lodge you."

"Oh!" Soamosa cried out in relief, and her heart filled to overflowing with gratitude.

She disconnected from her couch and flung herself at the nearest hand-hold. Scrambling towards the lock, all elbows and knees, Soamosa felt tears warming her cheeks. She reached the keypad, released the lock and flung herself into the suited arms of the woman who waited without. Their helmets knocked together with a resounding *clang*.

"Easy, girl!" Joat said, laughing. "These helmets cost a fortune." She held the girl awkwardly, feeling her trembling even through their suit's thickness. Joat gave Soamosa an occasional thump in the area of her shoulder blades in hopes the girl would soon feel comforted enough to release the death-grip she had on Joat's waist. "C'mon now," she said bracingly, "who've we got here." She gently but firmly pried Soamosa off and turned her towards the fighter's interior.

"It is Karak who is most in need of aid," Soamosa said urgently. "His fever is one hundred and four and he has been unconscious for over an hour." She began to tug Joat into the fighter.

"He the Kolnari?" Joat asked.

"Yes, he saved us."

"He *did?*"

Joat quickly saw that the Kolnari would have to be removed first, before the other figure in the lower seat could get out. Soamosa was lithe and slim and so could maneuver in that tight space with ease. But Captain Sung was both older and significantly thicker bodied. And one glance into his frightened, confused eyes told her that getting him out was going to be a project to remember.

"Okay," she said somewhat impatiently. "Karak goes first. Grab his other arm, Soamosa, then get at his feet and keep his rear end from catching on anything. Rand?"

"Yes Joat."

"Could you ask Seg to meet me at the air-lock with that cargo sled?"

"He's on his way."

Once in the *Wyal*'s gravity Karak seemed to weigh a ton. What with the thick, metal-heavy Kolnari bones and the great, muscled length of him, they nearly herniated themselves getting him onto the cargo sled.

Joat stood back and blew out an exhausted breath, put her hands on her hips. *I should have asked Rand to flux the gravity, like we did for the power suit.*

"Who did you say this osco was?" she asked aloud.

"He is Karak t'Marid," Soamosa answered in a tight, anxious voice, never taking her eyes off him.

"t'Marid?" Joat frowned.

Soamosa looked at her and licked her lips.

"He is Belazir's eldest son," she said, then she looked at him again.

"Can we use him as a hostage?" Seg whispered eagerly.

"No way," Joat told him with a dismissive gesture, "the Kolnari eat their young."

"Only very rarely," Soamosa protested. "For special ceremonies, Karak said, or under the most dire of circumstances." She looked up into their stunned silence and blushed. "In any case, you may be sure that if they did ransom him it would only be to destroy him. You must not return Karak to them," she cried passionately.

"He saved us, even the Captain, which was very awkward. Please help him! He is deserving of your aid, I promise you. He warned us of a plot to destroy Bethel and he was taking us there to thwart Belazir's plan when he was stricken." Her gaze turned defiant and she cradled Karak's massive paw in her own small hands. "And what is more, I love him."

Oh, wow! Joat thought *That oughta jump-start Amos. He'll probably come out of that box like he was spring loaded.*

She held her hands out at chest level in a soothing motion and said, half-laughing, "Look, if giving him back would make them happy, that's the *last* thing I'm going to do. So just relax and we'll get him into cargo hold C so that Seg here can take a look at him." *I should have put a revolving door on that place,* she thought uneasily.

Joat tapped in the destination on the cargo sled's keypad and they followed it down the corridor. Soamosa carrying the big Kolnari's hand and cooing reassurance, Seg dragging info out of the auto-doc that no one else she knew could either get or understand.

In years to come, she thought with a grin, *I'm going to wish I had a holo-snap of Joseph's face when he realizes just what her hero is.*

CHAPTER EIGHTEEN

BUSTER RAUCHFUSS READ the memo from Dana Sherman regarding Bros Sperin's request for one hundred and twenty thousand credits.

Is Sperin crazy? he thought. No *documentation, no explanation, no report of any kind? Just a bald-faced demand for more money than I'll ever see in my lifetime.* He couldn't authorize this. *Even if I wanted to!*

Besides, Sperin was on leave from his department, so this request shouldn't even have come to him.

I'll just kick it up to Mancini, Buster thought with sour satisfaction. *Let him lose sleep over it.*

He hadn't liked the way Sperin had been removed from his supervision without explanation. "Security reasons," Mancini had said. *Like I'm some kind of neo who can't be trusted.* Sperin had been his man, dammit. And he'd felt a certain cachet just being the supervisor of such a distinguished field agent.

Then Buster glanced at the memo in his hand, suddenly relieved that Bros Sperin wasn't *his* any longer. He hummed as he composed the memo he'd be sending.

Dear Paul, he began. *I'm sure you know more about this than I do* . . .

When the lock opened, Joseph rushed forward anxiously, his hands outstretched.

"Lady Sierra Nueva," his eyes appraised her, "you are well?"

"Quite well, thank you, Ser ben Said," Soamosa responded with automatic graciousness. "Though my savior is in sore distress, as you can see."

Joseph glanced down at the figure on the cargo sled and choked, his eyes fairly bulging. A tide of intense red swept from his neck to his hair line, making the blue of his eyes still more startling.

"A Kolnari?" he said, with a quiet viciousness more deadly than a shout. "I will not allow this creature to share a single molecule of air with me!" He glared at Joat. "Space him," he commanded.

Joat raised one eyebrow and pursed her lips. After a moment of strained silence he muttered: "If you would, Captain."

"I've done it before, Joe, so don't go thinking I'm squeamish. But apparently this boy rescued the lady *and* Captain Sung for no other reason than he loves her."

Joseph barked a high-pitched sound of disbelief.

"What's more, he was piloting her to Bethel to warn them about Belazir's plot."

"You cannot believe that!" Joseph protested. "I can see an innocent, inexperienced young girl falling for such nonsense. But Joat, you have seen and known a great deal more than *she* has. You cannot be such a fool."

Joat shrugged.

"I can't see any benefit to Belazir in this." She pointed at the body on the sled. "This is his son—according to Soamosa—his oldest son. You tell me, why would he sacrifice him?"

Joseph turned away with a disgusted sound, then he swung back and said in a low fierce voice, "We have only his word that he is Belazir's son. I do not call that proof."

"It's not like you to be blinded by prejudice, Joe. *Look* at him. If there's one thing I'm not likely to forget, it's what Belazir t'Marid looks like. That boy is a copy of him. In any event, the first time in recorded history that a Kolnari does a good deed, I don't think the proper response is to stuff him out the air-lock. So, you're just going to have to be patient with me and put up with him."

Without another word Joseph turned and walked over to Amos, leaning close to speak with him.

Joat rolled her eyes and clicked her tongue in dismay. The quarantine hold wasn't that big. *Hah!, the ship isn't big enough to hold this kind of rancor. Wake up, Amos! We need you.*

She strolled over to the sled and tapped Soamosa on the shoulder.

"I need you to help me get the Captain in here."

"Oh," the girl looked distressed. "Must I go?" She indicated Seg with a fluid gesture. "Could not your assistant aid you?"

"My friend is helping your friend," Joat explained patiently. "Besides, the Captain will know you, where he doesn't know us."

"No," Soamosa murmured, shaking her head sadly, "he will not. Nor does he recognize anyone else, or anything." Her eyes filled with sorrow: "It is truly terrible, what they have done to him."

"Yeah," Joat agreed. "The Kolnari specialize in that sort of thing. And I'm not too happy about what they've done to Amos, either."

"Amos? The Benisur Amos?"

For the first time the girl looked around her. Immediately, her eyes fell on Amos, laying deathly still in the rescue pod, looking like nothing so much as a man in his coffin.

She shrieked and fell to her knees, babbling, "No, oh no, oh no . . ." over and over.

Joseph walked over to her again and knelt beside her, putting a gentle hand on her shoulder.

"He is well, Lady. Only drugged, but the Benisur is conscious, he knows you are here. Will you come and speak to him?"

Soamosa looked at him in horror.

"He is well, I assure you. Dr. !T'sel here was looking for an antidote to the drug the Kolnari gave him. But then he was distracted." Joseph glared at Seg as he said this.

"This is a very sick man," Seg told him firmly, "I'm afraid that takes precedence. The Benisur will recover from the drug very nicely all on his own. Karak here is going to need some doctoring."

Joat watched Soamosa's distress grow, the girl's head whipped from Karak, to Joseph, to Amos and back again.

She laid her hand on Soamosa's shoulder and said briskly, "You'll have plenty of time later to talk to Amos, and Karak is in good hands with Seg. Meanwhile I need help with Captain Sung and you're already in a suit." She gave Soamosa a reassuring smile. "We'll only be a few minutes."

Soamosa closed her eyes and took a deep breath, releasing it slowly, she stood.

"Very well," she said calmly, her voice shaking only a little.

Joat raised a brow, impressed. *Not quite the sheltered Bethelite maiden she seems. I think this oasis rose was carved from steelite.*

Soamosa turned to Joseph and spoke with the hauteur of twenty generations of aristocrats: "Ser ben Said, if you can not reconcile your feelings for the Kolnari, then I suggest that you keep away from my friend. For I will not suffer him to be hurt." She narrowed her eyes. "Neither will I tolerate any insult being offered to him. Do I make myself clear?"

"Quite clear, Lady," Joseph answered quietly.

Well said, young cousin, Amos thought. *I am sorry that you have had this terrible experience, and yet, you have grown. You sound like a woman now and not a silly girl.*

To find her changed so much for the better, in spite of the pain and humiliation she had endured at Belazir's hands was nothing short of a miracle. Inside his mind he smiled. *I do not think your mother will find you very easy to manipulate after this.* He imagined her mother's face as Soamosa presented Karak as her dear friend and hero.

Oh child, he thought in amused dismay, *she will never speak to either of us again.* For that matter, they'd probably be stoned to death anywhere on Bethel, unless he put guards around them every hour of the day—and he would have to pick the guards carefully. No Bethelite would accept any Kolnari on equal terms; never mind as a potential son-in-law. They had lost too many loved ones to the Kolnari's casual cruelty. Not a family on the planet had been untouched by the brief but violent occupation. And the pirates had planned to sear the world down to bedrock when they finished looting it.

This will not be easy, he thought. *It may not even be possible. Child, child . . .*

Joat sank exhausted into her chair on the bridge. She didn't know what was worse: Sung's blank-eyed terror and the small shrill sounds he made when they'd suddenly passed into the *Wyal*'s gravity, or the infantile gratitude with which he'd hugged Soamosa when she took off her helmet.

She shuddered. Then she popped the top on the container of coffee she'd grabbed from the galley and gratefully took a sip of the hot, fragrant brew.

Kraig's nostrils flared at the scent, but he remained quiet, watching her carefully from the prison of his frozen suit.

"Rand, patch me through to Al, will you?"

In a moment Alvec's voice came through the com.

"Yo, boss. You wanted to talk to me?"

"Just wanted to know how it's going out there, buddy."

"Quiet. Nothin' to report, really. *Wyal*'s where the action is."

"You've got that right, Al. Would you believe Soamosa's in love with that Kolnari she brought in? Joe wants me to space him, Seg, I don't doubt, wants to study him, and Amos just lies there. Who knows what *he* wants."

She sighed wearily. "I think we should blow the fighter they came in. It's contaminated and we can't be bothered to salvage it, not with so much else to do. Can you manage that for us?"

"No problem, boss." By his voice Joat knew his eyes were gleaming. "You should see this weapons system ol' Kraig's got here."

"Yeah, when it comes to weapons there's no such thing as enough, for the Kolnari. Only things left regretfully behind."

Seg came quietly onto the bridge.

At Joat's questioning look he said, "I've got the young Kolnari stabilized. Fascinating reaction. I can't tell you how much I miss my lab!"

It was obvious from the passion in his voice. Joat smiled. Seg was a different being when he was in professional mode. As an espionage wannabe he might be a figure of fun, but as a scientist he was definitely a being to respect.

"I'm receiving a transmission from Central Worlds," Rand announced.

"Attention merchanter ship *Wyal*. Message received. Repeat, message received. We will act on your information immediately. Message ends."

"That's it?" Joat sat forward in outrage. "That's all they have to say?"

"Well, they wouldn't tell us anything that might be intercepted," Alvec mumbled. Under his breath: "I never did like those straight-leg bast . . . children of irregular origin."

"You can't intercept a tight-beam message," she snapped. She flung herself back in her seat. "It could be days. It's already *been* days." Her lips narrowed to an angry line, and her fingers beat a rapid tattoo on the arms of her chair. "We've got to do something or he's dead."

Her eyes strayed to her prisoner and met Kraig's. She smiled, showing her teeth and his Adam's apple bobbed prodigiously. "That's right," she murmured, "be afraid—be very afraid."

Seg cleared his throat.

"You're determined to carry through with this idea of rescuing Bros?"

She nodded.

"Al can take the rest of you in the *Wyal*," she said. "I assume Clenst has some sort of facility for this sort of thing? Decontamination, debriefing?"

"Yes, the very finest," Seg assured her. He drew himself up to his full height. "Um. I have . . . certain discretionary," he waved a hand uncertainly, "powers, I suppose you could say. I can authorize the engagement of up to a battalion of Yoered Family mercenaries."

He stood looking at her eagerly, his large eyes round, like a schoolboy awaiting praise and fearing censure.

Joat's smile was brilliant as she rose from her chair and gave a sweeping bow: "The com is yours."

"Joat," Rand said, "perhaps you should discuss this with Joseph. He will both need and want to know what decisions are being made here."

Joat blinked.

"Rand, that's downright sensitive! You're becoming more human every day."

"Thank you, Joat. I know you meant that as a compliment."

She blinked again and raised her brows. Then she went to Alvec's station.

"Rand, give me cargo hold C."

They'd brought in cots and a small store of self-heating food for their passengers' comfort, and they'd rigged up a curtained off area with a port-a-potty in it. Their passengers wouldn't be able to wash, but they'd survive that.

And even if I get my debt to Ciety cleaned up—amazing how unimportant that seemed now—*I still can't afford to have the whole ship decontaminated.* Viruses were nasty little things, even natural ones. Designed for durability, you might have to put the ship into a graving dock stationside and strip her to the hull to get them all.

Cargo hold C was designed for live cargo and was a self-contained, self-sterilizing facility. So even if they did impound the *Wyal* for a few months they'd be hard pressed to find an excuse for destroying her.

Of course it wouldn't matter then, because after a few months of not earning any income, *Wyal* wouldn't belong to her any more. *Come to think of it, legally, it already as good as belongs to dear old Uncle Nom.* Even if they returned from this mission, which he clearly didn't expect, she couldn't see him quietly writing off a hundred twenty thousand credits. *And who do I have for witnesses that he'll give* Wyal *back to me in exchange for running this errand?* No one the Yoered Family would pay attention to.

Joat frowned at the unwelcome thought, then brushed it aside. She sat forward, her eyes fixed on Joseph where he sat at Amos's side, glaring at Karak.

"Joe."

His head came up. "Yes, Captain."

Fardles! Still prickly. Aloud she said: "We've heard from Central Worlds. Basically all they did was acknowledge our message."

Joseph snorted. "What a great surprise that is. Did they at least imply that they were going to respond in any other way?"

She smiled bitterly. They'd both had experience with the ponderous bureaucracy of Central Worlds.

"In the broadest possible terms. Um. We're going to have Al destroy the fighter our friends came in. We can't bring it and we dare not leave it and risk the spread of this contagion."

"Wise," he said laconically. "Thank you for keeping me informed. Is there anything else?"

"Uh. Yes. Alvec will be taking all of you on to a quarantine facility where, hopefully, you'll be cleansed of any trace of this disease."

Seg nodded positively at her.

"At least Seg firmly believes so."

Joseph's eyes narrowed and the cant of his head became alert.

"And you, Joat? Where will you be while we are being purged?"

Back to Joat, she thought, *we're making progress.*

"I'm taking the other fighter and I'm going to get Bros Sperin."

His brows rose. "Just like that?"

"Suggestions are welcome," she said.

"I will go with you."

"Amos needs you," she said. "And so do Rachel and the children. This isn't like the SSS-900-C. You can't just act for yourself now; you're a father and a husband, Joe."

"I am also a man. And I have a great need to see this finished, Joat. If I can, I will kill Belazir. He has done too much to us. I cannot live with my hatred."

Joat sighed. She knew what he meant. If there was one thing she understood it was how unsated rage and hatred could poison your life.

"I wish Amos were awake to talk you out of this," she muttered.

I would not, Amos thought into the pause that followed. *I know my brother's heart too well. And he is right. He has a great need to take action. That is his destiny, Joat, do not fight him. You cannot forbid fate.*

"But he's not," Joat continued. "And I admit I'm selfish enough to be glad of your company, Joe. I've got some stuff to take care of first, then we'll suit up and meet at the air-lock." She cut off contact and sat back, her hand idly stroking her chin. Suddenly Al's voice startled her out of her reverie.

"Hey! You don't even ask me? I been watching your back for how long and you don't even ask me?"

"I'm asking you to take Amos and the rest to that Clenst facility. And who else would I let pilot the *Wyal*?"

"Rand," he said positively. "You know it can do it."

"You also know that I insist on at least two competent pilots aboard, including the AI. That's minimum safety rules, Al. I wouldn't leave this many lubbers with less. Especially since one of them is my adoptive mother's sweetheart. C'mon Al, don't give me a hard time over this. I need your support."

There was a long pause, redolent of ill temper and resentment. Then, "Okay," he mumbled, stabbing viciously at the firing stud.

His plasma gun fired an ultra-miniaturized, laser-triggered deuterium fusion pellet focused by magnetic fields. The abandoned fighter exploded in a brilliant burst of sun-hot violence, the whole mass of it reduced to gases in seconds.

Alvec's face-plate darkened to black automatically, protecting his eyes. He felt better, not perfect, but better. With a wry smile he maneuvered the fighter into position just over the air-lock and waited for Joat to grapple him.

"I don't want to do this," Seg mumbled mutinously.

Joat rolled her eyes with exasperation.

"Can you get Amos back on his feet?" she asked reasonably.

He shook his head. "No, not without more elaborate lab facilities. There are too many variables."

"Can you do anything else for Karak?"

Seg's mouth sphinctered shut in distress.

"No," he said at last. "The serum will either help him or it won't. Only time will tell."

"Well . . . you *can* help me. And you can help Bros Sperin by helping me. So do it," she said through gritted teeth.

"But it's wrong. Don't you understand?"

Joat's lips thinned to a straight line and she leaned forward in her chair, her eyes holding his.

"You wanted to be a part of Sperin's world. Well, now you are. Sometimes you're called on to do hard things, Seg. It's not like I'm asking you to kill him, for crying out loud!"

Kraig's eyes bugged and he flicked his gaze frantically between them. But his lips were compressed into a firm white line. As though he'd resist speech by sheer willpower.

"And if we don't get the codes and call signs from this man, an even more unethical bunch of people are going to rip Bros Sperin into little, screaming pieces!"

She sat glaring at Seg. "Meanwhile, I'm sitting here, captaining a blasted *hospital* ship, doing nothing! Oh, Central Worlds is sending help," she said quickly, cutting off Seg's protest.

"Just as soon as ever they can," she added sarcastically. "And you and Clenst are sending help, again, just as soon as they can. But I don't trust any of them, because they don't care! You know who cares?" She tapped her chest. "I do. They took him off *my* ship, and as far as I'm concerned that makes it my responsibility. So you choose one of those drugs and you inject him. Or I will."

In the end, Seg chose the drug that induced pleasure and an overwhelming desire to please. Kraig, awash with glorious sensations and having the time of his life, surrendered every secret he knew, up to and including the combination of his locker.

He even approved Joat's cobbled-together mercenary uniform.

"Oh yeah!" he enthused. "It's black an' it's tight. No one's going to look further than that."

Joat raised a brow. "Thanks," she drawled.

"No, problem, black and tight, way to go. Mmmmmmmm."

Joat looked uncertainly at Seg.

"He'll quiet down as the drug wears off," Seg assured her.

"Jeeeez, I hope so," Alvec growled. "I don't like the way he's lookin' at me."

"At everybody," Joat agreed. Then she shrugged. "Seg, would you join me in the galley please?"

Puzzled, and wondering if he was going to receive another lecture the Sondee followed her into the galley/lounge.

There was a display film covering the tabletop, and beside it was a box about a meter long and half as wide and deep.

Joat inserted a datahedron into a slot at the edge of the display film and a schematic blossomed upon the screen. Seg automatically leaned towards it and began to read. After a moment he glanced up at Joat, read a bit more, flipped through several more schematics and then straightened. He looked at her in perplexity, a most unhappy look on a Sondee face.

"This is top secret," he said.

"This is synchronicity," Joat said with a grin. "Simeon and I were working on this idea for a signal jammer and I'd almost finished the prototype when Clenst announced their own version. Talk about disappointed." She pursed her lips and shrugged. "All for the best though. If we'd sold it then we wouldn't have it here to use. What I need is help in finishing up the dispersal unit."

Seg checked her data.

"You manufactured ten thousand transmitter/receivers by yourself?" he asked in wonder.

"It's not that hard to make 'em," Joat said. "And as you've noticed it's a long way between systems. So time isn't a problem."

"It's amazingly like ours," Seg murmured. "Except . . . I think the sine-wave control function may be a little better. For some purposes."

"Well, the concept is identical. Lots of miniature receiver/transmitters catching signals and sending them back out with various time lags. Result; hopelessly garbled messages. Think it'll work?"

"Actually . . . in some ways it's more efficient than our design. Clenst might be willing to negotiate for those improvements."

"Music to my ears," Joat said, smiling. "Let's get to work, shall we?"

"I see you're using a rocket propulsion system."

"Keep it simple," she agreed, "that's my motto."

"Have you got rocket fuel?"

"You purists," Joat scoffed. "All we need is a volatile liquid." She put a couple of bottles of cleaning fluid on the table. "We'd never have gotten farther than the moon if we'd waited for guys like you. If it'll make you feel better I've got a form you can fill out before we begin."

Seg laughed nervously.

"There's no control-board indicated on your design," he objected.

"That's because there are cheap, readily available ones already on the market. Why reinvent the wheel?" Joat slapped a tiny control-board on the table beside the cleaning fluid. "That's a spare from the food processing unit. So, it'll think it's dicing carrots when it fires up the rocket. I won't tell it if you don't."

All of Seg's eyes were shining as he smiled delightedly at her.

"This is *real* hands-on, seat-of-your-pants stuff, isn't it?" he said enthusiastically.

"Hands on the seat of your *pants*?" Joat asked, bemused. *Jeeez, these Sondee have weird sayings.* "Whatever you say, Seg."

Joseph was fully suited when she met him at the lock, her helmet balanced atop the box in her arms. With a glance at the box he placed the helmet over her head and locked it down. She smiled her thanks nervously.

"Our suits look awful," he complained. "They *look* like they have been painted."

"Nothin' we could do about it," Joat said with a shrug. "Kraig said they had to be black." She snorted in disgust "Only the Kolnari would insist on black space suits. But then, I can't see them rescuing someone who managed to drift off. So why would they want to make them visible enough to pick up easily?"

Joseph grinned at her, his blue eyes alight with a fierce joy. "I am going to eat Belazir's beating heart," he said happily.

Absolute cold flashed over Joat's body and she stared at Joseph as if she'd never seen him before.

"Joe," she said quietly, like a patient mother addressing a particularly wanton five year old. "This is a rescue mission. We can't stop for lunch. Especially if we want to get away. So, we're not going on a Kolnari hunt, is that understood?"

His mouth twisted and his eyes flickered away as he nodded.

Joat kicked him in the shin.

"Don't you patronize me," she snapped. "Either it's understood that I am in command and that our mission, our *sole* mission, is the rescue of Bros Sperin, or you're not going. End of story."

"I need to finish this," he told her, his voice so rough it was almost a growl.

"But this isn't the time." Her eyes held his. After a moment she smiled. "If we can carry this off, Joe, Belazir will eat his heart out for us."

Twelve hours later they received a tight-beam message from the *Wyal.*

"Greetings, my brother," Amos's voice was husky from prolonged thirst, "and Joat, my friend."

"My Lord!" The joy in Joseph's voice seemed to brighten the inside of the cramped fighter.

"Good to hear from you, Amos," Joat said with a relieved grin.

"It is good to be able to speak, I assure you. I wanted to tell you that my prayers go with you."

"Every little bit helps," Joat assured him.

"Thank you, Benisur. Your blessing strengthens my purpose," Joseph said.

"So if you could clarify his purpose for him I'd appreciate it," Joat suggested. "He hasn't spoken to me since I told him he couldn't eat Belazir's heart this trip."

There was silence for a moment.

"Surely, my brother, you would not needlessly risk your life. There is Rachel to consider, and the children. And I would find it hard to bear if you were to die like a fool."

Wow! Joat thought, *I didn't think Amos knew how to be that blunt.* She had grown so used to his parables and subtle persuasions. Joat wasn't even the target of his remarks and she felt like she'd been hit with a rock.

Joseph gasped. Then: "I stand rebuked, Benisur. You are correct, of course. It is shameful to indulge myself at the cost of the greater good."

"I am pleased to hear it, my brother. This is an attitude that will serve you well in the coming years."

A contemplative silence followed. *And if that doesn't beg "C'mon, ask me what I mean," I'm a Shapelitic Nun,* Joat thought.

"What do you mean?" Joseph asked.

"My young cousin means to marry her Kolnari captive," Amos said. His voice seemed to smile.

"My Lord!" Joseph bellowed. "You cannot allow that!"

"Hey!" Joat snapped, her ears ringing.

"I am sorry, Joat. Benisur, you cannot be serious. The Lady's family will disown her. She shall be shunned. The shame will kill her mother."

Amos sighed. *I suspect my young cousin's mother is one of those who are immune to shame. Else she would be unable to use it so effectively as a weapon.*

Aloud: "Just before we were captured by the Kolnar I asked

Soamosa how she would like it if the people looked on her as a prophetess. And, of course, being a modest maid, she said she was no such thing and surely no one could take her for such. But now, I find myself seeing her in just such a light. For she truly loves this Karak and it is just as plain that he loves her. It seems to me, my brother, that she has given his humanity back to him. Perhaps we should try to join her in this task."

"My Lord!" Joseph groaned and then drew his breath in a great gasp. "Just because *one* of that demon breed shows signs of being human does not mean the rest are salvageable."

"He has a point, Amos," Joat said.

Amos didn't laugh, but the smile was still there in his voice,

"God does not challenge us by presenting us with circumstances that we welcome. And if Soamosa's family disowns her, I shall not. She shall be my heir, and I shall support her with all of my heart."

"She is too young to make such a decision, Benisur."

"Joseph, you would not be making such an objection if I had decided to marry the girl myself. Now would you? In fact, when it was arranged for her to accompany me, it was you who smoothed out so many of the details. Wasn't it?'

Joseph was so silent that Joat glanced down at him, wondering if his suit mike had broken down.

Then he said, "You would love having children, my brother," in a quiet voice filled with pained dignity.

Joat felt a little spurt of outrage. *Channa's not* that *old!* she thought. She'd always suspected that Channa was just working out her contract before she ran off to Bethel with Amos. *All she needs is a little time.*

"Prophet is not a comfortable family business," Amos observed. "I am not sure that I ought to have children. I might enjoy having them, but I am not so sure that they would enjoy being my offspring. Channa and I have discussed this and we feel that perhaps we should adopt our children."

Joseph was silent again. The kind of silence that fills a room with powerful, undefined emotion.

"On behalf of adopted children everywhere, Amos, go for it," Joat said with a smile.

"I shall," he said. "As I have said, I will adopt Soamosa. And her children and Karak's shall be my grandchildren. As she is my cousin, they will share the same blood as I." He paused. "Interesting. That would mean that Belazir and I would share the same blood."

"NO!" Joseph roared.

"Ow! Joe! Watch the volume control!"

"You go too far, my Lord."

Amos sighed. "Yes, perhaps you are right, my brother. But perhaps also, there are other Kolnari like Karak who do not wish only to kill and to steal. This could be a sign of hope for them and the beginnings of peace for both our peoples."

"Is it all right this trip if we at least hurt the Kolnari's feelings?" Joat asked dryly. "I'll really miss that sense of closure I'd get otherwise."

Amos laughed. "I have not lost my mind, Joat. I merely present a new idea. This may not be practical; and in any case, you have my cheerful permission—both of you—to annihilate Belazir t'Marid and as many of his followers as seems convenient, while you pursue your mission."

"Good luck, Amos." She shook her head in wonder.

"We will discuss this upon my return, Benisur," Joseph growled.

"It pleases me to think that I have given you still another reason to be cautious with your life, my friend. I look forward to our conversation."

"Joat?"

"Hey Rand, what's up?"

"Your ETA is twelve hours, correct?"

"Well, thereabouts, anyway. Depends on what we run into. Why?"

"Yoered Family anticipates being at those coordinates in fourteen hours."

Joat raised her brows. Not that she'd doubted Yoered's professionalism; but this kind of timing indicated a high level of commitment for what was a fairly casual contract.

"Well, I'm impressed. Clenst must be paying a premium."

"They are," Seg assured her. "It might be wise to coordinate your efforts with them."

Joat rolled her eyes. "You mean subordinate my efforts to theirs. No way, !T'sel. Two hours could make a major difference in Sperin's life span. You tell your flunkies to watch out for us. Out." She cut contact with the *Wyal* before anyone could protest.

"Give them back their humanity?" Joseph murmured in stunned tones.

"Poor Amos," Joat said. "The trouble with giving people back their humanity is that a lot of the time they don't want it returned." *Crikey, the last thing a thief and murderer wants is an active conscience. Poor Amos.*

"But the Kolnari? Has my lord gone mad?"

"No Joseph. You're just looking at the down-side of loving a living saint. They *will* do uncomfortable things."

"But the Kolnari?'

"Yeah. Let's plan what we're actually going to do when we find them," Joat said, cutting off what she recognized as an endless conversational loop.

"Perhaps we should try giving them back their humanity."

She laughed. "Yeah, then we'll shoot 'em while they stand there frozen in shock."

Joseph chuckled.

"I should not laugh at the Benisur," he said. "But truly, this is beyond everything."

"One thing at a time, Joe. You can talk him out of it when we get back."

She ran through the data again. Their plans were actually as set as they could be, on what amounted to—*It is* not *a suicide mission.* Joat had gone through her copy of Janes's *All the Galaxy's Spaceships,* a gift from Simeon, and found Belazir's flagship. It was not quite a light cruiser; a destroyer-leader, built to command a flotilla of lighter craft, a Central Worlds Navy vessel, heavily refitted for Kolnari use. Probably it had once been a Navy surplus ship owned by a planet the Kolnar had stripped, then destroyed.

She'd called up the schematic and Kraig had guided them through it.

"Avoid the A and B corridors if ya can, that's Kolnar territory, an' they like to hassle anyone that doesn't belong there."

He indicated where the brig was located. A fairly large section of the ship deep in its center. And he enthusiastically described what he knew about their security system.

"It's fantastic, man! If they ever went straight they could make a fortune designing security for rich guys."

He'd recited the security codes and their answers so that Rand could record them. And Rand had made up a program that would answer the question asked, regardless of the order in which the codes were presented.

"Security's pretty light on the decks the mercs use," Kraig had told them. "I mean who's going to be stupid enough to sneak . . ." He'd blinked at them. "Hey, I din't mean anything." He'd apologized for several minutes before they could convince him they weren't offended.

Joseph dubiously eyed the large ball of ice Joat held ready in front of the lock.

"*This* is your secret weapon?"

"Yup."

"A snowball?"

She chuckled. "The ice is imbedded with approximately ten thousand transmitter/receivers which will be dispersed at a controlled rate determined by the speed at which the *snowball* is traveling. We're going to push it right through Kolnari space and mess up their communications big time."

"They will blow it up, Joat."

"And if they do, some of the t/rs will be destroyed. The rest will be in a good position to do what they're designed for. It'll work, Joe. Trust me." She looked up at his scowling face. "Seg was really impressed."

He grunted and opened the lock.

Joat shoved her burden through the open hatch and Joseph closed it again. Then she picked up a control plaque and pressed the firing stud. The rocket ignited and her faux comet was off.

"You really like that alien, do you not?" Joseph asked as he strapped himself back into his seat.

"Yeah. He's a nice kid."

"He is a tactless, interfering busybody."

"But basically a sweetie."

"He is hideous to look upon and he is a fool."

"I knew you liked him."

Joseph growled. "It is hard not to. He is so much like a happy, bouncy little puppy."

They were silent a while, monitoring the discreet Kolnari signals. Kraig had warned them to linger just outside the Kolnar security perimeter and wait to be recognized.

Joat did and didn't mind.

The waiting was hard, largely because her excellent imagination kept conjuring possible disaster scenarios. Kraig might have left out something vital, or they might be given close escort to Belazir's ship. In which case they were sunk. The success of the whole plan depended on their being handled like a friendly.

Yet the longer they sat here, the more time her "snowball" had to do its work.

Suddenly there was a flurry of questions from the Kolnari. Rand's program answered as designed and they were given leave to proceed.

"Welcome back, Rendino du Pare," a woman's voice said.

"Thanks," Joseph muttered, "out."

"I hope that's not his girlfriend," Joat said.

"I would not worry," Joseph said quietly. "I am sure the Kolnar do not encourage chatter in their space."

They proceeded quietly on their way, watching the distant Kolnari fleet loom larger as they approached.

"Joat, may I ask you a question?"

"Sure."

"Your ship, the *Wyal,* what does its name mean? I have tried to find a reference to it everywhere that I can think of; without success. And knowing you, I am sure it has some significance."

"It's an acronym," she said with a grin. "Does that help?"

"Are you going to tell me or not?"

"It means While You Ain't Lookin'."

Joseph laughed silently. "Appropriate. It is pleasant to know that creeping respectability has not entirely obliterated the feral child I knew and loved."

They're not all watching me, Joat told herself. *This is normal. And this is the end of a normal mission.* Lights on the floor and ceiling guided her to a berth. She parked neatly and powered down. The hangar was cramped, nothing like the cavernous hold of an assault carrier. It was a little unusual for a ship of this displacement to carry fighters at all, but she supposed it was useful when you didn't have an elaborate military organization with specialized vessels. The tips of the fighter's weapons pods just barely cleared those of the other three; there was one empty berth—that would be the one Soamosa had taken—and a scurry of crew and robots, doing maintenance work.

No, they're arming up and fueling. Somebody's suspicious. Oh, joy.

"They're going to be expecting only one person to disembark," she said nervously.

"Kraig told you that security was light in the mercenaries' section, almost casual. My advice is to disembark with me, acting like you belong here. I doubt anyone will look twice, or bother to question us. As I said before, I am much more nervous about the paint on our suits."

"Don't worry," she said, "we'll shed them as fast as we can." *They do have a kinda orange undercast.*

Joat wondered if the suited figures servicing the fighters around them were mercenaries or Kolnar slaves. Either way, Joe was probably right. The ones who knew how many people should be returning from this mission sure as blazes weren't working on this deck. She grasped the strap on her black shoulder bag and followed Joseph across the floor to the locker area.

Joseph was keying in Kraig's locker combination when a message came through his suit's receiver.

"Rendino du Pare, you are to report to Captain Hobsbrowm for debriefing at fourteen hundred hours. Room C-780."

"Acknowledged, out."

Joseph finished the unlock code and pulled open the door. Then he took off his helmet and spoke to Joat.

"Now we know how much time we have. I am to meet with my debriefer at fourteen hundred."

Joat was already half out of her suit.

"It's twelve hundred now. They're not too eager to talk to you, are they?"

There were two uniforms in the locker, Joseph proceeded to put both on.

"It works to our advantage, of course. But I wonder what is going on."

Joat brushed her hair smooth and retted it in a ponytail.

"If we're lucky," she said, "Belazir's asleep and no one wants to wake him. If we're not . . . then he's with Bros."

"Or he is in conference with his captains, or working out, or just generally busy. Let us not worry about how Belazir is occupied until we must conclude otherwise."

"Joe," she said as she stuffed her suit into Kraig's locker beside his, "you're being reasonable. I really, really hate it when I'm being hysterically pessimistic and people insist on being reasonable."

"I shall try not to restrain myself," he promised with a smile.

"Well, all right," she said, "see that you don't." Joat looked him over, straightening his collar.

"Okay. Let's do it."

❖   ❖   ❖

The Kolnari had sealed a number of the access panels into the repair tunnel that ran between corridors C and B, no doubt for security reasons. The remaining few were carefully locked.

Joat pulled Sperin's override gizmo out of her shoulder bag and set it against the lock mechanism. It hadn't taken her long to figure it out. The thing was designed to be simple to use and she had a natural affinity for mechanical objects.

Still, she was nervous and her hands were slick with sweat. Even with Joseph's beefy body partially shielding her from view she felt conspicuous.

The fact that they'd sealed so many panels made her believe those that weren't sealed were under observation. That "everybody's watching you and they don't like what they see" feeling was raising chills up and down her spine.

The lock clicked open and she slipped through, half expecting to be met by a snarling crowd of armed Kolnari. *What are you doing here? Hands up! Behind your head! On your knees! March!*

There was no one there. She breathed a soft sigh of relief.

"How I wish we could use one of your little scramblers, Joat," Joseph murmured nostalgically. "I would feel so much more secure."

"You and me both," she said, smiling. "But they're just as likely to set off alarms these days as to get you by them."

They backtracked until they found the access panel they wanted. One that was located quite close to the Kolnari Brig. Predictably it was welded shut.

Joat pulled a roll of what looked like putty from her bag and began to stick it around the seam of the panel. When she was through she stuck a suction cup with a handle attached onto the center of the panel and pulled on it to test its grasp.

Then she and Joseph drew their sidearms and after carefully regulating the laser's temperature they melted the coil of heat activated acid they'd drawn around the seam. Slowly at first, and then more quickly, it liquefied and began to eat its way through the welds. Joat exerted a gentle outward pressure on the suction cup. What fumes there were stayed with them in the narrow tunnel, unpleasant, but nontoxic. For the most part. Kolnari would probably hardly notice them. A small alarm she'd built into her coverall was complaining about the *Dreadful Bride*'s toxic atmosphere in increasingly insistent tones anyway. She reached up and turned it off. *I know already!*

As the panel came free, Joseph reached out to support Joat's hand

and they lifted it slightly, but held it in place, not quite touching the frame it had once joined.

They listened tensely for sounds of voices or people walking by and were rewarded by silence.

Cautiously they lifted the panel outward and stepped into the deserted corridor. Then they fitted it back into place, reset their lasers and proceeded to the Brig.

CHAPTER NINETEEN

THE WOMAN BEHIND the Brig's reception desk was a heavy-worlder, no question. Her bones had been genetically altered for thickness and her height was somewhat below human norm. But her expression was curious, and relatively friendly.

"Yeah?" she asked. "Help you?"

"We're here to see a Mr. Bros Sperin," Joat purred.

Beside her Joseph stood impassively, eyes front, hands clutched behind his back in an automatic parade rest. Just so much muscle, ready to spring into action.

"Yeah? What for?"

Joat raised one brow.

"We have a specialty," she said smiling slightly.

"Oh?"

"Conversation. People can't seem to resist talking to us."

The woman chuckled evilly.

"Oh, yeah, I heard about that. I been expecting somebody like you. The Big Black Baddies tried with one of their creepy little medics and got nowhere. You'll have to leave your guns, though," she said.

Joat pursed her lips. "I don't mind leaving mine here, but I'd rather my companion kept his. Sperin is reputed to be an . . . educated man. I'd like to know he has a weapon pointed at him."

The woman was shaking her head and her expression was a lot less friendly.

"Or perhaps," Joat continued, "he could surrender it to the guard

597

on Sperin's door." She arched a brow. "I assume there *is* a guard on
his door?"

"Unh hunh. Let me see your ID."

A little hole appeared in the center of the woman's forehead and
intelligence ran out of her eyes as though escaping through it in a
narrow wisp of steam.

Joseph shook his hand, scorched by the backrush of burning gases
where the laser had burned its way through the holster. A scorched
smell insinuated itself through the sour chemical stink of Kolnar-
normal atmosphere.

"I did not want to do that," he said ruefully.

Joat frowned. She didn't like killing, didn't like the waste. And
like Joseph she hadn't wanted to see this almost-friendly hired
killer die.

"It couldn't be helped," she said grimly. "We don't have ID."

When at last they'd taken the deliriously happy Kraig out of his
suit, they'd checked his ID thoroughly. It was entirely too complex
to duplicate with the equipment they had. And as time was a factor, they'd decided to go without.

They arranged the mercenary's body so that it was turned slightly
away from the entryway, hiding the hole in its . . . her head. Even the
single second gained by the small deception might count.

"Let me get to work."

Joat went down on one knee behind the control console. *Ah . . .
dedicated system, just like Kraig said.* That was safer, in a warship
subject to viral attack; a worm program could be stopped by a series
of specialized interfaces, and it also made damage control in combat easier. The down side was that none of the subsystems was as
capable as one big one, and data transfer was slower.

"This will take a second."

She eased one of her tools out from behind the belt of her mercenary uniform and set to work, whistling silently between her teeth.
Ah, not too unusual. The Kolnar had been savages before the High
Clan left their planet—although it was a peculiar type of savagery,
you could mine raw metallic plutonium there with picks and shov-
els, they'd had nuclear-powered steamboats. The basic technology of
the space-going Kolnari clans was copied from Central Worlds-derived
models.

"Here." She snipped a fiber-optic line and spliced it into a con-
verter, then plugged a datahedron into the optico-magnetic device.

The screen before the dead woman cleared and began to show an uneventful corridor.

"There. That ought to keep the surveillance systems out of our hair, until someone notices the repeating pattern."

The main doors to the prison recognized them, routing though the intercept she'd placed on the computer. They proceeded through them as calmly as possible. The computer had indicated which of the cells was Sperin's and they moved confidently down the corridors.

There was a Kolnari standing guard outside the cell and Joat could feel Joseph going into high gear.

The guard showed no sign at all that he was aware of their approach. His posture had the relaxed alertness of a hunting beast.

Arrogant jerk! Joat thought. *Probably thinks there's no need to get excited about two* scumvermin *mercs. Oh baby, are you in for a surprise.*

"We are here to question the prisoner," she said, crisply, but with deference.

The Kolnari stared at the opposite wall, as though thinking deep thoughts that couldn't be disturbed.

After a full minute had elapsed Joseph said quietly, "We are here at the Great Lord's orders."

That got a reaction. The body remained rigidly in place, but a brass-yellow eye glanced in their direction. After a brief pause the guard spoke.

"I have received no orders that the prisoner is to be allowed visitors."

Then he returned to deep thought mode.

"Obviously the Great Lord has been detained," Joat observed, looking at Joseph.

"We will wait," he said grimly.

Joseph and the Kolnari stood like statues in contrasting colors, but after a few moments Joat began to pace.

She walked back and forth, spinning on her heel every four paces. Then she began to whistle through her teeth while clapping her hands before her and then behind her back.

Her fidgeting annoyed the guard. A very small wrinkle appeared between his brows. The equivalent of a full blown tantrum in any other people; he turned towards her, lips peeling back from his teeth.

Joseph's laser took him in the back of the skull, and the Kolnari collapsed, falling stiffly, like a giant tree.

Joe caught him before he hit the floor and Joat snatched the key from his utility belt. She aimed it at the door and it slid open obediently. Then she grabbed the Kolnari's feet and helped Joseph pull him into the cell.

Bros stood with his feet braced, swaying. He watched them enter with no reaction whatsoever, like a man viewing a holoshow.

Joat couldn't suppress an exclamation at her first good look at him. He was covered with burns. Some no more than reddened patches, but large areas were blistered and bleeding plasma. His face was slack with exhaustion, shadowed by his beard, his reddened eyes sunken in deep blue circles. He smelled awful; of infection and stale sweat and charred flesh.

Joseph's hand came over her shoulder, offering the shirt he'd just taken off and she jumped.

"Yeah," she said, as if Joseph had spoken. "Bros, you've got to put this on," she said clearly and calmly.

She took hold of one hand and slid the sleeve of the black shirt over it, ignoring the oozing wounds. He made a sudden sound of agony and began to struggle. Coaxing him to cooperate, she slid the other sleeve up and over his shoulder. Awareness flickered back into his eyes.

"Joat," Bros said, his voice hoarse, his breathing harsh. "I've been having this dream that you'd come for me since yesterday. But this is the first time you've worn something so sexy. Does it mean something?" he leered.

Good grief! Joat thought. *There's resilience for you.*

"I think it means your subconscious really, really wants you to get out of here. So why don't you just relax and go along with it?"

Fortunately the trousers were quite loose and slid over his boots with little trouble. Bros lost his balance at one point and started to fall, but Joe caught him. Blisters broke under Joseph's big hands and Bros gasped and cursed, but the pain seemed to make him more aware.

"Can you walk?" Joat asked anxiously.

"You're really here," he said and touched her face gently.

"Can you walk?" she repeated.

"Anything you can do I can do better," he quipped.

"If I'd known you were going to take that attitude I wouldn't have come," she grumbled.

He leaned forward.

"Give me a kiss, Joat, and I'll follow you anywhere."

Joat frowned and glanced at Joseph who nodded impatiently. She kissed Bros's lips gently, then smiled. *Like you'd have stayed with Belazir if I'd said no. Bros, you've got style even when you're nuts with pain and fatigue.*

"C'mon," she said.

They retraced their steps; Joat let the signal disrupting transmitter/receivers trickle from her pockets in their wake; Bros was stumbling forward in defiance of gravity, Joseph hovering nervously behind, ready to catch him if he fell.

When they reached the locker room Joat broke into the locker next to Kraig's with Sperin's lock pick and pulled out the suit it contained.

Then, she and Joseph stripped Bros of the mercenary uniform and shoved him into it without regard to his wounds.

Forgive me, Bros, Joat thought, *there's no time to go easy on you.*

She and Joseph hurried into their own suits, hearts pounding, waiting for an alarm klaxon to sound, waiting for discovery.

They sealed and checked each other's helmets and then marched out onto the flight deck, towards one of the green lighted fighters; fueled and ready for takeoff.

Joat boarded first and Joseph boosted Bros into her waiting arms. Between the two of them, they wrestled him into his seat, got him connected to life support and strapped down.

There were codes for taking a fighter out as well as in and Joat inserted the datahedron they'd made for it into its slot. Then she powered up and began rolling the big machine out of fine. *Ghu, but I've got to pee.* And she *hated* doing that with the catheters in. They hurt, and they always leaked a little. The universe was unfair to females.

Kraig's voice responded appropriately to every code and query until, at last, they were given permission to launch. And if there were any questions as to why someone who had just returned from a very long mission was going out again, they went unasked.

And that's the downside of disciplining the initiative right out of your troops, Joat thought with glee.

They launched and she keyed in a course that would lead them to Seg's Clenst facility. When she felt they'd traveled far enough, Joat brought out the control board for the signal jammer and turned it on. Communications chaos blossomed all around them.

S.M. Stirling

"It works!" Joat shouted. "I can't believe this, we're out! No one's following, no one's shooting, this is incredible." She wanted to dance and hug Sperin and hear Simeon tell her how smart she was. "We're going to make it! Prepare to go hyper!"

A high-energy particle beam flashed across their bow, causing their face-plates to darken.

"What the . . ." Joat said. She killed velocity and backed frantically until she could at least see who was firing on her.

A sleek, bright-yellow fighter with red markings hove into view and lined up to fire on them again.

"That is the symbol of the Yoered Family," Joseph said in astonishment.

Joat brought their fighter to a halt and dove, just as the Family fighter fired again. She grabbed the control board for the signal disrupter and hit the off control. Nothing happened.

"Fardles!" she snarled. "I can't turn it off."

"What?" Joseph asked.

"The signal disrupter. It's not receiving my signal to turn off. Apparently it's disrupting that too."

"You are joking!" Joseph said in disbelief. "This is not funny, Joat. Turn the cursed thing off!"

"It's just a prototype, Joe. It's never been used before. There are bound to be problems."

"We're being fired on by our *allies* because of one of your famous gadgets, Joat? Is that what I'm hearing here?" Bros asked.

"Yeah," she growled.

Bros started to laugh.

"It's not funny, Sperin."

"Truly, it is not," agreed Joseph.

"Now I'm sure this is really happening," Bros said. "I don't have this kind of an imagination."

"We've got to go back," Joat said.

The ship rocked as the Family fighter hit one of their fins with its beam.

Joat spun the ship 'round and ran flat out for the *Dreadful Bride*.

"I don't believe this!" she said. "I don't believe that Belazir t'Marid is my only hope of survival."

"He will kill us," Joseph predicted grimly.

"But not right away," Bros assured them.

Joat didn't deign to answer either of them.

The Family fighter hit one of their attitude-adjustment coils and the little craft tumbled helplessly for an agonizing minute before the gyroscopic system righted their ship. *At that it probably saved our lives.*

The sensors were showing multimegatonne explosions in a rapidly expanding pattern.

Joat gasped. "Well, that kills one option. I was hoping to linger outside the *Bride* for as long as possible and maybe escape in the excitement. But the Family has put *paid-in-full* to that idea, now hasn't it?"

"Joat, wait!" Joseph snapped. "If they cannot hear you they will not have the hangar doors open."

"For cryin' out loud, Joe. They can't hear us, but they can *see*. If they don't open the doors we're going to smash into them. They're not going to let that happen. Trust me."

"Trust . . . you?"

It's probably hard for him to talk with his heart in his mouth like that, Joat thought, as she aimed the fighter at the stubbornly shut hangar doors. *I know that's where mine is.*

"Pull up, Joat," Bros suggested tensely.

"Pull *UP!*" Joseph seconded at top volume.

"I can't steer," she said. "I'm hoping they can see that."

Just when she'd begun to give up hope, the huge doors began to move. She throttled back, trying to give them time to widen and flitted through the narrow gap with just meters to spare.

Two tears of relief rolled down her cheeks and she made a strange sound, half-laugh half-sob. Her male companions cursed imaginatively, particularly Joseph.

"Daughter of a mangy, limbless goatherd and a ruptured swine!" he shouted. "You little spawn of Shaithen! Don't you *ever* frighten me like that again."

She laughed outright.

"Blame the Family, buddy. Or Bros here, or Amos for that matter. None of this is my doing. I'm just reacting here and doing the best I can." She unstrapped herself from her seat. "People are going to be running around crazy out there. My advice is to run around with them until we can find a safe place to lie low."

"And then?" Bros asked dubiously.

"Hope the Family wins. But doesn't total the *Bride* while we're on it. And if they don't, try plan A again." She shrugged. "Woulda worked this time if the timing had been just a little better."

"I don't want to spoil your plans, Joat," Bros spoke carefully to avoid slurring his words, "but I'm not up to much running around."

"I know," she said, releasing his restraints. She pursed her lips. "Maybe we could stuff you into Kraig's locker."

He glared at her.

"I'm not that far gone," he said between clenched teeth.

"Be reasonable. It's nearby and I'm positive no one will look for you there."

"I'll keep up," he snarled.

Joat glanced over at Joseph, who shrugged.

"Suit yourself," she said briskly. "It's your funeral."

They descended from the fighter to a welcoming committee of battle-armored Kolnari and black-suited mercenaries.

"Who is your commander?" one of the Kolnari barked.

"Captain Hobsbrowm, Sir!" Joat snapped out.

"Report! What is the meaning of this?"

"Sir!" Joat said. Facing the Kolnari, she sketched a salute. "Yoered Family fighters have infiltrated the perimeter. Communications are down. There are indications that the Family people are affected by the jamming also."

There was the briefest pause, as though the Kolnari within the huge battle armor was taken by surprise.

"Very well," she said. "Report to your squad leader. Get another ship and join us outside."

"Yes sir!" Joat and her companions saluted and trotted off. After a moment they cut right behind the body of a fighter and out of sight of the Kolnari and her friends.

They paused a moment to look around and Joat saw a cluster of black-suited figures emerging from an elevator.

"There," she said and pointed. The others followed her and they slid in just as the doors were closing.

Bros leaned against the wall, gasping for breath. His face was pale and slick with sweat. Joat thought he looked ready to pass out. He opened his eyes and met hers. Then he straightened up a bit.

"I'm all right," he panted.

"Where are we going?" Joseph demanded of her.

"B corridor."

"*Kolnari* territory?' he asked in disbelief. "Surely you are joking?"

"Jeez! You really think my sense of humor is getting the better of me today, don't you?"

Bros grinned. "The Brig," he said. "Last place they'll look for us."

"We couldn't all fit into Kraig's locker," she muttered. The elevator doors opened onto B corridor and a scene of organized chaos. "And we couldn't very well slip into that repair tunnel without being seen, now could we? I figure the Brig's our best shot." She glanced at Joseph. "Suggestions are welcome."

"Speak with authority and behave as though we belong," he said.

"Don't I always?" she asked and lead the way.

They rounded a corner and blundered into a squad of Kolnari.

"YOU!" bellowed their leader. "What are you scumvermin doing here?"

"Sir!" Joat saluted. "We are to report to Captain Hobsbrowm. Sir!" All she could see in his black faceplate was her own reflection, looking determined. *Thank the powers-that-be for Captain Hobsbrowm,* her mind babbled. *I wonder if Hobsbrowm's a he or a she? How long can I keep referring to him/her without using a personal pronoun?*

"Hobsbrowm is not here," the Kolnari sneered. "You will fall in with us."

"With all due respect, Sir. I am under orders," Joat said.

"What is wrong with that man?" the Kolnari demanded unexpectedly, pointing at Bros.

"He's still getting used to the heavier gravity," Joat said. "He's a light-worlder."

"Phah! Weakling." He said it almost indifferently, as though thinking of something else.

He's wondering if he dares to interfere in the kind of "orders" that would allow me to defy him, Joat thought. *Make up your mind, creep!*

"Hobsbrowm does not need three of you. I will take this one." He pointed at Joseph. "Fall in!" he bellowed.

His face a blank, Joseph did so.

"What is your name, Sir?" Joat asked. "So that I can tell the Captain where this man is."

The Kolnari went very still. The way they did when they thought they might have made a mistake, but weren't certain yet what it might be.

"Skarik na Marid, petite-noble, commander of a section, is my name," he growled. "And I tremble at the thought of displeasing your captain. What is your name, scumvermin?"

"Rendino du Pare," Joat said crisply and rattled off Kraig's ID number. *It's not like he can check it out,* she thought nervously. *It just has to sound right.*

"On your way, scumvermin, before I change my mind."

Then the Kolnar barked an order and his squad marched off, Joseph bringing up the rear. Joat watched them out of sight. Joseph never looked back.

Silken jammed her fist into her mouth as though she would ram her scream back down her throat. She bit down until she broke the skin, and blood, hot and salty spurted onto her tongue. She flailed out with one hand, as though to clutch Belazir's green robe; only to have it whisk through thin air.

Nomik Ciety screamed. A hoarse bubbling scream like she'd never heard before. He was balanced on the crown of his head and his heels, his back arched in a great bow, arms held stiffly at his sides with his fingers clawing the air. Nomik's eyes were wild with disbelief and foam dribbled from his mouth.

Belazir watched with satisfaction, his heavy arms folded across his chest and his expression one of sensual enjoyment. Pleased that the drug was working as it should this time.

The med-tech stood by the hatch looking almost as aghast as Silken. The two Kolnari guards watched with academic interest.

"Please, Master and God," Silken begged, blood running down her chin, "make it stop, please! Whatever you want, we will do, I *swear.* Only make it stop!" She collapsed in incoherent sobs across the holo of Belazir's feet.

He looked down at her in mild interest.

"You are not as strong as I thought you would be," he remarked. "But I am generous to women, I will instruct you in the causes of my displeasure." He frowned slightly; it was difficult to make himself heard over Ciety's screaming.

"First," he said, raising his voice slightly. "You sent to me the daughter of our worst enemy to perform an important task for us. I cannot help but feel insulted by your lack of sensitivity." He sighed in exasperation as Nomik's screams reached new heights. "Kick him onto his face," he instructed the guards. "Perhaps it will stifle some of his noise."

He turned back to the wide-eyed Silken, who had her hands pressed against her mouth, as though that would somehow help to silence Nomik's cries.

"Where was I? Ah, yes. Second, as part of this woman's crew, what do I find? I find Bros Sperin! One of Central Worlds' most notable covert operatives." He spread his hands, raising his brows.

"What am I to make of this? One thing was bad enough—sending me the girl when I could not torture her to death without wrecking my greater scheme—but the other . . . ? It is intolerable. So . . . you are fools or you are enemies. Either way you must be punished. Surely you understand this? Incompetence and insults must always be addressed."

Nomik's body collapsed and he lay panting, whining slightly.

"Ah. It is over." He turned to Silken and said reassuringly, "There are supposed to be no permanent effects."

"You bastard," Nomik gasped, "you bastard."

Belazir compressed his lips.

"Of course," he drawled, "sometimes, with some individuals, a lesson must be repeated a number of times before its meaning is comprehended." He raised his hand to signal the med-tech.

Suddenly another Kolnari appeared beside Belazir.

"Great Lord!" he said excitedly.

Belazir backhanded him, knocking the man to his knees. His yellow eyes blazed.

"How *dare* you enter here? What is the meaning of this intrusion?"

"I abase myself before you Great Lord," a one word expression in Kolnari. The soldier bowed his head and placed both fists on the floor where he knelt. "Communications are down," he said urgently. "The fleet is under attack by Yoered Family fighters."

"What?"

"They've come because of us, you fool," Nomik lay on his side, glaring at Belazir. "You can't kidnap someone from Rohan and not answer to the Family for it. They're going to kick your butt, asshole."

Everyone went still, Belazir drew a deep angry breath, his nostrils grew pale and pinched.

"Give her the antidote," he snarled at the medtech, "give him the disease. Then report to your stations." Then he disappeared from the cell.

One of the guards grasped Silken's arm and raised it. The med-tech touched it with an injector. He moved over to Ciety and applied another to one of his arms. Then the three of them fled the cell and Silken crawled over to hold Nomik in her arms.

✧   ✧   ✧

Belazir threw off his silk robe and strapped on a utility belt, checking the charge in his plasma gun.

"Report," he barked.

"There is little more, Great Lord. Ships have been launched to meet the foe, the battleworthy ships have closed around the mother ship in protective formation. With communications out we can do little but wait."

"Fool!" Belazir snarled and marched out of his quarters moving towards the bridge.

Outside the door Skarik na Marid's small squad formed up around Belazir in a protective square.

Joseph strode along behind Belazir, eyes blazing, his heart full of hate. Amos's words rang in his head, "It would grieve me, my brother, to have you die like a fool."

Benisur, what am I to do? God has placed our enemy in my hands. Can I turn away in fear for myself and still call myself a man?

He could almost hear Amos's answer. "Wait for your best moment before you strike. And do not condemn yourself as a coward if no such moment arrives."

Before them an elevator opened and disgorged another crowd of Kolnari warriors running to their battle stations.

Joseph's whole body pounded with his heartbeat, it was all that he could feel, the blood raging through his veins. *Never have I felt such desire, not even in the arms of my beloved.*

He grabbed Belazir by the neck and flung him into the empty elevator with a mighty shove, drew his laser and threw himself in afterwards just as the door closed. He hit a floor at random, then spun and kicked Belazir's legs out from under him, bringing the butt of his pistol down on the back of the Kolnari's neck with a vicious crack.

Joseph fired on the elevator's control mechanism and they lurched to a halt. Then he turned back to his prey, his blue eyes alight with joy.

"*You!*" Belazir screamed, staggering to his feet. The blow would have killed any normal human. "*You!*"

The Bethelite cast his weapon aside and drew the long curved knife. He could hear Amos's voice again—this time condemning him for a fool. *And I do not care. Some things are beyond even loyalty, my prophet and friend.*

The lift cage was large, built to transport a section or more of troops in power armor. Belazir sidled crabwise, tearing off the remnants of his robe. His body was matte-black except where the dusty gray of scars seamed it, a gaunt thing of massive bones and muscles shrunken and knotted and still powerful enough to crack teak beams. There was no mind behind the golden eyes now, and a string of saliva dangled from one loose-curled lip.

"*You!*" he screamed, and leaped with his hands outstretched to tear.

Joat was relieved to see that the corpse she and Joseph had left behind was still on duty behind the reception desk. Bros labored along beside her and at last she felt safe enough to put his arm around her shoulder and give him some support.

"No," he said, resisting her. "Not until we're behind a locked door. There's no telling who we might run into."

She blushed and compressed her lips. He was right, and she was embarrassed. It wasn't like her to get soft like this.

They moved into the Brig and she started trying doors, looking for one that wasn't locked.

Around the corner came two Kolnari and a medtech, moving so fast they almost collided.

"What are you doing here?" one of the guards demanded.

"We've been sent to relieve Kolnari guards for duty elsewhere," Joat said.

"No," the other guard said, looking hard at Bros. "No, she lies. He is a prisoner."

"Ridiculous," Joat snapped. "We are heading *into* the Brig, not out of it."

"This is Bros Sperin," the guard insisted. "I know him."

The other guard and the med-tech began to grin.

Oh shit! Joat thought and went for her laser.

The first guard slapped her hand aside and kicked her legs out from under her. Joat lay for a single instant, stunned; she'd forgotten, over the years, the inhuman speed of the Kolnari.

Bros is unarmed! she thought as she crashed to the floor and she saw both guards moving in on him. Before she could get her stunned body back in action the medtech had her in a hold that immobilized her. He stripped off one of her gloves and pressed an injector against the inside of her wrist.

The last thing she saw as her vision darkened was Bros going down in a flurry of kicks from the two Kolnari guards. She heard something snap, and then there was nothing.

✧   ✧   ✧

She woke to the sensation of something heavy resting on her lap, holding her against a wall. Her eyes flickered open and she snapped them shut, the light in the room was so bright it drew tears. Cautiously, she slitted her eyes open and looked down to see what was so heavy.

Bros lay in her lap. He was perfectly still; blood trailed from his mouth. She snapped the locks on his helmet and tossed it aside, touched her bare hand to his pulse.

Chief Family Enforcer Vand looked down at her impassively.

"He is alive?" Vand asked.

Joat nodded wearily, then glanced up at him. Vand was much taller than she'd expected and twice as intimidating as he was on a screen.

"It would seem they questioned him very thoroughly," he observed. He looked away, his eyes never resting long on any place or thing.

Just as well, Joat thought. *When he looks at me I feel like I'm about to be dissected.*

"The Family would very much like to interrogate Mr. Sperin," Vand said, considering the notion.

Joat made a small flinging gesture and a knife slipped into her hand, she pressed it up under Bros's jaw.

"But you won't," she said with fierce determination.

"No," he said, his face still impassive, but a look of something like respect touched his cold eyes. "Of course not. In addition to restoring the Family's honor, the object of this mission was to rescue Mr. Sperin. It would hardly do to compromise Yoered's honor immediately after saving it. Now would it?" He smiled, and she wished he hadn't. "Our honor is an extremely valuable commercial property."

Joat had the impression she was being laughed at, though nothing visible backed it up.

"You must excuse me. We're in the process of teaching the Kolnari a rather sharp lesson on maintaining a certain standard of professional etiquette when in a Family port. Remain here," Vand commanded. "I have some medtechs on the way."

Then he was gone, moving lightly despite the bulky battle-armor.

As if I was about to scamper off and get into trouble, Joat thought sourly. She leaned her head wearily against the wall and closed her eyes. When she opened them she found herself looking into Silken's.

Silken sat on the floor across from her, with Nomik's head leaning against her breast, in a pose that mirrored her own.

Tears ran down Silken's cheeks and her expression was tired beyond all bearing. Her hair was wild and there was blood around her mouth, bruises on the porcelain skin.

Joat knew a moment's sympathy for her, realizing that Silken must be broken indeed if she was too weary to make threats.

Eventually the promised medtechs came and suited them up in quarantine outfits like the ones they were wearing. They lifted Nomik and Bros onto pallets. Each of the women walked beside one, looking down.

Joat wavered, wondering if she should try to find and destroy Belazir's store of stolen virus.

Then Bros opened his eyes and looked up at her and she found herself taking his hand and walking beside the pallet.

Ah well, she thought, *if I did find it Vand would only take it away from me. Whereas if they don't know about it then they're very unlikely to find it.* Joat was uncomfortably aware of how unlike her it was to hope for a miracle.

Then again, sometimes they happen, she thought dazedly.

There were other pallets waiting at the lock, with medtechs working around them. One in particular seized her gaze. A thick-bodied blond man lay on it; the uniform had been cut away from most of his body, and devices hummed over it. She could see broken bone on one flank where the ribs had been hammered as if with a maul, and the tech's fingers were straightening the left arm above and below the elbow, so that the positioning sleeves could be fastened. Inflatable casts already covered the whole lower half of his body, and it was only just possible to tell the color of his hair, because something had ripped half the scalp off his head as if it were a wig.

She walked to the side of the pallet. Incredibly, the blue eyes were open.

"Joe," she whispered.

He tried to smile. She bent closer.

"No . . . pain," he whispered. "Drugs . . ."

Joat closed her eyes. "Thank God you're alive."

"Thank . . . the God indeed."

"Who did this to you?"

"Belazir . . . t'Marid."

Joat's hands clenched. *That debt keeps building up and up!*

Joseph saw her expression, and tried to smile again. Blood ran down his chin and his eyes rolled sideways. Joat looked down on the floor.

The head was quite recognizable, despite the cuts. She could never forget those eyes, and they were open and staring.

CHAPTER TWENTY

BUSTER RAUCHFUSS CHEWED his lip and considered this second request for clarification and/or credits from their contact on New Destinies.

Mancini had never bothered to get back to him. Obviously he hadn't dealt with the situation either.

Typical, Buster sniffed. *Kick somebody up a notch and they think they're too good to answer their mail.*

Well, Paul would answer this one.

Dear Mr. Mancini, Buster wrote. *This matter is growing more urgent. Perhaps you should look into it yourself. Surely I shouldn't even know about this. After all, when Mr. Sperin was removed from my department you'll recall that I was told nothing for security reasons. I must say that it worries me, therefore, that I keep getting these messages.*

Let me know if I can be of any help on this.

That oughta shake Mancini up.

Buster received a reply that same afternoon, lightning speed for interoffice communications at CenSec.

Buster, it began.

All I know about your man Sperin is that he was taken off a Kolnari battle-cruiser in the company of Nomik Ciety and that he's in security quarantine.

You can tell your contact on New Destinies that we have no intention of giving that many credits to a station notorious for graft and bribery. Certainly not on the say-so of a man under that kind of a cloud. Word it however you like, but the answer is no.

I would hate to see you pursue this. Buster noticed the "your man Sperin" and the lack of signature and he felt a little frisson of alarm tickle the back of his neck.

I can't believe that Bros would have anything to do with the Kolnari, he thought dubiously. *The guy hated them.* But the bare facts were damning. He frowned. *It sure looks bad.* And it was rumored that Ciety could convert a saint to the devil's cause. He shook his head. *Enough credits can get to anybody.*

Certainly with this to go on he couldn't be expected to stick his neck out. Buster chewed his lip, then sighed and began composing a note for Dana to send to Sal on New Destinies.

Clal va Riguez was not authorized to make this kind of payment.

Short, sweet and to the point. *That oughta take care of that,* Buster thought with satisfaction. It had the virtue of being the absolute truth, too.

Joat left the *Wyal* glumly; she ignored the cluster of newshounds and floating pickups—even on Rohan, you couldn't avoid the media, lies and distortions would be flying all over the human part of the galaxy, many times faster than light. At least on Rohan, they didn't try to grab her arm to force an interview.

She smiled bleakly. Not with Enforcer Vand backing up *The Rules;* the bloody lesson taught the Kolnari had shown just how seriously the Family took them. She forced her legs onward.

Not a word since we got back to Rohan. She wondered uneasily whether Silken intended to honor Ciety's stated intention of canceling the *Wyal*'s debt; maybe she'd just been waiting to recover fully before putting in the knife.

Joat had been relieved that Silken hadn't required her to do anything blatantly illegal. Several times, she'd been ordered to ferry some rather creepy passengers to equally creepy destinations. And who knew what contraband they had in their personal luggage? But no outright smuggling.

Joat sighed. She'd been so sure that Bros—her mind shied away from the fierce disappointment she felt in him—or someone representing him at least, would have released her from the debt that bound her to her uncle and his concubine. So *much for being a hero. Not even a message.* Beyond the pain was a sadness that frightened her.

They'd been separated by the medtechs as soon as they were brought aboard the Family ship. Despite her protests she'd been taken into a cubicle to have her own wounds treated. Then a sedative had been pressed on her and she'd been escorted, dizzy and sleepy, to a berth and sealed in. She'd slept through most of the journey.

When they reached the quarantine facility she woke up in a Spartan room wearing nothing but a pair of plastic slippers and a disposable shift. They kept her locked up for three weeks, until her wounds were well healed and they were certain she carried no trace of contagion. She was able to communicate with Al and Seg, Amos and Soamosa right away. Then Joe, when he'd recovered sufficiently. But never Bros.

Joat sighed. Maybe he thought it was fair turnabout. She'd abandoned him on Belazir's ship, after all. *No! I went back!*

She'd attempted to relay messages, both directly to CenSec and through her old contact at The Anvil on New Destinies. To be blandly told that they had or would be forwarded to Sperin.

Not that she'd expected them to be eager to contribute that many credits to Nomik Ciety and Rohan's burgeoning economy. In fact, it would seem to go against their charter.

But *damn* this was like being a slave! Joat hung on, hoping that Silken was at least crediting the work she was doing against the debt. *At least that. If she won't return the* Wyal *to me outright, at least let me work it off.* Though so far, Joat was paying her own expenses.

She'd seriously considered enlisting Simeon's aid in getting through to Bros, but had been too ashamed to send her father anything from her Rohan address. Or from any of the other ports she'd been in lately.

I will not whine.

When she entered the bland waiting room at N. Ciety, Research and Development, there were two rather nondescript individuals seated in the lounge area, but no one was behind the reception desk.

She huffed impatiently and put her hands on her hips, frowning.

"Excuse me," one of the men in the lounge said, rising and coming over to her. "Are you Captain Joat Simeon-Hap?"

A sort of icy foreboding swept over her in a numbing tide.

"Who wants to know?"

They looked like accountants, mild and innocuous, with smooth, chubby faces. They smiled little, amused smiles at her response. Joat was willing to bet they were carrying weapons and that they weren't amused at all.

"Why don't we just cut the crap and get right to the point," the taller man said. "We represent New Destinies and we've come to repossess your ship in lieu of the debt you owe for a fine levied against the *Wyal*."

Her mouth went dry and it felt as though all her blood had run down into her extremities.

After what seemed a long time she croaked, "What?"

"We're foreclosing on your debt," the smaller one said slowly.

"But . . . Nomik Ciety bought the debt from New Destinies. I was working it off for him."

"I'm sorry," the tall man said. "We have no record of any such purchase." He actually did look marginally sympathetic. "You can file a complaint, and if there's been an error, you're certainly entitled to recompense." He paused. "Now, we'll require you to vacate the *Wyal* immediately. Obviously you'll only be allowed to take personal possessions. Any items which might be considered integral parts of the ship will naturally have to remain."

Rand! she thought for the first time. *What's going to happen to Rand?* This wasn't supposed to be happening. She'd never believed that CenSec would let her down like this, not once.

"Let me talk to Silken," she said, trying to keep her voice from shaking. "She's running things here, perhaps she can explain this." *And it had better be good or I'm going to rip her pretty, little face off.*

She sat behind the receptionist's desk and after a moment got the comp to release Silken's private number. A few moments later Silken's face, looking thinner, sharper and deeply annoyed filled the screen.

"You!" she said in astonishment.

"Me," Joat confirmed. "There are two men here claiming that there's no record of Ciety's purchase of my debt from New Destinies. Do you know what's going on?"

"Ah, yes," Silken murmured, leaning back with a half-smile. "I've been so busy that I'd forgotten. When Mik told you that he'd bought your debt he had every intention of doing so. But," she made a little moue, "your extremely negative reaction changed his mind." She shrugged and said indifferently, "Too bad. But it's not like it makes any difference. You never could have paid it off in any case."

"I notice you didn't forget to use me to ferry your friends around," Joat snapped.

"I told you, I forgot." Silken's eyes were disdainful, as yielding as stone. "Even you have to admit I have a great deal on my mind."

"Yeah, like how to keep my Uncle from drooling on the carpet."

Silken went white.

"You heartless, spiteful, cruel, vicious bitch," she said, each word a separate insult, sincerely meant.

"You're right," Joat said, ashamed. Suddenly, she understood Silken's malice so completely that she was utterly disarmed. Enough so that she couldn't forgive her own. "That was uncalled for, I'm sorry."

"There's nothing that could happen to you that would make you sorry enough to appease me," Silken told tightly. "That damn ship is the only thing you care about and I'm *glad* you're going to lose it. It's not enough, it's not nearly enough, but it will do for a start.

"I'll be watching you," she continued, fire beginning to kindle in her cold green eyes. "And whenever it goes sour for you, whenever you lose or miss out or get passed over," she tapped her chest with one slender finger, "—that's me. My work. I promise you. You don't know what sorry is, you slime-hag. But you will."

The screen went blank and Joat just sat there, staring at it.

One of the repo-men cleared his throat awkwardly and she looked up.

"We . . . might as well get this over with," he said.

She nodded, feeling freeze-dried inside, hard and brittle and shredded. Joat rose carefully, weirdly numbed, and began to ask pertinent questions as the three of them left the office, headed for the *Wyal.*

They gave her permission to download her logs and personal correspondence and to tell her crew herself.

Joat sat in her pilots couch for the last time, listening to Alvec curse.

"I never would've believed it," he said for the twelfth time at least. "Jeez, he seemed like an all-right guy. Y'know? This isn't right!"

"Excuse me," the taller repo-man said. "We'd like to get our own crew on as soon as possible. Could you speed this up a little, please?"

Joat started to speak and merely squawked, she cleared her throat. "I'd, ah, like to leave the *Wyal* as ship-shape as possible. You know, tidy her up."

He smiled knowingly.

"Yes, we get a lot of that kind of thoughtfulness. One of our debtors was so 'tidy' that his ship didn't blow up for three weeks.

Killed a family of five. So I'm afraid you'll just have to pack and go, leaving things just as they are."

She nodded coolly.

"Just a few more minutes," she said.

"Five," he said, holding up his spread hand for emphasis.

Alvec rose and walked directly towards him, as though he didn't exist, leaving the hapless debt collector to leap aside or get walked over.

"I'll meet you on the dock, Boss," Alvec called over his shoulder.

Joat turned her chair and looked at Rand's blinking "face."

"What about you, Rand?"

After a moments silence, it said, "Obviously I can't leave, can I?"

"No," Joat said, her voice soft with shame. Even if they would allow her to download Rand's personality she had no access to a computer powerful enough to receive it. Through all of their troubles and misadventures, she'd somehow managed to overlook *this*. She'd failed to protect a friend, one who had done far more than his share to help her.

Yes, his *share*. Rand was most certainly not an "it" any longer. *What a fardling stupid time to realize that!*

"I'm so sorry," she whispered, ashamed of her powerlessness and fighting to keep her tears from falling.

"Like you, Joat, I find I don't like the idea of a life of servitude."

"Oh," her voice creaked. "Might not be that bad. They'll probably declare you an AI ship and send you out on your own. You'd be making your own decisions and not getting yourself in the land of trouble I've lead you into."

"AI assignments tend to be the most tedious kind," Rand said. "No crew, no stimulation, not even an allowance for virtual reality in port—computers don't get paid. And I would scarcely be making my own decisions Joat, other than: "Should I allow myself to be hit by this rock or should I avoid it?" I'd scarcely call that autonomy," Rand said with scorn.

One side of her mouth crooked.

"You sound like me," she said.

"And why wouldn't I? You've put a great deal of yourself into me."

And children often resemble their parents, she thought morbidly.

"Excuse me," the tall one said, "are you through yet?'

"Just a minute!" she snapped. The repo-man glared, but withdrew. Joat thought she heard him say, " . . . think they've got an AI on board." Turning back to Rand, she said: "It's not over yet, buddy. Maybe there's still something we can do. At least now I'm free to move around."

"Correct me if I'm wrong. You have no credits."

"You're wrong. Little Silky owes us a considerable amount, and she *will* pay us."

"Why should she," Rand asked reasonably enough. "You can't make her."

"I may not love him, but I'm Nomik Ciety's niece. A quick genetic scan will prove our relationship, and the Family is very fond of backing family rights. Probably, all I have to do is make the claim and I could put his whole empire, such as it is, on hold."

"You can't hope to win such a claim," Rand's voice was almost surprised.

"Of course not. But it would cost more to hire an assassin than it would to pay me what she owes, and it would cost twice that to retain an attorney."

"She could challenge you to a duel."

"I can take her."

"If I were human, I would laugh. Silken hates you, Joat. To the point of obsession. I'm sure that nothing would give her greater pleasure than killing you herself. Probably she hasn't challenged you simply because it hasn't occurred to her."

Joat grinned savagely.

"Oh, it's occurred to her all right. But she won't risk leaving Ciety alone and at the mercy of the Family. If he were dead we'd have crossed swords long since."

"So you'll be able to leave."

"Yes. And I'll be able to call in favors, perhaps get a loan," she was silent a moment, "maybe even get through to Bros. So don't give up on me. Okay? I won't make that an order."

Philosophers might debate whether it was *possible* for a computer to commit suicide, since it wasn't certain that they could be self-aware in the first place. Rand's "impassive" face blinked multicolored lights for a few moments.

"Very well, I will abide. But, if I am sold to someone else, Joat, I won't serve them. If worst comes to worst I've saved a copy of Seg's worm program. Should some other bidder obtain the *Wyal*, I shall trigger it. If I don't fight it, it will be very quick."

"You can't be serious," Joat whispered. She couldn't believe her ears.

"Aren't you even willing to give a new owner a chance to prove their worth before taking such a drastic step?"

She wondered if she'd programmed him for self-preservation. *Of course I did! I couldn't possibly have left it out, it's too important.* Not that it was unknown for Rand to erase bits of programming he didn't want anymore. She'd never locked down any part of him, preferring to leave that . . . freedom, for himself.

"I am an individual," Rand insisted, "there is no more individual choice than this."

Joat sat still, too horrified to speak.

"All right, that's enough," the shorter repo-man struck the back of her chair, making it spin towards him. "Stop yakking to the computer, go pack up your belongings and get lost."

Her mind was wholly on Rand, or she would have kicked his tubby form through the bulkhead. Instead she gave him a disgusted look and headed off the bridge.

"Hey! Don't forget these," he said and handed her the collection of datahedrons she'd made.

"Personal files, erased," said Rand mechanically.

Joat sat in the auction room with her heart in her mouth.

It was an enormous hall, too brightly lit, with a strange sharp smell to it. The hall was furnished with ugly, uncomfortable chairs each having one arm that terminated in a small computer with a display screen. Currently it displayed the ship being bid on. There were a few controls that would call up information on the ship, schematics, history, and beside them a slot into which a successful bidder's credit chip would go. Almost every seat was filled with junk dealers, purchase agents, and bargain hunters.

She had with her every credit she could beg, borrow or earn and it was still forty thousand credits short of the fine.

Wyal was going on the block.

It was third on the list and the closer it got to the top the faster her heart beat. Her palms were sweating and she rubbed them surreptitiously on the fabric of her dark blue business suit. The strange, formal garment she wore in hope of looking more respectable only succeeded in making her feel obvious and awkward. *I should have robbed that bank. I should.* Robbing banks on Rohan . . .

The hammer went down and the *Wyal* moved one place closer to the block. Her breathing grew nervous and ragged.

She knew, she *knew* that she wouldn't get her ship back. Silken was certain to have agents among the bidders who would know to the credit how much she had. Agents who were, no doubt, instructed to bid just one credit more.

Alvec, who was working short, freelance hops, had offered his life savings.

"I can't take this," she'd told him, horrified and deeply touched, as well as terribly tempted.

"So make me a partner," he'd said.

And she'd smiled, hope blazing.

But it hadn't been enough. It had never been enough and Bros Sperin remained beyond her reach. So here she was, facing certain defeat, feeling humiliated before she even began.

How could I have been so stupid? she railed at herself. When had she grown so soft that she would put her freedom on the line, for someone else, mind you, with no expectation of cost or reward? *My own fault. Playing at spy,* she mocked, *I'm no better than Seg !T'sel.*

Alvec was furious with her for not asking Amos for help.

"I asked my father," she'd said. Though of course she hadn't told Simeon *why* she needed credits. "That's as much as my pride can take."

That was partially true, it had hurt to ask Simeon for help. Even though he gave it willingly and offered to take out a loan for more, no questions asked, it hurt. She'd felt like a complete failure. First Brawn school, and now this.

Nor did she dare to ask Amos for help. Bethel was a poor planet, most of her credits already committed for years to come. And though he was very rich, Amos was in the habit of pouring most of his wealth back into his world's struggling economy. She couldn't very well ask him to choose her needs over the good of his people. And she didn't think he would really understand about Rand.

Joat wondered if Joseph and Amos hovered in the same state of anxiety that tortured her, wanting to give, not daring to offer. Or if they even knew.

Either way she simply couldn't afford the time or the money it would cost to ask, only to be told no.

A deeper truth was that she felt Amos should have offered. Or Joseph should have. *He* knew all about the debt. Yet the total silence from all the powerful people she'd counted as friends—or more than friends—never varied. In the end she was just a forgotten detail, an unimportant loose end.

Joat frowned. *Oh, stop it,* she thought disgustedly, *there's no poison deadlier than self-pity. The mistake was yours and so's the punishment.*

Although that last wasn't completely true. Rand had made it very plain that he didn't count himself as part of the ship.

Rand's threat had certainly inspired her to new heights, and depths, in her fund-raising efforts. Sometimes, late at night when she couldn't get to sleep for thinking about it, Joat told herself that was why he'd made it. To get her over her shyness about asking friends for help.

Probably he doesn't mean to erase himself at all, she comforted herself. *Hah! A computer that plays with you. Somehow I don't think this idea will sell.*

Joat knew that if she lost the ship, and Rand erased himself, for the rest of her life, she was going to feel like a failure and a murderer.

There might still be time to get through to Amos on Bethel, she thought.

The next ship up was a tasty offering that seemed to have excited a lot of interest. Of course sometimes those were the ones that came on and off the block so fast you couldn't get a decent look at them.

Then there was the cost to consider.

A tight-beam interstellar com-link could cost me four percent of what I've got. On the other hand . . . On the other hand Silken's bidders wouldn't let her have the *Wyal* anyway unless she could exceed Nomik Ciety's entire fortune. And she couldn't even pay the fine.

She closed her eyes and took a deep breath. When she opened them she saw that she'd been right. The bidding was over and the ship had sold.

"I have an announcement," the auctioneer said. "The *Wyal,* which is the next ship on the list, has been withdrawn from bid. We're sorry for any inconvenience this may have caused. I'll repeat that. The *Wyal,* a merchant freighter ship, has been withdrawn from bid."

Joat's felt the bottom of her stomach lurch into zero-g. *My ship! What have they done with my ship?*

Absently she noted two bidders that turned to stare at her. Silken's people, no doubt. Well, they seemed satisfied by the look of white-faced horror that she knew she must be wearing. They'd be happy to report this disaster to their employer.

"They can't *do* that!" Joat said desperately.

The Sondee next to her looked up when she spoke.

"How can they do that?" she asked.

The Sondee shrugged. "Sometimes they get a private bid that more than meets the minimum price. In this case it wouldn't take much. The *Wyal* is a crummy little ship."

Joat raised an eyebrow and glared.

Instead of defending the honor or her ship she spoke: "What if you had questions about something like this? Where would you go to ask them?"

"Why, at the same office where you were assigned your seat. Through that door, down the hall, first door on the right," the Sondee said helpfully, then pointedly turned back to the auction.

Joat found the office empty, which infuriated her. She swore and muttered, pacing back and forth before the tall counter more and more rapidly.

At last frustrated beyond bearing she shouted, "Hello? Is *anyone* working here?"

No one answered.

She marched out into the hall, determined to open the first door she detected a being behind and demand service.

At the end of the corridor she turned left, at the end of that one, she found the president's office and went briskly in.

"I'd like to speak to someone in authority," she said to the surprised secretary.

"Do you have an appointment?" he asked politely.

"No, but I do have questions."

"Perhaps I can help you."

"I *said* someone in authority. That wouldn't be you." She marched over to the door of the inner sanctum and before the secretary could disengage himself from his desk, she was through it.

A well-dressed human in his mid-sixties sat behind the wide, wooden desk, a pleasant smile frozen on his face by her entrance. The younger man seated before him turned to see who had entered so precipitously.

It was Bros.

"You!" she said, her voice a near shriek.

He rose smiling and extended his arms as though to embrace her.

She backed up a pace and stood glaring at him, breathing hard, wanting to hit him and knowing that if she landed a blow it was because he let her.

No thank you, she thought, *I think I've been humiliated enough lately.* She turned and walked away thinking over and over, *I'm going to kill him, I'm going to* kill *him . . .*

"Excuse me," Bros said over his shoulder and followed her.

She was moving pretty fast when he caught her by the arm and pulled her through the first door they came to. It was an empty office. He shut the door behind him and leaned against it.

She paced back and forth, too furious to speak, glaring at him.

"I don't blame you for being angry," he said at last. "But there was nothing I could do until now. I didn't even know that this hadn't been acted on. I *told* them about it in my report, I insisted that we had an obligation to see that your debt was canceled, reduced or paid. But I didn't know it hadn't been done." He held out a datahedron.

"This is yours, *Wyal's* papers."

She took it carefully and swallowed hard.

"And where were you that you couldn't answer any of my messages? That you never attempted to get in contact with any of us?" She stood with her arms folded, looking him square in the face and asking with her eyes. *And how could you leave me believing that stuff about caring about me? How dare you make me believe in you like that?*

"You have to understand, Joat, I was interrogated by the enemy. It's customary to hold an agent incommunicado for at least two months afterwards. There are very solid reasons for it. If the Kolnari were a more sophisticated people, I wouldn't be free now." He frowned at her unchanging stare. "Look, I came as soon as I knew, okay?"

She nodded reluctantly.

"So, what happens now? Can I just leave? I've really got my ship back?"

He nodded and gravely watched Joat smile.

She couldn't help herself, the tension disappeared and joy broke over her face like a sunrise.

"How . . . how did you find out? You must have just been released. Was it the first question you asked?" She blushed "I mean, did you say: 'What's going on with the *Wyal*?' or what?"

"Simeon told me. He's the one who speeded up my release in fact. Officially, I should still be in quarantine for three days."

"My father?" she squeaked. "How could he possibly have known?"

"Rand sent a message blip to a passing brainship, who relayed it to a city manager and so on and so on."

"Oh fardles!" she clutched her hair. "They're the biggest gossips in Central Worlds. This means that literally everybody knows about this." Her voice had grown hollow and she leaned weakly against the desk. "I'll never be able to show my face in port again. And as for visiting the SSS-900-C . . ." She hid her face in her hands and groaned.

Bros grinned at her and shook his head.

"Talk about looking a gift horse in the mouth. It was a private letter and was treated as such. The problem your father had was wondering why you didn't ask him for help. You were certainly entitled to it."

"I did ask him for help. I asked him for a loan, a huge loan and he gave it to me, no questions asked."

"Oh, I wouldn't say that," Bros said, laughing. "He had a million of 'em for me."

Joat looked at him earnestly. "It simply never occurred to me to ask him for official help. You were the only one I thought could help me, because *you* guaranteed our expenses. I tried every avenue I could think of within CenSec." She shrugged helplessly. "But Simeon never occurred to me."

"And what about the Benisur?"

"I couldn't afford to go personally. Travel time was time I wasn't earning credits. I kept wanting to contact him, but time was short and I didn't dare risk the credits a tight-beam would cost. What if he couldn't afford to help me? What if he had to say no? Then I'd be out all those credits for nothing."

"Good thing Rand was thinking more clearly than you were."

She laughed. "Yes, it was. He's very bright, don't you think?"

Bros nodded, smiling.

"I brought this for you," he said and held out another datahedron.

"What is it?" she looked from the hedron to Bros.

He straightened.

"Well, after *this* and ten years, I've gone about as far as I'm going to with CenSec and still be allowed to do anything," he explained as he casually closed the distance between them. "But I've got a strong suspicion that Joat Simeon-Hap Enterprises is going to go far. And you'll definitely need a good security man."

Suddenly Joat found herself wrapped in a warm embrace. She stiffened and opened her mouth to object.

He kissed her lightly and smiled warmly down at her. Then gently pressed her head against his chest, resting his chin on her smooth blond hair.

"It's okay to lean on your friends, Joat. There's no harm in it."

"Oh, all right," she grumbled. "You're hired."

"Good." He kissed the top of her head.

She looked up. She could just see an earlobe beyond the curve of his lean jaw.

"Are you sure you want to do this? Silken could be a problem."

"I'm sure she will be."

"And some of the Kolnari got away. You know what they're like."

"Yes," he said comfortably and stroked her back. "I do."

Joat wriggled unhappily, enjoying the sensation but not trusting it. She couldn't help wondering what he really wanted.

Bros smiled. *I'd love to tell you that I bought* Wyal *back for you with my retirement fund, but I don't dare. You'd never let me get away with that.*

He'd also resigned from CenSec over their refusal to help Joat. Though to be honest, he'd been disappointed and surprised when they'd accepted it so quickly.

Still, it was the least I could do for you, he thought. *Considering what Belazir would have done to you if . . .* He let the thought slide, his embrace tightening unconsciously.

"And we can still work for Central Security sometimes. Right?" he asked. *After all, I'd hate to feel completely cast off.*

"Don't push your luck," she said and pulled away to grin up at him.

That's better, she thought, feeling more in control. All she'd needed was a handle, a reason behind his behavior. *Clearly CenSec thinks they can use me, so they've sent Bros along to be their agent-in-residence. Hah! Still . . . might be fun.* In fact, she was already looking forward to it. She'd enjoyed bargaining with Sperin. *Especially since, in the end, I got the better of him.*

Bros smiled down into her amused blue eyes, aware that she thought she had his number, and sighed in his mind. *This thing is going to take a lot of time,* he thought. *Good thing I've got plenty to spend.* There was a slight pang at the thought of his lost career.

"So," she said stepping out of his arms, "let's get going."

"Yes, Boss."

Joat snapped him a look.

"You realize that you're not going to be making big credits right away."

"Yes, Boss."

"I'll bet you expect me to make you a partner one day, don't you?"

"Yes, Boss."

"Don't count your chickens before they're hatched, Sperin. You'll have to earn it."

"Anything worthwhile has to be earned, one way or another," he said.

Joat let out a long breath, feeling the stiffness flow from muscles she hadn't known were tense. She smiled, and turned her head away.

"Yeah."

~ THE END ~